David Michie was born in Rhodesia, educated in South Africa, and has worked in public relations for fifteen years. Specialising in strategic planning, he has consulted for several of London's biggest public relations' agencies. His first two novels, *Conflict of Interest* and *Pure Deception*, quickly achieved international success. He now divides his time between London and Perth, Western Australia.

Visit the author's website at:
www.davidmichie.com

By the same author

CONFLICT OF INTEREST

DAVID MICHIE OMNIBUS

Pure Deception
Expiry Date

DAVID MICHIE

timewarner
paperbacks

A *Time Warner* Paperback

This omnibus edition first published in Great Britain by
Time Warner Paperbacks in June 2005

Copyright © David Michie 2005

First published separately:
Pure Deception first published in Great Britain by Little, Brown in 2000
Published by Time Warner Paperbacks in 2001
Copyright © David Michie 2000

Expiry Date first published in Great Britain by Little, Brown in 2002
Published by Time Warner Paperbacks in 2003
Copyright © David Michie 2002

A CIP catalogue record for this book
is available from the British Library.

ISBN 0 7515 3785 3

Printed and bound in Great Britain by
Mackays of Chatham plc, Chatham, Kent

Time Warner Paperbacks
An imprint of
Time Warner Book Group UK
Brettenham House
Lancaster Place
London WC2E 7EN

www.twbg.co.uk

Pure Deception

To my dear friend, Kay Paddon, with love.

Power today has little to do with how much property a person owns or commands, it is instead determined by how many minutes of prime-time television or pages of news-media attention he can access or occupy.

Douglas Rushkoff, Media Virus

PROLOGUE

Alan Brent had never felt such terror in his life. Even half an hour later, hurrying through the night with shoulders hunched and collar raised, he had to fight to control the nausea, to keep down the acid rising from his stomach. *Clink, clink, clink*, came the sound from his trouser pocket. Steel on glass. He tried blocking it from his mind.

In ten years undercover he'd seen some sights – all manner of depravities and perversions and horrors. But none like tonight. Christ, no! Even though it hadn't been him trussed up on the floor, subjected to Larson's barbaric surgery, he'd scarcely been able to comprehend the sheer, stupefying viciousness of it. Behind their thick lenses, his eyes were still wide with shock. In his jacket pockets, he'd clenched his hands into tight fists to stop them shaking.

They were moving as fast as possible without drawing undue attention. One of the dark shadows was fifty yards ahead; the other man, fifty behind. This was Alan's first time out and they were taking no chances. They had been ruthlessly effective from the start, their actions planned meticulously to cover all scenarios, drilling each sequence in rehearsal, again and again. So when it had come to the actual operation, they were doing it for the hundredth time, and had carried it out with digital precision. Searing, heart-stopping torment had been inflicted with Teutonic efficiency. No wonder Larson thought he was untouchable.

As they rushed past shop windows lit up in the night, Alan told himself he should derive some satisfaction from the fact that he had at least been accepted. He'd broken into the inner circle. They'd never have let him anywhere near this if they'd had the slightest doubt. Going operational was a mark of trust, recognition – he needed that if he was going to penetrate the highest level of the organisation, though he hadn't counted on the cost. What had happened tonight outstripped his most lurid expectations – and there was nothing he could do about it now. He was way past the point of no return. Bile rose to his throat. It was all he could do not to retch.

They turned into his street. He paused, as he'd been instructed, while the front escort checked the way before signalling all clear. Alibis had been established and weren't to be wrecked by chance encounters – that was their reasoning and he played along with the game, knowing that, if it came to it, he could get one of the women from HQ to pretend to be his girlfriend.

The house was a typical Victorian terrace, indistinguishable from the other sixty in the street. He made his way quickly from pavement to front door, keys in his hand, and as soon as he was inside he shed his jacket, threw it over a coat-hook and headed immediately for the stairs. The sound from his trouser pocket as he ascended was a loathsome reminder. *Clink, clink, clink.*

Alan's kitchen was large and scattered with the detritus

of bachelorhood, cast in sepia by the grubby yellow glow from the streetlamp outside. Standing in the centre of it, spectacles glinting, he raised shaking fingers to push back the dark, wiry locks that fell dishevelled about his face. This was his first moment alone since the attack. It felt surreal to be back in the midst of familiar territory after what he'd just been through. As he stood there, heart pounding, and mouth vile, he still found it hard to believe. God Almighty, what had he let himself in for? In all the time he'd been working his way into the group, they'd never gone this far.

As he took a step forward, there came the sound from his pocket again – a single, unbidden *clink* – and with it, the unavoidable knowledge that the moment had come for him to deal with it. Trying to ignore it just wasn't an option any more. Wearily, he picked up a paper serviette from among the salt and pepper sachets and other remnants of number-less fast-food meals scattered across the kitchen bench. Unfolding the serviette over his right hand, he reached down into his pocket.

An hour before, the jar had been empty and clear; now its glass sides were sickeningly smeared. He set it down at the far corner of the bench without looking at it. *He'd been down on his knees when they'd made him pick them up. His skin-tight gloves were so fine, it had been like touching them with his bare hands. He hadn't felt nausea at the time – only shock. His fingers had shaken so violently he'd only just got them in the jar and was screwing the lid tight when he'd been ordered out.*

Turning, Alan made his way from the kitchen, trying to dismiss the jar from his mind. He wanted, more than anything, to leave it all behind. To forget about it completely. Climbing a final flight of stairs, he made his way into the long attic room he used as his combined office and bedroom; the place where he spent most of his days and all his nights.

As always, it was lit by the ghostly purple glow of his screensaver, which was reflected in a series of Velux windows that ran along the ceiling.

He slumped on to the sofa and turned on the television with the remote control, at the same time picking up a half-empty can of Sprite from the floor and taking several, greedy swallows to flush the bitterness from his mouth and throat. He flicked through the television channels trying to find some absorbing distraction. But there was no distraction, he soon discovered, from his own raging turmoil. No matter what images appeared on television, he couldn't get what was in the jar out of his mind. Nor could he avoid the realisation, which came suddenly and nagged at him insistently, that he'd have to go back downstairs again. There was no way he could avoid it. He'd have to return to the kitchen, pick up the jar, and put it away in the fridge.

It was a warm night, after all. He couldn't risk the contents decomposing.

1

Right from the start, Mark Watson reckoned there had been a mistake. Making his way through the tinted glass doors leading off the pavement, he found himself in a vast, white atrium flooded with light from a domed glass ceiling six floors up. It was the kind of reception area that couldn't fail to impress, unexpected as it was completely incongruous. Most buildings in Soho were cramped and quirky – the offices of graphic designers and film producers and advertising agents to be found at the ends of dimly lit warrens and narrow staircases. GCM was utterly, improbably different. It was like stepping into an immense, bedazzling temple of glitz.

The reception desk, at the far end, was an endless curve of white, Egyptian marble, studded with clocks showing the time in every major entertainment market from Los Angeles to Tokyo. Behind it, four young women with supermodel good looks glowed, as though charged with post-gym endorphins. Above them, the GCM logo – a triumphal flourish in gold. Even before he'd got to the reception desk, Mark found himself thinking that someone, somewhere along the way had cocked it up. They'd got the wrong guy.

Promptly signed in, he was waved across to the seating area beside one of the chrome counters. Not that he was in any mood to sit. Instead, he walked around the walls, studying the float-framed photo-montages of famous actors and actresses holding aloft their glittering Oscars, superstar singers beaming with their Grammies, Broadway luminaries clutching luxuriant floral bouquets as they took their final bows. He picked up one of the glossy GCM brochures. Until that particular moment, he'd had no idea what GCM even stood for – but there it was, spelled out in embossed gilt lettering, Global Creative Management. And beneath the agency name, its client list.

As he scanned through it, he was increasingly impressed – and unfamiliarly self-conscious. Every single client listed was a major league player: pop stars whose records had gone platinum; household name actors. This was the 'A' league, no doubting it. There weren't any names here that were only vaguely familiar. No has-beens, wannabes or never-was-es. This was a list so star-studded, he could only be left wondering one thing: why the hell did they want to speak to *him*?

He'd received the phone call first thing this morning. Eight-thirty had found him behind his desk in the software support department of mobile phone company OmniCell, feeling less than bright-eyed and bushy-tailed; last night's *South Pacific* rehearsal in the Battersea Arts Centre had ended at half past ten, after which most of the cast had decamped to the nearby Slug and Lettuce for a swift one. But one had inevitably become two and even three in some cases – including his. He hadn't got to bed until the early hours.

So when the first call of the day had come through this morning, he hadn't bust a gut to get it. Instead, he'd let it ring awhile, hoping one of his colleagues would pick it up. Only when it became apparent they weren't going to, had he grabbed the receiver.

'Support,' he'd announced.

'Is Mark Watson available?' The voice at the other end was female, American and cool. Nothing like the usual Helpdesk callers, who phoned in various stages of desperation.

Mark sat up in his chair. 'That's me.'

Which was when Elizabeth Reynolds had said she was calling on behalf of Hilton Gallo from GCM. It was a blur after that, but the upshot was that he'd come to Hilton's attention and the GCM chief wanted to meet him. Would he be available later this morning?

Mark had felt sleepy numbness replaced instantly by sharp curiosity. He'd never heard of GCM – who were they, some record label? – and he assumed that Vinnie Dobson, his self-appointed manager, must have sent them a demo tape. But a high-powered meeting later this morning was the very last thing he felt up to.

'What about Wednesday?' he'd suggested.

The sleek voice on the phone swiftly cut that idea short: Mr Gallo was flying back to LA tomorrow morning. It was today, or nothing.

Mark had raised a hand to his brow, perplexed. He supposed he could wangle an early afternoon, but quite frankly, he didn't feel ready. He had no idea who this GCM crowd were, he was unprepared, and there was no way he was going to be briefed before he went in to see them – Vinnie was long weekending in France right now, stocking up on cheap booze. On the other hand, he guessed he owed it to Vinnie to go and see them – his manager had been sending out demo tapes for months. Eventually he told

Elizabeth, 'I might just manage four o'clock this afternoon.'

He didn't recognise the pause at the other end as arctic. Elizabeth Reynolds, every bit as smooth and svelte as she sounded, couldn't help pondering over the irony of it: Hilton Gallo represented more 'A-league' showbiz stars than any other agent in Los Angeles. He was a man with whom every studio head in Hollywood wanted to do lunch. Well-established celebrities of stage and screen would fly across America for the prospect of a mere twenty-minute slot in his notoriously crowded schedule. And here, she thought, was some complete zero, some London cybernerd, saying he *might just manage* four o'clock. She glanced down that afternoon's overloaded schedule. Hilton had made it very clear he wanted to see this guy. She couldn't afford to get heavy. Things would have to be shifted. After a while she said, 'Take down the address.'

Mark quickly unpeeled a yellow Post-It note and began writing.

For the rest of the morning, his mind very definitely wasn't on the job. He guessed he should be trying to dream up insightful analyses on the state of the music industry for when he went to GCM, or trenchant questions showing he kept up with the trade mags. Instead he kept wondering who this Hilton Gallo bloke was, and which demo tape he'd listened to. Mark had recorded a couple over the past year, about one of which he had decidedly mixed feelings.

He tried Vinnie a couple of times but, as he already knew, his mobile had poor reception in France. Mark understood that better than anyone – it was he who'd given Vinnie his mobile in the first place. OmniCell had been doing a discounted rate deal for staff and friends – and Vinnie had just had his mobile stolen. Mark also wondered what he was supposed to wear. Here he was, sitting in a Marks & Spencer suit and crumpled tie; he couldn't go to see some big shot from Los Angeles looking like a Helpdesk flunky.

It wasn't like Mark to get uptight. It was his easygoing self-assurance that drew people to him, a relaxed manner which came from not taking himself too seriously. Unexpected developments he took in his stride – with a job like his, he had to. But today's call from GCM was different; it was the first professional interest in his singing career he'd ever had.

At lunch-time he hurried back to his flat for a change of clothes so that when it was time to leave, he could head straight out to the Soho address he'd been given. In the end he decided to dress smart casual, and count on his broken-up face to see him through. While no one would have described Mark as handsome in the conventional sense, there was something about the way he looked which caught the attention – and held it. He was tall, rangy, with long, dark hair, but it was his face that was the reason for his popularity with women. Dominated by a long, prominent nose, jutting out at an angle as though once broken, Mark's craggy features gave him a battered, soulful look. Women responded to him as a man in need of loving. Macho, but at the same time vulnerable, he quite unconsciously provoked in them a surge of mixed feelings – intrigue, tenderness, lust. Men, taking in his height and rugged features, accorded him automatic respect.

Mark was aware of the impression he made on both sexes and hoped that today his natural bad looks would see him through. At least he could count on his hair, he thought as he left OmniCell shortly before three-thirty and headed to the nearby tube station. Thick, lustrous and down to his collar, his hair was his best asset – and women loved running their fingers through it. He'd opted for a dark linen jacket and black moleskin trousers, a deep-blue shirt and narrow tie, which he hoped did the business. As he descended the stairs to the Underground, he couldn't escape the irony. Here he was on his way to what could turn out to be the most important meeting of his performing career to date – the kind of meeting that would have got Vinnie all steamed up – and his 'manager' was nowhere in sight. After months of knocking on doors, sending out demos, trying to get in with the movers and shakers, now when someone was finally showing interest, Vinnie didn't even know it was happening.

It was Vinnie after all, who'd got him involved in the business. Mark had known Vinnie from way back, the two of them having grown up together on a council estate in Lewisham. After school they'd lost contact, Mark finding his way into computers through the guidance of his school's careers adviser, getting himself fixed up in a flat-share in Wimbledon and generally enjoying being a man about town. He'd always been close to his mum of course, and brother Lloyd, three years his junior. Growing up in a single-parent family, he'd felt a responsibility for them from an early age, and since he'd been earning, he'd enjoyed treating his mum to the kinds of things she'd never been able to afford when he and Lloyd were both kids, like dinners out, and weekend breaks, and indulgent gifts on her birthday.

And as the time approached for Lloyd to leave school, Mark had kept an eye out on the OmniCell internal appointments notice-board. When a trainee slot came up in new product development, Mark made sure that Lloyd's name was put on the interview list – and Lloyd had walked away with the job. That was three years ago, and since then Lloyd had advanced rapidly in the department, helped by his natural aptitude for computers combined with a creative mind.

Meanwhile, Mark's social life in Wimbledon had really taken off. A whole bunch of OmniCell's younger crowd lived in the area and used to get together at nights and over the weekends. There was a constant tide of people coming into town and going to parties and sleeping over. Discovering his own gregarious nature, not to mention his popularity with women, Mark had made the most of his independence – and it wasn't often that he woke up on a Sunday morning alone.

His singing career had started by accident just over a year ago. Mark had been out with a few friends at the Lamb in Balham where, by chance, Vinnie had organised a karaoke evening. Having been told in the past he had a good voice, and never lacking in confidence, it hadn't taken much egging on for Mark to be persuaded to take to the floor with Oasis's 'Wonderwall'. He'd been well received – extremely well received, Vinnie had thought, watching from the sidelines. It wasn't only the distinctive gravelly timbre he had to his voice, it was also his easy manner. He was clearly enjoying himself up there and good feeling was communicated effortlessly to the crowd. He had, Vinnie realised grimly, a lot more charisma than some of the 'professional' acts he managed.

Since leaving school, Vinnie had worked his way into the pub and club circuit as a music manager. Taking on guitarists and keyboard players who weren't too fussed about having to dodge the occasional beer can, he had a few acts on his books, ranging from acid-house artistes and late-night jazz crooners to mainstream rock groups who did covers of everyone else's music so that they could occasionally slip one of their own numbers into the mix. The hours were long, the pay was a joke and personal spats seemed endless. But Vinnie hadn't cared. He'd always believed in himself, and reading the music industry magazines – *Music Week* and *Billboard* – he would dream big dreams. It was only a matter of time until one of his groups came to the attention of music talent scouts. It was just a question of right place, right time, then he, Vinnie Dobson, would cash up big. He would come out from left of field and storm the industry. He knew he could do it – every week he read about guys heading in from nowhere to turn into major players. He'd get himself the Ferrari, the flash place in Hampstead. He'd be out at Stringfellows every night with a different woman on his arm. No doubt about it, Vinnie Dobson would be a name to be reckoned with.

Sure enough, his break had come when Swerve were signed up by Strobe Records, and 'She's My Lover' raced up the charts to number five. He'd created Swerve from the anaemic-looking, auburn-haired brothers, Oli and Steve Lamark, who hailed from a one-Porsche town in Lancashire. At a time when heroin chic was big on the catwalk, the Lamarks' look and their angst-rock sound had been perfectly in keeping with the times. It had been a first for all three of them and, when he looked back on it, there were things Vinnie would have done differently. But while it lasted, he'd been unstoppable. Okay, his commission hadn't stretched to the Ferrari, or the flash place in Hampstead – not yet. But he'd rented a flat in South Kensington and bought himself a second-hand Mercedes and all of that was a big step up. His confidence had been boosted as never before – people started calling his career 'meteoric'. Around that time he'd also signed up the Irish singer Siobhan O'Mara and Nigerian band Cha Punga, and music company executives started returning his calls. There was no doubting it, Vinnie Dobson was on his way to the top.

But when Swerve's follow-up number 'Wanting You' was

released, it barely made it into the top thirty, and after an initial burst of play-time, it was hardly heard of again. 'Too derivative' was the criticism that stuck – the Lamark brothers had imitated their own first hit too closely and that turned the punters off. Within days, Strobe Records were slow-pedalling the idea of an album – let's see how the next one flies, they said. And the initial buzz of excitement about Vinnie's other signings, Siobhan O'Mara and Cha Punga, died down into nothing.

Vinnie, who'd been spending money faster than it rolled in, quickly found himself staring down into the abyss. The Kensington flat had had to go, and he returned to his parents' place in Balham – 'while looking around for a place to buy' was how he played it. He'd fought to keep the car, as well as an aura of unassailable confidence – think big, talk big was how he operated. But, a year after Swerve's third single had flopped, and the two brothers had fallen out over some bimbo from Norwich, the big-time Vinnie front was getting harder and harder to keep up. Getting gigs in smoke-filled dens had never been a problem for him, but the real money was in record deals, and nobody on his books really stood out as a potential star. Nobody, that is, until he saw Mark Watson on stage.

Vinnie had bought Mark a beer after his karaoke performance and said he should think seriously about singing. Mark just laughed. That was the kind of stuff he'd dreamed about when he was fifteen. Standing in front of the bathroom mirror, hairbrush 'microphone' in hand, he'd had the same fantasy as every other teenage kid in the country. But that wasn't reality. Not the way he saw it.

Nonetheless a seed had been planted in his mind, and a couple of days later when Vinnie phoned to tell him a slot had become free next Saturday night in a club just round the corner from where he lived, and please wouldn't he consider it, Mark eventually said yes. It was only three songs with a back-up band. There'd be rehearsals on Saturday afternoon. Couldn't hurt.

That Saturday night Mark had enjoyed himself more than he'd ever imagined – and received a rapturous reception from the audience. He'd only ever thought of himself as just an ordinary bloke, but if he did have a musical talent, maybe he should develop it – he hadn't got such kicks from anything else before.

Which was why, over the next few months, he'd taken up proper singing lessons and started to perform. He found himself at folk evenings and in jazz back-ups and even in the bass of a baroque choir – his new singing teacher encouraged all his students to throw themselves into the widest range of musical experiences possible. In the meantime, at Vinnie's insistence, he let his former schoolmate book him in on a few gigs, and record a couple of numbers to send out on demo to various record companies. The idea of himself as a star in the making was a novelty to Mark, but Vinnie could be very persuasive, leaning against his sleek Mercedes puffing on a slim panatella. Vinnie who had got 'She's My Lover' to number five in the charts, and who always seemed to have a deal up his sleeve, Vinnie whose gregarious bonhomie was infectious – maybe he'd turn out to be right, thought Mark, glancing round the GCM atrium. Although he still couldn't avoid being sceptical about his present situation. Even if Vinnie *had* blustered him in to see Hilton Gallo, agent to the stars, Gallo would work out in an instant that Mark was nothing like all his other top-drawer clients.

'Mr Watson?' A voice sounded across GCM's magnificent reception area as he stood at a chromium counter, scrutinising the selection of crushed watermelon, mango and papaya. He turned to find an immaculately blonde woman in a black suit making her brisk way towards him.

'That's right.'

She delivered a crisp handshake before gesturing to a glass-walled lift at the side of the atrium. 'I'll take you up.'

The lift slid up the side of the atrium towards the glass ceiling, the reception desk rapidly dwindling in size below. Gliding all the way to the top, Mark realised that, despite his reservations about the meeting he was about to have, he was by now very curious indeed to meet this Hilton Gallo.

As the lift came to a halt, he was shown along the corridor of the penthouse floor, also brilliantly lit and expansive, its walls bedecked with autographed portraits of showbiz luminaries – actors, actresses, sitcom stars, directors and producers . . . who wasn't here? Then throwing open a door with a flourish, the black-suited woman gestured, saying, 'Do go in.'

The room was very long, and white, and all the way down its right side sliding doors opened out on to a garden glimpsed through muslin curtains, that were billowing like clouds in the late-afternoon sunshine. A polished, alabaster table gleamed down the length of the room, at its centre a vase containing the largest display of fresh-cut flowers Mark thought he'd ever seen. A hundred blossoms, exotic and multicoloured, splashed vividly against the pure whiteness of the room. At first, Mark thought he was alone. Then after a moment, two figures emerged towards him from the intense brightness at the far end. The first, a tall, lean, elegantly suited man, his dark hair cropped so short it was almost shaven, had a curiously monastic appearance. As he drew closer, Mark noted the narrow face, the acute eyes – he felt the man had summed him up even before he reached out with a strong handshake and said, 'Hilton Gallo. And this is my assistant, Elizabeth Reynolds. You spoke?'

'That's right.' Mark turned to shake her hand. Elizabeth was every bit as svelte as she'd sounded, with big, blonde hair and an azure dress, accentuating the unnerving dazzle of her blue eyes.

'Let's step outside,' suggested Hilton, 'nice day.' He brushed aside one of the curtains, to reveal the most extraordinary of gardens, green and lush, its central feature an Italianate fountain from which water cascaded into a round pond stocked with golden koi. At the far end, yellow honeysuckle foamed about a wooden pergola which overlooked the garden on one side, and Soho Square six floors below on the other. It was the most unlikely Arcadia in the centre of London.

'I heard your tape.' Hilton led him across to the pergola, in which a table and chairs had been set up, and a jug of iced orange crush with glasses. 'I was impressed. Very impressed.'

'Thank you.' Mark wondered which tape he was referring to – but decided to keep schtum about that for the moment.

'Drink?' Hilton was gesturing towards the jug.

'Thank you.'

As Elizabeth began pouring out drinks, Hilton looked over at him again, that same almost predatory observation, all-seeing, all-knowing. 'It would help if I told you something about us, yes?'

'It would.' Mark nodded.

'GCM is the most powerful talent agency in America, and therefore,' Gallo gave a small, dry smile, 'the world.' He handed Mark a glass of orange crush before picking up his own. Mark was about to take his first sip when Hilton asked him, unexpectedly, 'Any idea why that might be?'

Mark had half-expected to be grilled on the dynamics of agency power-plays and, quite frankly, didn't take kindly to it. But he'd go along with Gallo for the moment.

'I suppose all the stars you represent?'

'Exactly.' Hilton met his eyes with an expression of approval. 'And would you care to venture what it is that makes our clients so powerful?'

'Money?' He shrugged.

Hilton nodded once. 'I thought you might say that.' Taking Mark by the arm, he guided him on to paving stones which formed a border round the perimeter of the lawn. It looked as if they were going for an afternoon stroll.

'You know, Mark,' he began, his hand still resting on Mark's right arm, 'the world we live in, money isn't the issue any more.'

Oh, yeah? thought Mark, try telling his bank manager that. Or his mates. Or any of the people walking along the street outside. But of course the world Hilton Gallo was talking about was a completely different place. It was a world of Oscar-winning clients and transatlantic jet-setting, and assistants who looked as if they'd just stepped off the catwalk. And just for this incredible moment, he thought, it was his world too.

'There are those who have it,' Hilton was saying, 'and have it big. They sit managing their investment portfolios from their Holmby Hills mansions, or maybe out of town some place – the Aspen chalet, the château in France – and they're worth a hundred, maybe two hundred million. But,' he glanced over at Mark, his eyes lit with wry humour, 'so what?'

So what indeed, thought Mark.

'Did you know,' Hilton asked him, 'every year there are another ten thousand millionaires in the world?'

'I didn't.'

'Think of the effect. A million in the bank used to be the Holy Grail. Now being a millionaire is no big deal. It's the democratisation of wealth. No one cares what you say or do just because you have a few million.' Hilton halted and turned to him, fixing him with a look of searing conviction. 'Power isn't about money any more. It used to be, but no longer. Shall I tell you where the game's moved to now?' He took a step closer, as though about to disclose a thrilling secret known to only a select élite.

Engrossed, Mark nodded.

'Power,' Hilton's voice had lowered to one of compelling intimacy, 'is about how many minutes of prime-time television you command. It's about how many column inches of newspaper you can access. How much radio play-time you occupy. How many hits you get on your website. Media control is the new currency. Control the media, and you control the world.' He paused as though at the high altar of truth.

'You see, Mark, people out there,' he gestured to Soho Square and beyond, 'they have a voracious appetite for media. We're living through the biggest explosion of media channels in history. They just can't get enough of it. You know how powerful that makes our clients?'

Mark had never had things related to him this way before. But what Hilton was saying did make sense. It was so simple, so obvious – and the super-agent's zeal was self-evident.

'Because our clients are powerful,' he had started walking again, 'that gives us leverage. GCM has more muscle than any other agency to land the most lucrative endorsement deals, to hike up performance fees, to extract maximum value for intellectual property.' They were on the final length of their garden circuit, walking alongside the balcony railing which overlooked Soho Square. Then Hilton paused abruptly. 'Which brings me to you.'

Here we are, thought Mark, crunch time. The moment when he would be found out. Discovered as someone different from the person he was believed to be. But at least he'd got a walk round the penthouse garden with Hilton Gallo out of it, and a lecture on the true meaning of power.

'Like I say, we were very impressed with the tape.'

It couldn't have been that second tape Vinnie had persuaded him to do one Sunday afternoon when he had access to spare studio time. It must have been the first, thought Mark. But why had Gallo waited four months to respond to it?

'Few performances stand out like yours did.'

'Glad you liked it.'

'We more than just liked it. We found it very compelling.'

No need to over-egg the pudding, thought Mark wryly. But he supposed Hilton Gallo couldn't stop selling. That was what he did.

Hilton was studying him carefully, 'I sense a certain . . . reservation?'

He was tuned in all right, Mark had to admit, very observant.

'I s'pose I'm just surprised you think my demo tape—'

'It wasn't a demo tape,' Hilton cut in. 'GCM has a policy of returning all demos unplayed.'

Mark raised his eyebrows.

'We rely entirely on our own scouts. You were recorded at a charity concert a few weeks back.'

Well, this changed things! He knew the concert Hilton was referring to. An e-mail had gone round OmniCell asking for volunteer performers for a children's leukaemia charity supported by the staff association. Mark had put his name down for a singing slot, thinking it would be good practice. As it happened, the charity concert had provoked his one and only serious argument with Vinnie. Vinnie had been dead against it from the moment Mark told him about it and Mark hadn't been able to work out why. Until a few days later, when Vinnie had phoned to tell him he'd booked him a gig at The Three Troubadours in Notting Hill. Same day, same time as the charity do. Mark had told him, forget it, he was already taken. Raising his voice, Vinnie said he thought they'd agreed Mark would cancel the leukaemia thing. When Mark begged to differ, Vinnie threw a wobbly.

In the end, Mark had done the charity concert and Vinnie had growled at him for a week. But what else was Mark to do? He'd promised to do the concert, so he had to go through with it. What he hadn't realised until this moment was that there'd been talent scouts on the prowl.

'We prefer managing the search process ourselves,' Hilton was telling him now, 'avoids potential . . . complications.'

Mark guessed exactly what complications he was referring to.

'You had no contract regarding the concert?' Hilton confirmed now.

Mark shook his head.

'And you don't have any recording arrangement or agent at this time?'

'Not a recording deal. But a mate of mine has been setting up gigs and sending out demo tapes—'

'Does your management contract—' interjected Hilton.

'We don't have a management contract,' he returned, 'nothing official.'

There had never been any paperwork between Vinnie and him, and the fact was that Mark made a lot of his own arrangements which Vinnie disputed, like singing lessons ('Why bother? You can sing already'), *South Pacific* ('Different ball-game, mate') and charity concerts ('Total waste of time').

'Well, then,' Hilton raised his palms in front of him with a smile, 'we have nothing to worry about.'

You mean, you have nothing to worry about, thought Mark. He reckoned Vinnie would be none too pleased if GCM snapped him up for mega-stardom just like that.

'Anyway, it's not your representation we're here to discuss. It's you.'

Mark raised his eyebrows.

'Your voice. Your presence. The way you are. I think you could be exactly what we've been looking for.'

'What exactly is that?' Mark asked.

'Can't go into details right now,' Hilton was confidential, 'but let's just say that it's the kind of opportunity any male singer today would be very excited about.'

At that moment, Elizabeth's mobile phone sounded. She answered it before putting her hand over the mouthpiece. 'Julia,' she called over to them.

Hilton made a dismissive gesture. 'I'll call her back.' He frowned.

Hilton Gallo would rather speak to me than Julia Roberts? wondered Mark. Or was it some other Julia? Meeting Hilton's eyes now, he asked, 'I thought you only represented big-name celebrities?'

Hilton regarded him seriously. 'True. That's how we make them.'

Glancing away into the square below, he pointed to a large Peter Jones van crawling through the traffic.

'You see that truck down there,' he nodded towards it. 'Imagine a fleet of those pulling up outside our offices every night and loading up with celebrity. That's how it is. We *manufacture* the stuff. It's true you need to start off with the right material, but there's never been a shortage of that. Our expertise is in following the markets, predictive modelling, matching artistic resources to where the money's headed. We've been cross-referencing very intensively of late, and I think you could be the right guy,' he looked back at Mark, 'but I need to be certain. I'd like you to put down a couple of tracks for me in the studio.'

Mark had been following all this with mounting interest. For all his initial scepticism and his reservations about Hilton Gallo's super-cool style, there was no doubting what was going on: this man, on first-name terms with the world's biggest stars, was considering plucking him from obscurity. That was the deal.

'Now, if you're in agreement,' Hilton was leading him back to the pergola and putting down his empty glass, 'we've a studio round the corner on standby. Sound engineers, and keyboard back-up. What I'd like is for you to record a couple of songs, a ballad for sure, and maybe something fast. I'll take the tape back to LA with me tomorrow. I should have a response for you pretty soon.'

Less than ten minutes later, Mark was making his way back down the steps away from the white light of the GCM building. On his way to the biggest audition of his life, he felt his head spinning. Events of this afternoon had been like something out of a story-book, and as a council-house boy from Lewisham, Mark knew just how much story-books had to do with the real world. But for all his ingrained cynicism, his disbelief in sudden strokes of good fortune, that was exactly what was happening. So *this* was how it felt to be discovered? To find the world suddenly changed halfway through the afternoon? Of course, there were no guarantees. But what a ride he was having in the meantime!

The only dark shadow on the horizon was what to do

about Vinnie. If GCM signed him up, his self-appointed manager would be more than a little piqued. He'd be absolutely livid. Still, thought Mark, no use worrying about what might never happen.

2

'You've got your ballet shoes?' Isis brushed her daughter's hair into a pony-tail.

'Yes, Mommy,' replied Holly. Then, not wanting to be asked, 'And my tutu, and my leotard and stockings.'

'Good.' Isis snapped a bead band round her hair. 'And the stuff for Miss Adams's class?'

'That's changed to next week.'

'Okay.' She glanced at her watch.

'Are we going to be late?' Her five-year-old daughter was more conscientious about time-keeping than she was.

'Not if I have breakfast when I get back.' Isis flashed a guilty glance in the direction of the breakfast table with its wheatgrass juice, lactobacillus yoghurt and high-fibre muesli. Anything to delay that. 'Go brush your teeth. Quickly. I'll be downstairs.'

Making her way through the hallway of her Malibu home with its familiar, sweeping view of the Pacific Ocean rolling on to the private beach, Isis paused, giving herself the once-over in the mirror. The greatest sex icon in contemporary pop, according to this year's *Rolling Stone* magazine survey. Just as well they never saw her at seven-forty-five in the morning. Or any time, for that matter, in the past few weeks. Because although the blonde hair, the striking height, the leonine poise hadn't lost their impact, there was something else too – an uneasy apprehension which had come into her eyes of late and which she just didn't seem able to shift.

Isis had always operated on intuition. It was what had led her to her greatest successes. It was her guiding star. *Aphrodisia*, her massively successful album, had been a creation of her inspired sixth sense, the result of her understanding, at a premonitory level, what it was her audience most wanted to experience at that particular moment. Conversely, there had been times in the past when ignoring her inner voice had led to her undoing. When she'd pretended not to hear what wasn't convenient at the time – and had always lived to regret it.

In the past three weeks the sense that something was awry had returned with a disturbing intensity. What's more, she knew the cause of it; three weeks earlier, she had signed an endorsement with Berkeley Square, the global cosmetics manufacturer. The deal was to be made public when a male partner, promoting the men's products in the same range, had also been signed up. What Isis couldn't work out was, why the apprehension? The Berkeley Square deal had come up at exactly the time she'd needed it most. It had seemed like the answer to her every prayer. What could possibly be wrong with it? In particular, why the sense of terrible foreboding that seemed to threaten the most vulnerable part of her, something from her past she'd spent the last eighteen years of her life trying to put behind her?

Celebrity and secrets, she knew all too well, were a deadly cocktail. But despite a decade of intense media scrutiny, of journalists picking and prying into every corner of her existence, she had succeeded in keeping her most private secret to herself – and two trusted advisers. How could the Berkeley Square endorsement contract possibly lead her into danger?

Running a hand through her lustrous locks, she turned away from the hallway mirror. No point in dwelling on it now, she thought, pushing aside a tapestry wall-hanging and making her way through a concealed door, down a flight of stairs, past the bodyguard's living quarters.

'You ready to rock 'n' roll, Frank?' she called, as she walked past his door towards the semi-darkness of the garage.

'Coming right now, ma'am.'

Bodyguards were rostered for four weeks at a time – the security firm said that stopped them getting complacent. She could always tell what week they were in by how deferential they were. When they first arrived, they were always in total awe of her – the most famous female pop singer, who'd achieved icon status on account of her provocative sexuality. Whey-hey, she could almost see them thinking, this made a change for them from all those anonymous studio big-shots. Things changed pretty soon though. After a couple of weeks they had worked out she was just the same as anyone. Worse. She had a hellish temper.

Her current bodyguard, Frank Stenner, was still in his first week, so it didn't take him long to emerge from his quarters, resplendent in dark suit and tie, cellular phone and handgun tucked discreetly beneath his jacket. He hurried into the garage behind her.

'D'you want me to—'

'I'll drive. You sit in the back with Holly.'

'Yes, ma'am.'

Driving at least gave her something to do where she felt in control, she reflected, climbing her way up behind the wheel of the specially customised Range Rover. Its tinted glass windows were bullet-proofed. It was fully equipped with an automatic siren and tracking devices, and linked up to an instant alert centre which guaranteed helicopter gunship response anywhere in LA within twelve minutes. A microphone and loudspeaker had been built into the chassis behind the front wheel, through which to communicate without having to open any windows. It even had flamethrowers, operated by a red floor lever under each side, specially installed by a security expert from Johannesburg, car-jacking capital of the world. Having woken up one night to find a stalker in her bedroom, holding a gun to her head, she wasn't taking any chances.

She glanced in the rear-view mirror and saw Frank wearing sunglasses.

'Too bright for you in here, Frank?'

'Uh . . . no, ma'am.' It took him a moment to work it out, before he removed his shades and stuffed them in his pocket.

She didn't know why she got so tetchy with the staff. Even though her once-legendary retinue had been slimmed down to just a bodyguard and her housekeeper Juanita, she still felt awkward having them around. It went beyond the fact that she'd grown up poor. It was more that she worried if they hung around her long enough, maybe something in her long-distant past would communicate itself without her even being aware of it. Maybe they'd find her out.

In saner moments, she told herself she was being ridiculous. You couldn't tell about that kind of thing just by looking. Christ knew, she'd been ogled and leered at more than any woman in history apart from Princess Di. But there were only two people in LA who knew her secret, and she intended to keep it that way. Not even her former husband

and Hollywood heart-throb John Dettler knew. When she'd spoken to Hilton Gallo about it, Hilton had said best not to tell him. On a need-to-know basis, John hadn't needed to know.

Glancing at her watch again, she was about to hoot when Holly appeared, running down the steps into the garage, piling into the back of the car and slamming the door shut behind her. Noticing the smudge of toothpaste at the corner of her mouth, Isis tugged a handkerchief from her pocket and was dabbing it with saliva, but Holly, seeing the movement, had already licked the back of her hand and wiped her mouth. Then as Isis pressed the remote-control button to open the garage door, Holly looked up at Frank with a bright smile.

'Hi, Frank!'

'Hi, Holly! How're ya doing?'

'All right.'

She was tall for her five years and blonde, just like her mother. She had more manners than her mother had had at that age, and was a lot more mature. In fact, she was more grown up than most five-year-olds – she had to be, thought Isis, checking her daughter was belted in, before starting the engine and heading out into the driveway. Once outside, they went through the well-worn routine of waiting for the garage door to shut, before using another remote-control to open the two sets of eight-foot-high steel gates that led out to the street.

Isis was trying to give Holly as normal a childhood as possible, after all the interruptions. The dropping her off at school, the music classes twice a week, the friends who came round to play – in recent months they'd settled into a comfortable rhythm after the upsets of the past. During Holly's first three years, their family life had been one of relative normality, though John had frequently been away on location. But during the last two, Holly had been shuttled to and fro, not only because of the separation and divorce, but also because there'd been times Isis simply hadn't been capable of being a mother.

Glancing in the rear-view mirror, she noticed the child looking pensively out of the window. She was sure Holly sensed a lot more than she was capable of expressing, poor kid. It worried her when she went quiet. 'Doing anything special at school today, hon?' she asked to draw her out.

'Just the same.' Holly looked up at where Frank was scanning around them. 'I'm going to draw a picture of Frank.'

'That's cool.' Isis marvelled at how easily Holly adapted to their changing cast of guards, in contrast to her own uneasiness. Now Holly was looking at her in the rear-view mirror.

'Are you going out today?' She'd picked up on the make-up, thought Isis, and realised that leaving her home for a meeting was a big thing for her.

'Just to see Hilton about the new record.'

'Oh.' She was thoughtful again, before coming out with one of her disconcerting observations. 'Does Hilton think you're better?'

'Honey!' Isis glanced up in the mirror at Frank, resenting his presence even more. 'That's never been a problem.'

It was Hilton who'd found her that last time, bombed-out and comatose in her bedroom. She hadn't been responding to his calls and, by divine intervention, he had decided to take matters into his own hands, driving out to Malibu the morning after her accidental OD. Once he'd arrived, her bodyguard had confirmed she was in her bedroom. Receiving no reply to his persistent knocking, Hilton had ordered the guard to break down the door. And there she'd been, the

drugged-out wreckage of the former Queen of Charts,
minutes away from death.

That had been six months ago, though it felt like a lifetime. And it was only when she'd hit rock bottom that the
recovery process could begin. Only when she woke up in
the Betty Ford Center, washed up, washed out, an intravenous drip in her arm, that she realised she'd done exactly
what she'd vowed she never would – she had turned into a
cliché. Staring at the white walls of her private ward, the
white furniture and white sheets, the white coats of the
doctors and nurses, as she lay in her chemical strait-jacket,
she was too numb to feel anything, much less shed a tear.
All the same, she could hardly believe that she, of all people,
had fallen victim to the entertainment industry's most con-
tagious virus: fear of failure.

She hadn't exactly been a nobody before *Aphrodisia*. Her
début album, simply called *Isis*, had sold a very respectable
two million copies, its title track making it into the top ten
of the singles charts. Her newly appointed personal manager,
Alan Roberts, had generated hours of radio play-time and
her ten-city tour through America, with the accompanying
TV interviews, press hype and fan mobbings, had been not
so much her first taste of celebrity as her first sit-down, seven-
course, cordon bleu feast of fame. There'd been an effortlessness about it all which she'd taken for granted. Surprised
and delighted by her good fortune, when she'd scribbled a
few tracks for a new album it had been almost incidental to
her round of promotional concerts and interviews. Hilton
had said he loved the new compositions – and for her second
record had negotiated a major deal with Unum Music.

It hadn't been the only deal he'd swung. In those far-off,
carefree days, he'd also introduced her to the up-and-coming
Hollywood action adventure hero, John Dettler, and proposed

marriage. It had seemed a wonderful idea at the time and their Waikiki beach wedding had been followed, a year later, by the birth of Holly, an event that gave rise to one of the most widely circulated anecdotes proving just how ditsy the Queen of Charts could be. No sooner was she admitted to the labour room than Isis had ordered a telephone and had a nurse dial up John, who was on location in Italy. For the next hour and a half her screams of pain had echoed to Tuscany via satellite link-up – she'd insisted he stay on the line throughout her entire labour, so he would never be in any doubt about the agony of childbirth.

Later that year her second record had been released. *Aphrodisia* was the album that made her – and at the same time, paradoxically, led to her undoing. For all Hilton's enthusiasm and the lucrative Unum contract, nothing had prepared any of them for what was to happen. There'd been a massive tug from the retail chains within a day of the title track release – 'Aphrodisia' the song rocketed straight to the number one slot of the charts that week. Featuring Isis groaning her way to orgasm, above a sensual mix of Caribbean rhythm, orchestral sophistication and crooning sax, 'Aphrodisia' was novel, provocative, and instantly controversial. And the video, in which glimpses of her nakedness appeared in an erotically charged montage of settings from tropical to Egyptian occult, only pushed the line even further. Her record was instantly condemned by the fundamentalist right, taken before the censorship board in Australia, and championed by every gay club from San Francisco to Sydney. Best of all, it had been hotly debated on *Oprah* – thereby ensuring it remained the most played record in America.

As sales figures poured in from every world market, Unum executives had been ecstatic. With the release of the album, and its instant trajectory to the top of the charts, there had been feverish rounds of meetings, before the decision was taken to strip out a second track for single release; 'All I Need' was soon soaring up the charts. Over the next three months it had been an orgy of celebration as successive hit singles prompted Unum to keep pulling off tracks for single release. This was another *Thriller*, they declared. The album had already broken all Unum sales records and was on course to take a tilt at Michael Jackson's. One week, four of the top ten singles in America were *Aphrodisia* tracks – that same week, Isis appeared on the front cover of *Time* magazine.

The media, of course, just hadn't been able to get enough of Isis, and at GCM five agents were installed under Hilton to work full time on the avalanche of interviews, endorsements, concerts, and franchise requests that flooded through their doors. Isis had found herself at the centre of a whirlwind of activity, operating at a level she'd never have entertained in her wildest dreams. As she sat in meetings at GCM to have the latest sales reports presented, looking round at the dozen or more high-powered suits – producers, agents, lawyers, accountants – she could scarcely believe that all of this revolved around her. She realised that she'd turned into a one-woman industry.

She'd also become fabulously rich. Just how rich, she'd lost track of after the first fifty million – every time she discussed things with GCM, the figures had moved up. But there was more than she could possibly spend. Which was when she'd bought the ranch in Santa Ynez and the beachfront house in Malibu – a home next to the ocean had always been her dream, and here she was, having just turned twenty-eight, living it. There were the smart cars, the furnishings, the designer clothes. The never-ending stream of investment decisions. Overnight she had acquired a travelling opera of investment advisers, personal trainers, off-shore lawyers, interior designers, wardrobe consultants, personal shoppers. And at the centre of them all, like a maestro in black tails, Alan Roberts, her personal manager, conducted the entire performance.

The Aphrodisia World Tour had been a whirlwind of mass adulation, with capacity crowds packing out the largest entertainment venues of America, Britain and the rest of Europe. By the time it came to a close, four months after it started, Isis had become the most controversial pop icon in the world.

But even on tour, the doubts had set in. It was as though everything around her, from the weekly sales schedules to the acres of magazine coverage, served as a reminder of *Aphrodisia*'s overwhelming success. Driving through crowd after crowd of adoring fans, instead of revelling in their admiration, she had one thought and one thought alone: how on earth was she ever going to top this? Having ascended the giddying slopes of success with such easy nonchalance, finding herself as though by chance at the very pinnacle of achievement, it began to dawn on her that there was only one way she could go from here.

At first she didn't admit to herself that she was losing her nerve. She tried not even to think about it. Though on her return from tour, when she started work on some new songs, comparing them to the *Aphrodisia* tracks proved irresistible. How did they match up, she agonised. How different should they be, or how similar? What if they bombed? What if all the adulation over *Aphrodisia* turned to derision when she released her next album? Would she turn out to be a one-album wonder?

Hilton had tried helping her through her deepest concerns. All his biggest clients, he reassured her, suffered the same fear – it was one of the hazards of success nobody

ever told you about. Apart from offering his own advice, and
urging her in the direction of Transcendental Meditation,
he'd given her the names of several therapists who'd helped
other clients wrestling with the same demons. But Isis was
determined not to become another self-obsessed, southern
Californian earth muffin, who couldn't open her mouth without spewing psycho-babble. And she couldn't see the point
of sitting about cross-legged on the floor, repeating the same
mumbo-jumbo over and over.

Her third album, *Eros*, had been far from a flop. The title
track ascended rapidly through the charts, and the disc went
platinum after just ten weeks. The album would have been
celebrated as a stunning success if it hadn't followed
Aphrodisia. The problem was that it had. And contrary to
Hilton's frequent appeals to her sense of perspective, there
was no escaping the anticlimax she felt every time she visited
GCM for the latest sales updates. In her own mind, if
nowhere else, she was on a downer.

In retrospect, the Broadway débâcle had merely delayed
the inevitable. Musical impresario Patrick Denholme had
approached her with an invitation to play the lead role in
his new production, *Seventh Heaven*. Hilton had been against
the idea from the start, but she'd lectured him that critical
acclaim was as important to her as the commercial rewards
of another album. In her heart of hearts however she knew
that the appeal of *Seventh Heaven* went much deeper. She'd
believed that her performance in New York would be something that couldn't be measured in terms of record sales. She
wouldn't be living from day to day according to the latest
retail figures. She was putting herself in a position where
nothing she did could be compared to what she'd ever done
before.

The naïveté of this assumption became all too apparent

the morning after opening night. Following an unprecedented blaze of media hype, she found herself subjected to
the most vicious mauling of her life. Apart from the fact
that she had no acting skills whatsoever, wrote the New York
critics, the voice of *Seventh Heaven*'s leading lady lacked all
substance and depth. Its flimsiness betraying a lack of formal
training with every note, commentators were astounded she
had been cast in such an exposed role. Stripped of sound
engineering and special effects, they all concurred, Isis
couldn't sing. Evidently the public agreed. After an initial
six-week run, the show was boycotted by the New York
public, and ticket touts found it impossible to persuade even
Japanese tourists to see the show. Acrimonious publicity
ensued, as cast members fingered her as the cause of all their
troubles. The final indignity came when *Seventh Heaven*
closed its doors after just eight weeks, having lost $5 million;
it was Broadway's biggest flop in years.

She'd returned to LA, wearied and defeated, only to find
herself on the brink of bankruptcy thanks to her long-time
manager and confidant, Alan Roberts, who turned out to
have been systematically defrauding her. She'd had to give
up the ranch at Santa Ynez, the cars, the staff, all the trap-
pings on which she'd so quickly come to depend. The threat
of financial ruin had been accompanied by all the legal wran-
gles, and this collapse of her personal world had in turn
destroyed the last vestige of her inner confidence. She had
sought the fail-safe, white solace of Dr Coke, and for several
months spiralled downwards in sharp descent, before the
final drama of her rescue from death by Hilton Gallo.

The first time she and Hilton had met after her stay in
the substance abuse clinic had been several weeks later in
one of GCM's private dining rooms. He hadn't spared her
feelings, subjecting her to an in-depth grilling on her coke

habit, her rehab programme, her future intentions. She'd realised there was no place to hide, and had told him the whole, unedifying saga including a blow-by-blow account of the state of her finances. Getting back to work, she declared, wasn't just something she wanted to do – it was a necessity if she was to save her home.

Hilton had pretty much gathered most of this already, and in true Gallo style had already been active on her behalf. He'd begun though by lecturing her on a few home truths. Broadway had been a serious mistake. Quite apart from turning out to be the biggest PR disaster of her career, doing Broadway had also meant she'd been out of the music market for a while. And the markets had kept moving. The youth audience who'd made her so big with *Aphrodisia* was now three years older. She needed to be repackaged and relaunched if she was to appeal to former fans and the new record buyers who'd taken their place.

The solution he'd proposed, however, was audacious. A new Isis album was already in development which would carry entirely fresh material written specifically for her instead of by her. More than that, he was in negotiations with British beauty company Berkeley Square about a lucrative endorsement deal for a beauty product range which would have the same evocative name as her new album: Nile. As a brand, Nile was perfect. The name was inextricably linked with her own and it conveyed the same powerful images that had propelled *Aphrodisia* to such meteoric success. What's more, the commercial double-whammy he'd put together had never been attempted before. Nile products would appear on perfume counters amid a wave of endorsement advertising at the same time that *Nile*, the CD, went on sale in record stores worldwide. The endorsement deal alone would deliver enough up-front cash to ensure she could keep her Malibu home. What's more, Hilton had built in what she realised was an insurance policy; she'd be joined, both on the album and the endorsement deal, by an unknown male talent. While the beauty range was to include 'his' and 'hers' products, Hilton's intention was to broaden the market appeal of the new album. What he didn't say, but what she understood implicitly, was that if it all went terribly wrong, she wouldn't be left standing in the spotlight alone.

Not that she'd been wild about the idea of the 'unknown male talent'. Just how unknown was unknown? Hilton had argued that apart from following the well-established convention of a romantic duet, the singer would be British, giving the album extra sizzle in America and added impact in Britain. She wasn't to worry about being overshadowed, this guy would be a complete nobody. In fact, they didn't even know who he was yet, talent scouts were still scouring Britain trying to find someone suitable. In the meantime, he needed her help as he worked up to final contract stage on both the record and endorsement. She must stay clean, make a few carefully selected social appearances, and work to a carefully scripted story he'd devised for the media.

Which was why, in the past few months, she'd been going to parties like last night's *High Society* magazine bash, the kind of remorselessly pretentious ass-kissing *soirée* at which she wouldn't usually be seen dead. But there she'd been, bright-eyed and drug-free, circulating in a room of wall-to-wall celebrity, being seen by all the right people and, in particular, Ariel Alhadeff, CEO of Unum Music, with whom she'd had a brief but significant exchange, underlining her commercial credentials. Then there was the interview with the *Los Angeles Times*, her first in eighteen months, a back-from-the-brink, baring-of-the-soul portrait which had appeared last week and apparently sent out the right signals.

All this, the socialising, the media exposure, even the wheat-grass and lactobacillus yoghurt, she thought of as the Gallo Rehabilitation Programme. Much as it ran contrary to her nature to be little goody-two-shoes, she realised that right now she didn't have a choice.

'Mommy, when will Daddy be back in town?' Holly broke her from her thoughts as they approached school.

'Not till the weekend, honey,' she replied.

'Will he take me to Sea World?' The visit had been prom-ised for several weeks.

'You'll have to ask him. He said he would.'

'I want to see the walrus put his flippers over his face.' She'd seen the ads on TV and was entranced. 'He's so cute!'

Isis smiled at her daughter in the rear-view mirror. Even in her darkest hours, she'd never forgotten how lucky she was to have Holly. There'd been times, to her shame, when she'd been overwhelmed by doubts and fears about her own career. But she'd never gone for long without remembering her daughter and the joy of being her Mom. All her adult life what she'd wanted most of all was someone to love and nurture, someone who'd respond to her with unconditional love. After getting to LA and embarking on her career, the prospect of that had seemed increasingly remote. In fact, she'd almost given up the idea as a hopeless dream. Then Hilton had introduced her to John, and when Holly had been born it had meant far more to her than any amount of public acclaim or adulation; it had been her deepest and most fervent wish come true.

Since regaining control of her life, she and Holly had grown closer. She was doing her best to give her daughter all the love and self-assurance she'd been denied in her own childhood. More than anything, all she wanted was for Holly to grow up as a well-balanced kid.

As they pulled up at the school gates, Isis turned to kiss Holly goodbye.

'Be good,' she told her, 'we'll see you at twelve-thirty.'

'Okay.'

Frank was already out of the car and going round to Holly's side, scanning the area as always before opening her door, and seeing her the few yards to the school gates. The Early Development Centre in Brentwood wasn't exactly the most convenient school to get to, but it did offer the best security. Behind all the lush foliage surrounding the buildings, eight-foot-high walls topped with an electronic security alert provided fortress-like protection for all the celebrity offspring attending the school.

Once Frank was back in the car, Isis did a U-turn before heading back towards Sunset, turning on the radio as she did. She paid barely any attention to a newsreader who was running through the usual litany of politics and crime. Then, out from nowhere, an item suddenly caught her attention. Something about an attack on the Chief Executive Officer of Berkeley Square cosmetics.

'. . . we cross now for a live up-date from London,' the anchorman was saying. Quickly reaching over, Isis hiked up the volume.

'Yes, John,' the voice boomed through the car, 'this is undoubtedly one of the most terrifying attacks carried out in London in recent times and people here are still getting to grips with what happened. It was carried out late last night at Jacques Lefevre's home in Belgravia, an exclusive residential area in central London, not far from Buckingham Palace. Police haven't released all the details yet, but we do know that a gang of five men broke into Mr Lefevre's home and assaulted him. Many people will know that Mr Lefevre's wife is the Gossamer Girl, Helena Defoe.'

Transfixed as she listened to the news item, Isis's eyes were filled with horror.

'What happened next has left the police here visibly stunned,' the reporter's voice faltered. 'They aren't giving out any details at present, but it seems the gang carried out some form of mutilation on Mr Lefevre.'

'Mutilation?' echoed the anchor.

'That's right. As I say, police aren't saying exactly what yet . . .'

'Jesus Christ!' Isis couldn't contain herself.

The Los Angeles anchor was asking about motive, and the London reporter replying, 'So far nobody has claimed responsibility, but police suspect an animal liberation group.' Before the item had even finished, Isis had pulled over to the side of the road.

'Frank! You drive.'

'Right, ma'am.' He climbed out of the back as she slid over into the passenger seat, wrestling her cellphone from her handbag, and dialling. Of all the beauty companies in the world, the crazy bastards had to pick Berkeley Square!

The phone at the other end rang only twice before Hilton Gallo answered.

'I've just heard about Lefevre.' Isis didn't conceal her alarm.

In the back of a GCM limo, on his way directly to the office from Los Angeles International Airport, where he'd just arrived from London, Hilton raised a hand to his face, pinching the bridge of his nose. If there's ever bad news to break, get it out yourself, was his dictum. But he didn't always get there first. He'd only heard the news himself less than ten minutes ago on the car radio, and was still waiting for someone from the office to phone back with the full story.

'It's only just happened, so nobody knows yet who did it—'

'Oh, great!'

'—or why.' He paused for a moment. 'It's important not to jump to conclusions.'

'What other conclusions are there except that there's a bunch of animal rights nutsos on the warpath of Berkeley Square?' Even as she said it, she felt a return of the anxiety that had been at the fringes of her consciousness these past few weeks. Only this time the sensation was closer. It had become an urgent, insistent gnawing in her stomach.

'Like I said, let's wait for more information,' Hilton continued, businesslike. 'In the meantime, I have some extremely good news from London. We've found you a partner.'

In the passenger seat, Isis was weary. She knew the distraction technique. She used it herself. She realised Hilton was trying to get her mind off animal terrorists. But she was too shaken to care about anything else.

'I'll have a video and some photos in the next few days,' Hilton told her. He didn't add that he was looking over some black-and-whites right now, and intended running them past a few colleagues the moment he got to the office. 'I don't think there'll be any problem pulling him over here at short notice.'

'Who is this guy?' She was still to be convinced this was good news at all.

'One of our scouts found him playing at a charity concert in London. Never recorded a thing. I doubt more than a couple dozen people have ever heard of him.' He picked his way carefully across her sensitivities. 'The Berkeley Square people watched him in the studio when he was recording. They reckon he fits the brief. The two of you will be sensational together.'

They ended the conversation with Hilton promising to

call her within the hour for a full update on Berkeley Square. Snapping his cellular phone shut, and slipping it into his jacket pocket, Hilton glanced at his watch. He hoped Elizabeth would get back to him quickly with some reassuring information on the Lefevre incident. The Nile deal was of great personal importance to him, and he didn't intend to let it slip out of his grasp. Not only would it deliver him a pleasingly astronomical personal commission, but much more importantly, with its audacious scope, it would secure his position as the most outstanding agent of his generation. A guru in the world of creative management. It was a ruthless profession, and Hilton had honed his skills to perfection over the years – this endorsement would be the pinnacle of his achievements so far.

He looked again over the photographs of Mark Watson spread out beside him on the back seat. He was perfect, thought Hilton, just perfect. His looks and his voice couldn't have fit the brief any better. On his last night in London, at his Green's hotel suite, the video had been delivered to him by courier, and immediately he'd slipped it in the recorder and watched. Mark had been nervous, of course. There were rough edges to be knocked off – the hair, for starters, would definitely have to go. But the overall package was exactly what they'd been looking for; the guy's dark ruggedness contrasting with Isis's fair hair and feline beauty, his husky bass timbre supporting her mellifluous alto.

He smiled, recalling his meeting with Mark. He'd been much taken by the young man's humility, his gratitude. He wondered how long it would take before he changed. Because once he signed the Berkeley Square contract, he would become suddenly wealthy, and Hilton had had plenty of opportunity to observe at close hand the effect that sudden wealth had on people. There'd be at least a million in it for

Mark from the endorsement, and another million plus coming in from the recording contract, a deal already well advanced. In a very short space of time – call it a month – Mark's life would be transformed. There'd be more money than he'd ever wished for. He'd be the talk of every gossip column and celebrity magazine in the world. He and Isis would soon be splashed on big-city billboards and advertisements in all the top glossies – Berkeley Square was funding a massive awareness campaign, which would culminate in the release of the *Nile* title ballad, destined to be a number one hit single.

Critics sometimes accused Hilton Gallo of playing God with people's lives, dabbling his fingers in the stuff of their souls. That wasn't the way he saw it. Instead, he regarded himself as the facilitator, the mover operating behind the scenes to bring plans to fruition, to make dreams come true. And one thing he knew for certain was that all Mark Watson's most lavish fantasies were about to be realised. In just a few weeks, he was going to be a star.

London
Tuesday, 31 August

'It probably won't come to anything.' Mark swilled the Carlsberg in his glass, across the table from Vinnie.

'What won't?' Vinnie was lighting up a slim panatella.

'What I'm just about to tell you.'

'Well, spit it out.' Vinnie's mouth curled into a broad grin as he exhaled a plume of blue-grey smoke. 'Talk about keeping a man in suspense!'

Swarthy, leather-jacketed, his dark hair brushed back carelessly from his face, Vinnie's man-of-the-world confidence took some getting used to. And his reaction to what had

gone on yesterday afternoon was something Mark had
considered with care. The truth was, Mark was still bemused
by it all. Nothing so exciting had happened to him in, well,
ever.

But even on his way home from the studio yesterday
evening, returning to the familiar landscape after his recording session in Soho, as he looked out at the row upon row of
grey, terraced houses curving into the distance, it was like
coming out of a movie in which he'd played a walk-on part.
It was then that the phrase had come to him, 'It probably
won't come to anything.' Yeah, that was it. There was a certain
gritty realism about it. He couldn't pretend that what had
happened hadn't been wonderful while it lasted. It had been
fantastic! But he supposed he shouldn't count on it coming to
anything. After all, how many people did he know whose lives
had been changed out of all recognition during the course of
a single afternoon?

He'd got home to discover that Vinnie had responded to
one of the messages he'd left on his mobile phone voice-
mail. Then later that night, during the briefest of conversations on a very crackly line, they'd agreed to meet at
Vinnie's local haunt, the Lamb, the following evening.

And here they were. Vinnie had insisted on buying drinks
and sitting down before Mark told him about the events of
the day before.

'I called you in France yesterday,' Mark told him, 'because
I got the weirdest call. A woman from GCM said a bloke
called Hilton Gallo wanted to see me, pronto.' As he spoke,
he scanned Vinnie's face for signs of recognition. The name
Hilton Gallo didn't seem to register with him – but that of
GCM obviously did. Before the look of irritation crossing
Vinnie's face could develop into anything, Mark continued,
'I had no idea who GCM were. I thought they must be a

record company and I reckoned you must have posted them one of the demos—'

'Got to be joking!' snorted Vinnie. 'Wouldn't send out stuff to the competition.'

Mark took a sip of his beer. For a moment he couldn't help contrasting the room in Vinnie's parents' semi-detached in Balham which currently served as his office, with the six floors of glittering opulence in which he'd found himself yesterday afternoon.

'Yeah, well—'

'Just tell them to sod off,' Vinnie interrupted. 'In fact, don't bother. *I'll* tell them to sod off.'

'It's too late for that.'

'How d'you mean?'

'Like I said, they wanted to see me pronto. Like yesterday afternoon.'

Vinnie was leaning back in his seat, a look of incredulity on his face.

'I don't believe it.' He was shaking his head. 'You didn't *go*, did you?'

'Course I did.' Mark looked him in the eye. 'I assumed you'd sent in a demo.'

All Vinnie's customary joviality had evaporated. Now he was shaking his head severely. 'You shouldn't have gone in without speaking to me first.'

'I did try.' Mark was caustic.

'Anyway,' Vinnie shrugged his shoulders, 'complete waste of time. Those guys are major league. Don't waste their time with small fry.'

'Well, thanks for the vote of confidence!'

Oblivious to his sarcasm, Vinnie blew cigar smoke thoughtfully into the distance, before taking another sip of beer. For just a moment, Mark wondered if he was going to drop the subject. As far as he was concerned, he'd said his piece, told Vinnie what he needed to. But Vinnie wasn't letting go.

'So what did they want you for exactly?' Meeting Mark's gaze, his expression was hawkish.

'They were pretty vague.' No need, thought Mark, to tell him Hilton's comment about how it was the kind of opportunity any male vocalist would be excited about.

Vinnie was scrutinising him closely. 'But they must have said *something*!'

'They did mention a kind of duet.'

'Oh, yeah. Who with?'

'Wouldn't say.'

'See?' Vinnie's lips turned in disdain. 'Like I said, total waste of time.'

'Yeah,' nodded Mark. As he'd expected, Vinnie's reaction hadn't been one of effusive congratulation. So he repeated the phrase, 'Probably won't come to anything.'

That, he trusted, closed the subject – at least for the moment. But Vinnie had fixed him with a long, brooding, dark-eyed intensity.

'And if it does,' he said after a long pause, 'they'll have to come through me.'

Mark took a swig of his beer. He had no intention of leading the conversation down *there*.

'So where did they get your demo?' persisted Vinnie. 'One of the record companies?'

Christ, thought Mark, here we go. He shook his head. 'Took it themselves.'

'At one of my gigs?' He flushed with indignation.

'No. At the gig I did for the leukaemia charity—'

Vinnie instantly realised the implications. 'So they're trying to poach you?' he exploded, voice raised and eyes blazing.

'I don't think—'

'What d'you mean, you don't think?'

'They didn't even talk about—'

'The bastards are trying to fucking poach you!' he yelled so loud that people at the other tables were looking round. Not that that bothered Vinnie. 'Well, I hope you told them you already have a fucking manager!' He jabbed Mark in the chest with his forefinger.

'I did mention it.' Mark remained cool.

'And what did they say about *that*?' he demanded.

Mark hadn't wanted this – any of it. He just didn't see the point of arguing about something that probably wouldn't ever happen. But if Vinnie was going to try pushing him around, he wasn't about to cave in.

'They wanted to know about you.'

'They did, did they? Like what exactly?'

'Like what kind of arrangement we have.'

'Arrangement?' Vinnie bellowed. 'How d'you mean, arrangement?'

Mark met his seething expression evenly before saying the word, 'Contract.'

The effect was like unleashing a jet of oil into a raging fire.

'I'll tell you what kind of fucking contract we have!' Vinnie yelled. 'I get you the gigs and you do the fucking singing.'

'It's not me that needs to be persuaded.'

'Of course it is!' he retorted. 'This is all about you.'

Mark shook his head. 'It's about GCM. They're the guys with all the aces.'

On the other side of the table, Vinnie couldn't help himself. Shoving his chair noisily back from the table, he rose to his feet. Seizing Mark by the shoulders, he began to shake him. 'So you're saying you're on their side?'

'It's not that.' Mark pushed back his own chair. 'I can't make GCM—'

'Yes, you can!' Vinnie jabbed a forefinger in his face.

'How?'

'Tell them to go fuck themselves!'

Mark was aware of some of the regulars, including his brother Lloyd, coming over to their table as he stood up. 'Are you seriously saying that if GCM offer me a recording contract, I should tell them—'

'If I don't get my cut, you haven't any choice! You're contractually obliged!'

'Oh, really?' Mark felt his own temper quickly rising. 'You want a cut of something you didn't have anything to do with? Something you tried your level best to talk me out of? Fantastic judgement you've got!'

'That's not the point!' Vinnie ranted. 'I'm your fucking manager!'

Mark delivered a cold, hard stare. 'Then where's the contract?'

Vinnie attempted a lunge at him but was held back by Cyril, the Lamb's manager, who'd seized him by the arm and was telling him to leave off. Lloyd and some of his mates were calling out, 'Give it a break, Vinnie!'

But Vinnie's face was darkening to a deep, dangerous crimson. Despite the efforts of all those trying to restrain him, he'd grabbed hold of Mark's lapels and was pressing his face into Mark's. 'Listen to me, you little shit.' He was shaking him. 'I made you what you are today. You're *my* property. Cut me out of this deal and I promise I'll fucking kill you!'

3

He'd chosen an office block that had been deserted halfway through construction, a vacant concrete and steel tower twenty floors high that stood, a monolith of failure, among all the glittering high-rise office and apartment blocks of London's Docklands. Inside it was a wreckage of scaffolding and decayed boardwalks. Up to the sixth floor internal dividing walls had been constructed, forming a maze of concrete cubes and passages leading nowhere. It was perfect. No security guards on the building nor any closed-circuit television monitors in the area. Visitors could come and go unnoticed. Four possible exit routes from the building. And he'd familiarised himself with its layout. He didn't expect any difficulties today, but he'd planned for them anyway. He always did. Scrupulous preparation was one of the reasons Bengt Larson was wanted by police forces in four different European countries – but had never been caught. It was what would make One Commando the most feared fighting machine in the history of the animal liberation movement. It was why last night's operation against Jacques Lefevre had been such a spectacular success.

He glanced at the hands of his Breitling Aviator. A few minutes before eleven a.m. He was dressed in trademark black, which formed a sharp contrast to the short blond hair and pale blue eyes that belied his Swedish ancestry. Black jeans, black boots, black sunglasses and a black turtle-neck sweater followed the contours of his powerfully built shoulders and well-muscled chest. He spent an average of two hours a day in training to keep in peak physical condition. He always pushed himself to the limits of his endurance, knowing that one day that extra strength, that steel will, could make the difference between life and death.

Others in the movement had quickly recognised in Larson a level of commitment and discipline that was extraordinary. In organisations where fanatical ideologues held sway over constantly changing factions of supporters with big hearts but little stomach for real fighting, Larson had come sharply into focus as a man of action. Someone who could be counted on to make things happen.

Larson was as aware of his strengths as he was contemptuous of the inadequacies of others. His father – who had dreamed of a career in the military but had been rejected because of his asthma – had drilled into him as a child the importance of never showing any pain or fear. Tears were for silly little girls and punishable with a good hiding. It was important to be strong, logical and self-sufficient at all times, and to be better than everyone else at whatever task you were set. Larson had tried his best to live up to those high expectations. He despised all forms of weakness; it was the flabby complacency of his compatriots which had driven him, in his youth, out of Sweden and into the German army. Then when the end of the cold war deprived him of an enemy, he worked his way through various resistance organisations before determining that animal liberation was the last frontier. It was a cause where the battle lines were sharply drawn. A struggle equal to his leadership capabilities – a modern fight for a modern soldier. When he'd been approached by leaders of the Animal Freedom Lobby, a mainstream animal rights group, to set up a secret, paramilitary wing, Larson had agreed, on one condition; that he alone had total control over the organisation. The AFL had been in no position to argue.

He'd masterminded One Commando from the ground up, putting into practice all the lessons he'd learned during intelligence training with NATO forces. He'd begun with his own personal safety. Operating out of a network of safe houses across Europe, he seldom spent more than ten days in any one country, and was never in Britain for longer than three nights. All those he recruited to his élite corps were rigorously screened – he was well aware that the secret services, with too many agents on their hands, were now penetrating animal liberation cells. Which was why, even once they were recruited, he ensured that none of his commandos ever knew more than they absolutely had to. They didn't meet one another except in training for an operation. They didn't even know each other's names. At any one time Larson might be in touch with up to fifty contacts all over the world, none of whom knew the others, or how they fitted into his future plans. He was the master of compartmentalisation and took extreme care to ensure that nobody had any knowledge of the big picture – except for one. And that one was the only man in the movement Larson respected for being as smart as he was.

He'd seen the other man at meetings, not only of the Animal Freedom Lobby, but also of other animal rights and anti-vivisection groups. In the early days of One Commando, he'd gone incognito to the kinds of meetings where he was most likely to find recruits. Whether it was an anti-cruelty conference in Cologne, or a live-animal export protest in Dover, the other man always seemed to be there, his dark, elegant suits and clean-cut features setting him apart from most of the other animal rights sympathisers. Jasper Jones was what he called himself – an assumed name, Larson supposed – and through his contacts he discovered that Jones worked for some kind of advertising agency in London. And although he looked different from most of the AFL crowd, what wasn't in any doubt was Jones's standing among all the people who counted. He had no formal function in the main animal rights groups, but he was treated with evident respect.

Each man had noticed the other, but had deliberately held back until they'd both found themselves at the same meeting in Paris. Larson had taken the empty seat next to Jones's at the back of a crowded conference room, and struck up conversation. Things had progressed rapidly after that. Although both men were wary, Larson soon found that Jones was as driven by a strong desire to make his mark as he himself was. And while he, Larson, was the implementer, the doer, Jones seemed both willing and able to underwrite the cost of One Commando activities, as well as to suggest strategy. Each needing the other, they complemented one another perfectly.

The principled Jones had suggested they agree on certain rules from the beginning: they would only ever take action against a company when there was incontrovertible evidence that it was engaged in torturing 'or abusing animals. And they would only take action against those who were ultimately accountable for torture and abuse. Theirs would be an ethical campaign. A just campaign. The public might not always approve of their methods – but never would One Commando be open to accusations of falsifying evidence, or picking the wrong target.

Last night's operation, the Lefevre attack, had been their first joint effort – and the most daring operation in the animal liberation movement's history. Berkeley Square had become a One Commando 'project' after AFL activities failed; when anecdotal evidence had come to light, a few months earlier, of massive abuse of animals in a Berkeley Square laboratory in Spain, the AFL had written a letter of protest. Berkeley Square had responded with a swift and firm denial.

Realising that clear evidence was needed, it was Jones himself who had travelled to a laboratory outside Madrid and, posing as a delivery man, gained admittance for long enough to fire off some film. His photographs had shown the horribly mutilated and discarded bodies of two chimpanzees, and over a dozen rabbits on which the most barbaric vivisection had all too clearly been carried out. AFL activists had printed fliers with photographs, circulating them directly to the public outside Berkeley Square Head Office. Surely the company couldn't try to pretend now?

But the response from Berkeley Square had, once again, been instant rebuttal. Neither Berkeley Square nor any of its subsidiaries tested on animals, declared a statement issued by the company's media office. All such testing had been abandoned ten years before in accordance with the Code of Practice of the Ethical Pharmaceuticals Manufacturers' Association, to which Berkeley Square was a founding signatory. The mere repetition of such allegations was libellous, and Berkeley Square wouldn't hesitate to take action against irresponsible reporters.

To the AFL's consternation, the Berkeley Square statement had been enough to keep their evidence completely out of the media, with the exception of a few tabloid reports referring obliquely to 'allegations of animal testing'. How was it that photographic evidence could be so completely quashed? There it was in black and white – but no one would believe them! Frustrated at their lack of success, the AFL had asked One Commando to see what they could do.

Last night, One Commando had done just that. Never had such dramatic, direct action been taken. The response had been immediate and massive. The operation had dominated every evening news bulletin on radio and TV and had made the front-page headlines in every newspaper this morning. The work of a single night had created massive awareness – and it had been Jones's suggestion that had transformed what would have been an incident scarcely worth reporting into the most newsworthy event in the country. Jones, with his flair for the theatrical.

None of the group had known before the raid what had been planned. They hadn't needed to. And afterwards, they'd dispersed back to homes outside London and, in several cases, across the Channel. But there was one piece of unfinished business. A piece critical to the ultimate success of the operation, which was the reason he was here this morning.

At exactly eleven there was a noise from the main fire escape. From a secure vantage point he watched as Alan Brent climbed across a steel RSJ into the concrete tower. Slight of build, pale-faced and bespectacled, he seemed the most unlikely recruit to One Commando. But Larson hadn't brought him in for his physique – he'd hired him for his brains. Brent had a genius-level IQ rating and a photographic memory. But more important still was his special facility with information technology. Whether cracking advanced security codes or hacking into computer systems, Brent's abilities were unsurpassed – he was a cybernaut extraordinaire. Last night it had been Brent who'd disabled Lefevre's electronic alarm within thirty seconds, making the entire mission possible. And that hadn't been the only part he'd played. Because it had been his first operation, Larson had given him another assignment to test his mettle. A form of initiation. Brent had been shaken, that much had been plain to see – the shock had been visible in his trembling hands. But he'd gone through with it. He'd followed orders. And now, as instructed, he'd returned.

When Larson stepped out from behind a brick wall, Brent looked up with a start. Then in automatic response he pulled his shoulders straight and brushed a fallen lock of hair back from his face.

Larson nodded briskly, eyes concealed behind the black, reflective sunglasses.

'Good,' he murmured. Having learned to speak English from a series of American-trained teachers in Sweden his accent was a strange Scando-American. 'I have something for you.'

Behind his own thick lenses, Brent's face registered alarm as Larson reached into his bag. God Almighty, Brent wondered, had he walked straight into some trap? But as Larson extracted an envelope, he relaxed. It was of the brown, padded variety and an address had been printed on it. Accepting it, Brent stared at the address and the inscription beneath: 'From One Commando. Two eyes for many.' Realising what was to go inside, he asked, 'You want me to deliver this?' It was more an exclamation of astonishment than enquiry.

Larson acknowledged him with a brisk nod. 'The operation is all over the news. But not the reason. That needs to be changed.'

'But how will they know . . . ?'

This time, Larson extracted from his pocket a slim imitation-walnut case, wrapped in a veneer of protective cling-film. As Brent took it from him, he noticed the discreet gilt engraving, 'Jacques Lefevre', and remembered the case being extracted from Lefevre's jacket pocket the night before. Larson was also handing him a VHS tape labelled, 'Berkeley Square laboratories, Madrid'.

Staring down at the spectacles case and video, Brent swallowed. 'This . . .' he was shaking his head, 'this is going to . . .'

'Blow the place apart?' offered Larson, this time with a wry smile. 'My intention exactly.'

The afternoon editorial conference was already under way when the courier package arrived addressed to Patrick Harlow, Editor, *The Globe*. His secretary, Jenny, knew better than to let any such delivery sit on her desk for more than a minute while Patrick was in his office – conference or not. Tearing open the padded envelope, she found the spectacles case together with a videotape. The case was made of sleek imitation walnut, and she glanced at it briefly before standing to take both items in to Patrick. Glory, hallelujah! she thought. Patrick was always leaving his glasses in offices and sitting rooms – several times a week she'd have to get on the phone to track them down and have them biked back urgently. At last, it seemed, he'd responded to her frequent entreaties – not to mention those of his wife – and had bought a second pair.

She opened his office door without knocking. Around the large table extending from his desk, a spirited debate was going on about tomorrow's lead. Berkeley Square was the story of the week – the month! – and in the twenty-four hours since it had broken, *The Globe* and its tabloid competitors had been engaged in a frenetic scramble to track down family, friends, associates and acquaintances of the Lefevres, cheque-books at the ready, for any revelation – the more salacious the better – so long as it was exclusive. At this moment, *The Globe* had two options, both concerning Jacques Lefevre's wife, Gossamer Girl Helena Defoe, who'd been on a shoot in New York when her husband had been attacked. 'Helena: Supermodel. Mega-bitch' was based on the testimony of a model agency boss, and ex-boyfriend in Paris, who'd described her as a manipulative minx who'd set her sights on screwing her way to the top. 'The Heartbreak of Helena' was the alternative – a friend had described how desperately Helena had wanted Jacques' baby, but she'd had difficulties falling pregnant and was considering IVF treatment.

As Jenny slipped quietly into the room, Heather Samuels, News Editor, was arguing in favour of the IVF story.

'I agree it's a strong angle,' retorted Reg Frith, Deputy Editor, 'but that's not our market. Male readership, remember. They'll go for the "mega-bitch" story. We can run the IVF thing on page two.'

Jenny put the spectacles case and video down in front of Patrick.

'What's this?' Glancing away from Reg, he looked up with a querying expression.

'Just arrived for you. I assumed you'd ordered a new pair?'

Patrick shook his head, picking up the case, glancing at the polished veneer before catching sight of the fine calligraphic script. He opened the lid.

'What the—!' he exclaimed, recoiling from the contents in disgust as, beside him, Jenny's face turned into a portrait of revulsion.

Debate in the office ended abruptly as colleagues looked from Patrick to Jenny to the open spectacles cases. Then curiosity getting the better of them, they leaned or stood to get a glimpse of the cause of the consternation. Inside the spectacles case, gory with congealed blood, was, unmistakably, a pair of human eyeballs. Patrick regarded the horrified expressions of his colleagues for a moment before reaching for the tape. After a glance at its label, he leaned over to the TV in the corner of his office, slipped the tape into the video recorder and pressed 'Play'.

Bursting on to the screen shortly afterwards came images of whole batteries of cages containing rabbits in a laboratory-style warehouse. The date displayed in the corner of the screen was less than a month earlier. Close-up shots showed most of the rabbits had shaven fur and inflamed skin. The eyes of many were so damaged they were clotted with pus. Graphic, harrowing images, showing scenes of the most unspeakable suffering and pain, continued; an anti-vivisectionist's nightmare of stainless steel and surgical brutality. Shaking his head, Patrick fast-forwarded the video, his colleagues continuing to watch with him in stunned silence. The video continued its tour of the laboratory in relentless detail before freezing on a pile of dead rabbits which had been unceremoniously thrown into a plastic wheelie-bin.

Turning back to his colleagues, Patrick looked round at their shaken expressions.

'So much for Berkeley Square's denials.' His own expression was disparaging. 'I think we have our lead. And we'd best call Scotland Yard.'

Los Angeles
Tuesday, 31 August

Hilton Gallo's morning regime was always the same when at home in Los Angeles. He'd rise at five-thirty and swim thirty lengths of the Olympic-length swimming pool he'd had specially constructed in the garden of his Pacific

Palisades home. Having performed his ablutions, he'd spend forty minutes in meditation, focusing on nothing but his TM mantra. By seven-fifteen he'd be prepared for the day ahead, exercised and energised, every sinew in a state of finely tuned readiness, reflexes acute and focus concentrated. Like a samurai warrior, peak performance was what he sought, and the stamina to engage in relentless, bruising battle. Because as head of GCM, every day was a constant struggle in a war without end. Competition had never been more fierce. In Los Angeles alone ICM, CAA and William Morris were all chasing the same deals as GCM. And right across the globe wherever GCM had offices – New York, Toronto, London, Paris, Rome, Madrid, Berlin, Beijing, Tokyo – were theatres of war for which he, as Commander in Chief, had ultimate responsibility.

Over a fruit platter breakfast, Hilton would go through the press. There were the two daily trades, *Variety* and *Hollywood Reporter*, as well as the *Wall Street Journal* and *New York Times* from the east, and the local *Los Angeles Times*. And of course, there were the faxes his secretary Melissa Schwartz sent through first thing when she arrived at the office at six.

By seven-forty-five he'd be on the phone in the back of his chauffeured car, catching the European offices mid-afternoon. As a man of educated tastes and a confirmed Anglophile, despite the milieu in which he operated, Hilton had always believed stretch limousines to be the very epitome of vulgarity. Even Rolls-Royces smacked, to him, of the nouveau riche and the crass. German and Italian marques he found respectively lacking in charm and impossibly flash. Which was why he set out to work in a Bristol, that exceptionally rare and luxurious hand-crafted motorcar that was the very model of subtlety. He'd had his Bristol customised for the work he did – a phone and television screen in the back seat enabling him to video-conference with colleagues around the world. What it lacked in panache, he used to think – and many found its appearance bland – it more than made up for in the originality of its design, and its constant ability to surprise. It was a car with which he felt in complete accord.

Some mornings he might go to the Peninsula for a breakfast meeting. For those deals too covert to discuss even at the office, he'd be driven to any one of half a dozen hotels in which a suite had been booked using an alias. But this particular morning, as he headed towards GCM headquarters, he received his first telephone call of the day from Elizabeth.

'I've just had an early-warning call from Stan Shepherd,' she told him. Stan worked as Media Relations Chief in their London office.

'Yes?'

'The story's about to break over there that "One Commando" have claimed responsibility for the Lefevre attack.'

'Along with a dozen others.'

'They sent Lefevre's eyes to the Editor of *The Globe* along with a videotape showing scenes of rabbits being used in lab tests, allegedly by Berkeley Square in Madrid.'

Hilton didn't miss a beat as he pulled a grimace. He hadn't known about the eyes. Nobody had. So that was what the British police had been keeping under wraps. He instantly thought what Isis's reaction would be when she got *this* news. She'd beaten him to the phone when the story first broke. He couldn't let that happen a second time. He had to preempt anything she might pick up from the media. He was determined that this endorsement would be the success he'd planned. His personal stake in it was too great to let some adverse news spoil it now. He glanced at his watch,

'I want you to bring my nine-thirty forward an hour.'

'Ross, Andy, Neil,' she confirmed the attendees, her own presence a given.

'Plus Leo,' he added their head of global media relations – he would definitely be needed after this latest news. 'And pull together a risk assessment on One Commando, won't you.'

'Do I speak to the Metropolitan Police in London?'

'They won't speak to us. Try Francis Hanniford at Berkeley Square. Human Resources Director. Lefevre has seconded him to liaise with Scotland Yard. He's also supposed to keep us in the loop.'

'Understood.'

'Monitor all news broadcasts till I get in. Let me know the moment the story breaks over here.'

The GCM building on Sunset Boulevard was a massive six floor block in white marble and dark, reflective glass, fronted by eight huge fountains with extravagant, five-metre-high plumes. Royal palms swayed and the flags of a dozen GCM territories fluttered outside. Constructed in the late eighties as a deliberate, glittering statement of corporate machismo, a more triumphal totem of GCM's success would have been impossible for architects to conceive. No matter how much it offended his own sensibilities, Hilton knew that he wasn't the audience being played to. As the Bristol pulled to a halt inside the Director's entrance, next to the executive suite elevator, he opened the back door and stepped out. Less than thirty seconds later, he emerged from the elevator on the top floor, turning left and heading towards his private meeting room. It was exactly eight-thirty as he opened the door.

The meeting was tight but high-powered. Ross McCormack was head of endorsements, and Andy Murdoch his counterpart for music. Neil Ferreira, one of Andy's top people, was working on the Isis deal and Leo Lebowitz controlled the media machine that lay at the heart of all GCM activities. All conversation stopped as soon as Hilton came into the room. He nodded once to them all, before sitting down at the head of the table. Elizabeth was already on his right-hand side, briefing pad open for notes.

'Two issues here,' he began in his quiet, precise tones. Holding up a finger he said, 'One: the commercial fallout from the Berkeley Square deal. And', raising a second finger, 'two: the security implications for Isis.'

Across the table, his eyes met Ross McCormack's. Ross looked every inch the advertising man he used to be. His crew-cut hair was very blond, and his thick-rimmed glasses very red, giving him the appearance of someone out of a Roy Lichtenstein cartoon. When he spoke, he was strong and persuasive.

'The starting point is that we were conscious of the animal testing issue before we even negotiated. The legal team in London checked out Berkeley and all its subsidiaries as part of our usual ethical vetting procedure. There is no question that any of them use animal testing – they haven't for more than a decade.'

'What about the video?' asked Hilton.

McCormack shrugged. 'Who knows where that came from. Wherever it is, it's not a Berkeley Square facility. I double-checked the due diligence report before this meeting – Spain was cleared. Anyway, yesterday Lord Bullerton, Berkeley Square Chairman, read out their denial in person, outside Berkeley House, accompanied, at Leo's suggestion,' he nodded to his colleague, 'by his wife. Lady Bullerton is on the Council of the RSPCA, a fact that wasn't missed by the media covering the event.'

'So the Madrid video's just some hoax?'

'An attempt at justification,' nodded McCormack. 'Berkeley's version of events has been accepted by most commentators, including animal rights groups. They've also received powerful support from the Ethical Pharmaceuticals Manufacturers' Association. But the best thing they've done to validate their statement is to issue an open invitation to the media to visit any Berkeley Square production site anywhere in the world. That kind of transparency,' he shook his head, 'it's impossible to beat.'

Hilton looked over at Leo Lebowitz. 'Hasn't been much commentary over here. It's been a British thing so far?'

Lebowitz was nodding.

'How has it been playing in the UK?'

Lebowitz, forty-something, and the only bearded man in the agency, had the smiling, enigmatic air of a religious mystic.

'Immediately after the attack,' he replied, 'questions were raised about Berkeley. It seemed inconceivable that the attack could have gone ahead without any justification whatsoever. But things changed pretty quickly. Bullerton's statement laid to rest all but the hard-liners. Of course, the video could change things—'

'Has The Globe released it yet?'

Lebowitz was shaking his head. 'The police have it now. They're not letting anyone near it – say it's too disturbing.'

'How is this going to affect the timing of Nile?' Hilton asked Ross McCormack.

'If there is a delay we're talking a week, ten days max. Berkeley just want to get this whole thing behind them.'

'Does that gives us leverage to up the stakes?'

McCormack shook his head. 'There's no more room. We got a great deal out of Berkeley Square already. But I do think we need to add an addendum on security.'

Hilton was nodding, before looking over at Elizabeth.

'Where are we on a risk assessment?'

'Scotland Yard have appointed a Detective Inspector Bennett to the investigation – supposed to come highly recommended. Specialises in underground eco-terrorism.'

Hilton's expression was grave.

'Francis Hanniford was very helpful.' She glanced at Hilton. 'Turns out he was at Eton with the British Home Secretary and has been given direct access to someone high up in Scotland Yard – I would think Bennett or one of his reports.'

Around the table the others regarded her with intense expressions.

'Hanniford's faxing over the intelligence he's received on One Commando. Apparently they're led by a renegade former NATO army officer called Bengt Larson.'

'Danish?' prompted Lebowitz.

'Swedish. Hanniford says that Scandinavians dominate militant eco-terrorist groups in Britain.' Elizabeth recalled his authoritative public school accent. 'Larson is wanted by Interpol on previous charges, so this isn't a one-off.'

Hilton had raised his hands to his temples.

'Hanniford said the Lefevre operation was carried out so effectively the group didn't leave a trace of themselves behind.'

'Was there *any* reassuring stuff to come out?' Lebowitz wanted to know, exasperated.

Elizabeth nodded. 'Hanniford did say there's no evidence that One Commando's activities extend outside the UK. And Larson isn't known to have been involved in activity anywhere outside Europe.'

'Still doesn't give us much to reassure her,' remarked Lebowitz.

'Quite,' Hilton agreed looking round at his colleagues. 'In a few minutes I'm going to have to break the latest news to her before she hears it somewhere else.' He met their expressions gravely. 'She's not going to let this go.'

McCormack's eyebrows twitched with alarm. 'You're not seriously contemplating withdrawal—'

'Difficult to make a judgement call with what we've got so far.' Hilton regarded him evenly. 'But Isis's safety has to be our top priority.'

The meeting ended a short while later on an inconclusive note. Everyone knew what had to be done. But there was no getting away from the latest disturbing turn of events. They would proceed with caution, they decided, while trying to find out more about One Commando. Hilton had the hardest task, preparing Isis for the sensational news about to scandalise the US media and trying to persuade her not to pull the plug on Berkeley Square. Ross McCormack was dispatched to see Blake Horowitz, the company lawyer, to review security clauses in Isis's agreement with Berkeley Square. And Elizabeth Reynolds had a phone call to place to Mark Watson; she was to arrange for him to come to Los Angeles without delay.

4

Isis sank back into the plush cream sofa. On the table in front of her, in an intricately patterned Royal Doulton cup, was a drink of camomile tea. As always when she visited Hilton, she couldn't help responding to the air of tranquillity that always prevailed in his office, in marked contrast to the ferocious activity throughout the rest of the GCM building. The uncluttered spaces, fresh-cut flowers and clear light were part of it, but the real source of the calm was Hilton himself, sitting opposite, cool and dark in charcoal Armani, his expression serene. Not for the first time in the years he'd represented her, she felt more as though she were on a visit to her psychiatrist rather than in a meeting with her agent.

'I haven't told you this before,' she met his gaze, 'but ever since we first talked about the endorsement I was . . . anxious about it.'

Hilton raised his eyebrows. 'Was there a specific—'

'No,' she shook her head, 'nothing like that. It was more a deep-down feeling.'

Hilton brought his hands together and raised them, prayer-like, to his lips.

'Then all this blows up,' she continued, 'and it just seems to prove everything I'd picked up from the start.'

'What are you saying?' He was solicitous. 'That it was a mistake to sign the Berkeley Square endorsement?'

'Yes.' She met his eyes briefly before looking into the distance. 'Well, maybe,' she shrugged. 'Maybe it was a mistake. Maybe I should pull out now before it gets any closer.'

'It's understandable you feel this way,' he responded.

'But?'

'And I've always respected your intuition. You know that.'

'But?' she persisted.

'Well,' he met her eyes with a smile, 'you had very good reasons for signing the endorsement. What I must ask you now is if any of those reasons have changed?'

Leaning back in the sofa, she closed her eyes. Hilton always went for the analytical approach, but analysis was something she'd been incapable of ever since hearing of the Lefevre attack on the car radio. The news item had come as a hateful confirmation of her own uneasy feelings. Worse. While her emotions, until then, had been unfounded and ill-defined, now they had a clear and terrible focus.

Within hours, every news broadcast had been full of the gruesome twist to the Lefevre attack – the delivery to *The Globe* newspaper of the spectacles case containing Jacques Lefevre's eyes. The media revelled in the ghoulish horror of it, photographs or video-footage of the now-famous spectacles case carried in all the headlines. The footage of One Commando's video had also been described – only to have its implicit accusations fiercely rebutted by Berkeley Square who had arranged immediate media tours of its facility in Spain. While journalists had failed to find anything like the horrors depicted on the One Commando video, had Berkeley Square really disclosed the whole truth?

Isis's fax spewed out pages from Berkeley Square – copies of media releases about the condition of Jacques Lefevre, as well as categorical denials about the use of animals in product testing. Alone in Malibu, Isis had been absorbing all this in a state of growing terror, when Hilton phoned to say they should meet.

Now, in the reassuring serenity of his office, as he worked through the reasons they'd agreed to the endorsement, everything felt so different. He talked about how Berkeley Square had delivered the money she'd needed to hold on to her home. How the deal would deliver a huge publicity advantage to the launch of her new album. Neither of those reasons had changed, she had to agree. He then went into why she shouldn't over-react to news of the Lefevre attack; did it make sense to call off one of the most important deals of her career over an isolated incident on the other side of the Atlantic? One Commando was a London-based group whose past activities had all been carried out in Britain – there was no reason to suspect they were about to launch attacks in America. What's more, Lefevre was the only person they'd ever assaulted.

Hilton was, as always, immensely persuasive. By the time he'd finished, Isis felt foolish for even contemplating backing out. For a while she sat, regarding him in silence, before she murmured, 'What you're saying . . . I wouldn't disagree with any of it. From a rational point of view, of course I should stay in the game. It's just that this isn't about reason or logic.'

He raised his eyebrows, queryingly.

'It's about instinct. My instinct.' She shook her head. 'And that hasn't changed.'

'You don't seriously believe Berkeley Square actually does test on animals, do you?' he wanted to know.

'Maybe they do,' shrugged Isis, 'but I doubt it.'

'Perhaps you have a sense that what happened to Lefevre could happen to you?'

'Perhaps,' she nodded, 'or maybe worse.'

Hilton leaned back slightly in his chair, exhaling slowly. He'd already guessed that Isis's response might be bound up in her ultimate fear of having her traumatic past revealed. Just as he knew that, if it were so, no matter how compelling his arguments, they would be of little use.

Meeting his eyes, Isis tried to smile through her grim self-consciousness. She had told Hilton everything when he'd first taken her on as a client. He had insisted he needed to know if he was to protect her effectively – and he'd never let her down yet. When she'd come to LA, she'd wanted to leave her past way behind her, yet because Hilton was the man he was, she'd found the experience of telling him her story powerfully cathartic. Having been brought up as a Catholic, Isis understood the power of confession. And when she'd confessed to Hilton it was as though the act had itself been a form of expiation, and after it she'd been free to live her new life. Yet images of the past still haunted her. No matter how much she sought to exorcise them, they would return, unbidden, at odd moments of the day and night when they were least expected. One particular scene would play and replay, reaching out across nearly two decades to fill her with apprehension whenever it returned.

It was a baking mid-summer Sunday, the blazing sunshine exposing that run-down suburb of Miami in all its rank ugliness; the rusted cars, the boarded-up windows, the over-grown gardens and fetid stench of dog excrement. This was where the Carbonis had ended up after emigrating to the land of the Almighty Dollar six years before, encouraged by earlier émigrés from Lucca, Italy. There was money to be made in America, they'd been told – easy money. To Isis's father, whose dreams extended well beyond the suffocating city walls of Lucca, the invitation had been irresistible. After a few months of reality, broken promises of employment, and a labourer's wages, he'd started to realise the move had been a mistake. But Giovanni Carboni was too proud, too stub-born to go back. Instead, he'd gone to work for Amtrack, and his wife Marina had taken in ironing, and they learned to survive in the new country by acting as though they'd never left the old one.

They began to observe customs to which they'd paid little regard until then – like Mass on a Sunday. Isis's mem-ories of those Sundays were of endless, incomprehensible incantations while she sat on an uncomfortable pew, in tight, scratchy clothing, the sharp tang of naphthalene exuding from her father's only suit. Although he invoked the names of both Father and Son with exasperating frequency, her father had no religious feeling, and it was all her mother could do to keep up the daily grind, with-out troubling herself about metaphysical questions. But going to Mass reassured them both of their roots, gave them a chance to spend time afterwards with others from Lucca and Florence and beyond. Traditions that had been of little significance back home took on a special meaning here. Having failed to make his dreams of untold wealth come true, her father had retreated into the strict orthodoxy of the old country, where a man's job was to earn a living by the sweat of his brow, and the woman's was to take care of the family, and acknowledge her husband as her lord and master.

Giovanni didn't believe in lavishing affection – that was for women. He regarded himself instead as the one who set the rules and saw that they went unbroken, imposing all the authority at home that he was unable to express at work. His temper worn by ceaseless toil, he was a man whose fury was easily provoked – and nothing inflamed him more than sexual deceit, a characteristic he regarded as uniquely female. After a few glasses of Chianti he would rail at the fickleness of women, hammering on the table about how it was their treachery that wrecked marriages and tore families apart. Two of his friends from back home had lost their darkly attractive wives to rich, blond Americans – the women were nothing better than whores, he'd declare, challenging his wife with a furious expression she knew better than to contradict. Isis was left in no doubt that as long as she lived under his roof, her own behaviour would be watched with all the patriarchal zeal of an obdurate archbishop, and the faintest stirrings of sexuality would be subjected to her father's wrathful scrutiny.

On this particular Sunday, the Carbonis had been invited to the Bazzanis after Mass. Most Sundays, several of the families would get together, the women arriving with polenta, salami, gnocchi and torte – always torte! – and the men bringing bottles of cheap beer and wine. The afternoons would be whiled away in an alcoholic daze amid the reassuring buzz of Italian. Isis had always found these sessions tedious and now, at twelve, having reached that awkward stage between childhood and maturity, had begun to resent the endless hours sitting in the corner, gangly and uncomfortable. So this Sunday, when she pleaded a headache, to her relief and excitement her parents said she could stay at home. Her mother gave her an aspirin and prepared her lunch. Her father sternly warned her not to leave the house. She stood, looking woebegone and in pain, until the moment they closed the front door behind them, at which point she pranced through the house on her tiptoes with glee. All she wanted was time alone. Time unfettered. In particular, time to try out something new.

Two afternoons before, when the gym class at school had finished, she'd been walking past Gabby Trinci's locker. Beautiful Gabby, with the deeply tanned skin and sloe eyes and budding figure. As she'd walked by, she'd noticed that Gabby had left her locker door open and there, sticking out of it, was the end of her brassière strap. Gabby wasn't the only girl in the class already wearing a bra, but her intricately patterned black lace underwear was the most beautiful. Of all the girls in the class, she was the one Isis envied most – there was something effortless about her burgeoning womanhood that was far removed from Isis's own confused feelings of anxiety and guilt. The glimpse of the bra strap conjured up something irresistibly sophisticated; the tantalising promise of what might be. And alone beside the lockers, Isis had found herself doing something she'd never done before. She'd hardly been able to help herself. Opening the locker door, she'd quickly snatched the garment and shoved it in her pocket before continuing on her way.

She meant to return it, of course. She hero-worshipped Gabby and wouldn't want to do anything to upset her. Early next week she'd leave it somewhere it would be found and returned to its rightful owner. Meantime, it was hers to savour.

In the Carboni household, there was no question of her being allowed to wear a brassière. She knew better than to even suggest such a thing. Despite her desperate yearnings and prayers for her body to blossom like Gabby Trinci's, it hadn't yet happened. And until it did, she would be denied her sexuality. Not so long before, her father had returned home to find her putting away her mother's lingerie after a trip to the launderette. Even though it was baggy and discoloured and nothing like Gabby Trinci's pretty black underwear, perhaps there had been a certain longing in her eyes because her father, responding to her expression, had stormed over to where she was kneeling, picked her up and wordlessly thrown her out of the bedroom. The only time she'd put on make-up, two years ago, he'd marched her to the kitchen sink and rubbed her face raw with a dishcloth.

But today she had Gabby's beautiful brassière and her parents had gone out for the afternoon! Quickly stripping off, she went to her wardrobe and extracted the stolen treasure from where she'd hidden it inside a jersey. She held it awhile, caressing it with her fingertips, closing her eyes as she felt the touch of it on her cheeks. Then, with some difficulty, she put it on, hooking it at the back and using tissues to fill it out. Her body lacked Gabby's firm pertness, but as she looked at herself in the mirror above her mother's makeshift dressing table, she could still admire the way the fabric enclosed her body, the patterns where the black lace pressed close to her skin.

She brushed her hair, all the while imagining she was Gabby, before reaching inside a drawer to find her mother's special lipstick – the deep red one she only wore to go to church or on special occasions. She held the gold tube like the illicit treasure it was, before twisting up the lipstick and running it lightly over her lips, careful to avoid any smudging. She didn't get it exactly right first time, and had to tidy it up, but she was pleased with the effect. The blonde hair and the deep, red lipstick; the blackness of the bra against her pale skin. She was so absorbed in her reflection that she didn't hear the front door opening, or the footfall on the carpet. So engrossed in this thrilling, grown-up image of herself that she was only aware of the door opening when it was too late. She turned round to find her father and Mr Bazzani standing, staring at her. She knew, in that instant, there would be hell to pay.

She'd been right. One way or another, it had been pay-back time ever since the horrific events following the opening of that door. But no one else knew it – no one, that is, except Hilton and Leo Lebowitz, who needed to know all of GCM's clients' darkest secrets. Back in Florida, her father and Mr Bazzani were now both dead, their ugly secret gone with them to the grave. Her mother was living in a retirement village, slowly forgetting herself, a victim of Alzheimer's. And here in Los Angeles her own version of an uneventful childhood in an anonymous suburb of Miami had long been accepted as the truth.

Regarding Isis carefully across his office now, Hilton wondered how best to salvage the Berkeley Square deal which he still believed was in her best interests, but which had gone so shaky. When he did eventually speak his tone was entreating. 'Can we agree, at least, not to commit ourselves to any immediate course of action on Berkeley Square?'

'You're stalling?' There was a note of cynicism in her voice.

'Only until we get more information.'

There was a long pause before Isis sighed. 'I'm just not happy about it.'

It was, they both understood, a reluctant agreement.

'I know you're not happy,' Hilton tried his best to reassure her, 'and believe me, I want to get this resolved one way or the other as soon as possible. All I'm asking is for a little time to consider our options.'

Our options, thought Isis sceptically. There were some things that just couldn't be put neatly into boxes to be wrapped up and stashed away. Some things that were just too dark, too all-consuming, that would resist all attempts at containment. And for the first time since beginning her new life in California, twelve years ago, she couldn't avoid the visceral sensation that she was about to be engulfed by the afflictions of her own, troubled past.

Los Angeles
Wednesday, 8 September

Mark pushed the airport trolley carrying his single suitcase through the green route at Los Angeles airport. He'd always thought that when people flew halfway round the world they were supposed to end up jet-lagged. But he didn't feel tired at all. Right now he was more excited than he had been for years. This was the first time he'd flown transatlantic, the first time he'd been up at the front of the plane; two firsts in twenty-four hours and he'd loved every minute of it: the luxurious seats, as much champagne as you could drink, being waited on hand and foot by drop-dead-gorgeous hostesses. Now as he made his way through the chaos of passengers and trolleys in the Arrivals hall he saw a line of greeters holding boards, one of which had his name on it.

'This way.' The Hispanic driver took charge of his trolley when he announced himself. 'Only the one luggage?' He was surprised.

'Didn't have much time to pack.'

'Plenty stores in Beverly Hills,' grinned the other.

Mark laughed. Ever since he'd checked-in at Heathrow he'd been made to feel important. Very important. And he felt more important still as the driver pushed his trolley in the direction of a stretch Cadillac and began unlocking the boot. Mark stared at the car in astonishment. You hardly ever spotted cars like that in London – you only ever saw them on TV at the Oscars or Golden Globe awards. Picking up his suitcase, he began carrying it over to the boot of the car – but the driver insisted he put it down, and let him do the rest.

'You picking up a group of us?' asked Mark, staring at the car as if it was too much to hope for.

The driver looked confused, glancing about them. 'You come single?'

Mark nodded.

'Then just you,' he confirmed, opening the door for Mark to climb inside.

It was dark and cavernous and the back seat was plush as a sofa. Mark glanced about, taking in the dark glass, the telephone, the TV – already switched on with a control set into the side panel.

'You want a drink?' The driver was behind the wheel. 'Bar is under the table.'

He glanced down at the door under the table to the left before opening it curiously. A half bottle of champagne and miniatures of every conceivable alcoholic drink were crammed inside, together with cans of mixers. At three in the afternoon he didn't suppose he should be drinking anything more dangerous than Coke. Then he thought, why the hell not? This might be the only time he got to ride in one of these things, so he might as well celebrate. Cracking open the bottle of champagne, he helped himself to a glass – real crystal, he noticed – before settling back into his seat.

As he raised the champagne flute to his lips, he looked out of the window at the passing city and offered a silent toast to Los Angeles.

The last week had been like one of those thrilling roller-coaster rides that just got better and better. For all his innate wariness about events that seemed too good to be true, there was no doubting that things were happening in his life. He remembered how he'd taken his Mum and Lloyd out to dinner on his last night in London. They'd gone to Le Palais in Covent Garden, a restaurant his mother had always liked the look of, but believed was far too expensive for the likes of them. 'Aren't you being a bit extravagant, dear?' she'd asked, when he'd announced where he was taking them. Mark had just laughed. GCM had paid him the equivalent of four months' salary from OmniCell. Four months was what he'd told Elizabeth it would take him to find a similar job when he came back. All his expenses in Los Angeles were to be paid for and if he signed various contracts that were 'in negotiation', he stood to make big money, Elizabeth had assured him.

How much was big money, he'd wondered? Since he'd got into this singing business he'd often thought about how much he'd get for a first album. Of course, he was an unknown and any label would be taking a risk. But he reckoned he'd definitely make ten grand and possibly up to twenty. Mark had never been one to count his chickens – he had no idea if he'd make any money at all in LA. What he knew for sure was that GCM had deposited nearly five grand in his bank account. He'd never had so much money to his name and he intended to enjoy it – he might not have this kind of cash again.

As he sat in the back of the Cadillac sipping champagne, he looked out of the window at the unfamiliar city, and realised he was in a different world now. On first impressions, Los Angeles wasn't anything special – just a vast, bewildering sprawl of freeways and warehouses, commercial estates and unfamiliar road signs. Though as they got off the freeway and drove up Santa Monica Boulevard in the direction of Beverly Hills, things began to change. Towering royal palms swayed in the afternoon breeze, glitzy office blocks in black glass and white concrete rose from lush, manicured lawns, gigantic movie billboards and signposts to Century City communicated the unmistakable combination of movies and money and corporate power.

Leaning forward, he asked the driver, 'Which hotel am I staying at?'

'Mammon,' came the reply.

Unusual, thought Mark, to name a hotel after the much-maligned god of money. But, hey, this was Los Angeles.

'Good place?'

The driver was shaking his head. 'Heeeey! Lots of big stars there!' He grinned in the rear-view mirror.

Mark smiled, taking another glug of champagne. Perhaps he'd get to meet some big celebrities, he thought with a thrill of anticipation. That would be something to write home about.

He could hardly believe his eyes when they pulled up at the hotel which turned out to be called Chateau Marmont. Was this really where he was to stay? It was like a private castle at the end of its steep driveway, with its gates and turrets and secluded courtyard gardens. Shown to the second floor, he found himself not in a room, but a suite, with a lounge, balcony and well-equipped kitchen – this must be costing GCM a packet.

On his coffee table, after his porter had gone, he found an envelope from GCM awaiting him. If he'd like to take an hour to relax, Elizabeth had written, a car would be coming to collect him at four for a meeting with Hilton. And, almost as a PS, here was his five hundred dollars cash per diem. Mark hadn't done Latin at school, but right at this moment he didn't much care, studying the wad of unfamiliar dollar bills before undoing the paper clip that held them together and throwing them into the air above his bed. The fizz might have gone to his head, but he was enjoying this, he reckoned – every bloody minute of it!

By four-thirty that afternoon, showered, shaven and still waiting for jet-lag to kick in, he was being whisked up in the GCM elevator to Hilton Gallo's office. This time he'd been prepared for an impressive display of GCM agency testosterone, but all the same he hadn't been able to help marvelling at the building, with its massive fountains and towering blocks of marble and reflective glass – it made GCM's Soho offices seem modest by comparison. Hilton Gallo was sitting alone at a meeting table in the middle of an office the size of a tennis court. When Mark came in, Gallo rose to his feet, stepped across to him and shook his hand with that strangely priest-like manner of his. Once again, as Mark met his eyes, he couldn't avoid a disconcerting sensation of the man's omniscience – as though he could see right through Mark into his very soul.

'Was your flight comfortable?' Hilton was solicitous as he gestured towards a chair opposite where he'd been sitting.

Mark enthused about the champagne and the air hostesses for a while, and then Hilton was asking him about the hotel. He hoped everything was to his liking? Were his rooms all right? Was there anything else he needed? Mark found it hard to believe that the boss of GCM, a man who obviously had wealth and power beyond his comprehension, was bothering to take such a close interest in his personal well-being. Once again, he felt a return of the uncertainty he'd experienced during their roof-top chat, the feeling that he didn't really know where he stood with this super-smooth operator.

'Tell me,' Hilton asked, having confirmed that every aspect of his accommodation at Chateau Marmont was to his satisfaction, 'what do you make of Isis?'

The question caught him slightly by surprise. 'Well, I'm a big fan,' he said, though that was a given. 'I bought *Aphrodisia* when it came out. I used to do covers of some of the tracks – always goes down well with the punters.' He shrugged, finding it hard to put into words what he thought of Isis. 'She's a legend. Amazing. I wanted to see her when she came to Wembley, but the tickets were a bit steep. Forty-eight quid each!'

Hilton nodded sympathetically.

Mark chose not to mention the poster of Isis he'd had taped to his bedroom wall when he was a teenager – no need to sound adolescent. Plus, he reckoned, he'd been no different from any other young bloods in fantasising about her. Sexual fantasy was, after all, what Isis was all about.

'There was the Broadway thing,' Hilton was saying now.

'Oh, yeah, read about it. But that was Patrick Denholme. His music's crap and everyone's sick of him.' The words tumbled out unchecked, before he suddenly remembered who he was talking to. Hilton was probably Denholme's agent.

'I mean,' he quickly corrected himself, 'it's not so much that it's crap—'

A rare look of amusement passed over Hilton's features. 'It's all right,' he held up his hand, 'I don't want you to censor what you say.' Their eyes met for a moment before Hilton continued, 'Of course, you know about the personal problems Isis had. She's through them now.'

Mark was shaking his head. Why was Hilton so keen to shoot the breeze about Isis? He thought he was here to discuss a recording contract.

'There were some financial difficulties. Substance abuse. Often goes with the territory.'

'I didn't know about them.'

'Her last album, *Eros*, did very well, but didn't reach the same heights as *Aphrodisia*.' Hilton was looking for a response.

Mark shrugged. 'How could it? No one's ever produced two albums in a row with half a dozen number ones each.'

Hilton leaned back in his chair and regarded Mark thoughtfully for a moment. 'It's good that you think like that.'

'Just common sense.'

'Maybe. But when you've achieved an extraordinary level of success, it's easy to lose sight of these things, to get the feeling you're losing your grip.'

There was a long pause before Hilton asked, finally, in an even voice, 'So I take it you'd have no problem recording an album with her?'

For a while, Mark was disoriented, experiencing the mental equivalent of being swept up in a crowd of Chelsea supporters and hurtled, out of control, towards the barriers. 'Me?' he managed after a while, 'I mean . . . Isis!'

'Let me be candid with you,' Hilton remained soft spoken, 'and everything said between us remains inside these four walls.' He rested his perfectly manicured hands on the table in front of him. 'Since *Eros*, Isis has had a difficult time of it in America. In Britain and Europe, as you have observed, her star is still very much in the north. You'll recall our conversation about celebrity being a product we manufacture? Isis's is a classic case in point. She's a brand that needs to be repackaged and relaunched in the local market, and refreshed elsewhere. Which is where you come in.'

Mark was still floundering as he tried getting his mind round this one, his expression a mixture of shock and elation. 'But my voice isn't anything like hers.'

'Which is exactly why we believe you'd make such a successful partnership.'

'What if Isis doesn't agree?'

'She's already heard the tracks you recorded in London. She liked them very much.' He paused deliberately, waiting for any further concerns, before saying, 'And there's another deal we need to discuss. You're familiar with Berkeley Square, yes?'

'The perfume people?' Mark met his watchful expression. 'My Mum wears Nightingale. Always has.'

'Core brand,' confirmed Hilton, 'what they built the beauty division on. They make a whole range of Nightingale products which are very popular with mature women. They're also a major pharmaceutical drugs manufacturer, though that isn't something we need to concern ourselves with. What Berkeley Square want to do now with their beauty range is reach a much younger audience, broaden their market base, which is why they're about to launch a radically different product line called Nile. There are still a few territories where the name hasn't been registered so it's not to be mentioned to anyone. We can't risk it leaking – the name is just perfect. Especially,' Hilton's eyes were gleaming now, 'because it will also be the name of your new album.'

Mark felt a rush of adrenaline.

'Nile is an aspirational brand,' continued Hilton, 'targeting eighteen-to-forty-year-old upwardly mobiles. And it's being manufactured in "his" and "hers" ranges. Berkeley Square have planned a major advertising initiative to support

the launch, focusing on the endorsement by the hottest duo
in the pop world,' he gestured towards Mark, 'Isis and you.
We're talking three hundred prime site billboards across the
UK and Europe, and a further five hundred in the States.
Magazine ads running in fifty glossies from *Vogue* down, plus
blanket TV and cinema support. The media spend behind
Nile will be higher than for any beauty launch in history.
They've really got to make this endorsement work for them.'

Already overwhelmed by the prospect of recording an
album with Isis, these new revelations left Mark spinning.

'What would an endorsement of . . . Nile actually mean?'

Hilton nodded carefully. 'Strategically, it delivers an
unprecedented opportunity to raise awareness of Isis and you
at the launch of your album. We're talking here about the
equivalent of a fifty-million-dollar advertising campaign.'

Mark shook his head, scarcely able to take it all in.

'Practically, it'll mean several photo sessions with Isis and
you and a number of appearances – nothing onerous.'
Leaning forward he murmured, 'Of course, and this is only
if Isis and you decide to go ahead with it, it would also mean
good money, Mark, very good money. Your own share would
be something in the region of one point three, one point
five million. That's US,' he added quickly.

The conversation had long since left the stratosphere of
Mark's wildest fantasies. But this latest disclosure was just
too much for him. 'One point three million dollars?' he
almost stammered. 'I can't believe this!'

Hilton permitted himself a smile. 'I'll provide you with a
full breakdown of royalty rates in our main territories. But
by way of a ball-park figure you can expect at least another
million from the album – that's being very conservative. If
it goes off as we're planning, you'll be heading towards the
double digits within a few weeks of launch.'

Mark took a deep breath. All of this was more than amazing! Hilton had him hooked all right – it seemed like his whole life was about to be transformed more than he'd believed possible. But even in the heat of the moment, his old instincts came kicking in: one day he's sitting behind his desk at OmniCell where he never expected to earn much more than two grand a month. Then a couple of weeks later here he is in Los Angeles talking about multi-million dollar contracts. It all just seemed too easy. There was no doubting, Hilton was getting him keyed up. But there was something he just had to ask, a burning question to which he'd kept returning ever since that first roof-top meeting: 'Why me?' he demanded.

Hilton raised his eyebrows marginally. 'You're right for Isis. Right for the part. As I said last time we met, we've been looking for someone to fit a very tight brief. I don't want you to be in any doubt,' he nodded once, seriously, 'that you do.'

Mark glanced down. It was true, Hilton had said it before, and he wanted to believe him. But he couldn't avoid his natural suspicions.

'This Nile endorsement deal. Is it definite yet?'

'As far as Berkeley Square and Isis are concerned it is. But the agreement still requires your signature. Before you sign, I suggest you have a read through these.' He touched a pile of documents in front of him. 'They outline in full all terms of the contract, and I'm also giving you a Security Briefing to take away.' Hilton had no intention of concealing the possible risk posed by One Commando, but nor did he have any wish to dwell on it.

'Of course, there are other things you need to consider about both the endorsement and the recording contract. You very rarely get pay-outs at the level I've just been talking about, without there being strings attached.'

Oh yeah, thought Mark. Here comes the downside.

'How do you feel, for example, about having a different performance name? Having your image managed by GCM? Having the media dredge up everything in your past?'

Mark shifted uncomfortably in his chair. How could he know how he'd feel about it? He'd never experienced anything like it.

'It's not something I've ever seriously thought about.'

Hilton paused a moment before meeting Mark's eyes. 'Then I suggest you do.' There was no escaping his seriousness. 'Your whole life will change. Overnight you'll become the target of intense media scrutiny. There'll be security considerations. And while I very much hope you become our client, there are limits to what GCM can do on your behalf. You'll need to appoint accountants; in time, lawyers. We can point you in the right direction, but these decisions ultimately rest with you.'

He spoke, thought Mark, as though initiating a novice into some arcane sect.

'Now, I know I've thrown a lot at you and you'll need time to digest it. What I'd like to do,' he pushed the pile of documents towards him, standing as he did, 'is give you copies of the recording contract, endorsement contract, the security briefing, more information about GCM, our standard client contract, a copy of the recording timetable, and the music and lyrics of the first six tracks of *Nile*.'

Mark got up from the table, collecting up the documents under his arm, and following Hilton to a side door which led through to another office in which Elizabeth Reynolds and Hilton's secretary, Melissa Schwartz, were working.

'If you decide you want to commit to these deals,' Hilton was saying, 'the next step will be for you and I to exchange signed contracts, followed immediately by a meeting with our media head, Leo Lebowitz. In the meantime, this is all completely confidential and not to be divulged to anyone. Even the most casual aside in this town is tomorrow's headline news.'

Mark glanced up at him with a flash of impatience. Hilton's manner made him feel as if he was already responsible for some major news leak. What did the bloke take him for, thinking he was going to rush out of here and get on the blower to the *News of the World*?

'When do you want an answer from me?' he asked.

'Twenty-four hours?' Hilton was showing him across to Elizabeth's desk, before retrieving a cassette tape from it. 'And you'll want to listen to this. Composer demo of the ballad we intend to be the number one hit single: the *Nile* title track by Isis and Jordan.' Then, responding to Mark's look of surprise, he smiled. 'That's you, of course.'

An hour later, in the sitting room of his hotel suite, Mark was still trying to work out what to make of it all. Still in a state of elation, disbelief, uncertainty. Isis and him – he could hardly conceive of it! Until today he wouldn't have had the audacity to so much as dream of the possibility. Signed up with pop's greatest sex symbol was just incredible – but there it all was in black and white.

The documents Hilton had given him lay open, scattered about him. He'd tried reading a few, but he'd only get through a couple of paragraphs then the words wouldn't register as he was too distracted to take anything in. He kept jumping up and helping himself to another drink from the fridge, and pacing the room feeling in turns triumphant, doubtful, hardly able to take it all in. As well as recalling all the good things Hilton had said at their meeting, he also remembered the warnings: how his life would change when he became suddenly famous. The media scrutiny. How GCM would want to manage his image.

He had spent some time reading the Security Briefing on the Nile endorsement, and remembered seeing something on the news back home about animal liberation terrorists attacking the Chief Executive of Berkeley Square. The briefing contained a few paragraphs on One Commando, who'd claimed responsibility for the attack. Sounded like a bunch of right nutsos, he reckoned, and though their fanaticism made them dangerous, and he understood the theoretical risk, the idea that they'd suddenly get all hot under the collar about him just didn't seem very real.

In fact, none of this right now was nearly as real to him as the alternative – going back to London and returning to the OmniCell Helpdesk. And no way on earth was he going to do that. He'd have to be crazy! It'd take a lot more than a vague security threat and over-zealous news hacks to put him off. In fact, the idea of being pursued by the paparazzi gave him a buzz. It had to be a whole lot better than being a complete nobody, even if his new name was 'Jordan Hampshire' as it confirmed in one of the documents he'd have to sign.

Two point five million, Hilton had said. Up towards double figures within weeks if all went well. What kind of choice was that to someone who barely cleared a grand a month? He already knew, straight away, what he was going to do with the money. He'd buy his Mum a flat in one of those mansion blocks she'd always liked the look of on Prince of Wales Drive, across from Battersea Park. He'd set her up so she wouldn't have to work another day of her life and take her on a shopping spree to buy some expensive new clothes. He'd do something for Lloyd too – probably sort out a flat for him, so he could spend his wages on himself instead of handing them over to a landlord. And of course there'd be his own new home. He'd always fancied a place overlooking the river – maybe in one of those fashionable apartment blocks in Chelsea Harbour, a top-of-the-range penthouse. Why not? He'd easily be able to afford it! Hey – even if he never worked again, after these deals he'd be set up for life!

Suddenly he felt like speaking to someone – but everyone he knew lived in London. Glancing at his watch he made a mental calculation, adding eight hours and working out that it was just after one in the morning; there was only one person he dared call at that time of the night.

Lloyd protested vigorously when he finally answered the phone. He'd had a late night, he told Mark, and hadn't been asleep for long before being woken by his call. Didn't Mark know what the time was?

Mark told him he knew exactly, but this was important. Then he told his brother about the GCM deal. Riding a wave of excitement, he could hardly contain himself. Lloyd soon forgot the time too and was gratifyingly excited for him, thought Mark – not to mention envious. The two of them had always had an easy, mutually mocking relationship – each making sure the other didn't get too impressed with himself. Mark got a load of it from Lloyd tonight, of course, but he expected it – somehow it made the whole thing seem more real.

Then he asked Lloyd what was going on in London. Which was when the conversation took a disconcerting turn; Lloyd told Mark about his discovery, made the night before, in a Covent Garden wine bar. He and a few mates from work had gone there for a drink, and who should he spot in the corner but Siobhan O'Mara.

'Seeing as Vinnie's been so quiet about her,' said Lloyd, 'I thought I'd ask what she's up to.'

'Too right!' agreed Mark. When he'd asked Vinnie, of late, about other clients like Siobhan, or that Nigerian group he was looking after, Vinnie had gone all mysterious, hinting at advanced negotiations and imminent signings, but never committing to anything definite.

'Turns out she fired Vinnie eight weeks ago.'

'What? Who's she gone to?'

'Nobody.'

'She fired Vinnie without having anyone else lined up?'

'Exactly what I said,' chimed Lloyd. 'She said she'd just had enough of him. He was getting out of control. She thinks he's losing it.'

'Not the only one. Did he want to kill her too?'

'Worse. Seems the dark side of our Vinnie isn't all talk. A mate of hers at Strobe Records told her Strobe are suing him. They've got him on video in their car park smashing up a producer's Ferrari. Keyed the paintwork, smashed in the lights and slashed the soft-top.'

Mark was speechless with shock.

'He'd been getting agitated about some Swerve master tape he claimed Strobe had lost,' Lloyd explained grimly. 'Last time he gets a contract out of them.'

Both brothers knew how utterly at odds this was with Vinnie's oft-repeated assurances that he and Strobe Records couldn't be closer.

'That's not the worst of it,' continued Lloyd. 'He also had a go at Pete Kelly.'

'Got to be joking!' The Soho club owner, an eccentric bohemian who frequented the streets in the company of his golden retriever, wasn't only the most affectionately regarded owner on the London club circuit, his club was an institution among music talent scouts.

'Kelly docked a fifteen per cent management charge

from some performance fee. Vinnie wasn't expecting it—'

'It wasn't Vinnie—' Mark was already dreading what he thought would follow.

'—who did the dog. Yeah. He told Siobhan that Kelly deserved it.'

Two months before, Kelly had emerged from his regular watering-hole to find his dog gone from the lamp-post to which he always leashed him. The frantic search that ensued had been to no avail. Returning home, Kelly had found his dog dangling from the front door – strangled by its own leash.

'Christ Almighty!' Mark was shaking his head.

Alarmed though he was, in a perverse way the revelation made sense of Vinnie's recent behaviour. It followed a pattern. Vinnie had believed he'd arrived when he'd had his first big success with Swerve. He'd been quite the big shot with his chart-topping clients and his Mercedes and his slim panatellas. But this act had become harder and harder to keep up since Swerve collapsed. Vinnie didn't have any signings to replace them. He was getting desperate. Hence the Ferrari attack. Pete Kelly's dog. The way he'd reacted down at the Lamb. If he kept this up, Mark thought now, he'd soon find every door in the music industry slammed in his face.

'How's he been with you?' Mark asked, getting concerned about his brother's safety.

'Only seen him once down the Lamb and he completely ignored me.'

'Just watch out for him.'

'Hey, I can look after myself. Anyway, it's you he's mad at.'

'I'm a bit far away for him to do much.'

Lloyd didn't reply immediately. They both realised that

Vinnie had revealed a dangerous and previously unsuspected tendency. Vengefulness fuelled by desperation.

'Maybe he'll cool down,' Lloyd said, finally.

'Yeah,' said Mark, staring unseeing out of his window at Chateau Marmont. 'I really hope so.'

5

The e-mail Alan Brent received was short. Only one and a half lines to be exact. But the message it conveyed was cause for satisfaction. 'Congratulations' was the word Larson had used, referring to his special delivery to *The Globe* newspaper the week before. It was the first time Larson had sent him a personalised e-mail, instead of the terse, encrypted communiqués he usually issued to One Commando members. It was also the first time Larson had complimented him.

Every news bulletin on radio and TV last night and every national newspaper had reported his delivery of the eyes to *The Globe* newspaper the following day – an event that had given the Lefevre story a powerful impetus, providing, as it did, a shocking and savage revelatory twist. Until that moment the police had suppressed the details of exactly how Jacques Lefevre had been 'injured' – having first wanted to inform and advise Mrs Lefevre, who was flying in from New York.

But the genie had got out of the bottle now, and for over a week, One Commando had dominated the news media.

The contents of the video Brent had delivered had also been hotly debated – but despite the shocking scenes depicted, the media seemed strangely reluctant to accept that they had been shot in a Berkeley Square facility. Lord Bullerton's angry denials, together with threatened libel action, had had the usually accusatory tabloids siding with Berkeley Square. And when investigative teams from the broadsheet newspapers were unable to dig up anything to substantiate the One Commando video, it was assumed to be a hoax.

For all that, thought Alan, he was making progress. He'd almost got to the top. It had taken him six months, during which time he had closely scrutinised Larson's *modus operandi*, the clinical manner in which he kept every cell member separate and isolated. As military leader of One Commando, Bengt Larson was extremely significant, no doubting it. He was the most ruthless operator in the animal rights movement. But he wasn't the top man – of that Alan had been convinced from the start. There was someone above him who held sway.

For months, Alan's conviction about One Commando's unseen leader had been nothing more than a hunch. Then, last week, Larson had made a fleeting reference in a training session before the Lefevre operation. 'The powers that be,' he'd said, referring to the critical importance of the raid – confirming what Alan had suspected all along. And setting his ultimate objective. Alan didn't only need to win over Bengt Larson. He had to get right to the top of the organisation. If his mission was to be successful he needed to win the acceptance of 'the powers that be'.

Behind his computer, he glanced at his watch. Five to one. Just enough time to log on to the office intranet and file a report before his colleagues went off. They'd want to hear from him – and preferably without interrupting their lunch. Despite the nature of their work he'd long since discovered that most of the worker ants at HQ followed the same pedestrian regime of office workers the world over. In at nine, out at six. An hour off for lunch, at one. Endless meetings.

He never went into the office in person – under the terms of his contract he was specifically forbidden from going anywhere near the place. In fact, he'd only ever been allowed inside HQ once – ten years ago, when he'd been formally interviewed for the job.

They'd recruited him at the lowest point in his life. He'd just been fired from his first job, amid a welter of mutual recriminations, and he'd been feeling bitter, disillusioned, insecure. Having graduated from university cum laude five years before, he'd begun work full of big ideas and brave convictions. By the time he joined their operation, however, he'd been considerably more worldly wise.

His employers hadn't recruited him for his brains alone; apart from his near-genius-level intellectual prowess they also recognised in him a personality ideally suited to undercover work. Alan was a loner, always had been. He lived in his head, in the world of ideas, and working on his own suited him. It also kept things secure. Operating from home, he'd assembled, on his employers' budget, a collection of the most powerful computing and communications equipment available, all of which he'd installed in the large attic of his house which served both as office and bedroom. The vast majority of his assignments involved cyber-work, breaking through software encryption programs without being detected, as well as all the more routine stuff. Every day he'd spend hours at the keyboard, in an office lit by nothing but his customised purple screensaver, and which was crammed with equipment, as well as empty Coke cans and polystyrene Kentucky Fried Chicken cartons going back more meals than he cared to remember. He only ever went out of the house for food or other essential errands. His life was as sealed off, anonymous and self-contained as it was possible to be in a major city. All of which contributed to his effectiveness as an undercover agent.

He was also scrupulous about safety. He changed his cyber-ID and e-mail address constantly so that even if someone did succeed in hooking on to him they would never be able to track his presence for any length of time. He had people from work come in every month routinely to sweep his house for bugs. They'd go through the entire place, from top to bottom, checking for any recording or transmission equipment. Sensitive material arriving in hard copy form – and substantial quantities of it would arrive by special delivery – he'd store electronically, before feeding the originals into the industrial shredder. Non-sensitive stuff he stored. And because he'd been doing this work for ten years, it meant his house had, little by little, turned into a vast storage repository.

His involvement in One Commando wasn't like anything he'd ever done before. But from the start he'd kept his usual careful records detailing every contact that was made by e-mail or phone, as well as the content of every conversation. Having penetrated the organisation, he intended finding out all he could about it – in particular, the power structure and who made the decisions. He'd also realised that analysis and intellectual insight on its own were not enough. If he was to achieve what he'd set out to do, he also had to be accepted – all the way to the top. Larson's e-mail was an important recognition and he would build on it. He'd use the credibility he'd earned to get more information. And he knew he was getting there. Very much closer, in particular, to answering the question that had increasingly become his preoccupation: who exactly was the puppetmaster pulling One Commando's strings?

London
Thursday, 9 September

Jasper Jones got up from behind his desk and stepped out of his office, instructing his secretary to hold all calls for the next ten minutes before returning inside, closing the door behind him. A senior executive at the Euston Road offices of Love Smith Ben David, his office was elegantly appointed and currently in near-total darkness, lit only by his desk light. Several television awards glinted in a corner cabinet, but he'd otherwise eschewed the breast-beating of his colleagues in the industry, who usually bedecked their walls with framed posters of their latest productions. Instead, his own office walls were hung with a few favourite prints – a couple of Kleins and a Magritte. There was a comfortable black leather sofa for visitors, a drinks cabinet containing a few bottles of spirits including his preferred tipple – Bombay Sapphire Gin. But there was nothing that so much as hinted at where his personal pursuits really lay.

His colleagues had no inkling about his involvement in the animal rights movement. If they'd found out he had any involvement in the Lefevre attack, they would have been apoplectic. Consequently, this past week he'd had to keep his private exhilaration under wraps. Never could he remember such intense media coverage of an animal rights operation. It was the eyes that had done it. If One Commando had knocked Lefevre unconscious, or sliced his face open, or even shot him dead, the story wouldn't have merited more than a few column inches in the national press, or a brief mention on the main evening news. But the gouging of Lefevre's eyes had struck a chord that resonated with a deep, collective fear. The notion that a grotesque mutilation could be conducted in the hallowed privacy of one of London's most genteel squares was a nightmare scenario that had seized the public subconscious, and raised the game to a completely different level.

Whether it was the simple horror invoked by the ubiquitous image of Lefevre's spectacles case, or whether the symbolism was understood – the destroyer of countless animals' sight is, himself, blinded – what had happened had spawned more news stories and features than Jones had ever counted on. In the last seven days, Jacques Lefevre's spectacles case had been so photographed, so written about, that it had already become an icon of the animal liberation struggle. In future weeks and months, its mere appearance would be all that was required to inspire a profound, public gasp of disquiet.

Not that Bengt Larson was satisfied. Jones had just received an e-mail from wherever Larson was currently residing in Europe; he was extremely upset by the turning tide of the media. Initial news, first of the Lefevre attack, and then *The Globe* delivery, had done little more than report events in scandalised tones. Since then the full weight of Britain's gigantic media machine had been brought to bear on what had happened – and the rapidly growing consensus of all the features, analysis and editorials was that One Commando was using a hoax video to justify its actions. Journalists had already been through Berkeley Square plants, not only in Spain but in every country where the company operated, and nothing had been found. Commercial rivals had done their utmost to verify One Commando's claims – but to no avail. So where had the footage come from? Flipping open his Psion Organiser and switching on its green backlight in the gloom of his office, Jones accessed a coded entry containing Larson's secret contact details. Finding his mobile telephone number, he picked up his telephone and began dialling.

Larson was vital to the cause – he had to be looked after. It had taken Jones months both to identify and win the confidence of the commando leader. He had spent a substantial part of his 'extra-curricular' hours in the last year getting to know all the main players in the animal liberation movement. He'd sat through countless night-time meetings and for more weekends than he cared to remember had travelled to conferences, rallies and protests all over Britain and on the Continent. Focusing on more established activist groups, all run by cabals of career protesters, once he'd proved his commitment with a few donations, doors had been opened and confidences begun to be imparted; he'd identified the Animal Freedom Lobby as the organisation where his own ideas would be best received. It was there he'd heard the whispers of a paramilitary organisation – the ultimate goal of his quest. Around the same time he'd been making enquiries about the tall, well-muscled Swede who'd attended several of the rallies he'd been at himself. It didn't really surprise him when he learned that Larson was the leader of the nascent One Commando – he'd looked and sounded the part.

At the other end, Larson's phone rang just twice before he answered it.

'I just got your e-mail,' explained Jones. 'You're worried.'

'Worried!' Larson barked at the other end. The word was wholly inadequate as a description of his state of mind. 'You've seen the newspapers, the TV! They're saying we're a gang of unprincipled terrorists! They're saying Berkeley Square are innocent. This is destroying us!'

Jones listened patiently as, at the other end, Larson vented his frustration. Extracting a pack of Gauloise Lights from his desk, he drew one out between his lips before flicking it to life with his gold Dunhill lighter and exhaling a stream of grey smoke into the semi-shadows. He didn't even try to interrupt. Instead he listened while Larson let off steam, making the occasional note on the briefing pad in front of him, and puffing on his cigarette. Then, after the tirade had abated, he waited a long while before saying, deliberately, 'That's certainly one side to it.'

There was a pause of disbelief from the other end before Larson finally managed, 'There's another side?'

'For the last week One Commando has achieved massive high profile coverage in all the major national news media.'

'For all the wrong reasons.'

'What else were they going to say?' asked Jones. 'You know what keeps every news organisation in this country going? Advertising revenue. How much revenue has the Animal Freedom Lobby poured into media coffers in the last year? Zilch. And how much money have members of the Ethical Pharmaceutical Manufacturers' Association spent in the same time?' He glanced at one of the revenue spreadsheets scattered on his desk. 'Six hundred and fifty-two million pounds. So whose side d'you think they're going to take?'

'It's as blatant as that?'

'You better believe it.' Jones spoke with cool conviction. 'You have some of the most powerful forces in business ranged against you. And you can be sure they're leaning heavily on the media to get their side out. Just because editors write things, it doesn't mean they're telling the truth. It doesn't mean Berkeley Square isn't testing on animals. It only means that, right now, they've got the media by the balls.'

'Bastards!' At the other end of the line, Larson's voice was choked with anger.

'You talk about credibility,' continued Jones, 'what about

the credibility of the people saying there *isn't* any testing? Bullerton, the Chairman of Berkeley Square? The Ethical Pharmaceutical Manufacturers' Association?'

'But what about this open invitation to visit any Berkeley Square plant?'

'They close down the site in Spain. So what? They just set up a lab under a different name and get the results fed through to them that way.'

At the other end, Larson fumed silently. He'd learned a lot from Jones about the plotting and scheming of big business. It was Jones, with his acute business brain, who'd explained to him how shareholdings worked and subsidiaries operated. Before that, he'd never realised how devious big companies could be or what a hold they had over the media. But he knew, better than anyone, where the video footage had come from; it was he who'd broken into Berkeley Square's Madrid laboratory just a few weeks earlier. Now, the realisation of how the media were being paid to peddle lies began to sink in. And his despair was turning to resentment. The tide of energy was welling back inside him.

'When you think of all we're up against,' Jones spoke with feeling, 'you realise just how much we achieved with the Lefevre raid. It put One Commando on the map. It got major national media coverage that even a month ago would have been inconceivable.' For a few moments he focused on the operation – the success of its planning, strategy and execution. How One Commando had successfully evaded police detection. How they had become, overnight, the biggest name in the animal liberation movement.

'You've got them on the run. They don't know where to start looking for you and they're terrified you're going to strike again. That's what all these headlines *really* mean.'

'I don't know,' Larson was less certain, 'it just seems that whatever we do, no one's going to believe us. But I was there! I filmed it myself. How can they all pretend it isn't happening?'

'Believe me, Bengt, I share your frustration,' Jones said grimly after a while. 'And it seems to me we're going to have to come up with something else, something different to make them pay attention.'

'You have an idea?'

Jones's expression was grave. 'Let's just say, I've been working on something.'

'Like . . . Lefevre?'

Jones exhaled another thin stream of blue-grey smoke into the darkness.

'Like it,' he confirmed, 'except much, much bigger.'

6

Two days after arriving in LA, Mark was still buzzing. And still waiting for the jet-lag to set in. Yesterday afternoon, Elizabeth had phoned to ask if he'd had a chance to go through the contracts, and did he have any questions. Mark had said yes he had, and yes he did. But he would be signing. The truth was – not that he told Elizabeth – there'd never been any serious doubt in his mind. Once he'd convinced himself this whole story-book scenario was genuine, nothing else seemed to matter.

Elizabeth had sounded pleased with his reaction. He should sign the contracts, she told him, and bring them into GCM next day, where he'd meet Leo Lebowitz, head media honcho, so they could get the show on the road. Mark had put down the phone, amazed at the speed with which things were happening. Back in London, the major record labels took for ever to consider things. With GCM, the turnaround time on major deals seemed lightning quick.

Having waited in the GCM foyer for less than ten minutes, he saw Elizabeth step out of the lift wearing a white suit and looking very foxy. He found himself wondering about her, that way, but quickly checked himself. This was work, remember?

'Mark,' she reached out a welcoming hand. GCM people were always shaking hands, he'd noticed. He handed her over the envelope he'd had under his arm.

'They're signed?'

'Yeah,' he grinned.

'Good. I'll take them to Hilton and we'll get you counter-signed copies before you leave.'

He nodded, before asking the question that had been on his mind ever since Hilton had first told him about the record deal yesterday. 'When do I get to meet Isis?'

Elizabeth was hesitant. 'I'm not sure. We'll have to check your schedule.' Then, heading towards a door behind the reception desk, 'Seeing that you're now a client, would you like a quick agency tour?'

Mark nodded. 'I'd love that.'

She ushered him in, then through a steel security barrier, which slid open as she used a swipe card. Stepping forward, they came to a glass wall through which was visible a massive, open-plan office, with banks and banks of computer termi-nals stretching out into the distance. Smartly dressed exec-utive types were working at keyboards or speaking on phones in an industrious buzz of activity that reminded Mark of one of those exhibits you saw at the zoo, where you looked through a slab of glass into an insect hive.

'Accounts department,' she explained.

'Right.'

'We pride ourselves on having the quickest turnaround time in the industry. Four working days from cheques arriv-ing from the principals – that's the average turnaround time.'

He nodded. 'Reminds me of something,' he said, reaching into the breast pocket of his jacket and extracting an envelope addressed to himself. It had been sent by courier the day before and had contained nothing but a GCM compliments slip – and five hundred dollars in cash. 'There was a mistake.'

'Really?' A look of sudden concern crossed her face.

'You duplicated.' He was holding out the envelope. 'You already paid me.'

She looked puzzled, as she accepted the envelope. 'You mean?'

'When I got here. Then this came yesterday.'

Suddenly understanding, she smiled. 'That's right. No mistake. Five hundred is your per diem.' Then, responding to his confusion, 'Your daily allowance.'

'Five hundred dollars . . . *every* day?' He looked astonished for a moment. Then, 'That'll be for the hotel and everything.'

'GCM meets accommodation expenses.'

'So what am I supposed to spend five hundred dollars a day on?'

She couldn't help smiling. 'Oh, I'm sure if you practise, you'll get pretty good at it.' She stretched over, squeezing his arm. 'Most of our clients do.'

He was shaking his head ruefully as he accepted the envelope back. Then, glancing across to the other end of the Accounts department, he noticed for the first time that the entire far wall was the side of a vast aquarium containing golden koi – the same fish he'd seen in the fountain at the top of the GCM building in London.

'Biggest fish tank I've ever seen,' he remarked.

Elizabeth nodded, leading him back to the door. 'The building was designed by a feng shui expert. You know when you go to Chinese restaurants, they often have fish tanks near the cash register? The idea is to attract wealth.' She was leading him up a flight of stairs to the first floor.

'People here don't actually believe all that bollocks, do they?' he asked, astonished.

She raised a finger to her lips, and gave him a significant look. 'I wouldn't let Hilton hear you speak like that, if I were you.'

'You mean he really thinks—?'

'He believes in experimenting with anything that stacks the odds in our favour. You've got to admit, it's worked pretty well up to now.'

The stairs and lifts were at the centre of the rectangular GCM building. Arriving on the first floor, Elizabeth gestured towards the two wings to each side of them, clearly marked 'Film' and 'Television'. 'Like our main competitors,' she explained, 'GCM is divided into four main divisions – Film, TV, Music and Multimedia. Then we have services that run across all four divisions, like Media Relations and Endorsements.' She had led him into the Television offices, a maze of corridors with glass-walled offices behind which elegantly attired agents and their assistants were gesticulating on the phones, or talking in meetings with TVs playing. There was a palpable charge of energy about the place, thought Mark as he followed Elizabeth, a purposeful buzz of expectation.

'As of this week,' she was explaining, leading him on a brisk round-circuit, 'we have a hundred and eighty clients working on seventy different shows.'

'Actors, you mean?'

'Actors, producers, writers, directors. Sometimes the full package.'

Mark raised his eyebrows. 'How does that all work? How do you put things together?'

'Different in every case,' Elizabeth told him. 'Sometimes we'll pitch a sitcom concept to one of the networks, and they'll give us the go-ahead for development. Or they might have given creative approval to somebody else's idea, but come to us for casting. The start of it is always information.' They were heading out of Television now and into Film. 'You see this?' From one of the desks, as they passed by, she picked up a large, leather-bound file embossed with the GCM logo.

Mark nodded. He'd noticed a few files like it scattered about and had just assumed they were fancy telephone directories.

'This is the Film Bible. A database of every movie in English which is in development or production. Television, Music and Multimedia have their Bibles too.' She flipped open the cover to reveal a four-inch-thick wedge of computer printout carrying endless lists of names and titles and telephone numbers. 'Twice a week each division has full staff meetings, with video hook-ups to all our main offices around the globe. The meetings are part information exchanges, part brainstorms. We look at new books coming on the market available for adaptation, projects that studios are looking to develop, maybe a script which a producer client wants to get commissioned. Which directors want to work with which actors, or which actors have projects for which writers.' She tapped the file before replacing it on a desk. 'After meetings, all these files are updated, hard copy and intranet.' Then, leading him off round the Film offices which, to Mark, didn't look much different from Television, 'We guard our leads jealously – they're the lifeblood of the business.'

'Where do you get the information from?'

'Agents are out there all the time – breakfast, lunch and dinner meetings, industry bashes, private parties – and when they're not out circulating, they're on the phone.'

Glancing about at all the suited men and women, Mark noticed how many of them were wearing headsets with microphone transmitters as they strode about their offices.

'Two things done at once?' He pointed.

'Never enough hours in the day,' agreed Elizabeth, 'but we took medical advice after one of our top TV guys got a tumour in his ear.'

Mark looked at her in surprise.

'Agents make an average of a hundred and fifty calls a day. Sometimes we're on the phone for seven, eight hours.'

It was all a lot different from how Mark had pictured Hollywood agents. He'd always imagined their lives consisted of endless lunches with the rich and famous in chichi restaurants, after which they spent the day by the swimming pool in sunglasses and bathing trunks, sipping pina coladas with little umbrellas in them.

Looking around him he remarked, 'I always thought things in Los Angeles were more laid back.'

'In the bad old days. Now, most people in our industry work twelve- to sixteen-hour shifts.'

'How do you get to be an agent in the first place?'

'Interviews and psychometric tests like anyone else,' said Elizabeth. 'There are two hundred applicants for every one trainee job, and when you do get in, you literally start in the mail room.'

Walking through a maze of passages, Mark couldn't get over the scale of all this. Offices and meeting rooms and screening rooms seemed to go on for ever.

'After a while, once you get an idea how things work, with any luck you'll be taken on by one of the agents as an assistant. You shadow everything they do.'

'Like you and Hilton?' he risked.

'Exactly. But even when you get to be an agent, there's

no guarantee you'll stay. You have to bring in the deals –
and this is the most fiercely competitive business in the
world.'

'Sounds high pressure.'

'Which is why agencies attract a certain type of personality. It's not good enough just to be a super-salesman, you
also have to have the right instinct.'

'Killer instinct?'

She turned, smiling wryly. 'You could say that.' Then as
she led him back in the direction of the lifts, 'Some of our
people eat a stem of garlic every day to maintain their aggres-
sion levels.'

'Bit off-putting for clients?' he guffawed.

'Not if you eat enough parsley.' Then sotto voce, as they
waited for the lift, 'A few of my male colleagues say they
practise semen-retention techniques to keep their edge.'

Mark had to laugh at the absurdity of all this.
Testosterone-charged super-agents in their Armani suits and
goldfish in the Accounts department – he'd heard it all now.
Once they were in the lift, Elizabeth pressed the third-floor
button.

'Music and Multimedia are on the second floor,' she told
him as they ascended, 'same format you've just seen.'

'No chance of running into any celebrities then?' He'd
been in Beverly Hills more than forty-eight hours and *still*
hadn't seen anyone famous.

'Lord, no! It's the engine room down here – I just thought
you'd like a peek. Regular client meetings are on the fifth
floor.'

He nodded.

'We're going to level three, Media Relations.'

'All of it?' He was surprised. 'Must be a huge department.'

'Needs to be. It's the heart of our business.'

At that point the lift doors slid open on to a scene that was mesmerising for its sheer scale. A massive sprawl of open-plan desks ran the full length of the building, with glass-walled offices stretching down either side, like a vast airport terminal that had been converted into offices. Unlike the Accounts department, where executives busied themselves like worker ants, this place was a madhouse of yelled instructions and frantic arm gesturing, huddle-meetings around desks littered with media releases and, Mark noticed now, at least a dozen sound-proofed booths for live TV and radio interviews, all with their red 'Recording' lights on.

He was taking all this in with wide-eyed amazement when next to him Elizabeth said, 'About a third of all the world's biggest celebrity stories concern our clients.'

'I can believe it.'

'We have media contacts in every capital city on the planet and can get news out to them all within half an hour.'

'"Control the media and you control the world,"' mused Mark, recalling his first encounter with Hilton on GCM London's rooftop.

'One of Hilton's favourites,' she agreed.

'But how can GCM force journalists to say things?'

'We can't directly. It's a more subtle understanding than that. You see, when we contact journalists with news about our clients, or to arrange client interviews, we're always very clear about the information we're presenting and the spin we want on it. It's up to the journalist what happens next. If he turns in a hostile piece, we mark his card. Two strikes and he's out. He never gets another piece of news out of our offices again – not about any of our clients. Nor will he ever be allowed to interview them. When you look after as many clients as we do, a journalist is going to think very hard before slamming the door on GCM.'

Mark took all this in as Elizabeth led him through the flurry of the media relations offices towards the far corner.

'You said this department is at the heart of the business?'

She nodded. 'GCM trades on the reputation of its clients. Their appeal and ability to attract a large following. Those are all intangibles. They can be destroyed by the media virtually overnight. A well-managed image on the other hand . . .'

'What happens if you don't have an image?' he wondered, applying this information to himself.

She turned, smiling. 'Then you come here to get one.'

'You do?'

'That's exactly why Hilton wants you to spend time in Lebo-land. Leo Lebowitz is the best in the business.'

They had arrived at the doorway to a very large corner office, its high, white walls hung with sweeping and vivid abstract canvases, and from its window, a panoramic vista of Santa Monica Boulevard with its swaying royal palms. To Mark's surprise, there was no desk in the office. In fact, there was no furniture at all except a highly polished meeting table and, around it, a number of black leather chairs. On the far side of the office, headset strapped on, the bearded Lebowitz was on the phone – but gestured them inside.

'This is where I head back upstairs,' Elizabeth told Mark, 'but I'll see you before you leave.'

'Right,' he met her eyes and that impenetrable expression of professional cordiality, 'see you later.'

He stood at the door for a few moments while Lebowitz ended his conversation, removed the headset and turned to face him with a thoughtful smile.

'You must be Jordan Hampshire,' he offered his hand.

'Mark Watson is my real name,' he replied with a handshake.

'Reality's best left outside.' Lebowitz waved him towards the table, reaching behind him to close his office door. 'Let's stick to Jordan. Less confusing that way.'

Mark took a seat at the table opposite him and for a moment the two of them sized each other up. Lebowitz's intellectual authority, like Hilton's, was instantly self-evident, but unlike Hilton, whose manner lent him a certain detachment, Lebowitz was altogether more engaged.

'Hilton told you the purpose of this meeting?'

'Something about media management.'

'Whenever we take on a new client, we have a session like this to lay down the ground rules.' Lebowitz was stroking his beard reflectively. 'You see, we're all working as a team now, and it's important you know what your moves are, and what our moves are, when we engage the media.'

'Sounds military.'

'Has to be. When you're in the public eye, whether you like it or not, you have an image. Your only choice is whether to manage that image, or let the media manage it for you.'

Mark nodded. 'This image thing, why did you come up with the name Jordan Hampshire?' It was the first time he'd said the name out loud and as he said it, he didn't feel as if it had anything to do with him.

'My development team conducted extensive research using brand development instruments. An analysis of birth registers in ten major US cities shows that Jordan is the most popular name among eighteen-to-thirty-year-old A/B/C1 women. We also trialled twenty surnames, in focus groups, then using a quant. study, to find which was most closely identified with England. Hampshire topped it.'

Mark was astonished at how calculated it had been.

'We put the whole package into research, not just the name,' Lebowitz continued. 'Our psychographics came up with clear steers on image, wardrobe, hairstyle . . .'

Mark raised a hand to his hair automatically as Lebowitz opened up a flat box in front of him. This was something he hadn't thought about, he realised, feeling suddenly exposed. But of course, if these guys had come up with a name for him, they'd also have worked out an image, using all their fancy techniques.

Lebowitz was pulling out a selection of concept boards and sliding them across the table. To Mark's further concern, each board carried sketches of him – but not the way he looked right now, and definitely not the way he'd ever appeared on stage in London. The clothes Jordan Hampshire wore were altogether younger, a combination of retro flares and wide lapels with collarless shirts and crumpled linen jackets. The kinds of clothes only a real jerk would wear. And worst of all was the hairstyle. Gone was the lustrous mane of dark hair which he knew women went for, and instead was a short back and sides, so short he'd be almost bald, topped by a short, gelatined mass that looked like he'd just got out of bed. Walk into the pubs he used to frequent back home looking like that, he thought, and he'd find himself on the pavement in about ten seconds. Glancing up, he realised that Lebowitz had been watching his reaction closely.

'I'd feel a right dick looking like that.' He shook his head firmly.

Lebowitz seemed unperturbed. 'It usually takes time to adjust,' he said.

Something in his attitude nettled Mark. 'Maybe I don't want to adjust!'

'What, specifically, do you object to?'

'My hair, for starters. I've tried a lot of different styles. I know what women like and I know what suits me—'

'Suits *you*,' Lebowitz retorted. 'If it was thirtysomethings we were after, it'd be perfect. But that's not where the money is. The primary market is eighteen to thirty.'

'So you manipulate *all* your stars—'

'This isn't about manipulation,' Lebowitz was calm, his tone laced with a hint of humour, 'it's about accessibility. If you're not accessible to your market, you might as well pack up and go home.'

Mark wondered if Lebowitz's choice of expression had been deliberate, before deciding it was. Everything about this operation seemed calculated.

'So Isis's different looks . . . ?'

'Driven by the market. *Aphrodisia* was a flawless piece of packaging work. Exhaustive image engineering work. Pre-testing. We're going to do the same for you.'

Mark was disconcerted by his penetrating gaze. 'Pre-testing?'

'Before the CD and video release we run pilots. Get kids into observation rooms across the country and play them the stuff. If we've got the brief right in the first place there shouldn't be a need for fundamental changes. But there's usually some fine-tuning, maybe a revision of imagery or visual emphasis. Maybe some studio re-engineering. We need to be sure we've created a product with optimum impact.'

Mark was staring down at the concept boards in silence. None of this was anything like he'd imagined. After all the euphoria of the last few days, it was like flying into a wall at a hundred miles an hour. He thought GCM had signed him up because they believed he had something to offer. The way Lebowitz was explaining things now it seemed as if he was just to play a part, act a role that had nothing to do with him.

'This is all so . . . made up,' he was shaking his head, 'so artificial. Why can't someone just write bloody good music and be themselves?'

Lebowitz seemed amused by the proposition. 'They can,' his mouth formed a half smile, 'they usually do when they start out. But that's a pretty hit-and-miss way of continuing.'

'I s'pose you even use research to write the music?'

'We analyse what's worked well on the charts in the last six months and combine it with predictive modelling. On the back of that we briefed a couple of composers and they came up with several options which we played to our music panel – that's five hundred people nationwide. The *Nile* lead track is right on the button. Went down a treat.'

'What if Isis came up with a few songs of her own?'

'Oh, we'd test them. But we can't just let her do what she likes.'

'It worked for *Aphrodisia*.'

Lebowitz sighed. '*Aphrodisia* was three years ago. Isis was perfectly tuned in then. But the market's moved on and we can't risk her getting it wrong – there's too much at stake.' Then regarding his unconvinced expression, he looked serious. 'Unum Music is spending two million dollars on the video, eight hundred thousand dollars buying airtime and has an advertising budget of one point five million. *Nile* is going to be a number one hit. It can't be left to chance.'

So this was what Hilton had meant when he'd warned him about GCM having full artistic control. At the time it hadn't seemed a big deal, not when he was being paid over a million dollars for it. But now he realised just how much he'd be following orders. In reality, he was nothing more than a puppet on a string.

'The same goes for media relations,' Lebowitz was telling him. 'We have to avoid nasty surprises.' His expression was serious. 'The reason I kept this meeting private is so you'd feel free getting anything off your chest I need to know about.'

'What d'you mean?' Mark felt his heckles rise again.

'Anything that a tabloid newspaper or gossip columnist would consider interesting. I'm thinking along the lines of drugs, crime, sexual peccadilloes, domestic violence, unwanted children—'

Mark was once again infuriated by the way Lebowitz sat there, calmly reeling off a catalogue of intimate perversities. 'What if I've never done any of that stuff?' he protested, voice rising. 'What if I'm just a regular bloke—'

'Hey! Jordan!' Lebowitz leaned back in his chair and fixed him with a contemplative smile. 'I'm on your side, remember. If there are no skeletons in the cupboard, that makes my life a whole lot easier. But I have to say it would be a first. I've never signed up anyone who hasn't had some issue to manage.' Then as he met Mark's embarrassed expression his eyes turned earnest. 'One thing I don't want you to be in any doubt about is that in a few days' time your entire life will become public property. Journalists will be interviewing anyone who's ever known you – family, friends, enemies, ex-lovers, you name it. They'll be out after the dirt, waving their cheque-books, because that's what sells newspapers. If the first time I get to know that you were having an affair with your stepmother is when a journalist phones me for a quote, frankly, it's too damned late to save you. But if I know these things beforehand, I can put defences in place.'

The moment he'd started talking about friends and enemies and cheque-books, Mark instantly thought of Vinnie. If a journalist got on to him he didn't doubt that Vinnie would come out with the most twisted tale of duplicity and betrayal. You didn't have to imagine too hard to see the headlines.

'One thing I can guarantee,' Lebowitz continued, 'is that you'll be amazed what creeps out the woodwork. People you were at school with you don't even remember will come out saying you were best buddies. Girls you got in the sack will tell the most outrageous lies – even girls you didn't get in the sack—'

'There is someone you should know about.' Mark knew there was no point holding back.

Lebowitz gave him an enquiring look.

'Vinnie Dobson,' said Mark, 'used to act as my manager.'

Lebowitz unscrewed the top of his handsome Mont Blanc Meisterstück and held it poised on a briefing pad. Meeting Mark's eyes he said gravely, 'I need you to tell me everything.'

Mark finished fifteen minutes later, recounting his most recent conversation with Lloyd. Although there was no doubt in his mind that Lebowitz had to know, he didn't like having to do this. It made him feel like the school sneak who'd just been in the headmaster's office.

'Well, if that's the worst you've got,' Lebowitz looked up from his note-taking, 'we shouldn't have too many problems.' He scratched his beard thoughtfully. 'I'm sure we'll find a way to keep Mr Dobson out of mischief.' Then, looking up and meeting Mark in the eye, 'Are you sure there's nothing else we need to know about – embittered ex-girl-friends? Youthful indiscretions?'

Mark shook his head.

'On the subject of women – or indeed men,' Lebowitz leaned over, handing him a business card, 'here's the number to ring if you feel the need.'

Mark took one look at the shiny black card, with the

pink and gold lettering, before flashing back up at Lebowitz in annoyance, 'I'm not so desperate I've got to pay for it!' Was Lebowitz deliberately trying to piss him off, or was this just his style? He was about to flick the card back across the table when Lebowitz held up his hand.

'Keep it,' he ordered. 'Don't forget, everything is about to change for you. You're going to be a big star. You'll have to be wary of entrapment—'

'So for the rest of my life,' flashed Mark, 'whenever I feel like company I have to—'

'Georgia Klune is held in very high regard by this agency. She and those in her employ operate with the utmost discretion.'

'You mean, you refer all your clients to—'

'A lot of them.' He was nodding. Then, leaning back in his seat, he fixed Mark with that irksome, enigmatic half-smile. 'We all have our drives and our juices. Georgia provides what we think of as an insurance service. If any of our clients feel the need for relief, we prefer that they use Georgia's services, than be caught getting blow jobs from hookers on the Strip, or cottaging in the public lavatories. Whatever you're into, Georgia can provide it, and nobody will ever find out. That counts for a lot in my business.'

Mark regarded him, aggravated. This was all getting beyond weird.

'The deals will be announced in two days' time, and we're expecting serious media take-up. Before then, we've got a lot of work to get through. You'll also be needing a bodyguard.'

'Is that—?'

'Non-negotiable.' Lebowitz met his eyes. 'There's a lot of crazies out there who'd do anything to get on the news, including shoot someone famous.'

So this was what he'd signed himself into. A name and image that weren't his. Sex with women he'd never met. Security arrangements he didn't want. And none of it had anything to do with the main reason he was here – to record an album with Isis. So when Lebowitz said, 'Is there anything you'd like to ask?' he was quick to repeat the question he'd already asked Elizabeth,

'When do I get to meet Isis?'

'I've no idea,' the other was candid, 'is there any particular reason you need to?'

'Need to? If we're going to be working together, I'd like to get to know her.'

Lebowitz looked at him blankly.

'Or is that a quaint idea?'

The other shrugged – was that a trace of condescension? – before murmuring, 'It's a subjective thing.'

Mark shook his head, frustrated. 'Next you're going to tell me she's nothing like her image.'

Lebowitz grimaced. 'That's not a question I feel competent answering. Her image is all that concerns me.'

Then he was outlining everything that needed to be done in the following few days – clothes, hair, photo shoots for media pack development. An intensive schedule had been set up – there'd be no time now to enjoy the delights of Chateau Marmont.

Then, pausing, he regarded Mark carefully for a long while before saying, 'If I can offer you one piece of advice,' his tone signalled significance, 'you're going to see a lot of stuff about yourself in the media that I can tell you, right now, will be complete bullshit. Everything you say will be reported out of context, twisted and turned to support someone else's point of view. It'll help if you don't take it personally. Think of it as a game, a battle of wits.

When it gets really bad, and I can promise you it will, just try to remember it's not really you they're talking about. In fact, it's got nothing to do with you. It's a Jordan Hampshire thing.'

It was just after five that evening when Lebowitz was summoned by Hilton. Sitting on one of his large cream sofas, lighting subdued and the scene, out of the floor-to-ceiling window beside him, a panoramic night-time vista of Sunset Boulevard, Hilton looked like a man who'd just stepped out of his dressing room. As always, he had that air of calm order about him as though he'd recently emerged from an hour's meditation. Sitting, sipping his usual drink – hot water with a twist of lemon – he was the very picture of serenity.

'By close of play Monday,' he told Lebowitz once he was seated opposite, 'we'll be ready to go public. I'll have contracts signed by all parties to both deals. This afternoon Berkeley Square confirmed that Nile has been registered in every territory that matters.'

Lebowitz nodded.

'You've given some thought to how we're going to handle the announcement?' It wasn't so much a question, on Hilton's part, as an assumption.

'I believe a degree of unbundling is called for. I think we can take a couple of runs at this.'

'I thought you might.' A dry smile appeared on Hilton's face as he leaned back in his chair. Unbundling news into its component parts, to create several announcements instead of just one, was a strategy at which Lebowitz was Hollywood's master.

'First off is a major press conference. We go out with the record and endorsement deal fielding only the GCM media team.'

'No client appearances?' Hilton was surprised.

'Just photos in the media pack.'

Lebowitz's cavalier management of the media amused him.

'We want them to focus on the double-whammy. Same name record-signing and endorsement. Nile and Nile. Plus Isis and the new mystery man. There's plenty of news in there to keep them going a few days. Meantime every paparazzi in town will be hunting down Jordan—'

'We'll have to get him out of Chateau—'

'I've already put him in one of the guest houses. Nice and safe and also close to Unum.'

'Good.'

'When the time's right, we tip off the media for a joint Isis/Jordan photo-op. Script and package it for TV and tabloid front pages. By then there'll be a huge bounty riding on Jordan's head – every newspaper will be screaming for pictures. What we're looking at really is a global teaser campaign with a high-impact ending.'

Hilton regarded him with an appreciative expression. 'Excellent,' he said, 'the mileage we'll get out of this . . .'

'Biggest job we've ever done,' agreed Lebowitz.

Hilton paused for a moment. He always knew he could rely on Lebowitz to maintain tight control of the media. But there were other aspects of this operation where control would be more difficult. As he mused, his smile began to fade. 'What thoughts on Dobson?' he asked after a moment. The two of them had discussed the Dobson issue earlier on the phone, and come to a decision.

'Unum London will play ball.' Lebowitz nodded. 'Dobson will be getting an offer to sign a heavy-metal duo he represents on a session contract. Letter's going out in tonight's post.'

'Will remuneration be detailed?'

Lebowitz nodded. 'Forty grand sterling for a one-month contract.'

'Generous.'

'Unum are paying standard rate. We're topping it up fifty per cent. Small price to pay to neutralise—'

'Of course.'

'I'll have a follow-up call put in to him if we don't get a response on Monday. Unum have been co-operative.'

'I'll remember next time I speak to Ariel,' nodded Hilton, ever-conscious of the detail. The scheme to limit Vinnie Dobson's potential for damage had been straightforward; if he took the Unum money there was no way he could go whining to the media about being hard done by. If necessary, Lebowitz could make sure every news channel was aware that it was only Jordan's efforts that had secured his former musical partner a contract. Dobson would have painted himself out of the picture: end of story. The question was: would he take it?

'We'll have to see which way he's going to jump it before doing anything else.' Lebowitz reflected his own thoughts.

Hilton nodded, thinking this through for a while. Outside, the darkness was complete, bumper-to-bumper traffic down on Sunset forming an untidy line of moving red lights between floodlit office blocks and billboards. Then, turning to eyeball Lebowitz with a penetrating expression, 'Tell me, you haven't mentioned how your session with Watson went today?'

Lebowitz's eyes flicked over Hilton's shoulder and out of the window. 'Bumpy ride,' he murmured. Then, looking back to where Hilton continued to scrutinise him closely, 'If you want to know the truth, there's something about him I don't trust.'

Hilton absorbed this carefully. 'It's not just a matter of house-training?'

The other shook his head, adamant. 'No. It's more than that.' Meeting Hilton's gaze across the darkness of his office, for a long while he regarded him with a grave expression before saying finally, 'The problem is, the guy just asks too many questions.'

7

It was a quarter to eight in the evening when Jasper Jones slipped into his black Kenzo suit jacket, turned off the light in his office, and headed down the dimly lit corridor towards the lifts. Earlier that month, Love Smith Ben David had landed a new commission with fees worth in excess of two million pounds. Timing was tight, however, which meant all hands to the pumps. For ten out of the past fourteen days, he'd worked from eight in the morning straight through till midnight. Now as he headed out, even though he knew he'd done his fair share, he couldn't avoid a twinge of guilt knowing that most of his colleagues would still be here in another four hours. But it wasn't every day he had such a promising dinner party to attend. One of his fellow guests was to be Gail Sinclair, tall, blonde and beautiful. They'd first met at a Models Against Mink fashion show only a few weeks before. He'd instantly been attracted, and to his very great pleasure, the interest had been reciprocated. Which was why he'd prevailed on mutual friends to set up tonight's dinner.

Walking past the finance department, he called out

goodnight to Daniel Croom, who was always around long after everyone else had left. Receiving no reply, he slipped his head round the door. Daniel wasn't at his desk, though his light was still on, as was his computer, showing the Reuters screen-saver. It was more than Jones could resist; a news junkie through and through, he stepped across to scan the latest updates.

And then he saw it: just in from Los Angeles, the announcement from celebrity agency GCM that Isis and co-star Jordan Hampshire had signed an endorsement contract with British firm Berkeley Square cosmetics, to coincide with the launch of their new joint album, *Nile*. Jordan Hampshire, an unknown male vocalist, discovered by GCM, hailed from Wimbledon, south London. Jones had to reread the story three times to believe it. This was incredible, he thought, his mind spinning with the implications – the most astonishing turn of events. And One Commando could only benefit.

There was a sound behind him. Jones turned to find Croom at the door.

'Oh. Dan. Just popped in to say goodnight.'

The other stepped past him to his desk. 'Looking very pleased with yourself,' he observed Jones's smile.

'Oh,' Jones nodded towards the screen, 'just some interesting news.'

Making his way down to ground level in the lift a few moments later, he reflected that he'd planned to take a couple of bottles of chardonnay with him tonight. Scratch that idea, he decided. Make it two bottles of Dom Perignon.

But before he went anywhere, he'd be placing a call to Bengt Larson; this new, unknown star, Jordan Hampshire, had just stepped into One Commando's firing line. The sooner they knew a lot more about him, the better.

Mark stood in his bathrobe on the verandah of the Beverly Hills residence that was now his home, overlooking the lush green lawns, feather-leafed palms and glorious fuchsia baskets. 'Guest house' was the phrase Elizabeth had used. 'Mansion' would have been more appropriate. A double storey palazzo with four huge bedrooms, sumptuous entertaining areas, and a dazzlingly blue swimming pool, the place was equipped with every toy a man could wish for – spa, sauna, mini-golf course, billiard room, satellite TV, and a video library that occupied two entire walls of the viewing room. Situated high up in the hills, the GCM guest house had one of the most prestigious addresses in the suburb – and faced across the road to another home with a massive Italianate marble entry owned by a Hollywood studio.

At eight o'clock on a sun-drenched California morning, breakfast had just been served by his housekeeper. A dab hand in the kitchen, Mrs Martinez had prepared a trayload of fruit crushes and freshly baked croissants, accompanied by preserves and a percolator of full-roasted Columbia coffee. Not that he was in any mood to eat breakfast today. As he continued to pace about his multi-million dollar surroundings, Mark had never felt so angry in all his life. Exasperated was the way he was feeling. And, most of all, used.

The cause of his upset was sitting on the glass verandah table. It had arrived by courier at seven twenty-five this morning, a three-inch-thick pile of press cuttings, showing how the GCM announcement had been reported in that day's papers around the world. Most articles were dominated by photos of Isis and headlines about the double-whammy Nile endorsement and album release. All tied the news in

with the One Commando attack on Lefevre: in signing up
to Berkeley Square, were Isis and he putting their lives on
the line, the tabloids sensationally demanded.

But it was all the stuff about Jordan Hampshire that was
driving him crazy. Most of the papers had used those awful
photos GCM had shot of him a few days ago, leaning against
a Rolls-Royce, arm draped about the Spirit of Ecstasy and
wearing a dreadful smirk and the even more dreadful haircut. As if the pictures weren't bad enough, the captions were
worse. And all of them followed the same theme: 'Rags to
Rollses,' trumpeted *LA People*; 'Lewisham to LA,' proclaimed
the *Mirror*. According to the tabloids, he'd been down and
out in London, living in an inner-city sink estate when he
got his big break. He'd been abandoned by his father as a
two-year-old, said most of the papers, while they all
announced that his mother had brought up the family on
the dole.

It was outrageous! You got the impression he'd been a
no-hoper, a member of the economic underclass before
Hilton Gallo had shown up on his white charger. And as
for his mother – what an insult! What did they think she'd
been doing for the last thirty years, working her fingers to
the bone? He was especially disgusted to see the famous LA
syndicated columnist Inky Mostyn repeating all that crap.
Inky, whose column in a British tabloid he'd devoured every
week, believing the dapper, bow-tied author to be the
authentic voice of Hollywood. So much for authentic! He'd
turned out to be just as much of a sleaze-bucket as the rest
of them.

But that wasn't where the crap ended – not by a long
shot. Continuing the rags-to-riches hysteria, some of the
papers reported on his arrival in LA, how he was living a
'champagne lifestyle' at the Chateau Marmont where his

suite was just down the corridor from Leonardo di Caprio's.
Some determined hack from *The Globe* had interviewed
Chateau Marmont staff who, the very model of discretion,
had refused to divulge any information at all about him
except that his favourite room service order had been smoked
salmon bagels with cream cheese, and Cadbury's Fruit 'n'
Nut chocolate. That was enough for *The Globe* to make out
that the 'reclusive' Jordan Hampshire – where did they get
that from? – led a solitary, Howard Hughes-like existence,
alone in his luxury hotel suite, living off room service. They'd
even commissioned a psychologist to analyse his eating
habits. He was clearly insecure in his new environment, said
the shrink, pointing out that bagels with cream cheese was
classic 'comfort food'. He'd probably been suffering badly
from jet-lag too – using the chocolate to pep up his energy
levels.

If it hadn't been about him, he'd have laughed out loud
at what a total aberration of reality it all was. He'd known
before that you shouldn't believe everything you read in the
papers, but he'd never had any idea it was this bad! And it
was all very well for Lebowitz to tell him he shouldn't take
it personally – but it wasn't Lebowitz they were writing about.
Just laughing it off was a lot easier said than done. Anyway,
there were other people involved. What about his mother?
What about Lloyd?

Flicking through the press coverage – page after page of
it – wondering what to do, Mark quickly became increasingly vexed. All of this made him feel as though he was
nothing more than someone out of a second-rate soap opera,
a character whose whole life could be fictionalised according to whatever story-line editors had decided on. They'd
twisted so much about him already – and he hadn't even
opened his mouth yet!

He was still wondering what to do when, behind him, there was a knocking on the glass verandah door. Mrs Martinez was pointing at her watch.

'Your driver is ready in ten minutes,' she reminded him.

He looked up at her, nodding blankly. He recalled the advice Lebowitz had given him: 'When it gets really bad, and I can promise you it will, just try to remember it's not really you they're talking about. In fact, it's got nothing to do with you. It's a Jordan Hampshire thing.' He couldn't say he hadn't been warned, he thought as he glanced over the verandah table one last time, before making his way inside and upstairs to his bedroom. He couldn't say he hadn't been briefed to expect it.

As he got dressed in Levis and a YSL shirt, all the unsavoury press details whirling through his mind, he was struck by a different thought; he could understand how the gutter press would sensationalise and exaggerate any story they were given. But there were some things they'd *all* got wrong. Like the thing about his Mum – that made him more furious than anything – saying the family had lived on the dole, when all the years they'd been growing up she used to come home grey with exhaustion from her long hours in the dry cleaner's. So why had all the papers run that crap? And where had they got the line about him living in some inner-city sink estate? Where had that come from? It was as though GCM had put out the angles and the press had all faithfully repeated the stories. But he'd given one of Lebowitz's sharp-suited henchmen, Philip Kaylis, his full life story during a briefing session, and anyway he'd seen the announcement media release when it went out, and it hadn't carried any lurid personal details.

Hurrying through to the bathroom, he brushed his teeth and tried not to look at his hair. Then returning downstairs and grabbing the lyrics and music for today's session he headed towards the garage, where Denzil, his large black bodyguard-cum-driver was waiting.

'We've got company today,' announced Denzil as he arrived, nodding in the direction of the gates.

'How d'you know?'

'Two of them have been up ladders already.'

After all the coverage he guessed it shouldn't be surprising paparazzi were covering all the options. One of the papers had said there was a bounty riding on his head – the media had been screaming out for a joint appearance by Isis and him at the press conference, but no such opportunity had been forthcoming.

'So what do we do?' he asked Denzil.

'Same as usual.' The bodyguard was opening the back door of the Lincoln limo. 'Maybe get under the blanket.' Then, seeing his expression, 'Just till we get out the gates.'

He felt more than stupid crouching behind Denzil's seat, shrouded in a black light-proof wrap. But he'd had his orders from Lebowitz: he was to stay strictly out of sight.

No sooner had the electric gates started sliding open than there was a flurry of activity. He could hear the clamour of shouted questions and clank of hastily moved aluminium ladders as the limo shot down the driveway, climaxing in a chorus of noise and flashing as they went through the gates, photographers holding flash cameras right up to the tinted glass and shooting off exposures. Denzil cursed under his breath as they accelerated down the street.

'What's going on?' Mark wanted to know.

'Bastards on scooters.'

'How far behind?'

'All around. 'Bout five of them.'

Mark was keen to shrug off the blanket. 'D'you reckon they'll—'

'Best you stay under there . . . sir.'

It was a less than comfortable journey into Unum that morning. Thirty-five minutes under a shroud while paparazzi weaved and curved alongside the limo. Then when they reached the studio, there was another media encampment to contend with. So this was how life was to be, thought Mark, until Lebowitz and the boys had decided the time was right: hiding behind security walls and under blankets in the back of cars while all the time those bastards printed whatever they liked about him.

When he finally got out at the other end he was disoriented and shaken. Denzil saw him into the studios, which were the usual hive of industry, with technicians, musicians, couriers and assorted suits moving about the corridors of the sprawling complex. In the last three days he'd learned to find his way through the labyrinthine maze to Studio 18, where 'the Isis album', as it was generally known, was being recorded. He was still adjusting to the light, after the pitch-blackness of the last half hour, as he made his way down a passage, when he noticed the group of people coming towards him from the opposite direction. Sound engineers and studio executives were jostling about someone at the centre of the group, every one of them with a line to pitch, or so it seemed. Until that moment, Mark's only thought had been getting to the studio – on his very first day, an Unum exec had been at pains to explain the punitive costs of every studio minute. But he couldn't help paying close attention as the group drew nearer, and he caught a first glimpse of the person who was attracting all the attention.

Amazingly, he didn't get it at first. Her very familiarity made her difficult to place. For a few instants he was trying to compute where he knew her from. Then just as they were about to pass, he realised! And halted. The next few moments happened in slow motion. He found himself saying her name out loud, half in surprise, half in greeting. Looking up from where she had been engaged in conversation, she turned to make eye contact. There was recognition – he could tell immediately. He was poised, focusing on her every action. It was the moment he'd imagined for so long, for years as nothing more than a daydream, but in the last few days as a far more tangible reality. He was stepping into the presence of his idol. The supernova with whom his name, as of yesterday evening, had become inextricably linked.

As they drew closer, he wondered what he should say – what she would say; this unexpected encounter had caught him unawares. But Isis was raising her right hand, her fingers straightening. He stood, as though mesmerised, taking in every frame of the action. Her hand drew closer to her face, her motion slowing as she came directly opposite him. Even so, it had happened before he'd fully realised it; she'd delivered him a salute. A salute! That casual gesture of acknowledgement you made to a neighbourhood acquaintance or while encountering someone vaguely known to you in the street. Before she'd even passed him, she was already glancing away.

He leaned against the wall, turning his head to follow the progress of the small group down the corridor. He could hardly believe it! She hadn't stopped! Hadn't even deigned to greet him by name. However insignificant he was compared to her, they were still partners in this album! But she'd treated him with the kind of flip casualness she might show towards a delivery man or the garbage collector. He watched the group as it reached the end of the passage and turned out of view. Not for the first time this morning he found himself wondering what in Christ's name he was doing in Los Angeles.

Moments later, he strode into the Studio 18 mixing room.

'Jordan!' Sam Bach greeted him, gesturing through to the studio. 'We're ready to start rolling.'

'I need to make a call first.'

Bach glanced pointedly at his watch. Mark pointedly ignored him. He'd just begun to realise what he hadn't fully realised before this morning – that despite the big deals and big money, he was just a commodity. A story for the papers. A voice to support Isis's. If he didn't stand up for himself, no one else was going to.

A short while later, he'd obtained from Unum switchboard the number of *LA News*, and was demanding to speak to Inky Mostyn. When Mostyn answered the phone, his voice was every bit as loftily acerbic as his writing suggested.

'This is Jordan Hampshire,' announced Mark, 'and I'm extremely pissed off about what you wrote today.'

Bach and several sound engineers had turned, and were looking at Mark in astonishment.

'You know, I actually used to be a fan of yours,' Mark continued, indifferent to their startled expressions. 'I used to read your column every week in London. I reckoned you had the inside track, you told things straight. Then this morning I open the paper and find you've written all this unadulterated crap—'

'Whatever do you mean?' prickled Inky.

'The stuff about my mother bringing us up on the dole. And me living in some "sink" estate.'

'To which details, precisely, do you object?' Inky seemed not to understand.

Mark shook his head. 'All of it! It's just not true!'

There was a pause at the other end, and the sounds of paper being shuffled, before Inky responded, 'If it's not true, then you shouldn't authorise your publicity agents to circulate it.'

'Publicity agents?' repeated Mark, taken aback.

'Global Creative Management,' Inky rumbled. 'It's all here, quite clearly—'

'But they showed me the media release.' His voice rose in indignation. 'It didn't say anything—'

'Wasn't in the release. It was in the Biographical Notes.' Then, responding to the silence at the other end, Inky sighed rather grandly. 'My dear boy, *this* kind of media release is merely the "hors d'oeuvres". It seems to me that GCM have passed you by on the entrée.'

Mark heard the click at the other end with a spasm of anger. Face darkening, he reached into his Levis, took out his wallet and extracted a card from it, before dialling the number printed there. Meeting Bach's gaze across the mixing room, his eyes challenged the man to raise objection to this second telephone call.

'Leo Lebowitz's office,' came the brisk voice at the other end.

'I need to speak to him right away.' Mark's voice was staccato with rage.

'He's in a meeting at this time—'

'Then get him out of the meeting.'

'He's not in the GCM building.'

'I want him to call me at Unum studios the moment he gets back—'

'Aren't you involved in recording? That's Jordan Hampshire, isn't it?'

'No. It's Mark Watson. And I don't care if we're in the middle of a track, I want to speak to him *immediately*!'

* * *

London
Thursday, 16 September

It had been a crazy twenty-four hours for Vinnie Dobson. The craziness had begun that morning with the letter from Unum Music. Completely out of the blue and signed by some guy he'd never even heard of, Unum were offering him a forty grand session deal for 'The Holy Black', a heavy-metal duo who played the South London pub and club circuit. The deal was worth eight grand to him in commission.

Usually any breakthrough like this would have him on his mobile within minutes, making sure all his industry contacts knew that Vinnie Dobson was moving and shaking, and still a force to be reckoned with. In other circumstances, he'd have been behind the wheel of his Merc heading directly round to see Rick and Headley, aka 'The Holy Black', a magnum of Dom Perignon at the ready.

But Vinnie smelled a rat. Unum was one of the world's largest music companies, and despite marketing through a dozen different labels, it was notoriously hard to penetrate, especially for new artists. He'd even read once that it was Unum's policy only to take on musicians who'd already made it with other labels – Unum had no interest in developing new talent. Which was why Unum was one of the few music companies Vinnie hadn't ever bothered to contact. So why this unsolicited offer? And why 'The Holy Black', who were virtually unknown outside their South London beat? Just exactly what was going on, and who was behind it?

He hadn't had long to wait. Within hours of getting the letter, mid-way through that afternoon, had come the phone call from the *Mirror*. It was the first Vinnie had heard about Mark Watson's record deal with Unum; the first he knew of his début with Isis. 'No comment' was all he'd managed, too

shaken to say anything else. He hadn't known that GCM
had even been in touch with Mark again – let alone that
Mark had left London and was now in LA calling himself
'Jordan Hampshire' and signing up endorsement contracts!

No sooner had he hung up than the phone was ringing
again – this time the *News of the World*. Repeating his 'no
comment' line, this time with a flash of anger, he slammed
the hall phone down, then reckoned he'd better go into his
office and work out what to do next. But to get to the office
he had to walk through the lounge, where his parents were
watching TV.

'What's all this about?' his mother asked, regarding his
furious expression as the phone began ringing yet again. It
was exactly the wrong question at the wrong time. Because
the full impact of what had just happened unleashed an
anger Vinnie didn't even try to contain.

'That bastard Mark Watson! He's taken me to the fucking cleaners!'

'Language!' his father rebuked, as his mother got up to
answer the phone.

But Vinnie was in no mood for parental edicts. Storming
towards his office door, he raged about Mark's duplicity, going
behind his back and cutting him out of deals, even though
he owed his entire singing career to him.

When Vinnie's mother appeared at the door saying, 'It's
the *Daily Telegraph*. They want to interview you', his father
retorted sharply, 'He won't speak to them!'

Vinnie glared angrily at his father. 'Maybe I should!' he
blazed, making his way back towards the hallway, 'Maybe I
should tell them what a two-timing bastard—'

'You speak to any journalist,' his father roared across him,
'and you can pack your bags and get out right now. I won't
have my family's name dragged through the press!'

The row that followed had been more acrimonious than any before. While Vinnie and his father raged, his mother had taken three calls from two more papers and a newswire before unplugging the phone in exasperation. Meantime, Vinnie's mobile was ringing insistently in his office. Such was his father's wrath that for a while it seemed as though the two of them might even come to blows – then it all got too much for Mrs Dobson who broke down. Leaving his father to comfort her, Vinnie strode back into the hall, seized his coat and left the house, slamming the door behind him.

That afternoon, Vinnie was sickened to find the *Evening Standard* full of the Isis and 'Jordan Hampshire' story. His mother tried plugging the phone back in the wall – but for only half an hour before pulling it out again. The media hadn't given up the chase. If anything, they seemed even more desperate to speak to Vinnie. Holed up in his office, sullen and resentful, he kept his mobile phone diverted to voicemail, receiving no fewer than twenty-eight messages from hacks wanting to speak to him. Much as he longed to vent his feelings, to tell the whole world the truth about the double-dealing shithead, he knew that he'd have to find a new place to shift out to first. The moment he did, he reckoned – like in a couple of hours' time – he'd get hold of that kiss-and-tell bloke to auction off his story to the highest bidder.

He still hadn't worked anything out when he went down to the Lamb that evening. To his surprise, the moment he walked in the door he was treated like a celebrity. The local hero. It caught him completely unawares; people just started standing up and clapping and calling out to him – even though they knew he'd had nothing to do with it, it was as though he'd pulled off the deal of the century. It was like he was a Mafia don strolling up to the bar as a wave of hand-clapping burst out around him and all the regulars surged forwards to greet him.

After all the hype in the *Standard*, Vinnie had relished the opportunity of telling things the way they *really* were. Mark Watson might have been one of the more popular performers at the Lamb, and his brother might be playing snooker less than ten yards away in the corner of the pub, but Vinnie had soon put everyone straight on just what a double-dealing bastard Watson had turned out to be. He reminded them how it was he who'd first recognised Mark's talents and given him his break in showbiz. It was he who'd given Mark a platform, and arranged the gigs and sent out countless demo tapes at huge expense. And how had he been rewarded? Mr High-and-Mighty only goes behind his back to GCM, doesn't he? He meets Hilton Gallo, cuts Vinnie out of the deal, and next thing they all know, he's jetting off to LA, leaving a trail of unfinished business and unpaid bills behind him.

Everyone remembered the row between Mark and Vinnie two weeks before. Once they'd heard Vinnie's side of the story, they were as pissed off as he was. Not that they needed any prompting. Torn out pages from the *Standard* had been circulating round the bar, showing photos of Mark in Los Angeles, standing next to a Rolls-Royce and sporting a new haircut. Everyone agreed he looked a right dickhead with his hair carved up that way, trying to be oh so cool and trendy. His clothes were even worse, producing hoots of derision – didn't he know what a complete ponce he was making of himself, dressed up like some yo-man pimp. As for the name, just who in Christ's name did he think he was? Regulars down at the Lamb didn't have any time for those who got ahead of themselves, and tall poppies were very definitely there to be cut down. Mark Watson might have acted like he was their mate once, but he'd obviously been taking them for a ride; he hadn't been the person they thought they'd known at all.

Downing a few pints before ordering a plate of curry, Vinnie revelled in being centre of attention and having everyone agree with him – made a pleasant change from all the crap he was getting at home. He didn't tell anyone about the Unum letter, currently safely folded in his leather jacket pocket. He still hadn't worked out how to play that one.

By nine o'clock, and a few more beers later, Vinnie was feeling better than he had so far that day. Watching some of his mates take over the snooker tables, he'd studiously ignored Lloyd Watson before managing a couple of sets himself. He was returning his snooker cue to its rack and was about to head back to the bar, when he was approached by a bloke from one of the other tables who asked him for a game.

'You're Vinnie Dobson, aren't you?'

Vinnie glanced up at the tall, solidly built foreigner with the red hair and beard and serious, slate-grey eyes. Although his accent sounded European, there was also a trace of an American twang. He extended his hand – Vinnie shook it briefly.

'It's a privilege to meet you,' the stranger said, with a respect in his voice that sounded as if he meant it. Vinnie just nodded. The bloke was a bit different, and while he felt flattered, he was also on guard.

'You a journalist?' he asked, suspiciously.

'Definitely not,' the other looked offended, 'what makes you think that?' He walked round the side of the table and slotted some coins into the ball release. The balls tumbled out in a noisy volley.

'Can't be too careful,' muttered Vinnie.

'Wise,' agreed the other, 'very wise.'

They began setting up the balls when the stranger continued, 'The real reason I came here tonight was to congratulate you on your judgement.'

Vinnie raised his eyebrows. He didn't know what the bloke was getting at, and he was still suspicious about who he was, but there was something intriguing about him, a powerful magnetism. The two of them began their game, Vinnie breaking, before pocketing a few balls with ease. Then, leaning over the table with his cue, the other said, 'You've a lot of supporters, you know.'

'Yeah,' Vinnie watched him pot a ball, 'the blokes have been great.'

'I don't just mean here. I mean all over the country.'

'Oh, sure, I've had hacks on the phone all the time.'

The other glanced up at him. 'I bet you have,' he said in that admiring tone.

'I've been keeping well schtum.' Vinnie was back on the table, clearing it with ease. 'You only need to open your mouth,' he said importantly, 'and these guys twist every word you say.'

The other nodded. 'That's what I mean about judgement,' he told him.

'Yeah?'

'A lot of other people would have been persuaded to sell their story to the *News of the World* or something.'

'Wankers!' declared Vinnie.

'Very few people understand you can be more effective keeping out of sight.'

Vinnie got the feeling this was more than just some casual chat. The other bloke seemed to be making a point, but he couldn't work out yet exactly what.

'When you say more effective?' he asked, rapping the table

with his cue to indicate which pocket he was potting into.

Moving closer, the other leaned across the table, voice lowered. 'You're not the only one disgusted by Watson. It would be understandable if you decided you wanted some . . . compensation.'

Vinnie looked up at him sharply. The possibility still lingered in his mind that this bloke might be a journalist trying to catch him off guard, or hoodwink him into saying something that would be turned against him. Although his manner was a lot different from any journalist Vinnie had encountered before. In a strange way, he came across like someone out of the army. After a pause, Vinnie replied, 'Do you have anything particular in mind?'

The other met his scrutiny as he murmured, 'Like I said before, you're very perceptive.' It was the stranger's turn again, but Vinnie, having almost cleared the table, had left him snookered. The black ball rolled across the table directly into the far pocket.

'What I want to know is, why are you worried about what Mark's done to me?' Vinnie removed the ball, and prepared to clear up.

'I'm not.' The other surprised him with his frankness. 'It's him signing up with Isis that I find . . . distasteful.' He watched Vinnie effortlessly pocket the two last balls, before saying, 'So you see, we find ourselves in the same corner.'

'We?' Vinnie turned to face him, curiosity now as strong as his suspicion. 'I don't even know who you are.'

Bengt Larson regarded him carefully. Vinnie Dobson had been a lot easier to isolate than he had expected. And although as prickly as he'd been warned, he'd also proven susceptible to flattery. What's more, while absorbed in his previous games of snooker, he'd left his leather jacket thrown over a bar stool. Conducting a routine search of its pockets,

Larson had discovered a letter he knew would make his job very much easier. He nodded in the direction of a quiet corner of the pub. 'Why don't we . . . ?' he suggested.

Vinnie followed, glass in hand, to a badly lit table at a bay window, concealed from the rest of the pub by a fruit machine. No one would see them talking. Standing in the semi-darkness, Larson continued in confidential tones. 'My name is Alex Heindl,' he said, 'but that's not important. What is important is the group of people I work with. And my backers. You'd be surprised how powerful they are.'

Vinnie regarded him carefully. 'What don't you like about Isis?'

Larson's eyes narrowed. 'She's just taken three million dollars off Berkeley Square to endorse their products. She should know better. So should your former client.'

Vinnie instantly recalled the attack on the Berkeley Square's boss just a few weeks ago – it had been mentioned again in this morning's papers. In particular, there were the descriptions of how the bloke had had his eyes gouged out. The attack had made a big impression on Vinnie. He vividly remembered the TV coverage. Now he met Larson's expression with a sudden, new respect.

'Are you the ones—'

'You're probably thinking along the right lines,' Larson interrupted him, 'but I can't tell you anything about who we are.' Then as Vinnie was about to protest he continued, 'Not here. Not now. Just like I wouldn't expect you to tell everything about yourself to a complete stranger. But we do have a common enemy.'

Vinnie was following him very carefully, remembering the way the police detective had described the activists on TV. They were extremely dangerous, was what he'd said, and highly likely to strike again. The idea of having a commando group take revenge on Big-Shot Watson was one that suddenly seized his imagination. His mind was a tumult of excitement as he stared at Larson with even greater compulsion.

'I'm sure you would like to see some harm come to him.' Larson spoke with assurance. 'What I need to know is – how badly?'

Vinnie took a swig from his beer glass. Nothing would give him greater pleasure than waking up to read that Mark Watson had returned to his luxury Hollywood bolt-hole one night to have his dick chopped off and shoved in his mouth – like in that movie he'd seen. There again, he didn't want to have anything to do with it if it meant putting himself at risk. 'Depends, doesn't it?' he said to Larson.

'Of course it does.' Larson held his stare. 'We wouldn't expect you to get your hands dirty.'

'No?'

'It would help us more if you pretended that all was forgiven.'

'You've got to be . . . !'

Larson stepped closer towards him. 'What we need, more than anything, is information. Intelligence. And you can get it for us. But no one must ever make the connection.'

Vinnie's thoughts were racing again, only this time not with images of vengeance – but cash in the bank. Eight grand. This could be the perfect arrangement! He'd sign the Unum deal and take the money. Make out that he'd put the past behind him. Meantime, Mark Watson wouldn't have any idea what was about to hit him.

'So what happens next?' he asked Larson, the breathlessness of his voice betraying his excitement.

'You and my group have to trust each other,' Larson's eyes darted about the pub, making sure they were still alone and unnoticed, 'and trust must be earned. First, we take one simple step. You obtain a piece of information for us. In return, I tell you our plans.'

Vinnie nodded. It seemed reasonable. Regarding the other's cool blue eyes with a sharp intensity he asked, 'What information would that be, then?'

8

It was Hilton Gallo himself who returned Mark's angry telephone call from Studio 18. Minutes after Mark had demanded Lebowitz call him, he was summoned from the studio, where he'd been running through initial sound level checks.

'I understand you were after Leo, urgently?' Hilton was cool as ever. Lebowitz's secretary, Mark realised, must have reacted to his tone and gone directly to the boss.

'Too right. I'm pissed off about all the crap in the media. I thought it was just the papers at first, but Inky Mostyn says you guys are putting it out.'

'Let me understand this correctly,' Hilton's voice notched up a tone, 'you're saying there are distortions in the material GCM released to the media?'

'I am.'

'I understood you had reviewed that material?'

'Only the media release. But all the personal stuff was in the Biographical Notes which I never saw. I phoned Inky Mostyn to complain about his column and he told me he was only repeating what GCM put out.'

'Well, in the first case, the Biographical Notes were prepared on the basis of your briefing of Philip Kaylis. Second, the notes would have been sent to you for approval if you'd requested them—'

'How could I request something I didn't know existed?'

'—and third, the terms of your contract specifically preclude you from talking to reporters without GCM's authorisation. Fortunately, we enjoy a very good relationship with Inky who I'm sure can be persuaded to ... overlook your conversation. If you'd spoken to the wrong journalist it could have been disastrous.' His tone was accusatory. 'Did you speak to anybody else?'

'No, I didn't, but—'

'Don't you see, in the wrong hands the media could present us as being at odds—'

'That's because we are!'

'Mark.' It was one of the rare occasions Hilton called him by name, and he used it now to convey a powerful combination of purported sympathy – and steely determination. 'It's possible that Philip misunderstood what you told him, or misstated some of the details, but we never intended knowingly to circulate false information about you – who would benefit from it?'

That wasn't something Mark was able to answer.

'You know, the worst of it is all the stuff they're publishing in Britain about my mother living off the dole.' There could be no doubting the strength of his feeling. 'I don't know anyone who works harder. I've never known her *not* to work. For three years when we were growing up she never took more than a four-day holiday. Couldn't afford to. How d'you reckon she's supposed to feel with everyone she knows reading about her being some welfare couch potato?'

There was a pause before Hilton responded, 'I understand

you're reacting from the noblest motives. And I want you to realise we are also concerned about your best interests and want to sort this out. That's why I'm calling you personally.'

'I just don't see where Kaylis got this stuff—'

'Nor do I. But you have my assurance that the moment I put the phone down, I will be asking questions.'

'Good, because my family will want answers. I haven't spoken to them yet and probably won't today because of the time difference. But it's not going to be easy—'

'Rest assured, I'll be back in touch before close of play.' Hilton paused before reverting to his usual businesslike tone. 'On the subject of media coverage, GCM is concerned by the strong reference to the One Commando issue. We were expecting some mention, of course, but the level isn't helpful. Not to us, nor to Berkeley Square.'

With his own preoccupations, Mark hadn't paid too much attention to One Commando. But the animal rights group had been mentioned in most articles. He could see why the papers were doing it – it was a good chance for them to repeat the details of the Lefevre assault with lip-smacking relish.

'We need to shake them off the news agenda,' Hilton was saying.

'How can you stop journalists writing about them?'

'They've already milked the connection for as much as it's worth. They've said everything about One Commando there is to say.'

'So why are you worried about them?'

'Worry isn't the word I'd use,' Hilton corrected him. 'It's more *concern* that the market doesn't buy into all the tabloid hysteria. Our feeling is that if we put a different spin on the endorsement deal, the media will find it hard to keep on plugging away at One Commando.'

'That's something GCM will do, is it?'

'We'll provide the back-up, certainly,' Hilton told him, 'but you'll need to drive it.'

'How do you mean?' The warning bells were sounding. What did GCM want from him this time? Were they setting him up again for the media to make some ridiculous parody of his life? And was this why Hilton Gallo was calling him personally?

'I have no doubt,' Hilton's tone was significant as he looked over to where Lebowitz had been following the conversation from across his desk, 'you'll find the proposition, very, very interesting.'

London

Alan rushed up the staircase of his Clapham home, taking the stairs two at a time. Summoned unexpectedly by Larson just three hours before, his head was spinning from the events of the afternoon.

To begin with, when he'd arrived at the disused Kennington warehouse – donning a ski mask, as instructed, before entering – he'd found himself among a group of five masked commandos. He couldn't tell if any of the others had been involved in the Lefevre operation. In the fetid darkness of the vast corrugated aluminium shed, which was evidently used to store market stalls, they had assembled wordlessly before Larson who, powerful and dominating, explained One Commando's new purpose.

As he listened to the One Commando leader's extraordinarily audacious plans, he'd realised that Larson's ambition went way beyond another Lefevre-style operation. His new scheme would drive One Commando's objectives to a climactic conclusion. It would be the end-game, the final showdown; after the national furore following the Lefevre attack, he could scarcely conceive what fallout would follow Larson's latest plans.

As if all of that weren't enough, at the end of the briefing, Larson had pulled him aside from the others, leading him behind an ancient creaking market stall.

'I don't need to involve you directly in these operations,' he'd said. 'As a footsoldier your skills are surplus to requirements.' For one heart-stopping moment, Alan wondered if Larson doubted him. But surely he wouldn't have summoned him to the meeting if he didn't trust him? He stared up at where Larson's sunglasses glinted in a shard of light that fell from a hole in the roof, high above.

'What we need you for is intelligence.' He squeezed Alan's shoulder so hard it was all he could do not to grimace. 'We need all the information we can get – especially on our main targets. Do you understand?'

Alan nodded.

'Any contribution you make will be specially appreciated by the powers that be.'

There was that phrase again. And this time with a direct link to him.

'It is an opportunity for you to make your mark,' Larson told him, as though reflecting his thoughts. 'You'll be doing something for the movement which no one else can.'

All the way home, Alan had wondered how he'd play things. Larson was entrusting him with exactly what he sought – a project that would bring him to the attention of whoever really ran One Commando. The ideological force behind the group. The ultimate decision-maker. If he could deliver, Alan knew, he'd have set himself up as a key player. He'd be ideally placed to conclude his mission. But how could he give Larson what he wanted without opening up a whole new dimension of risk?

Reaching his attic workroom, he quickly logged on to his computer, opened up his e-mail package, and began to type.

Malibu, California

Isis was in her home studio when the phone call came through from Hilton. Standing, watching the sun slipping down behind the Pacific Ocean through the soundproofed glass, rehearsing her songs again and again, she'd been absorbed in her work when the phone introduced an unwelcome dose of reality. Something had come up, Hilton had told her quickly, and he needed to discuss it with her face to face. Might he visit her at home in, say, an hour? Isis had felt her chest tightening. She knew this must be serious. Hilton guarded his time jealously, and for him to come out to Malibu . . .

'Is it something to do with the Lefevre attack?' she'd wanted to know immediately.

'No. There haven't been any developments. This is more personal—'

'Christ!'

'Nothing you need worry about,' he reassured her hurriedly. 'It's actually very positive. But I think we should discuss it urgently.'

He'd arrived just over an hour later. Isis led him out to her balcony where they could sit in the shadows looking across to where the waves rolled in, washing the beach with silver.

'You got the press cuttings this morning, yes?' Hilton began, never one to waste time with small talk.

Isis nodded.

'Very strong coverage.'

'I know.' She didn't need Hilton to point out that the announcement had already generated at least three times the pre-publicity of her last album, *Eros*. Nor did she need to be told how all the hype was going to translate into sales. It was encouraging – extremely encouraging. Only, with the threat of One Commando given prominence in all the media, it was hard to feel upbeat.

'While all of that is very gratifying,' Hilton quickly read Isis's mood, 'Leo and I have also been giving a lot more thought to your concerns. In the last few days we've met several times for discussions. Leo's come up with a suggestion I think's well worth pursuing.'

In the shadows, Isis followed Hilton sceptically. Leo Lebowitz was indisputably the most ingenious PR spinner in LA, but she was highly doubtful he'd come up with any 'suggestion' that wasn't simply calculated to generate more air time and column inches.

'What we're looking at here is the issue of risk. You're worried about the risk of exposure.'

Isis didn't respond. She first wanted to see where this analysis was leading.

'As with any other risk,' Hilton continued, 'what Lebowitz is suggesting is that we do what we can to minimise the chances of your worst fears being realised.'

'This is starting to sound familiar,' her tone was cynical.

'Just hear me out,' he told her. 'If your name were to be romantically linked to someone, the result would be a highly effective diversion—'

'That would depend who that someone was.' There was a long pause before she demanded, 'Don't tell me you haven't got a name—'

'We do, of course.'

'Well?'

Hilton realised in her present frame of mind she was far from receptive. But there was no turning back now. Meeting her eyes in the darkness he murmured, 'Jordan Hampshire.' His expression was serious. 'Nothing long term.'

'Are you fucking crazy?' she exploded.

'We're talking six, eight weeks.'

'You're expecting me to let him stick his tongue down my throat—'

'It won't be necessary to go that far.'

But Isis wasn't listening to him. 'Make out with a goddam cellphone geek for a bit of publicity.'

'No,' Hilton countered, 'for the removal of risk.'

'You could at least have paired me off with someone a little more my type.'

'I know you don't like the idea of sharing the limelight—'

'It's not that.'

'I think it is. But you can't deny there's a certain logic to you and Jordan—'

'Oh, perfect logic if all you're looking for is constant media intrusion and harassment!' Her eyes blazed in the shadows. 'Why don't we just start a soap opera of my life and be done with it!'

Hilton waited a few moments before saying in measured tones, 'I've met Jordan several times and in my view he's a very personable young man. I would imagine he's been reticent in my company – no doubt in his own space he'd be a lively companion. If you were to meet him—'

'I already have.'

Hilton raised his eyebrows.

'I passed him at the studios this morning.' She remembered walking out from her early-morning session, in the midst of the usual retinue of sound engineers, Unum staff and security. The moment he'd appeared at the end of the corridor she'd recognised him. He was better in the flesh than the photographs she'd seen of him — bar the silly hair-cut. He'd looked spaced out, and as they'd got closer he'd slowed down with that jaw-on-the-ground groupie expression. Hilton was still scrutinising her carefully.

'Avoiding tough decisions has never been part of the deal,' he told her now.

'Hilton you're so persuasive.' She was facetious.

He shrugged. 'I'm just giving you an option. The rest is entirely up to you.'

She lowered her eyes, before glancing out to the surging breakers. Suddenly she felt like a wayward schoolgirl being carpeted by the headmaster. Hilton was the only one who ever made her feel this way. It was something in his detached style, she supposed, that made her face up to her own anger and suspicion. She supposed he *was* only trying to help.

'The point is,' he was saying, 'this is the risk we've had to live with ever since the beginning. There always has been the possibility that your secret—'

'I know! I know!' She was shaking her head. 'And most of the time I'm okay about it. But lately I've just felt threatened. The past few nights I've hardly been able to sleep.'

Hilton didn't respond, deciding instead to give Isis the opportunity to think over what he'd suggested. It was a long time before she spoke again, and when she did, her tone was fragile. 'What exactly would this . . . relationship entail?'

Bringing his hands together, he raised his fingers to his lips. 'A few dates. We'd want you to be seen out in each other's company at a couple of industry events.' Then, regarding her carefully, 'Timing is everything. The sooner the two of you are out somewhere together, the better.'

She absorbed this in silence for a long while before she asked, 'You think it'll be enough?'

He looked over at her imploring expression and wished he could give her the reassurance she sought. But there were no guarantees he could provide – she'd always known that. And it would have been wrong of him to pretend. So instead he answered, 'I think it's a good idea. And until we find out more about One Commando, it's the only real option we've got.'

London
Friday, 17 September

Lloyd Watson glanced at his watch in surprise when the doorbell rang. Just after ten in the evening. He wondered if his girlfriend Heidi had wangled an early shift at the hospital and come round to surprise him. Getting up from his chair, where he'd been sitting engrossed in *Inspector Morse*, he cast a critical eye across the sitting room: sleeping bags and crumpled pillows were strewn across the carpet from where two of his mates had been camping over. The remnants of his supper – a Domino's pizza box and several empty beer cans – littered the glass coffee table. Worst of all – Heidi's pet hate – all the ashtrays were still loaded from last night's post-pub party. He had to admit, it wasn't a pretty picture.

He walked through to the tiny hall, bracing himself for a tongue-lashing. The Banham front door had a security chain and fish-eye lens installed, although he never used them: why bother? But tonight, as he unlocked the catch, swung open the door, and caught sight of his visitor he felt a sudden tension in his throat. It wasn't Heidi on his doorstep. It was the very last person he'd expected to receive a visit from.

He instantly recalled his last conversation with Mark on the subject of Vinnie's vengeful streak. And his last encounter with Vinnie at the Lamb. He'd been among the group of regulars trying to calm him down – he hadn't doubted that Vinnie would have gone for Mark if it wasn't for all the blokes holding him back. Not that he'd have got very far; Mark could look after himself, Lloyd knew, just like he himself might have to right now.

But Vinnie was standing there with an embarrassed grimace on his face.

'Lloy-boy!' he greeted Lloyd with forced joviality, using the name he'd given him years before.

'Didn't think you'd want to come visiting?' Lloyd was direct. Looking him in the eye, he tried to figure out exactly what Vinnie was up to. He seemed calm enough though he'd probably had a few pints.

'Yeah, bit unexpected,' shrugged Vinnie. 'Can I come in?' He'd already stepped into the hall and was heading for the lounge, leaving Lloyd without much choice. Closing the front door, Lloyd followed him through.

'You know Mark's not here?' The thought occurred to him that perhaps Vinnie was after his older brother. 'He's—'

'In America. Yeah. I read the papers.' Vinnie sat back in the sofa, propping his feet up on the coffee table as he had dozens of times before.

Picking up the remote, Lloyd pressed the TV 'Mute' button, glancing at the screen as he did and wondering how long Vinnie planned hanging around. He decided not to offer him a beer. Lowering himself carefully into an ancient armchair, he looked over at Vinnie. 'You were pretty pissed off last time—'

'Oh. That!' Vinnie smirked. 'Yeah, well, that was then. This is now.'

It was a very different Vinnie from the one who'd been about to attack his brother. Very different too from the Vinnie that Siobhan O'Mara had told him about. Lloyd didn't try to hide his surprise.

'What's happened to change things?'

Vinnie shifted in the sofa before delivering one of his Big-Shot Music Producer looks. That had always irked Lloyd about Vinnie – he patronised him. Still treated him like Mark's kid brother, talking down to him and bragging about his exploits, expecting him to accept everything hook, line and sinker.

'This is to go no further than you and me.' Vinnie spoke conspiratorially, waving a finger between them.

Lloyd raised his eyebrows.

'I've just landed "The Holy Black" a forty grand recording contract.'

'That's amazing!' Lloyd exclaimed, thinking how pleased Rick and Headley would be. They'd been bashing away at the talent club circuit for years.

'So when's it coming out?'

Vinnie made a face. 'Session contract, not a record.'

'Who with?'

'That's the thing,' Vinnie eyeballed him, 'Unum Music.'

Then before Lloyd could react, 'I wasn't born yesterday. I know how things work. Let's face it, Mark probably put a word in for me.'

There was no 'probably' about it, so far as Lloyd could see. And Vinnie hadn't landed 'The Holy Black' a contract at all – Mark had got the Unum guys to throw it his way. Looking back at Vinnie, Lloyd said, 'Yeah. Mark's good that way.' He thought about his own job – he'd never have got his break into OmniCell if it hadn't been for Mark.

'So—' Vinnie was digging about in his pocket for a packet

of slim panatellas, before extracting one, removing the Cellophane wrapper, and lighting up, '—things have moved on a bit for me, you see.'

'I bet.' Lloyd eyed the panatella with distaste but decided not to be provocative by demanding Vinnie smoke it on the balcony.

'Foot in the door with Unum.' Vinnie was oblivious to Lloyd's expression. 'This is a first contract and I can build on it.'

'Sounds great.'

'Oh yes,' Vinnie couldn't resist it, 'just one of all kinds of new opportunities coming my way.'

'You mean, you've got other deals on the go?'

Vinnie gave him a secretive smile, thinking about his meeting with Larson. 'Like you wouldn't believe. New people, new deals – world's really opening up for me.'

Vinnie wouldn't divulge anything more and Lloyd wasn't going to give him the satisfaction of asking. Though he could hazard a guess about the 'new people' bit. Last time he'd seen him down the Lamb, Vinnie had been talking intently to a tall, bearded bloke with a strange accent. The pub got a lot of visitors, but the foreign man had sought Vinnie out. He'd played a few rounds of snooker with some of Lloyd's mates and, during the course of conversation, got to ask about Vinnie. Later, Lloyd had noticed the pair of them slipping out of the main section of the pub thick as thieves. Probably some hack wanting to buy Vinnie's story, thought Lloyd. Despite all Vinnie's bluster about not talking to reporters, it surprised Lloyd that he still hadn't cashed in on his former association with Mark. Even he had received calls from journalists promising large cheques in exchange for 'colour stories' about his brother. Had the foreign guy signed up Vinnie for some sort of exclusive?

'Way I see things,' Vinnie sucked on his panatella, 'I probably owe your brother an apology.'

He wasn't looking at Lloyd when he said it – which was just as well. This was so un-Vinnie that Lloyd couldn't conceal his scepticism.

'And thanks,' Vinnie continued, exhaling thoughtfully.

Well, those were two new words in his vocabulary, thought Lloyd. Next he was going to say he'd given his life to Jesus.

'Which is why I'm here.' He looked across at Lloyd's bemused expression. 'I tried to phone Mark, speak to him personally. Only problem is, when I called him at that hotel he was supposed to be staying in, they said he'd moved.'

'That's right. He's moved to a house somewhere.' Lloyd knew better than to say a mansion in Beverly Hills.

'You've got his number?'

Lloyd shook his head. 'Only spoken to him once since he moved and he called me. I reckon he can afford the long-distance rates.'

'Yeah.' Vinnie grinned, though his eyes weren't smiling. 'But, I mean, you could get his number for me?'

'Oh, sure,' Lloyd held his gaze. Of course he had Mark's number, but he had no intention of handing it over to Vinnie. Suspicions aroused, he didn't know what to make of Vinnie, except that he was up to something. Had his own agenda.

'He'll probably call me in the next week sometime. I'll ask him for it then.'

'Good.' Vinnie sat forward, tapping his ash into the opening of an empty beer can, before rising to his feet, mission accomplished.

'Coming down for a quick one?' he asked Lloyd, on the return to the front door, jerking his head in the general direction of the Lamb.

'It's all right, thanks. Need an early night.'

'Fair enough.'

Closing the door behind him, Lloyd returned to the lounge. He usually found Inspector Morse's investigations utterly engrossing, but tonight as he regarded the silent action, he had the unavoidable sensation that sinister events in real life had suddenly overtaken those on the screen.

9

Mark climbed into the back seat of the luxury Lincoln Town Car, pulled the dark blanket over his head, and braced himself for another round of flash cubes, car-thumping and yelled questions. He was less than ecstatic at being forced into discomfort once again by the very people at whose hands he and his family had received such a mauling. But it was for the last time. Hilton had promised him that.

'Less of them outside now,' Denzil tried keeping things upbeat as he closed the door behind him, 'the odds are stacked against them after dark.'

'Yeah.' Having laid his jacket out on the back seat, Mark was careful to avoid crushing his linen trousers. His clothes had been picked out for him by a wardrobe consultant sent over late that afternoon by GCM. And a stylist had spent twenty minutes fiddling with his hair, before applying various lotions and cosmetics to his face – none, he noted, manufactured by Berkeley Square – in preparation for what Hilton had described earlier in the day as the photo-opportunity of his life.

The GCM chief had phoned him, as agreed, after speaking to Kaylis about the Biographical Notes. It seemed there had been a genuine misunderstanding, he said. Mark had told Kaylis his mother lived in a council house. Not conversant with social services in Britain, Kaylis understood that to mean she was welfare dependent. As for the line about Mark living in an inner-city tenement, that's what Kaylis had taken him to mean by his use of the phrase 'housing estate'. Things had got lost in translation, concluded Hilton – and to prevent the possibility of such a thing ever happening again, he had instructed Lebowitz to ensure Mark received *all* media material in future, before distribution.

Mark hadn't said anything. Maybe it *had* just been a case of crossed wires. Then again, perhaps Lebowitz had deliberately sensationalised his past for the purpose of mass titillation. The fact was, he didn't think he could completely believe anything GCM came out with again. Meantime, Hilton's proposals to lose One Commando from the news agenda – and, at the same time, end his life in hiding – had taken him by surprise.

'We have in mind a photo-op,' he'd said.

'Hasn't that been on the cards?'

'Not the one we envisaged. We're planning to move things on a bit.'

'Yeah?'

'Leo and I have discussed this at length, and we believe it would be in your interests, as well as Isis's, for the two of you to be seen out together.'

'You mean,' Mark responded to his tone of voice, 'romantically?'

'Yes.'

Mark's astonishment was exceeded only by his certainty

about Isis's reaction to this. 'She'll never do it,' he told Hilton after a pause, 'she doesn't even like me.'

'What makes you say that?' Hilton moved automatically into damage-limitation mode.

'When I saw her at Unum she completely ignored me.'

'She's running to a tight schedule.'

'Not that tight!'

'I've already spoken to Isis and she's very willing.'

Quite the little cupid, Mark thought, but didn't say, still taken aback by the suggestion. After the current assault of half-truths and bare-faced lies, the prospect of another blaze of publicity in the near future didn't exactly thrill him. Especially seeing that it involved engineering his love life – or at least the appearance of it.

'Just think about it,' Hilton tried to enthuse him, 'intimate candle-lit dinners with the most famous pop chick in the world.'

Yeah, right, thought Mark. A few weeks ago he'd have been enthralled by the prospect. But now he knew nothing came without a pay-off.

'It's also a great way for you to make your first public appearance.' Hilton noted the silence. 'We'll put you into the right restaurant and by the time you come out every news organisation in the world will be waiting for you.'

For the first time in his life, Mark was beginning to realise why it was that famous people so often turned reclusive. After a lengthy pause he found himself asking, without really wanting to hear the answer, 'When did you want all this to happen?'

At the other end of the phone, Hilton was brisk. 'We've booked the two of you a table at Bianco Verdi tonight at eight.'

Now, as they drove out to Malibu, Denzil shaking off the

paparazzi, on the back seat Mark followed their progress on a Los Angeles street map. Looking at the map, it seemed hardly any distance at all from Beverly Hills to Malibu – but on the ground, the streets seemed to go on for ever, block after block of city that to an outsider's eyes formed an endless, anonymous sprawl. Once they'd got out to Malibu, however, it was something different, the affluence of the beachside community almost tangible. Denzil turned into a private driveway that led into what seemed like a fortress – he had to use his mobile phone to get the maid to open up the electronically controlled gates. Once inside, they found themselves sealed within a high-walled courtyard, requiring more security doors to be opened. While Denzil stayed outside with the car, Mark was shown inside to the lounge, where he was told to wait.

It was a strange sensation, finding himself in the home of the woman who'd been his idol, his fantasy. This view – a panoramic sweep over to where the silver breakers washed up on the beach – was the view that Isis looked out on during her private hours. These sumptuous damask chairs were the chairs she sat in. There was something voyeuristically thrilling but at the same time curiously matter-of-fact about being here. The room itself was long, cream carpeted and softly lit, opening out on to a balcony that overlooked the beach. Float-framed platinum discs bedecked its tangerine walls, and two Grammy awards stood on a corner shelf. On his way over here this evening, Mark had wondered if Isis would treat him any differently tonight than with the cool indifference of their studio encounter. But now as he stopped in front of each platinum disc, reading its inscription, he found himself wondering why he should have expected to be treated any differently. What was he to her, anyway?

When Isis did make her appearance, it was anything but grand. Rushing into the room, shoes in her hand, the first words she said to him were, 'Running late.' She was stylish in sculpted black, her blonde hair swept back, cleavage carefully revealed, and diamonds glinting at her ears and round her neck.

'We'll use the Mercedes.' She glanced over at him briefly, gesturing with the shoes that he should follow her. Obediently, he crossed the room, catching her scent as he did so – a warm, ambrosial fragrance that trailed after her in the hallway, through a door concealed by a large, tapestry wall-hanging and down some stairs towards the garage. By the time he'd stepped into the far side of the customised stretch Mercedes, Isis was already talking to someone on her mobile phone. Her driver, Frank, took them through security, first into the courtyard, then out through the gates. Mark sat silently as Isis ended one call before promptly beginning another, and the car glided back towards the city in the direction from which he'd so recently come. Any hopes he might have had of a tête-à-tête en route were soon ended. And while a powerful impulse made him want to just stare at Isis now that he was sitting so close to her, he didn't want to seem like a star-struck fan. So he just looked out of the front and side windows instead. Not for the first time since arriving in LA he felt that he was caught in some bizarre dream he had yet to categorise as fantasy or nightmare.

A short while before reaching the restaurant, Isis abruptly ended a call and turned to him.

'Now, how are we going to do the entrance?' she wanted to know.

It took him a moment to work out what she meant. Then he said, 'I thought the media will only get there later.'

'Bianco Verdi is one of the places you go to be seen,' she explained, making him feel awkwardly self-conscious. 'People there notice *everything*. They'll be interpreting every action.' As she met his eyes for the first time, her expression, thought Mark, was impenetrable.

'The restaurant's on my side of the street. When we pull up, the driver will open my door. You should get out your side, come round and give me a hand up – my left hand – then accompany me into the restaurant on my left side.'

He nodded.

'We'll hold hands, your right, my left,' she held hers out across the back seat and he reached out in response, 'fingers like this.' She demonstrated, before letting his hand drop. Mark had never choreographed his entrance into a restaurant before – he found the detail of it astonishing – though he was glad of the briefing when the time came. Bianco Verdi had a raised verandah overlooking the pavement, and behind the immaculately sculpted Luma shrubs interspersed in ceramic tubs along the railings, tables were packed out at this time of the night. He was aware of the theatre being created from the moment Isis emerged from the back seat of her car. He took her hand in his with an assumed ease of familiarity and, as they made their way towards the restaurant entrance, he noted the turning heads and interrupted conversations, the sudden movement of waiters towards a corner of the restaurant, quickly followed by the emergence of the impossibly named Romeo Casablanca, bouffant-haired, sports-jacketed and mincing over towards them with extravagant arm movements. 'Darling!' He approached Isis. 'So good to see you.'

Air kissing her on both sides, he stood back for a moment, still holding her arms, evidently enraptured by the spectacle of having her to dine in his restaurant. When he acknowledged Mark, it was almost as an afterthought, extending his hand while his gaze remained fixed all the time on Isis's face. Then he was hustling them to the most visible table in the restaurant, revelling in all the attention being generated. As they walked through the restaurant Mark couldn't fail to observe the unaffected gawping, as dozens of eyes focused intently on Isis, before taking him in too – he had never been the subject of such comprehensive eyeballing in his life before. And along with all the gawping, were smiles and waves from people Isis seemed to know, judging by the way she returned their greetings.

'You know a lot of people,' Mark murmured beside her.

'Mostly ass-creeps.' She turned to him, with a glued-on smile. 'Every time I come to a place like this I remember why I don't come more often.'

Then as they got to their table, 'Let's give them something to choke on their oysters about.' She tugged him towards her so he knew to lean over and kiss her. It was a brief kiss and felt perfectly natural, the kind of kiss any couple in love might exchange in a restaurant. They sat down at their table as waiters fussed with napkins and menus while the *maître d'* snapped his fingers for a complimentary bottle of Taittinger. When it had arrived, Isis made a fuss of inviting the manager to join them to toast Nile. After he'd finally left them on their own she told Mark, 'Ninety seconds and he'll have tipped off every major news channel in town.'

Mark's smile was wry. 'You're good at this.'

She shrugged. 'Practice.' Reaching out to where his hand was on the table, she slipped her fingers between his. 'Remember, it's all a performance now. Just keep it light. Plenty of bedroom eyes and stolen glances.'

'That doesn't need much acting.'

'Oh, very arch.' She laughed flirtatiously. 'Nothing saying you can't sometimes enjoy the performance.'

'Good,' said Mark, 'I plan to.'

Sitting opposite her for the first time, he was surprised how comfortable he felt in her company. After the way she'd ignored him at the studio, he'd come prepared for the worst kind of prima donna behaviour. But Isis was warm, engaged – even if it was all an act – and he found himself responding to her.

'How d'you feel the recording's going?' he asked.

'Mm,' she nodded. 'Pretty much on track. Recording's the easiest part.'

'Oh, yeah?'

'Media reaction – that's something else.'

Mark instantly reached up towards his hair.

'I had no idea what a circus I was getting myself into when I signed up.' He'd been wondering if he should get this off his chest, but it seemed all right now. Necessary, even. He didn't want Isis to get the wrong impression of him. 'It's been bad enough getting used to the silly clothes and even sillier haircut without having to read all the crap about my family and myself in the papers.'

She was following him intently.

'All that stuff about "Rags to Rollses,"' he was shaking his head, 'it's all such trash.' Pausing a moment, he leaned back in his seat. 'Sorry if I'm ranting. It's just so unexpected.'

'That's not ranting.' Her eyes glinted. 'Believe me, I *know* about ranting!'

'I s'pose you must be used to the media putting out rubbish about you?'

She shook her head. 'You never really get used to it.'

'So, what, I mean, d'you do?'

'You just keep going. You don't have any choice. Anonymity is no longer an option.'

She'd expressed something he wouldn't have been able to understand himself till a short while ago. In all the years he'd idolised the Queen of Charts, he'd never so much as guessed at the bizarre existence she had to lead, nor at how far removed from her public persona the real Isis might be. Small wonder she kept outsiders at bay. Remembering how she'd moved down the corridor at the studios, surrounded by the group of Unum executives, he realised now that the reason she'd ignored him had probably been nothing more than self-defence.

'It's inevitable you go a bit mad,' she said, sipping her champagne. 'I know there's plenty of people think I'm crazy with all my security gates and alarms. But you only need to wake up once with a blade to your throat, and you realise you just can't live normally. Too many nutsos out there.'

He thought of the Lefevre attack and his conversation with Hilton that morning. Not that One Commando was a subject he thought he should pursue.

Regarding him with an expression of enquiry, Isis asked now, 'I want to know what you were doing before.'

'Before Hilton?'

She nodded.

This was another thing he'd wondered how best to package. But he'd realised by now that she had a well-developed bullshit detector – there was no point pretending to be anything he wasn't.

'I was doing weekend gigs in clubs and pubs around South London. Like the papers say, no one had ever heard of me – that much is true. But it's not true that I was living in poverty on some council sink estate. And my mother wasn't living off social security. We've always been a hard-working family. We didn't have much,' he levelled with her, 'but at least I had my hair.'

He told her about how his father had left the family when Lloyd was only two years old, how his mother had worked in a dry cleaning shop and he'd had to take on responsibilities from an early age. It had been such an ordinary background he wouldn't have thought it would be of the slightest interest to Isis. But her questions revealed more than casual curiosity. She told him that she, too, came from a very ordinary family of Italian emigrants who'd settled in Miami. She hadn't always lived in a multi-million dollar home in Malibu. Mark felt a connection had been made between them – one he least expected. Recounting some family anecdotes from his childhood, and laughing with her, he forgot for a while that he was sitting opposite the world's sexiest pop chick.

Forty-five minutes later, Isis was in the powder room tidying up her make-up in preparation for the photo-frenzy that would accompany their departure from Bianco Verdi. The evening had gone better than she had expected, she found herself thinking through a blur of champagne. She'd been pleasantly surprised by Mark Watson's lack of pretension and his English humour. Unlike most pop star wannabes she'd met, he didn't come across as a self-absorbed boof-head. Instead, there was an all-round self-sufficiency about him that she thought was sweet. She supposed his looks helped; she was by no means oblivious to their powerful appeal. It might be easier to get through this make-believe romance than she had originally feared.

On her way back to the table, Romeo Casablanca hurried towards her, a-flutter with the news that a very large contingent of photographers were now encamped outside the restaurant. Was there anything he could do? He wrung his hands in dramatised anguish. Isis announced that she and Mr Hampshire would make their escape through the kitchen.

Back at the table, she explained the change of plan to Mark as he stood up and slipped into his jacket.

'But isn't the whole point of tonight—'

'They'll be waiting. Why d'you think I tipped off Casablanca? There'll be far more interest in the pictures if it's thought they're illicit instead of some PR job.'

Mark shook his head. He was still new to this.

'It'll also help if they have something to write about,' she said, pausing in the short passage that led through to the kitchen. Ahead of them, Romeo Casablanca was fussing and fretting, but now as she raised her face to Mark, he leaned down towards her, feeling her arms round his shoulders. This time as their lips met, to his surprise he felt her mouth parting. This wasn't something choreographed in advance and he didn't know if he should be taking liberties. But as she held him to her, he decided it should be treated like a moment of unrehearsed desire. Bodies pressed tightly together, his mouth searched hers. He was aware of several waitering staff passing by, but tried to ignore them, just like he was trying to ignore the fact that it was the world's greatest sex icon whose tongue was in his mouth. It felt good, no doubting it, the two of them melting together. But he'd hardly had any time to get used to it and she'd broken away from him and was stepping back. For a single instant their eyes met and he sensed a significance in her expression, though he couldn't place whether it was admonition or lust. Then she was directing him, ahead of her, into the kitchen, past a wide-eyed galley of chefs to the back exit.

Just as Isis had predicted, the moment they emerged their appearance was greeted with a flurry of flash cubes and excited calls from photographers. Doing their best to seem caught unawares, they hurried, hand-in-hand, to where the Mercedes was parked near by, engine already started for a quick escape. They pulled away with a squeal of wheels and several paparazzi photographers on scooters in hot pursuit. Mark glanced about at them.

'D'you think we'll lose them?'

'We don't want to. We came in this car for maximum exposure,' Isis replied, moving closer towards him on the back seat. Responding, he draped his arm around her shoulders amid another blaze of flash cubes. As the Mercedes purred out towards Malibu on that warm Los Angeles night with the Queen of Charts snuggled into his shoulder and the world's media in hot pursuit, Mark couldn't help but wonder at how quickly his life was changing.

Back in Isis's home, the garage door sliding shut behind them, Isis got out of the car and led the way back up the stairs and through the concealed entrance to the hallway.

'What happens next?' he asked her.

She turned. 'Hilton suggested you wait for an appropriate time before leaving,' she told him with a droll smile.

'Oh, yes?' he responded with a grin. 'And how long, I wonder, is appropriate?'

'Well, not five minutes.' She was leading him into her sitting room. 'So would you like a nightcap?'

'A Scotch would be nice, thanks.' He eyed her loaded drinks cabinet. Then as she poured them both drinks, 'I don't s'pose he gave you any other instructions, did he? Like, am I supposed to walk out of here with a big smile on my face?'

Turning, she met his eyes with an impish expression, handing him a tumbler. 'We could tousle your hair.'

'Ruffle up my clothes.'

'Lipstick and lovebites?' She snorted with amusement.

'I'll drink to that.'

They clinked their glasses and took first sips before meeting each other's eyes. Once again, he didn't know quite what to make of her. This evening may have been all role play, but he couldn't help sensing a tug of genuine attraction. Or was that simply wishful thinking? Here he was, late at night, with the world's most famous pop star looking into his eyes across the sofa of her soft-lit Malibu home. Of course he wanted to have those thoughts.

They continued their effortless conversation from the restaurant, Isis recalling the lighter side of her Broadway experiences, then after he'd finished his drink, Mark glanced at his watch.

'I've been here forty minutes. Do you think that's an "appropriate" time?'

'I guess.' Isis got up from where she was sitting. 'I'll leave you to head out the front door.'

Denzil was waiting with his car outside – and a bank of telephoto lenses, doubtless, already trained on the door.

'It's been a . . . great evening,' he approached her, 'thank you.'

Again, he sensed an energy between them, an intimacy that went beyond simple friendliness. He wondered if she'd show she sensed it too. Now was the time in the evening. This was the moment. He leaned to kiss her, preparing for embrace. But as he moved closer she turned, offering him her cheek. Then she was quickly breaking apart.

'I enjoyed the evening too.' She smiled enigmatically, squeezing his arm. Then stepping back, she gestured towards the hall. 'See you in the papers.'

Later that night, back at Beverly Hills, Mark noted from the array of clocks in the hallway that it was just after eight a.m. London time. He hadn't spoken to his family since the papers had come out. He reckoned he'd better make a couple of calls before turning in for bed.

He spoke to his mother first, concerned about how she'd been affected. She'd been at home the previous morning when the paper was delivered – the Watsons had always been a *Daily Mail* household. As it happened, the *Mail*'s article hadn't been too bad, but no sooner were they reading it than the telephone was ringing with reporters from other papers. Mrs Watson had been outraged by some of their questions – she'd let them have a piece of her mind, she told Mark. And when she arrived at work later, her colleagues were similarly indignant about what they'd read in the press. Any journalists calling the dry cleaner's were soon told where to go – none of the women there had any doubt that it was the papers who were twisting the truth, sensationalising what had happened 'just so they can sell a few more copies', as Mark's mother put it.

Mark hadn't been able to help smiling to himself when his Mum had said that – he should have known he could count on her sound common sense. No, she was very proud of him, his mother lectured him firmly, turning the tables on the conversation, and he wasn't to let the gutter press upset him.

Next he'd called Lloyd who, to his further relief, regarded the whole affair with droll amusement. The first he'd known about it was looking over fellow commuters' shoulders on the tube on his way to work the previous day. Arriving at the office, it was to find his e-mail 'In' tray swamped with notes from colleagues, with many ribbing references to one of the newspaper articles which referred to him as having been 'rescued from the dole queue by his generous big brother'. Later in the day, the publicity manager had put her head round the door and made a wisecrack about his older brother doing a celebrity endorsement for OmniCell.

Mark told Lloyd what he'd already warned his mother about – that a new wave of publicity was about to break, making Isis and him out to be an item. 'It's all just a scam,' he said, 'but for God's sake don't tell anyone that.'

'Just trying to stir up more publicity?' had been his mother's reaction earlier.

'Something like that.'

'Bummer having to get it on with Isis.' Lloyd had been facetious. 'Just how much selfless fucking is involved?'

'Keep your filthy little thoughts to yourself.'

They'd joshed about for a short while, then Lloyd had something to tell him. 'You'll never guess who came sniffing round after you last night.'

'Who was that, then?'

'Only your former "manager".'

'What?' exclaimed Mark. 'Round to your flat?'

'Yeah.'

'Did he give you a hard time?' Mark immediately thought back to their last conversation, and the revelations about Vinnie's increasingly violent tendencies.

'Nothing like that,' Lloyd replied. 'Came to tell me he'd just landed some deal with Unum.'

Mark was astonished. 'Would have thought that's the last thing he'd want you to know about. Anyway, I thought he wasn't speaking to you?'

'He wasn't. Not till his social call. Completely ignored me down the Lamb. Then he came round saying he wants to thank you and—'

'Thank me?' interjected Mark.

'—and apologise . . .'

Mark was beyond surprise. Unum deal or no Unum deal, Vinnie's nocturnal visit was way out of character.

'He wants something,' he told Lloyd after a moment's pause.

'Yeah. Your contact details.'

Mark absorbed this in silence.

'I didn't give them to him,' Lloyd added quickly.

'Why did he say he needed them?'

'Says he's planning to look you up. He's thinking of heading to LA.'

'Uh-huh?' That didn't ring true either. None of this did. Vinnie had always had a lot of front, but gushing thanks and gratitude had never been a part of it. And as for a visit to LA. It just didn't make sense, thought Mark – unless Vinnie was now working to a different agenda. In cahoots with someone else.

'Tell me,' he asked his brother, 'have you noticed anything else about Vinnie acting different?'

'Not really,' Lloyd shrugged at the other end, 'same old, same old.'

'He's not hanging out with a new crowd?'

Lloyd recalled Vinnie bragging about new people and doing new deals and remembered he'd seen him in the company of that foreign hack. He hadn't planned telling Mark about the journo – first of all he didn't know for sure that he *was* a journo, and second, even if he was, what could Mark do about it?

'There's been a few new people sniffing around for him,' was all he said now.

'What kind of people?' Mark sounded serious.

'Well . . . *a* person,' Lloyd corrected himself, 'and it might've been just nothing.'

At the other end, Mark wondered why Lloyd was being so evasive.

'Just tell me about the guy!'

'Well, I think he may have been a foreign reporter.'
Sensing Mark's determination, Lloyd decided to get the bad
news out of the way first. 'He and Vinnie were in a huddle
behind the fruit machines for about twenty minutes two
nights ago.' After a brief pause he added, 'I wasn't going to
mention it 'cause I don't know if the guy even is a journalist—'

'Hey, I'm way past worrying about what some foreign
language newspaper writes about me. The stuff in English is
bad enough.' Mark was pacing up and down.

'But if they paid Vinnie enough—'

'He'd say anything – I know,' agreed Mark. The Unum
deal had been planned as a damage-limitation exercise, not
that anyone was under the illusion it would stop Vinnie
taking a few snipes.

'What makes you think this guy was up to something with
Vinnie?' he persisted.

'He came looking for him. I was playing a few sets of
snooker with the boys when he sidles up and takes an interest, and before you know it he's asking questions about is
this Vinnie Dobson's local, and which one is he.'

'When you say foreign – was he a frog or something?'

'That's the thing, he had this weird accent, like half
American and half something else – German, or maybe
Scandinavian.'

Mark halted in his tracks. Euro-American accent. He
remembered reading the words, and though he couldn't place
where, he instantly sensed an uneasy recognition.

'Looked different, too. Really tall gym-boy – must pump
iron for hours a day – red hair and this goatee beard.'

As Lloyd continued, Mark's mind was whirring – until it
all suddenly slotted into place: the 'Security Briefing' on
Berkeley Square. The stuff Hilton Gallo had given him that

first day. The three-line profile of someone called Bengt Larson, he remembered, described him as being muscular in build, a master of disguise, and having a 'Euro-American accent.'

Aware of the pause at the other end, Mark's thoughts raced ahead. No need to tell Lloyd of his sudden suspicions, he reckoned, though an idea was starting to form. Breaking the silence he asked his brother, 'If you saw a photo of this bloke, d'you think you'd recognise him?'

'Oh, sure,' Lloyd was breezy. 'I spoke to him for a while and—'

'The thing is, he may have been in disguise.'

At the other end, Lloyd was surprised. He knew there was no end to what journalists would do for a celebrity scoop but he hadn't realised that dressing up incognito was one of them.

'You reckon you know who he is?' he asked now.

It was a while before Mark responded in a determined voice. 'No. But I mean to find out.'

Minutes later, Mark had walked through to the study, an expansive, book-lined affair, with shelves ranged from floor to ceiling down two whole walls, and the feel about it of a gentleman's club. In the lockable filing cabinet under the large, leather-topped desk, he kept all his most valuable documents – his contracts with GCM, Unum Music, Berkeley Square – together with anything else he considered important, including the Security Briefing. He'd soon found it, and was flicking through the pages to the paragraph about Larson. He remembered reading it that first day at Chateau Marmont, and how, at the time, Bengt Larson and One Commando had seemed an abstract concept, a theoretical threat if he signed the Berkeley Square endorsement. He hadn't had any idea that Larson might acquire a sudden significance in his own life. Could it be that within just ten days a violent terrorist, wanted by police forces of four European countries, was now trailing through his old London haunts?

This time as he focused on the paragraph about Larson he did so intently – there was nothing hypothetical about him now. It was only a short paragraph and didn't say much more than he remembered; as he read and reread it, he didn't know exactly what he was looking for, except for some clue, something that might signal where he could find out more about Larson, what he looked like – and what was being done to arrest him. The police of those four European countries must have photos of him, he thought. Identikit portraits at the very least.

He stared at the screen of his Compaq desktop, and a thought was suddenly triggered. The Compaq, complete with modem and dedicated phone line, had already been useful for exchanging e-mails with some of his mates back at OmniCell. Now he switched it on, impatiently waiting for it to boot up. Clicking on 'Internet' from a screen crowded with icons, as soon as he was connected he headed for the Alta Vista search engine, tapping a single word into the search field the moment it appeared.

On the support desk at OmniCell he'd had to be net-literate – most OmniCell product manufacturers kept detailed specifications on their websites, and responding to customer queries invariably required trawling through pages of electronic data. Mark had learned that the answers to most things could be found on the Net, if you had the patience to look, and now as a navy blue page with an impressive logo appeared, he wondered how far this would get him in his search for Bengt Larson.

The Interpol website, with its distinctive sword and scales logo surrounding the globe, had buttons ranged down both sides of the page. Glancing across them, Mark found one headed 'International Terrorism' which he opened up. It carried nothing more revealing than a few bland pages of definitions about differences between terrorism and crime – but at the bottom was a link to 'Current investigations'. This proved equally unexciting, providing nothing more than a round-up of major terrorist activities, all of which had already been well publicised. But once again there was an intriguing link – to 'Most Wanted International Terrorists'.

Hitting the button, Mark was soon looking at an A to Z of individuals, each accompanied by a photograph, as well as a summary list of the terrorism for which they were believed to be responsible. He scrolled rapidly down, hardly daring to hope for what he might find.

But there he was – Bengt Erik Larson, thirty-five, currently leader of One Commando animal terrorist group, but connected to a catalogue of previous terrorist activities which hadn't been so much as mentioned in GCM's Security Briefing. Prior to One Commando, Larson had been a member of a neo-Nazi anti-immigrants group in Munich responsible for a campaign of bombings, including the implosion of an entire four-floor apartment block, killing thirty-nine people, and the assassination of three Turkish community leaders. After apparently running to ground for eighteen months, his career in international terrorism had continued, bizarrely, with the Green Warriors, a militant eco-group. Mark vividly recalled the John F. Kennedy-style assassination of the high-profile Chief Executive Officer of one of the world's largest oil companies, gunned down in the back of his limousine while being driven through the streets of Amsterdam. That story had been all over the news media for weeks – though at the time there'd been no connection between Green Warriors, who'd claimed responsibility for the killing, and Bengt Larson, whom police had only subsequently identified as Green Warrior's mastermind.

The idea that Larson who, to date, had eluded the most strenuous efforts of Europe's police to catch him, might now have turned his attentions to him, just seemed too much to believe. And despite the Security Briefing, Mark had never imagined that signing a commercial endorsement deal could lead to such consequences. Now he looked at the photograph of Larson, taken nearly ten years before, when he was still an officer in the German army. He took in the direct blue gaze, the short-cropped fair hair, the straight, unsmiling mouth. He hoped to God he was jumping to conclusions, that Lloyd was right and the Lamb's foreign visitor had just been some Continental hack. But he couldn't afford to take any chances.

Within moments he'd sent an e-mail to Lloyd with Larson's photograph as an attachment. He asked Lloyd to get back to him a.s.a.p.

10

Isis's unexpected coolness towards Mark at the end of the evening had been far more apparent than real – a defence concealing her true feelings. In her private suite, she hurried through to check on Holly. Her daughter was sound asleep, lying in her customary foetal position, the sheet clutched to her chest and her long blonde tresses sweeping across the pillow beside her. Sitting on the edge of the bed, Isis reached out, stroking her daughter's hair back into place in an automatic gesture, before tracing down Holly's cheek with her fingertips. Looking down at the child's sleeping features, untroubled and at peace, seemed only to heighten her own feelings – a turmoil she had unwittingly provoked that evening. Because as much as she had enjoyed it at the time, her encounter with Mark, first in the restaurant and later at home, had snared her on a memory she wished to forget. A recollection that had carried her remorselessly back into the past.

* * *

That Sunday afternoon's humiliation, with her father and Mr Bazzani, was the turning-point. Afterwards, nothing was ever the same again. Her relationship with her father was irrevocably damaged and she tried to make sure she was never again left alone in the house with him. Even when her mother and other people were about, she couldn't escape the expression that sometimes came into his eyes when he looked at her. So she retreated into silence and lived, more and more, in the world of her own imagination, instead of the one she shared with her family. It was a double life; no matter how worried or at risk she felt, there was always another place she could escape to, a place of safety where she could be who she wanted to be, and no one could get at her.

She found a co-conspirator in her safe other world in Gabby – the girl whose beautiful lingerie had led to her undoing. Her father had, of course, destroyed the lace brassière. It had been his first act on catching sight of Isis as she'd sat in front of the mirror – he'd torn the bra from her body, ripping its delicate fabric. Isis had planned to return it to Gabby the following Monday, but now that wouldn't be possible, and there was no way she would have been able to afford to buy a new one. So she decided to take a chance and she confessed. Catching Gabby alone in the locker room, she explained that her beautiful black brassière had been a temptation Isis had been unable to resist; that she'd only wanted to take it home before returning it. She didn't tell her everything about her father – not then. All she said was that he'd found the bra in her school case, assumed she'd stolen it, and destroyed it to teach her a lesson.

Gabby had listened to all this without anger or recrimination. To Isis's tearful relief, she hadn't been at all upset that Isis had 'borrowed' her bra without her knowledge, and even less concerned about having it replaced – for a fifteen-year-old she had been wonderfully understanding. In fact Isis's confession had the effect of cementing their friendship. They hadn't been close friends in the past, yet they quickly became so. Inviting Isis home after school, Gabby had opened the door to the kind of family life she yearned for herself – a warm and generous home where childish pranks were regarded with indulgence, and exciting plans for weekends and holidays were constantly being hatched.

Isis's parents approved of the increasing lengths of time she spent with the Trinci family. Mr Trinci was a well-to-do businessman with two handsome sons as well as the pretty Gabriella – a love-match could prove very auspicious indeed. Meanwhile, Isis's adventures with Gabby were a lot different from the sedate, chaperoned outings she led her parents to imagine. Often, when Gabby's parents were away on one of their frequent nights out of town, she would invite Isis over after homework, and the two of them would pick out pert, sassy dresses from her extensive wardrobe, and spend ages applying make-up before blow-drying their hair. Then they'd go out to parties where they knew their presence would be kept secret, or to beachfront bars across town where they wouldn't be recognised. There were so many firsts for Isis from those clandestine excursions: her first drink – a frozen banana daiquiri; the first time she was chatted up by a man; her first kiss. She and Gabby would arrive back at the Trincis' house, high with teenage exuberance or crying with laughter as they recollected the excitement of the night's events. On rare occasions, Isis stayed over at the Trincis', and those nights she liked best, sleeping in the spare room beside Gabby's with the wonderful knowledge, as she closed her eyes, that she wouldn't be woken up by her father. But most times she found herself having to take off all her make-up, brush out her hair, and replace Gabby's pretty dresses with her own unflattering clothes before returning to the oppressive atmosphere of her own home. The Midnight Pumpkin, she used to call herself.

The most important 'first' from that period was one she didn't recognise at the time: even though she and Gabby used to set out in search of nothing more complicated than simply having fun, Isis felt, for the first time, an implicit acceptance of who she was. While her father continued to cast a dark shadow over her life at home, he was unable, she discovered, to extinguish her own sense of identity or to destroy her capacity to be happy.

Her friendship with Gabby meant more than simply the pursuit of high jinks. Gabby helped her in very practical ways too. Isis would never forget how it was Gabby who slipped a magazine into her desk, one morning at school, pointing out the title of a feature she ought to read. At lunch-time that day Isis sat in the playground, engrossed in the article which seemed to have been written especially with her in mind. It was all about girls who'd gone through exactly what she had, teenagers who were experiencing exactly the same trauma at home, and who faced the same feelings of isolation and despair. There were interviews with some of them and colour photographs. Psychologists and care workers gave their views – all of which Isis quickly devoured, before going back to the beginning of the article and reading it a second time. But best of all were the two lines at the end of the piece which gave the number of a telephone helpline which people like her could ring to get help.

She had, by then, opened up completely to Gabby, telling her all about her father, and her own emotions of unworthiness and self-blame. Knowing now that there was an authority, other than her father, to whom she could turn, and that she could take action to change things whether he liked it or not, held out the hope of an intoxicating freedom. But it was also terrifying. What if she picked up the telephone and called the helpline? What if she set in motion the things she now knew were possible? Nothing would ever be the same again. Even though she hated the way things were, changing her world completely would take special courage.

After school she discussed things with Gabby, and as usual her friend's confidence was persuasive. The way Gabby saw it, she simply had no choice but to act: she should call the helpline people as soon as she could. Whatever hardships might follow, they would be as nothing compared to the horrors she had already suffered. Besides, said Gabby, you'll always have me around to see you through.

If only that had been true. Later that same day when Gabby was walking home from school, a speeding driver had swerved to avoid a cyclist – and run directly into her. She'd been rushed away by ambulance, but her internal injuries were so severe that nothing could be done; Gabby had died within minutes of arrival at hospital.

A late night telephone call had broken the news to Isis, who had put down the receiver numb with shock. It just didn't seem possible – she'd been speaking to Gabby only hours before! That night, in defiance of her father, she locked her bedroom door. She knew she'd be unable to sleep, and as she sat, bereft, at the edge of her bed, face in her hands and tears sliding silently through her fingers, in her devastation she knew she couldn't carry on like this any longer. Gabby's final advice to her had been that she should make that telephone call. Tomorrow, she would do it, even though it meant ending her world.

*   *   *

Now as Isis looked down at Holly, she thought that she would probably never have made the call if she'd known the course of events that would follow. Ultimately, of course, it had been her salvation. She had learned to blossom as a woman and a singer, to fulfil a musical talent that had remained unexplored until her late teens. And of course the ultimate prize was Holly herself who was now the centre of her existence. But all this had only come at a price, and one she was still paying. Intimations of her past would catch up with her when she was least expecting them, bringing her face to face with the vulnerability she had never overcome. That kiss with Mark in the restaurant, and the moment of promised intimacy with him back at home were such reminders. Behind the worldly disregard that served as her persona, what she really felt was a silent, but insistent fear. Nothing terrified her more than the prospect of seeing exposed the pain that lay at the heart of her past.

London
Monday, 20 September

It was early afternoon when Jones's mobile telephone rang. Excusing himself from the informal meeting in his office, he answered it briskly.

'Checking in for the last time,' came Larson's distinctive voice.

'You're ready to go?'

'Ten-fifteen p.m.'

'Good.' In front of his colleagues, Jones dared not sound too enthused, even though Larson had, once again, demonstrated singular efficiency.

'This time tomorrow you will be watching it on the BBC and I shall be reading about it in *Le Soir*.'

'Excellent.'

Jones glanced over at where his colleagues were talking among themselves, coffee mugs in hand. It was at moments like these, amid day-to-day mundanity, that his involvement in One Commando gave him a particular charge of excitement, a thrill of clandestine pleasure.

'And if tonight's mission isn't ... persuasive enough,' continued Larson, 'I am planning the final onslaught.'

'You mean you've recruited that manager?'

'Dobson. He's playing ball.'

'I'd like to meet him.'

'I'm sure we can arrange it. I've also got Brent doing some research for us.'

'Oh.' Jones hesitated. 'I see.' He'd always been suspicious of Brent. It worried him that the intense young man might find out too much, get beyond himself. Mensa-intelligent Brent who could hack his way into any computer system in the world.

'You'll let me know when it's over?' he confirmed.

'I'll call from Eurostar tonight.'

Beverly Hills

Mark knew he was running late as he scrambled into his clothes. Seven-forty-five according to the bedside clock – he was due in at Unum by eight-thirty. The recording schedule was more intense than he'd ever imagined. He'd even had to put in a few studio sessions over the weekend – not to mention the informal rehearsals back home. Still – just as well, he reckoned. Recording *Nile* helped take his mind off everything else that was happening.

He hadn't heard back from Lloyd on the photo of Bengt Larson, though he needed to check this morning's e-mail.

As for Isis and their phoney romance, that had been all over the TV news over the weekend, and he reckoned there'd be another inch-thick delivery of press cuttings from Lebowitz waiting for him when he got downstairs. Not that the media coverage interested him nearly so much as what had actually gone on. He'd kept going back over everything that had happened between Isis and him, asking himself if it was possible any part of what they'd done for the cameras had been spontaneous, for real. There had been moments which had certainly felt like that to him. And what had happened later when he was leaving her home? Why the sudden withdrawal, the deliberate distancing?

He hurried downstairs to the kitchen. Mrs Martinez had prepared her usual fry-up, but there wasn't time for it. Grabbing a slice of toast and a mug of coffee, he headed in the direction of the study. Denzil was standing in the hallway, looking severe in dark sunglasses and gesticulating at his watch.

'Yeah, yeah,' Mark muttered through a mouthful of toast, 'give me five.'

He'd become far less enamoured and intimidated by The System than when he'd first arrived. Big names and big money had meant a lot to him then, but he'd realised, pretty soon, that if he didn't stand up for himself, he'd be treated like a doormat. Years on the OmniCell helpdesk had made him instinctively obliging – but now that he'd realised what he'd let himself in for, signing the Berkeley Square endorsement, it was no more Mr Nice Guy.

Behind the study desk he logged in quickly, opening up Eudora Light and entering his password. The eight-hour time lag between LA and London had some benefits, he supposed. If he sent an e-mail last thing at night, he could be pretty certain Lloyd would have replied by the time he got up next morning.

Up came the connector monitor, with five messages to download, followed in seconds by a bleep announcing that he had mail. Lloyd's was one of the e-mails and he opened it straight away.

'*The photo you sent me – that's the bloke from the Lamb!*' Lloyd had responded, unaware of the seriousness of his confirmation. '*He was older than in the picture and had red hair and a beard. Even if you hadn't warned me about the disguise, I reckon I'd have recognised those eyes anywhere! So who is this guy and what paper does he work for? And should I give Vinnie your contact details? I'll be seeing him in the next few days.*'

Shoving himself back from the desk, Mark felt giddy. Putting his head in his hands, he closed his eyes and took in a few deep breaths. Get a grip, he told himself. You have to think quickly!

He'd already decided that if this happened he must tell GCM; for all his suspicions about the agency's media agenda, surely he could trust Hilton when it came to security? Besides, this discovery wasn't only about him – it concerned Isis too. GCM would have to get on to the police – in Britain they'd put someone on Vinnie's tail.

Still feeling dazed, Mark sat up again in his chair and, leaning over, picked up the cordless telephone. He dialled GCM – the only number in America he knew by heart. When he asked for Hilton, he was put through to his secretary Melissa Schwartz who, recognising Mark's voice, told him that Hilton was currently in London.

'Shit!' he murmured under his breath. He hadn't considered that Hilton might be in London, but of course the GCM boss was frequently out of town.

'Is it something Elizabeth can help you with?' she suggested.

'No,' he was emphatic, 'it needs to be Hilton.'

There was a pause at the other end before Melissa told him, 'I'm looking at his diary now. He's in a client meeting for the next hour, then he's at a book launch in Piccadilly. If it's extremely urgent, we can interrupt the client meeting. Or we can get him to call you after the launch, which will be around eight o'clock – noon our time.'

'Only trouble is, I might still be over at Unum—'

'Studio eighteen,' Melissa confirmed briskly. 'I can get him to call you there directly?'

'Or I might have finished for the day.'

'What if I was to get him to call you later at your home. By then you'll definitely be wrapped up at Unum?'

Melissa was steering him away from interrupting the meeting, and maybe it would be better having Hilton's undivided attention. Alarmed though he was by his discovery, would it make any difference if Hilton only got the news about Larson later in the day?

'Okay,' he agreed with Melissa, 'get him to call me at home. But tell him it's serious.'

London

Hilton Gallo sat in his tastefully appointed suite at Green's, going through financials from GCM's European offices. He always stayed in the same fourth-floor suite, having found it, like the private hotel itself, through trial and error and, once found, returning to it every time he was in London, which was at least once a month. Simon Dubois, the Poirot-like character who presided over the hotel with his immaculate moustache, all-seeing eyes and Gallic charm, always made sure that every detail of Hilton's stay was to his client's satisfaction. Over many trips, Hilton's preferences had been noted and accommodated on each subsequent visit. Ahead of his arrival, direct telephone and fax lines were installed in the suite. The second bedroom was cleared of furniture, providing a quiet and spacious meditation retreat. And the sitting room walls were hung with the pride of Green's art collection, which included several Constables and a Stubbs. Whenever changes in furniture or décor were being considered, Simon Dubois always made a point of consulting Hilton, not only for the purposes of customer relations, but because, over the years, he'd come to respect the soft-spoken Californian's finely honed sensibilities and flawless taste.

This evening though, aesthetic matters were far from Hilton's mind. Rather, as he sat at the Boulle desk, shuffling through computer printouts from GCM's offices in Paris and Rome, he was unusually distracted by figures, wishing, for the umpteenth time that the French and Italian agencies would follow the rest of the network in adopting Excel software, instead of the chaotic accounting package he found so difficult to make sense of.

Glancing at his watch, he saw it was just after ten. Often, when he was in London, he'd enjoy an evening stroll before turning in. It was a private pleasure he'd discovered several years before – he'd take in the arboured squares and terraced houses of Chelsea, the cobbled mews streets and restaurants whose understated entrances belied their Michelin-star chefs. London, he often used to think, was far more his spiritual home than Los Angeles – it was so much more cultivated, restrained, civilised. If things had been different he would have moved here years ago. As it happened, his personal enjoyment of the city was restricted to those precious few hours when, business commitments discharged, he could afford the luxury of time to himself. His evening strolls fell into this category, but tonight, alas, there was no question of getting out for a walk. Thanks to One Commando he was considered high on the 'at risk' list, and his new security arrangements were particularly draconian when he visited London. They applied to every aspect of his activities, from his arrival at Heathrow, to the opening of his mail. Much against his own preferences, he was now accompanied round the clock by a security guard – currently watching *Wycliffe* in the hallway of his suite. So instead of a walk, Hilton went through to the bathroom, and splashed his face with cold water.

Just another half hour of maddening accounts, he promised himself, towelling his face dry and meeting his eyes in the mirror, then he'd call it a day. As always, when faced by a particularly irksome task, he tried to step back from the immediate difficulties and get a grip on the bigger picture. Whatever the frustrations of trying to understand French accounting, there was no question that, as an agency, GCM had got through the last week far better than he had feared.

Lebowitz's solution to One Commando's continuing media presence had been a great success. The joint appearance of Isis and Jordan at Bianco Verdi had pushed the terrorist group off the news pages. Media attention now switched to the burgeoning love affair between America's most famous sex icon and the tall, dark stranger from London. Video clips of the two of them had been flighted on all the celebrity news slots. Photographs of them sneaking out of the back entrance of the restaurant were plastered all over the press. There was much feverish speculation about the romance, with body language experts noting the powerful bond between the two of them, restaurant staff commenting that they'd hardly been able to keep their hands off each other, and astrologers divided on the issue of compatibility. Meticulously choreographed 'friends' of both parties were reported as saying how crazy they were for each other.

In the light of this latest victory, Hilton thought as he returned from the bathroom to his desk, his current difficulties with the European accounts were nothing if not trivial. Sitting down, he'd no sooner started work once again when he heard a knock at the suite door, followed by the sound of his bodyguard opening it.

'We have a delivery.'

Recognising Simon Dubois's distinctive French accent, Hilton got up from behind his desk and made his way through to the hallway. Simon stood, immaculately groomed as ever, accompanied by a young lad from room service carrying two hefty-looking documents. Hilton was surprised, but not greatly. He hadn't been expecting a delivery, but unsolicited scripts were a constant feature of his life.

'Good evening, sir,' Simon greeted him as he approached.

'Simon?' Hilton raised his eyebrows.

In all the years he'd been coming to Green's, he couldn't remember a single occasion when Simon hadn't greeted him by name. Now, as he met the hotel manager's eyes, he tried to place the expression. He seemed agitated, even angry. But why?

'You'd better bring them in,' Hilton nodded towards the documents.

Simon's assistant carried the parcels over towards the hallway table. Following him, Hilton reached into his trouser pocket, searching for some change, when he became aware of heavy footsteps down the corridor. Glancing over his shoulder he was aghast to see Simon shoved out of the way by a dark-clad, masked gunman. Four other figures, all brandishing pistols, followed immediately behind. Hilton's bodyguard barely had time to reach his own pistol before he was struck to the floor. He fell, heavy and unconscious, while two of the intruders made directly for Hilton.

'No noise, or you're dead,' one of them barked. They collected him up as though he were weightless and hustled him into the bedroom where they flung him on the bed, face first. Heart pounding, Hilton told himself to try not to panic. But he instantly guessed who his attackers were with a wave of sickening dread.

Time seemed to stretch out for an eternity as one of the men, standing over him, retrieved a roll of electric wire from his pocket while the other pinned him down to the bed, arms tugged behind him. They quickly rolled the tape round Hilton's wrists and ankles. Meanwhile, two of the other intruders were slipping round the side of the room, closing all the curtains. Behind him, Hilton could hear the man who was evidently the gang leader giving orders to Simon Dubois.

'Now, directly to the hotel entrance. Leave immediately, speaking to no one. Go to this address and wait. If there are no problems, we return your family.' Hilton recognised the accent from the Security Briefing – confirming his worst fears.

'When?' Dubois was asking.

'Go!' The suite door was locked behind Simon, then there were the hurried sounds of footsteps. Hilton, rolled over and jerked up by the shoulders, found himself staring up at a tall, well-built figure in a mask, wearing baggy, military-style trousers and a black jersey.

'So this is what a Hollywood super-agent looks like?' Larson loomed over him.

'Two hundred million dollars a year going through your hands, Mr Gallo. All that money must make you feel invincible. But look at you now.'

Hilton felt his heart pump so hard it threatened his whole system. *Stay calm*, he ordered himself. *Keep your head and*

work this out. But cool composure became even more difficult as the man pulled out a hunting knife and, with the tip
of the six-inch blade, traced a line around first his right eye,
then his left, before flicking the skin next to his ear. A thin
scratch line welled up, instant red.

'You're going to persuade your famous clients to cancel
the Berkeley Square endorsement,' he said as a statement of
fact. 'They will give up because of the violation of animal
rights by Berkeley Square in Madrid.'

On the floor next door, Hilton's bodyguard had come
round and was starting to groan. Ordering his men to secure
him, the leader glanced back at Hilton.

'No amount of security and bodyguards can protect Isis
and her lover from us.'

Hilton knew he had to keep this man talking. Create
delay however he could and hope that someone, somewhere
had worked out that things were amiss.

'If Berkeley Square really is torturing animals in Madrid,
why can't anyone else find the facility?'

'Maybe they closed it down,' Larson retorted angrily.
'Maybe people aren't looking in the right place.'

'I think you underestimate their efforts,' Hilton risked
further provocation. 'There are investigative journalists and
cosmetics companies who'd love nothing better than to
prove you're right.'

'I am right,' Larson's voice grew more heavily accented.
'I went there myself. I made the video!'

'Then help us find this place.'

Larson was shaking his head. 'You think I'm that stupid?
You know exactly where it is! You're part of the cover-up.'

Hilton shifted his position on the bed. The electric wire
was cutting into his wrists. Arms behind him, his back was
arched with pain. He had to keep Larson talking.

'Isis and Jordan only signed the endorsement after due diligence. They'd drop the contract instantly if there was evidence—'

'You,' Larson was wagging the knife at him, shaking his head as he did, 'you already have evidence.'

'The whole world believes the video is a hoax.'

Larson's eyes flashed angrily behind the mask. 'Then I'll have to persuade you it's not!' His voice rose.

Seizing Hilton's face, he thrust him back against the bed, his grip like a vice about Hilton's forehead.

'This . . . persuasion,' Hilton choked, 'it could backfire. Isis and Jordan . . . may refuse.'

The other was leaning over him, the blade of his knife just inches away from his eyes. 'They won't refuse,' he snarled, 'not after they've seen you.'

11

'Trouble!' the radio on Larson's belt crackled to life.

Quickly standing, he seized it to his ear, pressing the red transmission button. 'What kind of trouble?'

'Company.'

All the commando members stared at Larson who stood, frozen for a moment, before rushing to the window, carefully lifting back the curtain, and staring outside. Everything appeared quiet. But through the stillness came the sounds of approaching police sirens. They weren't far off. Larson glanced quickly round, before ordering, 'Balcony exit!'

On the bed, Hilton wondered what they were going to do with him now. The now loudly advertised approach of the police could be a disaster! Every moment seemed to last an eternity as he struggled to watch what was happening. Would this precipitate a hasty end, he wondered? Would they shoot him dead?

Black-clad figures were running to where curtains concealed doors leading out to a narrow balcony at the side of the room away from the street. Pushing aside the curtains, they opened the doors. Now they were standing, in pairs, on the balcony, seizing the railings one floor above and hauling themselves up. Where was Larson, Hilton wondered? Moment by moment he waited, dry-mouthed, for a final act of retribution. Would it be some searing, unimaginable horror? Or simple, instant death?

The longer he waited, the more he felt he'd been completely forgotten. But after the tension, that seemed impossible! Weren't any of them left behind? After a few moments he raised his head to glance around him; had they all just gone?

Downstairs, the One Commando lookout monitoring police radio activity got out of his car, and walked directly, but not with undue haste, in the direction of where a back-up vehicle was parked one street away. It was a routine call that had alerted him. A police car had been sent out to investigate a barking dog disturbance in the same street as Green's. Moments later it had been instructed to disregard the previous order – PT 19 were on an operation in the area.

To his astonishment, Hilton found himself alone. He rolled over on his side, taking the pressure off his wrists. After all the adrenaline released into his system, the sudden calmness felt as surreal as the drama that had preceded it. Would they come back for him, he wondered quickly. How should he try to escape?

One floor above, Larson and his group were going through a well-rehearsed drill, collecting Green's letterheaded paper and envelopes from inside a drawer, and setting them alight before throwing them in a waste-paper bin and holding the burning papers up to a smoke detector. They triggered the fire alarm. As panic engulfed the hotel, they were quickly stripping off their black jerseys, masks and boots, rifling through wardrobes to find coats and bathrobes. Hotel staff could be heard running round each floor from room to room, hammering on doors and calling out for all guests to evacuate using the fire escape. The five terrorists were soon in the corridor, joining in the mêlée of guests, chambermaids, porters and kitchen staff making their way down the steel stairs behind the hotel.

The police arrived at the hotel in four rapid-response vehicles, two pulling up directly outside the front door and two squealing to a halt round the back. The tip-off had come less than five minutes earlier, and there'd been no doubting its seriousness. Firstly, the informant's credentials were impeccable – it was an inside job. Secondly, precise information had been provided on what action was being taken, where, when and by whom. Twelve police officers were soon scrambling from the cars and pounding through the usually hushed corridors, currently engulfed in chaos.

Two police officers had soon broken through the door to find Hilton sitting on his bed, working on the tape around his wrists, the left side of his face flecked with blood.

'Thank God!' he cried out with feeling as they rushed over to him.

'Are you all right?' The WPC was studying his face with concern.

Hilton was no longer even aware of the cut. 'They would have got my eyes,' he told them. Relief flooded through his body. He felt his jaw tremble from delayed shock.

The WPC was behind him, working quickly at the electric wire on his wrists, while the other policeman was at his ankles.

'How long were they in your room?' the WPC asked.

'Couple of minutes. I tried to keep Larson talking. If you'd been any later—'

'We were here within three minutes of the tip-off.'

'Tip-off?' His wrists freed, Hilton brought them round in front of him and was massaging them.

'That's right,' the PC confirmed.

'You mean?'

'Can't say more than that.'

Hilton raised his eyebrows. The policeman obviously knew more than he was letting on. Like why they had responded to the tip-off in the first place. He knew the police didn't react to every crank call that came in.

Ankles unfastened, he stretched his legs, before going over to the window where he stood for a moment, drawing back the curtain. Looking down at the gathering chaos of people – diners, residents, service staff, passers-by, a few policemen combing through them, in vain – he shook his head.

'They've got away.'

The PC joined him at the window, pulling a notepad from his pocket. 'It would help if we had some descriptions, sir.'

Hilton delivered a sideways glance. 'They're not going to march outside in military fatigues and ski masks.'

Then as the PC looked at him in surprise, he continued, 'They took control of the situation the moment they set off the fire alarm.'

'Perhaps you could tell us exactly what happened, right from the beginning.'

'Yeah.' Feeling his composure begin to return, Hilton's mind raced to assimilate all that had happened. Looking over at the policeman, he raised a hand to the muscle that twitched in his cheek. 'But I've got a couple of questions for you first. Like what in God's name are you going to tell the media?'

Los Angeles

'Elizabeth, it's me.' The voice at the other end of the phone was cool and crisp as ever. But Elizabeth Reynolds was startled.

'Hilton?' Both she and Leo Lebowitz, standing on the other side of the desk from her, looked up at the clock faces ranged across the office wall. London time was 1.30 a.m.

'Can't you sleep?' She was concerned. Hilton had caught the red-eye to London the night before and had, as usual, planned a full day's work at GCM offices in Soho. She would have thought he'd be exhausted by now.

'Haven't got to bed yet,' there was a droll note in his voice, 'we've had an . . . incident here. I need to speak to you and Leo. Conference call.'

'Leo's standing right opposite. I'll transfer to your office.'

Moments later they were sitting on either side of Hilton's meeting table, expressions aghast as Hilton smoothly recounted events of the evening, beginning with the ploy of the 'unsolicited manuscripts', the break-in by One Commando, and the eleventh-hour tip-off which had saved him. He told them about his midnight meeting with Detective Inspector Bennett of Scotland Yard, the investigating officer in charge, who had assured him that the police would respond to any media enquiries about events at Green's only with a standard form of words along the lines that an incident at the hotel had been investigated. After the meeting with the police, Hilton had returned to his fourth-floor suite at Green's, a replacement bodyguard in tow, where he planned to spend what remained of the night before catching the early-morning Eurostar to Paris.

Despite all the trauma, his equilibrium had evidently been quickly restored. Speaking with a calm detachment, it was as though he was describing a sequence from an action-thriller movie, rather than speaking as the victim of a terrifying attack. In fact, the only emotion he betrayed was one of concern about the outcome of the Berkeley Square endorsement.

'I've secured a news ban on what happened tonight,' he told Lebowitz and Elizabeth now, 'but One Commando is escalating this thing. They're after the endorsement contract, and Isis and Jordan are top of their list.' There was a lengthy pause before he answered the question that had begun to form in all their minds. 'The two of them will have to be told.'

Across the table from Elizabeth, Lebowitz put his face in his hands. 'She's gonna completely flip,' he groaned. 'It was bad enough with the Lefevre thing.'

'Do you see we have any option?' Hilton asked coolly.

Exhaling heavily, Lebowitz shook his head. 'No. We can't keep it from them. At least, not for long.'

'I think it would be best if I deal with the news myself, face to face, as soon as I get back,' said Hilton.

'Not a conversation I would relish,' responded Lebowitz. 'We're going to have to come up with something incredible to keep her in the deal.'

'Our only hope is a police breakthrough. But I couldn't get anything from the turkeys at Scotland Yard I spoke to tonight.'

It was rarely that Hilton signalled his disapproval so forcefully. Elizabeth and Lebowitz exchanged glances.

'Elizabeth, I need you to follow up tomorrow. I'm tied up in meetings all morning – I've told the police you'll be calling on my behalf.'

'Right.'

'We have to get a grip on what progress they're making with One Commando.'

'I'll speak to Hanniford again.'

'Find out what police briefings he's received.'

'Will do.'

'We need something tangible.'

There was silence for a moment before Lebowitz said, 'What if she wants to pull out?'

'You'd better discuss it with legal,' Hilton's voice was grim. 'Map out the options.'

All three of them were thinking about the Berkeley Square production cycle that was currently running at full throttle. Graphic design concepts had been signed off weeks before and with the photography now completed, the first colour proofs to be used in magazine advertisements, and on billboards, packaging and an array of promotional material were due any day. Intensive media schedules had been booked, and special guest appearances by Isis and Jordan already set up. For Isis and Jordan to pull the plug now would be a devastating blow, not only to Berkeley Square. GCM would suffer from massive and damaging fallout. Whatever the reasons given, Isis would be shunned by commercial sponsors for the rest of her days, and GCM would acquire an unenviable reputation as the agency that pulled out of the world's biggest endorsement deal at the eleventh hour. Plus, Berkeley Square would want to be handsomely compensated. It was the kind of scenario that was every agency executive's worst nightmare.

Signalling the end of the conversation, Hilton was about to hang up when Elizabeth told him, 'I've had a message from Melissa. Mark Watson wants you to call him at home.'

'Can't it wait till tomorrow?' After the events of the evening he was hardly in any mood for client calls.

'He said it was serious.'

*   *   *

Mark's recording session ended much later than scheduled, and it wasn't till mid-afternoon that he got back from Unum. Having been so completely absorbed in *Nile* had been good for him – he hadn't had a moment to dwell on that morning's e-mail from Lloyd. Though on his way home, he remembered his call to Melissa Schwartz and glanced at his watch; he wondered when he'd hear from Hilton.

As they reached the top of his street in Beverly Hills, he was astounded to see that the huge marble entry across the road from his house had been replaced by mediaeval-style gates. Gone were the white-plastered walls, replaced by towering ramparts.

'What's going on there?' he asked Denzil, staring across the road.

'New movie.' Denzil was blasé. 'Situational shots.'

'You mean,' he remembered the house was owned by a movie studio, 'none of that stuff over there is real?'

'Shit, no!' laughed Denzil.

'Had me fooled.'

'Would fool anyone who didn't know better.'

Back home, he took a swim before relaxing by the poolside with a bottle of Rolling Rock, and sheets of lyrics for the next day's recording. He had quickly learned the value of preparation and became so immersed in the music that the next time he glanced at his watch, it was after four-thirty. Which made it half-past midnight in London. Highly unlikely that Hilton was going to call him now, he thought, picking up his towel and making his way back indoors. For all Melissa Schwartz's promises, he thought bitterly, he obviously wasn't important enough to merit a transatlantic phone call from the venerable Hilton Gallo.

After another hour had ticked by, he became convinced this was the case. He was on the verge of phoning Melissa again to give her a piece of his mind when the telephone rang.

'I understand you need to speak to me?'

Mark looked at his watch. 'It's two o'clock over there!'

'Busy night,' Hilton was laconic. 'I would have called earlier but I've been unavoidably detained. Something . . . serious?'

'That's right,' nodded Mark. 'One Commando.'

There was a pause at the other end. 'What about them?'

'I don't know what's going on, but Larson has been in contact with Vinnie Dobson.'

'How, precisely?'

Mark told Hilton of his telephone conversation with Lloyd – of Vinnie's uncharacteristic visit to his brother's flat, and how the stranger Lloyd had seen in the local pub had triggered a memory from GCM's Security Briefing. He explained about the Interpol file and how Lloyd had identified Larson.

After listening intently, Hilton replied, 'Quite a piece of detective work.'

'If you pass the information on to Scotland Yard,' Mark continued, 'they'll put a tail on Dobson—'

'Of course,' agreed Hilton. 'In the meantime, if your brother sees Larson again—'

'Believe me, I've taken care of that. If Larson shows his face down the Lamb, the police will be down there before he's got his first pint.'

Hilton reflected on this soberly. 'You'll let me know—'

'Sure,' Mark was impatient. 'So what do you have on One Commando?' It was a while before Hilton replied, 'I was going to wait to tell you this, face to face, but there is something and it's not good, I'm afraid. Earlier this evening they attacked again—'

'Oh, my God! Who?'

'Me. In my hotel suite.'

'I don't believe—!' Mark was incredulous. 'You mean . . . Are you all right?'

'Just. The police arrived minutes after One Commando. Apparently they'd had a tip off.'

'I don't . . . !' Mark struggled to take it in.

'Still getting over it myself.'

Even in his state of shock, Mark registered the connection between Jacques Lefevre and Hilton Gallo – and in that instant realised that all the sensational tabloid predictions had proved to be right. One Commando *were* after the endorsement deal. And if they'd already tried getting to Hilton Gallo, their ultimate targets had to be Isis and him. No wonder Bengt Larson had been on his tracks in London.

'Did they say anything about the endorsement?' he asked Hilton.

'They want you to drop it.'

'Christ! Does Isis—?'

'Not yet.'

Mark hesitated for a moment. Isis had made no secret of her security fears. When she heard about this she'd go off the deep end.

'So, what happens next?' he asked.

'I don't want to rush a decision. The police here are taking this very seriously – they're under huge pressure to act. Your information could also be a breakthrough.'

'You said something about a tip-off?'

'That's right.'

'Well, I mean, do they know who it was? Or why?'

Hilton drew breath before saying, 'I intend to have more on that by the time we speak again.'

'When will that be?'
'I get back to LA in two days' time.'

London

The emergency exit had been a textbook operation. As it should have been, thought Larson. He'd drilled the team through it, just like he'd drilled them through every step of the operation, planning for every contingency then rehearsing, rehearsing, rehearsing till they responded like clockwork.

They'd encountered no difficulties escaping down the fire escape of the hotel and down into the street below. There, bewildered hotel staff, most of whom had never been through a fire drill, were doing their best to appear in control as they rounded up equally bewildered residents and diners. When the police cars, blue lights flashing, screeched to a halt outside the hotel, most of the uniformed officers had hurried indoors though several of them had begun combing through the gathering crowd of hotel guests, employees and curious onlookers. But Larson and his team had no difficulty slipping round a corner into the quiet mews street where the fallback getaway vehicle was waiting, engine already started.

It was a Federal Express van stolen from a depot late that afternoon, and its absence wouldn't be noticed till the following day. In the meantime, its passage through town aroused no suspicions as it duly made its way up Old Brompton Road, past where Harrods was lit up like a birthday cake, and towards Piccadilly. Not long afterwards, it pulled into a cul-de-sac just a few hundred yards from Leicester Square, where there were no closed-circuit television cameras to record the occupants emerging, now dressed in anonymous jeans and sweaters. They'd kept their surgical gloves on, of course, until the very end. The police didn't have prints of any of them – and they didn't want to start a collection. Within twenty seconds they'd dispersed in half a dozen different directions, mingling with the late-night West End crowds of teenagers and tourists.

Larson himself made directly for a public telephone where he soon set up the present meeting. As he walked along the Islington terrace now, the door to one of the blocks of flats opened and a figure emerged, crossing the street.

'What went wrong?' asked Jones a few moments later, pulling out his Gauloise Lights and offering him one.

Larson waved the pack away. 'We'd just got into Gallo's room,' he said, 'then we had to abort. Long stop warned us the police had been scrambled.'

The two men were walking along the street.

'Tip-off,' said the other, exhaling a stream of smoke. It was more a statement of fact than a question.

'Had to be. But who? Couldn't have been anyone at the hotel. We got right in there without being seen.'

'Are you sure about CCTVs?'

'First thing I checked out on our recce. The place was clean.'

'Which leaves only one possibility.'

Larson glanced over at him. 'That's what worries me. But I checked them all out.'

'How many people knew about tonight?'

'Six. The four I took with me, and the two who took care of Dubois. Brent also sat in on the first briefing, but I stood him down. I need him to take care of the research.'

Jones looked at him challengingly.

'I'm cultivating him. The guy's a genius when it comes to electronic security systems.' He felt the need to justify his decision. 'He can hack into anything on the internet – he can even break into Scotland Yard files and access police records. He's useful.'

Then, irritated that Jones wasn't agreeing, 'Look,' he wore a determined expression, 'I know Brent. He's rock solid.'

'I don't like it,' Jones was shaking his head.

'You think I do?'

'Got to be Brent. Where else could the tip-off come from?'

It was the question that worried Larson most. The one to which he had no answer.

'What d'you want me to do,' he retorted angrily, 'blow him away when we don't know for sure—'

'I'm not saying that,' Jones sucked on his Gauloise, 'I'm not saying you should blow him away.'

They walked on in silence for quite a while, Jones finishing his cigarette and flicking the butt into a drain in the roadside before he turned back to Larson again. 'All I'm thinking is that you should double-check. You want to believe Brent. I want to believe Brent. Let's double-check.'

'How?'

'Have him in for an interview. A formal interview.' Jones nodded meaningfully. 'See what comes up.'

'Yes?' Larson met his eye.

'Sure. We hope he's clean, but if he's not . . .' It didn't need spelling out.

As they walked on, Larson realised he didn't have any choice. Tonight's operation had gone belly up because of a security leak. It was up to him to fix it. He couldn't afford to lose Jones's support. And what Jones suggested wasn't unreasonable. He nodded once. 'I'll talk to Brent.'

'Good man.' Jones was brisk.

'Do you want to . . . assist in the interview? Second opinion?'

Jones considered this for a moment. 'I would, of course.

But best we keep things as we agreed, with me behind the scenes.'

They turned down a road to the left, and shortly afterwards, left again, making their way back in the direction of Jones's flat.

'I tell you what I *would* like,' he nodded to Larson. 'I'd like to see a recording of the interview. See for myself.'

'Of course,' Larson shrugged, 'I can arrange it.'

Los Angeles
Tuesday, 21 September

At three a.m. the morning after Hilton was attacked, Elizabeth Reynolds was woken by her alarm clock. Getting out of bed, she made her way through to the kitchen and poured herself a glass of milk before dialling the number she'd brought home from the office. In London, DI Bennett sounded unsurprised to be hearing from her – time difference or not. No, he didn't have any fresh information for Mr Gallo. But he would keep her posted, he assured her.

Later that morning at the office, when she still hadn't heard back from him by ten a.m. – six in the evening, London time, she called him again. He gave her the same message again – this time delivered in brusque tones. So she phoned Francis Hanniford.

Put through by his secretary, she heard the Berkeley Square director get up to close the door of his office before returning to the phone. Greetings exchanged, she began to explain what had happened to Hilton, before Hanniford cut her off in mid-sentence.

'So I've heard.' Hanniford's cut-glass accent conveyed a natural authority.

'DI Bennett?' She was surprised.

'Good heavens, no. Hilton spoke directly to Jacques earlier today.'

Elizabeth shook her head. 'Hilton's asked me to follow up on his behalf. But Bennett,' she was frustrated, 'he just won't tell me anything!'

'He wouldn't,' Hanniford was direct. 'With all due respect, my dear, he isn't going to reveal himself to a publicity assistant in Los Angeles. But that doesn't mean investigations aren't well under way.'

'Well, what *is* happening?' Elizabeth's voice rose in exasperation.

'I'm not as close to this one as I am to the Lefevre follow-up,' confided Hanniford. 'But, fortunately for both of us, there's a common element emerging.'

At the other end of the line, Elizabeth was listening intently.

'Confidentially, what we are seeing here bears all the hallmarks of a classic MI5 operation.'

'You mean there's someone—'

'Inside the group.'

'The source of the tip-off?'

'Exactly.'

'Scotland Yard have confirmed this?'

'Absolutely not. And they never would – directly. It's more insinuated than that. One has to understand the signals. My Yard connection went to considerable lengths lecturing me on how, after the cold war, the secret services were redeployed, and that included tracking more extreme animal rights organisations. He also said the services would be highly responsive to incidents like the attack on our CEO.'

'But if this is true,' asked Elizabeth, 'and there's an MI5 agent in One Commando, why weren't the police waiting for them at Green's?'

'This is where it gets interesting. It is probable that the police, our DI Bennett included, have no authority to close them down. Not their operation. It may well be that MI5's man on the inside has only recently been accepted by One Commando and has been charged with the task of finding out something specifically—'

'And until he does, One Commando can do what the hell they like!'

'Oh, it's not quite as bad as all that,' Hanniford replied with wry amusement. 'There may be a few close shaves, but they can't risk another Lefevre-style attack going ahead. Nor another Green's. Not again.'

Los Angeles
Thursday, 23 September

Mark and Isis strode down the corridor at Unum Music. The moment they had been summoned from the studio, Mark saw apprehension cloud Isis's face. During the past two days behind the microphones, they had deliberately banished all conversation about One Commando and had focused instead on their work; what was going on in London couldn't be allowed to interfere with the recording of *Nile*.

Studio 18 had become like an oasis amid all the anxieties following Hilton's attack. Having recorded most of the album separately, there were several tracks Isis and Mark needed to sing together – including the duet ballad designed to become the hit single 'Nile'. They'd done most of this work in the last few days. For Mark, it had been the most intense experience of his singing career. Even as he and Isis performed, he'd catch himself out wondering how it was that he had come to be in a Los Angeles studio, singing with his pop-star idol. More than that, how was it that as they rehearsed and performed 'Nile', he felt a return of that same connection he'd experienced the first time they'd met – except this time, even more powerful. They gazed intently at each other, voices rising and falling with the ebb and swell of the melody, and it felt, to Mark, as though there was an intuitive force at work. Surely Isis must be feeling it too? During the breaks in their recording sessions they had relaxed together in the lounge area, and Mark had realised that all the hype surrounding Isis and her career had fooled him into believing that she was some kind of superwoman. But over the past forty-eight hours his wariness and shyness in her presence had evaporated, and a tentative trust had been established. They had chatted and laughed over silly articles in the glossy magazines laid out for them on the table along with the mineral water, and Mark had discovered that Isis was just a human being like him, with her own everyday concerns. He was intrigued by the way she didn't really talk about her past, as he did, and he respected how she was trying to bring up her daughter with as much normality as was possible under the glare of the media spotlight. And he had to admit, the more he saw of her, the more beautiful she seemed. Her blonde hair and feline blue eyes were in complete contrast to his own dark looks. He was captivated by the difference.

Mark wondered if the growing closeness between them was all the more powerful *because* of the danger that threatened them both. No longer simply partners in an album, they were now also the joint targets of One Commando. Carried by the lyrics of the song, powerful and poignant, and the melody that brought their voices together and lifted them apart with an intensity that grew and grew, each inspired the other as they reached towards the final, thrilling climax. There was a charge going on in the studio, a sensuality that was potent, undeniable – Mark knew he wasn't the only one aware of it. He'd seen it in the way Isis held his eyes as they performed together – and avoided them afterwards, as though self-conscious about what she'd revealed of herself. He could see it on the faces of the sound engineers when they went into the mixing room to hear their takes. It was as though they'd been caught, like embarrassed voyeurs, witnessing a private intimacy; it took them all a few moments of chair shuffling and averted glances to get back to usual.

It was during their final playback session of the day that Hilton arrived – and the mood suddenly changed. As they walked through to the meeting rooms, it seemed to Mark that with every step they took, the sense of apprehension was heightened. Hilton had come to Unum directly from LAX, and was waiting for them in his dark Hugo Boss suit, crisp, white shirt and Hermès tie. Looking up at him as they shook hands, they could hardly avoid the narrow red scar to the side of his left eye.

'I know you wanted to pull the endorsement last time we spoke,' he got down to business right away, looking Isis in the eye, before glancing over at Mark, 'and that remains your prerogative. However, I thought I should let you know that we have some new information.'

'Arrests?' asked Mark.

'Not as yet.' Then, reacting to Isis's dismissive shrug, 'What we have found is that the British secret service, MI5, seem to have an agent in the group. That explains the police tip-off when I was attacked. It should also give us all a measure of reassurance that even if an attack was being planned against both of you, it would never be allowed to go ahead.'

'You mean, like the attack on you wasn't allowed to go ahead?' Isis was sardonic.

'It didn't get very far.'

'Well, pardon me if I'm not crazy about having armed terrorists rampaging through the house while I wait for the police to arrive—'

'I'm not saying we're in the clear—'

'What about Vinnie?' asked Mark. 'Are they following that up?'

'I gave the lead to Bennett—'

'This is hopeless!' Isis interjected, shaking her head firmly. 'Berkeley Square isn't worth it. Nothing's worth it!'

'We need to consider—'

'I'm sick of considering!' she snapped. 'I'm sick of weighing up the options. Putting my life on hold. This endorsement has been a nightmare right from the start, and I want out.'

'Isis, you know that's not true,' Hilton's tone was even. 'You shouldn't forget the benefits that came with the signing.'

'What are you saying,' demanded Isis, 'that I should ask Berkeley Square to sign up for another ten years?'

Hilton gave her time to cool off before saying in a low voice, 'I know you're not going to like my advice. But I don't think you should pull out because of what happened to me.'

'How many more attacks do you want me to wait for?'

'Don't forget there's an MI5 agent in this group.'

'Very reassuring!'

'It should be. And there's no suggestion One Commando even operate outside of London, let alone in Los Angeles. You need to be aware of all the implications – both of you,' he added, fixing Mark with a severe expression. 'The production process for the endorsement advertisements is way down the line. If you decide to withdraw now, Berkeley Square won't just be looking to you to return the money.

They'll be suing for production costs and commercial damages.'

'Just wonderful!' exclaimed Isis.

'Obviously, we'd have a very strong case with direct terrorist intimidation, but it would all go legal.'

She collapsed back in her chair, hands pressed to her eyes.

'What you're saying,' Mark resented Hilton's tone, 'is that we can sit and wait to be attacked by terrorists, or get taken to the cleaners by Berkeley Square?'

'What I'm saying,' Hilton replied sharply, 'is that while there's a lesson to be learned from my own ... disturbing encounter, it's to keep a grip.'

Isis was shaking her head slowly. 'That's what you said last time,' her voice was choked, 'when Lefevre was attacked. But things haven't gotten better. They just keep getting worse. And what if they start delving into my background?' she blurted. 'They could destroy me without coming anywhere near Los Angeles!'

'What background?' Mark demanded. 'How could they destroy—'

'That's got nothing to do with One Commando.' An uncharacteristic heat came into Hilton's voice as he flashed an angry glance first at Isis, then Mark. 'It's not at all relevant.'

'If it's relevant to the endorsement,' Mark wasn't going to be bamboozled, 'it's relevant to me. What's this "background"?'

Isis was staring down at the floor, unusually self-conscious.

Hilton exhaled slowly before regaining his usual expression of calm detachment. 'Isis gets confused about something that happened a long time ago, which doesn't mean anything to anyone any more. What she seems to forget' – although he addressed Mark, he continued gazing at Isis, unwaveringly

– 'is that she's been the biggest name in pop for years. People have been trying to dish the dirt on her from the minute she got to be famous. Why should anyone start looking there now?'

12

Alan Brent worked on the research assignment the way he always worked on any project that compelled him – the only way he knew *how* to work at things: obsessively. *The powers that be*, the phrase had kept on running through his mind like a mantra since his last meeting with Larson. This was the break he'd been waiting for, his chance to find out who really ran One Commando. To make himself useful, gain acceptance, accomplish his mission.

He had no idea where his investigations on their behalf would lead him. But his brief was simple: to dig up anything and everything that might help One Commando in their mission against Isis. And he had the most powerful information technology equipment with which to do it. As a student, working with an ageing IBM in the university library, he'd managed to break through meticulously constructed fire-walls into the most advanced security systems in the world to penetrate classified files at Los Alamos National Laboratory in America, the Bank of England – he'd even hacked into Paramount Studios to play around with scripts for episodes of his favourite sitcom *Cheers*.

The Isis project was far from straightforward. For starters he didn't even have Isis's real name to go on. Not that he was daunted. The only thing that really bothered him was what he'd do with any information he did retrieve. He supposed that if he dug up anything really interesting, his first duty would be to notify his boss before he contacted Larson. It would be up to him to decide how to play it.

He'd started by trawling the archives of US counter-culture music e-zines. He knew none of the mainstream music titles ever mentioned the name she'd been born with – her publicists had succeeded in keeping that out of common currency. But he'd come across a few self-styled 'cult' e-zines in the past; sporadic and usually short-lived publications run out of bedrooms and public housing basements by disaffected twentysomethings who'd failed to make it into the mainstream music industry, and who'd turned their critical abilities instead into undermining it. His search through back issues confirmed that the 'crass commercialism' of Isis's music was a core target. In themselves the vitriolic critiques were of no interest to him; what he sought, quite simply, was a name.

It had taken him several hours to get it. Eventually he found it in a 1993 issue of the *Beat Meat* edited by one A. Henkshaw of Baton Rouge, who related a conspiracy theory to conceal Isis's past and even her real name. Henkshaw claimed to have evidence that her family name was Carboni and she'd been brought up in a middle-class Italian household, in Miami, Florida.

Alan quickly established that *Beat Meat* had been through a number of ownership changes since 1993, and that A. Henkshaw had long-since ceased to have anything to do with the title. He doubted that speaking to him about an article researched so long ago would be of the slightest use. But he needed corroboration. Using a search combining both 'Isis' and 'Carboni' he found confirmation sooner than he'd expected, and from the unlikeliest of sources; a piece on contemporary culture and 'Who influences the influencers' had appeared in the *Wall Street Journal* two years ago. It carried a pen-sketch of Isis including the information that her real surname was Carboni and that she hailed from a 'down-scale suburb of Miami'. The revelation that she had been born into an unexceptional Italian émigré family carried with it the full weight of the *WSJ*'s authority.

Alan left that lead, he could come back to it later, and looked up the on-line telephone directory for Miami. It included over two hundred Carbonis. Trying to find a link in that lot was virtually impossible. Even if she had a family out there, they were probably ex-directory and almost certainly wouldn't speak to him. So he printed off the list before turning his attention to locating the Registry of Births for Miami Dade County. That was plain sailing; the county had its own website, and he clicked his way directly into public records – only to find that they went back no further than 1990.

Births, births, births, he thought, where else would they be recorded? Swiftly accessing a media-list directory from a press-cutting bureau in New York, he surveyed a complete list of publications for the state of Florida, from the *Miami Herald* to the most obscure trade and hobby journals. But as he looked through the list he was already discounting it – if her family really had come from a slum, they were hardly going to announce the birth of their child in the *Miami Herald*.

Baptisms. If they were Catholic Italians they would have

had her baptised – there had probably been at least one exclusively Italian Roman Catholic church in Miami in the late sixties to early seventies. He was already searching for names of Christian churches in Miami. It was a long shot, he realised – most of them probably weren't mentioned on the internet. But his search revealed one overtly Italian Catholic church site, St Columbus, presided over by Father Marvin Robieri. The Catholic priest was evidently a big fan of the net – links to St Columbus, the Italian Family Church, appeared over a dozen times in search results under different references. And his church's own website bore an impressive logo, as well as a full-colour photograph of a beaming Marvin in all his ecclesiastical glory, with a gold crucifix, white doves and blue-clad Mary Mother of God, all in lurid hues. There were links on the site to a whole range of activities – church events, fellowship groups, fund-raising activities, mission work and a host of others, signposted in either English or Italian.

Alan glanced over them all, more amused than anything. On the surface, Father Marvin's Italian Family Church was exactly what he was looking for. But there was nothing that suggested baptismal records could be accessed – though they might be, he supposed, if he phoned. He was scanning down the links when the word 'Bollettino' caught his eye – probably worth a click, he supposed.

'Bollettino' was an electronic e-zine, no less. It was in Italian and appeared to serve as a kind of notice-board of events in the parish community of St Columbus. He couldn't understand very much, but scrolling down several pages, his eye was caught by subtitles 'Battesimi', 'Matrimoni', 'Funerali', with names and dates recorded beneath. Raising his eyebrows, he glanced along the list of links at the bottom of the page. Were any of these archives, he wondered, clicking one after the other. Did 'Bollettino' go back any further than Father Marvin's all-singing, all-dancing website?

Moving his cursor on to 'Archivi', he clicked into what was clearly an archive retrieval mechanism, and keyed in a date at random – February 1969 – before entering 'Search' and holding his breath. The down-load indicator of his computer was flashing, and Alan shifted his chair closer to the screen. It was such a long shot he didn't dare hope for anything. But to his astonishment up came 'Bollettino' for that month. A poorly reproduced and dog-eared image of a typewritten newsletter. But it was legible – and Alan was astonished that it was available at all. Father Marvin had evidently spent days, if not weeks, painstakingly scanning in all the past editions for posterity.

For the next few hours, Alan went through every one of the newsletters from 1968 to 1974 – no one knew Isis's age for certain – writing down the names of every Carboni ever baptised at St Columbus's. There had been eight in all, five boys and three girls, and Alan immediately set about trying to find the girls, beginning with his favourite tracing technique – the tax return records of the Internal Revenue Service. It was a method with which he was thoroughly familiar, and he had soon hacked effortlessly through the encryption devices designed specifically to keep out unauthorised visitors. Because of the strong possibility that the women he sought would have married, Alan searched through tax records from the period of their early twenties, before following through. And it wasn't long before he'd tracked down two of them, one a teacher in Delaware, the other a police officer in Florida. There was no trace of the third, Maria Chiara Carboni. Could she be Isis? Knowing the inadequacies of the Internal Revenue Service systems, Alan decided to look elsewhere, hacking into the files of educational institutions and police departments to track down Maria Chiara.

Later, Alan thought how ironic it was that when he'd made his discovery about Isis, the really big discovery, he hadn't even recognised it. The full significance of what he'd hit upon continued to elude him. Turning to medical institutions, in and around Miami, he hacked his way, with only a minimum of trouble, into the computer records of the Salmacis Hospital – one of those he'd found listed on an on-line directory. He had no idea if Salmacis was a private or public institution, and the records, such as they were, revealed little. But he did find, in 1984, several entries for patient M.C. Carboni, treated by Dr Robert Weiner. Alan printed off the page. Right then he didn't attribute any special significance to it – there was no telling if this was Maria, or Mirella, or for that matter Marco, and even if it was a Maria, was it *his* Maria or not?

It was only after a number of his more sophisticated tracking techniques hit dead ends, that Alan realised he'd failed to try the most basic. Going to the Yahoo homepage of an internet search engine, he keyed in the name Maria Carboni. There were dozens of matches, but within minutes he'd found one Maria Carboni in Miami and with her own website, advertising 'Paws on Miami Beach – offering both pooches and pussies the Purrrfect Pampering'. There was a photograph of a beaming Maria, holding a closely cropped, pink-rinsed poodle to her cheek and surrounded by red heart cat cushions and designer leashes. It was a gaudy, tacky image, but he had no doubt that this was the Maria he'd been searching for. Flopping back in his chair, he let out a low sigh. So this was the upshot of over ten hours on the net – a poodle parlour in Miami Beach!

As he sat, slumped in his chair, staring at this Maria, he

wondered though if there was not something about her face that was reminiscent of Isis. Was it an Italian gene-pool thing, he asked himself, or was it that after too many hours in front of the screen his eyes were just playing tricks with him? Leaning forward, he concentrated harder. The more he stared, the closer he could see a resemblance. Were they sisters, he wondered – but if so, what had happened to the record of Isis's baptism? And what exactly was it about Maria Carboni's face that held the key?

Lloyd spotted Vinnie the moment he stepped into the Lamb. A creature of habit, Vinnie was propping up the bar in his usual corner, talking to the manager and a few of his usual associates. As he busied himself ordering a round of drinks and taking them back to his table, Lloyd didn't pay him any special attention, though their eyes met across the pub and Vinnie delivered a nod. Lloyd still found it hard to believe: Vinnie Dobson in cahoots with one of Interpol's Most Wanted Terrorists. When Mark had given him the news, he had dismissed it at first as impossible. But he'd checked out the Interpol website for himself, and there it all was – including a photograph of Larson minus the red beard. Mark had asked him to try getting information out of Vinnie on the sly. Play it low key, he'd insisted. Give him my mobile number and tell him I'd like to hear from him. Find out *anything* you can about his new 'business contact', but whatever you do, don't let him think we're on to him. It's got to be casual.

Lloyd reckoned Vinnie would come over to him during the course of the evening. They hadn't seen each other since the surprise visit to his flat last Friday; he reckoned Mark's 'grateful' former manager wouldn't be able to resist approaching him. And sure enough, about half an hour later, he felt a tap on his shoulder.

'Thought you'd been avoiding me.' Vinnie cocked his head.

'Nothing like that.' Lloyd noted the surprised expressions round the table. Last time he and Vinnie had had anything to do with each other, the latter had been threatening his brother's life. Now he was motioning that Lloyd should get up and speak to him alone. He was doing his Swerve-manager, wheeler-dealer act which Lloyd usually resented, but which tonight he reckoned could be useful.

'Speak to him?' Vinnie wanted to know.

'Couple of days ago. Told him about your visit.' Lloyd was aware of Vinnie's impatient expression, and thought he'd play along with him for a while. 'He knew about your Unum deal—'

Vinnie raised a confidential finger to his lips.

'Oh, sorry. Yeah, he's pleased things are going so well for you. He asked how you were doing. I told him you were pretty flat out at the moment. That's right, isn't it?'

'Sure, sure.' Vinnie glowered before prompting, 'What about the phone number?'

Lloyd nodded innocently. 'Oh, I got that.' He touched his breast pocket. 'Right here, in fact.'

Vinnie visibly relaxed. 'Did he say anything else?'

'Just that he'd like to hear from you.'

'I'll be calling him all right,' the other said and took a swig of his bitter.

'You must be doing really well, heading out to LA?'

Vinnie nodded. 'Part of the jet-set now,' he said, only half in jest.

Lloyd looked suitably deferential. 'That's with the new business contact you mentioned?'

Vinnie shot him a sidelong glance. 'Pretty much.' Then,

unable to contain himself, 'You're talking big league. Seriously big league.'

'What – big league in London?'

'Christ, no. All over the place. He flies in. Does the business. Flies out again. Never in the same place more than a couple of days at a time.'

'Bit difficult to do business with if he's always on a plane?' he prompted.

'Oh, he stays in touch.' Vinnie patted the jacket pocket in which he kept his mobile.

'Sounds intriguing? What line is he in?' No harm in asking, thought Lloyd.

'Now that, Lloy-boy,' Vinnie touched his nose conspiratorially, 'is what you'd call classified information. And you know me. I like to keep things under wraps.'

Los Angeles
Friday, 24 September

Twenty-four hours after getting back to Los Angeles, Hilton Gallo was showing uncharacteristic signs of frustration: there'd been no further news from Scotland Yard on One Commando. DI Bennett was maintaining his wall of silence, despite the eleventh hour tip-off which had put the police hot on the heels of the group; despite the presence of an MI5 agent within it; despite the Vinnie Dobson lead. There was not so much as an inkling that arrests were imminent or that the group was about to be closed down.

And that meant he was going into this afternoon's meeting with far less certainty than he would have preferred. Ranged about him in the GCM Boardroom were the endorsements head Ross McCormack, and his counterpart in music

Andy Murdoch, plus GCM's in-house lawyer, Blake Horowitz, and Leo Lebowitz. Across the table from him Elizabeth was ready to take notes.

'The endorsement,' began Hilton, eyeballing Ross McCormack, 'where are we on the critical path?'

McCormack fiddled with the bright red frames of his spectacles. The prospect of Isis and Jordan Hampshire pulling out of the biggest deal he'd negotiated in his life was more than alarming. It had been giving him sleepless nights. If this deal went pear-shaped, no matter what the reason, he might as well kiss goodbye to his job and his career.

'Production's finished and artwork has been sent by Berkeley Square's agency to fifteen of the thirty magazines on the media schedule.' He tried hard to project his usual, brisk efficiency. 'The forty-eight-sheet posters have been sent to media agents in each of the twelve participating countries for installation. We're all on schedule for the campaign to break in a fortnight's time.'

Hilton nodded. Usually he would have been reassured that McCormack and his team was so well on top of production, but on this occasion the prospect that the endorsement was now slipping beyond control was less reassuring.

'And what about the matter we discussed last night?' He turned to Blake Horowitz.

Blake hadn't got to bed last night till three, after a marathon session at the offices of GCM's attorneys Mitchell & Curtin. Now he massaged his tired eyelids.

'There are three main points to this,' he began in measured tones. 'The first is the very practical one that at some point this campaign reaches the point of no return.'

All eyes turned to McCormack.

'As I said, the artwork's already gone.' He raised his shoulders.

'Artwork can be recalled.' Hilton looked over at him, steel-eyed.

McCormack's eyebrows twitched nervously. 'The posters, sure, we can pull those out even a few days before. But the magazines will be going to print any day now.'

'I want you to find out which day, specifically.'

'For all thirty of them?' McCormack's pale cheeks were rapidly colouring to the shade of his spectacle-frames.

'Yes,' retorted Hilton, glancing back to Horowitz. 'Carry on, Blake.'

'The second point is the basis on which our clients would revoke their endorsement contract. Having carefully checked the articles of the Berkeley Square contract,' he fingered a thick document in front of him, 'I find there is no specific clause that explicitly or implicitly allows for withdrawal on the basis of intimidation. I've discussed matters with Mitchell & Curtin and we believe there *is* precedent for such a withdrawal. However,' he looked up significantly, 'we would need to establish a threat. Evidence of terrorist intimidation would have to be provided to substantiate our clients' actions. And as far as I'm aware, we have no evidence as yet beyond your own experience,' he nodded at Hilton, 'which would be regarded by the courts as hearsay.'

Hilton looked down at the table, tight-lipped.

'The only other way out,' Horowitz continued, 'is to establish that Berkeley Square has, in fact, been testing on animals, and that our clients' reputations would be damaged by association ...' That was a line he didn't need to continue. 'The third issue to raise is that of commercial damages. Berkeley Square would seek the three point five million they've paid our clients. Production costs we estimate at half a million, and media costs at nearly eight million.' He glanced over at where Ross McCormack was nodding in agreement. 'Damages would be significant, especially having already announced the clients' endorsement. Depending on jurisdiction, and looking at the scale of awards paid out in past endorsement disputes, we're looking at damages equivalent to the endorsement cost, at the very least. Then there's the potential legal costs of the other side should we not succeed. In round terms we could be looking at twenty million plus.'

Hilton looked up to find all eyes on him.

Ross McCormack was shaking his head. 'That's some hit.'

'It's a monstrous penalty to pay,' retorted Hilton, '*if* there's no danger posed to our clients. But if it's the only way we can guarantee their survival . . .' He glanced round the table seriously. 'What we need right now is more information.'

Heads were nodding, though not McCormack's; the man wore a dyspeptic expression.

'Elizabeth, can you get Bennett on a conference call. You'll have to get him at home.'

A short while later, Elizabeth had brought a telephone over to the table, having dialled the policeman.

'Detective Inspector Bennett. Hilton Gallo. I'm with several colleagues wanting to know where you are with One Commando?'

Bennett sounded surprised. 'As I told your assistant yesterday, we're using every means at our disposal to bring this to a swift conclusion.'

'Just how swift? I got the impression, after my attack, we were talking hours?'

'It could be hours,' the voice at the other end was even, 'but it could be weeks.'

'Weeks?' Hilton's voice was choked. 'How could it be weeks? You know who these people are!'

'There are extenuating circumstances.'

'What extenuating circumstances?'

'I'm not in a position to divulge that information.'

There was a lengthy pause before, at the end of the table, Hilton drew himself up to his full height, clasped his hands in front of him, elbows on the table.

'Inspector Bennett,' his voice was sharp with authority, 'allow me to outline our position. Our two clients top the target list of a violent terrorist organisation. The terrorists are threatening them unless they cancel their endorsement contracts. It seems to me there are only two solutions. One is to apprehend the terrorists. The other is to cancel the endorsement contracts. I'd like to share with you, confidentially, the figure just passed on by a colleague, who tells me that any such cancellation will cost my clients twenty million dollars. Now perhaps you understand why I'm so eager for any information which will help resolve this problem?'

'Indeed,' came an unimpressed-sounding Bennett from the other end after a pause, 'and you must understand I am equally committed to protecting the means by which I have come to acquire certain information—'

'You're talking about the MI5 agent?'

'I'm unable to confirm or deny—'

'Let's cut the crap, Bennett.' His colleagues had never witnessed Hilton in such wrath. 'We know about the agent, no thanks to you. So, what are these "extenuating circumstances" that prevent you from arresting the group?'

'That's not something I'm allowed to divulge.'

'And what about Dobson? Has he led you anywhere?'

'The Metropolitan Police run a very tight ship. We have few enough staff to conduct surveillance of known criminals without committing our resources to following individuals in London pubs who have *allegedly* been seen in the company of Interpol suspects—'

'You mean, you're doing nothing about it?'

'I mean, we're pursuing the most fruitful lines of enquiry.'

'But you're not prepared to tell us what those lines are?'

'Mr Gallo, we're in the business of saving people's lives, not saving Hollywood money.'

Hilton jabbed the speaker phone off, furious. It was rare, in his negotiations with others, that he wasn't able to advance the interests of GCM and its clients – or at least leave the door open to the possibility of future advancement. But Bennett was in a separate category from those with whom he generally did business. GCM's dominance in the entertainment industry meant nothing to the policeman. Exasperated, Hilton was wondering where to take things next when Melissa Schwartz came through with a note: Mark Watson wanted to speak to him urgently.

'Put him through,' Hilton was curt.

Lloyd had phoned Mark to report on his conversation with Vinnie as soon as he got home from the pub. Mark had insisted that he relate to him every detail. The revelation that Larson was so highly mobile was extremely disturbing, and even though Lloyd and he didn't discuss it, they both realised the implications: Bengt Larson could be in America, even as they spoke. Right now he might be holed up somewhere in Los Angeles, planning the next attack. Despite what Hilton had said to Isis and him the day before, One Commando wasn't just a UK-only group. They were international.

For the first time since arriving in Los Angeles, Mark had felt at risk. Looking out of the windows of his Beverly Hills home, across the lush lawns to the flower beds lining the perimeter walls, he found himself wondering just how secure his home really was.

Now he reported back to Hilton on Lloyd's conversation with Vinnie. Hilton, who had him on speakerphone, sounded tense from the start of the conversation, and was even more uptight by the end of it. He *had* to realise, thought Mark, that this latest revelation meant the end of the endorsement. Last time they'd spoken to Isis, it had taken all Hilton's powers of persuasion to keep her in the deal – and even then she'd been far from happy. If she'd known that Larson's activities were global, she would have *insisted* on bailing out; Mark had no doubt that the end of this whole débâcle was only one phone call away for Hilton. As soon as he got on the line to Malibu, that would be it.

But there didn't seem any foregone conclusion as far as Hilton was concerned. Far from acknowledging that the time had come to draw a line under the whole Berkeley Square fiasco, he was moving the conversation smoothly on to security arrangements. He would instruct security specialists employed by GCM to conduct an immediate assessment of Mark's protection, he told him. They would be ordered to upgrade all necessary measures. No expense would be spared to ensure his safety. It was all very well, thought Mark, but why bother if they were going to call off the endorsement?

His suspicions growing, he waited until Hilton had ended before asking expectantly, 'And what news on Vinnie Dobson? Has he led them anywhere useful yet?'

There was a snort of impatience from the other end before Hilton admitted, 'I've just been on the phone to Bennett at Scotland Yard. They're not keeping Dobson under surveillance.'

'You've got to be—!'

'Bennett claims they don't have the resources. I think there's a very different reason.'

'But he's a direct lead to Larson!'

'So is their inside man. That's what they're not saying. It's my belief,' Hilton tried to convey more certainty than hope, 'they've got an operation under way they don't want to compromise—'

'I'd say it's more a case of the Plods not knowing their arses from their elbows,' retorted Mark. It wasn't a sentiment he'd expressed yesterday in front of Isis, but the fact was he'd lost all confidence in the Met when he was twelve; there'd been a break-in at home in Lewisham, and even though the police knew the suspects, and confirmed their fingerprints, they said they didn't have enough to go on to secure a conviction. He'd realised then, you couldn't count on the Met.

'This really is the end of it,' he was exasperated.

There was only silence from Hilton.

'Let's face it, when Isis hears that Larson's mobile she'll pull the plug.'

'That's by no means a certainty,' Hilton's tone was clipped.

'Come on, Hilton, I was there. I saw her face. She wants out.'

'There are good reasons for her to stay in.'

'Oh, sure. But as soon as I tell her about Larson—'

'As you'll have gathered by now,' Hilton swiftly interjected, 'she's a very . . . complex lady. This needs to be treated with sensitivity.'

'Meaning you don't want me to tell her?' He was sardonic.

'It's difficult news.' Hilton's response was frosty. 'It's best if I break it to her.'

'So in the land of the brave and the free, you can't talk to people about direct threats to their lives?' Mark's cynicism about Hilton's information control was now complete.

'That's not what I said.'

'Sounded like it to me.'

'All I said was—'

'That I shouldn't mention it,' his voice rose, 'so you can cover the whole thing up!'

'Let me spell this out,' Hilton's voice had sunk to sub-zero, 'I've known Isis since she arrived in Los Angeles fourteen years ago. You've known her a few weeks. I've worked closely with her. I understand her. I know her strengths – and her blind spots. When it comes to breaking difficult news so as not to cause undue distress, I'm better placed than you to do it.'

'So long as you *do* "break the difficult news,"' retorted Mark.

'I've already said that I will.'

'Oh, yeah,' Mark sounded disbelieving.

'You have my word,' Hilton intoned deliberately, 'and if I can give you some advice, I suggest you be a little less hasty in the judgements you form about people.'

13

For Alan Brent, the timing couldn't have been worse. Shortly after six in the morning he got the phone call from Larson; the One Commando boss wanted to see him. A taxi would be coming to collect him from his flat in ten minutes.

It was typical Larson – urgent and unpredictable. For security reasons Alan supposed it had to be that way. But following the revelations of just a few hours ago, he wasn't sure what to do; how much of his discovery should he reveal?

He hadn't been able to let go of the Isis riddle. It had got under his skin. The mystery of her identity – who she was and where she came from – had had him intrigued, infuriated, utterly absorbed. It was an intellectual puzzle he was determined to solve. The fact that he'd been commissioned to dig up this stuff by Bengt Larson, that he planned to use it to come to the attention of *the powers that be* became almost secondary to his main purpose; he *had* to discover the enigma of her past.

As it happened, the key that unlocked the door had come to him when he'd stopped looking. At the end of a long session of fruitless hacking that had gone on until one this morning, he'd shoved himself back from the computer desk, walked across the attic room, stripped down to his underpants and collapsed into bed. He had lain there, physically tired, but mentally perplexed, his mind performing high-wire gymnastics with the unrelated bits of data he'd assembled so far, but getting nowhere; 'Paws of Miami Beach'. Maria Carboni. Salmacis Hospital.

It had been as he was falling asleep, when his subconscious took over the problem that his conscious mind had failed to solve, that the realisation had come about. It was only once he'd stopped trying too hard, as he drifted between consciousness and sleep, that it came without any effort at all, jolting him awake.

Suddenly, he was too excited to sleep. In the dark, he glanced at the hands of his watch – a quarter to two in London made it a quarter to nine in Miami. He was soon up at his desk, getting phone numbers from international directory enquiries, and placing calls. He didn't get far by phoning Salmacis Hospital direct – Dr Weiner was no longer full time at the hospital, he was told, having set up his own practice elsewhere. No, they didn't have the number for that practice right now, but if he'd like to call back during normal working hours . . .

Back at his computer, Alan chased down several more dead alleys before finally getting his breakthrough shortly after three in the morning. He'd succeeded in tracking down Robert Weiner through the American Medical Association website. Now fifty-four, Weiner was still practising in Miami, operating a practice with two other specialists in downtown Miami. Short résumés of all three doctors were provided. Hardly daring to breathe, Alan scanned down their details. All worked in complementary disciplines. Any one of them may, or may not, be required to attend to a particular case. But each of them was a specialist in the same field of counselling, and treated patients emerging from the same tunnel of horrors. Alan found it hard to believe. But there it was, right in front of him, staring him in the face.

Surely Isis hadn't been through that?

'I want you to tell me about the Gallo operation,' demanded Larson, tugging him through the door almost as soon as he'd knocked. The flat was on the first floor of a derelict council block in Kensington Olympia. Stark, graffiti-sprayed walls were lit from a single naked bulb dangling from the ceiling. Even paler and more dishevelled than usual after a sleepless night, Alan blinked in bewilderment behind his thick lenses.

'But I – I wasn't even involved. Why me?'

On the way over, he'd wondered what was going on, tried to work out the significance of Larson's latest, and typically unanticipated, demand.

'You tell me.' Larson was accusatory. Dangerous.

'I'm n-not sure what you mean. I don't know anything about it.' He felt his mouth go suddenly dry. He should have seen this coming. Having got this far into the organisation, he should have prepared for confrontation. But he hadn't. He'd been so absorbed in the Isis assignment he'd forgotten about most other things. Now he felt alarmingly deficient.

'That is strange,' Larson began to circle him slowly, all the while staring intently at him. 'Your mates seemed to know all about it.'

'What mates?'

'Don't fuck with me, Brent,' Larson growled in his ear, 'you know who I'm talking about.'

'I don't.'

'All this while you've been tagging along with us, making

yourself useful, you must have thought you were being very clever,' Larson had returned to face him, and was eyeballing him from six inches away. 'Meantime, it turns out you're nothing but a spy. A snoop.'

It was then that Alan became aware of the red light of the camera. Installed in one corner of the room, it dangled from a hook that had been screwed into the ceiling. What was going on? Was this a set-up? He tried remembering what he'd learned about conflict resolution. He took a deep breath.

'There's obviously been a mistake,' he began. Appeal to reason, he recalled. Always appeal to reason in the first instance – and introduce an element of surprise. Yeah, well, he could do that all right.

'The Gallo operation – I don't know what you're talking about. And I'm not a spy. How could I be? Why would I spend hours getting incredible stuff on Isis if I was a spy?'

'What "incredible stuff"?'

'The research I've been doing.' He wished he could come across more confident. More controlled. But a nervous tic had developed under his eye. He felt his whole cheek twitching.

Larson met his eyes with a long, cold stare.

'I th-thought that was why you wanted to see me.'

Larson was leaning back with his arms crossed. 'Oh, yes?' His tone was disdainful. 'Exactly the kind of answer I'd expect from an undercover agent. There's only one problem with what you say. This information you talk about – I never got it.'

'That's because I only had the breakthrough last night.'

'How *very* convenient for you,' snorted Larson.

'But if you let me tell you now you'll see there's no way—'

'I think you'd better.'

Alan swallowed hard. He was radically revising his plans

by the second. The proper procedure would have been for him to relay his findings to HQ for their considerations before even hinting at their existence to anyone else. And in this instance he was in no doubt that his discoveries would have astounded all the head honchos there. But there was no way he could follow standard procedures right now. He didn't doubt for a second that Larson meant business.

So he told Larson everything. From the tracing of Maria Carboni right through the detection process to his final, astounding discovery. It was the first time he'd put his findings into words and said them out loud, and as he spoke he was aware how bizarre they must seem.

Larson stood listening to him, expressionless. When he was done, he glanced up at the ceiling for a few moments before saying, 'Well, either that is the most incredible thing I've ever heard, or it's the desperate tale of a worm wriggling on its hook.'

Alan felt beads of perspiration starting to slide down his forehead. 'I d-don't know where you get the idea of a . . . spy from.'

'The police were tipped off.' Larson's voice was steely. 'I didn't tip them off. It wasn't anyone in the group. Only one other person knew—'

'But you're missing a motive!' protested Alan.

'There'd be a motive if you were a spy.'

'But I'm not. You vetted my b-background. You know how committed I am to the cause—'

'Do I?' Larson was disbelieving.

'Well, you know how much I hate Berkeley Square.'

'Oh, yes. You joined them as a graduate,' his tone was mockingly schmaltzy, 'and they stole your big idea. They made you change departments. Such a sad story.'

'It's true! You know it!'

'It seemed to be true. Just like your discovery about Isis seems to be an amazing piece of detective work.'

'Go ahead. Ch-check it out!'

Larson leaned over him. 'I will,' he said, staring into Alan's eyes from just a few inches away, 'because you know what I'm going to do if it's not true, don't you?' He was nodding slowly. 'That's right Alan. I'm going to kill you.'

Jasper Jones sat on the kilim-patterned sofa of his well-upholstered sitting room, poring over the Sunday papers, while breakfast news pumped out of the TV. He seldom bought only one newspaper at the weekends. And this morning he'd bought the lot. Slipping out of bed carefully so as not to disturb Gail, who'd stayed over with him last night for only the second time, he'd gone down to his local newsagent just after eight o'clock. There he'd bought the *Sunday Times, Sunday Telegraph, Sunday Herald, Independent on Sunday, Observer, Mail on Sunday, Sunday Express, Sunday Mirror* and *News of the World*. With all their supplements and colour magazines, they stood over eight inches high on his coffee table. But Jones was not interested in anything but the news coverage – and particularly that on the front page.

He'd first become aware of it last night as he and Gail had returned from a party at the home of PR agency boss Mark Maritz in Hampstead. The radio of his Saab convertible was tuned in as usual to Capital Radio. During an advertisement break had come the unexpected announcement that tomorrow's *Sunday Herald* would carry an exclusive account of a second attack in central London by animal terrorist group One Commando. Included was an interview with Simon Dubois, a hotel manager whose family had been held hostage in the attack. Read out in breathless tones and making much of the police news blackout that had prevented reporting of the incident before now, the *Sunday Herald* puff-piece was tailor-made for sensation.

Jones had had a hard time keeping his feelings concealed from Gail. Having closely monitored the media immediately after the failed attack, he'd quickly realised the police had blanketed the whole thing. Monday night's disruption at Green's had evidently been explained to all those involved as a false fire alert. And that had suited him fine; he hardly wanted to see One Commando's failure trumpeted in the press.

As the week wore on and there was still no word of the attack, he'd begun to think the story might never surface. But thinking hard as he'd sped through the mild Saturday night, he had realised that this could only be wishful thinking. All it took was a casual exchange in the supermarket, a playground conversation, and the media, with eyes and ears everywhere and cheque-books at the ready, would pounce. Word had evidently got out from the Dubois family: had it been a calculated cash-in by Simon Dubois, or something more accidental? How much would be revealed? And now the cat was out of the bag, how many other Sunday papers would be hurriedly remaking their front pages?

He wanted, urgently, to get on the phone and find out just how this story was breaking. That was, of course, out of the question with Gail sitting right beside him. Slim, blonde, beautiful Gail with whom a new and very gratifying relationship had begun after the dinner party they'd both attended ten days earlier. But even as he drove her back to Islington, the inviting prospect of a night of passion ahead, he thought that, if the truth be told, he'd rather be heading for Wapping to pick up an early edition of the *Sunday Herald*, or spending the next few hours monitoring the twenty-four-hour news channels he received by satellite TV. He'd rather be getting a grip on what was going on; the One

Commando project meant a lot to him. He'd invested too much time, money and energy in it to see it all go belly up.

This morning as he'd flicked through the papers on his way home from the newsagent, he'd soon confirmed that all the late editions carried news of the Dubois interview, with the *Sunday Herald* adding to their front-page headline splash with a double-page spread on pages two and three. Back in his flat, he'd closed the sitting room door and turned the television on, volume low, as he continued to scan through each of the newspapers, tearing out any articles referring to the attack. He didn't have long to wait until an ITN news round-up repeated news of the attack, together with a clip of Dubois climbing into his car the night before, remarking that he had nothing more to say.

Recording all this on video, Jones took in every word in a state of total absorption. Then came his detailed reading of the *Sunday Herald*. They'd covered it as a human drama piece, with much made of the 'terrifying ordeal' suffered by Dubois's wife and two children, photographed looking traumatised on one page, with Simon Dubois appearing every bit as gaunt on the other. The family had been at home on an ordinary school-day afternoon when masked gunmen had burst through both the front and back doors simultaneously and ordered them, face down, on to the carpet. Shock had initially prevented them from doing anything but obey orders. But as soon as she'd recovered the power of speech, Mrs Dubois reported that she'd told the intruders they must have the wrong house: what interest could they, an ordinary middle-class family, be to a group of evidently organised militia?

But the gunmen hadn't been inclined to make conversation. They had apparently been highly disciplined and kept communication to a minimum. Mrs Dubois and her two children had been ordered to collect warm clothes and coats, before being handcuffed and bundled into a panel van which arrived down a laneway at the back of their house. In the darkness of the van, being driven through South London, Mrs Dubois had remembered the One Commando attack on Jacques Lefevre – or so she claimed. Clutching her children to her it was all she could do, she'd told reporters, to keep herself from breaking down, to stay brave for her kids' sake.

Scanning the rest of the piece, Jones turned to the interview with Dubois himself. There was nothing in here that hinted of One Commando's real target. The *Sunday Herald* – presumably at Dubois's request – hadn't even mentioned Green's by name, although none of the other papers had felt any such compunction. All that was reported of the main event was how Dubois, held to ransom over his family, had provided access to the hotel in an attack that had been foiled by the early intervention of the police. No mention was made of One Commando's intended target, though it was stated that Hollywood celebrities frequently stayed at the hotel.

Jones quickly recognised the *Sunday Herald*'s ploy: sensational though it was, what they'd launched here was a teaser. They'd deliberately kept back enough revelations to feed to readers, piecemeal. Rather than use up all their ammunition in one hit, they'd started a *Herald*-exclusive soap documentary which they'd use to beat down their opponents over the next week in the unending circulation wars. This was a story set to run and run. Jones was livid.

It was only moments after this recognition that the sitting room door opened and in came Gail wearing his bathrobe. Clear-eyed, hair brushed and even, if he wasn't mistaken, wearing a touch of make-up, she came over behind where he was sitting and put her arms around his chest. 'You work too hard,' she whispered, kissing his cheek.

'Not usually.'

Her hands roamed down his chest. 'Only since you met me then, eh?' she smiled.

He put his hands over her arms, as though to massage them but in reality to prevent them descending any further.

'I expect you've worked up quite an appetite?' she asked knowingly. 'I thought I might cook some breakfast. That is, if there's anything in your kitchen to cook?'

'Very nice,' replied Jones, relieved to be free of any further encumbrances. 'There should be some eggs and bacon and ... things.' Then, glancing over the papers strewn all over the floor, 'I've got an important phone call to make.'

Bengt Larson was surprised when Jasper Jones's number showed up on the display of his cellular telephone. It was rare for Jones to initiate contact between the two of them, and unprecedented for him to call early on a Sunday. Stepping out of the derelict West London flat, he flipped open the phone.

'So, what do you make of the papers?' Jones exploded at the other end.

Larson had never heard him so angry. 'What d'you mean?'

'The *Sunday Herald*!'

'What are you talking about?'

'Christ Almighty! It's even worse than I thought. You haven't seen it?'

'No.'

Jones let out a long, steady stream of smoke from his Gaulois before telling Larson what had happened.

Larson paced up and down the corridor of the derelict council block.

'This is terrible!' he kept repeating, as Jones explained how the story was being played out in the media.

'You'd better believe it!' There was no mistaking Jones's accusatory tone. 'It goes completely against our strategy! We agreed, right at the beginning, we'd only act against direct targets. Now the whole world knows that civilians have been hurt – it plays into enemy hands.'

'But you agreed to the Dubois operation!' protested the other.

'I considered it acceptable collateral in securing Gallo.'

'But we never got that far—'

'And why not, Bengt – that's the point I'm making. Because of Alan Brent, that's why. Because he's a spy. He tipped off the police. And what have you done about him?'

'As a matter of interest,' Larson's usually impeccable English was cracking under pressure, 'I'm interviewing him right now.'

'What d'you mean?' Jones was caught unawares.

'Only that he's sitting, strapped into a chair, and I'm asking him . . . difficult questions. I've had him here for the last three hours.'

'You're filming it?' confirmed the other.

'Yes.'

'And?'

Larson paused a moment before exhaling heavily. 'You were right. He's guilty.' It took a lot for him to admit, but he couldn't ignore the evidence. Brent had looked like he was going to piss himself from the moment he'd arrived. 'He's the spy. The mole. I'm sure of it.' He paused before going on. He hadn't planned getting on to the next bit until he'd had time to follow up Brent's claims. Investigate first, he'd thought, before telling Jones. But with Jones about to spontaneously combust at the other end of the phone, he decided he'd better tell him right away. 'But there's something else,' he murmured. 'It may be misleading – I still need to check out the story.'

He told Jones about how he'd commissioned Brent to investigate Isis's background, and what Brent had found out about Maria Carboni, Salmacis Hospital, Dr Robert Weiner. As he spoke he detected a change in attitude at the other end of the line.

'This . . . information,' when Jones finally responded his voice was low, 'if there's any truth to it at all—'

'Of course,' Larson didn't need to be told, 'very useful.'

Useful? Jones's mind was going into overdrive.

'He told you this morning?'

'Correct.'

'Who else has he told?'

'No one.'

'You're sure?'

'He only found out himself a few hours ago.'

'Hmm,' mused Jones.

'There are only three of us who know about it. Brent. Me. And now you.'

There was a long pause before Jones finally retorted, 'Strikes me that's one person too many.'

Looking back to the door of the flat in which Brent sat cowering on a chair, Larson agreed with Jones's implied edict in just four words. 'Yeah,' he grunted eventually, 'he's gotta go.'

Minutes later, Jones emerged from his study to where Gail was standing in the kitchen frying up a mixture of onions and tomatoes.

'Smells delicious,' he observed, coming up behind her and slipping his hands into the bathrobe. 'Looks delicious too. After breakfast I'm going to have to reward you. One good turn . . .'

She turned with a grin. 'I'm pleased you're not working

all day. All work and no play makes Jack a dull boy.'

'True. But there are some things in life,' running his finger-tips up her taut silky thighs, 'you just can't ignore.'

Across town Bengt Larson slipped the mobile phone into his pocket and extracted a pair of black leather gloves which he tugged over his hands before opening the door.

Alan Brent squinted myopically at him in the semi-dark. Earlier, Larson had dashed his spectacles to the ground and stamped on them in a fit of rage.

'What's happening?' he wanted to know.

Larson stepped over to him and was lifting him to his feet.

'Interview terminated,' he told Alan.

'What does that mean?' The voice was so thin it sounded about to break.

Summoning his assistant with a jerk of the head, Larson dragged Alan off his chair by the scruff of his neck, and thrust his back against the wall.

'Guilty as charged.'

14

Flight BA2
Monday, 27 September

Mark sat near the back of First Class, sipping orange juice
and flicking distractedly through the latest issue of *Men's
Health* magazine. In the past, before Los Angeles, he'd
always thought that flying up front must be one of the
most glamorous experiences in the world. Now as he sat
among a passenger roster of anonymous businessmen and
the odd semi-celebrity, he reflected wryly on how times
changed.

He'd travelled to New York earlier in the day, and this
flight would get him to London just before five in the afternoon, local time. Lloyd would be out at Heathrow to collect
him, then they would make their way down the M4 and
through rush-hour traffic towards South London. With any
luck, they'd be ordering their first pint down at the Lamb
before eight. It was a high-risk visit; if things didn't go well
for them tonight, they wouldn't have a second bite of the
apple. He had to return to LA to continue his recording
schedule on Wednesday; as he'd soon discovered, session work
was a twenty-four-hours-a-day, seven-day-a-week business in

tinseltown. He'd had to get permission to leave from GCM – it was like being back at school.

It was a radical idea, he supposed, but drastic times called for drastic measures; this seemed his best and maybe only option. After his terse exchange with Hilton Gallo it had become all too apparent to him that no one had any grip at all on One Commando. The MI5 insider had come up with sweet FA. The Met weren't even following up the lead he and Lloyd had given them. It was disarray all round. Meantime, Isis was hiding out back in Malibu while Hilton was up to his usual control freakery, trying to avoid telling anyone what the hell was going on.

There was nothing for it, he'd decided, but to take matters further into his own hands. So that was why he was heading back to London, with a very specific aim in mind. The idea had been triggered when Lloyd was telling him about his encounter with Vinnie down in the pub – Vinnie had remarked on how Larson stayed in touch with him by phone, and gestured towards his mobile. The OmniCell mobile.

From his days on OmniCell Customer Support line, Mark was intimately acquainted with every aspect of mobile phone operations – he'd had to be. Thinking about how they might be able to track down Larson's whereabouts using Vinnie's mobile, he soon realised how difficult that would be. Even if Vinnie *did* have a contact number for Larson – and that was unlikely – and even if Lloyd could get hold of his call log, trying to identify one number among the dozens of other mobile numbers would be like looking for a needle in a haystack; Vinnie was what OmniCell termed a 'high-traffic user'.

It was only later, when the thought of the mobile returned, niggling at his mind, that he recalled Lloyd telling him, not so long ago, about something the software boys had developed, which enabled up to three hours of conversation to be recorded and downloaded on to a computer file. From there it could be played back, as if through a tape recorder, or alternatively a voice recognition programme could be used to generate a written transcript. The idea was being developed for the business market, but Mark began to wonder about an altogether different application.

Late on Friday night, Mark had phoned Lloyd to ask him more about the device. Bleary-eyed and heavy-headed on a Saturday morning, Lloyd had been surprised by Mark's interest in software development stuff – but the reason had soon become apparent. And when Lloyd confirmed that Vinnie was still in London, there seemed to be no option.

It was just after seven-forty-five when the two brothers stepped into the Lamb. Within moments the place was bedlam. Lloyd hadn't told anyone about Mark's visit – it had only been confirmed the day before – so his appearance was a bolt from the blue. Just the way they'd planned it.

Everyone in the pub was suddenly crowding around Mark; friends, drinking mates, Lamb regulars, all wanting to shake him by the hand, slap him on the back, buy him a drink. Those who had been most outspoken against him when stirred up by Vinnie were, Lloyd noticed, among the first to lead the rush to welcome their showbiz celebrity back to Balham. There was no mention of 'moronic' hairstyles or 'oikish' clothing now. Instead, it was all Mark this, and Mark that, and won't you sign my sweatshirt, Jordan Hampshire, ha, ha?

Lloyd had picked him up from the airport, on schedule, and they'd made good progress on the roads. They'd have been much quicker by Underground, but Mark hadn't wanted to get caught up with people. Besides, they needed to discuss plans for the evening in private. They'd already worked out the overall strategy on the phone, but as they drove into town, turning south down Earl's Court Road, they talked through the detail. What they were attempting was highly illegal and used leading-edge kit but, Lloyd assured Mark, wasn't technically difficult. Using a welter of jargon which Mark used to spend his working hours translating for the benefit of the public, Lloyd evidently regarded this evening's operation as presenting only a minor challenge to his capabilities. What's more, he'd left work that evening fully prepared for all eventualities, as was evident from the bulge in his coat pocket.

The technical side was, however, only one aspect of the overall plan, and the most straightforward. The practicalities were different, and would require opportunism, meticulous timing and a great deal of care if the whole operation – the only reason for Mark's trip back to London – wasn't to be blown. Vinnie couldn't be allowed to suspect, for so much as a minute, that they knew he was involved with One Commando, much less that they were about to turn him into an unwitting double agent. And the only card they had to play was the element of surprise.

In the Lamb, Mark looked round the sea of eager faces. In other circumstances he guessed he would have found the adoration and inevitable wisecracks a real ego buzz. He would have pushed the boat out, enjoyed a few drinks and just let go. But tonight's visit to the Lamb wasn't social. Scanning through the group that had formed around him, it took him a while before he caught sight of Vinnie who was perched at his usual place, pretending not to notice his arrival.

'Vinnie!' He headed in his direction, taking the still-forming entourage with him. Some of the regulars, remembering the last furious encounter between Mark and his 'manager', followed proceedings bright-eyed with expectation.

Vinnie turned to meet him, a droll smile appearing on his face. 'Mr Hampshire!' He shook Mark's outstretched hand and thumped him on the shoulder, 'The hero returns!'

'Yeah, well, don't feel much of a hero with this haircut.' Mark raised a hand to his head.

'Oi! Vin, aren't you going to punch his lights out?' demanded one of the Lamb's stalwarts provocatively.

Vinnie just laughed. 'Hey, I'm proud of this man.' He thumped Mark on the shoulder again before turning to the manager. 'Line up a pint for him, will you, Cyril.'

A group had formed around them, just like they'd figured. Lloyd had moved into position on Vinnie's immediate right, although Vinnie had not acknowledged him – there was too much else going on.

I only need twelve clear minutes, Lloyd had said. *Fifteen at the outside.*

Mark reckoned it wouldn't be too difficult to keep Vinnie occupied that long. After his visit to Lloyd's flat, and the whole story about how grateful he was to Mark over the Unum deal, Vinnie was hardly going to change his line. He needed to keep in with the Watson brothers to be any use to One Commando. No matter how much he hated it, he'd have to keep up the act.

Vinnie was a creature of habit, so they'd counted on him behaving true to form tonight, and he hadn't let them down. Monday nights had always been quiet for him. 'The showbiz man's Sunday,' he used to quip, and he customarily spent it down the pub. What's more he was wearing his trademark leather jacket – a designer garment bought from a leather shop on King's Road, with pockets which, though deep, were easily accessible from where it hung loose at his sides.

In the first few moments after Mark had approached Vinnie, while his attention was firmly elsewhere, Lloyd took advantage of the jostling crowd and hearty handshakes, to slip his hand into Vinnie's pocket, find and extract his mobile.

The movement escaped the attention of nearly everyone else – most of them were too focused on what was going on between Vinnie and his former protégé. But Mark noticed his brother stepping back from where he'd been pressed beside Vinnie and retreat behind the crowd. So far, so good, he thought.

In the Gents', Lloyd quickly shut himself inside a cubicle, kneeled on the floor and, closing the toilet lid, used it as a surface to work on Vinnie's phone. Opening up mobile phones was all in a day's work and he knew precisely what needed doing. Whip off the housing, install the chip. A couple of minutes reprogramming then on goes the housing again and it's back to the pub. The chip he'd brought with him was in a small, sealed plastic pouch and when the time came he inserted it using the pair of tungsten-tipped tweezers he'd brought specially for the purpose. The chip had been customised to store both incoming and outgoing conversations, and the reprogramming that followed ensured that every time the 'End' button was pressed, the file containing the most recent call would be automatically transmitted back to a computer at OmniCell. This would mean an enforced three-second delay between calls. But nothing on the display would register that anything unusual was happening. And meanwhile, back at OmniCell, Lloyd had already ensured that every incoming file from the phone would be securely stored on computer and instantly accessible by Mark, wherever in the world he happened to be, via the Net.

Back in the pub, Vinnie handed Mark the drink he'd just bought him, before raising his own glass and clinking 'Cheers'.

'What about your drink?' Mark asked, as Vinnie swilled down what remained in his glass.

Vinnie pointed at his watch. 'Got to go, mate,' he explained. 'Session in Soho with a talent scout. Eight-thirty. Could be worth a lot of money.'

Oh, Christ, thought Mark. *This is all we need!*

'Lloyd tells me things are looking up?' He had to keep him talking.

'Too right!' Vinnie thrust his glass down on the counter.

'I'd like to hear about it.'

'Yeah, sure. When are you leaving town?' Vinnie's eyes were bearing into his.

Mark shrugged. 'Can't say. All depends when they want me back.'

'You're staying with Lloyd?'

'That's right,' he lied. He had no intention of issuing One Commando a gilt-edged invitation.

'Tell you what,' Vinnie turned away from the bar, 'I'll buzz you tomorrow. We'll set something up.' Thrusting his hands in his pockets, Vinnie searched for his keys. Mark watched, trying not to appear transfixed, as he fished about for them. They were a large bunch attached by a sturdy chain to a silver Mercedes logo, and having taken them out of his pocket Vinnie threw them up in the air before catching them again – one of his little habits. Glancing back at Mark, he was about to head out when a look of sudden alarm crossed his face. Dumping his keys on the bar top, he dived into both pockets again before confirming his suspicions.

'My mobile!' he exclaimed.

Now he was checking his breast pockets, and trousers. 'I always keep it . . .'

Across the bar Cyril asked, 'Maybe you left it at home?'

'No,' Vinnie was shaking his head vigorously, 'called someone on the way here.'

As he quickly became desperate, Mark was working out
the best way to keep him from going.

'Why don't you phone your mobile number?' someone
was suggesting. 'You'll soon find where—'

'Some bastard's probably nicked it!' Vinnie was resentful.
'Wouldn't be the first time either. Last time this happened
it cost me big-time. *All* my contacts call me—'

'Try phoning it,' the suggestion was repeated.

'Yeah! Not a bad idea. Cyril!' Vinnie was turning.

Mark knew he had to interrupt. This couldn't be allowed
to go on. Lloyd hadn't been long gone – if he was at the
reprogramming stage and the mobile rang, that would
completely screw things up!

He grabbed Vinnie's arm. 'Your car. What about checking there first? Probably find it just slipped out of your pocket,
you know how things do . . .'

Vinnie looked over, with a doubtful expression.

'Where are you parked?' persisted Mark.

'Just outside,' he gestured.

'If you're going anyway—'

'I might have to cancel the fucking thing. Last time some
bastard rang up a hundred quid of calls!'

'No need to panic,' Mark tried humouring him, 'it's probably sitting on the floor of your car.'

Some of the others were agreeing with their newly
returned celebrity.

Looking round at their expressions, Vinnie shrugged. 'I
guess it's worth . . .' he started in the direction of the pub
door.

A few of them, led by Mark, followed him. Glancing at
his watch, Mark wondered how long Lloyd had had. It didn't

feel like any time at all. *He had to keep Vinnie occupied for another ten minutes.*

The Mercedes was parked almost directly outside, and Vinnie had soon pressed the automatic unlock switch. As he opened the driver's door and was leaning inside, some of the others looked beside the passenger seat.

'Nothing here,' Vinnie was tight-lipped. Having checked the floor and side, he now had his hand under the driver's seat. 'Not a fucking thing!'

Elsewhere around the car, the others were saying the same thing. They rummaged about, increasingly hopeless, until Vinnie ordered them out.

'Forget it!' He slammed his front door shut. 'This is a fucking waste of time.'

'When did you last use it?' someone was asking.

'I told you!' he barked, 'I called someone on the way here. I parked the car and we talked for a while. Then I finished and came inside. It's been nicked!' he looked directly at Mark.

'Sure looks that way,' Mark agreed.

'Best phone yourself up,' someone was repeating.

'What's the point? It's been nicked!'

'Yeah,' agreed Mark, 'they're not going to answer it, are they? And even if they do, what's he going to say?'

'But it might be lying about somewhere?'

'Can't do no harm, can it?'

'Just give it a go!'

The group was moving back inside, Vinnie with a face like thunder. Trying his mobile number was the best thing he could do and Mark realised he couldn't keep up the argument against it – not without seeming daft. Back at the bar, Vinnie was asking Cyril for the payphone he kept behind the bar and rifling through his pockets again – this time for change. Before he'd found any, however, one of the regulars was offering him his own mobile to use.

Distancing himself from the group, Mark made his way across to the Gents'. Inside, the place was empty – except for the one cubicle.

'Are you finished in there?' he asked in an urgent whisper.

'Just about.'

'He knows it's missing! He's trying to ring the bloody thing!'

'No worries—'

Mark heard a jangle of instruments as Lloyd got up from where he'd been kneeling.

'—volume's right down, mate.'

Less than two minutes later Vinnie was, once again, leaving the pub in high dudgeon. This time, Mark and Lloyd were the only ones following him.

'I'm going to be late!' he fumed, thrusting the pub door open with far more force than was needed. 'Late for my appointment and no mobile. What a fucking joke!'

'Yeah, well . . .' Mark watched him climb in the car and shove his key in the ignition.

The car had roared to life when, beside the driver's window, Lloyd called out, 'Hey! What's that?' and was gesturing under the car.

Moments later, Vinnie took back possession of his mobile. Still angry and upset, he managed only muttered thanks.

'Don't know how that happened!' he grunted, glancing at Lloyd only briefly.

'Or how we missed it before.' Mark adopted a bewildered expression.

'Yeah. Speak soon.' Vinnie jerked his head, before pulling away into the night traffic.

The two brothers watched him head down the road, and turn left at the first set of traffic lights.

'Sorted?' Mark turned to Lloyd.

'Oh, yes. Mr Dobson is now upgraded with the very latest cellular technology.'

'Good man.' Mark put an arm round his shoulders and gave him a squeeze. They were turning back towards the pub when he continued warily, 'I wonder if he's calling them right now?'

'We'll know about it, soon enough.'

Pausing before opening the pub door Mark continued, 'And what's with the eight-thirty appointment on a Monday night?'

'Yeah.' Lloyd shared his questioning expression. 'Don't reckon we should stick around here too long.'

15

It was social services who alerted the police to the problem on the derelict Olympia housing block. Drugs and gangs had destroyed much of the surrounding estate. Most flats had been trashed and were boarded up. There were, however, a few residents who hadn't been able to leave, who had no other place to go and the council hadn't been able to relocate them. Old Mrs Mills was one. She lived with half a dozen padlocks on the front door and only ventured out of her home twice a week when her son came to visit. But meals on wheels called by, regular as clockwork, and it was one of their ladies she first mentioned it to.

'There's something funny going on upstairs,' she'd told the volunteer.

'Yes, yes, dear.' The meals-on-wheels lady didn't pay too much attention to Mrs Mills's ramblings. She was losing her mind, poor thing, and after five years living behind bars was given to paranoia.

But when the social worker came round to check on her that same afternoon, he paid closer attention to Mrs Mills's complaint, and noticed something the meals-on-wheels lady hadn't. It was an odour, as faint as it was unmistakable to someone who'd smelled it before.

'That funny smell is probably from where someone has illegally dumped rubbish round the side of the block,' he told Mrs Mills, not wanting to alarm her. 'As for the noises you heard upstairs at the weekend, well, people are using these places for squats all the time.' It was, they both agreed, a disgrace she still had to live there.

As soon as he was back at the office, the social worker called the police, who dispatched two young PCs in a car to investigate. The social worker didn't give precise directions to the flat above Mrs Mills's, but none was needed – the PCs' sense of smell was all that was required. Nor did they need any equipment to break into the flat. Making their way along an exposed outside passage, they found the door unlocked and ajar. After stepping through a small hallway, they entered what had once been the main living room. There they halted in their tracks. They'd come here expecting a corpse – a corpse in a slum block. But what they were looking at was very much more complicated. The man's body dangled from a noose, head slumped forward and face hidden behind a mass of dark, unruly hair. Around his neck, the crude, cardboard placard attached to a piece of electric cable bore the single word 'SPY'.

One of the PCs turned to speak into the radio strapped to his shoulder.

'We're at the flat. Bit pongy,' he told the control room, viewing with distaste the excrement spattered on the floor beneath the dangling body. 'Our chum here's been dangling from a rope for two, three days?' he glanced at the other PC who nodded back, expressionless. 'Best send over a SOCO.'

Alerted to a suspicious death, within minutes a scenes-of-crime officer was dispatched to the flat, which was quickly taped off. Donning white overalls, he was soon photographing the body, before cutting it down, then going carefully through every room in the derelict flat. A police surgeon arrived, and shortly afterwards, a team from Forensic with a zip-up body bag.

Detective Sergeant Morris, large, hardboiled, and short-tempered, was put in charge of the case; several hours later he was reading through the pathologist's report for the benefit of his two subordinates in his office back at the station. The report wasn't long. The victim had died of a broken neck, consistent with the circumstances in which he'd been found. The victim's clothes were now sealed in plastic bags on the DS's desk, along with the placard which had been found around his neck.

'Spy,' mused the DS after finishing the pathology report. 'But for whom?'

'Drugs operation?' ventured White, the older of the two DC's.

'Forensics checked all the clothing and scene of the crime. No evidence of drugs contact. And the MO . . . too ritualistic for a drugs killing.' The DS leaned back in his seat. 'Looks to me like a gangland killing. But something's not quite right.'

'ID?' queried Detective Constable Brewer, new to Morris's team.

'D'you think I'd be sitting here now if we'd found a passport in his back pocket?' glowered the DS, jerking his head at the plastic bags. 'This is all we've got to go on.'

DC Brewer sifted through the bags, before picking up one that contained a pair of spectacles, one lens of which had been smashed, and the other badly cracked.

'Thick lenses,' he remarked.

The DS leaned forward in his chair with a grunt. As he

turned over the bag in his hands, he noticed the manufacturer's name down the side of the glasses, but nothing to
distinguish the spectacles from a million others – except for
the thickness of the lenses. In the meantime, Brewer was
glancing at all the other bags on the DS's desk, before he
noticed one containing a spectacles wallet. It was a cheap,
black plastic sleeve without any markings on the outside,
the kind that was handed out by high street opticians
throughout Britain to purchasers of glasses of all kinds.

'Can I open . . . ?'

The DS nodded.

It was unlikely, but worth a look. Unsealing the clear
plastic bag and extracting the spectacles wallet, he opened
it up and glanced inside. There *was* a white lint cloth at
the bottom, the kind used for polishing lenses. He tugged it
out between his fingers and when he unfurled it he found,
printed in faded green ink, the name of a well-known retail
chain – Super-Specs – together with the address and phone
number of the Clapham branch. Meeting the DS's eyes,
Brewer said, 'They couldn't prescribe too many glasses with
lenses this thick.'

'Well done,' the DS's face was dour. 'Now check it out.'

The manager of Clapham Super-Specs was overworked,
harassed and had no easy answers. Customer computer
records were ordered by name, not prescription, he
explained. And while the lenses were more powerful than
most, they were by no means unique; he'd have to go through
all 3,500 customer records to pull out the two dozen or so
which closely matched the prescription. Plus, of course, it
was quite possible that the customer had acquired the case
and polishing cloth when buying a pair of sunglasses.

That night the Super-Specs manager worked into the
early hours, clicking through every computerised index card

in his customer records. It was a chore he could do without, he'd told the police. The hours were bad enough just trying to run this place without having extra stuff dumped on him. But they'd told him they were investigating a murder. He and he alone had the means by which to make a critical identification. He was legally obliged to assist.

When his list of twenty-eight names came through the next morning, the two DCs immediately began checking them off one by one. It was the least rewarding and most tedious line of enquiry. But they had no choice; the spectacles were their only lead.

Just before knocking off time, DS Morris summoned them for a status meeting. The list of names to be eliminated was down to five, the two DC's reported. They'd printed them out in alphabetical order.

'Before beating down any doors,' Brewer regarded Morris's testy features, 'we ran their names through the computer.'

Morris raised an eyebrow, questioningly.

'Nothing on four of them. But we picked up something on the first one. He had a restraint order slapped on him a few years ago. It might be nothing; we're still waiting for the full report.'

As Brewer continued, Morris glanced back at the list of names, focusing on the one at the top: Alan George Brent. Should it mean anything to him, he wondered?

Los Angeles
Wednesday, 29 September

Isis hadn't moved from the security of her home since Hilton's visit to Unum music studios over a week earlier. She'd needed no further warning to take extreme care, both of Holly's security as well as her own. Confining herself to her home studio, she focused on her music, rehearsing the few tracks she still had to record and spending a lot of time on the phone to her producer Sam Bach. Holly took the stay-at-home routine in her stride, Isis explaining that the unscheduled break from school would only be for a few days; her daughter soon had Juanita and Frank running round in circles at her bidding.

Despite the feeling of normality in the house, however, Isis's thoughts were haunted by One Commando. It was the first thing that entered her consciousness when she woke in the mornings – and the same thing that made it so hard getting to sleep at nights. Apart from the hours she spent with Holly, or rehearsing her music, or in some other convenient distraction, she couldn't drive the fear from her mind. They were after her – there could be no doubt of that now. The Berkeley Square endorsement had put her top of One Commando's list.

What Hilton had told her about the undercover agent *did* make a difference. It was her one consolation, her one hope that something could still be salvaged from this ordeal. Now it seemed that One Commando were no longer only the pursuers – they were also the pursued. How long would it be before they were closed down? She put calls into GCM every few hours, where Hilton and Elizabeth were in constant touch with the UK. It's only a matter of time, Hilton kept repeating the same phrase. Don't make any precipitous decision. There's a massive police operation in play.

In the meantime, life in the outside world went on and she knew she couldn't stay in limbo-land very long. Sam Bach had rescheduled an already intensive recording timetable to accommodate her and couldn't hold out much longer – she'd have to go into Unum early next week, to complete all the stuff Mark was doing. Ross McCormack and Andy Murdoch had been on the phone to discuss meetings and travel arrangements leading up to the launch of *Nile* in just a few weeks' time.

Most of all, Leo Lebowitz was becoming increasingly anxious about all the pre-launch publicity she would lose if she remained reclusive. She'd already passed up on a high-profile modelling agency launch the night before, which Lebowitz had wanted her and Mark to attend. She could just imagine the GCM boys hammering their calculators as they worked out the future sales she was losing through reduced visibility. She and Lebowitz had had a long conversation when he'd tried to persuade her to go to the function; yes, she knew One Commando were hardly likely to attack her in a room that was awash with celebrities. And she had no doubt that the vehicle escort GCM could provide would ensure her safety. It was, more than anything else, that she didn't feel up to circulating with the shiny set when she was just so worried, so hollow. Anxiety, she told Lebowitz, was an emotion very difficult to conceal.

That was when he'd suggested Panama Jacks instead. A casual family diner in Malibu, it was a short drive from her home. He'd have it vetted thoroughly by security immediately before the visit. She could be there and back within an hour and she wouldn't have to see anyone – it would just be Mark and Holly and her, dropping by for a weekend brunch – though he'd make sure a few photographers had been alerted in advance. The proposition was hard to turn down, especially as Panama Jacks was Holly's favourite, and Isis knew she couldn't keep her daughter cooped up at home much longer without respite.

Mark would play ball, Lebowitz assured her. He'd been on the phone to her singing partner who had just returned from an unscheduled supersonic trip to London. Back in town to continue his recording schedule, Mark was worried about her, said Lebowitz. Isis remembered how Mark had reacted last time they'd been together. She'd let slip about her 'background' and he'd instantly wanted to know all about it. It had been a foolish mistake, but in the heat of the moment, with Hilton pressuring her into staying in the endorsement contract, the words had come tumbling out before she could stop herself.

And that, she supposed, was exactly why she needed to keep Mark at arm's length. She had done her best to suppress the mutual attraction she'd sensed since their very first 'date' at Bianco Verdi. There had been times, especially in the last week as they worked in the studio together, when she had felt they were sharing an intimacy almost as great as love-making. But letting anything develop with Mark would be dangerous. Life could not be allowed to imitate art. If it did, and in a moment of tenderness she allowed all the barriers to come down, she knew she risked revealing the terrors of her past. And once she did that, once she'd confided her secret, she'd no longer be able to control it.

It was the same burden of emotion she'd had to carry ever since arriving in California. While in certain relationships she'd succeeded in enjoying sexual intimacy without having to give of her innermost thoughts and feelings, there were some men, she knew, with whom that couldn't happen. Mark was one of those men. His most attractive quality, his sensitivity, was also the greatest threat to her composure. If she gave herself to him, she knew she'd end up giving away much more than she should. For that reason she had no intention of getting romantically involved with him; it wasn't even a possibility.

*　　*　　*

Panama Jacks was a casual family diner on the opposite side of the road from Malibu beach, on the ground floor of a small ribbon of shops. Decorated in maritime theme, its walls were washed sea-green, and suspended from the ceiling was a low canopy of fishermen's nets, gathered up about brass lamps. Artifacts from shipwrecks had been placed about a room which buzzed with families, mostly local, but a few tourists as well.

Mark, whose body was still on transatlantic time, had reluctantly agreed to come when summoned by Lebowitz. Eager though he was to spend time with Isis, he was feeling fatigued – and knew he had to conserve his energies for a demanding studio session later in the day. What's more, lunch out with Isis accompanied by her daughter and both their bodyguards wasn't exactly the kind of encounter he had in mind. But Lebowitz had been insistent. It was critical to the publicity effort, he'd said. And what was forty-five minutes in the rest of his life?

Arriving at Panama Jacks with Isis, Mark couldn't help comparing their arrival here with the entrance Isis and he had made at the irredeemably self-infatuated Bianco Verdi. There there was no mistaking the whispered excitement and turning heads when they were ushered in by their body-guards – who had spent ten minutes reconnoitring the place beforehand in the company of other security experts – but after they were shown to a back table by a bug-eyed teenage waiter, the place soon calmed down. Apart from the occasional sidelong glance, and a couple of photographers' flashes – business done – people seemed happy just to leave them to their meal undisturbed. This was Malibu, thought Mark, where seeing stars in your local restaurant wasn't a big deal. He only wished they didn't have to sit down accompanied by two bodyguards in black suits with conspicuous bulges at their hips – but it was a whole lot better than not going out at all. Holly certainly thought so, excitedly demanding that the children's menu be read out to her twice before demanding her favourite potato wedges with garlic and chives.

A couple of times he met Isis's eyes across the table and tried to work out the expression in them – friendly, but distant. 'A complex lady,' Hilton had said about her the day before – that was no exaggeration. In fact, he was half-surprised she was still in the Berkeley Square deal at all after the discovery of the day before. Hilton's well-honed powers of persuasion had obviously kept her in play, though for how much longer he wouldn't care to speculate. Despite her efforts to appear at ease, he could detect she was anxious and on edge, and he didn't think he was just projecting his own feelings. The fact was, they were both caught up in a waiting game – waiting for the British police, or for MI5 to announce a breakthrough. But as every hour passed, and still nothing happened, how much longer were they expected to wait?

They were taking first sips of their drinks when their waiter returned to them, kneeling at their table, his striped pinafore clustered with buttons.

'Sorry to disturb you, Isis, ma'am,' he began, 'but you have a phone call.' He pointed towards the bar at the back of the restaurant, where cash tills and a telephone was also located.

Isis raised her eyebrows. 'It can't be for me. No one even knows I'm here.'

'He definitely asked for you,' the waiter nodded earnestly, 'I can bring the phone over here, or would you like to come . . . ?'

Isis glanced over at Frank before shrugging. 'Just take a message.'

'Right.'

Mark was glancing about the restaurant. 'Could be some-one here on a cellphone.'

'Yeah, but why?' Isis looked suddenly worried.

The two bodyguards were glancing about them. 'Kind of strange,' was all Frank would say.

Then the waiter was returning. 'I asked to take a message but he cut off.'

Isis looked up. 'Did he say anything at all?'

The waiter pulled a face. 'He said, "This is for Isis and Jordan Hampshire", but then he just hung up.'

At that moment the whole restaurant exploded in a crash of glass. Both of the large front windows shattered, with jagged shards of glass flying far back into the restaurant and flames leaping from table to table. Suddenly everyone was screaming. For a moment, Mark was too bewildered to move. It was as though some invisible, destructive tidal wave had burst through the window at the front of the restaurant, throwing whole tables of people on to the floor, leaving them lacerated, bloodied, crying out in shock. Further back, diners were scrambling from their tables in panic, looking about, wild-eyed, confused about what was happening and where to flee.

The two bodyguards instantly sprang into action. Frank picked up Holly, Denzil had his arms round Isis and Mark. They were running towards the rest rooms. Others in the restaurant were starting to move quickly too, as fire spread rapidly. The low canopy of fishermen's nets was ablaze, smoky flames leaping up to the ceiling, setting off the shrill clang-ing of a fire alarm. Hustled through the restaurant, Mark noticed a smashed wine bottle on the floor in a fast-growing puddle of paraffin fire.

They were soon in the corridor leading to the rest rooms, then out through a fire escape door through which several of the waitering staff had already fled. Outside, in the blazing sunshine, the bodyguards kept on running.

'Gotta get out of here!' Frank shouted over his shoulder, keeping Holly's face pressed firmly into his neck.

Mark looked about at the bloodied faces and hysterical screaming people as bedazed diners scrambled outside. It seemed wrong to be running away from all of this, doing nothing to help. But the bodyguards were heading directly back to Isis's Range Rover in which they'd all come.

Sensing his hesitation, Denzil kept tugging him by the arm. 'They might be waiting out here to pick you off.' Denzil couldn't get the door opened fast enough, thrusting the two of them inside.

'Mommy!' cried out Holly, scrambling from the front into the back seat, between Isis and Mark. Isis clasped her tight, as Frank quickly checked under the car, and its bonnet. Then he was back inside, engine started and pulling away at high speed. Isis closed her eyes, her face drawn and pale. Mark looked back at all the people they were leaving behind, standing in groups of pain and shock. Holly started to cry. While Frank concentrated on getting away as fast as possible, Denzil was keeping up 360-degree scans. There was a strange silence in the car, with the three of them huddled together like survivors from a shipwreck, while the two bodyguards constantly searched about them on high alert. Then as they got back to Isis's house and the gates began to open, she looked up at Mark, eyes filled with fear.

'Better call Hilton.'

He nodded.

'Tell him they're in LA.'

Hilton was round at Isis's within an hour. He'd been working at his Pacific Palisades home and when Mark called he'd got into his car and come over straight away. En route, he'd put in a call to the Los Angeles Police Department, telling them what had happened.

He arrived to find Isis hugging Holly on the sitting room sofa, Mark pacing up and down, and bodyguards stationed both out at the front and at the back. Wordlessly Hilton walked over to Isis and Holly, giving them both a hug, before turning to Mark and squeezing his arm. Even in casual attire he was immaculately groomed, sporting a linen jacket, deep blue shirt and beige Daks flannels.

'What about the special agent,' Mark was wry, 'who was going to tell us everything before it happened?'

'I know,' he acknowledged Mark's disappointment, perching on the arm of a sofa opposite.

'So much,' added Isis, 'for One Commando only operating in Britain.'

There was a tense pause which seemed to go on for ever. Mark flashed a glance, first at Isis, then Hilton, then back to Isis again.

'What?' demanded Isis.

'You didn't tell her, did you?' Mark blazed at the other. 'You gave me your word – that's what you said! And you didn't tell her!'

'Tell me what?' Isis's voice rose as she clutched Holly to her.

Hilton had fixed Mark with an impenetrable stare.

'Last Friday, before I went to London, I found out that Larson operates an international network. I told him.' He nodded towards Hilton. 'He promised me he'd talk to you about it. Said it was better coming from him.'

'I had every—' began Hilton, only to be cut short by Isis, face flushed and eyes blazing.

'You kept that information—'

'I had every—' repeated Hilton, voice raised.

'You bastard! You knew damned well I would have dropped Berkeley Square.' Isis was anger incarnate. 'Instead you put Holly's life and my life at risk for some photo-opportunity—'

'It's not like that!' Hilton managed.

'Oh yes, it is like that!' At her side, Holly began to sob.

'I had every intention of telling you.' Hilton got up from the sofa arm and began pacing the room.

'When?' demanded Isis. 'When we were both lying on a mortuary slab?'

'Today's incident was very unfortunate.'

Eyes ablaze, Isis was shaking her head vigorously.

Mark's voice, furious but controlled, cut in beneath both of theirs. 'It was also completely avoidable.' He regarded Hilton bitterly. 'You lied to me. You told me not to speak to Isis. You said you'd do that yourself. I trusted you and you let all three of us down.' He glanced at Holly and Isis. 'It makes me wonder what other lies you've been peddling—'

'Now let's get real—'

'Like your story about the Biographical Notes. All an innocent misunderstanding, you said.'

'As it was!' Hilton regarded him with piqued indignation.

'Which just happened to generate acres of press coverage. Is there nothing you won't stoop to for media space?'

'You're way out of line!' Hilton's voice was raised so high he was almost shouting. 'Something difficult has happened and now you're fantasising about other stuff that just isn't there.'

'If there's no "other stuff" why won't you tell me about Isis?'

Hilton and Isis exchanged furious expressions before Hilton replied, 'That's an entirely separate issue.'

'I don't think it's separate. It's all part of you and your information control. And I'm sick of it! You feed me a line here and a line there to shut me up. You treat me like some goddam puppet that'll dress and sing and shave its head and do any damned thing you choose.'

Hilton's expression was withering. 'I did warn you about image management.'

'Managing my image is one thing. But I won't be patronised!'

'And you're being paid rather a lot of money.'

'Yeah,' snorted Mark, 'danger money. But as far as I'm concerned, you can shove it! This endorsement isn't worth all the money in the world.'

'That goes for me too,' chimed Isis.

Across the room, Hilton struggled to regain his customary poise. 'I hope you've both thought very hard about what this means—'

'I've been thinking about nothing else,' Mark nodded towards Isis, 'her neither.'

'Don't forget the police are working on this.'

'Exactly,' turning for the door, Mark nodded towards Denzil, 'and look how bloody hopeless they've been.' At the door he looked back, fixing Hilton with a challenging stare. 'Seems to me if there are any answers to be found out, I'm going to have to keep looking for them myself!'

16

Hilton Gallo had put phone calls in to Blake Horowitz, Ross McCormack and Leo Lebowitz and of course Elizabeth before he'd even got on to the Pacific Highway into town. They must drop whatever plans they had for the evening, he told them. They had a huge amount to do in a very short space of time; tonight was going to be a late one.

'You've all heard the news.' He glanced round the sombre assembly in his office an hour later.

'Last straw?' asked Ross McCormack in a tone of resignation.

'She wants out and there's nothing I can do to stop her. I've played my hand. Overplayed it.' Hilton shrugged, in an uncharacteristic gesture of helplessness, remembering Mark's furious expression as he'd stormed out of Isis's house a short while earlier. He could hardly believe that his masterpiece – this spectacular deal – was crumbling before his eyes. Then nodding towards the plastic file on McCormack's lap, 'Where are we on timing?'

'We've already missed the deadline on some of the editions in South East Asia and two mainstream European titles. We could pull out of the rest first thing tomorrow, but it'll be a bloodbath.'

Hilton was glancing up at the clocks ranged about his office wall. 'It already is tomorrow in Europe. You'll get on the case when they start getting in to work?'

Nodding wearily, McCormack wondered what kind of career he'd have left in a few hours' time.

Catching his eye, Hilton responded, 'At least what happened this afternoon satisfies the requirement Blake noted last time.'

'Evidence of intimidation?' Blake looked grim. 'I'd say so.'

'You're putting out the withdrawal announcement immediately?' asked McCormack.

Hilton shook his head. 'I have a better idea.' Then observing the surprised expressions of his colleagues, 'I've spent months putting together this deal. I don't want GCM to be the agency that pulled out of the world's biggest endorsement – firebomb or not.'

They had all fixed him with expressions of intense concentration.

'The solution I have in mind,' he continued, 'is to turn the tables. Get Berkeley Square to release them from the deal—'

'Why would they do that?' McCormack's very blond eyebrows were raised.

Lebowitz had already seen where Hilton was heading. 'Public opinion?' he queried.

Hilton nodded. 'We'll pile on the pain in the next twenty-four hours. Bring overwhelming pressure to bear on the Berkeley Square Board so it becomes . . . an easier decision for them to withdraw the contract than to continue it.'

'Going to take some doing,' McCormack couldn't help observing.

'Of course. But the best result under the circumstances, no?'

They worked frenetically for the next five hours, fuelled only by hastily eaten Thai take-outs and strong black coffee couriered in by security. In his office, Blake Horowitz burned the midnight oil drafting new documents that would replace Isis and Jordan's current endorsement agreement and that would be legally binding in both USA and UK jurisdictions. The new documents provided for all options from the best-case scenario – Berkeley Square releases the two clients from all obligations, no strings attached – through to postponing the arrangement contingent on the arrest of the One Commando hierarchy.

Ross McCormack meanwhile was reviewing agreements with each of the twenty-five magazine titles yet to go to print with Nile advertisements. Having scrutinised the details of terms and conditions relating to postponement and withdrawal penalties, he was drafting alternative faxes and e-mails to each title, one of which was to be sent to each in twenty-four hours' time. Hilton's get-out was, he had to admit, an inspired piece of opportunism. If it came off, and Berkeley Square could be persuaded to withdraw, he'd be the happiest man in Hollywood – spared to fight another day. But could Hilton do it?

Up on the sixth floor, he and Leo Lebowitz were pulling out all stops to ensure that it did. The psychology was simple: to create such a powerful tide of opinion against what had happened, that by the time it came for Hilton to speak to Jacques Lefevre, Berkeley Square would get a huge benefit in PR terms from making the grand gesture. Carving up GCM's client list between them, Hilton and Lebowitz placed calls to all the biggest names in Hollywood, asking if they'd be prepared to give a reaction to the media about what had happened to Isis that day. Even though it was late on Wednesday night, most of their clients felt an undisguised, vicarious horror about what had happened to Isis and Jordan, and they were only too happy to oblige.

Within an hour, Lebowitz was contacting all the major media networks, offering quotations, down-the-line interviews and TV appearances for a gathering line-up of A-league movie stars, music performers, TV show celebrities and other showbiz luminaries. Provided with a ready-to-run celebrity story on a plate, the media were soon swinging into action.

Shortly after ten p.m., the focus of Hilton's attention switched to GCM London. Rousing a sleepy Stan Shepherd from his bed, just after six on Thursday morning UK time, he quickly updated him on developments and asked him to prepare a hit-list of GCM clients in the UK and Europe. It was too late to get into the Thursday morning papers, of course, but TV and radio were a different prospect altogether. While taking on for himself the unhappy task of having to wake up most of his biggest British clients from their slumbers, Hilton had Shepherd begin contacting major UK radio and TV stations, offering big names from Hollywood for live interviews.

It didn't take long for the momentum to develop. The limitless appetite of the media for any kind of celebrity news was always a certainty. When half a dozen or more major celebrities were prepared to be interviewed – doing their own careers no harm in the process – the result was guaranteed. Shepherd's track record of relentless networking also paid off. Speaking to a contact in one of the television news rooms, he discovered that the Home Secretary, the person with ultimate responsibility for law and order in Britain, was being interviewed on *Breakfast News*, Britain's most watched early morning news programme. Calls to the Minister's private secretary, and the hasty drafting of an appropriate soundbite, ensured that the Home Secretary himself weighed in against 'the utterly vile and reprehensible terror campaign of One Commando'.

In recent weeks, Shepherd had also been making friends with the PROs of mainstream animal rights lobbies, most of whom were desperate to distance themselves from the terrible damage One Commando was inflicting on the public image of their cause; Presidents and spokespeople from as diverse a range as Animals First, the RSPCA and even the Animal Liberation Army were coming forward to protest against One Commando's activities. Soon after ten-thirty, Hilton looked at his watch. Things were progressing well, but he could see he was still going to be tied up for several hours, drumming up support in Europe.

He called in Elizabeth.

'I need you to liaise with the police here to find out what in God's name they're doing. The Sheriff in charge is George Varley. Check with Mark to see if he's been in touch with them.'

'Shall I try Bennett in London as well, for an update?'

'Don't even bother,' he was dismissive, 'but keep Hanniford in the loop.'

Elizabeth tried Varley's phone several times, finding it engaged, before dialling London. Hanniford was unperturbed to be called so early in the morning. Before Elizabeth had even spoken, he was commiserating with her on the latest news which he'd heard on Radio 4 earlier that morning.

'So you've heard,' she was brief. 'I just wanted to keep you updated – and find out if you had any more news.'

'Not at this end. What are the police saying in LA?'

'We're still waiting for them.'

'They'll be liaising with Scotland Yard—'

'Who'll be liaising with MI5.' Elizabeth let out a sigh of frustration. 'Surely someone must know what's going on?'

She meant it as a rhetorical question. But Hanniford replied with assurance, 'Oh, someone knows very well.'

'Home Secretary?' she ventured.

'Close,' replied the other. 'He doesn't have time to keep up with the progress of every single case, but his spin-doctor is sure to know about prickly media issues. Try Peter Campbell. He's the only one with the whole picture.'

Elizabeth registered the name. She was sure she'd heard Hilton mention Campbell in the past. 'Can't you ask him?'

'Only about Lefevre.' Hanniford anticipated her request. 'It would be wrong of him to disclose anything beyond that and I wouldn't want to ask it of him.' There followed a considered pause. 'But I suppose I could give you his direct line. Hilton Gallo could call him directly. I shouldn't really be doing this, but in the circumstances . . .'

After taking down the spin-doctor's telephone number and finishing her call to Hanniford, Elizabeth tried Varley again. This time, his phone rang.

'I've just been on the line to Isis,' said Varley after she'd announced herself. 'I was about to call Mr Gallo. We've got them.'

'You've got the bombers?' Elizabeth raised her voice for Hilton's benefit, before switching her phone on to loudspeaker. Hilton made his way swiftly into her office.

'Booked them just over forty-five minutes ago in Culver City.'

'Was one of them Bengt Larson?'

'No. Why should that be?'

'He's the guy that attacked me.' Hilton spoke now.

'These punks aren't One Commando.' Varley was dismissive. 'Never been to London. Don't even have passports.'

Elizabeth and Hilton exchanged looks of disbelief.

'I've just come out from interviewing them. Fall into what I call the "social misfit" category. Spoiled kids who've had it too easy and wanted to do something to get themselves noticed.'

· 'Are you saying,' Hilton spoke carefully, 'these people have no connection at all with One Commando?'

'That's exactly what I'm saying. It's a copycat.'

'You're sure,' asked Elizabeth, 'they're not just covering for him?'

'Believe me, they're not covering for anyone. I've put the frighteners on them and they're not holding back. Their parents made sure of that.'

'Parents?' asked Hilton. 'How old are they?'

'Didn't I mention? They're both seventeen.'

Hilton exchanged a look of bewilderment with Elizabeth before asking, 'But – why Isis and Jordan?'

Varley let out a grunt of contempt. 'They've seen all the One Commando stuff on TV. Decided they wanted to get into the headlines themselves.'

'And how did they know they'd gone to Panama Jacks?' asked Elizabeth.

'Followed her from home. They've been staking out her house for the past two days.'

London
Thursday, 30 September

Jasper Jones's footsteps were brisk as he walked back to his flat from the Angel Underground station. Having spent the day in Paris on business, he'd returned to Heathrow on an early evening flight. It had been after changing at Paddington from the Heathrow Express to the Circle Line that he'd unfolded his copy of the *Evening Standard* to discover, right in the middle of the front page, the Jacques Lefevre announcement. The headline had electrified him. We've *done* it! had been his initial, triumphant reaction, as he'd glanced round at his fellow passengers, many of whom were reading the same article with inscrutable expressions. We've just forced Berkeley Square to walk away from the biggest endorsement deal in the history of the beauty industry. What a coup! What a triumph! He'd had to suppress the sudden rush of adrenaline as he'd stared at the ghoulish photograph of Jacques Lefevre in his black suit and black sunglasses, the white of the bandages showing down the sides of his face. It was the kind of image picture editors from every national newspaper would be sure to plaster all over tomorrow morning's editions. An image which would be seared into the public consciousness.

Once he started reading the article, however, Jones's initial excitement quickly changed. It wasn't Isis and Jordan Hampshire who'd abandoned the endorsement, he realised; Berkeley Square had ended it themselves. Far from suffering the humiliation of a major celebrity walk-out, Berkeley Square were being portrayed as the good guys, releasing stars from their contracts to spare them 'future intimidation'.

One Commando had yet again been outmanoeuvred in the media by Berkeley Square. While a litany of 'One Commando violence' was repeated, there was no detail about the systematic abuse and torture of animals by Berkeley Square as evidenced in all the AFL material distributed to the media. The only reference to that was a sentence to the effect that 'alleged evidence of animal rights abuse was generally accepted as faked'.

Jones wondered how Larson would react to this latest turn of events. The two would have to speak soon. Since yesterday morning, Jones had given considerable thought to that biggest and most unexpected twist of all – Larson's revelations about Isis. In a journey through an Aladdin's cave of surprises, that had been the most staggering surprise of them all. How best to use the new information was something Jones had thought about without coming to any certain conclusion – but the Lefevre announcement put a very different perspective on things; now he had no doubt at all about what needed to be done. If *Rolling Stone* magazine's 'Pop Queen of the Year' thought she didn't need to bother about One Commando again, she was very much mistaken.

Making his way swiftly home, eager to get in touch with Larson, it was only when he had the front door key in the lock that he remembered. Christ, yes! Gail would be upstairs, waiting for him. Yesterday afternoon as they lay together in a state of post-coital bliss, she'd suggested they spend the next evening together. If he lent her a spare key, just this once, she'd come round in the early evening and prepare something for supper – she'd give him a nice surprise, she'd suggested meaningfully. He'd been in no mood to refuse. Gazing across the satin sheets at her delicious nakedness, Jones had been thinking that she was the woman of his dreams – or almost. His only regret was her deficiency in the intellectual firepower department. She had no interest in current affairs and didn't appear to read anything more demanding than *Hello!* magazine – her casual acceptance of the status quo really couldn't be more different from his own focused intensity.

He made his way upstairs, and before he'd even got to

the first floor he could smell the results of her labours in the kitchen – a delicious aroma of garlic and coriander wafted through the house.

'Hello, darling!' he called out, not wanting to startle her. He needn't have bothered. In the kitchen she was oblivious to his arrival, all other noises drowned out by the hissing of the frying pan and the music blaring from his Sony portable which she'd retuned from Radio 4 to Melody FM.

Opening the kitchen door, he looked across to where she was standing at the bench dressed in his red silk bathrobe – and under it, a set of lacy black underwear designed with only one purpose in mind. Despite the urgency of his wish to speak to Larson, he couldn't help grinning.

'Hello, darling!' he repeated from the kitchen door.

She turned with a smile. 'My poor baby!' She pulled the pan off the stove and hurried over to him. 'So late! I was getting worried about you.'

They kissed hungrily, Gail pressing her body against his and running her fingers through his hair. When they pulled apart, she asked him, 'I hope Paris put you in a romantic mood?'

'I'll be feeling more . . . romantic after a drink and a shower,' he replied.

She beamed at him. 'I'm sure that can be arranged,' she murmured, walking over to the cupboard where he kept his Laphroaig. Taking out the bottle she splashed a generous measure into one of his crystal tumblers.

As she did, he glanced round the kitchen. 'You've found everything?'

She nodded. 'Brought some stuff over myself.'

Then, as he looked back at her, 'Don't worry, I'm not about to move in. Spare key's back in your study.'

He shrugged. 'I'm not complaining.'

As she handed him his drink, he regarded her appreciatively – his red gown wrapped about her perfect figure; the tantalising glimpse of cleavage clad in black lace; her flawless features, made up to perfection, and the mane of tousled blonde hair. All this, and she wanted to cook for him too.

'While you're busy here, I'll just . . .' He gestured upstairs.

'Fine.'

'I've got to make a couple of calls as well.'

'Just don't be too long.'

Then as he was leaving the room, 'Oh. I brought the mail up from downstairs when I got in.' She motioned towards a pile of envelopes. Glancing over it, Jones's attention was immediately attracted by a large padded envelope which had evidently been personally delivered. His name was printed on it in Larson's distinctive hand. Collecting the envelope, he continued on his way upstairs to his study where he closed the door, put the glass of whisky down on his desk, and turned to the video player in the corner. It must be the Alan Brent video. Larson's interrogation of the secret service spy. Fumbling with excitement, Jones ripped open the stapled envelope and seized the video inside. He was in so much of a hurry to watch it, he didn't notice that the envelope had been opened and re-stapled. The holes of the new staples matched, but not exactly, those of the originals.

He was soon watching the tape, which was indeed the interview of Alan Brent. He marvelled at the quality of the recording. Larson had done an extremely good job of it – the light and camera angle could hardly have been improved on. As Larson had already told him, Brent had been sweating like a pig while Larson strode about him, clad in black. His answers to Larson's questions were weak, evasive – and Larson had shown no mercy. Why had he tipped off the police about the Gallo operation? How long had he been an informant? Was he an undercover agent for the police or a secret service? Jones watched, utterly engrossed as Brent squirmed under pressure, rivulets of perspiration pouring down the sides of his face and neck, heavy spectacles repeatedly slipping down his nose.

Now Larson was beating Brent around the head. Brent's glasses had slipped off again, one time too many for Larson, who angrily flung them to the floor, stamping on them with the heel of his boot. Brent cried out in protest, only to be struck heavily across the face. His terror was visible after that. His already pallid features had gone white as a sheet and his lips were quivering with fear. Taking a sip of his single malt, Jones watched intently as Larson told Brent he'd been found guilty and was to be executed.

Jones had thought Larson would have switched off the video camera at that point. The agreed purpose of the taping had, after all, been to give Jones a chance to see how Brent reacted to questioning, to provide a second opinion on whether or not he posed a security threat. But events had got ahead of themselves. Now the video showed one of Larson's sidekicks armed with handcuffs and a sturdy rope. There was a final desperate struggle as Brent tried to flee – not that he had a hope in hell. Then he was being trussed up like an animal about to be put on the spit.

'Be grateful we're not cutting your tongue out first,' Larson said, quite audibly.

There was a chilling theatre to the hanging. Brent pleading, crying out for help, which earned him another crack across the face and a heavy knee to the stomach. Then they had taped his mouth up. He was forced to climb up on the execution chair, where the knot of the rope was carefully adjusted about his neck. When the chair was kicked out from under him, he fell with an unceremonious crack, and dangled, limp, from the end of the rope.

It was one of the most intensely engaging pieces of action he'd ever seen, thought Jones, taking another long gulp of Scotch, and switching the video player off, before collecting up his study phone and dialling the latest contact number Larson had given him.

In Helsinki, where he'd spent the evening pumping iron at the local gymnasium, Larson had just returned to his safe house, a small flat in a high-rise apartment block, when his phone rang. He checked the display for the number of the incoming call, before answering.

'You've seen the news?' asked Jones.

'We wanted Isis to end it,' the other replied, 'not Lefevre.'

'Exactly.' Larson's frustration with Berkeley Square was self-evident. Even so, Jones thought he should be explicit. 'There's still been no acknowledgement of animal testing, let alone a promise to change things. It's the most ruthless cover-up I've ever seen.'

'So what do we do now?' Larson asked, voice flat. 'Tell the AFL we have failed as badly as they did?'

Jones searched his pocket before pulling out his cigarettes. 'Oh, I don't think we have to do that just yet. There's also the Isis information.'

'What use is it to us now? She's no longer involved.'

'Then we'll just have to re-involve her.'

'You mean—'

'Quite simple, the way I see it.' Jones extracted a cigarette. 'She tells the truth about Berkeley Square, or we tell the truth about her.'

Larson thought about this for a moment. 'Sounds very simple,' he responded, eventually.

'The best ideas always are.' Jones lit up.

Larson realised Isis would be desperate to keep secret the dramatic revelations about her private life which Brent had discovered and he had subsequently confirmed. And with no further obligations to Berkeley Square, why shouldn't she come out and tell the world what was going on?

'Just imagine the headlines,' Jones prompted him. '"Isis condemns animal torture in Spain. Berkeley Square forced to close Madrid operations." *Then* we'll see the tables turned. All of a sudden Berkeley Square will be in the corner and then you'll see the media turn.'

'But what about our agreement?' Larson asked. 'Only to go for targets who are ultimately accountable?'

Jones had wondered if Larson would go there. It was a subject to which he'd already given serious thought.

'You're right to ask,' he said now. 'The way I see it, Isis and Jordan Hampshire might not be directly responsible for torture. But they are for joining the conspiracy to hide the truth about it. In my book, that amounts to the same thing.'

So absorbed was he in his conversation with Larson, Jones hadn't heard the creak on the landing as Gail made her way, barefoot, upstairs. He had no idea she'd been hovering outside his door, listening intently to his conversation. Though the moment he'd put the phone down, having discussed plans with Larson in detail, she'd returned downstairs, waiting for the sound of his study door to open before calling out, 'Would you like another drink, Jas?' She appeared at the bottom of the stairs, the bottle of Laphroaig in her hand.

Jones paused, glancing into his empty tumbler. 'That would be good.' He decided he did have something to celebrate – not that he was about to tell Gail. Far from being floored by Berkeley Square's tactical advantage, he'd persuaded Larson that while Lefevre had won a battle, he had yet to win the war.

'Actually,' he reached out for Gail's shoulders before she'd reached the top of the stairs, admiring all six feet of her pure, blonde perfection, 'there's something I'd like even more than another drink.' As he leaned to kiss her, she responded, trailing one hand down his front to his crotch.

'You've finished for this evening, then?' she whispered, putting down the bottle of whisky.

'Not quite.' Pulling the cord around her waist to unfasten the knot, he'd soon brushed the bathrobe off her shoulders so that it fell in a wreath of crimson about her bare feet. She stepped up beside him, a voracious expression on her face. Taking his glass and putting it on the carpet, she stood before him in her designer underwear and began unbuckling his belt. His breathing quickened as he looked down at where she was bending in front of him, the outlines of her beige nipples showing through the intricate pattern of black silk. Undoing the buttons of his trousers and tugging them down his legs, as she slipped under his final layer and took him in her hand, she met his eyes with a look of unabashed lust.

17

The fax came through on Isis's private fax line sometime between two and three in the morning. The fax machine was in the mixing room of her studio, downstairs and through two closed doors from her bedroom. A light sleeper, Isis was aware of the sound of paper feeding through the machine. But she didn't fully awaken. Having registered what the noise was, she simply went back to sleep. It wasn't unusual for her to get faxes overnight; GCM offices in London and Europe frequently sent over stuff. When she woke up the following morning, she didn't even remember that she'd heard it.

After too many nights of troubled sleep, the last two had been blissful; eight hours right through, with no tossing and turning waiting for sleep to come, no wakening in the middle of the night, unable to banish her fears till dawn. Jacques Lefevre had banished them for her. She would never forget his appearance on TV: there'd been an audible gasp of shock from the media corps, accompanied by a flurry of flash cameras as he'd appeared through the door of the Berkeley

Square boardroom. It was his first public appearance since the attack and he was dressed in a dark suit and wearing large black glasses, the bandages covering his eyes clearly visible beneath. Led to a microphone by his secretary, his steps had been slow and tentative. Once he'd been introduced, there was nothing faltering in his voice, however. In the briefest announcement, he outlined the One Commando threat against Isis and Jordan Hampshire, and explained that he had concluded that nothing could justify allowing a continued risk to their well-being.

All the world's media knew it was an admission of defeat. But Lefevre's tone had been one of defiance. He had implored police forces to use every means at their disposal to arrest One Commando. Never, he declared, had corporate Britain been so held to ransom by a small group of militant extremists. This was about more than simply the protection of a handful of individuals, or even one company. One only needed to visit Russia and other Eastern European states to see what happened when terrorism and blackmail were allowed into the economy; the preservation of the free market system was at stake.

It wouldn't have mattered what Lefevre said; his sheer presence, standing there in his black glasses and white bandages, was enough to evoke powerful feelings of sympathy and outrage. But his speech was stirring and impressive, spoken to a media corps which had been unnaturally silent, hanging on his every word.

And his words had a specially profound meaning for Isis. She watched, heart in her mouth, taking it all in with complete absorption. When the news item had finished, she'd raised her hands to her eyes, silent tears of relief and exhaustion trickling between her fingers. Her oppressive burden lifted, for the first time since signing the endorsement deal she'd felt free. Her own long, dark night, she thought, was over.

Since that release yesterday, she'd felt very different. She'd had her first 'normal' day in weeks. It had been like having her life back again.

She'd gone into Unum for a hastily arranged final recording session. Then on impulse, she'd booked a hair appointment and had Frank drive her to her favourite beauty salon for the full treatment; facial, manicure and massage. She'd just lost one and a half million dollars and she was going to have to be extremely persuasive next time she met the bank manager. But she also felt invigorated, renewed.

She'd set up a series of business meetings for today, Friday. She planned to spend time with her accountant, her lawyer, her financial adviser. But as it turned out, she never got to see them. Having dressed and put on her make up, she'd gone through to her office to get together the papers she needed for her meetings, when she noticed the fax on the machine. She picked it up. Although it took her only a few seconds to read, she stared at it as though in disbelief for a full half minute. Then she walked over to the telephone, picked it up and began dialling.

The worst had happened. The discovery she'd feared for her entire professional career had finally been made. And yet a curious calm had come over her – almost as though she was watching all this happen to somebody else.

Hilton had been finishing off a breakfast meeting at the Mondrian when her call came through. Hastily excusing himself, he stepped out of the room. Isis told him about the overnight fax, before reading it out: '"Tell the truth about Berkeley Square's animal testing,"' she read out, '"or we will tell the truth about you. You have forty-eight hours."'

But it was the two words at the top of the page which

carried the impact. Two words pointing to the secret she'd successfully kept hidden from view for the past eighteen years. One Commando had found it out and now there seemed no escaping from it.

At the other end of the phone Hilton paused, deep in thought, considering the situation before Isis murmured, 'Just when I thought it had gone away. But it's never really gone away, has it? Not from the day I started out.'

'You're right,' he answered, realising that denial would serve no purpose, 'it has always been a possibility.'

In her sitting room she turned to face the sea. 'After all that's happened these past few weeks, I just wish I could lose myself. I don't feel I can cope with this any more—'

'You've done exactly the right thing calling me,' he said. Having reached a decision, his voice was now charged with resolve. 'And this is something we're going to handle together.'

She was still in a state of shock, he realised. Probably still anaesthetised to the full force of the news. That would hit her later. In the meantime, it seemed to him they now had only one remaining option, one last resort; he had to make sure she didn't do anything to blow it.

'There's just no end to it!' she was saying. 'Every time we close a door, they find another way in. And now the genie's out of the bottle.'

'It isn't yet,' he was firm.

'You think I should make a statement about Berkeley Square?'

'Even if they did test on animals, which they don't, you can't give in to blackmailers. They'd only come back for you.'

'Then what . . . what am I to do?'

'Last time I was in London,' Hilton's tone was serious,

'when they had me all bound up and lying on the bed, I thought – this is it. End of the line. There's no way I'm going to get out of this. But,' he paused, significantly, 'I *did* escape. I got out unhurt. The secret service agent in One Commando tipped off the police. I was only moments away from serious injury or death. But it wasn't allowed to happen.'

'The point being?'

'The point being that with an MI5 guy active in One Commando it's way too soon to give up. He saved me from . . . a fate worse than death. We can count on him to make sure this information about you stays under wraps.'

'We can?' She was distracted.

'Yes. I'm calling the British Home Office right away.'

Within moments of Hilton getting back to his office, Elizabeth had placed the call on his behalf. She'd been right in thinking her boss knew Peter Campbell. The two had attended an image management conference in Berne several years earlier, and had kept in occasional contact ever since. Not that she expected Campbell to do Hilton any favours; his reputation as an information control freak preceded him.

'Peter Campbell's on his way to a cocktail function at Downing Street,' she told him before putting through the call. 'I managed to track down his car phone number with Hanniford's help.'

'Thanks,' Hilton's face was sharply etched with worry, 'put him through.'

'Peter, its Hilton Gallo from GCM, Los Angeles. Francis Hanniford suggested we call you.'

'Ah, the Berkeley Square issue.' Fresh from a party to celebrate four years in power, and seated in the back of the Home Secretary's chauffeured Daimler, his spin-doctor, resplendent in an evening suit and sipping a glass of hot water with a twist of lemon, was his customary acerbic self.

'We need to know what progress is being made on One Commando,' continued Hilton. 'Scotland Yard are telling us nothing.'

'Procedural guidelines,' responded the other.

'And in the meantime, my client, Isis, is under threat.'

'But I was given to believe,' Campbell was puzzled, 'that the endorsement matter was settled?'

'Berkeley Square walked away from it – only because One Commando are still at large.' Hilton was firm. 'Now they're trying to blackmail Isis into supporting their ridiculous claims about animal testing. They have uncovered personal information about her which they're threatening to release. They must be stopped.'

Campbell blew on his glass of hot water thoughtfully, before replying, 'Regrettably, Hilton, neither the Met nor Interpol have reported any great progress. Larson and his cohorts are highly mobile and extremely difficult to detect given their constant changes of disguise and identity.'

'But what about Intelligence?' At the other end, Hilton found his frustration hard to conceal.

'Rear-view mirror stuff. Very little that's predictive.'

'Surely your agent can give you a steer?'

'Agent?' queried the other.

'Your undercover agent!' Hilton was exasperated. 'The MI5 guy.'

'I'm not sure I understand.'

'Francis Hanniford has already told us,' Hilton's tone was weary, 'there's no need to keep up this charade.'

'What charade?'

'I personally was attacked by these thugs—' his voice rose in anger, 'now my client is directly at risk—'

'Look, Hilton,' Campbell audibly pulled rank, 'I can assure

you there is no obfuscation going on from my side. Let me be quite categorical about this. There is no intelligence agent working inside One Commando.'

Hilton was shaking his head. 'But Francis Hanniford told us—'

'If dear old Francis has chosen to believe that, it's very much his affair. He's never brought the subject up with me or I would have put him straight.'

Hilton's unusual display of anger turned into an even more extraordinary desperation. 'But there's *got* to be an agent,' he insisted, 'who else tipped off the police when they tried to attack me?'

'That's something being investigated. It certainly wasn't Intelligence.'

'Are you saying,' he was finding all this too incredible to believe, 'there has never been an agent?'

'That's exactly what I'm saying.'

'And you're no closer now to apprehending One Commando than you were after the Lefevre attack?'

'Regrettably, no.'

'So what in God's name are we supposed to be doing?'

'That's really not for me to advise.' In the back of the Daimler, Campbell took another sip of his lemon water. 'All I would say is that we are dealing here with extremely dangerous criminals.'

When Hilton ended, he sank his head into his hands. Across the desk from him, having listened to every word of his conversation, Elizabeth felt, by turns, guilt and a rising nausea. It was she who'd originally been misled by Hanniford into believing in the existence of a secret service operation. Hanniford had seemed so certain, so confident. Now she realised how much of GCM's strategy had been founded on a fundamental error.

'No agent?' Her voice was barely a whisper.

Hilton shook his head without looking up.

'When Isis finds out—'

'She can't,' Hilton looked up, directly into her eyes. She didn't know if it was undisguised anger or ferocious determination in that gaze – but she knew he must not be crossed.

'If we tell her, we take away her hope.' His eyes bored into hers. 'And that's all she has left.'

Mark emerged from the swimming pool of his Beverly Hills home, seizing a beach towel from a nearby chair and drying himself briskly, before squeezing the water from his hair. He'd never thought of himself as a keep-fit fanatic. But this morning as soon as he woke up he knew he needed to do something, anything, to burn off the nervous energy he felt building up inside him.

Ever since his row with Hilton he'd been edgy and uptight. In spite of Lefevre's announcing that the Berkeley Square deal was off he'd felt in his gut that he hadn't heard the last of One Commando. There was just too much going on. For one thing, what was this 'background' of Isis's and why wouldn't they tell him? What would Vinnie do with the rug pulled out from under him by Lefevre? And the biggest puzzler of all: why was One Commando so convinced that Berkeley Square tested on animals, when the rest of the world accepted they didn't?

Lloyd had paid an unsolicited call on AFL offices posing as a potential recruit, and picked up anything and everything they'd ever published on Berkeley Square. He'd given the handful of fliers to Mark when he'd dropped him off at Heathrow on Monday night.

'Take a look at these,' he'd suggested, 'interesting reading.'

The photos were disturbing all right. Close-ups of rabbits, scarcely recognisable with their shaven fur, inflamed eyes and bodies punctured with tubes and needles. The pictures of chimpanzees were even worse – Mark found himself averting his gaze from the scenes of grotesque cruelty. Around these images, the accusations were equally sensational; all these photographs had been taken inside the laboratories of Berkeley Square's Research and Development unit, located in an industrial suburb of Madrid. An unnamed AFL activist gave a full, first-person account of his visit to the facility, including how he'd circumvented lax security measures, getting close enough to shoot dozens of photographs.

A different leaflet comprised first-hand interviews with former workers from the plant. Photographed in silhouette to protect their anonymity, in every case they had left the laboratory as soon as they had been transferred to the animal testing unit, nauseated by the systematic mass suffering inflicted on animals.

Taken as a whole, the evidence seemed compelling. Photographs, interviews – plus there was a video, Mark knew. Could it really all be just a hoax, he wondered? If so, what sick kind of individual would spend hours faking photographs of animal torture, and making up horror stories? And why pick on Berkeley Square? None of it made any sense.

Lloyd had also picked up stuff from Berkeley Square, like glossy brochures devoted to Berkeley Square R & D. Flicking it open, he encountered the genial face of Dr Andrew Craig, Head of Research and Development, described as an eminent bio-pharmacist, who'd formerly held senior positions in several major pharmaceutical companies as well as serving on British Government advisory committees. His introduction to the brochure was upbeat without being self-important, describing methodologies used by Berkeley

Square as 'leading edge' and emphasising the principled
nature of the company's policies on genetic modification
and other contentious issues. 'It is a source of personal
pride', he noted, 'that Berkeley Square's laboratories in
Madrid are not only at the very forefront of technological
development, but that the Company's endeavours are
informed by an enlightened philosophy of corporate responsibility and ethical leadership.'

Looking from the AFL leaflets to the Berkeley Square
stuff and back again, for a long while Mark wondered what
to make of it. Either Berkeley Square had succeeded in
putting up an elaborate smokescreen, he decided eventually,
or One Commando were motivated by reasons which just
seemed inexplicable.

Now as he headed back up to the house, he found Mrs
Martinez in the kitchen preparing a late breakfast. A full
English fry-up would be ready in half an hour, she told him.
In the meantime, he decided to check out his internet access
to the OmniCell computer on which all Vinnie's telephone
conversations were being recorded. Wouldn't do any harm
keeping tabs.

In the study he logged on, quickly finding his way to the
address Lloyd had given him, and entering the security passwords they'd agreed. A file log opened up showing that since
the chip had been installed, Vinnie had made no fewer than
forty-seven calls! Taking a swig of his beer, Mark wondered
wearily if it was even worth trawling through them. Clicking
open the first one, he was surprised, however, by the quality of the recording. All of a sudden his study was filled with
a call Vinnie had evidently made from his car, after leaving
the Lamb two nights ago, warning the manager of some club
he could be slightly late – he'd been with an important
client. Yeah, yeah, thought Mark, pull the other one. He

didn't recognise the manager's voice, but the music in the background was Metallica and the recording was so clear he could even hear Vinnie shifting gear. He read the time label – 8.28 p.m., Monday, 27 September.

Mark found to his relief that by simply moving the cursor down the page, he could click open the next message without having to listen to all of the first. And it didn't take long to assess if a call was going to be of any interest. He wasn't surprised to confirm that most of Vinnie's conversations were purely social, with a few business calls thrown in. But the fourteenth call was very different. It was an incoming call. And as soon as he heard the accent he knew it could only be one person. The conversation, at nine-thirty a.m. this morning, London time, was brief:

Larson: I am putting you on standby.

Vinnie: (*Bitterly*) Oh, yeah? Like there's still something happening.

Larson: Why shouldn't there be?

Vinnie: Berkeley Square have pulled out! It's all over the papers!

Larson: They can't walk away from it as easy as that. There's still no admission of guilt.

Vinnie: You're the only one who seems to think they're guilty.

Larson: (*Growing heated*) How can I deny what I've seen with my own eyes?

Vinnie: They've cancelled the endorsement so I don't see what you've got on them now.

Larson: Let's just say I have some very powerful material on one of our targets. Information that's been kept hidden for many years and would be highly damaging if it came to light . . . (*Dryly*) . . . as

> damaging as if the truth is told about Berkeley
> Square.
>
> Vinnie: You must be talking about Isis. But it's not her
> that interests me, mate. It's that fuckhead, 'Jordan
> Hampshire'.
>
> Larson: (*After a long pause*) Believe me, if there's no Isis,
> there'll be no 'Jordan Hampshire'. And there'll
> be no Isis after this.

Minutes later Mark was sitting in the back of the Lincoln. He ordered Denzil to get out to Malibu immediately. He didn't care what he did. How many speeding tickets he picked up. Just get the hell out there as soon as he could. Unlike the last piece of information he'd got on One Commando, this time he wasn't trusting it to Hilton. There weren't going to be any delayed reactions or PR spin. This time he'd make sure Isis got it straight. The recorded conversation with Larson was all he needed to know that Isis and he were caught up in something that went way beyond an endorsement. As much as he was attracted to her, he wasn't going to let her take him for a fool. There was another whole dimension to this, something that Isis and Hilton were concealing. But the time for game-playing was over. He needed to know, right now, just what the hell was going on.

Isis was alone in her sitting room when he arrived, and she'd looked up in surprise when Juanita showed him into the room.

'One Commando have got something on you and they're threatening to use it,' he told Isis urgently, the moment they were left alone.

'Hilton spoke to you?' she queried.

Mark stopped in his tracks. 'No. I found out myself. Less than an hour ago.'

Isis turned away. She was more traumatised by the fax earlier that day than by anything that had happened during her entire singing career, and the timing of Mark's visit couldn't have been worse.

'It happened this morning,' she told him.

'What happened?'

'The blackmail,' her voice was taut. 'It's not good enough that we're no longer endorsing Berkeley Square products. Now they want us to tell the world that Berkeley Square tortures animals. If we don't, they're threatening to release information.'

So events had already overtaken them, thought Mark. All the more reason he should know the whole truth.

'What information, exactly?' He stepped closer towards where she was sitting.

She averted her eyes. 'Personal stuff. Stuff about me.'

'You mean, the stuff you and Hilton don't want me to know about?'

When she didn't answer he continued, 'It's not just about you. It's about me, too.'

She flashed an irritated glance. 'What *are* you talking about?'

'About our CD, Isis. And about my career.' He met her eyes and held them as he tried to reason. 'I've moved countries for it. I quit my job for it. I've put everything into it and now it's being threatened. I think I have the right to know—'

'The right?' she demanded, rising from the sofa. 'Don't lecture me about rights. Nothing, and I mean *nothing* gives you the *right* to meddle in my private life!'

'I'm not talking about *meddling*!' The sudden heat of her anger made him resentful. 'I just want to *know*—'

'And I'm telling you you can't know!' she told him. 'My private life remains private!'

Their eyes locked in blazing exchange before he lashed out. 'Just as bad as Hilton, aren't you?' he was furious. 'Keeping me in the dark—'

'That's not true!'

'"Managing information",' he taunted.

His criticism stung – because she knew it to be true. But what choice did she have? She couldn't tell him now, in a moment of crisis. If she told him, she'd spend the rest of her life wondering if he could keep the secret.

'I've done a lot for Hilton and you. Changed my name. My appearance. I've played along with the sham romance. I didn't want any of that. And you're quite happy to take, take, take—'

'I don't have to listen to any more of this!' Isis marched past him towards the door.

'Spent your whole career running away from the truth, have you?'

'You know what the problem with you is?' At the door she wheeled round with an accusatory gesture. 'You're out of your depth. Out of your league. You're like a small boy in short pants with no idea what you're into.'

'Oh yeah?' Mark shouted after her receding figure, 'And what about you, Isis? Tagging me along and dumping me when it suits you! All your fans might think you're something special, but I know different – I know better! When it comes down to it, you're nothing but the bitch from hell!'

18

Moments later, Mark heard the door to her bedroom wing slam shut. Standing alone in the lounge, after she'd stormed out, he trembled with rage. How dare she treat him like this? After the lengths he'd gone to – for both their sakes – trying to get a fix on One Commando. And this was his reward!

The very last thing he'd have expected was a reaction like this. And the news that One Commando had already issued a blackmail fax had taken him completely by surprise. What did it all mean? If One Commando was intent on blackmail, why had Larson put Vinnie on standby? And surely the secret service agent inside One Commando must know what this information was? Most of all, Mark just wanted to know what they had on Isis that was supposed to be so threatening.

He paced up and down the sitting room for some time, thoughts in turmoil, trying to make sense of the senseless. Gradually he began to calm down. 'My private life remains private,' he mused. She was terrified about whatever it was

coming to light. The fax from One Commando must have
come as a huge shock. Even though he felt completely justified in wanting to know what was going on, he began to
wonder if he should have handled things differently. Maybe
he could have been more sympathetic? Perhaps he needed
to make more of an effort to understand what was going on
in her head?

Hoping to make amends, Mark set off along the passage
in the direction of the bedrooms. He'd never been down this
end of the house before and didn't really know what was
there, except bedrooms and a staircase leading down to Isis's
basement studio. Reaching the bedroom wing door, he
knocked loudly, but receiving no response, opened it and
continued. On the right side of the corridor, a series of
windows gave panoramic views of the ocean, while rooms
led off to the left – a couple that seemed to be guest rooms,
then Holly's, then a master suite he took to be Isis's. Yet
again receiving no reply to his knocking, he put his head
round the open door of the bedroom and found it empty.

Continuing further down the corridor he came to a small
sitting room – evidently her personal retreat. In contrast to
the opulence of her main sitting room, this place was decorated with rustic simplicity – deep red walls, kilim-style rugs
and rattan furniture including a large cushioned armchair
drawn over to a balcony overlooking the sea. There was still
no sign of Isis. Glancing about the room, Mark took in the
carelessly scattered cushions, the basket of seashells, the pine
shelves cluttered with silver-framed photographs, mostly of
Holly. There was a row of books too, including the Betty
Bailey biography of Isis, together with a selection of music
and showbiz titles and some fiction. A large, wide tome with
'ISIS' running in glitzy capitals down the side stuck out from
the others; curious, he pulled it out, discovering it was a

photo album of her *Aphrodisia* world tour, specially presented to her by GCM.

He was about to slip it back on to the shelf, when he noticed behind the first row was a second line of books. He could see a few of the titles: *Child Abuse in America: Fact v. Fiction*; *A Sob in the Dark: Coping with Physical and Emotional Abuse*; *Why Hurt People Hurt People*. Instead of putting back the Isis book, he leaned over and lifted out *Journey out of Darkness – A Manual for Self-Realisation*. The book fell open on its title page, on which he found a dedication written, in an elegant hand, at the front: 'For Isis – Never forget: As you think, so you become. With sincere good wishes, Dr Robert Weiner, Salmacis Hospital.'

Staring down at the book, Mark flicked through its pages. It felt wrong to be nosing around in this way but neither Hilton nor Isis would tell him anything. Perhaps this book was the key. The hidden books all pointed to the same subject, and as he glanced at the chapter headings of *Journey out of Darkness* he wondered if he'd discovered something of significance. Then something slipped out from between the pages of the book and fell to the floor. He leaned down to collect a single-page letter. It was written on fine bond paper, yellowed and brittle with age, and signed 'Mom'. As he picked it up a few phrases caught his eye: *I know I have failed you . . . tried to keep your father from you . . . recover from surgery*.

'What the hell d'you think you're doing in here!'

Mark jumped back guiltily and looked up to find Isis striding down the passage towards him.

'I came looking for you.' It sounded unconvincing as he said it. 'I thought we should—'

Isis was already upon him, grabbing the book and letter from his hands and pointing to the door. 'Get out!' she demanded, mighty with rage.

'Isis! We're both in this together!'

'Just get out of my house!' She pointed to the door. 'And don't you ever, *ever* let me find you in here again!'

London
Friday, 1 October

DCs Brewer and White had received a reply from Records, and soon discovered more about the restraint order, now eight years old, against Alan George Brent. According to the terms of the court order, Brent was forbidden from going within one hundred yards of any Berkeley Square building, director, or senior executive. The homes of a number of executives were also included in the ban.

The moment DC White saw Berkeley Square on the printout, he hurried through to report to DS Morris who, in turn, contacted DI Bennett. Bennett instructed Morris to check Brent's home, while he pursued other lines of enquiry. As soon as he hung up from speaking to Morris, Bennett picked up the phone to Berkeley Square's Human Resources Director, Francis Hanniford.

'Mr Hanniford, it's DI Bennett, Scotland Yard,' he announced himself. 'During the course of our enquiries, we have come across someone who we have reason to believe may be involved in One Commando activities against your company. Does the name Alan Brent mean anything to you?'

At the other end of the line, Hanniford groaned.

Brent's house had only one bell. There was no response when the policemen rang, not from Brent's place nor from either of the neighbours. They decided to break in through the bay window at the front. It was standard, covert police procedure; easy to get into, and no trouble to repair. Using the roll of thick, sticky paper and the collapsible steel baton they'd brought specially for the purpose, they soon rolled over the glass, and smashed round the edges of the window before removing the paper and hauling themselves through the now-open frame.

They found themselves in a large front room which, in most homes in the area, would have been used as either a lounge or a large bedroom. This one though was piled from floor to ceiling with brown cardboard boxes. They were neatly arranged with code numbers written in thick black pen on the outside of each box, as well as a month and a year. Some of the dates went back over ten years, noticed DC Brewer. Squeezing through the narrow space between rows of boxes, the policemen made their way into the main corridor leading through the flat, opening the door into another room which proved to be similarly stacked with boxes. DC White led the way through to a kitchen and bathroom – even these rooms had been turned into warehousing. Raising his eyebrows he murmured, 'Expensive storage facility. Rents for two-bedroom flats in this area are anything from two hundred a week up.'

DC Brewer was already unfolding the flaps of a cardboard box on the floor beside him. When he'd got it open, he let out a low whistle. DC White soon made his way over. Inside there appeared to be a pile of publications, the top one a pornographic magazine – X-Cess – its cover a lurid portrait of two women dressed in black latex, squatting above a man who was manacled and spreadeagled in what looked like a sado-masochist torture chamber. Lifting up the magazine, Brewer found more editions of X-Cess – in fact, the box was packed full of them. The two detectives quickly carried out random checks of other cardboard boxes in the room, and in other rooms of the downstairs flat. It soon became apparent that all of them contained hard-core pornography, magazines and videos going back more than a decade.

Climbing upstairs to the upper flat, past shelves stacked with yet more cardboard boxes, they called out several times before forcing their way through the locked door. Making their way inside, it was only to encounter yet more rooms of brown cardboard boxes, stacked from floor to ceiling.

In silence, the two detectives surveyed the kitchen, a squalid mess of fast-food cartons and condiments, before ascending the final flight of stairs to the attic room. There they discovered a double bed shoved into one corner, a creased, grey duvet flung to one side to reveal stained yellow sheets. On one side of the bed was a digital alarm clock with a red button that flashed every second. DC White wrinkled his nose as he glanced from the bed to the clothes strewn across the floor, a few stashed in a black bin liner which evidently served as a washing bag. Other clothes and belongings had been discarded carelessly on a threadbare carpet. A torn leather sofa and lava lamp gave the place the feel of a student dive that had been caught in a time-warp. Several empty bottles of vodka and cans of Sprite lined up beside the sofa confirmed the impression.

But the other end of the room was a different matter entirely. The whole facing wall was a mass of electronic equipment, the purpose of which was suggested by the tangle of wires leading from them to a row of five telephone sockets in the wall. A black, imitation-ash desk sagged under the weight of further equipment – scanners, a printer, fax machines and modems, all co-ordinated through a state-of-the-art keyboard and monitor.

DC White turned to his colleague. 'Quite a set-up he had here,' he mused.

'We'll have to dust the place for prints.' Brewer was more

cautious about confirming this as the home address of the murder victim they'd found in Olympia.

The other shrugged, 'Yeah, yeah. Classic underground porn operation. I've seen this kind of thing before, down the East End.' He gave Brewer the benefit of his extra years of experience. 'They assemble more electronic equipment than you can shake a stick at, then steal mountains of videos and photos from other internet operators and load it on to their own sites.'

Brewer glanced about him in surprise. 'You mean one bloke can run the whole thing out of his bedroom.'

'Technically speaking,' the other nodded, 'but you'll probably find he was just an agent for a larger underground set-up.'

Glancing at a pile of 'First Fist' videos, DC Brewer thought aloud, 'Wonder if there's any kiddy stuff in here.'

'Doubt it.' White was opening a desk drawer, rummaging through the contents. 'Mainstream operators don't tend to get mixed up with paedophile rings. Don't need to. Can cash up big time without going so high-risk.'

'So why d'you think he was strung up?'

'That, old son, is one of life's great mysteries.' Then, enigmatically, 'My guess is that it had nothing to do with his . . . money-making activities.' He glanced about with a caustic expression.

White had opened a desk drawer and was flicking through some of Alan Brent's papers, while Brewer looked about the room more closely. Behind a ceiling-high wall of boxes, Brewer found a filing cabinet and quickly had it open. The Berkeley Square files were meticulously ordered at the back of the second drawer. They included a company organisational chart, showing its different divisions, with photographs of the executives in charge. Several of these had been

circled in red, including Jacques Lefevre's. Calling out to
White, Brewer looked through the other files. Brent had an
'assassination list' of half a dozen Berkeley Square executives. Further information on each target included all contact
details including home addresses. The two policemen
exchanged a wordless glance before collecting up all the files
from the cabinet, bagging them carefully, and heading back
for the police station. There, they reported to DS Morris.

'Looks like our Alan Brent ran an underground porn operation on the Net,' White told his boss when the three of
them were in his office, behind closed doors. 'Unbelievable
operation. Three floors of hard porn.'

'What about Berkeley Square?' Morris was impatient.

'Found an assassination list.' Brewer gestured to the bulge
of files. 'Berkeley Square corporate structure. The lot. No
doubt he wanted to persuade his lords and masters to settle
a few old scores.'

Morris raised his eyebrows. 'Now we've got Bennett and
the whole of Scotland Yard breathing down our necks.'

'So what's the story with Brent and Berkeley Square?'
asked White.

'Former employee. Seems he was recruited by the
company to develop an IT idea he dreamed up at university
– some sort of allergy diagnoses using a computer. After a
few years, when the program was about to be marketed, he
and Berkeley Square had a falling out over who owned it.
He said the idea was his, but Berkeley Square held the patent
and collected all the cash.'

'Did he take it to court?'

'Tried to. His lawyers told him to settle out of court – he
didn't have a case. Berkeley Square paid out a hundred grand
in goodwill.'

Brewer's eyebrows twitched.

'Brent wanted more. He started threatening directors. Phoning them at home in the middle of the night – that sort of thing. Which is when they slapped the restraining order on him.'

'And he signed up with One Commando?'

'Seems so.' He paused before continuing, 'Bennett's convinced One Commando hanged him.'

'Motive?' asked Brewer.

'Round his neck,' shrugged Morris. '"Spy". They may have thought he tipped off Scotland Yard about Gallo. Maybe they were worried that his day job would compromise their activities.'

'Doubtful.' White was shaking his head. 'He still wanted to get One Commando to go for his own targets in Berkeley Square.'

While DC White exchanged a thoughtful expression with his boss, it was young Brewer who scratched his head. 'But, sir, if Alan Brent didn't tip off Scotland Yard,' he asked, 'then who did?'

Helsinki
Friday, 1 October

'What if they don't say anything?' demanded Larson. It was coming up for twenty-four hours since he'd faxed the demand note to Los Angeles and there had still been no response. Not so much as a word from either Isis or Jordan Hampshire on the subject of animal rights abuse by Berkeley Square.

'That's something we need to take very seriously,' replied Jones, who'd taken care to close his study door when Larson came through on the mobile. Gail was along the corridor in the bathroom, getting ready for a dinner party to which they'd both been invited.

Larson digested Jones's observation in silence. Persuasive though he believed his demand idea had been, ever since he'd sent the fax to Isis from a cellular telephone, he'd found himself wondering – what if they refused to play ball? What if they said nothing at all? Now he told Jones, 'I want to make a plan of action if we don't hear from them by the end of the deadline.'

'Sensible,' nodded Jones, slipping a hand in the pocket of his red dressing-gown as he paced the semi-darkness of his study.

'I can drop an envelope off to the local Reuters office. In an hour the whole world will know the truth about Isis.'

'An interesting thought.' Jones paused, meeting his own eyes, reflected in a gilt-framed mirror, with a hard stare. 'But what would that do for the cause?'

At the other end, Larson hadn't anticipated this reaction. 'I thought the whole point of the information was—'

'To trade a truth for a truth,' interjected Jones. 'But if, like Monsieur Lefevre, they find themselves incapable of telling the truth, then I would suggest we are left with only one alternative.'

As Larson absorbed this he added, 'If I can make a suggestion, Bengt, it is that we consider playing from our strengths. We've tried reason. We've done our utmost to persuade them. Maybe it's time, again, to do what we do best.'

Larson stared out of the window of the high-rise apartment, to where the sun was still high on the horizon even though it was eight in the evening. It was a long while before he spoke, but when he eventually did, it was in that tone of sardonic certainty that had drawn Jones to him at the very beginning.

'Yes,' mused Larson, 'I would enjoy a bit of foreign travel.'

Los Angeles
Friday, 1 October

Staff at GCM had never seen Hilton Gallo so agitated. Their CEO's legendary serenity had turned out not to be disaster-proof after all – but no one knew the reason for his current disquiet. Elizabeth Reynolds knew the discovery that there wasn't an MI5 agent working inside One Commando after all had a lot to do with it. And she felt a heavy burden of responsibility for having passed on Francis Hanniford's assumption that there was an agent as a statement of fact. But she knew that there was something else troubling Hilton; something had happened out at Malibu he wasn't telling her about.

Instead, he'd summoned Leo Lebowitz to his office. As Lebowitz made his way through Elizabeth's office, he'd raised his eyebrows. She shook her head. 'I'm out of the loop on this one,' she admitted, as he knocked on Hilton's door and walked in.

Inside, Hilton was pacing up and down by the windows.

'You guys have worked out some options?' he demanded, the moment Lebowitz appeared.

The other nodded. 'Dusted down the crisis strategy we worked out years ago for just this kind of eventuality. We're pretty much boxed into reactive mode.'

'Reactive? Shouldn't we be out there doing something?'

Lebowitz regarded his boss's agitation with concern. He'd never seen Hilton so perturbed.

'Very simply, we have two options in dealing with the media,' he began to explain, deliberately calm. 'The first is to hunker down in reactive mode – which isn't to say we do nothing, but we keep all the action under the surface. We prepare for a revelation of the full facts and have all our ammunition prepared and targeted in case we need it. The second option is to go proactive. Get the news out ourselves on the basis that we *theoretically* have more spin control.' He held Hilton's gaze steadily. 'Now, we can go that route, sure, but I would very, very strongly advise against it. Too high risk,' he said, shrugging. 'What if it turns out One Commando don't have the full story?'

'They've got enough,' countered Hilton, 'they could work out the rest.'

'Maybe. Maybe not. I know it's tenuous, but what if they don't know the significance of the discovery themselves?'

'Leo, please. Remember who we're dealing with.'

'Or what if', Lebowitz persisted, 'Interpol close down One Commando before they've had a chance to get the story out.'

Again, Hilton was shaking his head. 'Cloud cuckoo land.'

'The point being that once we've gone out with the story, we can't reel it back in.' He paused, looking over to where Hilton was staring out of the window, 'There's a terrible finality to it. We can't unsay what's been said. Ever. And the benefit of getting this particular story out ourselves is marginal to say the least. The basic facts are sensational enough before journalists even get—'

'Do we have to put out . . . the whole story?'

Lebowitz was shaking his head. 'It's the whole story or it's nothing. We can't go out with a fudge. That would be courting disaster.'

'Surely there must be a sympathy card?'

'Believe me, Hilton, if the need arises we've got the full sympathy *pack* to play, but the only way it'll work is if the other side put out the story first.'

'The other side.' Hilton was shaking his head. 'If . . .' then shrugging, 'when One Commando put the story out, just how bad d'you think the damage will be?'

Lebowitz nodded. 'I've put just that question into research this morning. The panel results so far aren't looking good. In fact, they're terrible. We're getting a strong sense of disappointment about the lack of trust . . .'

Hilton was following him intensely, Lebowitz's words seeming to affect him viscerally.

'What that research doesn't take into account—' he started.

'I know,' Lebowitz nodded, 'it's different when it's for real. But even allowing for all that,' he sighed heavily, 'it's the very worst piece of news that could come out prior to a record launch. There wouldn't be anything of a record launch left.'

Lebowitz's words were heavy with significance; it was as though with every word he spoke, Hilton was diminished. Folding his arms against the back of a sofa, Hilton leaned down to rest his head against it.

'Can't you give me anything, Leo?'

Lebowitz knew he must not allow Hilton any illusions.

'All the feedback I'm getting is that if the full story comes to light,' he hesitated only slightly, 'it's curtains for Isis, and for Jordan Hampshire,' he exhaled heavily, 'over before it began.'

19

Vinnie wasn't sure this was the right bloke, to begin with. They'd agreed to meet outside the open-air theatre in Regent's Park at one-fifteen p.m. Hurrying along a path, he spotted the figure sitting on the bench, reading that day's copy of the *Financial Times*, as he'd said he would be. Right place, right time, thought Vinnie, but something about the man he was due to meet struck him as odd. Wearing chichi sunglasses and a designer suit under an elegant Burberry, he wasn't anything like Alexander Heindl. Vinnie had been imagining someone a lot bigger and tougher and more military in appearance. This guy looked like a yuppie.

As he approached him, his footsteps were less certain. The other man looked up.

'Vinnie Dobson?'

'That's right.' Vinnie paused, hesitant.

Then the other man was getting up from the park bench. 'Let's take a walk. Hedges have ears.'

He was only half-joking, thought Vinnie, glancing at the thick bushes behind him. There was something very earnest about this guy. Intense.

'I've heard a lot about you,' Jasper Jones said now as they made their way among the lunch-time strollers in Regent's Park.

'From Alexander Heindl?'

Jones paused a moment before replying, 'Yes. From Alexander. He tells me you've been very helpful.'

Vinnie had no idea where this was leading. He didn't know why this bloke wanted to meet him and was irked at being ordered across town on some mystery mission. No sooner had Heindl told him about this guy, than the man had phoned himself to set up the meeting.

'So you're about to go to America?'

'So Alexander keeps saying.'

His irritation didn't escape Jones. They walked on a few more yards before he asked, 'Looking forward to it?'

Vinnie thought about Mark making all that money – a multi-millionaire overnight. Plus he was screwing Isis into the bargain. The prick thought he'd got away with it. Like he could just turn his back, cut Vinnie out of the deal and everything would be hunky dory.

'Oh, yeah,' Vinnie turned to Jones, 'very much.'

The other smiled. 'Good,' he murmured. 'Good.' Then, pausing, he turned to face Vinnie. 'Tell me, what are you looking forward to most of all?'

Vinnie shook his head. 'Getting that prick Watson.'

'That's Jordan Hampshire's real name is it?'

'Yeah.'

'And you used to be his manager?'

'Damned right I was.'

'What have you got against him?'

'Did the dirty on me, didn't he? I was his manager for years, right? Worked hard to get him known on the local circuit. Then along comes GCM and their recording deal with Isis and that's it. Kaput.'

'But you can't blame him for accepting a deal like that.'

'I can blame him for cutting me out of it.'

'You mean, you didn't get—'

'Not a bloody thing,' Vinnie snorted. 'They cut me out completely.'

'How much do you think you should have been paid?'

'Three hundred and fifty grand, maybe more.'

Jones raised his eyebrows. 'That's a lot of money.'

'You're not joking, mate.'

'Surely,' he regarded Vinnie intently, 'you should be taking legal action.'

'Get real!' snorted Vinnie. 'What chance do I have against GCM?'

'There's legal aid available.'

Vinnie was shaking his head vigorously. Whose side was this bloke on anyway? 'Too complicated for that.'

'But surely a contract is a contract. If Jordan Hampshire broke the terms—'

'That's the whole point. We didn't have a contract, did we?' whined Vinnie. It was the first time he'd admitted it to anybody, but it didn't matter so much telling this bloke who he'd never even met before.

'You managed his business affairs, but you didn't have a contract?' the other was incredulous.

'Not written down or anything. What we had was a gentleman's agreement. An understanding.'

'Has he offered to pay you—'

'Nothing.'

'No form of . . . compensation?'

'Nothing!' Vinnie repeated, louder. He could feel the

anger building up in him. The violent, all-consuming hatred which came to him every time he thought about Mark Watson. And something in this bloke's manner gave him the feeling that the other wanted to know just how mad he was right now with his famous former client.

Jones regarded Dobson's visibly rising anger with satisfaction. His face was colouring and fury coming into his eyes. All he needed was a gentle push.

'Tell me,' he asked Dobson in a sympathetic tone, 'how do you feel about Jordan Hampshire right now?'

'How am I supposed to feel?' Vinnie exploded. 'After all he's done to me I hate the prick! He's stabbed me in the back. Stolen my money. He's turned my life into a fucking nightmare!'

Jones nodded encouragingly. 'And seeing that he hasn't paid you money you feel is rightfully yours . . . ?'

'He's going to pay for it all right,' Vinnie menaced. 'I'm going over to LA and One Commando will be right behind me. They'll get that son of a bitch and by the time they're finished with him and Isis they'll both wish they'd never even heard of GCM!'

'What are you planning to do to them?'

'You'll have to ask Alexander Heindl that, but you know what happened to that French bloke?' He smirked. 'That was just the warm-up.'

Less than fifteen minutes later, Jones left Regent's Park alone, heading in the direction of Marylebone Road, while Vinnie Dobson made towards Baker Street. Slipping his hand in the pocket of his Burberry, Jones felt the video recorder stashed in his pocket and turned it off, before removing the cord that led from the back of his overcoat to the camera concealed behind his glasses. A most productive session, he thought, strolling the short distance to the main road, and waiting for a cab heading east. Dobson had been an easy turn. Larson had primed him well for the meeting and he hadn't held back. It was all there: the motivation, the planning, but most of all the emotion, turbulent, vindictive, in your face – and nothing whatever to do with the cause of animal liberation.

Beverly Hills

Mark spent most of the car trip back to Beverly Hills in silence. Eyes closed and expression weary, he reflected that his visit to Malibu had been a complete disaster. He felt bad, very bad, about how Isis had caught him in her private sitting room, going through her personal library. But he felt completely justified in trying to seek her out. And just as he owed her an apology for intruding into her privacy, she still owed him an explanation about exactly what One Commando had on her. But after what had just happened, he reckoned his chances of getting it weren't too good.

The moment he'd got in the car, he'd written down the name of that doctor so he wouldn't forget it: Dr Robert Weiner, Salmacis Hospital. He'd also noted the names of some of the book titles while he still remembered them. And the phrases from her mother's letter: *I know I have failed you . . . tried to keep your father from you . . . recover from surgery.*

It all seemed to point in only one direction: Isis had been abused as a child. The man who, more than any other, was responsible for her protection, had instead betrayed both instinct and his daughter's trust, his treatment of her so savage that she'd required hospitalisation. Hardly surprising, Mark supposed, that Isis was so much on edge, her emotions running so close to the surface. It was hard even to imagine her feelings.

The more he thought about it, the more his discovery seemed to explain things. Like the moments of closeness they'd shared, first at the restaurant, then later at Unum studios, moments when he'd felt the overwhelming, intuitive force of mutual attraction – only to be rebuffed with a casualness that denied the slightest hint of involvement. Isis had conveniently hidden behind the on-camera, off-camera explanation. But it seemed to Mark that the real reason was far more complex and had to do with Isis's feelings about intimacy, which took her far back into her past.

What he couldn't understand, right now, was her paranoid fear of having her past revealed. Of course it would be traumatic to have the whole world find out about the part of her life that made her most vulnerable. But it wasn't as though she was the perpetrator of some terrible crime. She was the victim, for God's sake! Wouldn't the public response be a wave of sympathy and support. Surely it wouldn't mean the end of her career!

Mark just couldn't work it out. Try as he might, he could think of no explanation for her desperate desire for concealment. Unless, of course, she was trying to protect her father. But who was her father, and what kind of power did he have that both Isis and GCM were so determined that the truth should never come to light?

Deep in thought, Mark paid no attention to their progress from Malibu back home. Though in the front, Denzil was clearly in a conversational mood. Oblivious of Mark's discovery earlier in the day, not to mention events at Isis's home, he was irrepressibly upbeat.

'So, you must be feeling safer now with the endorsement

deal behind you?' he asked, the moment Mark opened his eyes and glanced out of the window.

'I guess.'

'Those punks, they have to be pretty damned crazy, unhinged, to do what they did to that French guy!'

Mark nodded. He wasn't exactly in any mood to be reminded of One Commando's exploits.

'What I don't get,' Denzil chattered on, oblivious to his expression, 'is why those guys think Berkeley Square do things to animals. No one else does, do they?'

'No,' agreed Mark, 'they don't.'

'The whole world's gone looking at this factory down in Spain, and they ain't found nothing.'

Mark thought about the AFL fliers he'd had scattered across the coffee table earlier in the day. The gruesome photographs of the rabbits and the chimpanzees. The photo of the laboratory gate with the Berkeley Square sign outside it – the laboratory that Berkeley Square denied had anything to do with them.

Turning into his street, the Lincoln cruised up the winding tarmac towards the top of the hill. As they neared the top, Mark couldn't help noticing that, during the course of just a few hours, the neighbouring property across the road had changed yet again. Gone was the mediaeval castle look, and instead it had been transformed to a Southern horse stud. White palisades were driven into the ground, giving an impression of ageless permanence, and over the recently erected traditional pole gates hung the authentic-looking estate sign 'Bluegrass Creek'. Viewed in isolation, it looked exactly as though it had been transported here directly from Kentucky.

'Changed again,' Mark nodded across the road.

'Amazing what a piece of fence and a sign can do,' agreed Denzil. 'Creates this whole idea . . .'

He carried on chattily as he brought the car to a pause, waiting for the electric gates to open. But Mark wasn't listening. Instead he paused, transfixed by what Denzil had just said: *Amazing what a piece of fence and a sign can do.*

Suddenly it struck him: what if there *was* a lab near Madrid, testing on animals? And what if someone had put up the Berkeley Square sign outside? Maybe One Commando had set the whole thing up to *look* like a Berkeley Square facility. Maybe the sign shot they'd used on their video wasn't anywhere near Madrid. But then Bengt Larson and his cohorts were smart operators. Surely they would have realised they'd never convince anyone? And why continue to go for Berkeley Square, when they'd failed to convince anyone about their torture claims?

As soon as he was back in the house he hurried to the study where he switched on the computer. The moment Eudora Light was open, he was tapping out an urgent letter to Dr Andrew Craig, whose e-mail address he'd found in one of the Berkeley Square brochures. Explaining who he was, Mark hurriedly related the new idea he'd just had, before scanning in the photo of the 'Berkeley Square laboratory' from one of the AFL leaflets he'd brought back with him from London. Was there anything that identified the building in the photo as a place near Berkeley Square's real Madrid laboratories, he wanted to know? Were there any distinguishing features suggesting where this plant, if it existed, really was to be found?

Checking to make sure the e-mail went through, Mark stared at the screen as he worked through the implications. It seemed a long shot, but what, he began to wonder, if One Commando were themselves the victims of deception?

Las Vegas
Sunday, 3 October

The gym of the Golden Millennium Hotel was large, anonymous and well-equipped. Bengt Larson had been on the treadmill for the last twenty minutes, the speed gear shifted to maximum. When he ran he tried to clear his mind of everything but running. Focus, he always ordered himself, whenever he found his mind caught up in thoughts. Keep your focus!

Since last Tuesday it had been harder than usual to retain a steel mental discipline. He'd been living for an item on TV or radio news. A piece in the papers perhaps. But the forty-eight-hour deadline he'd given Isis had come and gone – and still no statement on Berkeley Square. Despite all the evidence, the leaflets and the video, a copy of which had been sent direct to GCM. Despite the photos which demonstrated, beyond any shadow of doubt, the systematic abuses of Berkeley Square. In the end he'd had no choice. He'd had to come to America, to play out the final act.

If his detailed planning had been meticulous before, this time round it was even more rigorous – it had to be. His carefully chosen team of just three others were not only One Commando veterans who could be trusted and who were in peak physical condition. Each of them also had a specialist expertise. De Clerque from Amsterdam was the explosives guru. Guittard from Marseilles knew everything there was to know about security systems. And Harris, in Washington State, was highly trained in martial arts and had the kind of underground network in the US required for procurement. Not to forget their special guest.

As always, Larson had assembled as much detail about the operation as possible, though several important factors were still unknowns. This operation, he'd never been in any doubt, would be the most challenging since One Commando had begun. It was the most high risk, and the potential for things to go wrong was greater than on any mission he'd organised in his life. But unlike any other operation before, the potential impact of this one was huge. So huge, in fact, it went way beyond his imagination.

20

Who was Isis's father? Why was she trying to protect him?
Mark had been working on the questions since late last week.
And he reckoned he knew a way to get them answered. Back
home in London on the OmniCell helpdesk, he'd had a lot
to do with the debt collection department. Businessmen and
private individuals who ratcheted up huge loan accounts or
overdrafts which they couldn't repay, were sometimes
tempted to 'disappear', change their names, leave the country, go underground. It was the debt collection department's
job to track them down. Speaking to the blokes in the department, Mark had got to know the ways they traced people,
using paper trails, computer systems, old-fashioned sleuth
work on the telephone. The more difficult jobs, he knew,
the company had subcontracted to tracing agencies. Those
agencies were international. They were able to track down
debtors who lived in the most remote corners of the world,
sometimes years after they'd left Britain. If he could get a
tracing agency on to the job of tracking down Isis's father,
he reckoned he'd soon find out why his daughter and GCM

were so desperate to protect him. He speculated a bit himself. What if her father turned out to be a politician, or some big business tycoon? Then he thought of the Italian name; it would be scarier, much scarier, he supposed, if he turned out to be some figure from the Mafia underworld.

He'd had to wait out the weekend before getting hold of his mate in OmniCell's debt collecting department. To his intense frustration, it was still more time before he had the name and telephone number of the tracing agency OmniCell used in Florida.

In the meantime, he'd had two e-mails from Dr Andrew Craig at Berkeley Square's facility in Madrid. In the first one, Craig had thanked him for his 'interesting idea', saying he'd circulated to all staff the photo from the AFL leaflet which One Commando claimed was Berkeley Square's. Should anyone be able to identify the building, he assured Mark, he'd let him know. Craig's second e-mail, sent on Monday morning, consisted of just two lines; a secretary in R & D thought she knew the building; it was opposite where her husband worked. Craig had sent her out with a digital camera.

Then there were the recordings of Vinnie's endless telephone calls. Painstakingly sifting through them all each morning, Mark had come across only one that alerted his suspicions. An incoming call from someone who didn't give his name, but only said that Alexander Heindl had said they should meet. They'd made an arrangement to get together in Regent's Park. Mark had never heard Vinnie mention this Heindl bloke before and it all seemed very mysterious. But maybe it was just Vinnie wheeler-dealering. Maybe it had nothing to do with Isis and him.

Mulling over his different lines of enquiry, Mark also kept wondering about Dr Weiner of the Salmacis Hospital. Might he be worth putting in a call to, he mused, if only to confirm his area of medical expertise? Mark supposed he'd find Salmacis somewhere in Miami, where Isis had grown up, and he wasn't wrong. Operator enquiries had soon given him the number of the hospital.

'Does Dr Weiner work there?' he asked, sitting behind the desk of his study. It must be many years, he realised, since the doctor had treated Isis.

'Dr Weiner sometimes consults at this hospital, but he has his own practice,' the receptionist told him.

'Do you have the telephone number there?'

'Please hold, sir.'

A short while later he was dialling a different number. As it rang, he glanced at his watch. He didn't know exactly how many hours Miami was ahead of LA, but it was now nearly three, so he guessed it must be early evening over there. He doubted very much if he'd catch Dr Weiner in. He'd probably have to call back or leave a message.

'Weiner,' replied a brisk voice at the other end, almost immediately.

'Oh,' Mark was taken aback, 'hello . . . Dr Weiner.'

'Yes?'

He hadn't expected to be speaking to him, not directly or so soon. Now that he was, he realised he hadn't worked out what to say to him. 'Actually, I'm phoning about a friend.'

'Ah.' Robert Weiner's tone changed in an instant into counselling mode. 'Does this . . . friend want to see me professionally?'

'You see, I need to find out what you do first, I mean, your area—'

'I know what you mean,' the other responded smoothly, well used to dealing with nervous patients. In a few jargon-free sentences, he explained before asking, 'Now, was it something along those lines?'

At the other end, Mark sat for a few moments, shocked to the core. He'd had his suspicions, from the titles of the books in Isis's private library. But hearing Dr Weiner tell him out loud, listening to him use those words with the fluent ease of practice made him realise just how very little he really understood.

Putting down the receiver Mark took a great sob of air before burying his face in his hands. It was a long time before he emerged from the study.

Las Vegas

Vinnie fiddled with the worry beads in the pocket of his leather jacket as he strode through the lobby of the Lucky Nugget Hotel. It was filled with fruit-machines. Glancing about at the tacky surroundings, he viewed with disdain all the fat Americans perched on stools, feeding quarters into the machines. Bunch of dumb fucks, he thought. Didn't they know you could never win against a one-armed bandit? He, meantime, had seen what he was looking for. Flashing red and gold signs had arrows pointing in the direction of the gaming salon – a vast, dimly lit expanse of tables, where people were playing roulette and poker and blackjack. The cool, air-conditioned interior was heavy with cigar smoke interlaced with ribbons of perfume. Cocktail glasses clinked from the nearby bar. There was money here – the place was filthy with it. And by the time he'd finished, a whole wedge of it was going to end up in his back pocket, of that he was certain. He knew a system. One of the regulars down at the Lamb had shown it to him. Apparently, the bloke who'd invented it had bust so many casinos, he was banned from all the main gambling houses in Monte Carlo. Plus there was the fact that Vinnie was feeling lucky. Very lucky. The kind of feeling that made him believe that things had finally started turning his way.

Heindl had called him about the trip late the week before.

'We need you to fly out in twenty-four hours. Do the recce,' he'd said.

At the other end of the phone, Vinnie had decided to try out the plan he'd been working on.

'Twenty-four hours.' His tone was sharp. 'You gotta be joking, mate.'

Heindl had assured him this was no joke. And he was on standby.

'But I can't just . . . take off at such short notice,' he'd blustered.

'Why not?' Heindl had asked.

'Something's come up – a deal. I need to be here. If I don't I could lose big money.'

At the other end Larson's expression hardened. So that was the game. He should have guessed.

'Like how much?' he asked Vinnie.

'Five grand.'

'That is a lot of money.'

'Exactly my point.' Vinnie admired his own negotiating position.

Then Heindl was saying calmly, 'I'll have five thousand pounds in cash for you when you check in at Heathrow airport tomorrow night.'

Hanging up, Vinnie had punched a fist into the air with a yell of triumph. Yes! Five big grand in less than five minutes. Plus the satisfaction of knowing Mark Watson was about to see his ass – bigtime. He was back on a roll!

True to his word, Heindl had left five grand in an envelope together with his ticket, which he collected from an American Airlines desk at Heathrow. Vinnie had been surprised to find he wasn't flying direct to Los Angeles. His ticket took him to New York instead, where he'd been instructed to take a cab into the city, then a train to Boston, before catching another flight west.

When he'd finally arrived in Las Vegas, it had been nothing like he'd imagined. As he'd been driven into town from the airport, the taxi driver had taken him past all the famous hotels and gambling palaces, all emblazoned with flashing signs and spectacular special effects, from erupting volcanoes to cascading waterfalls. This place was dedicated solely to twenty-four-hour entertainment, mostly of the gaming variety – Vinnie reckoned he could get used to it. He was blown over by his hotel room – massive, deep-pile carpet and with two king-size beds all to himself. Heindl had left him a note. He was to keep a low profile until he appeared down in the lobby next morning at nine sharp.

Now as he swaggered across the casino, he headed for the money exchange to cash in some of his freshly minted cash for a pile of roulette chips. 'Make it a thousand dollars,' he bragged to the dark-suited woman behind the desk, who shoved a pile of counters in his direction. Then he was glancing round for a table to play at, before checking out one with a few spaces free. Double or quit, that was the game he'd learned. Keep it simple and get out when you're ahead.

He'd no sooner sat down than one of the cocktail waitresses in a black, crotch-length skirt and leather tassel top was offering him a glass of champagne. He hadn't realised it was free. Ooh, Mama, he could get used to this, he reckoned, taking a slug. After he'd made his pile, he might cruise the bar. Everyone knew American women just loved an English accent. The croupier, an ageing Oriental with a gold tooth and glittering rhinestone waistcoat, was spinning the wheel.

'Place bets!' he ordered in a shrill voice Vinnie didn't

much like the sound of. Well, fuck him, thought Vinnie, fuck them all. He shunted fifty bucks on to red. Start as you mean to continue, that was his line, he reckoned, downing another mouthful of champagne. He was in with the big time boys now, and nothing could stop him. Vinnie Dobson was invincible.

Pacific Palisades

Hilton Gallo was sitting at his bedroom escritoire, putting the finishing touches to a GCM Tokyo takeover proposal, when the telephone rang. Varley announced himself.

'There's been a development you should know about.'

'What's that?'

'In the past twenty-four hours, three forged EU passports have been used at different entry points into the US. The French think all three documents were commissioned by Larson.'

'How come?'

'For the past three months they've been monitoring the activities of Barend Rousseau, master forger in Paris. Specialises in providing fake ID. Last week he prepared forged EU passports for three men. The gendarmerie believe they were collected by Larson.'

'When you say "believe"?'

'They have CCTV bugs in Rousseau's offices. Picture quality isn't great, but the image of last week's visitor is an eighty per cent match to Larson.'

Hilton considered this for a moment before asking, 'If the passports were fake, why weren't the terrorists arrested?'

'The fake passport numbers were only loaded on to the computer *after* the men were inside the country.' Varley was clearly embarrassed. 'But by then . . .'

'D'you know where they're heading?' he could hardly bear to hear the answer.

'Got a trace on one of them. He had a connecting flight to Denver almost immediately.'

'Denver?'

'Unlikely that was his final destination.'

'He's heading west,' observed Hilton, 'which means the other two are headed this way too.'

Varley didn't argue.

'You have some way of tracking them?'

'No, sir. I think it's safe to assume they will all have booked onward flights in different names. The only reason we got the one in DC was because we caught him on airport cameras. He was late for his onward flight and was in such a hurry it made him easy to follow.'

'Well, what if—?'

'Viewing tapes from Denver?' Varley pre-empted his next question. 'That would be an overwhelming task.'

There was a long pause before Hilton said, 'So all we know is that the three of them, who *might* be members of One Commando, *might* be heading to Denver?'

'I know it's tentative, but in the circumstances . . .'

Hilton walked across the white carpet of his bedroom to where his window looked out into the darkness of the ocean. Only a few distant lights signalled the presence of ships in the night. Hilton thought quickly.

'Have you spoken to Isis?' he asked Varley.

'Not yet.'

'I don't think you should. It would be better coming from me.'

The police officer was hesitant.

'Her psychological state right now is very fragile,' continued Hilton. 'My concern is that if this news isn't pitched a particular way, it could push her over the edge.'

'Right.' Varley had read all the newspaper stories about Isis, the same as everybody else. He knew she lived in Lalaland, and like other big-name stars was to be treated with extreme caution. The last thing in the world he needed was to wake up to the headlines that she'd been admitted to some clinic with a nervous breakdown because he'd passed on the latest inconclusive Interpol report.

'In that case, I'll leave it to you.'

'Good,' nodded Hilton, 'and you'll let me know as soon as you have more news?'

'You can be sure of it.'

Hilton replaced the telephone receiver, but didn't go back to his writing desk, pausing instead, deep in thought. In the game of information management, timing was everything – and right now he didn't have time on his side. It would be another twelve hours before Unum Records gave *Nile* the final sign-off, and although all the noises coming out of Sam Bach's office were positive, the show wasn't over until Ariel Alhadeff had given the record the official thumbs up. He couldn't risk Isis high-tailing it out of town – if she did, and was unable to fulfil any final changes Unum demanded, then everything they'd both worked to achieve in the past six months would be put at risk.

He hadn't told her about the non-existence of the MI5 agent because he hadn't wanted to take away her hope. Now the ethics of disclosure loomed in his mind yet again. He'd always regarded himself as a straight-shooter. In a town in which every truth was relative, he'd made every effort to be punctilious in his client relations. But he pondered on Varley's latest news; Isis was anxious enough already, he reflected, without getting more alarming calls with information she couldn't do anything about. How was she supposed to react? Leave Los Angeles every time people with fake passports came into the country? And even if she did take off to some high-security bolthole, how much safer would she really be anywhere else, compared to her Malibu fortress?

All the same, he couldn't pretend the information didn't add yet a further disturbing dimension to the blackmail crisis – one he didn't much care to think about. If he could just get over tomorrow's Unum meeting, he decided, then he'd pay her a personal visit and get everything out in the open.

It was only a few hours away, after all.

Beverly Hills

Mark sat in the upstairs bar of his Beverly Hills mansion. Perched on one of the leather-padded bar stools, he flicked restlessly through the fifty-eight channels of his TV set while sipping on a vodka. After his short exchange with Dr Weiner, he didn't know what to think. As soon as he'd recovered from the initial shock of confirmation, he'd picked up the phone again and had started to dial Isis's number before reconsidering the whole idea. He wasn't ready yet, he decided. What exactly was he going to say to her? He needed to get his head round things first. He needed a drink.

That had been a couple of hours earlier and he'd been unable to focus on anything since. The more he thought about it, the stranger it seemed, but time and time again his thoughts kept coming back to the same point: why? He found it impossible to make sense of. His own family background and experiences were so far removed he just couldn't understand it. And he reckoned there was no way he was ever going to unless she explained it to him – and in her current frame of mind he couldn't see her doing that.

He wondered how he'd be next time they met. Tomorrow morning they had the meeting down at Unum to listen to the final mix of *Nile*. He'd been told it was an important meeting. Leo Lebowitz had phoned to advise him that the top Unum brass would be there and recommended he go 'in character', wearing some of the garments already picked out for the Jordan Hampshire wardrobe. He wondered how he'd react when he saw Isis. He played through their last scene in his mind. He'd have to carry on as though nothing had happened, at least while all the others were about. But would there be time alone with her afterwards? And what should he say? He wanted it out in the open between the two of them. But getting to that point was just too difficult and right now the very thought of it overwhelmed him. Pouring himself another drink, he walked over to one of the armchairs and dropped into it. *Seinfeld* was on TV and waves of studio laughter only confirmed his exhaustion.

When the telephone rang it took him a while to get to it. The secretary of Dr Andrew Craig was putting her boss through.

'I thought you'd be interested to know,' the brisk brogue of Craig's voice also conveyed excitement, 'the secretary I referred to in my e-mail visited the facility. And I've just been there myself – less than ten minutes away. It *is* the same place as in the AFL flier.'

Mark raised a hand to his forehead. 'And the animal testing?' he asked wearily.

'Nothing to identify the site from outside,' reported Craig, 'but the owner of the plant next door says it belongs to Voisier Laboratories.' His tone was acerbic.

'You know Voisier?'

'Oh, aye,' confirmed Craig. 'Monsieur Voisier is well known in the industry for his . . . methods. Notorious, one might say.'

Tuesday, 5 October

Isis could tell something was different from the moment she saw him. And it wasn't just the Jordan Hampshire clothes which he'd doubtless been ordered to wear by GCM. The difference had more to do with the way he was hardly meeting her eyes. Was it guilt, she wondered – or resentment? Since she'd ordered him out of her house last Wednesday, her own feelings had been running high. More than anything though she'd felt anxiety knotting her stomach as she worried about what he might have seen.

She'd been walking down the corridor as he'd been about to return the Isis photo album to the shelf and caught sight of the second, concealed row of books. As though viewing it all in slow motion she had seen him reach behind for the book that Robert had given her, flick it open, and then her mother's letter had fallen to the floor.

It had all happened in a few instants. Not enough time for Mark to have read any of the text. But had he realised the significance of the second row of books? Had it got him wondering? The possibility of it was added to her already deep concerns about blackmail and the more she thought about it, the more agitated she became. It seemed to her that she was finally about to lose control of her secret. After years of keeping the lid on, of relentless and rigorous management by GCM, she now had the deep-down sense that everything in her past was about to burst into view.

With Holly back from a visit to her father's though, there had been no question of Isis revealing any of her true feelings – she didn't have the luxury of being able to fall apart. Instead she'd just had to pretend, as she was pretending now in this roomful of suits. All the Unum big guns were here from Ariel Alhadeff downwards, not to mention the GCM team – Hilton, Leo, Andy Murdoch and even Blake Horowitz which was unusual for a final-mix session. They'd all had copies of the final-mix since the weekend, so the purpose of today's meeting was as much to finalise launch plans as to showcase the music.

As Sam Bach skipped selectively through the tracks, highlighting different aspects of the CD and emphasising its inbuilt market appeal, there were appreciative nods from around the table towards where she was sitting with Mark at one end. The two of them had, of course, heard this stuff so many, many times over the past few weeks that they were way past the point of being objective. The initial excitement they'd felt about the music itself had long since been replaced by concerns about phrasing, acquainted as they were with every nuance of melody, every syllable of the lyrics. All the same, seeing the effect the music had on the gathered suits from Unum and GCM was encouraging. Isis thought back to her first pre-release meeting just before the album *Isis* had come out and remembered how, after weeks of intensive work, it had felt, finally, that everything was coming together.

Glancing briefly at where Mark was concentrating on some remark by Ariel Alhadeff, she felt a pang of remorse. If it hadn't been for the dark cloud hanging over them right now, she thought, Mark would be feeling that same excitement. If it wasn't for all the trauma that arose from her past he would also have been feeling the same sense of achievement, anticipation, even mild euphoria that she'd felt when she'd first sat in on a meeting like this. It was impossible to guess what he really was thinking at this moment. He had deliberately withdrawn into his own world. If only they could return to the carefree intimacy they'd shared at the recording studio.

When the meeting ended, all the Unum suits dispersed in a rapid flurry of handshakes and congratulations. Walking down the corridor to the secure parking facility behind the Unum building, Isis asked Hilton if there'd been any news from the police. He glanced down at the floor, shaking his head. Nothing substantive, he told her, but, delivering a meaningful gaze, said he'd be in touch with her later in the day.

During this time Mark was walking behind them, appearing to be absorbed in the cover of the *Nile* CD. Outside in the parking lot they donned sunglasses, Hilton and Lebowitz making their way towards a stretch limousine, Isis heading across towards where Frank was standing beside the open door of her Range Rover. Mark's limo was parked near hers, Denzil behind the wheel. But they were still some distance away when he said, 'We need to talk.'

She glanced over at him. His voice was tight, almost choked. It was hard to tell what emotions were going on behind those dark lenses. Her footsteps slowed. 'You hardly said anything back there. What's the matter?'

'It's, uh, it's . . . important.' How was he to put this? Ever since he'd stirred from his armchair, early this morning, he'd been wondering what words to use. He still hadn't come up with any ideas by the time he had to leave for the meeting. Maybe there was no nice way of saying what he so desperately needed to say. As the two of them crossed the tarmac, the sun blazing down on them, he battled for expression, before finally blurting out, 'I know what they've found out about you. Your . . . past, I mean.'

Isis halted. Her instant reaction was one of disbelief. How could he know? Turning to him, she found herself replying, 'That's impossible!' She was shaking her head determinedly.

'No, it's not.'

'You *can't* know. Hilton and Lebowitz wouldn't tell anyone – not in a thousand years.'

'It wasn't Hilton or Lebowitz who told me.'

'Then who did?'

Denial was one thing he hadn't expected. He realised warily he was going to have to get into the detail he'd most hoped to avoid.

'Well . . . no one exactly. I kind of worked it out for myself.'

'Oh, yeah,' she allowed herself a grim smile, 'and what conclusion did you come up with?'

'I spoke to Dr Weiner.'

Isis's expression suddenly froze. As she fixed on Mark from behind her sunglasses, her face rapidly darkened.

'You got his name from the book?' Her anger was quickly building. This was even worse than she'd feared.

Mark stepped back. 'You weren't going to tell me, were you?' he tried, defensively.

'So you snooped?'

'You didn't give me much choice—'

'You snooped!'

'I didn't want to, but—'

'Do you realise you've just put my entire professional career on the line?' In fury, Isis was vehement. Terrifying. 'Your spying could destroy everything I've worked for my entire life. And blow away your chance of a career with it!'

'But I haven't spoken to anyone!' he protested.

'So it was all telepathy?'

'Not even Weiner knows I found out about you.'

'You're talking in riddles, Mark.' She stepped closer, prodding him in the chest with her index finger. Although she'd lowered her voice he was in no doubt about the ferocity of her anger. 'You'd better tell me how you *did* find out.'

'Okay,' he held his hands up, 'I did get his name from the book. I saw the other books you had there. I put two and two together. I phoned to ask him about what sort of work he does—'

'I trusted you,' Isis managed between clenched teeth, 'and this is how you reward my trust.'

'That's why we need to talk!' He was desperate.

'There's nothing left to talk about.'

'But there's so much other stuff—'

'Why don't you keep on snooping then? See what else you dredge up!' She about-turned and stormed away from him.

Mark hurried after her. 'Isis, please!' he was begging her, 'be reasonable!'

Shaking her head, sunglasses flashing in the midday sun, it was impossible to get through to her. He'd expected her to get upset – but he'd hoped for a very different outcome. He'd wanted them to talk about it, for Isis to realise there was no point in blocking him out any longer. Most of all, he'd wanted her to tell him why. Why had she done it? What had been such an irresistible compulsion eighteen years before? He wanted to understand this woman who so intrigued him. But she was already stepping into the back seat of her Range Rover, with Frank slamming the door behind her. She wasn't looking at him as the car pulled away with a screech.

21

In the Range Rover, Isis fought to keep back the tears until they'd left the Unum lot. The desperate fury of her reaction to Mark concealed an even greater turmoil of anguish beneath. Already pushed to the brink by One Commando and their blackmail demand, now came the confirmation that Mark knew her secret too!

When she'd arrived in Los Angeles fourteen years ago, she'd had only one simple wish; to put the past behind her. But it seemed to her now that everything she'd done since getting here had been building to this moment. It was as though some perverse power beyond had conspired to return her to that time in her life she most wanted to forget, forcing her to confront what she so desperately wished to leave behind.

She had stashed Gabby's magazine article in her locker. During breaks in class and after school she would return to the locker again and again to read the article, especially all the stuff about the other girls who'd been through the same ordeal as she had. Every time she read it, she felt the same heady mixture of emotions: surging, liberating relief at the discovery that she wasn't the only one in the world suffering this torment; deep fascination at the description of how doctors and psychologists had helped others like her to recover. But there was a terrible fear, too; she knew that once she'd decided to do something about it, there could be no turning back. And at the age of fifteen, despite all the suffering, it was hard, very hard, to turn your back on everything you knew.

What really prompted her to make the call was Gabby's funeral. Five days after the accident it was held at St Columbus's and everyone was there from school, from church, from the Italian community. Because she and Gabby had been such good friends, the Carboni family sat near the front. Isis could see Gabby's sisters and parents and grandparents sobbing during the Mass, which set her off too. She stood there, throughout the service, tears streaming down her cheeks, and there was nothing she could do to stop it. The worst was when the headmaster stood at the front of the church and spoke about how everyone felt about Gabby at school. He told the mourners that Gabby had been more than simply a conscientious student and athlete; what had made her exceptional was that she'd gone out of her way to help others. He talked about some of the things Gabby had done, things that Isis and most of the other kids had no idea about. In those few short minutes during the funeral the whole congregation came to realise just how special Gabby had been. And after the headmaster had finished speaking, Isis made a promise to herself; she was going to make the telephone call to the people mentioned in the article. She was going to do it, not just for her own sake, but because she felt she owed it to Gabby as well. Gabby had pointed her in that direction, and the fact that she'd died so soon afterwards seemed, to Isis, like a kind of omen. A sign that she should do something.

The following day at lunch-time, instead of sitting under the trees in the courtyard waiting for the two o'clock bell to summon her back to class, she finished her sandwich, went to her locker, wrote down the telephone number in Biro on the back of her hand, took a few coins and slipped out of the school gates. There was a telephone box a few hundred yards down the road and it was working – she knew, because she'd tested it on the way into school this morning. Fortunately it was empty when she arrived. Heart pounding in her chest, she felt shaky as she picked up the receiver and began dialling. This was the most daring, the scariest thing she'd ever done in her life. And how was she going to explain herself? She could hardly find the words.

She was a little breathless when a woman answered the helpline. And relieved to be asked only where she was calling from. This was a national helpline, explained the woman, and she put Isis's call through to someone in her local area. There was a bit of a wait as she was transferred, then another ringing tone. A male voice came on the line. Isis would have preferred to speak to a woman. In fact she was thinking of hanging up and phoning back some other time. But the man sounded very gentle. And he didn't ask her any questions except whether she could arrange to come into an information centre in downtown Miami. He didn't even start to talk about her problem. He told Isis when advisers would be at the centre and said he hoped they'd see her there. And that was it. No pressure. No need for her life story. Just the offer of help. Walking back to the school gates, Isis had felt suddenly lighter, as though a heavy burden she hadn't even been aware she was carrying had been lifted from her shoulders.

'Thank you, Gabby!' she whispered, looking up at the sky. 'Thank you, thank you, thank you!'

Her first chance to go to the centre came the following Tuesday afternoon. Her mother had taken a part-time job at the local delicatessen, and her father never got home from work before six. School ended early, so she'd be able to make it into town and back home before either of her parents returned. She thought carefully about what clothes she should wear, before opting for her best jeans and a sweatshirt. The man on the phone had told her where the centre was – she could picture it exactly in her mind – so she hadn't needed to write it down. She simply caught a bus that took her straight there.

The centre itself was up two flights of steps on the first floor above a hairdressing salon. The reception room had a warm, cushioned feel about it with pastel-coloured walls and soft, comfortable furniture. As she walked across to the receptionist, she noticed posters on the walls to do with drug problems and unwanted pregnancies – and realised this centre wasn't only for people with problems like hers.

The woman at Reception looked up with a friendly smile. 'Is this your first visit?' she asked.

Isis nodded.

'You'll need to fill in one of these. It's completely confidential,' she assured Isis, handing over a form on a clipboard. On the form was a list of subjects on which you could receive counselling. Isis ticked the appropriate one for her, filling in her age and a few other details before handing the form back to the receptionist with a blush. Even though she hadn't actually spoken, it was the first time she'd admitted her problem to anyone apart from Gabby.

The woman glanced briefly at the form. 'If you sit down, someone will see you soon,' she said.

About twenty minutes later she met Robert Weiner for the first time. Although she had no idea what to expect, when the woman at Reception showed her along a corridor and told her to take the first door on the right, what she found wasn't like anything she had imagined. It was a large room that seemed like every teenager's fantasy. There were no chairs or desks – it was all beanbags and deep-pile rugs, posters on the walls of the big names in pop, an impressive-looking stereo system covered in flashing lights, and even a billiard table at the other end of the room. Standing in the middle, dressed casually in jeans and a checked shirt, was a man who introduced himself as Robert Weiner. He had a friendly look about him and a sensitive face. It was only much later that she discovered he was one of the leading experts in his field. It was just as well she didn't know it this first time, because she was intimidated enough by just being here. Though Robert immediately began to put her at ease, offering her a cool drink and then, as he went to get it, suggesting she pick out a record from the collection by the stereo. She browsed through the records in the rack before pulling out one by Abba which had long been her favourite LP.

When Robert returned to the room they both sat on bean-bags facing each other. They chatted a bit about music, what she liked and what she didn't. She was amazed he seemed so up to date with all the groups and the records that were doing well in the charts – he seemed genuinely interested in it all. But she also knew that, sooner or later, they'd have to get on to the reason she was visiting. Studying Robert's features carefully, she decided he was all right. Even though she was still embarrassed to be here, she reckoned she could trust him – he made her feel safe.

'You're probably feeling a bit nervous,' he said finally, glancing down the form which the woman from Reception must have given him. Then, meeting her anxious expression with an encouraging smile, 'Well, congratulations! Just coming here takes a lot of courage. There are plenty of people out there who would like to come, maybe even know they should come, but they put it off because it's such a difficult thing to do.'

She looked down at her hands. She was glad he realised that. It *was* difficult – not so much getting away from school and her parents, but having to speak to an expert, someone she'd never met before, about the most intimate part of her, the dark horror that had dominated every day of her existence for more years than she cared to remember. As though reflecting her own thoughts, he continued, 'For most people I see, this isn't a subject they can talk to anyone else about.'

Isis nodded vigorously. 'I had a friend, and she knew, and we used to do a lot of stuff together. But she died in a car accident ten days ago.'

'I'm very sorry,' Robert spoke softly.

'She was the only one.' Isis bowed her head. 'She was the one who showed me the article.'

There was a pause before Robert said, 'And you don't want her to die in vain, right?'

Looking up, she met his eyes. She hadn't put her feelings into those words, but what he said was exactly how it was.

'Right now you're probably feeling all alone with this,' he continued, holding her gaze, 'but it's important you realise that there are plenty of people who have exactly the same issues to deal with that you do.'

She looked at him in disbelief.

'You haven't ever talked to anyone about this except your friend, right?' he confirmed. 'So how do you know there aren't lots of other girls out there, maybe even girls you know, who are also not talking about it? Keeping it to themselves?'

He had a point – in theory. But thinking about all the kids she knew at school . . .

'Every day I see at least five different people who feel just like you do. Multiply that by twenty days a month and twelve months a year, that's twelve hundred women every year. And I'm only one practitioner – there are at least half a dozen like me in Florida alone.' He gave her a few moments to let the information sink in. That was a lot of people, thought Isis, and she never would have guessed. She was sure he wasn't lying to her – why would he? – but it just went against everything she'd ever thought about herself. Until Gabby had shown her that article she'd imagined she was the only one in the whole world with this problem. She'd always thought of the situation at home as being one that was hers alone.

'When did it first start—?'

'It's always been like this.'

Robert hadn't even needed to finish the question. He was making a note, nodding. 'With most people there's a turning point.'

Isis immediately thought back to the day when her father and Mr Bazzani had arrived back home unexpectedly.

'When I was twelve,' she said.

'Do you want to tell me about it?'

Isis had never told anyone the full story, not even Gabby. She'd only told her a part because she'd been so ashamed. Now, just thinking about it, the colour rushed to her cheeks.

'You can take all the time you need,' Robert told her.

It *did* take her a while to get started. To explain about Gabby's locker and how she'd seen the brassière – but had always intended to give it back. Once she started, though, the words came out in a torrent as she relived the scene in her mind, experiencing again the emotions she'd felt all those years ago: the erotic self-indulgence as she'd savoured the forbidden pleasures of Gabby's black lace bra and her mother's crimson lipstick – like living in a dream as she'd sat in front of her mother's dressing mirror. Then the visceral shock as she'd looked up to discover her father and Mr Bazzani standing at the door. Time standing still as their eyes met in the mirror, hers shamefully self-conscious and fearful, her father's blazing with a powerful mix of devastating fury and unbridled reproach. Then he'd swooped down upon her, ripping the brassière from her body and using it roughly to wipe the make-up off her face. Next, he'd flung her on the bed, face down. Mr Bazzani had pinned her by the shoulders as her father wrenched her pants down her legs. Not a sound had been uttered until that moment. Not a word exchanged, or necessary, as she'd struggled hopelessly to escape from their clutches. Then the screaming had begun.

Tears rose to her eyes as she recalled what had happened. Robert gently reached over to take her hand. The simple act of remembering had unleashed all her pent-up emotions. Every detail of that primal horror flooded back through her in cruel, vivid detail as she relived the terrible experience of that afternoon – and all the experiences that had followed. Tears rolled silently down her cheeks, before Robert handed her a box of tissues.

'Don't hold back,' he advised her in that serene, authoritative voice to which she was to become so accustomed in future months. 'Let all the hurt come out.'

It was the first time she'd ever been told by an adult it was okay to cry. In her family weeping, except in grief, was regarded as a sign of pathetic weakness. Her father was forever castigating her for her sensitivity, her inability to conceal the fragility of her emotions. But different rules applied with Robert, she was beginning to learn. Robert not only understood her vulnerabilities, he wanted to see them; it was the first time she'd felt fully accepted for who she was.

It was the first time, too, she began to see her family with a detachment of which she'd been incapable until then. Robert asked her a lot of questions about her parents, and in so doing made her realise that their idea of the world wasn't the only way it could be seen.

'The clients I see who have it hardest usually come from families who are very conservative, or where there is a deeply engrained ethnic culture, or whose education is lower than the national average. When these factors combine, in cases such as yours, it makes the issue extremely difficult to deal with.'

Isis nodded. She was still feeling shaky after the catharsis of reliving her ordeal, still getting used to the novel idea that instead of being all alone and taking the blame for her situation on herself, she was part of a much larger group of people going through the same private agonies.

'What about your mother?' Robert asked.

Isis shook her head. 'I think . . . she wants to change things. She tried to pretend it wasn't happening at first. She doesn't understand.'

'Of course. And there are divided loyalties. No matter how much she might want to help you, she probably feels that taking sides against your father won't help matters.'

Isis looked at Robert hopelessly. 'So what must I do?'

Robert reached over to give her shoulder a reassuring squeeze. 'Coming to see me is the best possible thing you could have done. You see, my job is to provide my clients with choices. And you do have choices. You can either carry on as you are—'

Isis was shaking her head defiantly.

'Or we can help you change things. But I must warn you, when I talk about change, I mean complete change. A change in almost every single aspect of your life, not just things at home.' His gravity was inescapable as his eyes held her gaze. 'You need to be completely sure that's something you can cope with.'

'Mind if we swing past Varley's office for an update?' Hilton looked across the expansive back seat of the GCM stretch limo.

'Sure,' nodded Lebowitz, already dialling the office to find out what news had broken during his two-hour absence. 'Good meeting,' he gestured in the direction of Unum Music as he raised the cellphone to his ear.

'Very good.' Hilton looked out of the tinted glass window before adding in an ironic tone, 'Leaves us free to play cat and mouse with One Commando.'

Lebowitz was soon talking to one of his colleagues, while Hilton checked his pager for messages. Traffic was light and it wasn't long before they were heading down Santa Monica Boulevard in the direction of the LAPD building. Though before they got there, Lebowitz had come off the line and looked up at Hilton sharply.

'Seems like there's been a breakthrough at the Berkeley Square end. The lab where they're supposed to be testing on animals? Belongs to a private company called Voisier Laboratories. Not ten minutes from Berkeley's own facility in Madrid.'

'One Commando set it up to look like Berkeley Square?' asked Hilton.

'Seems so.'

'But why would they want to do that? Why not just go after Voisier?'

'Who's ever heard of Voisier?' Lebowitz shrugged.

'I guess.' Hilton remembered Bengt Larson's face pressed

closely into his at his Green's suite. For all Larson's highly drilled efficiency, there had been a fanatical desperation in his expression, a genuine anger. It hadn't seemed like an act on his part; somehow the notion that Larson was pursuing Berkeley Square in full knowledge of the company's innocence didn't ring true.

'So what's being done?' he asked after a pause.

'They're setting up a press conference in Madrid tomorrow – Lefevre and Lord Bullerton double act. It'll be held at the Berkeley Square facility and the media will no doubt make a stampede for Voisier immediately afterwards.' He pulled a droll expression. 'Wouldn't like to be their PR man.' Then as Hilton absorbed this, 'Oh, and you'll never guess where the supersleuth work came from.'

'Not Bennett?'

Lebowitz shook his head. 'No. Our Mr Watson.'

'You're saying—'

'Shrewd cookie. Worked out that maybe there was something going on, but it was being dressed up to be misleading.'

'Nice of him to tell us.'

'Went direct to Andrew Craig.' Lebowitz shook his head, his tone sardonic. 'We pay him all that money and still he doesn't love us.'

'I think he stopped loving us when we put him into play.'

'Always the way.' Lebowitz shrugged, matter-of-factly. 'They never understand the price of fame.'

Sheriff Varley had little new to report when they stepped into his office. The fake passport holders hadn't been tracked beyond Denver. In Britain the police were still far from making any arrests. And latest Interpol computer reports had generated little of real value.

Lebowitz quickly updated him on the latest discovery about Voisier. 'After tomorrow,' he declared, 'the whole world will know One Commando's game.'

'Not that that will stop them,' added Hilton. 'They still have the information on Isis which they could release at any time unless', he fixed Varley with a purposeful stare, 'you do something.'

Varley sighed heavily. 'Mr Gallo, you know that black-mail is an issue we take very seriously. But my main concern right now is the safety of your clients.'

'Precisely,' returned Hilton. 'And even though you have a group of dangerous, armed terrorists headed directly towards them, you appear incapable of action.' This conversation, Hilton couldn't help thinking, was becoming strongly reminiscent of his fruitless discussions with DI Bennett at Scotland Yard.

'That's just not true,' Varley looked him in the eye, 'all squad cars in the vicinity of Malibu and Beverly Hills have been put on special alert. They're watching your client's home—'

'I was thinking in terms of arrests.' Hilton's gaze was hard.

'How can we arrest them when we don't even know for sure they're in the country?'

At that moment Hilton's phone rang. Extracting it from his jacket pocket, he recognised the number of GCM's guest house on the display.

'Mark Watson,' he murmured, before answering.

After Unum, Mark had returned home where he checked the OmniCell computer for an update of Vinnie's latest calls. That was when he'd heard the one from Larson saying he was to be sent on a recce to Los Angeles. Vinnie had got five grand out of the deal – that would have pleased him no end, thought

Mark grimly – but there were no other details about when he was flying out, or what this 'recce' was to involve.

And there had been one other thing. 'Alex', Mark noted, was what Vinnie had called Bengt Larson. Could this be the 'Alexander Heindl' alluded to in a previous conversation – the one setting up that mysterious meeting in Regent's Park?

One thing he was sure of was that he must tell the police. He needed protection. And he wanted to know how to handle Vinnie's arrival. This was the first definite evidence that One Commando were on their way to LA – but exactly why, he couldn't work out; they had tried to blackmail Isis and had failed. So why didn't they tell the world about her dark secret? What was stopping them shooting down her career overnight? Unless, of course, it had all been a bluff.

Hilton Gallo was his first stop, to get the details of his LAPD contact. As it turned out, Hilton was meeting Sheriff Varley when he called. After swiftly explaining the situation, Mark heard Hilton relay his discovery to Varley.

'Where is your client at this moment?' Varley reacted instantly.

'Beverly Hills. GCM guest house,' responded Hilton.

'We've got to get him out of there. Put him somewhere secure.'

'Like where?' asked Hilton.

'A safe house.'

'Can't get safer than Isis's,' proposed Lebowitz.

'What kind of security does she have out there?' Varley demanded.

'High-level electronic security systems. Armed-response crews within five minutes. She's had every security firm in town go over the place,' Hilton told him.

'She wouldn't want me under her roof,' Mark said down the phone.

'Oh, I think we could persuade her.'

'Damned right,' nodded Lebowitz, 'it'll play well in the media: "Jordan and Isis are à *deux*".'

'Just great!' Mark's tone was bitter. 'My life's under threat and, still, the only thing he's worried about is what the papers say.'

'I don't think that's strictly true.'

'Ask Varley what I'm supposed to do when I get the inevitable call from Vinnie Dobson?'

A few minutes later, Mark slammed down the phone, heading upstairs to his bedroom to pack a suitcase. He'd agreed to go over to Isis's until Varley and his men had made alternative arrangements – probably a safe house out of town.

They'd discussed, in detail, what they'd do if Vinnie called. They'd gone over the conversation between Vinnie and Larson, detailing what had been said. If Vinnie was being sent on a 'recce' they didn't want to alert his suspicions, said Varley. Mark should invite him round. Fix a time – and tell the police immediately. They would then set up an operation and have people in place so that once they knew where Vinnie was, they'd close in on him.

By the time One Commando arrived in town, Varley told Mark confidently, they'd find themselves with an LAPD welcoming committee.

The two-car convoy sped down the Interstate 15 from Las Vegas to Los Angeles. Chevrolet Luminas from the same car-hire firm, they were unremarkable and attracted no attention during the six-hour trip through the desert, then through the Los Angeles sprawl; Arcadia, Pasadena, Riverside, en route to the apartment in Santa Monica. In the first car, Harris and de Clerque sat in silence almost the

entire duration of the trip, Harris driving while de Clerque
sat up front with him. Behind them on the back seat, two
small suitcases contained nothing more suspicious than
clothing and toiletry bags.

As the only US-based member of the team, Harris had
been in charge of procurement for the whole operation and
everything they needed had already been installed in the
safe apartment. A former Marine who'd been dismissed from
the armed forces after being court-marshalled for 'imposing
undue discipline' during a mission in Somalia – he'd shot
dead five tribespeople who'd refused to play ball – Harris
was now a furniture salesman in Seattle. The job was the
perfect cover; people came in to see him, and he went out
for frequent 'measurings' without arousing the slightest suspicion. Often to be found at the back of the showroom behind
the closed glass door of his office, on the phone or sending
and receiving faxes, Harris had never moved many sofas.

De Clerque's requirements had been the most challenging. He'd sent through specifications for Pentolite deton-
ators, Cordex, P4 plastic explosives and a timing device.
Harris's long-established underground network had come up
with nearly everything on the list, but certain items of South
African manufacture had been more difficult. In the end, de
Clerque had been forced to source the devices in Holland,
disassemble them and courier them over to Harris, for
reassembly and testing.

As for Guittard, most of his list of electronic equipment
had been readily available. Harris hadn't had any difficulty
with the shopping list, picking up a lot of it over the counter
from Radio Shack. The telephone interceptor had been more
difficult, but available from a counter-surveillance operator
in Boston. Also in the Santa Monica apartment was the
small but carefully selected arsenal of weapons ordered by

Larson: four Glock 17 automatic pistols and two MP5s; six-inch-blade hunting knives in leather sheaths; two-wave radio sets; dark-coloured trousers, shirts and jerseys bought from Sears; ski masks and combat boots.

Preparations had been made far beyond the apartment. Harris had made arrangements to scramble getaway vehicles with a single telephone call, ensuring a range of several routes was available at any one time. Like every other One Commando operation, Larson had emphasised, this one was to be surgical. They were to penetrate all defences to the target, do the business, and get out again before anyone knew what was happening. The Lefevre mission was a textbook example. Gallo's would have been too, had it not been for a spy in their midst. But this time, Larson told Harris coldly, there was no Alan Brent.

Harris had also carried out the reconnaissance. Ever since Isis and Jordan Hampshire had become targets, he'd been keeping their two residences under close surveillance. All their movements were monitored, particularly security arrangements, the drill followed by security personnel, the location of CCTV cameras, and everything else there was to know about how the two stars were protected. Jordan Hampshire's Beverly Hills home was, Harris had soon discovered, an open book. The rudimentary alarm system could be disabled simply by cutting off the electricity mains. The security guard's quarters were easily isolated. There were no bars or security glass in any of the windows.

By contrast, Isis's home had the reputation for being a fortress of security arrangements – a reputation well-deserved from what he'd been able to detect through the Szirowski Optic binoculars from out to sea. Apart from employing an on-site guard whose living quarters were inside the house, she was also linked to an armed-response service, which guar-

anteed a fully mobilised cadre of crack security personnel
within twelve minutes of her pressing any one of a number
of panic buttons located throughout the house, or of key
entry points being breached. The link to the service was by
radio, not landline; deactivating the system would require
elaborate planning. Then there were the on-site challenges.
Two alarm systems in different parts of the house. The
double-gate entry intended to isolate all visitors between
outer and inner grilles before they gained access to the house.
Steel security screens controlling access to various corridors.
Plus Isis had once told an interviewer she was well armed –
if that was true, the locations of her weapons were unknown.

Harris's big surveillance breakthrough had come ten days
earlier as he was pacing about the furniture showroom.
Playing on one of the televisions was one of the endless
documentaries on celebrity – this one about the homes of
the rich and famous. Harris had looked up when there had
been a mention of Isis's house and how she'd transformed it
from a modest beachfront cottage into a sprawling mansion
split over several different levels, and including her own studio.
There'd followed interviews with the architect and some camp
interior designer who'd discussed the creative dimensions of
the job amid much limp-wristed arm waving. The thought
had suddenly hit him: Isis would have required planning
permission from the City Hall Planning Department to carry
out all this work. Surely they would have required full details
of the project, including floor plans? A telephone call to the
Planning Department quickly confirmed this. When he was
told records of previous planning applications were confidential, he wasn't concerned. He simply had several of the
clerks in the planning department tailed for a few days, before
choosing the one whose lifestyle aspirations appeared most
out of proportion to his modest salary. An offer was made

and a deal done: it wasn't long before he had in his possession a detailed floor layout of Isis's house, which he e-mailed Larson. From there, the plans had gone to de Clerque and Guittard. By now, all four of them were intimately acquainted with her house.

During their time in Las Vegas, Larson had gone through his usual rigorous pre-op training, focusing on the main challenge of this operation – Isis's security systems. They faced the most complex logistical problems ever and, equipped with floor plans, photographs and videos of relevant interview clips, in Larson's suite at the Lucky Nugget they'd mapped out as many different scenarios as they could foresee, working out their *modus operandi*, roles for each of them that were flexible enough to be adapted to whatever circumstances they faced.

As usual, Larson's outward demeanour had been one of implacable calm. But beneath the impenetrable expression he harboured a concern that had never troubled him on previous operations. This was One Commando's biggest and most daring mission to date, with its highest-profile targets ever. It would have a much, much greater impact than the attack on an anonymous businessman in central London. When the bodies of Isis and Jordan Hampshire were found in her Malibu home, a global tidal wave of hysteria would follow. The story would dominate the world's media. There would be condemnations and condolences, weeping fans depositing a mountain of bouquets at her gates; endless tributes would be played on radio and TV stations. It would become one of those pivotal events, like the assassination of John F. Kennedy or the death of Princess Diana – people would always remember where they were when they heard about the double murder of pop's greatest sex icon and her lover. And he, Bengt Larson, their executioner, would inherit their fame. One Commando's notoriety would become as powerful as their celebrity had been, making him the most feared guerrilla leader in the world – a man of whom even his father would be in awe.

It was ironic, he thought as he sat hidden behind his reflective Ray-Bans in the back seat of the second car, that the key to his ambitions and this whole raid came in the form of the undisciplined, self-opinionated loser sitting in the passenger seat of his car.

Vinnie Dobson had been in a state of sullen bitterness since being escorted from the roulette table the night before. His instinctive reaction had been outrage: he could do what he liked, he complained loudly to the man he knew as Alexander Heindl, his voice raised. This was a free country. The croupier was staring across at him and others round the table were looking up, bemused. Then Larson had seized him by one arm and Harris by the other, and he remembered being told how plain-clothed security men patrolled casinos all the time, and how he couldn't afford to attract their attention because he was staying at the hotel under a false name and using a false passport.

He'd allowed himself to be escorted back through the lobby and up in a crowded lift till they came to Larson's floor, where they were the only ones to step out.

'That's a thousand bucks you made me leave behind!' He turned to Larson in undisguised fury as he was led down the corridor.

Larson ignored him.

'What the fuck d'you think you're playing at?'

Harris's American voice was cool and cautioning. 'Mind what you say.'

'*You* mind what *you* say!' snapped Vinnie as Larson pulled out his card key and opened the door of his suite.

Once inside, there was no holding Vinnie back. 'I'm doing you fuckwits one hell of a favour coming here. If I back out of this, you're stuffed. Completely stuffed.' He glowered first at Larson, then Harris, both of whom watched him without expression. 'You both know that,' he interpreted their silence as deference. 'You need me a whole lot more than I need you.'

'Is that so?' Larson came towards him, stopping less than a foot away so that his tall, muscled body towered over Vinnie's. 'I think you've completely misjudged the situation,' he said in that strangely contorted accent of his.

Vinnie was forced to raise his head so that he could meet Larson's eyes.

'You did us no favour coming here. We paid you five thousand pounds to release you from non-existent contracts.'

'What d'you mean, non-existent—!'

'We looked into your activities in London.' There was contempt in his voice. 'There was no big deal in the wings. Since Swerve you haven't cut anything except a sympathy contract from GCM.'

'That's not true!' Vinnie's voice quavered between anger and fear.

'Don't tell me what's true and what's not true. Your demand for money from us was extortion.'

'Get out of my face.' Vinnie tried brazening it out, reaching out to Larson with his arm. But Larson wouldn't budge.

'Just because I'm here doesn't mean you own me.' He tried pushing Larson away with both arms now.

'It means you'll do exactly as we say.' Larson's voice was toneless. 'And I don't tolerate indiscipline. Harris?'

In a single motion Harris, who had acquired a black belt in judo after three years' intensive study in Japan, had seized Vinnie by the arm, brought it up behind his back and forced him to the ground where he yelped in agony.

'Stop it!' he cried. 'You're going to bust my arm!'

'So what if we do?' asked Larson.

Vinnie hadn't stepped out of line since. He'd sat in one room of Larson's suite while the others planned the operation in the other, occasionally having him order in something from room service for them. Larson had given him a book to study, *Close that Tele-sale*; he expected Dobson to have thoroughly familiarised himself with the techniques it covered by the time they left Las Vegas, he said. Vinnie had protested, saying he didn't know anything about tele-sales and didn't need to. To which Larson had replied that he was about to close the sale of his life: when he phoned Mark Watson, wanting to visit him in Isis's home, the answer must be 'yes'.

Larson had been staring out of the car window at the barren landscape for most of the trip. Up front, in the passenger seat, Dobson continued to flick through the tele-sales book, distracted. He'd been left in no doubt how important it was that Mark should agree to meet him. Everything else depended on it – all One Commando's elaborate preparations would be as nothing if he didn't play his part. But that wasn't something directly within his control. Although he'd left Mark on cordial terms outside the Lamb in London, he couldn't guarantee how he'd behave in LA. For once, Vinnie felt his bluster desert him.

Finally, unable to take the silence any longer, he turned round to face Larson, his voice rising in desperation. 'What if, I mean, what if he doesn't say yes?'

It was a while before Larson responded. 'He must,' he said in a level voice. 'If he doesn't, you won't be going home. You won't be going . . . anywhere.'

*   *   *

Mark had only just stepped into the hallway of Isis's home when his mobile phone went off.

'Mark, me old son,' came the voice from the other end.

'Vinnie!' He didn't have to feign surprise. While he and Varley had discussed what he'd do when this call came through, he hadn't been expecting it nearly so soon.

'Didn't really think I'd call, did you?'

'Well, I—'

'Only joking!' Vinnie acted out his usual life-and-soul persona. 'So guess what? I've just made my first transatlantic crossing. First of many.'

'You're in America?'

'Even better. I'm in LA!'

'Really?' Mark was aghast as he looked through the open front door to where Denzil was parking the Lincoln, oblivious to his conversation.

'Too right,' Vinnie was saying. 'And I'd like to see you.'

'Sure!' Mark tried to project enthusiasm. 'Would be good.'

'So what are you up to?'

'Well, we've just had the album signed off,' began Mark, 'we'll soon be in rehearsals for the tour—'

'No. Now, I mean.'

'Right now?' This was happening too fast! He wasn't ready for this and, more to the point, were the police? They hadn't been expecting the call for a day or two, maybe more. Deep down, he supposed, he'd hoped that if he and Isis disappeared from view for a while the One Commando problem would go away; how could their cause be sustainable once the Voisier scam was publicly revealed?

But there was no escaping the voice at the other end of the phone.

'Right now,' he said cautiously, 'I'm in Malibu.'

'You're at Isis's then?'

'Yeah, why?'

'You know how much I'd love to meet her.'

'I don't know if that's such a good idea.' Mark made a play for time. 'She's not feeling too good at the moment. In fact she's in bed.'

'Sick, huh?'

Mark paused before saying, 'That time of the month.'

'But *we* could still meet,' persisted Vinnie.

'I'd like that, Vin. But I've got to be at a function in town at six. By the time I get home, I'll have to head right out again.'

'Oh,' Vinnie digested this in silence before saying, 'the thing is, I'm only here for a couple of hours.'

'How do you mean?'

'Heading to Las Vegas.'

'You flew all the way here just to play blackjack?'

'I've got some business to attend to as well.'

That'd be right, thought Mark. Maybe Vinnie had been sent on his recce so they could all hole up somewhere and work out their operation. Maybe that was the plan.

As though confirming his suspicions, Vinnie continued, 'We can meet up properly, in a few days when I get back. I was just hoping to see you quickly. Couldn't I drop in to see you, just for ten minutes?'

Mark thought of his conversation with Varley. Surely it wasn't beyond the capabilities of the LAPD to get some plain-clothes cops out to Malibu in half an hour? Someone who could trail Vinnie back to wherever his new-found friends were hiding?

For a moment as he paused, mind racing, he thought that the timing of Vinnie's call couldn't have been worse. He hadn't seen Isis since earlier in the day at Unum – Christ knew what kind of reception he was going to get.

And he could just imagine what her reaction would be when he told her he'd invited a known One Commando spy for afternoon tea. But right now, it seemed the best thing to do. Hadn't Varley himself told him that when Vinnie asked to meet him, he should say yes?

Eventually he said, 'Well, I guess if this is the only chance we have . . . Do you know Isis's address?'

22

Malibu, California
Tuesday, 5 October

When Isis emerged from the bedroom wing to find that Mark had arrived, and that a One Commando agent was on his way to her home, her already dark mood grew rapidly worse.

'Why the hell—?'

'Just following orders,' he said with a bleak grimace. He didn't much care that he was on her home ground. Vinnie's imminent arrival and the accompanying police operation were far too important to get hung up with her mood swings. Besides, after her temper tantrum outside Unum Music, he reckoned he didn't owe her any favours.

'I've got to tell Varley what's happening.' He picked up her hallway phone, extracted the policeman's number from his wallet and commenced dialling.

'Is that Sheriff Varley's office?' Mark didn't recognise the voice at the other end.

'No, Simmo, a colleague,' replied the other. 'Varley's stepped away from his desk for five minutes.'

Mark exhaled heavily. 'It's Mark Watson. Do you know about One Commando?'

'Fully briefed.'

'I'm at Isis's and have just had the call from Dobson,' he said quickly. 'He's coming here in thirty minutes.'

'You're both in the house?' confirmed the other.

'All three of us – there's also Holly, Isis's daughter.'

'Stay where you are.' His voice was imperative.

'You'll be able to send in—?'

'Of course. Just stay where you are,' the other repeated. 'We have the situation under control.'

Mark hung up, looking over at Isis's expression – a mix of anger and apprehension.

In the back of the specially equipped courier van heading out towards Malibu, Harris switched the microphone off his headset, before leaning forward to where Larson was sitting in the driver's compartment.

'I've just intercepted a call. They're on to Dobson.'

Larson flashed a look of urgent enquiry.

'It's okay, it's okay.' Harris nodded. 'I told them to stay put.'

When the buzzer of the gate intercom sounded, Mark looked into the monitor by the front door. Vinnie was standing alone – he must have come out by taxi, thought Mark, picking up the intercom before letting him through both sets of gates. Then he opened the front door and stood waiting for him to appear, unlocking the steel grille behind the door with the key kept next to the gate monitor.

'Jordan Hampshire!' Vinnie greeted him in a facetious tone as he approached the front door. 'So here we are, both of us in Lalaland together.' He extended his hand as he stepped towards Mark.

Mark played along with the put-on joviality as best he could.

Then Vinnie was exclaiming, 'This place is like Fort Knox!'

'Yeah, well, has to be.'

'Electronic controls for everything, right?'

'Something like that.' Mark waved in the direction of the gate intercom as he led him through the hallway into Isis's sitting room. 'You're in luck. Isis got up a short while ago.'

'Oh, great!' responded Vinnie, though Mark didn't miss the twitchiness about him, the distracted expression on his face as he glanced about a hallway crammed to the rafters with security equipment. He could look all he liked, thought Mark, it wasn't going to help. Even if he'd cased out every device in the house, in just a few minutes Varley and his men were going to arrive – the beginning of the end for One Commando.

In the meantime, they were to play along with the pretence of normality.

'Come through to meet her.'

'Yeah.' Vinnie followed him, scanning round the room.

Leading him out on to the balcony, Mark watched Vinnie carefully as he reacted to the presence of Isis, whose expression was hidden behind large Versace sunglasses. Standing a short distance away, Frank was watching Holly who had gone down to the beach immediately below.

'Isis, this is Vinnie Dobson from London,' said Mark.

Vinnie extended his arm and was shaking her hand more vigorously than was polite. 'I'm your number one fan,' he said.

How many times had she heard that, Mark couldn't help wondering. Aloud he said, 'Vinnie's only here for a short while, then he goes to Las Vegas.' He turned to Vinnie.

'That's right,' Vinnie was nodding, 'I've got to be out of here soon. But I couldn't pass through LA without looking up me old mate. I was the one who discovered him, you know?' he couldn't resist.

'Really?' Isis's eyebrows darted above her sunglasses briefly.

'Oh, yes. Knew he was going to turn into a star!'

There was an awkward pause while Isis regarded her unwelcome guest coolly through her sunglasses. Then Vinnie was saying, 'You know, right now,' he was apologetic, 'I need a loo.'

For just a moment, Mark and Isis exchanged a look of mutual bemusement before Mark was saying, 'Sure.'

Turning Vinnie away he led him back through the sitting room into the hallway.

'It's called the bathroom over here,' he said, pointing him in the direction of the visitors' bathroom. 'Second on the right.'

Hilton Gallo was in the Columbia boardroom pitching a major new motion picture development to the assembled suits when, back at GCM, the phone call came through from Varley. With neither Hilton nor Elizabeth in the office, it was his secretary, Melissa Schwartz, who picked up the call. Was his message urgent, she asked Varley, having explained that Hilton was out of the office. There was no mistaking the seriousness of Varley's tone when he replied. This was extremely urgent and of critical importance too.

Moments later Melissa was typing a message to appear on the pager Elizabeth carried with her at all times. Only in the most extraordinary of circumstances would she consider interrupting a meeting as important to the agency as this one. But these were extraordinary circumstances.

Elizabeth felt the pager vibrating in the pocket of the handbag pressed against her leg under the boardroom table.

While one of the Columbia execs was engaged in a spirited defence of the studio's latest budget-busting space movie, she leaned down, slipped the pager from her handbag and read the message, before scribbling it on a piece of paper which she slipped to Hilton, sitting beside her.

Hilton quickly excused himself from the meeting, to the evident astonishment of both the Columbia and GCM teams.

'Life or death issue,' he explained, heading for the door.

Outside, he commandeered the nearest phone and quickly dialled Varley.

'What is it?' he demanded.

'We got a fix on one of the group – the guy who changed at Denver? He terminated in Las Vegas. From that we back-checked and picked up another guy, also in Vegas.'

'So they're all there.'

'That's our assumption,' Varley spoke quickly. 'There's something else you should know. We've run ID on both men. De Clerque's wanted by Russian police, he's heavily involved with a St Petersburg Mafia group. He had explosives train-ing from a former KGB sabotage team, and has blown his way into three banks in the last eight months. The other guy, Guittard, is a digital security wonk. Ex-Marconi and a technology runner between the IRA and Tripoli. Someone wealthy must be bankrolling these guys.'

Hilton listened to Varley with a hard-eyed intensity. 'What's being done?'

'We're searching for them, of course. But trying to find four men in Las Vegas . . .' Then, after a pause, 'We need to get this information to—'

'Of course,' Hilton replied swiftly. 'And protection?'

'I've fixed a safe house for both your clients. Santa Ynez. It's being prepared to take them tonight.'

'In the meantime—?'

'Our squad cars are patrolling Broadbeach—'

'We're way past that stage.'

'Only a few hours ago you assured me she had the highest level security of any home in California?'

'We can't just leave them like sitting ducks!'

'Get your clients to pack their bags,' Varley didn't disguise his impatience, 'and we'll be round to collect them.'

Vinnie Dobson had a good look at the gate entry and intercom console as he walked through the hall to the bathroom. As soon as he heard Mark out on the balcony talking to Isis, he about-turned and went back to it, quickly scanning the CCTV image, the intercom receiver, the array of buttons and lights on the panel.

Walking in here had been dead easy! Straight through the open gates and in through the front door. After all the contingency planning bullshit One Commando had gone on about, he'd expected masked gunmen and razor-wire at every turn. Instead, it had been like stepping into the home of any other multi-millionaire. He'd quickly noticed where the two bodyguards were standing – he'd been warned to expect them and told that under no circumstances was he to attempt a gate opening if either of them was around. But one was out on the balcony right now, and the other floating about like a spare part in the sitting room. 'If you can't perform the gate opening from inside, cut your visit to less than ten minutes then leave,' the man he now knew as Larson had ordered him. 'We'll get in when they open up to let you out.'

No need for that, thought Vinnie, trying to decide which button to push. As soon as the gates had opened, he knew, they would cut off all the electricity and phone lines so that none of the security systems would function. It wouldn't take them long to get up the driveway and into the house. They had the whole thing drilled down to split-second timing.

Suddenly the phone was ringing and he felt under pressure. He couldn't hang around here – he could hear footsteps heading in his direction. Taking a chance he pushed both green buttons on the entry console before stepping away. Mark was in the sitting room picking up the phone.

'Mark. I need Isis.' Hilton's voice was imperative.

'Hold on a second.' Mark was about to put the receiver down when he heard a click on the line. The unmistakable sound of another receiver being lifted. But how could that be? Denzil and Isis were on the balcony. Frank was downstairs. The other two lines went into the hall and Isis's bedroom. His bemusement turned to outrage, however, as Vinnie appeared in the doorway holding the cordless receiver from the hall.

There was a smirk on Vinnie's face as he came towards him – a sly, challenging expression. About to shout at him to put the phone down, Mark heard the telephone line click dead – and instants later was aware of movement out of the corner of his eye. Glancing out of the window, he saw to his horror the gates opening and four men in dark clothing pounding up the driveway.

Vinnie pounced, knocking the receiver to the floor and shoving Mark against a bookcase. Hearing a noise from inside, Denzil was already storming in from the balcony, seizing Vinnie by the shoulders and throwing him off Mark, on to the floor.

'They're coming through the gates!' gasped Mark.

Denzil looked up to see figures nearing the house.

'Frank!' he screamed as he ran to the balcony door, 'bring her up!'

Mark was scrambling over to Isis who'd jumped up from where she'd been sitting, her face frozen with terror. Frank rushed up the steps from the beach carrying Holly, and shoved the child into Mark's arms.

'Behind the security barrier!' Frank ordered, hurrying to join Denzil.

Mark led Isis into the house, carrying Holly and shielding her eyes. To get behind the security barrier, which could be lowered to isolate the bedroom wing, they had to go through the hallway – immediately outside which their bodyguards were now in hand-to-hand combat with two dark-clad intruders. For a moment in the sitting room, Mark paused in indecision. Then he decided they should get through while they still had access. He and Isis had hardly started their dash through the hall when they both found themselves twisted back and falling to the floor. As they fell, they caught sight of a tall man with short-cropped blond hair and cool blue eyes. He must have come in from the balcony. Holly had fallen on top of Mark and rolled on to the carpet.

'Run to your secret place!' screamed Isis.

Above them, Larson barely glanced as she sprinted out of the room.

'We get her later,' he told Isis, expressionless, poking her in the chest with his boot, pointing his automatic pistol from her face to Mark's and back again.

Outside the front door, Denzil had defied Harris's judo training with several well-placed blows to the head – but Harris now had him on the floor where the two were locked in struggle. Meanwhile Frank's brawn had been too much for Guittard whom he'd sent reeling down the steps. Then,

catching sight of where Larson had Isis and Mark pinned
down, he moved stealthily through the hallway and up
behind Larson, delivering a powerful blow to the small of
his back, sending him buckling across the sitting room. Isis
sprang up immediately, running through the hallway and
down the corridor to the bedroom wing. Scrambling to his
feet, Mark found his escape blocked by Larson who'd seized
him by the ankle. Frank began hammering Larson's
outstretched arms. Seeing that Mark was about to escape,
Vinnie, who'd watched Larson's capture of Isis and Mark
from the corner with a smug satisfaction, grabbed the nearest weapon he could find – an oak fruit bowl – and ran over,
intending to bring it down heavily on Frank. Frank ducked
out of the way, so that the full force of Vinnie's blow struck
Larson on the shoulder. Larson yelped with pain in the same
instant that Mark broke free, following Isis into the bedroom
wing. Immediately he was in the corridor, he pressed the
button operating the steel security grille which began to slide
down from the ceiling. Then he ran to find Isis.

Isis had rushed to Holly's bedroom. They had regular security drills, once every two or three months. They'd pretend
the house was under attack and they'd follow the directions
of the security firm that had installed their systems. Behind
the steel security grille, the bedroom wing was safe, with
windows providing an escape route out. As a last resort, they
could bunker downstairs in the studio, access to which was
protected by additional security measures. Now Isis sought
Holly in her special hiding place – a cupboard in her bedroom
which had a false bottom. But she wasn't there! Nor was she
in any of her other cupboards or under the bed. Hurrying to
her own room, Isis had called out for her daughter, searching in every place she could think, before trying the guest
bedrooms.

By the time Mark appeared, Isis was desperate.

'I can't find her anywhere! She's not here!' She glanced about, wild-eyed. 'Unless—' She looked behind where the steel grille was descending, to the guest bathroom. As a game, Holly sometimes hid in the washing basket, pretending to have gone missing. Following Isis's gaze, Mark ducked beneath where the steel security screen was already more than halfway to the floor. As he hurried across the hall he could hear the sounds of combat from the sitting room. In the guest bathroom, Mark called out for Holly, opening several cupboards, before finding her huddled up and trembling with fear, in the washing basket. Seizing her, he carried her outside. The grille was getting closer and closer to the floor. He wouldn't have time to clamber under it with Holly in his arms. Instead he put her down on the floor, held her by the wrists and swung her in an arc that sent her flying across the polished wooden floor under the gate to where Isis was waiting, just moments before the grille lurched to a halt inches above the floor – and lights went out throughout the house. Sweeping Holly up in her arms, Isis looked through the steel bars at Mark with a mixture of profound gratitude and anguish, just as Larson stormed through from the sitting room.

'Like a rat caught outside its cage.' He seized Mark by the back of his shirt, flinging him heavily on to the floor.

For a moment, Mark lay paralysed on his stomach, all the air forced out of his body. As he lay there, gasping and unable to breathe, he looked out towards the front door, where Larson's three dark-clad accomplices had overwhelmed Denzil and Frank, and were dragging their two unconscious forms into the house.

Larson had Mark's hands behind his back and was taping up his wrists while shouting out something to one of the others about the inside security barrier. De Clerque quickly moved over to the grille and was packing plastic explosives on to the four steel bars from which it was suspended. Dragging Mark away from the area, Larson tugged him along the hallway and into the kitchen, where he began taping up his ankles.

'You're wasting your time,' Mark gasped. 'Whatever you do, the whole world will know the truth tomorrow.'

'You speak nonsense.'

'Berkeley Square are holding a press conference. Madrid. Tomorrow.'

Larson flipped him over so that his back arched painfully over his bound hands.

'That's good.' He'd seized Mark's ankles and was wrapping them tight with tape.

'How can it be good? They'll know you framed Berkeley Square! They'll know the testing went on at Voisier.'

'What is this Voisier?' Task completed, Larson shoved Mark's feet away in contempt, flashing an angry glance at him. 'The video was of Berkeley Square!'

As Larson stalked out of the room Mark stared after him. Was it all a bluff? he wondered. But why would he bother? Larson's anger seemed like a flash of fervent outrage. It wasn't put on.

He could hear them in the hallway fixing explosives in place. With the two bodyguards inside and the front door closed, there'd be no sign from the outside of the house that anything was amiss. Despite the hitches, the operation was running with clean, surgical efficiency. With both electricity and phone lines cut, there was no way he or Isis could contact people outside – even if they could get to a phone or panic button. But surely Hilton would have raised the alarm after his abruptly curtailed phone call?

Raising his head as far as he was able, and taking short,

panting breaths, he glanced about the kitchen searching for something, anything, with which to free himself. Drawing up on to his knees, he found that he could shuffle backwards very slowly. Behind him, next to the space under the kitchen sink, was a unit of drawers. He didn't know what was in them, but it was worth a try.

From outside came the sound of a muffled crack, followed by a great reverberating clanging which shook the whole house, as the steel grille fell from its supports on to the floor.

'Bring them here!' Larson ordered, before darting back to the kitchen to check up on Mark.

The cacophony of the steel gate crashing had made Mark lose his balance and tumble once again on his face. When Larson looked into the kitchen he was lying, prostrate and gasping.

Within seconds of the grille coming down, there was an ominous hissing. Two of Larson's men quickly returned, clutching their faces.

'Tear gas!' screamed Harris, hurrying out of the corridor into the hall. He and Guittard who had run in first and had taken lungfuls of it, were doubled up in agony, faces in their hands. Glancing about him, Larson tried to keep his rapidly rising anger in check. If he'd known she'd had gas installed, it would have been very, very easy to have brought masks. One gap in intelligence and now he had two men incapacitated and a no-go zone created, while his target was free to escape from the other end of the house.

Seizing dishtowels from the kitchen, he handed one to de Clerque.

'You and I go in and get them,' he ordered.

Then, glancing into the sitting room, where Vinnie was sitting sullenly in one corner, 'You look after your friend.'

Mark was back on his knees as soon as they'd left, and

inching back towards the drawers. He didn't know how long he would have before Vinnie appeared. Only moments. But he had to get there – it was his only chance.

He could feel one of the drawer handles against his knuckles. He managed to pull it towards him without falling forward, and search inside with his fingertips. There were linen napkins and napkin rings, other smooth round objects he couldn't identify. Then the handle of a knife. Seizing it hurriedly, he fell on his side, sliding his legs from under him so that he was sitting with his back to the drawers and legs out in front of him, the knife clasped in his hands behind him.

Running his fingertips up the blade, however, he soon discovered that what he'd retrieved was a cheese knife. Its only sharpness was at the twin tips of the blade. Nonetheless he began jabbing through the tape that wrapped his wrists together, piercing and tearing and working frantically at the bindings, until Vinnie appeared in the doorway.

Vinnie had a bruise all the way across his left cheek from where Larson had thrown him against a table. It had come up in a dark, crimson weal and had started to bleed though he affected not to notice.

'So, Jordan Hampshire,' he leaned against the kitchen door-frame, 'bet you don't feel such a big-shot now, do you?'

Behind his back, Mark kept working on the tape. But he had to keep his movements carefully controlled.

'You just don't get it,' he shook his head.

'Oh, I get it all right,' sneered Vinnie, 'thought you were so clever using me to get what you wanted. Big money. Big house. The Queen of Pop. But I'm the one who put you there.' He pointed to himself. He was on a roll now – which was just what Mark needed. He was ranting on about how much he'd done for Mark, how he'd put him on the map.

All the while he was talking, Mark kept up the piercing and tearing. Piercing and tearing. He was making progress, he could feel it. The bindings were getting looser.

As Vinnie vented his spleen, Mark hastily glanced around him. It was one thing getting his hands free, but with his feet still bound, how was he going to get past Vinnie? He needed to work things out – to use his brains. He knew that with the tear gas canisters off, Isis and Holly could be in only one place. She had explained to him how they'd only ever use the gas as a last resort, before bunkering in the downstairs studio, which was not only soundproof, but airtight too. But how to reach the two of them? And how to get them all out of here?

After a while he interrupted Vinnie's monologue, 'It's not all how it seems, you know.'

'Oh, yeah?'

'The clothes I wear. The haircut. None of that's my stuff. They make me do that for the media.'

'Oh, sure, like you've got no control.'

'Too right!'

'You're the big star but you've got no say.'

'Not a lot of say.'

'Why do I find that so hard to believe?'

'D'you think I'd go and stick a fucking stud in my tongue, then?'

'That'd be right,' said Vinnie.

'It's the truth.'

'Get out of it!'

'Well, what d'you think this is, then?' He opened his mouth.

Shaking his head, Vinnie walked over towards where he was sitting, 'Where is it, then?' he demanded, leaning down to look in Mark's mouth.

In that same instant, Mark reached over, his hands now free, to a spray can of industrial bleach that Juanita kept under the kitchen sink. He squirted the contents in Vinnie's eyes. Staggering back, Vinnie howled in pain as Mark quickly pulled himself to his feet, seized a carving knife from the top drawer, and slashed through the tape around his ankles. With Vinnie doubled up in the corner, Mark thought quickly. Isis and Holly would have locked themselves into the downstairs studio. Larson and the other man searching for them in the bedroom wing would quickly realise they'd gone down there. Secure as the studio was, it couldn't withstand plastic explosives. If they tried to escape by car, that would only prompt Larson and the other one to wait outside and attack the moment they emerged from the garage. Suddenly he had an idea.

Five minutes later, the garage door started to judder open. Larson and Guittard scrambled outside to halt a getaway. Inside, they could hear the Range Rover kicking into life. Meanwhile Harris and de Clerque, recovered from the tear gas, had seized Holly and, despite her futile efforts to break free, emerged from the house and were running up the driveway with her struggling form. Or so it appeared. Larson didn't notice the two dark-clad figures immediately, focused as he was on the opening garage door. But once alerted, he shouted for them to stop. This wasn't part of their plan! The three targets were to be isolated *inside* the house. Something was going wrong!

But his two comrades continued to the top of the driveway. The first one disappeared from view and the second, carrying Holly, was about to turn the corner out of view, when he suddenly collapsed to the ground. The bullet had been a clean shot, directly through his left shoulder. As he fell, he released his grip of Holly, who scrambled away from him, rushing towards the first dark-clad figure. Ripping off the ski mask and black hood, Isis faced the rapidly approaching line of police officers.

'Don't!' she cried out, grabbing Holly to her. 'It's us!'

As Mark lay on the ground, bullet wound bleeding, he looked back at where the remote-operated garage door had opened sufficiently to allow room to climb under it. Guittard was already scrambling inside. Urging him on, Larson glanced up the driveway when he suddenly saw Mark's prostrate body – and realised he'd been duped.

Abruptly, he turned from the garage, setting off swiftly down the beach towards the neighbouring property. It was only moments before the line of police reached the top of the driveway. A volley of fire pursued Larson as he dodged and weaved between Isis's house and her neighbours. Then, struck by a bullet, he was thrown off his feet and collapsed in a heap on the sand. Watching all this from where he lay on the ground, Mark felt his face wet with blood, and a strange, pounding sensation in his shoulder. Moments later, he blacked out.

By the time Hilton and Lebowitz arrived on the scene, a dozen squad cars with flashing lights already blocked the entrance to the street, a hundred yards up from Isis's house. Two ambulances were at the gates and a fire engine down the driveway. Rapid-response media vehicles jammed the street and two TV helicopters were circling overhead – police had already cordoned off the property to a fast-gathering crowd of reporters, neighbours and prying passers-by. Explaining who he was, Hilton demanded to be taken to his clients.

He'd been suspicious the moment Mark answered the phone. Something in the other man's voice hadn't sounded right. Then he'd been disconnected and the moment he called back he got an extended ringing tone. Realising the phone line had been cut, he immediately dialled up Varley, telling him what had happened. Varley promised to take immediate action.

Hilton had taken the lift downstairs, ordering Elizabeth to get Lebowitz to join him. The two of them had headed out frantically through the traffic, Hilton phoning Isis's place continually, but to no avail.

As he and Lebowitz appeared, escorted by a reluctant police officer, Varley came out towards them.

'Are they okay?' Hilton's face registered an uncharacteristic tumult of emotion.

'Thank God, yes,' nodded Varley. 'Mark Watson's taken a hit in the shoulder – on his way to hospital, but nothing serious. Isis and Holly, they're being treated for shock.' He gestured towards the house.

'What the hell happened?' demanded Lebowitz as they strode towards it.

'One Commando took out the bodyguards and disabled the security systems.' He glanced behind him. 'Survival in those circumstances,' he was shaking his head, 'quite frankly, it's a miracle—'

'So how—?'

'Two of them were badly teargassed. Crawling on the floor apparently, when Mark Watson knocked them out and grabbed their uniforms.'

'When did your boys get here?' asked Hilton.

'As soon as you phoned I got on to control,' said Varley, 'but they already had six squad cars on the way. You should have told me you'd already—'

Hilton was shaking his head vigorously. 'You were the first person I called.'

The two men halted abruptly, exchanging a long, hard stare that seemed to last an eternity. Before, finally, Varley whispered the question that had stopped them both:

'Then who tipped them off?'

23

Elizabeth Reynolds was at his bedside when Mark came round from the general anaesthetic. He'd been rushed to Emergency where surgeons had operated immediately on his shoulder. He'd suffered only minor damage; the bullet had passed under his skin and through his biceps before exiting, only just missing his humerus bone and brachial artery. It would be several months before the muscles knitted back together and he'd have to wear a sling for the first few days as a precaution. But no lasting damage had been done.

As he blinked open his eyes and focused on Elizabeth's face, she reached out and squeezed his hand.

'Take it easy,' she murmured.

He felt his eyelids close heavily.

'They cleaned you all up and stitched you back together. You're going to be fine.'

He smiled, exhaling slowly before asking, 'How's . . . Isis and . . . ?'

'They're both okay. Shaken. But okay. It's all over now.'

She took his hand again. 'Larson's dead. The others are in jail.'

He opened his eyes to look up at her flawless features and the blonde hair that framed her face. He was still floating from the anaesthetic and Elizabeth appeared dreamily angelic amid the white walls and white sheets of the hospital room. Taking in what she'd just told him, he recalled the events of the afternoon like a sequence out of a movie. The arrival of One Commando through the gates. The desperate struggle in the house. How he had realised the only possible escape route was through diversion and disguise.

'It's all . . . surreal,' he managed, after a while.

'Don't think about it – you don't have to. Just relax.'

But closing his eyes again Mark found that he *wanted* to think about it. He didn't want to 'just relax'. Even if Larson had been killed and the rest of One Commando were out of action, there was still too much that was unexplained. Even in his drowsy, drugged-up state, he recalled Larson's anger when he'd told him, while struggling on Isis's kitchen floor, about Voisier Laboratories. It hadn't been the anger of being caught out or proven wrong, Mark had thought even at the time – but the anger of being contradicted. Larson passionately believed he *had* videotaped Berkeley Square's labs in Madrid. It wasn't just a cynical set-up; it was the real thing. And no doubt that was how he justified the attack on Lefevre – and the horrors he'd planned to inflict on Isis and himself.

Which was another thing Mark didn't get: One Commando had the inside story on Isis and had threatened to use it. So why hadn't they gone ahead and carried out the threat? Why hadn't they told the world about her private past and left it to the media to tear her apart. Flying out to LA on a military adventure was a risk he just couldn't understand them taking.

The key to all his questions, Mark thought in his anaesthetic haze, was bound up in the biggest mystery of all: who had tipped off the Los Angeles police? While being loaded into the ambulance, he'd been told of the eleventh-hour alert – exactly the same as the British police had received just before Hilton Gallo was attacked in Green's. Someone outside One Commando knew what was going on. And for reasons Mark couldn't fathom, he'd decided to tell the police – not far enough in advance to prevent the attack from happening, but with enough time to ensure they were quickly on the scene.

Thoughts giddy and disordered, Mark moved restlessly on the hospital bed before he looked up directly at the ceiling. There *was* another person outside of One Commando! There had been the conversation when that guy with the made-up-sounding name had set up the meeting with Vinnie in Regent's Park. If the call could be traced . . .

'I need to get to a phone.' He felt down his body with his right hand, and found he was wearing some kind of gown, as he looked over at Elizabeth again.

'We've spoken to your mother,' she reassured him. 'She knows you're going to be fine—'

'No it's – it's something else. I must get hold of Lloyd, my brother.'

Elizabeth was glancing at her watch. 'But it'll be the middle of the night—'

'Doesn't matter.' He was already struggling to get up. 'This is important.'

'All right, wait.' She sensed his determination. 'I'll call a nurse and see if we can put some pillows behind your back. You can use my cellphone.'

*   *   *

London
Thursday, 7 October

It was after midnight when the sleek convertible pulled up in the quiet Islington street and from out of the driver's door stepped the dark-suited figure of Jasper Jones. Since Malibu he'd been working even more intensely than ever. He hadn't had much sleep and the long hours and frenetic pace had put dark bags under his eyes. But the lack of sleep hadn't bothered him. Almost every waking moment for the past two days had been spent focused on One Commando and the Isis secret. Adrenaline charging through his system, he'd seldom felt so driven, so close to his goal.

He let himself into his house and made his way up the stairs, stepped into the sitting room and threw his jacket over the back of the sofa before switching on the TV news channel through force of habit. The drama at Isis's house had been all over the media, of course, the final end-game like something out of a mega-budget Hollywood blockbuster. With Jordan Hampshire lying wounded in a hospital bed and a One Commando trial inevitable, the whole saga was set to run and run.

In the meantime, Isis's secret, undoubtedly the most explosive confidence to which he'd ever gained access, had yet to be revealed; he was the only one now who knew it. Because the only other person with any idea about his real involvement in One Commando was now lying in a mortuary in California. All in all, thought Jones, he couldn't have scripted the whole thing better himself.

In fact his only cause of regret was the end of his budding romance with Gail. Last night he'd been at home, fixated on CNN, when the doorbell had rung and in came Gail, with two bags from Marks & Spencer replete with food.

'Surprise visit!' she announced cheerily. 'I thought I'd cook us both supper.'

He'd barely been able to suppress his irritation – or keep his eyes off the TV screen.

'Don't look so ecstatic.' There'd been an ironic note in her voice he'd never heard before.

'Sorry.' He turned back to her. 'It's just that I have a lot of work to do tonight.'

'Oh, work, schmurk. Can't you give it a break for once?'

Jones had felt the heat rising to his face. 'Don't presume to tell me how I should spend my time!' he snapped.

She stood, staring at him open-mouthed, bags of groceries dangling from both hands, before about-turning and walking back to the front door.

'Look, I'm sorry,' he went after her, 'that came out—'

'It's all right, Jas, perfectly all right,' she glanced over her shoulder with a toxic smile, 'I'd rather find out sooner than later.'

'Find out what?' Alarm was added to his mixed emotions.

'Don't play the innocent.' At the front door she swivelled round and pointed a long, exquisitely manicured finger in his face. 'You're seeing someone else, aren't you?'

He reacted to the accusation with amusement and relief. 'Seeing someone else?' he repeated, incredulous. 'I don't have time to see you, so when the hell am I supposed to be seeing someone else?'

'If you weren't such a two-timing bastard you would have time to see me!' she argued, tears in her eyes.

For a moment he looked her up and down, taking her all in. She was perfect, he thought yet again. Just the look he went for, and tailor-made for the passenger seat of his Saab. Pity he had to let her go, but if she wanted to believe in her outlandish fantasies, then good luck to her. He didn't have the time or the inclination to whisk her upstairs and molly-coddle her and tell her that everything was going to be fine.

'Look, Gail,' he began, 'I'm not seeing anyone else. I've no *desire* to see anyone else. I think you're a great girl and that we've got a wonderful thing going between us. You just have to understand that sometimes I have to work incredibly long hours.'

'I thought you were an agency director?' She was suspicious.

'I *am* a director.'

'So, you must have a choice?'

He shrugged. 'You'd think I would but—'

'And you choose to put your work above me?'

'It's not like that!'

'Then how is it?'

'It's—' he stood before her, spluttering, trying desperately to think of something to say.

'You know,' she'd opened the front door, composure having returned, 'I think I'd prefer it if you *were* seeing somebody else. At least I'd have the satisfaction of knowing I'd dated a man with balls!'

She turned, slamming the door behind her, and stalked down the pavement at high speed. He hadn't made any effort to go after her. What was the point? Within moments he was back in front of the TV, completely absorbed in a live report from LA.

Tonight he hadn't long been home when the phone rang. Even for Jasper Jones, calls at half past midnight were outside the ordinary. It crossed his mind that this might be Gail. But from the other end came the panic-stricken tones of Lindy Laburne, Animal Liberation Front's key spokesperson.

'I've been trying you all night,' her words came out in a

torrent, 'something terrible's happening and I just don't know what to do.'

'Why don't you tell me?' he asked, his tone cool and condescending.

'I've heard on the grapevine that Berkeley Square have set up a media conference in Madrid tomorrow. The lab we've been campaigning about – turns out it belongs to Voisier.'

'How unfortunate.'

'We've staked everything on this,' her voice rose, agitated. 'I just don't understand how it happened.' She ranted on for quite some time before demanding, her voice near the point of hysteria, 'So what do we do?'

'Nothing we *can* do,' Jones told her, crisply. 'We can't stop Berkeley Square holding a media conference.'

'But I mean, surely . . . how could we have got it so wrong? You went there yourself!'

'I did indeed.'

'So did Alexander when he took the video.'

'Exactly.' Then, after a pause, 'I don't understand it at all.'

Laburne let off steam for a few more minutes before realising that any further discussion was futile. Putting down the receiver at the other end, Jones shook his head. Silly bitch! The only surprise, so far as he was concerned, was how long it had taken them to work it out.

The decision to pick Berkeley Square had been quite fortuitous. In his early days in the animal rights movement he'd invested considerable time checking out animal testing allegations, and one of his searches had taken him to Madrid. Rumours had been circulating of a laboratory carrying out the most evil excesses, and with the help of local sympathisers, and relentless questioning, he'd eventually tracked it down in a sprawling industrial zone. Far behind an outer security fence, the building was heavily fortified and regularly patrolled by a private security firm. He'd gained access posing as an out-of-hours delivery operator for long enough to fire off half a dozen surreptitious photographs. While there he had also caught sight of a package addressed to Voisier Laboratories.

It hadn't surprised him. Jean Voisier had already been run out of his native Belgium by anti-vivisection campaigners. Having had to close down in Bruges, it looked as if he'd simply decamped to Spain where he'd continued his lucrative and barbarous testing. Returning for a few external shots the next day, Jones had been on the way back to his hotel when he'd got hopelessly lost in the unfamiliar, anonymous maze of factories and chimneys and security fences. He'd paused to consult a map, and when he'd looked up he'd found himself directly outside a Berkeley Square plant.

That had got him thinking. A campaign against Voisier Laboratories back home in London wouldn't be exactly headline-stopping. No one outside the animal rights movement had ever heard of Voisier, a tiny sub-contractor in the vast machine of the cosmetics industry. Plus there was the fact that Voisier was in Madrid, not Manchester. And what were the rights-sensitive chattering classes of Britain supposed to do, apart from write stern letters to their MEPs? They couldn't boycott Voisier products. They couldn't protest outside Voisier offices – there weren't any. All in all, his photos would provoke nothing more than a storm in a teacup.

Berkeley Square, on the other hand, offered limitless possibilities. It was synonymous with middle England – the Nightingale product range had been much loved by generations of ladies of a certain age. The company's glossy advertising promoted all the values – sensuality, gentility, refinement

– that his photographs most sensationally contested. The idea that all those many litres of eau de toilette and parfum had their genesis in this cruel, clinical hell on earth was an outrage.

So the decision had been easy. He'd photographed Berkeley Square's own sign and, on his return to Britain, he'd commissioned a duplicate to be made. Then, hours before Larson's subsequent video break-in, he'd personally attached it to the anonymous external fence of the Voisier plant, before removing it afterwards.

He hadn't, of course, been at all surprised by the media's reluctance to accept AFL allegations. His main challenge, as he'd always known, had been to keep Bengt Larson determined, motivated, and in the game. But it had been easier than he'd feared; in the face of universal condemnation, Larson had continued to believe his own eyes. No one's fool, he had *seen* the sign. He *knew* the plant was Berkeley Square's. Outright denials by Lefevre and Bullerton only inflamed his passions all the more.

Right from the very start, Jones had expected revelations about Voisier's Madrid facility to bring an abrupt halt to the One Commando campaign. But until that happened, he'd been only too happy to run with the show as far as it went – which, as things turned out, had been beyond his most wildly optimistic expectations. Tomorrow's Berkeley Square media conference was, he considered now, the icing on the cake. Making his way across to the drinks cabinet, he selected a twenty-five-year-old bottle of port, before pouring out a glass for himself. Time for a celebratory nightcap, he decided. Berkeley Square would be setting the scene for him, with One Commando revealed in the very worst and most duplicitous light. It was all just perfect for his purposes.

Wednesday, 6 October

Lloyd got into work early, and spent the morning going through Vinnie's telephone conversations. Mark had told him about the call setting up a meeting in Regent's Park, but hadn't been able to give him a date; Lloyd was having to screen through every single call on the computer.

As he got into the routine of listening to the first few seconds of each, he thought about how Vinnie himself was now sitting five thousand miles away in a police cell. He'd read the details of his part of the attack in the paper on the way into work. Taking part in an armed break-in with the intention of committing grievous bodily harm carried penalties of several years in jail which, the paper's legal experts were saying, would almost certainly be spent in America.

Mark, meanwhile, was being lauded as the hero of the day, whose quick thinking had saved not only himself, but Isis and Holly from an unimaginable fate. An enterprising paparazzi photographer had, with the aid of his telephoto lens, snapped a photograph of Mark, arm in a sling, while in hospital – a photo which had been plastered all over today's tabloids.

Head bent as he listened to each sound-bite, clicking the cursor forward, Lloyd worked with unusual intensity and speed. On the phone, Mark had gone to great lengths to stress the urgency. Although the media seemed to believe the show was over for One Commando, according to Mark there was something much bigger than the future of One Commando at stake. There was someone, right here in London he believed, who had a particular knowledge he could use to achieve everything that One Commando had failed to achieve – and without any of the risk. He could knock Isis off her pedestal and destroy her career by making known a particular piece of information. Just who this bloke was, and what motivated him, wasn't something Lloyd had discussed on the phone, but he thought about it a lot as he went through all the recordings. If there wasn't any risk involved to this man, why had One Commando launched their high-risk strike in Malibu? Just how closely was this guy working with One Commando? And had he been known to everyone in the group, or just the now-dead Larson?

He found the recording eventually. The conversation itself was of less interest than the telephone number of the incoming caller, also digitally recorded. Having copied the call on to a floppy disk, and written down the incoming telephone number, Lloyd quickly typed a code on the keyboard – and watched the entire directory being deleted. In less than a minute, he'd wiped out all trace of his illicit operation.

The Regent's Park caller didn't use an OmniCell number – that would have been just too easy, reflected Lloyd. Not that he was especially perturbed. Many of the industry's 'propeller heads' like himself knew each other. They met at exhibitions and conferences. They moved from one company to another. They traded information. With the caller signed up to a rival network, Lloyd realised it was time to call in a few favours.

It was halfway through the afternoon before his call into SatLink was returned. His SatLink mate, a former OmniCell colleague who'd moved companies, had been tied up in meetings. Lloyd had to do a lot of grovelling; confidentiality of customer records was the Holy Grail of the industry and never to be passed off lightly. Assuring his contact that his interests were entirely non-commercial, Lloyd had had to pull out all stops to persuade him. But the information did come through shortly before five; the user name was one

Jasper Jones. The phone was registered for personal use, with a billing address in Islington. The moment he had the information, Lloyd logged out of his computer and headed for the door.

Los Angeles
Wednesday, 6 October

Isis emerged from the bathroom of the lavish Peninsula Hotel suite, glancing across to where Holly was kneeling at the coffee table in the sitting room, with a colouring-in book. Hair still wrapped in a towel, and wearing a hotel dressing-gown, she made her way over to her daughter.

'Darling!' She sat on a sofa behind her. Turning, Holly climbed up and nuzzled into her lap.

'Did you sleep okay?'

'Snug as a bug in a rug,' replied Holly.

'Good.' She hugged her tight.

They had the whole floor to themselves, no one knew they were here, and there were police guarding the lift doors to make sure it stayed that way. After the attack, emergency medics from the ambulance had treated Holly and her for shock, then they'd gone back inside the house, but only for long enough to pack a few bags; they needed to get out of there. Hilton had made arrangements with the Peninsula, and the police had blocked off the media convoy. Arriving at the hotel they'd made their way, under protection, directly to the lifts and come straight up. Her doctor had arrived within half an hour and prescribed her some pills they might both need to get to sleep, as well as mild tranquillisers. But neither of them had taken any medication – they hadn't needed to.

Traumatic though the events of the previous day had

been, they had also been powerfully cathartic. For the first time Isis felt free of a direct threat to her life. The prospect of physical horror which had been with her ever since she'd heard of the Lefevre attack, was now gone. Although there was no escaping the intuitive sensation that things weren't completely over. That foreboding which she'd sensed ever since signing the Berkeley Square endorsement was still present in her consciousness, leaving her with the strange sensation of a life 'on hold'. She no longer felt directly threatened – but nor did she feel completely free. She had no desire to return home, but she wasn't sure whether she wanted to take off on holiday either – something that Hilton kept suggesting. As for Holly, it was hard to tell. She seemed to have taken it all in her stride – she'd even made a joke about it, as though the One Commando attack had had all the reality of a computer game. But what was really going on beneath that irrepressible exterior might not reveal itself, Isis knew, for some time.

Isis had also kept wondering about Mark. She'd tried calling him in hospital – only to find that he'd discharged himself. His cellphone had been switched off and it was only when she finally got hold of Mrs Martinez that she was told he was on his way back to England to see his family. She badly wanted to speak to him. Her feelings for him had gone through a profound change with the attack – she knew she owed him both Holly's life and her own. She recalled vividly every detail of what had happened – the risk he'd put himself under to rescue Holly from her hiding place; the way his escape plan had been the means of their release from siege.

She recalled too, with remorse, her own fury when he'd told her, outside Unum Music, how he'd discovered her secret. She'd been guilty, she realised now, of extreme selfishness. Even before the attack he'd deserved some kind of explanation; after the way he'd acted during it, she really felt the need to explain herself.

When the telephone rang, it was answered for her by their hotel butler.

'Message from Mr Lebowitz,' he said, coming through a short while later. 'He says you should watch CBS.'

The Berkeley Square item had already begun on the news by the time she'd switched on the television. In the foyer of Berkeley Square's much-publicised Madrid facility, the media corps was evidently larger than had been expected, judging by the crush; Lord Bullerton, Jacques Lefevre, and Andrew Craig were pressed against a white wall, while television lights blazed and flash cameras caught their every gesture. The purpose of today's session, Bullerton told the tightly packed assembly, was to clarify recent allegations made against the company. What had been billed as an executive briefing, however, soon dissolved into a witch hunt; no sooner had Craig announced that the laboratory featured in AFL leaflets had recently been identified as one within a few minutes' drive of Berkeley Square than pandemonium ensued.

Clutching Holly to her lap, Isis and her daughter both watched as journalists bayed for the address of Voisier Laboratories – which Craig was only too happy to supply. Whereupon there was an instant exodus out of the door. The female CBS reporter announced that over twenty teams of reporters and TV crews had made their way in convoy to Voisier Laboratories. Reaching the inside security fence, their demands to speak to the owner resulted only in the rapid exit, a short while later, of a white Mercedes from the back of the factory. This had provoked the media corps even further; in less than a minute they'd forced open the gates and, ignoring the two dazed security guards, had made their way inside the factory.

'Some viewers,' the CBS lady said, 'will find the following scenes distressing, but they are by no means among the worst that we found.'

Isis turned Holly's face away from the TV as there followed the same vision of hell that Bengt Larson had videotaped – but which the British police had never allowed into public circulation. As cameras panned over the row upon row of tortured animals, the CBS reporter, barely able to maintain her composure, described how Voisier Laboratories had perpetuated this same horror once before in Belgium – before being forced to close down.

Mercifully, the next footage showed rescue teams, as well as volunteer vets and other animal welfare groups, removing the lab animals and driving them away to new and more hopeful futures. Some, explained an animal welfare worker, would have to be put down, their diseased eyes and infected wounds too ravaged to treat. But for the others, new homes would be found. One of the most heart-wrenching sights was a baby chimpanzee being reunited with the tortured mother from which she had been separated, apparently for weeks. The two of them, clutching desperately at each other, were said to be bound for a primate sanctuary in Zimbabwe.

'Will they be all right now, Mummy?' Holly wanted to know.

'Yes, my baby,' Isis cuddled her. 'For ever and ever.'

Now the CBS reporter was wrapping up with an interview with Andrew Craig. 'Tell me, Dr Craig, how did you find out that Voisier Laboratories were One Commando's real targets?'

'Jordan Hampshire worked it out,' Craig told the cameras in his bluff brogue. 'He wondered if animal testing was going on in a facility nearby. After that, it was easy.'

'You never knew before,' the CBS reporter asked in disbelief, 'that this was going on in a laboratory just a few kilometres from here?'

Craig delivered a stony-eyed glance. 'Do *you* know everything that goes on in your business district?'

'So,' she had to roll with the blow, 'One Commando attempted deliberately to mislead people?'

'Unless they were, themselves, misled.' Craig was dry.

The reporter looked astounded. 'You must admit, Dr Craig, that's a far-fetched proposition?'

'I must admit nothing of the kind. It is one possibility.'

'But who would want to mislead an animal rights group? And for what reason?'

Craig was looking into the distance contemplatively, before musing, 'For what reason, indeed?'

24

At the wheel of the hire car, Lloyd headed out in the direction of Ealing, Mark sitting beside him in the passenger seat. He'd arrived back in London the afternoon before and had gone straight to the family home in Lewisham. Their mother had been extremely anxious since the attack, and even though they'd spoken on the phone and he'd reassured her that he was all right, she couldn't wait to see him. She'd fussed and flapped about him, not letting him pick anything up and frequently asking him how he felt – 'It's just a damaged muscle, Mum,' he found himself telling her sharply after he'd been home a few hours.

But he knew he'd done the right thing coming back. Last night the three of them had sat down to his favourite childhood meal – grilled cutlets followed by strawberry cheesecake – and he'd produced a bottle of champagne he'd bought duty free. His Mum had toasted his health and success with *Nile* but, thought Mark, what they knew she was really toasting was the end of the One Commando threat.

Lloyd had taken today off work. Earlier this morning he'd

picked up the hire car – Mark had decided to treat himself to a BMW – before collecting his brother. Last night, as soon as their mother had gone to bed, Mark had looked at Lloyd and asked, 'Traced that number?'

Speaking quickly in a low voice, Lloyd had told him about his investigations. After getting hold of Jasper Jones's address, Lloyd had set out on a recce, directly from work. He hadn't really known, in his own mind, what he was expecting by staking out Jones's home. He supposed he hoped to catch sight of him. But by the time he got there, he wondered if he was too late. From what he could gather, walking past the street number, Jones occupied both floors of a terrace house; sitting on a concealed doorstep opposite and slightly down the street, Lloyd observed a light being switched on. Someone was at home, and unless Jones had a partner or housemate, that someone must be him.

It was cold and dark outside and, huddled up, pressing his knees to his chest, Lloyd had stared up at the house, and observed the occasional passer-by. He could never be a private eye, he'd reckoned, glancing frequently at his watch as the minutes ticked slowly past. After over an hour of this he wondered if he should just go home. It seemed pointless hanging round waiting for nothing to happen. Besides, Jones was probably settled in for the night and had no plans of going anywhere. He was about to get up when he heard the sharp click of stilettos on the pavement followed, a short while later, by the appearance of a tall, striking woman making her way purposefully along the opposite side of the street. She wasn't only highly attractive, as Lloyd observed when she walked under the streetlights, but even though she was carrying a couple of M&S grocery bags she conveyed an indefinable glamour, as though she was used to being watched. She had to be a model, he decided.

As her footsteps slowed, he was wondering casually which house she lived in, when she made her way directly towards Jones's front door. Halting, she pressed the buzzer; from across the street, Lloyd heard the sound of footsteps descending the stairs. Would he get a glimpse of Jones, he wondered? When the door swung open, would he stand in the entrance to greet her? But there were no hugs and kisses for public display. The woman was inside the moment the door had opened.

Outside, Lloyd had reflected that Jasper Jones was a lucky man. The woman had come armed with M&S bags and looked like she was set to cook supper – all very cosy. Was she a girlfriend? She didn't have keys to his house, so maybe things were still fairly new. Mulling over the possibilities, Lloyd heard raised voices only moments before Jones's door was opening again and out came the woman, still with the groceries, slamming the door behind her. The crashing of the door reverberated all the way up the quiet street as she stormed back in the direction from which she'd come only minutes earlier. Lloyd glanced between the girl and Jones's front door, expecting it to swing open at any instant, and for Jones to make an appearance. But there was no sign of him.

Lloyd thought quickly about what he should do: he could continue on here, staking out Jones's house. But if he did that, he'd lose the girl – and she could be useful. Besides, he decided, he could always come back tomorrow morning and catch Jones on his way to work.

Quickly getting up from where he'd been huddled in the shadows, he headed down the street in hot pursuit. She was easy to follow and completely oblivious to what was going on around her, absorbed no doubt in the row she'd just had with Jones. She caught the Underground at the Angel and he trailed her movements as she switched to the Piccadilly

Line, finding a seat and burying her head in a *Marie Claire* magazine for what was evidently to be a long trip. Sitting just two seats away from her, close up he appreciated her blonde good looks all the more – the high cheekbones, narrow chin, and radiant blueness of her eyes. He noted how she attracted a lot of attention in the train – she must be used to being stared at, he guessed, although she showed no sign of being aware of anyone else.

She got off at Ealing Common and, making her way down to the Broadway, turned left. Evening diners as well as visitors to the pub on the corner gave him cover as he tracked her into a residential street. Falling well back, he watched carefully as she extracted a bunch of keys from her handbag, making her way to the front door of a semi-detached house, and let herself in.

'I'm not sure if she's anyone useful . . .' Lloyd told Mark, after reporting this.

Mark met his eyes with a determined glance. 'You've done a great job!' he told him. 'And right now, we need all the leads we can get.'

Then, observing Lloyd's surprise, he got up from where he'd been sitting and paced the room, gesturing with his free hand while he spoke.

'The way I see it, what we've got right now is a real bugger's muddle. I'm having trouble trying to make sense of it all. Why did One Commando launch a high-risk operation in California, when they could have done far more commercial damage releasing the information they have about Isis?'

Lloyd followed his brother intently.

'How come Larson didn't know about the Voisier thing?'

'Are you sure he didn't?' Lloyd interjected.

'As sure as I can be,' he said. 'I was on the floor. He was

tying me up. I told him about Voisier. He just went mad—'

'Maybe—'

'Uh-uh,' Mark anticipated him. 'Not that kind of mad. More like he was angry I could even suggest it.' Mark paused, staring into the mid-distance before turning back to Lloyd.

'Then there's the biggest question of all.'

'Who tipped the police off?'

'Exactly.' Mark nodded soberly. 'Had to be an insider.'

Now, as they curved round the Chiswick roundabout, heading north towards Ealing, the two of them talked tactics. The way Mark saw it, they had only two options. They could follow up Lloyd's leads themselves. Or they could go to the police. Mark wasn't in any hurry to see all their own investigative work come to nothing – besides which, if they went to the police they'd have had to admit how Lloyd had broken the law bugging Vinnie's phone, which would get him into serious trouble at OmniCell. Going to see Jasper Jones's evening visitor seemed the best thing to do right now – though they both had their reservations; what if she slammed the door in their faces and refused to speak? Worse, what if she told Jones that they'd been round asking questions? All they could count on was the row Lloyd had witnessed two evenings before – and the impact of her opening the door to find Jordan Hampshire on her front step.

They parked the car a few metres from her home in the wide, tree-lined street. It was mid-afternoon and they knew that if 'the model', as Lloyd referred to her, had an office job, they'd have to hang around – and just hope she made her way straight home. But something about her made Lloyd think she wasn't a regular office worker – she'd just didn't seem the type.

They climbed out of the car into the chill afternoon. The sun was weak behind smudged banks of grey cloud, but at least it was dry. Making their way to the front door, Mark reached for the round, brass knocker and hammered three times. The two brothers exchanged a tense glance. Then there was a sound coming from inside, and a shadow appeared behind the frosted-glass panels of the door.

'Who is it?' came a woman's voice.

'Jordan Hampshire,' announced Mark.

'Yeah. That'd be right. And I'm Isis.' The voice was young and clear, and had the intonation of recently acquired refinement. As she moved closer, they saw blonde hair dappled through the frosted glass.

'Seriously! It's me.'

Evidently curious, and perhaps recognising his voice from TV, she carefully opened the door – on the chain – and peered out. Mark took a step back so she could see him, meeting the two wide blue eyes.

'Did the agency send you round?' she seemed not to believe what she was seeing.

He shook his head. 'Found my own way round. This is my brother, Lloyd,' he said, pointing. 'We need to ask you a couple of quick questions.'

She paused. 'What about?'

'A guy who lives in Islington. We only know him as Jasper Jones—'

'I've nothing to say about that tosser,' she snorted. 'I chucked him two nights ago.'

Relieved to hear this, Mark decided to risk it, 'The thing is, he may have been caught up in criminal activity—'

'Why don't you go to the police?' The eyes glanced from Mark to Lloyd.

He shook his head, 'I'm afraid it's not that simple.'

The door closed and they heard the chain being slipped back before she was opening the door. Mark had to agree with Lloyd – she *was* spectacular. About-turning, she took their entrance for granted and was leading the way through to the lounge. 'I can't believe it's you here,' she told Mark.

'It's me all right.'

'So what's she like?'

'Who?'

'Isis!' she replied, sitting on a black leather sofa and looking for all the world as if she'd just stepped out of a glossy magazine. 'Is she a moody cow like they make out?'

Mark remembered that, as far as 'the model' was concerned, Isis and he were an item. 'You know how it goes,' he and Lloyd sat down opposite, 'we have our moments.' He met her eyes. 'What couples don't?'

'That's not how it was with Jas,' she picked up on the cue.

'No?'

'I don't know what you want to know about him,' eyes narrowing she leaned forward in her seat, 'but I'll give it to you straight: he's a two-timing bastard.'

To their surprise, she didn't enquire further about criminal activity before launching into a tirade about Jasper Jones. How they'd met at Models Against Mink, and how he'd subsequently courted her. Clearly a girl that demanded drama, she told them of her suspicions right from the start. The furtive phone calls from behind closed doors. The unexplained absences.

'He might even be married for all I know!' Her mercurial gaze flicked from one to the other. She was enjoying the celebrity audience. 'I could tell you a few stories about men, believe me. A girl can't be too careful. She has to keep a close eye.'

Mark was nodding in agreement. As she'd been speaking

he'd already realised: at the very least, this girl was highly volatile, unhinged. He had a pretty good idea Lloyd was thinking the same thing too; this one was a 'rabbit-boiler'. Now he asked her, 'You kept . . . a close eye?'

'Have to, don't you? I listened to his phone calls—'

'How d'you do that?' Lloyd was surprised.

She shrugged. 'Changed the mode of his answerphone so it recorded incoming calls. There was nothing on the tapes – at least no female callers – but that doesn't mean a lot by itself, does it?'

'These tapes—?' Mark probed.

'I s'pose you'll be wanting them?' She tilted her head, coquettish.

'Well, it would be—'

'Only if you promise you'll give me your autograph.'

'That's not a problem.'

'And a photo!' She glanced over at Lloyd. 'Will you take a photo of the two of us. The girls will never believe this!'

She stepped across the lounge and was going through a cabinet drawer.

'Doesn't surprise me you think he's a crook,' she shuddered, collecting up a handful of micro-cassettes.

'No?'

'Always had his mind on something else. Always plotting and scheming. And people used to send in the most . . . kinky videos.'

Giving Mark the handful of micro-cassettes, she resumed her seat opposite.

'Sex videos?' asked Lloyd.

She screwed her face up, 'Just . . . kinky. S&M, I suppose. There was one I saw, and this bloke was being strung up by a rope by these thugs in black outfits and masks. Acted like he was being hanged. At least – I think it was acting.'

Mark gave Lloyd a sideways glance. 'But why, I mean, would people send that sort of thing to him?'

'It was his job, wasn't it? Videos.'

Mark shook his head, bemused. 'I've no idea what his job is.'

'Well, just shows you, doesn't it?' She rolled her eyes, leaning back in the sofa. 'He told me he was well known. Like, everyone in the industry was supposed to know his work.'

'So, what *does* he do?' Lloyd could barely contain himself.

'He makes documentaries. He calls himself,' she grimaced, 'the *master* of the exposé. He goes into things, undercover, and makes these fly-on-the-wall programmes . . .'

Opposite, Mark buried his face in his hands. It was a long, long time before he murmured, 'Of course!' His voice was husky. 'It had to be.'

Jasper Jones worked in the editing suite under the offices of Love Smith Ben David. It was late – after eleven, and he was pale and drawn as he sat going through video footage on several different monitors, an annotated script in front of him. Tonight, like the past few nights, would be a late one as he rushed the production through, but he wasn't worried by the lack of sleep – he was still living on adrenaline.

What had started as an idea for an engaging insider documentary had quickly developed way beyond that. The One Commando activity had burgeoned beyond his most fanciful dreams. Then, when he'd made the discovery about Isis's secret, that had been transformational. He'd no longer be hawking round a fly-on-the-wall series to the major TV channels. Christ, no! They'd be scrambling to buy not just the documentary, but the book rights too. This thing would be a multi-media extravaganza. Of course, there'd be rich pickings from the newspaper exclusive. He'd be able to expand his already sizeable investment portfolio. Yes, he'd be rolling in it. All the expense so far had definitely been worth it. And then there'd be TV awards, the talk-show circuit – overnight, he would become the most celebrated director and author in Britain.

He didn't look up immediately when he heard a noise at the door. Too absorbed in his work, it took him a moment to register that the last person had gone home an hour before. When he did look up, he half expected to find the night watchman, on one of his routine patrols. Instead, there was a young man in his mid-twenties in jeans and a jacket, standing eyeing him from the door.

'Mr Jones?'

'Who are you?' He was irritated by the distraction.

'The name doesn't matter,' the other stood, hands in his pockets, cocky. 'I'm with the AFL.'

'Who let you in?' Jones's annoyance grew. 'How did you get past security?'

The other pulled a droll expression. 'Your old boy wanted a smoke, didn't he? So he stepped outside for a while.' He shrugged. 'Open house.'

Jones's eyes flashed from the intruder back to the monitor. 'Well. Now's not a good time.'

'I bet it's not.' The other's tone was laced with sarcasm. Jerking his head towards the monitors he asked, 'Making your One Commando documentary, are you?'

Jones responded with a disdainful stare.

'No need to pretend with me, Mr Jones. You see, some of the others at AFL might be idiots, but I'm not.' He tapped his head. 'Worked it out, you see.'

'Did you really?'

'I reckon this Voisier thing didn't catch you by surprise at all. I reckon you knew about it all along—'

'Don't be so stupid!' snarled Jones. 'How on earth could I have known?'

'Maybe you put the Berkeley Square sign there yourself?'

Jones glared contemptuously across the room at the young intruder. He'd been prepared for all kinds of contingencies, but this had caught him unawares. Though he supposed he shouldn't be surprised by some kind of backlash from the AFL.

'Now look here,' his tone was imperious, 'you're welcome to your own opinions, but the fact of the matter is that I'm as shocked as you are by what has happened. This completely destroys everything we've been working so hard to achieve.'

'Not from where I'm sitting it doesn't.' The other took a step closer. 'The way I see it – it all makes for great TV. I mean, who's ever heard of Voisier? Who cares what they do to cute, fluffy animals? But Berkeley Square—'

'This isn't about TV!'

'Isn't it?'

'My involvement in the animal rights movement has nothing whatsoever to do with my professional career.'

The young man was shaking his head. 'Wish I could believe you, mate, but it doesn't add up, does it? I mean, take that Lefevre guy. He could have been knocked over the head, or shot or something and no one would have given a damn. But gouge his eyes out, well, that's a different kettle of fish, ain't it? That's prime-time TV. That was your idea, wasn't it?'

'I had no influence at all on what One Commando planned for Lefevre!' Jones blustered.

'Same with that attack in Malibu. It couldn't work, could it. It was never going to work—'

'Larson was the most capable commander I'd ever met. If anyone was going to do it—'

'Yeah, but not with the police coming after him,' suggested Lloyd.

'What on earth—'

'Both times,' he pointed at Jones. 'Hilton Gallo. And Malibu. Both times the police are tipped off just before the attack. Too much of a coincidence to my way of thinking.'

Jones felt his heart pound, his mouth go dry. This guy knew far more than he could have just picked up. He'd been working on it.

'Look, Mr Whatever-your-name-is,' he tried to brazen it out, 'this is all a wonderful conspiracy theory. Quite magnificent. The only problem with it is that it's complete rubbish.'

'I'll tell you why I know you're lying,' Lloyd continued calmly as he came towards him. 'What happened to the single most powerful weapon One Commando ever had? And don't pretend you don't know what I'm talking about.' He glanced at one of the monitors which had a frozen image of Isis in performance. 'Yes,' he nodded, 'her. What happened to *that* information?'

Jones sat back in his seat. It was impossible to assert himself as the other leaned over him.

'I'll tell you what happened,' continued Lloyd. 'Nothing. It was never used. You thought you'd keep it for yourself, didn't you? Make sure your production was the most sensational exposé ever seen?'

He stared down at Jones's face, only a few inches from his own.

'Got to hand it to you,' he smiled mirthlessly. 'You've had half the AFL dancing to your tune for the last twelve months. Larson's dead and his guys have been put away, and all this time you've been sitting here in your Director's chair choreographing the whole thing. They didn't know they were just actors. While they were all taking it for real, all you were interested in was a prime-time TV series!'

Sliding further down in his chair, Jones was becoming even more alarmed by the outpouring of discoveries. This intruder posed a serious threat to his plans. Arguing with him wasn't going to work. He had to be neutralised. Jones hadn't come all this way, paid out all that cash, for his plans to be ruined now. For a long while the two stared, unblinking, at each other as Jones tried to figure it out. Then he glanced away at an anglepoise lamp, before he asked in a businesslike tone: 'Why have you come here?'

Lloyd cocked his head. 'Why d'you think?'

'You're not like the others,' said Jones as though thinking aloud. 'I think you're here to cut a deal.'

Lloyd nodded. 'Keep talking.'

'You're looking for a pay-out.'

'Silence money, right?'

'Yes.'

'What kind of deal?'

'Fifty thousand pounds.'

'Puh-lease,' Lloyd was shaking his head. 'I'd get more than that from the papers. I want a cut.'

Jones looked alarmed. 'What kind of—'

'I'd say keeping all your secrets is quite a big job. I reckon it's worth about fifty per cent of takings.'

Jones looked up into Lloyd's face with an expression of undisguised loathing. As though he was going to hand over half his earnings to some self-styled sleuth from the AFL. Especially after he'd spent so much on this project already. Did this arrogant little upstart really think it came that easy? Eventually he said, 'Okay. Fifty per cent.'

'You can start by advancing me a payment right now.'

Jones held his gaze. 'It'd have to be a cheque. We don't keep—'

'A cheque's fine,' the other stepped back from him. 'I'm sure you wouldn't want it to bounce.'

'My office.' Jones gestured towards the door, rising from his chair.

Nodding, Lloyd made his way out of the editing suite. No sooner had he got to the door, however, than he felt a swingeing arc of pain in his shoulder and he was slumping down to the floor. Behind him, Jones had seized the anglepoise lamp. Using it as a club, he'd brought its heavy base crashing down on Lloyd with all his strength. Aiming for Lloyd's head, he'd missed and struck his shoulder instead. Now Lloyd was trying to scramble across the floor, away from him.

'You don't really think I'm going to hand over half my hard-earned cash to some jumped-up Sherlock Holmes do you?' he sneered at Lloyd who was jammed in a corner between the photocopier and a dustbin. 'Larson's been my lackey all this time – what makes you think I'm going to let a nobody like you—'

'It's too late!' cried Lloyd.

'Oh, I don't think so.' Jones pressed down his foot on Lloyd's chest.

He already had a plan. There was a service elevator just outside. Once he'd knocked this one out cold, he could get him down to basement parking and into the boot of his car with no one around to notice a thing. He'd make sure the offices were left neat and tidy before heading for the municipal dump. Larson had once given him a lecture about body disposal. There was a Glock pistol concealed beneath the driver's seat of his Saab. In less than an hour, this whole unpleasant incident would be over.

Now as he raised the anglepoise again, Lloyd screamed out, 'I'm wired!'

'Nice try, sunshine.'

Jones was bringing the lamp smashing down towards where Lloyd was trapped, when he suddenly buckled, the anglepoise smashing through the glass panel of the open photocopier as he stumbled forward.

'He's right.' Jones heard a familiar voice behind him.

Lurching round he found himself face to face with Mark Watson.

'Yeah, it's me.' Mark noted Jones's aghast expression with grim satisfaction. Then gesturing towards Lloyd, 'Quite an actor, isn't he, my kid brother?'

Jones glared from Mark to Lloyd and back again. 'What's this?' He was bewildered.

'You should know.' Mark regarded him coolly. 'It's what you do best, Mr Jones. It's a sting.'

Jones stepped forward, seizing Mark by his shirt. Using his good arm, Mark pushed him back. 'I wouldn't do anything more if I were you.' He met his eyes with a grim smile. 'The boys in blue are already on their way up.'

When the lift door opened downstairs ten minutes later, the night watchman didn't immediately grasp what had happened. All he knew was that the police had arrived half an hour earlier with a warrant for access to several floors of the building. Nothing like this had ever happened on his shift before.

Of course, he knew who Jasper Jones was; many nights Jones had been the last one out of the building. 'All locked up, sir?' he'd ask if Jones left by the front door. Jones would generally grunt some form of acknowledgement.

Tonight, when Jones stepped out of the lift, the watchman

didn't notice that he was attached to a policeman by a pair of cuffs.

'All locked up, sir?' he called out as usual.

But tonight, Jones didn't reply. Quick as a flash, the policeman answered on his behalf. 'He will be, for about fifteen years.'

Maldives
Monday, 11 October

On the verandah of the beachside bungalow, Isis reached out her hand to where Mark was sitting opposite. They had just finished a delicious dinner, and as they sat relaxing in the sultry night, the only light came from a bowl of floating candles on the table – and the turquoise glow of phosphorescence from the coral reef offshore. Palm fronds rustled gently along the beachfront and from the darkness of the vegetation all about them came the ethereal cadences of crickets.

'Four days.' Isis's eyes glinted in the darkness. 'Feels more like four weeks. It's like LA was a different era.'

Mark leaned back in his cane chair. 'I s'pose in some ways it was. It'll be a very different LA we return to, thank God.'

Soon after the Jones arrest, Hilton Gallo had dispatched them both for a week's rest and recuperation. A hurried consultation with GCM's travel agency had produced this private chalet in the Maldives, where they were guaranteed seclusion. There was no radio or television to intrude into their thoughts. And only with some reluctance had Isis agreed to leave the telephone connected. For one whole week, it was just the three of them.

They had spent the first three days on the beach, soaking up the sunshine, unwinding from all the tension and drama of the past weeks. Mark and Isis had helped Holly build extravagant sandcastles and, as the days wore on, the three of them had become closer and closer. Holly would march into Mark's bedroom in the morning and drag him blinking into the sunshine to play games on the sand. Isis would look on in amusement from the verandah, glad that her daughter seemed to be emotionally unscathed by the traumatic events at their home, and impressed at Mark's easy way with her child. They had taken a boat trip out to look at the corals and exotic fish. There had been something magical about swimming among beautiful, vividly coloured creatures with Holly and this man who had saved their lives.

She wished that she hadn't put up so many barriers when she and Mark had first met – it was because she had felt attracted to him and feared the consequences. When they had been recording *Nile* the sexual tension between them had been electric, but she had felt powerless to act on it. Threatened by it even. For those two days in the studio they had enjoyed a fleeting intimacy but then the whole nightmare with the AFL had taken off, and their uneasy alliance had been tested to breaking point. She had treated him badly, she knew, and as she got to know him better now, she realised how lucky she was that he hadn't just turned his back on her. It was a sign of their feelings for each other that they had managed to come through it all together. And under the blue skies of this tropical paradise, they were gradually rediscovering their earlier closeness – a friendship that was daily growing into something deeper.

Last night, their third night together, after Holly had gone to bed, Isis finally found the strength to tell Mark what she knew he'd been so desperate to hear. She had already made her mind up, of course; a sense of obligation. Besides, he already knew her secret; what he deserved to understand was *why*.

It hadn't been easy going back into it, revisiting the trauma she'd spent her whole adult life trying to put behind her. But for Mark, hearing Isis's side of the story had been revelatory. His gaze had been unfaltering as she'd related the most extraordinary experience of anyone he'd ever been close to – made all the more extraordinary by the spectacular heights of achievement she'd subsequently reached. The private agonies she'd suffered gave him a new understanding. And as he knew more, as she'd told him of her most intimate fears of the past, her father's brutality and her mother's silent acquiescence, he'd been ashamed of his own initial reaction to the discovery. Instead of aversion, he'd felt a welling up of admiration at her courage.

'There's something I don't understand,' he'd said, earlier in the evening. 'Holly.'

'John and I adopted her.'

'So that whole thing about phoning John when you were in labour—'

Isis smiled, shrugging. 'Leo Lebowitz. Who else?'

They had spoken for hours and from the heart. Now that there were no barriers from Isis's side, their conversation flowed with an easy effortlessness – there suddenly seemed so much to talk about. After they'd finished, in the early hours of the morning, and Isis had fallen asleep, exhausted, on the chalet sofa, Mark had picked her up in his arms, and taken her through to her bedroom. Putting her to bed and drawing the covers over her, he'd looked down at where she slept with an overwhelming tenderness.

Tonight, he felt a return of that same tenderness as he held her eyes across the table. And not only tenderness. Lifting Isis's hand to his lips, he kissed it.

'You're so beautiful, Isis,' he told her. 'You've always done it for me.'

She looked over at him questioningly. 'Even now?'

'Even now.'

Getting up from the table, he came round beside her and she rose to her feet. They kissed, with searching, passionate kisses, his hands descending her back as he held her to him.

'So,' he broke apart after a moment, 'I'm not just some small boy in short pants any more, caught up in something out of his league?'

She met his grin with a chuckle. 'Yeah? And what happened to the bitch from hell?'

They both laughed before he kissed her again, then reminded her, 'There are no cameras here.'

'This isn't for the cameras,' she replied, her hands roving down his body. Then, eyes meeting his, 'And it never was . . . only for the cameras.'

'Now there's an admission!'

There could be no mistaking his arousal – or hers – as they clung together in their awakening desire. Wordlessly, he put his hand round her waist, and led her across the verandah, to her bedroom.

Los Angeles

'One never likes owning up to a mistake, but I have to eat my words, Leo,' Hilton faced Lebowitz, who was sitting opposite him on one of his cream sofas.

Lebowitz returned a quizzical expression.

'There was a time back there, just ten days ago, when I was convinced we'd be unable to contain the Isis story. Remember you said we shouldn't be pre-emptive because you never knew what was round the corner. Well, you were right and I was wrong.'

Lebowitz shrugged with a wry smile as Hilton put aside

the report he'd been sent by Scotland Yard, detailing Jasper Jones's arrest.

Hilton was shaking his head. 'Who would have thought the enemy was a documentary maker?' Then, after a reflective pause, 'D'you reckon he can do us any harm from behind bars?'

Lebowitz shook his head. 'Zero credibility,' he replied. 'No one will believe a word he says now.'

'Meantime he's just delivered us more pre-launch publicity than we could have dreamed of,' beamed Hilton.

The arrest of Jones had given the One Commando story yet another unexpected twist to which the media, on both sides of the Atlantic, hadn't failed to respond. With the launch of Isis and Jordan's album less than ten days away, public obsession with the couple had never been greater.

'I've stood the crisis team down,' Lebowitz told him, 'and the Isis files are back in secure holding.'

Hilton met his eyes. 'No need for damage limitation after all.'

'None,' agreed Lebowitz, 'her secret is still safe. You know, after this, I can't help thinking it always will be.'

EPILOGUE

Father Marvin Robieri was proud of what had been achieved at St Columbus's. During the past decade the Italian community, to which the church belonged, had prospered. And St Columbus had prospered with it. The church roof appeal had been the start of the transformation, though the urgently needed replacement of the dilapidated roof had soon been followed by other construction work, which Father Marvin had, for a very long time, been offering up for Divine Blessing.

It was living proof of prayer in action, Father Marvin would frequently remind his congregation. First there had been the new St Columbus Hall, where youth group meetings, community events and other informal gatherings were held, giving the church an even more active part in the life of the community. Then there was the Outreach centre in town, where trained counsellors were on duty, twenty-four hours a day, to help those whose lives were being torn apart by drugs, alcohol and domestic violence. Most recently, a suite of offices had been added behind the Hall, to accommodate the growing number of pastoral and administrative staff required by the burgeoning activities run by St Columbus.

The development of the St Columbus website had been one of Father Marvin's more rewarding projects. Always technologically minded, he had been inspired by a visit to St Columbus's by a group of pupils from Milan to create a forum within which his local congregation could stay in touch with friends and family in the old country. He'd been amazed by the number of visitors to the site from all over the world, starting on the very day of its inception. The two terminals he had installed at the back of St Columbus Hall for e-mail purposes had proved so popular that he'd swiftly ordered another three, and a Communications Room had been created. Adding to the website in every way he knew how, Father Marvin had come to regard it not merely as a tool for communication, but also as a repository for everything that was important to the life of the Church. All its activities and history were now instantly accessible to anyone, wherever in the world they might be; it was a way of putting his own community on the virtual map.

It had been a long and onerous task, going through records since the Church had begun, collecting information and either keying it or scanning it into his computer. But there would be people, out there, who would find his work of value, he had no doubt. And if, through his labours, he drew just one single person into the fold, all his efforts, he would remind himself, would have been worthwhile.

Having inputted all the community records – baptisms, marriages and funerals – since St Columbus had begun, he found himself beginning to wonder if there was any further need to keep the many boxes of ageing files and papers which were now easily accessible by computer. What was the point? While he was required by law to keep certain records, most of the material cluttering up the new admin offices fell way outside that category.

In the end he decided to make his own rule; any records that were over ten years old which he wasn't required to keep, he would discard. It was an important task and one that required discretion – which was why he'd taken it upon himself to go through every single one of the ageing records.

The job had already taken several months, and he was less than halfway through. It was something he fitted in between all his other more urgent activities, and he'd usually find himself in the admin offices late in the evening, after a function in the Hall, spending an hour or two clearing out more boxes. He would go through every page of each file. Not a single document was to be consigned to the black bin-liner at his feet until he had looked at it to make sure it shouldn't be kept. And whenever he doubted the relevance of a piece of information, he kept it.

While Father Marvin was sometimes to be heard describing his task of clearing out the archives in wearied tones, it was one that wasn't entirely a burden. Much of the work was routine, but there were plenty of memories and nostalgic reflections too as he sifted through the paperwork: a baptismal notice which conjured up the image of anxious parents sitting outside the vestry; names which recalled faces of those in the community with whom he'd had dealings in the long-distant past, forgotten till now.

This particular night he came upon a set of programmes for a carol concert held at the church twenty years before. There must have been thirty of them wrapped around with an elastic band. Extracting one, he opened it up and glanced through it. He supposed he must have had a hand in producing it, though he couldn't really remember. Below the list of carols were printed the names of all those who had appeared, including the organist who'd been at the church for thirty years – now, sadly, passed away, several members of the congregation – had they really all been together for that long? And of course the children. They were mostly just a blur of names – even for Father Marvin who was well known for his excellent memory. One or two names did stand out. Those kids who'd gone on to achieve great things with their lives. And those whom he remembered for less grati-fying reasons – problems with the law, parents, authority of all kinds.

Now as he scanned down the list he paused at a name which instantly brought an altogether different memory; he could remember watching the poor kid walking past St Columbus's on the way home from school, day after day. Always alone. It had been there from the start to those sensi-tive enough to notice it, but as the child reached puberty, the differentness was inescapable. Father Marvin had felt his heart go out, his compassion aroused – though he had a policy of never directly intervening in the lives of his congre-gation unless asked. Instead, he'd suggested the idea of the carol concert to the mother, Rosa Carboni, who'd duly sent her child to take part in the choir. Father Marvin had looked for opportunities to nurture the poor kid, whom, he remem-bered now, had possessed a remarkably good singing voice. He'd hoped, perhaps to open a door, to create a point of contact. But after the carol concert, the child hadn't returned to choir.

Now that he thought about it, Father Marvin realised he had no idea what had happened after that Christmas. The father, a tyrannical brute by all accounts, had died some years ago. The mother suffered from Alzheimer's and he'd visited her in hospital several times though she hadn't remembered him. But what had become of the child? Father

Marvin searched his memory; no, he couldn't remember anything, though he could recall the blank faces of friends of the family whom he'd once asked. It was, he reflected, just one of life's many mysteries which he'd continue to live with – what had happened to little Marco Corrado Carboni?

Expiry Date

To my very dear friends
Alec Berber, Tom Curtin, and Adrian and Marlene Mitchell,
and to my darling wife Koala, with love.

Acknowledgements

My special thanks to Kate Davidson of the University of Surrey's Centre for Research on Ageing and Gender for her invaluable support while researching this book; Dr Douglas Robbie for providing such clear direction on medical matters and Alex Singleton, whose encyclopaedic knowledge of criminal activity and police procedure has, once again, been extremely helpful.

This existence of ours is as transient as autumn clouds.
To watch the birth and death of beings is like looking at
the movements of a dance.
A lifetime is like a flash of lightning in the sky,
Rushing by, like a torrent down a steep mountain.

BUDDHA (from the Extensive Sport Sutra)

I don't want to achieve immortality through my work . . . I
want to achieve it through not dying.

WOODY ALLEN

Prologue

It would have been just another suburban tragedy – except for one thing.

That afternoon, Andrew Norton left his City office early, catching the 2.20 train from Waterloo. On arrival at Weybridge station, he walked out to the car park, climbed into his Honda CRV, and began the three-mile drive through the curving arboured lanes to Matthew's school.

This was a twice-weekly ritual. On a good day, Matt and he would be home by three. After settling his son with homework and a mug of tea, Andrew would head down the corridor to his study. His PC was linked to the office intranet and he'd resume work, keeping an eye on Matt till Jess got home from her graphic design job just after six.

Andrew's bosses at Glencoe Asset Management liked to hold him up as a glowing example of their own enlightened working practices. But the truth was that for three of the past five years, Glencoe's North American Fund had yielded the highest returns in its sector making Andrew, at forty-three, one of the most sought-after fund managers in

1

the City. Glencoe had no intention of losing him for the sake of a few hours of teleworking. And for his part, the afternoons at home made him feel more engaged in his son's life, which was important to him. Time, after all, was fast running out.

That particular afternoon, Andrew passed between the ivy-clad gateposts of Greendale Primary, and headed for the covered courtyard outside the school offices. He pulled up directly in front of the 'No Parking' sign – a special dispensation of the Headmaster's – and waved over to where Matt was, as usual, at the centre of a group of kids messing about outside the hall.

Jess and he had been worried when Matt joined the school two years before. Even though his celebrity preceded him, there was no guarantee he'd be accepted by the kids in Primary 4. But within days they'd realised all would be well. Matt's sunny optimism led to rapid popularity and his sharp wit made detractors think twice about teasing. He hadn't been at Greendale a month before a request had come from Primary 6 asking for his attendance at an interschool athletics meeting; Matt had already acquired mascot status.

Getting out of the CRV, Andrew opened the tailgate. Whizzing towards him from across the courtyard, Matt came to a halt before climbing out of his wheelchair and gingerly making his way into the passenger seat of the car. With ease of practice, Andrew folded the chair, slid it in the car and closed the door, before returning to the driver's seat. Matt's leg had come out of its plaster cast two weeks before. Even though he was capable of walking, doctors thought it best he should stick to his wheelchair, especially at school. They didn't want to risk another fall.

The drive home that day had been uneventful. Andrew asked about the morning's spelling test. Matt talked excitedly about a forthcoming trip to the Natural History Museum. Would he be allowed out of his chair for the visit, he'd wanted to know?

Once home, they followed their familiar routine, Andrew putting the kettle on for tea, and Matt collecting a few slices out of the breadbin for the ducks. Their home, acquired after several years of six-figure Glencoe bonuses, was a bungalow with a lawn that rolled gently down to the water's edge. Living on a river had always been a dream of Jess's, one Andrew had come to share after nearly ten years of suffocation in a Clerkenwell loft. Down at the bottom of the garden, a sturdy wooden landing made for an excellent vantage point both up and down the river. Around three in the afternoon, without fail, the ducks would assemble in noisy anticipation of Matt's arrival.

Because he was still wheelchair-bound, Andrew pushed him down the lawn to the landing, a Cellophane wrapper of bread in his lap. More than fearful of water, Matt had always shrunk from the river bank, even though his parents had long since installed protective railings. But up on the landing he felt steady and secure.

There was the usual fracas as he began tearing off pieces for the mêlée of gathering mallards and teals. Andrew delighted in the expression on his son's face as he dispensed largesse to the flapping, clucking flock. Matt was always careful to ensure that the smaller, less aggressive birds got their share.

The telephone ringing up in the house sounded above the quacking.

'Won't be a minute,' Andrew told his son.

3

Matt nodded, too absorbed in the activity even to look up.

As things turned out, the one minute extended to eight. Andrew had to search through his filing cabinet to check the details of an application form. And when he emerged from the house, Matt was nowhere to be seen. His empty wheelchair on the landing was a silhouette of shining steel against the rippling blue-grey river.

'Matt?' he called, more surprised than worried that his son had left the landing. Usually, he had difficulty persuading Matt to come back inside. He glanced up and down the river front, but there was no sign of him. He called again, wondering if Matt had gone up the side of the house. But why would he have left his ducks?

Suddenly alarmed, Andrew rushed around the side of the house. The narrow strip of land leading to the front was deserted. *Where the hell was he?* He pounded down to the landing, screaming out Matt's name. He glanced around, wild-eyed, at the calm surface of the water.

It was *possible* Matt had fallen in. He could have got out of his chair. He might have stood on the four-inch ledge that ran round the bottom of the landing. If he'd slipped, he could have floundered. He'd never been a strong swimmer. And in his condition . . .

Andrew ran up and down the waterfront. He scanned the bank, bellowing Matt's name. Grabbing the mobile phone out of his pocket, he frantically dialled 999, demanding an ambulance. As he did so, he was kicking off his shoes. Throwing down his jacket. Tugging the tie from round his neck.

As soon as he'd blurted out the address, he dived in the river.

*

4

Chief Inspector Hardwick of the Weybridge police was immediately informed by the Duty Officer. As he looked up from behind his desk, his face filled with grave concern. He didn't need to be told who Matthew Norton was. Everyone in town knew that. Even though Weybridge had the reputation – undeserved in his opinion – of being part of the anonymous commuter belt, there were local characters who stood out from the crowd. And Matthew Norton would have stood out anywhere. He'd been in the papers, including the nationals, more times than Hardwick could remember. There'd been a BBC documentary about him just a few months back. Whenever he was seen out in the streets, or down at the station, people would wave and yell at him. Matthew would wave and yell right back. He was like that; friendly, open-natured. He was Weybridge's local hero.

Everyone loved Matt Norton, despite his appearance. In the street Hardwick would overhear parents telling their children not to stare. Matthew looked unusual, they'd say, but that didn't affect who he was inside.

For there was no denying he was very different. Unlike all the other kids in Primary 4, Matt Norton had the body of a seventy-five-year-old.

1

The Ming-blue Audi TT coupé roared across the tarmac of Zonmark science park. Behind its wheel, Dr Lorna Reid glanced at her watch in irritation. She'd been in too much of a hurry to change out of her white lab coat. And the collection of files and print-outs she'd hastily flung on the passenger seat beside her scattered across the floor as she curved round a corner towards the main administration building.

Moments earlier she'd been ordered by Spencer Drake to the Zonmark media suite. She was supposed to be in an interview that should have started seven minutes before. Yet another interview in which, today of all days, she was in no mood to participate. She resented being dangled, like bait, in front of journalists. Nothing in her scientific training had prepared her for it. But following the media leak about NP3 ten weeks before, she'd been at the heart of an all-consuming feeding frenzy. Newspapers were hyping her work as 'the single, biggest medical advance since the discovery of penicillin'.

Spencer Drake, Zonmark's ever-present spin-doctor, had of course demanded that she play the game. And she knew his exhortations to 'maximise impact' and 'accentuate the positive' didn't just apply to what she said. For the first time in her career as a research pharmacologist she would survey herself in the mirror each morning, casting a critical eye over her wardrobe, wondering how she'd come across in the papers or on TV. It was bad enough feeling like a performing monkey, she thought grimly. But her concerns right now ran far deeper. Only a few minutes before, she had received a phone call that had shaken her both professionally and personally. But there was no time to digest the news in private. No chance even to discuss it with her boss, Zonmark's Chief Executive Officer, Armand Kuesterman. Right now she had no option but to wear a brave face and squander yet more precious time in the service of her lords and masters.

Slamming on the brakes, she brought the TT to an abrupt halt outside admin. She swung her long legs out of the car, strode through the automatic doors, and headed directly through Reception.

'Can I help you?' A youthful security guard, who'd just started with Zonmark that week, asked politely as she showed no signs of stopping.

'I doubt it.' Her Scots accent was clipped as she swept past his desk.

'But you have to sign in!' he called after her.

'Lorna Reid. Doctor. R-E-I-D. Get that?' she responded over her shoulder, shoving through a pair of swing doors.

She was a woman who inspired strong feelings among her co-workers. Male colleagues were far from impervious to her feminine allure. Tall, svelte and mid-thirties, every-

7

thing about her – from the long dark hair swept back over her shoulders, to the aqua-blue eyes – communicated energy. Purpose. Determination.

There were those who were in awe of her intellectual prowess, her Calvinistic work ethic, and most especially, that rarest of gifts among research pharmacologists – her creativity. To these admirers Lorna Reid was one of the most brilliant biotechnologists on the planet: 'Super-Scot' to use the sobriquet recently bestowed on her by the *Wall Street Journal*.

But she had plenty of detractors. They despised her impatience; the high-handedness with which she'd react to messages unanswered and jobs undone; her hectoring of those whose performance didn't meet her own stringent standards. Such people disdained Lorna Reid and all the glory showered upon her. As far as they were concerned, she was just a first-class bitch.

Stepping into the media lounge, a room furnished with comfortable armchairs and decorated in soothing pastels, she made her way towards where her visitor was standing in the opposite corner. Extending her hand, she introduced herself: 'I'm Lorna Reid.' She tried a smile.

'Judith Laing,' greeted the other. Petite, attractive, with inquisitive, dark eyes, she had an engaging presence, but Lorna knew not to judge by appearances; Spencer Drake had already e-mailed her Judith's biography. Despite her diminutive frame, Judith Laing was a heavy hitter. Shortly before being appointed Washington, DC correspondent of Britain's *Daily Sentinel*, she'd choreographed an exposé on crooked business practices at sportswear manufacturer Starwear. Those revelations had triggered one of the most spectacular corporate collapses in recent times. Starwear, once the

8

world's biggest brand after Coca-Cola, no longer existed, and its CEO, Jacob Strauss, was still languishing behind prison bars. Such was the power of Judith Laing, remembered Lorna warily, offering the journalist a coffee before sitting.

'I'm just doing a profile piece,' Judith told her, setting down a micro-cassette recorder on the table in front of her. '"British brains lead America" – you know the kind of thing.'

Lorna nodded. It sounded innocuous enough, but she wasn't going to be lulled into complacency.

'Why don't we start off with the celebrated footnote?'

'That old chestnut?'

'It *was* the starting point.' Judith regarded her with a perky smile. 'I think it can take another airing.'

Lorna never ceased to be amazed by journalists' appetite for the story of her original discovery. No matter how many times she told it, they wanted her to replay the tale about when, as a PhD student at Wolfson College, Cambridge, she'd been attached to a pharmacology research centre presided over by the illustrious Professor Ron Hall. How she'd spent weeks conducting a literary review on Professor Hall's behalf, poring over endless papers and research reports on his field of expertise – anti-psychotic drugs. And how she'd stumbled upon an asterisk at the end of a yellowing paper about a non-mainstream drug trial that had occurred twenty-four years earlier in Louisiana, USA.

Most other researchers would have paid scant attention to it. But Lorna Reid wasn't like most other researchers, which was precisely why Professor Hall had hired her. Methodical, meticulous, and possessed of terrier-like tenacity, Lorna wasn't one to overlook the apparently disconnected, the marginal or the obscure.

9

Neuropazine, the drug in question, had never been developed beyond the experimental phase. Making use of several active metabolites which had been superseded by other schizophrenia treatments like clozapine and respiridone, its importance was tenuous to say the least. But Lorna had wanted to know more. She'd written to the Canadian consultant psychiatrist who'd contributed the article all those years ago, but he'd long-since forgotten the details of the drug trial. Never one to take 'no' for an answer, she'd made enquiries about research facilities in Louisiana, establishing that little primary work was carried out, but that the pharmacology faculty at Lafayette State University was the pride of the South. Following a hunch, she'd contacted the faculty head – and had been duly rewarded with a reply providing a full clinical scope of the trial. After studying it carefully, Lorna had concluded there was nothing to be gleaned from this study after all. No undiscovered pearl lurked at the heart of this particular oyster.

But all that changed dramatically when, a full year later, she came across the work of Copenhagen-based antipsychotic expert Arne Gelthaus who hypothesised, *en passant*, that a number of untested biochemical agents, including NP3, suppressed the production of enzymes associated with genes linked to ageing. This was only conjecture, Gelthaus noted. Ageing research wasn't his field of expertise. And besides, no experiment had ever been conducted using NP3 drugs.

But Lorna knew differently: Neuropazine's active metabolites had included NP3. And a particular memory stirred. Within moments she'd retrieved the Lafayette papers from her filing cabinet. Standing over her desk, she'd

10

gone through the documents with the speed of familiarity – and the urgent realisation that she had, in her possession, two separate parts of the same puzzle. In particular there was a chart she could recall distinctly. It was on the top corner of a right-hand page. It detailed patient profiles – including age. She remembered looking at it, a year earlier. She also remembered noting that most of the patients were older than the average clinical profile. Her concentration never more focused, she'd felt her heart pounding as she swiftly progressed through one document after another. It had to be here. Surely she hadn't just imagined it?

Sure enough, she'd found it. And it confirmed what she'd known: most of the 150 patients had been geriatric; some had been in their seventies; a dozen in their eighties. What's more, a post-experimental review gave a full profile of study-group participants five years on. Lorna had quickly worked out that the average mortality age of Neuropazine patients was three years higher than the usual average. Not a startling figure in itself. But because the group had taken Neuropazine only for five years, it was hugely significant. What if they'd taken a more extensive course? How much longer would they have lived then?

Even though the Lafayette trials had failed to develop an anti-psychotic drug, the side effect of Neuropazine was nothing short of revolutionary. Could she have happened, quite by chance, on the most sought-after remedy of her profession since mediaeval times: *elixir vitae*?

'After writing up my findings in *Science* magazine,' she explained now, 'I found myself with more sponsorship and job offers than I could handle.'

Judith nodded. 'Why Zonmark?'

'They made me an offer I couldn't refuse.' Lorna met her

eyes evenly. 'Armand Kuesterman took all my research proposals on board. There were no funding problems.'

'The same could be said, surely, for any number of biotech companies?'

'Maybe,' she shrugged. 'There were also other reasons I wanted to be in Washington, DC. Personal reasons.'

Judith paused a moment before enquiring, 'Millar Kirkbrian?'

Lorna's eyes widened momentarily. Judith Laing had evidently done her homework. 'Yes,' she nodded. 'Millar had a lot to do with it.'

The reality, although she wasn't proud of it, went further than that. Millar had *everything* to do with it. The man she'd been in love with at Cambridge, Millar had been offered a position at the International Institute for Democracy, in Washington, DC, at the same time that she'd been on the receiving end of the Zonmark offer. Their future together had seemed divinely ordained.

Meeting Judith's enquiring glance she told her now, 'As you may know, things didn't work out between Millar and me. It didn't last six months. Quite frankly, it's ancient history.'

Judith continued briskly, 'NP3. In layman's terms – how does it actually work?'

'You'll be familiar with the pianola?' Lorna used her favourite metaphor. 'You know, those automatic pianos that are played using rotating rolls, like a child's musical box?'

Then as Judith nodded, 'A human being's genetic possibilities are rather like the keyboard of a pianola – in theory, any tune at all can be played on it. But hormones are like the music roll. Once they engage with the keyboard, only certain notes will be expressed.'

12

'Most people believe we are our genes.'

'That's only true up to a point. Think about thalidomide babies. They inherited from their parents the genes for perfect limbs. But the thalidomide taken by their mothers acted on those genes at an early stage of development, changing the instructions.'

'So, NP3 changes the instructions to genes that dictate ageing?'

'That's right. Even relatively short exposure to NP3 can modify genetic behaviour and slow down ageing. The exciting possibility I'm working on is that, over a longer period of time, genes themselves will mutate, so that long life can be passed down from one generation to the next.'

'Ethically controversial, isn't it?' Judith shot her a sharp-eyed look. 'As is testing on children?'

Lorna was familiar with these provocations. 'I prefer to think of NP3 as an elegant dual-solution methodology.'

Judith smiled wryly, recognising a well-rehearsed answer.

'The problem with all anti-ageing therapies is obvious, really; they take a very long time to test. Lab rats live for thirty months and anti-ageing treatment takes four or five years to test on them fully. So what about humans? Even initial findings could take a minimum of twenty years. For conclusive evidence, including a full study of side effects, you're talking two or three times that long. I realised I needed to find another way through the problem. Which was when I decided on progeria.'

Judith nodded. She'd seen photos of children who suffered from the disorder that caused them to age ten times faster than normal. By seven, kids with progeria would start suffering from illnesses that usually occur only in people in their seventies or eighties. By twelve, all the features of

13

old age – hair loss, disappearance of cheek fat, impaired mobility and arteriosclerosis – were shockingly pronounced. Often they would have had their first stroke or heart attack by the age of fifteen.

'I was looking through all these progeria cases, wondering what could be done to help them, when I suddenly thought – instead of testing anti-ageing therapies on people growing old at the normal rate, what if progeria volunteers could be found? They'd not only benefit directly, but the whole testing process would also be speeded up.'

'You weren't worried about the ethical issues?'

'I don't see that denying progeria victims the chance to lengthen their all too short lives could be described as "ethical".'

'But the bigger picture, the age retardation,' persisted Judith, 'there are some who believe this kind of genetic engineering is a step too far.'

'The search for the elixir of life is as old as medicine itself.' Lorna was unapologetic. 'What scientist would walk away from an opportunity like this?'

Judith didn't suppress a smile. She'd always preferred interviewees who were unafraid of controversy, and Lorna was a feisty one all right. But how much further would she go? 'Your NP3 programme was one of Washington's best-kept secrets for over three years. Then the recent media-leak made you suddenly very visible. How do you feel about having fame thrust upon you?'

Furious, would have been the honest answer. Resentful about all the hours she spent talking into microphones while work piled up back at the lab. And, after this morning's news, having to project a bright-eyed assurance that couldn't be further from her own true emotions, she was

14

deeply weary. But she couldn't so much as hint at all that to Judith. 'Media commitments are really just part of the job.'

'So you don't mind the added burden—'

'In the biotech industry,' she tried to halt the line of questioning, 'it's by no means unusual—'

'Nonetheless, the leak must have come as a rude awakening?'

'With a major programme like NP3,' she parroted the Spencer Drake line, 'it was always a possibility.'

'And NP3 *is* Zonmark's flagship programme, isn't it?' Judith met her gaze evenly. 'It must make you feel very exposed having Zonmark's share price riding on your shoulders?'

'I wouldn't say that. Zonmark does other things too. The company's core product, Zondrax, is the market leader in anti-inflammatories . . .'

Judith listened to Lorna's switch into management speak with curiosity. Earlier, talking about her research, Lorna had been straightforward, uncontrived. Why was she being so defensive now?

Meanwhile Lorna, dutifully peddling the Zonmark angle, felt trapped by Judith's irrefutable logic, and worse, by the need to project an image that was completely out of kilter with reality. For the simple fact was that Judith's questions were striking perilously close to the truth. Had she been sitting opposite any other journalist, Lorna wouldn't have been so concerned. But Judith came with a daunting reputation. And her reference to Millar Kirkbrian showed she'd come fully briefed. All of which made Lorna wonder just how much of events behind the scenes at Zonmark Judith already knew.

Her problems at Zonmark had started even before the

15

recent media leak. Along with every other Nasdaq-listed biotech firm, Zonmark had seen its share price wiped out after the collapse of biotech giant Advance Gene Technologies. The effect on Lorna's programme had been direct and instant: her programme budget was cut by thirty per cent. With her spending already tightly stretched, the deep budget cut had been a source of rankling discontent, as well as causing outright clashes between her and the Zonmark Board.

But things had really changed the morning she'd opened up the *New York Post* and discovered, to her horror, a major article on page three entitled 'Wonderdrug Leap in Anti-Ageing Treatment'. Underneath was a photograph of a very much younger version of herself, lifted from the *Science* magazine piece that had appeared ten years before.

Mind reeling, she'd scanned down the piece, scarcely able to believe what she was reading. The article noted her progress from Cambridge to Zonmark – a move that had passed without notice anywhere else in the media. Then it went on to say that she was on the brink of a major breakthrough that could prolong lifespan by thirty years. Enough details of her work were given to confirm that her research was both significant and advanced – but without any of the caveats she always emphasised.

She read through the piece with stunned disbelief. Much of the information it carried could only have come from inside Zonmark. But who had leaked it?

It was also the question that preoccupied Armand Kuesterman. Summoned to his office the moment she'd arrived at work that morning, she'd had her first, major, stand-up row with Kuesterman, Finance Director Eli Schwartz, and Spencer Drake. Schwartz had led the attack, accusing her of a deliberate media leak. She had flatly denied this. He'd switched the charge to negligence. Still seething after her budget cut, she'd found his accusations more than she could take; she'd let him have it with both barrels.

It had all got very ugly before Kuesterman intervened, trying to calm things down. The problem, he told them, was that the genie was out of the bottle. It wasn't yet nine in the morning and the switchboard was already jammed with calls. NP3 had turned into a media issue, which was why he'd invited Spencer Drake to the meeting.

Until that time Lorna had never heard Drake utter more than two sentences. Appointed Zonmark's first Corporate Affairs Director within days of the biotech market crash, he'd rarely left Kuesterman's elbow. Tall, ascetic, a man of notoriously few words, that morning he'd explained that if Zonmark didn't manage the NP3 issue themselves, the media would manage it for them. He proposed a full media conference. A broker roadshow. An NP3 website. In all of these Lorna was to play a central part. Dropping a long-arranged trip to Europe to interview half a dozen potential panel recruits, she'd reluctantly taken on a new role as media personality.

And the media had loved her. The stunning good looks, the articulate confidence, the Scottish cadences. Despite her aversion for journalistic hype, they couldn't get enough of her. Investors were evidently impressed too. Within days, Zonmark's share price was back to pre-crash levels. Within a week, it had soared to a ten-dollar high. It was all smiles from Armand Kuesterman and Eli Schwartz. More than anything else, they told her with assurance, what mattered now was open communication.

17

Ironically, it was when media obsession about NP3 was at its greatest, two months ago, that things started going badly wrong. Panel recruitment began to falter. Fifty was the minimum number of progeria kids they required for findings to be statistically significant. Fifty was what they needed to get to first base. But recruitment had slowed right down when they reached the mid-thirties. Steve Manzini, her newly appointed head of panel recruitment, had lost both assistants in the budget cuts, and was having to do all the legwork himself. And locating children with progeria, especially outside America and Europe, was proving a challenge. Numbers had dwindled to just one new panel member a month.

As if all this wasn't bad enough, they began losing panel members. They'd always known that, even if NP3 was spectacularly successful, there would be natural attrition. If you had kids ageing at ten times the usual rate, even if you halved that rate, they would still fall victim to illnesses, especially heart disease. The deaths of two children in Europe around the time of the leak was regrettable enough. But in the last month, Ouyang Wing had died in the garden outside his Beijing apartment; Darryl Barker of Sydney, Australia had suffered a fatal heart attack during a funfair ride. The media knew none of this – Spencer Drake had been in full suppression mode. As far as the outside world was aware, the full panel of fifty children was all but complete. The reality was, they were still struggling to find thirty.

Anxious about the widening gap between perception and reality, Lorna had been trying persistently to get hold of Kuesterman for the past week. The problems she faced with the NP3 programme were bad enough without the knowledge that if they became known to the media, their effects would be devastating.

But Kuesterman had been difficult to get hold of. First it was back-to-back meetings. Then it was a last-minute trip to London. Eventually she'd interrupted his meetings with venture partners in Frankfurt last Friday to tell him they needed to speak urgently. Kuesterman had been responsive. 'You have the first slot in my diary when I'm back next Wednesday,' he'd said, 'I promise.'

'Next Wednesday' was this morning – when she'd received the worst news of all: the death of Matt Norton. Little Matt, whom she'd last seen only a fortnight earlier during his quarterly visit to Washington, DC. She'd had no time to dwell on the personal tragedy of it, or the feelings of his parents, Andrew and Jess, who had become friends. Surveying the impact of his death on her NP3 trial data she'd felt an overwhelming sense of futility. Now her panel was down to twenty-nine. And there wasn't a single new recruit on the horizon.

She'd phoned Kuesterman's office, seeking him out, but the harridan he employed as his gatekeeper denied he was in the office yet and was exasperatingly vague about his expected time of arrival.

'There've been stories about friction between you and Zonmark management,' Judith probed now. 'Would you care to comment?'

Lorna raised her eyebrows, wondering exactly what Judith had heard and where she'd heard it. Before hazarding a guess, she said, 'You don't want to believe everything you hear on the expat cocktail circuit.' Her smile felt like a grimace as she shifted uncomfortably in her chair.

In fact, Judith hadn't heard anything about problems

between Lorna and Zonmark management – she'd merely been fishing. But she'd evidently stumbled on something, although she wasn't planning to pursue it now. She wasn't here under false pretences, and had been telling the truth about only wanting material for a profile piece. Already an admirer of Lorna's, she *had* heard stories about her on the cocktail circuit suggesting that her compatriot was possessed of a single-minded conviction she could relate to. But the interview had revealed something else, a dichotomy between the real Lorna, and the Lorna that was staying determinedly 'on message'.

'Progeria is very rare, isn't it?'

'About one in ten million.'

'And you're looking to recruit fifty to your panel, plus a control group?'

Lorna nodded.

'Big job?'

'I have a great team. The best.'

It was the area of attack that Lorna feared most of all, but after Judith's questions about 'friction', it seemed altogether inevitable. As did the next question: 'So, how many panel members are you up to now?'

She daren't tell the truth. She couldn't come out and say 'twenty-nine'. Instead she said, 'We're making very good progress.'

Judith regarded her, clear-eyed, evidently expecting more.

'It's difficult to be specific,' she continued. 'At any one time we're evaluating a number of potential panel candidates.' She reached up to brush back an imaginary lock of hair.

It was a gesture of concealment Judith didn't miss. 'Close to fifty, then?' she persisted.

'I'd prefer just to say, we're on course—'

At that moment, her pager bleeped loudly from her lab coat pocket. Reaching over for it, she glanced at the message flashed up on the display. She'd made her secretary, Gail, promise to forward Kuesterman's whereabouts as soon as she'd tracked him down. '*AK in meeting with SD & ES,*' read the pager.

In an instant, Lorna's eyes darkened to a deep cobalt. Anger rising inside her, powerful and unstoppable, her face flushed several shades darker.

'I'm sorry,' she rose to her feet, 'I have to end this meeting.'

Observing her rapidly changing demeanour, Judith was intrigued.

'I'm needed elsewhere,' Lorna explained.

It didn't matter that she was being interviewed by the *Daily Sentinel*; it could have been a guest appearance on Larry King for all she cared. She wasn't going to stand back while the Zonmark Board dissected her programme behind her back.

'I'd like to finish off by phone.' Judith was collecting up her recorder and briefcase. 'Would this afternoon suit?'

Moments later, Lorna was striding down the corridor of the executive wing towards the corner suite, presided over by Beryl Hattingh, Kuesterman's Personal Assistant. Beryl was matronly, in her mid-forties and permanently swathed in a cloud of cloying scent. She and Lorna had never even pretended to be friends. Lorna was heading directly towards Kuesterman's office door when Beryl rose regally from behind her desk. 'You can't go in there,' she commanded, 'he's in a meeting!'

'Watch me.' Lorna was curt.

About to block her path, Beryl saw the expression on Lorna's face and evidently thought better of the idea.

'So much for the first available slot in your diary!' Bursting into the room, Lorna glared over at where Kuesterman sat at his highly polished mahogany meeting table, flanked by Schwartz and Drake. With his broad, Slavic features, dark jowls and heavy horn-rims, Kuesterman had the perpetual look about him of a jaded businessman straight off a long-haul flight.

'I'm not accountable to you for my schedule.' His glasses flashed in her direction.

'Cut the crap, Armand. This is obviously about NP3.'

Removing his spectacles, he looked up at her flatly. 'What if it is?'

'First of all, it goes completely against what you *promised* me last week.' She stepped over to the meeting table so that she was facing him directly across it. 'Second, what happened to all the talk about "open communication"?' Glaring now at Schwartz and Drake, she continued, 'In case it isn't obvious, I deeply resent having the NP3 programme discussed without me.'

'And I reserve the right to manage this company any way I please.' Kuesterman's expression was severe. 'I had every intention of asking you to join us once we'd covered a few issues.'

Lorna regarded him cynically.

Despite the permanent appearance of dishevelment, Kuesterman was no walkover. Fixing Lorna with a severe expression he told her now, 'I'm worried about the results coming through and I'm worried about recruitment.'

'You're not the only one.'

'So what do you propose to do about it?'

'All that I'm able to,' she sparred, 'on a much reduced budget.'

Kuesterman pushed back in his chair. 'You're not claiming that budget cuts have something to do—'

'That's exactly what I'm *claiming*.' Her ire up, Lorna was making no concessions. 'I lost two full-time staff in the budget cuts. We now have limited scope to analyse data, to undertake predictive modelling, to amend formulation. We have no staff dedicated to panel recruitment. My team are working twelve-, thirteen-, fourteen-hour days. I can't press them any harder.'

'I don't think your dedication is in any way being questioned.' Drake's voice was smooth and dark in counterpoint to her Scots pique. 'What the market's looking for are some good news angles.'

'I shouldn't be having to worry about "good news angles",' she retorted.

'If your recruitment was on schedule you wouldn't have to. We could issue a simple progress update.'

She glared across the table at him.

'This is the new reality, Lorna.' Kuesterman rubbed his five o'clock shadow. 'You know the deal as well as any of us.'

'Too bloody right! But I can't just manufacture "good news angles" on demand.'

'All right,' Drake persisted, as Kuesterman leaned back in his chair with a splenetic sigh, 'let's take recruitment and headline results out of the equation—'

'What are we left with?' she regarded the spin-doctor, bemused.

'That's what I want to know,' he pushed. 'There must be some individual case studies? Some positive stories?'

She regarded the serious expressions round the table. Meeting Drake's questioning expression she said evenly, 'It's all very well pulling out individual stories, but every single one of the kids on my panel has a serious illness. Even if we slow the rate of ageing by fifty per cent, they will still die young. Today's good news story will be tomorrow's tragedy – that's guaranteed.' Then, as the PR man returned her gaze, 'The only unexplored terrain is the Lafayette trials.'

Lorna and Kuesterman had discussed these frequently since she'd joined Zonmark. They'd agreed on the value of further analysis of the Neuropazine data, but her priority was to set up Zonmark's own panel. The Lafayette stuff could wait till later down the line. At least, that was what they had thought before the media leak. Before things started going awry.

Kuesterman exchanged a significant glance with Drake. Then he was shaking his head. 'I don't think that's such a good idea.'

'The work has to be done. We've been putting it off and putting it off for years. And it's a positive story.' She glanced at Drake, who was averting his eyes. 'It's the only story I know which will distract media attention long enough for me to get NP3 back on track—'

'It's just not where I want to go,' Kuesterman repeated his objection.

'But the final analysis has to be done sometime.'

'That's not a view I necessarily share.' Kuesterman spoke firmly, as though closing the subject.

Lorna was flabbergasted. He'd never expressed the least reservation in the past. What game was he playing now? Looking from where Schwartz contemplated the grain of

24

the mahogany table, to Drake's studious avoidance, to Kuesterman's scowl, all the frustration she'd been feeling about NP3 for the past month came to a head. All the helplessness and anger and despair-inducing sense of futility. When she spoke again, her tone was no longer heated; it had fallen to sub-zero. 'When I brought the NP3 programme to Zonmark,' she said, eyeballing Kuesterman, 'you promised me confidentiality. You agreed a level of funding. Most of all, there was never any question about my autonomy as Research Director of the programme.'

Her presence was so powerful, her emotion so palpable, that none of the men could avoid looking up at her.

'But where am I now?' She gestured, hands raised. 'Let me remind you. You've put me in the full glare of the international media. You've cut back my funding. And what I resent most of all,' she pointed at Kuesterman, 'is that you're now questioning my judgement. You're trying to tell me how to run my own programme.' As she stepped back from the table, all three men were transfixed. 'Well, I'm sorry,' she continued, 'this is not the way I conduct my work. It seems to me that what you *really* need is a new programme director – and I won't stand in your way.' Striding over to the door, she reached for the handle. 'When my contract comes up in four months' time, I shan't be renewing it. You have my resignation.'

She swept back through Kuesterman's ante-room, Beryl staring at her, goggle-eyed, and headed swiftly back down the executive wing corridor. By the time she reached the lobby, the uniformed security guard was hovering awkwardly in the middle to intercept her, radio phone in his hand.

'Mr Kuesterman just called.' He could barely get the

words out quickly enough the moment she appeared round the corner. 'He says, please won't you go back?'

Half an hour later, Lorna swung her car into Du Cane Plaza Hotel on Pennsylvania Avenue. Driving towards the short, covered portico, she pulled up at the hotel's imposing main entrance. Her car door was opened by a valet in navy and gold livery, and she stepped out, making her way hurriedly up the short flight of marble stairs into the lobby.

Stepping inside she immediately felt different. Everything from the vaulted ceiling mouldings, to the sumptuous gilt-wood furnishings and the lush, baroque string quartet, conveyed congeniality, a refinement that couldn't be further removed from things back at Zonmark. Making her way past the concierge's desk, she stepped inside a lift the size of a small room, and pressed for Penthouse Level.

It was rare for her to interrupt her working day for personal matters. And in her three-month-old relationship with Jack Hennessy, she'd never paid him a surprise visit. But there was nothing that was usual about today. After her stormy encounter with the Zonmark management team, she'd never felt more in need of Jack.

She checked her appearance in the lift mirror, which, like every other fitting in the hotel, was exquisitely appointed. An elaborate, Louise XIV frame was flanked on either side by ebony-and-gold sarcophagi lamp holders. Beneath it, on a polished Boulle bureau, a collection of perfumes was ranged about a vase of vivid Columbian orchids which were flown in daily from Bogota. In the flattering semi-light, Lorna touched the dark hair back from her face and checked her lipstick, before meeting her

26

eyes in the mirror – still a dark shade of blue. She turned, as the lift doors opened, and walked down a rosewood-panelled corridor until she reached a door on which a brass plaque was engraved 'The Hennessy Foundation'. She knocked just twice before being summoned from inside.

Jack Hennessy looked up from his desk in surprise. In his mid-forties he was darkly handsome, with a high forehead and strong jaw suggesting intelligence and conviction, while the silvering of his immaculately groomed hair lent him a particular gravitas.

'Lorna! Wonderful surprise!' As he rose and moved across his office to greet her, he carried with him the quiet assumption of status.

They embraced with all the ardour of new lovers. Then, taking her arm, he led her over to a Chesterfield and sat her down, fixing her with an enquiring expression. 'You came to tell me something?'

She nodded. His ability to read her moods had been one of the things that drew her to him. As was his involvement in her work. Now she met his eyes with a flash of exasperation. 'I've just had my worst morning ever at Zonmark. This morning I hear that Matt Norton died. Accident. Then I find Kuesterman's back from Europe. You know how he promised me the first available slot in his diary? Turns out he's in a huddle with Schwartz and Drake.'

Jack raised his eyebrows.

'So I just marched in,' she continued. 'They hauled me over the coals. Recruitment. Results. You name it.'

'What did you do?'

'What could I do?' She shrugged. 'I quit.'

Regarding her with surprise, before he could say anything he noted the start of a smile about her lips.

'Oh, they came begging,' she beamed. 'Didn't get as far as Reception and they wanted me back.'

'But is that what *you* really want?' He'd heard all the Zonmark stories and knew how rapidly things had spiralled out of control in the past four weeks.

'It is *now*.'

'You mean—'

'I renegotiated terms.'

'Your budget?'

'Back to what was agreed. And not just that. No more questions about where I'm taking the programme.'

A smile crept over his face as he shared in her triumph. '*You!*' Reaching out, he seized her shoulders, shaking her. 'I'm so proud of you!'

They kissed again before, breaking apart, their expressions turned intimate.

'How about lunch?' proposed Jack.

She glanced down involuntarily at her watch. 'I've an appointment up at the Gene Science Institute.'

'Sole *meunière* from Chez Roget?' He tempted her with her favourite from the restaurant downstairs.

'I'd love to, but I know what'd happen.' She met his eyes meaningfully. Only last Saturday morning when she'd stopped by to visit him, they'd soon found themselves in bed – which was where they'd spent the rest of the day, making love and discovering all the details about each other's lives and past loves, their fears and phobias, their dreams for the future.

'How about dinner?' she suggested.

'Done.'

'You'll come to my place?'

'Seven-thirty.'

'I'm looking forward to it already.'

Moments later she was back inside the lift, Jack Hennessy holding the doors open as they kissed goodbye. Returning to his office, he moved across to the window and looked down at the hotel entrance, his eyes narrowing when the dark blue TT curved out from the covered parking and into the traffic on Pennsylvania Avenue. Dr Lorna Reid, he mused. In the past few weeks he'd found out a great deal about her. He'd made it his business to. She was way more important to his future than she could ever have guessed.

2

Matt's funeral was held at St Mark's on the Tuesday after his death. A large congregation from Weybridge joined family and friends for the service. Teachers from his school, parents of other children in his class, local shopkeepers and an assortment of other semi-familiar faces crowded the small church. Such was the crush that the vicar had to arrange extra chairs to be added to each pew. Standing at the front, as Mozart's *Panis Angelicus* filled the church, Andrew and Jess were only dimly aware of what was happening. Trying as best they could to support one another, both were unable to contain their grief.

The short cremation service afterwards was attended only by family and a few close friends. Afterwards, in the sanctuary attached to the crematorium, Andrew and Jess found themselves having to speak to those who'd come. It was an ordeal they would have preferred to avoid. For there was no feeling, at this wake, of a life lived to the full, no celebration for many years of shared memories. Instead, only a benumbed sense of injustice. Desolation at the inexplicable cruelty of it all. Later, driving home through the grey afternoon, Andrew and Jess didn't exchange a single word.

Matt's body had been found within an hour of Andrew raising the alarm. It wasn't the first time the Weybridge police had had a 'missing, feared drowned' alert. They knew the procedure. Two groups combed the area – one from the furthest point downriver that a body could possibly have reached, the other starting from the Nortons' landing. Andrew had called Jess home from work, and the two of them had joined in the search. As it happened, his body was found only slightly downstream, tangled in vegetation at the side of the river. Later, the coroner had found water in his lungs, consistent with drowning. There were no suspicious marks on his body. 'Accidental death' had been certified.

It was the verdict they had expected. But Andrew was bewildered. And struggling not to be dragged under by the current of his own overwhelming guilt. Trying to cope with the shock of what had happened, he felt strangely disbelieving of the sequence of events that seemed to have taken place. Matt must have got up, out of his wheelchair, walked to the edge of the landing, and somehow lost his balance, falling under the handrail and into the river.

Andrew didn't doubt his son's mobility. Only half an hour earlier, Matt had been walking at school. And he knew, only too well, that Matt was like a jack-in-a-box in his chair, constantly wanting to get up and out.

But the simple fact was that Matt had a fear of water. He hated going anywhere near it. He'd be content enough on the landing, which was several feet above the water and rock solid. Up there he felt sufficiently distanced not to be threatened – 'I'm the king of the castle,' he used to proclaim as he hurled bread crusts down for the ducks. But on the landing he couldn't be coaxed from his wheelchair, not by anything. And he never wanted to go anywhere near the edge.

Andrew and Jess hadn't understood his fear. But on the evening of the accident it had seemed as though he'd had some prescient knowledge of his fate. Sitting at the kitchen table, with darkness falling, they'd been too shocked for tears, too numb to move. There just didn't seem anything to say.

Chief Inspector Hardwick had called by to tell them the coroner would be conducting his examination the following day. Given Matthew's special circumstances, he'd explained delicately, the coroner would be in touch with his doctor. But was there anything else that either parent wanted to say?

Andrew had told him how out of character it was for Matt to step close to the edge of the landing, given his fear of the river. How hard it was to believe that he'd got out of the wheelchair and, of his own accord, walked to the landing rail. Hardwick had listened gravely, taking notes. Could they remember other occasions when Matthew had walked by himself on the landing? Had he been particularly excitable that day? They went over things again and again, every detail Andrew could remember, before Hardwick asked him evenly, 'Mr Norton, are you saying that the circumstances of Matthew's accident were suspicious?'

It was Jess who'd finally answered, 'No.' There was obviously nothing to investigate, she said. It had just been a tragic accident. As she'd spoken she'd looked directly at

32

Andrew. There could be no mistaking the message in her eyes. She didn't want him to take it any further.

After they got back from the crematorium, Andrew went to their bedroom and changed out of his black coat and trousers. Jess retreated to her dressing room. There had been a terrible separateness between them since the accident, a silence so loud it seemed at times to roar about them. They still exchanged everyday endearments, keeping up the pretence of normality. But it was as though they were only going through the motions while the chasm between them opened up deeper and deeper.

Andrew put on a tracksuit and trainers and pocketed a front door key before making his way out into the cold grey evening. He walked briskly up the driveway, and once he was out on the road he started to jog, his breath creating steamy clouds in the icy air as he went. Up the curving road to the top of the hill, then bearing left along a path that went through a copse of pines before wending past a smallholding and a row of allotments. As a younger man he'd been a keen athlete. He'd played rugby for his university second side and had been an enthusiastic rower. A large part of the attraction of the Weybridge house for him had been the opportunity to resume rowing. That plan, like his other good intentions to exercise, had lapsed in recent years. Simply trying to keep on top of his job at Glencoe was exhausting enough. After meeting his family obligations, he rarely had much energy left.

But now he felt the urge to run in a way that he hadn't for a long time. Unfit, he ached from the unfamiliar exertions, yet he kept pushing forward, driven by an unknown energy, an urgent need to put everything behind him. He ran and ran in the falling light. He was oblivious to the low, swirling clouds, the scent of rain, before he finally turned back towards home on a path that followed the course of the river. It was as though he couldn't keep away from the scene of the accident. Every bend and twist of the grey water now had a bitter association: the place where they'd found the sodden notebook from Matt's blazer pocket; the house where he remembered seeing a local policeman pounding vigorously on the door; the eddy created by the enormous, gnarled roots of an ancient weeping willow where Matt's body had been caught, choked in weeds.

And eventually, of course, the landing. The view from the house down his garden to the river was one that, until last Wednesday, he had regarded as among his most precious. It was the reason he worked as hard as he did. It was his haven of tranquillity away from the harsh demands and deadlines of the City. But in the moment he'd realised the significance of the empty wheelchair, his feelings had abruptly changed. Now, as he approached the landing from the riverside, his footsteps slowed. A heaviness overcame him as he gasped for air. He no longer felt any fondness for the river. It held no charm, no sense of rural peacefulness. In the last few days the scene had become, for him, one of cruel alienation, the impassive face of nature which had robbed him of his son. He'd even begun to wonder if they should move house, although he'd said nothing about it to Jess yet. It was still too soon.

He walked along the last stretch of the river, coming up off the path onto the lawn. For a while he bent over, hands on his hips, as he recovered his breath. He hadn't realised that Mrs Hayes, his neighbour, was already standing near the bottom of her garden, looking out across the river. Then he heard the crunch of twigs underfoot.

'Very sorry about your loss, Mr Norton.' She spoke with a strong West Country brogue.

'Thanks,' he grunted, with only a glance in her direction.

Mrs Hayes had been a difficult neighbour ever since they'd moved into the house, ten years before. A professional complainer, she'd written to the local council whingeing about everything from their construction of a carport to the speed with which they reversed down their driveway. But, bizarrely, there were also occasions when she'd gone out of her way to help, signing for Royal Mail deliveries when they were out, or leaving home-made pickle on their doorstep. She was probably just a disturbed old woman, they'd decided. Though today of all days Andrew didn't have the patience for her.

'Hard to take, isn't it?' The familiar indignation rose in her voice. 'There he was one minute, so full of life, and the next . . .'

He waited for the inevitable phrase. And sure enough, she came out with it. 'Poor little mite.' She was shaking her head.

He knew she didn't mean any harm by it, but the words had always grated on him. Both Jess and he had made sure that Matt never felt hard-done-by. Neither of them had permitted themselves – or him – the idea of victimisation. Now Mrs Hayes was rambling on about how Matt had never let his frailty stop him.

'I saw him that last afternoon, I did,' she couldn't resist telling him. 'Happy as Larry feeding the ducks.'

Standing upright, Andrew looked over at her sharply.

'You didn't see him falling in?' he asked pointedly. Chief Inspector Hardwick said he'd interviewed all the neighbours, but had been unable to find any witnesses.

'No. I just happened to be looking out of the window and there he was, feeding the ducks.' Then, as though responding to an unspoken accusation, 'I didn't think he'd come to any harm seeing as he was being supervised.'

'So you didn't see me go back inside the house?' he persisted.

'Oh, yes. I heard the phone. But when you came out again I took myself off to make a cup of tea.'

'When I came out?' he was surprised.

She nodded. 'You and the other gentleman.'

'But there wasn't another . . . gentleman.'

'Oh, no!' Mrs Hayes was having none of it. 'There was the two of you, I remember distinctly.'

Andrew paused, thoughts suddenly racing, before asking her carefully, 'You mean, later, when I came outside with Chief Inspector Hardwick . . .'

'No. Before that. When Matt was feeding the ducks.'

'And you saw two men come out to the landing.'

'Like I said, seeing as he was being supervised—'

'You're sure you're talking about last Wednesday afternoon?'

'Of course I'm sure. It was the same afternoon Martin and that little tart had a blazing row.'

'Martin?' he was bewildered.

'On the box. *Coronation Street*.'

'Oh.' He was finding it hard keeping up with her, but felt compelled to probe further. 'This other . . . gentleman I was with. Did you see what he looked like?'

*

When he went back into the house a few minutes later, he found Jess sitting with the TV on, the volume so low it was barely audible. She wasn't watching, but sat staring ahead, her long blonde hair drawn back from her face with an Alice band, and an inconsolable emptiness in her wounded eyes. In the days that had followed Matt's death, she'd swung between periods of heart-wrenching anguish and frozen inaccessibility. To his growing despair, her periods of withdrawal were becoming increasingly frequent. He knew better than to try to comfort her right now. Frustrating though it was, he realised that at moments like these she was lost to him. Instead he made his way through the house to their bathroom where he showered, thoughts racing with what Mrs Hayes had just told him.

When he'd dressed again he found Jess in the kitchen. 'There's some lasagne in the freezer I could warm up,' she told him, tonelessly.

'I'm not really hungry.'

'No.'

He wanted so much to reach out to her, to take her in his arms. For her to say she didn't blame him. That it wasn't his fault. That things would be all right. But he knew she'd only break away, leaving him all the more thwarted. He stood a moment, hesitating while she put on the kettle, before deciding just to come out with it. 'I saw Mrs Hayes down near the river. Says she saw Matt that afternoon and there were two men with him. Seemed to think one of them was me.'

Taking two mugs off a shelf and putting them on the kitchen bench, Jess didn't react immediately. Instead, she opened the fridge door before she said, eventually, 'Obviously just confused.'

'Maybe,' he replied. A bit too quickly. 'But it's worth mentioning to Hardwick, don't you think?'

She had her back to him as she poured milk into the mugs. And he found himself wanting her approval badly. She had always been so supportive in the past. Both of them used to talk about how well they complemented each other. Their closeness had been the envy of many of their friends. But her only response now was to shrug.

He knew he should leave it there – but he couldn't. What Mrs Hayes had said gave credence to a different possibility, one that had preoccupied him since Matt's death, but for which he'd blamed himself for being a ludicrous conspiracist. Perhaps Mrs Hayes had got it wrong. But what if she hadn't?

'I really think I should phone to tell him,' he persisted.

When Jess turned to face him, she was wearing an expression he couldn't place. But it was more, much more than wearied despair. If anything, it seemed like cold fury.

'Whatever you do, it's not going to bring Matt back,' she said.

Baur au Lac Hotel
Zürich, Switzerland
Wednesday, 12 April

The four American businessmen in the private dining room of the exclusive Swiss hotel kept their conversation to anodyne small talk until the silver service staff had served their Chateaubriand and withdrawn. This meeting had been meticulously planned to guarantee discretion. The room had been reserved under an assumed name, arrivals choreographed at different times through separate entrances. As far as even their closest work colleagues were concerned, each of them was here to attend the European Medical Insurance Conference. All four had made a point of attending at least two or three EMIC sessions. But EMIC was merely a cover. The real purpose of their visit to Switzerland began only when the Dom Perignon gave way to a 1982 Gruaud Larose Bordeaux.

They could have made their different ways to a secret location in America, only the risk of being seen together didn't bear thinking about. Had word got out that the chief spin-doctors of Mayflower, H&S and Virtual Health, three of America's most powerful health insurers, had been seen in a huddle with the Managing Director of Corporate Forensics, a Wall Street corporate detective agency, it would have well and truly blown their cover. As far as the rest of the world was concerned, their three companies were direct, aggressive competitors. That was the perception they needed to preserve – even if it did mean the occasional transatlantic sortie.

Mayflower, H&S and Virtual Health weren't the largest health insurers in America – but they were the most profitable by far. Carving up the most lucrative, up-market sector between them, they controlled more than $30 billion in funds and their twenty million policyholders included everybody who was anybody in America. After all, health insurance wasn't optional for society's more affluent members. They regarded access to private treatment as a necessity.

The group's covert deliberations occurred several times a year and they'd met only a month before in Montreal. They frequently held teleconferences. And while running negative advertising campaigns fiercely critical of each other's companies, the three men were on the most cordial of terms. Over the years they'd got to know each other well, having long worked out a strategy to ensure their mutual survival and prosperity. For while those who didn't know any better – including all their respective staffs, and most of their Boards of Directors – might believe they were bitter rivals for the upper end of America's healthcare market, the reality was that through constant monitoring and research, the three men ensured that they appealed to subtly different groups within the market. 'Segmentation' was the marketing word for it; 'divide and rule' was a phrase others might have used.

Julius Lupine, the tallest and, at 54, oldest of the three, took the lead. The large and immensely grand communications head of Mayflower was known both for his perverse intellect as well as a lifestyle that epitomised everything to which Mayflower policyholders aspired, with his chalet at Aspen and his penchant for fast foreign cars. When H&S and Virtual Health lambasted Mayflower for its sky-high premiums, their attacks only emphasised Mayflower's blatant appeals to élitism and ostentation. Because Mayflower offered more than mere health insurance. It also provided stretch-limo collections from airports for policyholders and interstate visitors, and recuperative weekend breaks in five-star resorts after surgical procedures. Mayflower had even pioneered medical care facilities in the grounds of de luxe golf estates, where clients could be cared for while their partners enjoyed private tuition and buggy rides with leading golf pros.

Campbell McIntyre's H&S society, meantime, was attacked for 'cherry picking'. Its exclusions list meant that only those people who presented low health risks qualified as clients. But the 'cherry-picking' accusation was simple reverse psychology. H&S's exclusions were no worse than most insurers – but the idea that being accepted by H&S meant you were somehow fit and healthy was a compelling sales proposition. And McIntyre, younger than Julius Lupine by four years, had the eternally youthful appearance of one of his 'cherry-picked' clients through judicious use of plastic surgery and a wife twenty years his junior.

George Pollos, slim, Greek and sallow-skinned, ran the marketing for Virtual Health, the first online service to provide health cover over the Net. When Virtual Health's profit-to-earnings ratios came in for harsh censure from his colleagues, the criticism only underlined the cost advantages of joining an innovative e-surer. Tens of thousands of thirtysomethings had clicked their way to Virtual Health's online application form in the past three years.

Just as the three marketing men had long since divided the healthcare market to maximum advantage, they were also quick to respond to new threats. And the very day that the *New York Post* piece about NP3 had appeared, they knew they needed to find out more. Lupine had quickly commissioned a biotech analyst to get onto the case. The analyst had had just a fortnight, but his findings had been as disturbing as all three men had feared.

A source in one of Zonmark's several research satellites had been persuaded to make certain disclosures about the activities of his headstrong colleague, Dr Lorna Reid. As Lupine had reported back to his three colleagues during the American Medical Association conference in Montreal, Reid's NP3 trials were already well underway. The *New*

York Post hadn't been exaggerating when they reported on the potential of the gene therapy to increase average life-span by twenty to thirty years. Within a decade it was possible that the American population could be divided into two groups – those who were taking NP3 and those who weren't.

This wasn't the first time they'd been confronted by some anti-ageing wonderdrug. Californian biotech firms were coming out with spectacular claims all the time. What they didn't like to talk about was the length of time it would take for human testing of therapies. NP3 was different because of Zonmark's methodology. By testing the stuff on progeria children, Lorna Reid had cut the R & D time-lag down to a fraction.

In Montreal, Lupine had confirmed that NP3 presented the most serious threat they had ever faced. All the actuarial tables, on which they turned a profit, might just as well be thrown out of the window. The three men had soon decided to pursue things further. In particular, they must find out what the rest of the health insurance industry was doing about NP3. Which was why Corporate Forensics had been commissioned.

Meeting all three of them for the first time, Peter Durne, angular, bespectacled, with thinning grey hair, waited for his cue from Lupine. As soon as the waiters had closed the dining suite door, all three men turned to him expectantly.

'So, Peter,' prompted Lupine, 'what can you tell us about our peers?'

Used to dealing with the most testosterone-charged Wall Street buccaneers, Durne knew he had to deliver this head-on. 'The news isn't good. The industry is completely divided on the issue of genetic discrimination. There are some taking the moral high ground saying there must be no sharing of genetic information—'

McIntyre rolled his eyes at the naivety of the notion.

'—while most believe we're sliding into information sharing already. That's one problem. Another problem is no one's sure how this NP3 therapy works. We're in uncharted waters. NP3 might promote longevity, but what about dread diseases like cancer? Does it stop them being triggered?'

'That's what the progeria panel's about, isn't it?' challenged Pollos.

Durne's spectacles flashed in his direction. 'Progeria imitates the ageing process, but it's not ageing.'

'How do you mean?'

'The kids she's testing on don't get all the illnesses old people get. They don't develop prostate problems, cataracts, Alzheimer's. But they do get arteriosclerosis and heart problems.'

There was a pause while they digested this. Then Lupine wanted to know, 'And what's been the effect of NP3 on them?'

'Significant delays. The development of all terminal conditions has been pushed way back—'

'Creating another fifteen years of early old age?' interjected McIntyre.

'Exactly.' Durne nodded sharply.

Expressions round the dining table were bleak. This was precisely the age period when the biggest medical claims came rolling in for hip ops, prostate trouble – the whole gamut of non-fatal geriatric conditions.

'I've made a lot of enquiries in the last month, you'll find a list in the back of my report.' Durne gestured towards his briefcase in the corner of the room. 'My opinion is that this issue's going to take the industry years to deal with. What it comes down to is basically two things. One, will it be legal to discriminate against people taking NP3, by charging them higher premiums? And, two, even if it is legal, can you prove clients are on the stuff from standard blood tests? The answer to both questions, right now, would appear to be "no".'

The debrief continued for the next twenty minutes, as the men grilled Durne. When a waiter came back to clear away their plates at the end of the course, the Corporate Forensics chief made his excuses and departed, leaving behind three bound copies of his report.

Retiring to a sitting room replete with overstuffed armchairs and Empire furnishings – Lupine had chosen Baur au Lac specifically because of its scrupulous attendance to creature comforts, a point on which he placed the highest premium – the three men ordered coffee and cognac, and spent time perusing the report in silence.

Then Lupine stood, moving over to a picture window with its spectacular view over Lake Zürich. The lake in April was postcard perfect, its tranquil blue waters fringed by trees budding with the first green intimations of spring. Absorbed in his own reflections, he stared out, unseeing, before turning finally, cigar in hand, and exhaling a blue-grey cloud of Davidoff.

'Do we tell our shareholders?' he wanted to know.

McIntyre and Pollos looked up from their copies of the report. Pollos was pensive before remarking, 'Don't see we have much choice. It's all going to get out, sometime or other.'

McIntyre nodded. 'If they ever found out later and knew

we'd been sitting on it . . .' Then, flicking through his report again, 'Names have been named,' he noted with approval. There were lists of every major health insurer in North America, together with the position, where known, of every CEO on issues of genetic discrimination and information sharing. 'Before breaking the news,' he mused, 'what about some low-key lobbying . . .'

McIntyre's response to crisis was always to work out a solution behind the scenes before presenting it to the world as a *fait accompli*. But Lupine was shaking his head. 'It'd be like wrestling with clouds. The publicly owned companies daren't commit themselves to a position. Unless we got all the majors on board, there wouldn't be an industry solution, and like Durne said, getting them to agree on something as divisive as this . . .'

McIntyre exhaled heavily, the closest he ever came to admitting that someone else was right.

'So what action *do* we take?' enquired Pollos.

'You know me,' Lupine was swift to respond, 'I like to go for first prize.'

The two other men regarded him closely before Pollos confirmed, 'You mean . . .?'

'Shut down NP3. Why settle for less?'

McIntyre raised his eyebrows. 'That would take some doing, Julius. Lorna Reid isn't your standard research pharmacologist.'

'That's as may be.' Lupine cocked his head with a sardonic expression. 'But then, we're not your standard health insurers, are we?'

Looking up at him, McIntyre found it hard not to share Lupine's dry humour. Though even as he smiled he was struck, and not for the first time, by the disconcerting

45

notion that this entire exercise – the trip to Switzerland, the meeting, the briefing by Peter Durne – was nothing more than window dressing to support a course of action that Julius Lupine had already decided on quite some time before.

3

Lorna had chosen from her wardrobe with special care. Her standard business attire was strictly professional – dark, sensible, no nonsense. But that morning, turning to the other, more interesting side of her wardrobe, she had selected her Armani suit; it showed off her figure to perfection. Lorna wasn't above revealing something in the way of cleavage or thigh if she thought it would serve a purpose. Arresting and seductive, without appearing in any way undignified, she'd decided her much-loved Armani would fit the bill: today she was on the charm offensive.

All the way through the four-hour flight from Dulles airport to New Orleans she'd worked on her laptop. There, she'd collected a hire car, consulted a street map, and made her way up Route 10 to St Augusta Hospital, arriving shortly after noon.

She had considered sending her deputy Greg Merrit down to New Orleans. But when he'd made enquiries about the Lafayette trials, he'd been given the runaround. Then her own two e-mails to Ray Barnett, Hospital Chief

47

at St Augusta, had gone unreplied. As always, when confronted by a confusing muddle, Lorna's response had been a reflex decision: she'd get down to New Orleans and sort things out herself.

The Lafayette trials, which had sparked her interest in Neuropazine all those years ago at Cambridge, had never been anything more than a starting point, a launch pad for her own research. Once her NP3 programme was underway, it had always been her intention to follow up on the detail of the Lafayette tests, not because she expected to learn anything more, but from a deeply engrained sense of clinical rigour.

As things had turned out, the demands of the NP3 trial had been so great that she hadn't had time for anything outside the progeria panel. Greg had tried to locate the trial documentation, but after learning that Lafayette State University archives had been destroyed by a basement flooding five years before, his enquiries had run aground. No one at the university's pharmacology department, it seemed, could be bothered to help them with some long-forgotten experiment carried out thirty years before.

But Lorna knew that while Lafayette University had conducted the experiment, the Neuropazine drug had been administered at St Augusta Hospital. Even if Lafayette had lost all their archive material, surely St Augusta or the Louisiana Department of Health and Hospitals would have retained records?

She pulled up in front of the stately but creaking administration block of St Augusta, a two-storey building with Corinthian columns and wrought-iron latticework, all in evident need of repair. Stepping inside the large, dim-lit lobby, she was surprised to find it strangely deserted, except for two black families sitting motionless on bare wooden benches. Visitors, she wondered, of hospital patients?

It didn't even occur to her to wait around in the deserted shabbiness of the foyer for someone to appear. Instead, she followed a faded sign pointing in the direction of 'Hospital Chief', and make her way, unchallenged, through to Barnett's office at the end of the ground-floor passage. On the way she passed only one other person, a harassed-looking nurse, hurrying down the corridor, eyes averted, face creased in a frown.

Hospital Chief Barnett's office was empty, as was an adjacent room she assumed was used by his secretary. Taking a seat on one of the scuffed visitors' chairs opposite his desk, she pulled out a report from her patent leather briefcase, crossed her legs, and began reading.

She'd already confirmed Barnett would be here. Calling the night before, using the pretext of a personal delivery, she'd established he was free of engagements between noon and 3 pm. She planned to ambush him after an 11.30 meeting with his senior registrars. She had no idea what Barnett was like, except for his unresponsiveness. Perhaps he was a genuine victim of the overstretched public health system, but she had her doubts. Six years working for Zonmark had been all she needed to experience the resistance that happened when Nasdaq-financed biotech wizards bumped up against state-funded institutions. There was a four-letter word to describe it: envy.

Braced for the worst that Barnett might throw at her, even though she'd come down here prepared to charm the pants off him, she was ready to go in heavy with the 'right to public records' line. Whatever it took, she intended getting her hands on the rest of the Lafayette data and taking a copy of it back for analysis. Whatever Kuesterman's inexplicable reservations, she had no doubt a fresh analysis would give Spencer Drake something to feed the media. And with him off her back, she'd be able to get on with her real work on NP3.

She'd been waiting less than ten minutes before a dapper man in a dark suit and tie hurried into the office.

'Dr Barnett.' She rose to greet him, noting his gaze linger down her body for just a moment longer than was strictly polite. 'Lorna Reid.'

She'd been expecting a crusty Southern administrator with greying hair and intemperate features, but Ray Barnett was early forties and briskly businesslike. As they shook hands she could see him trying to work out how he knew her name.

'Zonmark Biotech,' she prompted.

'Oh, *Dr* Reid.' He was gesturing for her to sit as he pulled up his own desk chair. 'I feel I owe you an apology. I know you've been trying to get hold of me, but we've had a very bumpy ride in the past few weeks and I'm seriously understaffed.' He made a frustrated gesture towards the door.

An apology was the last thing she'd been expecting. Had it really been time, rather than reluctance, that had kept him from replying?

'Unfortunately, I don't think I can help,' he continued briskly. 'I did make enquiries about the records you requested. But the archive at Lafayette State University was flooded—'

'Five years ago,' nodded Lorna, 'I know.'

'We kept no data at the hospital.' He was matter-of-fact.

'For trials as extensive as Neuropazine there must have been at least one set of data?'

'Quite probably. But the participants were all treated as

outpatients. And until we were computerised, outpatient records were only kept a few years.'

Lorna regarded Barnett closely, still wondering if he was working to some hidden agenda.

'What about doctors involved?' she probed.

'Thirty years ago? If there are any still practising here they would have been very junior at the time. But I can make enquiries.'

'And the man who headed up the trials?'

'Doc Krauss.' He nodded. 'Retired some time back. Before I joined, so at least three years ago.'

'I could speak to him?'

'Don't see why not.' He shrugged. 'He's moved out of the state. Somewhere up in New England, I believe.'

'You're in touch?'

'Not personally. He writes some of his colleagues from time to time.' Then, meeting her gaze, 'He's all there,' he tapped his head, 'if that's what you're thinking.' Leaning across his desk, Barnett pressed the button on an intercom to summon his secretary.

There came the sounds of movement from the office next door before a woman appeared in the doorway. Thin, pale, hatchet-faced, she wore a dress that looked as if it had come out of the black and white era. She acknowledged Lorna's presence without a smile.

'Mrs Lane, I need Doc Krauss's contact details for Dr Reid.'

'You know staff records are confidential,' she admonished Barnett with a sharpness of tone that startled Lorna.

'That may be so—'

'I'd have to clear it with Personnel.' There was no mistaking the hostility.

'On this occasion I think we can make an exception.' He ignored the tone. 'I'm sure Doc Krauss would be only too happy to share his experiences with Dr Reid.'

'If State Inspectorate find that we're handing out confidential information—'

'Put them right onto me,' commanded Barnett.

Mrs Lane remained in the doorway, regarding Lorna, stony-eyed.

'Do we have an address for Dr Reid?' she asked after a pause.

'Mrs Lane,' Barnett's voice betrayed irritation for the first time, 'I want Doc Krauss's details *right now*.'

Turning on her heel with an audible gasp of resentment, Mrs Lane retreated down the passage.

'I was brought into this place to change working practices,' Barnett told Lorna, rolling his eyes. 'But changing people . . .'

She glanced at him in sympathy.

For a few minutes he spoke about the culture of secrecy at St Augusta, before conversation returned to the Lafayette trials. Scanning down a staff list, Barnett considered it unlikely that any of his senior consultants would have worked at the hospital at the time of the trials, though he offered to put out a note of enquiry on her behalf. Doc Krauss, it seemed, was her only lead.

When Mrs Lane still hadn't returned ten minutes later, Barnett suggested they make their way to the records office themselves. There they found a male nurse eating his sandwich lunch. 'Any sign of Mrs Lane?' asked Barnett.

'Just two minutes back,' nodded the other, 'heading to the canteen. Always takes her lunch hour at one.'

Checking his watch, Barnett muttered with exasperation about having to administer the whole hospital singlehandedly, before he began to make his way through towering shelves of filing cabinets. 'Former personnel records . . . somewhere right down the back,' he mused, making his way through the maze of dank shelving. Lorna followed closely behind as he worked towards the back of the archives that were lit only by a few naked bulbs hanging from exposed cables. A sudden chill in the air made her shiver. Hugging herself she glanced about at the mildewing cardboard box files lined up on steel shelves, the dark shadows in the gaps between them.

There was a disturbing undercurrent about this place she'd detected from the moment she'd stepped in. Not just the archive – the whole hospital. There seemed an almost palpable sense of despair, as though something had once happened here so terrible that the misery of it had become engrained in the very fabric of the institution. A place of lost souls, she mused, before pulling herself up. There were times her imagination would get ahead of her, before her rational, scientific side ordered her mind back in line. Just because it was cold and musky, she decided, she was getting spooked. She decided to follow Barnett more closely.

The hospital chief had to pull out a number of drawers before finding his way to archive files of former employees. These had been placed in date order, and it took him a while before he worked back to the year of Krauss's departure. But he found his way there eventually, and returned to the front of the records office, where an ancient Xerox machine ground noisily to itself in the corner. He'd soon run off a copy of a page showing Krauss's contact address and phone number in Campden, New Hampshire.

Handing her the sheet he met her eyes again. 'I'm just sorry you had to come all the way out here to get it,' he said.

A short while later he was showing her through to the hospital foyer. As they made their way down the corridor Lorna was struck, again, by the emptiness of the building – and its gloominess. The two black families who had been there when she arrived were still slumped on wooden benches like surreal statues caught in a time-warp, or some baleful movie about the bad old days in the Deep South.

Suddenly, her imagination was racing again. 'The patients here,' she asked Barnett, her expression intense. 'They're mostly black, are they?'

He nodded. 'Pretty much. But our catchment area is wide and we take all comers. We even do Wilson State Penitentiary – almost all as outpatients, for obvious reasons.'

'And it's always been this way?'

'For the last twenty-five years or so. Until then it was exclusively Afro-American.' He regarded her shining eyes with curiosity. 'Why d'you ask?'

'The Lafayette trials – none of the documentation noted that.'

'Is race relevant in a psychiatric trial?'

Lorna was shaking her head. That was the whole point! Krauss hadn't noted race in the Neuropazine trials. It hadn't been an experimental factor. But it was directly relevant to ageing.

On the steps of the administration building, she exchanged a crisp handshake with Barnett, before heading down to her hire car. Swinging her briefcase onto the passenger seat, she climbed behind the wheel and started the engine, little realising she wasn't alone in the car. As she drove past the building, something made her turn to glance back up. And that was when she realised she was being watched. Mrs Lane was standing on the upstairs balcony. A lone figure with pallid features, she stood motionless in her dark dress, staring down at Lorna's car. In the midday sun, the balcony shadows hung heavy and oppressive. With its crumbling plaster and decayed handrails, the once-majestic building now stood stark and eerie, as though choked into silence. There was something creepy about the whole place, decided Lorna, pulling her gaze away from the rear-view mirror. She was relieved she wouldn't be coming back.

On her way down the lengthy driveway, she was passed by a van heading towards the hospital, steel bars covering its windows. 'Wilson State Penitentiary,' she read as the van drove by. She recalled mention of a secure ward attached to St Augusta in papers about the Neuropazine trials. Could that be the source of the darkness that seemed to permeate St Augusta Hospital, she wondered? 'The criminally insane' – the phrase came unbidden to her consciousness in all its Dickensian horror. Perhaps that was at the heart of it.

She'd soon dismissed St Augusta and Mrs Lane from her mind as she turned out onto Route 10. Unaware of movement behind her, her thoughts returned excitedly to the discovery that the Lafayette trials had quite probably been conducted on black patients. Back in Cambridge, for all her scientific intelligence, she'd been incredibly naive about world affairs. In particular, she'd been oblivious of American history, and the racial profile of Southern states like Louisiana. No doubt if she'd studied at Harvard or Yale, she would have been more aware. But she realised now what a mistake she'd made in a fundamental assumption about the Neuropazine trial. The statistical reality was that life expectancy for black Americans had always been lower than for whites. Poorer diet, living conditions and access to medical care were some of the reasons that black people died younger.

But all the original calculations she'd made for her *Science* magazine article had been based on an average life expectancy age for *all* Americans. The same calculations, based on black life expectancy, would produce a very different set of figures – an even stronger endorsement for the life-extending properties of NP3!

Her mind churned with the implications for her research. The revelation wouldn't change in any way what she was doing on her programme. But after all the setbacks of the past months it would give Spencer Drake something to spin about. She wondered if she should call Greg Merrit to share her discovery. Or what about Jack? She had her cellphone on the seat right beside her.

Then, taking a deep breath in, she told herself to calm down. Although it seemed highly likely the Lafayette patients had all been black, she wouldn't know for sure until she'd spoken to Dr Krauss. As soon as she got to her hotel, she decided, she'd phone him. Even allowing for the one-hour time difference, it wouldn't be too late to call him in New Hampshire.

She was booked into a de luxe suite at the Du Cane Plaza that night. Jack had made the reservation personally. When she'd told him about her trip, he'd insisted she stay at the hotel as a family guest and he hadn't needed to work hard to persuade her. In the three months they'd been seeing each other, she'd come to appreciate the high elegance and discreet, personal service provided by Du Cane Plaza hotels. As Jack's partner, she felt almost a sense of belonging.

Mulling over her discovery at St Augusta, she was deep in thought when she felt the movement against her left heel. Unfamiliar with the Chrysler she was driving, she paid little attention at first. Without looking down, she brushed off what she assumed was the floor-mat with her right foot and continued driving.

Several moments later the movement came again, but this time against her right foot. Rubbing her leg she tried dislodging the mat, but it only started riding up her shin. With some irritation she glanced down to see what was happening. And instantly froze. It wasn't a mat. It was a snake!

She stared down for a few moments, mesmerised, before the terror hit her. Lurching nausea induced by her phobia. Dizziness threatening her consciousness. The creature's shiny-scaled thickness uncoiling stealthily from under her seat, its blunt head protruding from the shadows. Flicking its tongue up the back of her legs.

Adrenaline was flooding through her system. Her heart raced out of control. Transfixed, she felt that the snake was looking directly at her. Evil menace filled those eyes.

She was incapable of any thought, rational or otherwise. Caught up in surreal slow motion, time became meaningless. She remained transfixed. Cars were swerving to avoid the veering Chrysler amid a chorus of angry horns. Some instinct for survival made her take her left foot off the accelerator. She moved it slowly, away from the snake, towards the door. Giddy with terror and gasping for breath, she was oblivious of everything else. She had no sense of where she was or what she was doing. It was only visceral impulse that made her grab hold of the handbrake and tug it slowly upwards.

As the car skidded to a halt at the side of the road, spinning round ninety degrees with a shower of loose stones, she was fumbling at the door handle. The snake was curling up her right leg, head raised, tongue darting. As she slid her foot out from under it, both snake and shoe slipped onto the floor.

Then it was all she could do to scramble out. Slam the door shut behind her. Arms and legs were trembling uncontrollably. Within moments she was slumped against the bonnet, heaving for breath, silent tears flowing down her cheeks.

Her rescuers were two agricultural reps, making their way from Jackson to New Orleans. On the road some distance behind, they'd witnessed the car's erratic weaving through the traffic, followed by her hasty exit from the vehicle, one shoe on, one shoe off. It hadn't looked right.

They pulled up behind where she was leaning against the car, hugging herself while she cried uncontrollably. And at first they hadn't been able to get any sense out of her, except a gesture towards the driver's seat. Looking through the window, shielding his eyes from the sun, the first rep, who'd introduced himself to her as Harvey, soon spotted the cause of her upset. 'A flathead!' he exclaimed, summoning his colleague to look at where the snake was now coiled around the handbrake. Then, observing the hire car key-tag, he turned to Lorna.

'Real nasty-looking, but pretty harmless, ma'am. Get quite a few of them in these parts. D'you want me to get rid of him?'

Minutes later, after Lorna had recovered her speech, she explained her snake phobia. Even with the snake long gone, and the car checked over to confirm there were no further unwanted passengers, she couldn't bring herself to go near it, not even to collect her belongings. As it was getting late and they were all heading into New Orleans, the reps offered to take her into town in convoy. She could ride with Harvey in his car, while his colleague followed in hers. Traumatised and tearful, Lorna gratefully accepted.

The rest of the journey into the French quarter of New Orleans took just over thirty minutes. During this time, Harvey, a large, amiable man in his early fifties, speculated on how the flathead could have got into her car. He had no idea how just talking about snakes scared her. Instead he wondered, aloud, if it was possible the snake could have somehow entered through an open window. It seemed unlikely, he reckoned, so was she quite certain she'd shut the door when she'd gone inside St Augusta Hospital?

All things considered, he decided after further ruminating, there were only two possible explanations. Either the snake had been in the car from the time she collected it – and who knew how long it had been curled right up there, under the front seat, made you think, didn't it? – or someone must have deliberately put it in the car when she'd been visiting Ray Barnett. 'Someone with a very sick sense of humour.' Harvey had glanced over at her with a paternal eye.

Lorna had tried looking grateful. She'd long since reached the same conclusion, although she failed to see how sense of humour came into it. Trying to block out all thought of the car journey, and Harvey's continuing analysis, she turned her thoughts instead to her suite at the Du

Cane Plaza. She couldn't wait to change out of the clothes that were tainted by her snake experience. She relished the prospect of being alone in comfortable surroundings, removed from all of this. She'd have a glass of gin and tonic to steady her nerves. A nice, hot bath. She'd put the whole, harrowing ordeal behind her.

The lobby of the Du Cane Plaza in New Orleans was every bit as luxurious as the Washington, DC hotel, but instead of cosmopolitan sophistication, its décor was evocative of traditional Southern grandeur. A sweeping double staircase led to wide upstairs galleries lit by stately chandeliers. Thanking her rescuers, she made her way over to the concierge's desk with some relief, a bellboy wheeling her luggage behind.

The concierge, an elegant Swedish woman, checked her computer when Lorna gave her name. 'We don't have you on the computer, Dr Reid.' She looked up after a moment. 'Might the reservation be under another name?'

Lorna shook her head. She'd been with Jack when he made the call. She remembered his specific instructions that the suite was to be reserved in her name.

'I suppose you could try Jack Hennessy,' she suggested.

The other woman reacted – and not only with recognition. A sudden scepticism clouded her features when she tapped into the computer, as though she'd decided she was dealing with some kind of nutcase. Then she was shaking her head again. 'I'm sorry. There's nothing here.'

'This is ridiculous!' Shaken and exhausted, Lorna felt pushed to the end of her endurance. Seizing the telephone on the concierge's desk, she lifted the receiver before dialling. 'I'm phoning him, right now.'

The concierge resisted her usual admonition that the

telephone was for use by hotel guests only, regarding Lorna with an uncertain expression.

Trying Jack's cellphone first, Lorna found it switched off. Dialling him at home, she only got the answerphone.

'God Almighty!' she cried out, slamming down the receiver. Emotions running between nervous exhaustion and rising impatience, she struggled to check her tears.

'Look, I'll reserve something myself. We can sort out payment when I leave tomorrow.'

The concierge was shaking her head. 'I'm afraid we're fully booked, Dr Reid.'

'*Every* suite? *Every* room in the hotel?'

'It's conference season down here. And with the jazz festival . . .'

Another concierge, a fresh-faced trainee, stopped from where he had been walking past. 'Did you say "Dr Reid"?' he enquired. Then as Lorna nodded, 'Someone from your office called this morning to cancel your reservation.'

Bewildered, Lorna took a moment to react. 'But they couldn't have,' she insisted, 'none of them knew I was staying here.'

'They definitely said they were from your office.'

Then the first concierge reached under the desk for a leaflet. 'There seems to have been a mix-up.' She tried smoothing things over. 'We can recommend a few places nearby.'

But Lorna was shaking her head. 'Just forget it.' She about-turned, retrieved her luggage and made her way back through the lobby. Outside she stepped into a waiting taxi, and told the driver to take her to the airport. She'd had quite enough of New Orleans. She wasn't going to stick around for another dose of it tomorrow.

As they passed the throbbing carnival that was Bourbon Street, with its jazz and its voodoo shops and its endless bars, she reflected on her unnerving experiences: St Augusta Hospital with its portentous atmosphere and toxic staff; the snake horror – just how likely was that to have been chance? *And* the mix-up over the hotel reservation. It all seemed like too much of a coincidence. As if there was someone out there who had gone out of their way to make this trip a complete nightmare for her. Someone who wanted to make her pack up and go home.

Was she just being paranoid, she wondered? Reading too much into a sequence of unconnected events? Or was it possible she was being scared off? Chased away by someone who didn't want her poking around the Lafayette trials. It was hard to make sense of it. Quite simply, who would bother? What would *anyone* have to lose from her opening up the records of a drug trial carried out thirty years before?

Two days after Matt's funeral, Andrew left the office early. He planned taking the 2.20 to Weybridge as he had on previous afternoons, though for very different reasons. As he made his way through the office in his tan Burberry trenchcoat, several of his colleagues nodded across at him sympathetically. But it didn't escape him when Bob Bowler glanced around, askance.

Bowler reported to him, although his behaviour in the office sometimes gave the impression that the opposite was the case. Late twenties and a workaholic, having nimbly sidestepped the high-tech collapse of early 2000, since then Bowler had believed himself to be invincible. Now, in a single moment's glance, he seemed to be questioning

Andrew's motive for leaving early. Andrew ignored him, taking the lift down to ground floor before making his way towards Waterloo Bridge.

Until that moment, everyone at Glencoe had been sympathetic about his situation. Dozens of sympathy cards and letters had been sent to his office. A handful of colleagues had attended the funeral and a large wreath had been presented on behalf of the company. Glencoe's Chairman, Sir Stuart Jamieson, had made a rare appearance on the eighth floor to pass on his personal condolences. 'I'm sorry, Andrew. Very, very sorry. Absolutely awful.' Stuart always gave the impression of a large, amiable, Eton-educated Teddy bear. But for all the charm, he possessed a shrewd judgement. 'If there's anything we can do for you . . .?'

Andrew had nodded.

'If you need to take off a few . . . some time.'

The correction was noted, 'a few weeks' deleted midsentence, to be replaced by something more open to reinterpretation later.

'Thank you, Sir Stuart.' They had shaken hands.

His closer colleagues couldn't have been more supportive. Both Tony Faber, who ran Vector Fund Management, and his secretary Ruth, a mature lady in her mid-fifties, had been down for the funeral. Between the two of them they'd done what they could to ease his workload, keeping his involvement in routine bureaucracy to a miminum. All in all, he was very lucky working where he did, he mused, as his train pulled out of the station. As for the Bob Bowlers of this world, there was one in every office.

The reason for his early departure this afternoon had to do with his conversation with Mrs Hayes two days earlier.

No matter how much he tried, he just couldn't ignore what she had told him. As soon as he arrived home, he started on what he regarded as the real business of the day. Picking up the photograph of Matt he kept on his desk – a favourite of his taken at a picnic in the grounds of Blenheim Palace the summer before – he removed it from its ornate Addison Ross frame, put it on his scanner, and downloaded the image into an ordinary Word file. Then he began the message he'd already written in his mind countless times already today. 'PLEASE HELP!' he typed, in capital letters, above Matt's photograph. Then beneath it: 'Matt Norton died on Wednesday, 5th April, after falling in the river near Basset Road, Weybridge. Two men may have witnessed the accident. Information is sought about these witnesses URGENTLY. Reward offered. Please contact Andrew Norton.' He gave his mobile phone number.

The message was simple, though stark. It felt surreal typing out the words 'Matt Norton died'. Seeing them printed out in black and white. He still couldn't quite believe them. There were moments during the afternoon, as there had been every day in the last week, when he half expected Matt to appear in the doorway, or hear his voice from the other end of the corridor.

Andrew experimented with different font sizes and lay-outs before printing off a version he was satisfied with. Of course Jess, with her graphic design skills, would have done a far better job, but he hadn't asked her. She would have refused. And it was her attitude that troubled him more than anything. She'd already said what she felt about Andrew's doubts – no matter what he discovered, he wasn't going to bring Matt back. It was as though she'd closed the door on events of that Wednesday and had no further interest in revisiting them. He could understand why she might want to do that. Perhaps putting the past behind her was her way of coping. But it wasn't his.

He had, of course, discussed things with Chief Inspector Hardwick. Calling him first thing this morning for an off-the-record conversation, he'd told the policeman about his conversation with Mrs Hayes. He hadn't had to explain who Mrs Hayes was. Hardwick had received countless letters of complaint from her over the years on all manner of subjects, from the noise disturbance of motor cruisers passing up the river, to security worries during the annual Weybridge Regatta; the Weybridge Police Force had grave doubts about her reliability as a witness. Hardwick had explained to Andrew how, if he wished to lodge a formal request to open a murder enquiry, this would be done, but that the resources the police allocated to the case would have to reflect the evidence available. And Mrs Hayes's testimony, even if she cared to repeat it to the police, would not be regarded as substantive.

Andrew had guessed this, which was why he suggested putting out a local notice, asking for any information. Hardwick had replied he could see no harm in this activity – so long as Andrew didn't make any allegations of wrongdoing. His notice, the policeman warned him, should be phrased as a solicitation for witnesses – not murder suspects.

Now Andrew sent two hundred copies of the notice to print. As they were coming over his laserjet, he went through to the bedroom and changed out of his suit into jeans and a polo-neck sweatshirt.

A short while later he was making his way out of the

house and up the driveway, a thick pile of notices in his hand.

Response to his leafleting was rapid – though not of the kind he had hoped for. He had returned from posting a large batch through letterboxes when Jess's Rover pulled in the driveway. She'd been into Casey-Bothwell's gourmet pie-makers, and picked up a Duck à l'Orange pie for herself, as well as Andrew's favourite, a chilli plum beef. She often did this on a Thursday – they regarded the pies as something of an end-of-week treat.

Jess started on the supper soon after getting in and, as in the past few days, they kept up a routine of pseudo-normality. As she worked in the kitchen, he opened a bottle of wine from the cellar, put on a CD of Chopin *Ballades* and lit the dining-room fire. He offered her some wine and when she accepted, poured out a glass and put it beside where she was preparing a salad. Slipping an arm around her waist, he squeezed her to him for a moment. She didn't reciprocate the tenderness, and carried on chopping a cucumber. He released her, making his way through to the sitting room where he picked up a copy of the *Evening Standard*, and began leafing through it.

Conversation over supper was desultory. Andrew began to wish he'd suggested they eat it off their laps in front of the TV. Then after she'd finished eating Jess looked up and told him, 'I got a call from Sally, on my mobile this evening.' A senior designer at her company, Sally was younger than Jess and extremely talented. She and Jess had always got on well, but although Andrew had only ever met her twice at work functions, he hadn't taken to her. To him she had appeared hard-bitten and world-weary, and he hadn't understood what Jess saw in her. Still, his wife's workplace friends were no business of his.

'She got your leaflet.' Jess eyed him across the table.

'Oh.' He remembered that Sally lived not far away, in a cul-de-sac opposite The Highwayman.

'You didn't tell me.' Her voice was as flat and empty of expression as her eyes.

He'd already thought about the probability that Jess would find out about the notice. He'd planned to introduce it into their conversation – if they'd had one. But now that she'd brought it up, he had a reply. 'When I told you what Mrs Hayes said, you gave me the impression you weren't much interested in investigating things further.'

'You might at least have asked,' she reproached him.

He was still wondering how to respond when she continued, 'When did you decide to stop talking to me?'

'Jess, it isn't like that.' Leaning back in his chair, he dabbed his lips with his napkin as he struggled to control his impatience.

'So what other little surprises do you have planned?' Her lips were pursed.

'I don't have anything *planned*.' His voice rose before, checking himself, he continued in a reasonable tone, 'All I want is to make absolutely sure that Mrs Hayes got it wrong.' Then meeting her glacial gaze, 'If nothing comes of it . . .' He shrugged. 'I just didn't think you wanted to be involved.'

'I didn't *what*?' It was apparently the very worst thing he could have said. 'How could I possibly be *more* involved?' She was scraping back her chair and flinging her napkin on the table. Storming down the corridor to their bedroom.

'I didn't mean it like that – and you know I didn't!'

Andrew couldn't conceal his anger as he got up to follow her. Then when she didn't reply, 'This hasn't been easy for me either, you know!'

She slammed the bedroom door shut. He knew better than to go after her, but tonight he couldn't help himself. Following her down the corridor, he burst through the bedroom door. 'What d'you expect me to do? Forget Mrs Hayes said anything?'

She was sitting on her side of the bed with her back to him, face in her hands.

'Well? Tell me!' he persisted, hands on his hips. 'What do *you* think I should be doing?'

'Just leave me alone.' She shook her head.

'That's the whole point!' he cried, exasperated. 'I did leave you alone. I left you well alone. I didn't involve you in the flyer. Then you criticise me for it. Seems to me I'm damned if I don't and damned if I do! Whatever happens, I can't win.'

'For God's sake, Andrew!' She rose from the bed, voice choked and cheeks wet with tears. 'Matt's only been gone a week –' her eyes were defiant, '– and here you are talking about "winning".'

'But it might not have *been* an accident,' he protested, thinking that however sure he was of himself, however right, Jess could always make him feel selfish and mean-spirited.

She strode right past him. 'When are you going to stop clutching at straws?' she demanded, at the door.

'I don't see what's wrong—'

'No. Of course you don't. You can't bear the truth, can you?'

'What's that supposed to mean?' he challenged.

For a moment they paused, eyes interlocked in an intensity of emotion unmatched by any that had passed between them during their entire married life. So, finally, they'd come to the heart of it. The subject they'd been avoiding ever since the police had found Matt's body choked in the riverside weeds. He felt his heart race, charged by anger and dread.

At last she said, 'You were the one who left him by the riverside.'

When she left the room, he didn't follow her. He knew the accusation shouldn't surprise him, but he still felt overwhelmed by the enormity of it. Slumped against the bedroom wall, he heard her go back up the corridor and into the spare bedroom. She slammed the door shut behind her and turned the key.

His mobile phone rang shortly after nine. The voice at the other end was unfamiliar. 'Taylor here. We live about ten houses from you – quite a way downstream. I'm calling about your leaflet.'

'I see.'

'Look, it's probably nothing at all,' continued the other, after expressing condolences, 'but I thought I should at least mention what we saw last Wednesday afternoon.'

4

At first he thought the flames were fireflies. They visited sometimes, though usually not till summer, clouds of peripatetic light playing on the surface of the lake outside. Awakened by the motion of light filtering down the corridor, it took him some moments, between sleep and full consciousness, to register. There was too much mist for fireflies, was his first recognition. Then he realised that the thick stream pouring into their bedroom wasn't mist at all. Horrified, he reached over, shaking his wife awake. 'Hannah!' he cried out urgently. 'Fire!'

The old man scrambled from the bedclothes and hurried, in his pyjamas, to the bedroom door. Opening it wider, he was shocked by the size of the conflagration at the end of the short corridor. Had he forgotten to check the embers in the fireplace before going to bed? How could it have got this big without him sensing a thing? Raising a hand to his ear, he involuntarily touched the place where he usually wore his hearing aid.

Hannah hurried over, clutching her nightgown as she looked down the passage.

'Fire Department!' He turned away from her, retreating back into the bedroom towards the phone. But she reached out, seizing his hand,

'Don't! It's a waste of time!'

The nearest fire station was ten miles away in Campden. By the time rescue services got here, the place would be razed to the ground. Eyes meeting, they exchanged a horrified look of understanding. Was the isolation they so greatly treasured about to engulf them? Could the very seclusion of their retirement idyll destroy everything they owned?

He seized his bunch of keys from the bedside table and rushed towards the steel grid at the end of the corridor. The blast of heat struck him physically, like a wave, slowing his movements. Behind him, smoke billowing into the bedroom sent Hannah into another coughing fit, her lungs weakened by a bout of pneumonia last year. Making his way through the smoke and heat, Albert worked through escape routes. Which way out? And what to do about the fire? He dimly recalled the two extinguishers they'd bought years before. Stored under the kitchen sink, they would be no use at all on something this size.

Reaching the grille, he could see through the haze of acrid smoke flames leaping off the living-room furniture. Even without his hearing aid, he heard the crash as a large picture fell to the floor with a shatter of glass. Inserting the security door key, from force of habit he reached out to hold one of the steel bars – before letting go in an instant, with a howl of pain. He tried to ignore the burn to his hand, the stinging in his eyes as he quickly unlocked the middle deadlock. It was while he was crouching to undo the lock at the base that there was an almighty explosion as the drinks cabinet caught alight. Litres of alcohol gushed across the room in rapidly spreading plumes of fire.

At that moment he realised that whatever half-formed ideas he might have had about rescuing valuables and escaping out of the front were just hopeless. The place was an inferno. He couldn't even see the front door. And even if he got to it without being consumed by flames, by the time he had undone each of its three locks, he would have no chance of survival. He cursed the security measures he'd installed to protect them when they'd moved here from New Orleans. Turning back, he saw Hannah standing at the bedroom door, a cloth over her mouth, gesturing frantically that he should return.

'The storeroom!' she shouted as he came back.

Behind the bathroom was a small room created by the back extension. In it was the original rear entrance, a basic steel door leading out to the back porch, with a solid padlock inside.

'I'll get the key!' he called, hurrying past her to a corridor cupboard. He didn't keep it with all his others as the storeroom door was used so infrequently. In fact, they hadn't opened the door for years. But he knew exactly where the key for it was to be found. He'd always been careful about such things. On the second shelf of the cupboard was a small card index box in which he kept spares to the car, boat and bank safe. He was fumbling through it, when he was thrown to the ground as another almighty crash reverberated through the cottage. Even before he'd clambered back on his knees, he

72

realised that the whole ceiling had caved in. Up in the roof space, fire was racing through from the front of the house.

He screamed to Hannah who'd fallen under a length of ceiling board, and was struggling to her feet. She stumbled over towards him.

'The padlock key!' he cried frantically, looking about him at the chaos of dust and smoke and collapsed ceiling. The heat of the fire was drawing terrifyingly close, the smoke so dense it was nearly impossible to keep their eyes open. Scrabbling through the mess on the floor, they searched for the contents of the index box. It was a race against time. The thought passed through Albert's mind that he might try unpicking the padlock. Under normal circumstances it wouldn't be hard. But he'd dismissed the idea within a moment of thinking it. His hands were so shaky he could barely control them.

The fire, fuelled by all the oxygen in the roof space, became all-consuming. The steel grille where he'd been standing less than a minute before was obscured behind leaping flames. Splinters of burning wood rained down on them. Eyes reduced to narrow slits, they moved their hands across the floor in a desperate, frenzied search.

It was Hannah who found it. Pressing it into his hand, she bent over, succumbing to another bout of coughing. The burning acidity of the smoke had scorched her lungs. Albert jerked her to her feet. He felt awful doing it, but there was no alternative. The intensity of the fire was growing by the second. Dragging her into the storeroom, he was confronted by another surreal scene. Everything was on fire. The suitcases, the rolls of leftover carpet, all the papers from his medical career at St Augusta Hospital, were now licked with blue-green flames. He scrambled across the room as fast as he was able with Hannah slumped against him. This time as he approached the door, he was prepared. Grabbing the sleeve of his pyjama – it wasn't much, but it provided some insulation at least – he seized the padlock.

The moment he grabbed it, he knew something was wrong. Bending so that it was only inches away from him, as he raised the key he realised. It wasn't the old padlock. It was a new, combination lock. 'Hannah!' he shouted above the noise of the fire. Sick from coughing, she lurched towards him. 'Did you put this on?' His eyes bulged, bloodshot. Dizzy, she shook her head.

At that moment a burning rafter crashed down between them. They flung themselves to either side, and the flames leapt up several feet. Staring at the padlock with its unknown combination, Albert suddenly remembered the delivery man from Liquorland who'd made a surprise delivery early that evening. Not the usual delivery man. A different youth whose smooth, bland features were memorable only because of a deep, red blemish under his left eye. He'd arrived with a 'loyalty bonus' bottle of bourbon and had asked to use the bathroom.

As he recalled their unexpected visitor, Albert Krauss suddenly thought back to his early days at St Augusta Hospital. And in that moment he knew his greatest fear was being realised. It had been a threat throughout his medical career. A dark horror that could have destroyed his reputation at any moment. By the time he retired, he'd thought he'd got away with it. But now he realised the truth. The past had finally caught up with him, and he and Hannah were going to be burned alive.

Lorna arrived at Zonmark for her usual 8 am start, restless and weary before the day had even begun. She hadn't had much sleep the night before. Her plane back to Washington had been kept on the tarmac of New Orleans airport a full hour after scheduled take-off. It had been late by the time she'd got back into Washington, but she'd phoned Jack, who she knew would be expecting to hear from her. He'd been bewildered by her experience at the Du Cane Plaza in New Orleans. And even more dismayed by what she'd been through earlier that day. Then as they were discussing the situation back at Zonmark, he'd dropped a bombshell of his own. He'd only intended it as a casual aside, she was sure, but the implications were dramatic. What if, Jack had mused, news of NP3 had reached the media because of a deliberate leak authorised by Kuesterman? What if her programme had been used to bump up Zonmark's flagging share price after the biotech crash?

By the time she'd crawled to bed, it had been after two in the morning, and even then she hadn't managed any sleep. She'd tossed and turned, replaying events in New Orleans, and thinking about what Jack had said, imagining darkly where this all might lead. And she couldn't stop wondering about Dr Krauss. What if he *did* confirm that the entire Neuropazine panel had been black?

She was still wondering when she got to work next morning. The NP3 building was one of half a dozen satellites arranged around a Zonmark administration block housing research and production facilities. Lorna's operations occupied the entire ground floor. Stepping through a revolving door, she stood for a moment, as all arrivals must, in a white, cell-shaped entry cubicle, before being cleared by an unseen guard using CCTV surveillance. Then a steel door slid open and, in marked contrast to the bland security area, ahead of her was an expansive lounge, with gaily coloured armchairs and sofas, deep-pile rugs, toy-barrels and desks kitted out with computer games. This was the waiting area for panel kids who visited Zonmark for six-monthly assessments. It was designed as a place of relaxation for parents as well as children, and as Lorna walked through she took in the rich aroma of Brazilian coffee from the percolator in the corner, and glanced over the headlines of that morning's batch of daily newspapers laid out on the coffee table.

Beyond the bright murals of the waiting room was a small suite of open-plan offices, much like those in any other corporate building, except for the plethora of IT equipment. This was the NP3 data processing department presided over by Chen Samuki, part of her five-strong team.

Chen wasn't in yet, but along the corridor Steve Manzini was already behind his desk. Lorna's newest employee, Steve had been appointed to head up panel recruitment. But no sooner had he put his two assistants in place than he lost them in the budget cut.

Lorna felt bad about the upheaval. Though something in Steve's manner made it hard for her to express herself to him fully on this, or any other subject. He was intense and hard to fathom. Dark-haired and bespectacled, he came with a dazzling track record and glowing references from a pharmacology centre in California. His earnestness had been much in evidence during his job interviews, but so, too, had his intellectual brilliance. Lorna had assumed that after he'd settled in, he'd relax a tad. As it happened, relaxation didn't seem a concept in Steve's experience. He seemed to spend his entire life at work.

The next office after Steve's belonged to her personal assistant, Gail, who ran the admin side of NP3. Her own corner office had picture windows in both walls facing out across the landscaped lawns of the science park. A third, internal window overlooked Greg's domain – the glistening steel laboratory equipment in which all panel samples were subjected to a comprehensive battery of tests. Access to the multi-million-dollar laboratory was available only from the corner office at the other end of the block, which Kuesterman had assumed she'd take for herself, but which she'd insisted that Greg have. She'd always intended her second-in-command to have hands-on responsibility for operations. That way, she was free to deal with strategy.

Greg had been her first recruit five years ago. She'd taken him on just months after starting NP3. More than just her second-in-command, he knew as much as she did about the programme, and in the case of specific test procedures, more. She knew she could count on him to keep things on track. He wasn't simply her deputy, he was her alter ego, her confidant.

Often on a Friday lunchtime they'd go out to a local Italian and discuss progress over pasta and Chianti. During the week they'd frequently stay late to talk through detail. Greg had learned to read her moods and knew exactly when to calm her, if she was feeling fraught – and when to leave her alone to her own reflections. Both had been single for a lot of the past five years. From time to time they

77

would commiserate with each other about their mutual lack of a love life.

Two years her junior, Greg was tall and rangy-looking with long, fair hair and a ready smile. Lorna had always been mystified at his bachelor status, believing many women would find him highly attractive. She certainly did, although she'd never allowed their professional relationship to be compromised. Or at least, not seriously.

There had been one occasion, about a year before, when they'd both attended a seminar in New York addressed by the high-profile genomics expert, Craig Venter. Returning to their hotel after a post-seminar cocktail party, instead of the chaste goodbye pecks they sometimes exchanged, Greg had kissed her on the mouth – and she had yielded. There had been no mistaking what they both wanted. Their arousal had been mutual – as had their recognition that this wasn't a good idea. After a few moments they had broken apart. Their embarrassment hadn't required a voice, they'd simply said goodnight, and gone their separate ways. Nothing more had been said about the kiss – no words had been needed.

Now Lorna stepped across her office and sat at her desk. It was, as always in the morning, gleaming and uncluttered – Zonmark ran a strict clear-desk policy as part of its tight security regime. The first thing she did was to reach down into her briefcase and retrieve a sheet of paper which she placed in front of her. It was the document Barnett had copied for her the day before containing the full contact details of Dr Albert Krauss.

Picking up the phone, she dialled his number. She had been wanting to do this since yesterday afternoon. She'd even thought of phoning from home this morning, before deciding that 8 am was the earliest she could call.

There was a strange tone at the other end, different from the regular ringing sound, but perhaps the doctor was on some rural telephone exchange. Checking her watch, she saw it was a few minutes after eight. Surely he'd be out of bed by now? It was late enough on a spring morning, she'd thought, for him to be up and about, but still early enough to catch him before he'd gone out anywhere.

As the phone continued to ring, she wondered about his house. Was it one of those great, rambling places in the countryside which took an age to walk through, and with only one phone in the whole house? He and his wife would be elderly, she reasoned. It might take them a while to answer.

But after another half minute of ringing, she realised there was to be no answer. Nor did he have an answerphone. Putting down the phone, she reached over to her computer mouse and automatically clicked onto Microsoft Outlook, checking what she had on today – and when she'd have a chance to call back Krauss. As usual she had a busy schedule, but as she scanned through everything she needed to do over the next ten hours, it all seemed so much less important than her phone call. She needed to do this before she went any further.

She clicked into her e-mail server, intending to get on with some work, but she couldn't help herself. Within moments, she'd picked up the phone and was dialling Krauss's number again. Perhaps she'd dialled the wrong number the first time, she told herself, trying to justify her distraction.

The response was just the same, and after a full minute of waiting, she hung up briefly before trying directory assistance. Maybe the number was no longer current, she figured. It couldn't hurt to check.

She gave the name and address to an operator and waited, half expecting to be told the number was unlisted. But to her surprise, the operator came back to her immediately – with the same digits she had just been dialling.

Perhaps Krauss had simply gone out for a walk. Or a day trip somewhere. What if he'd gone for longer – away on holiday? She might not be able to contact him for a while.

Frustrated, she tried putting Krauss out of her mind. Checking her In-box, she found over sixty new items waiting for her after her day out. As she scanned down one immediately caught her eye. It was the NP3 programme report for the first quarter of the year.

Greg had sent it to her late the night before. The e-mail itself consisted of only a single line: 'We need to speak about these results', followed by three exclamation marks. Lorna immediately opened the attachment and scanned through the results.

Spreadsheets summarised the results of all analyses conducted, with each child represented by a separate row on the table. Deterioration rates for each ageing indicator were compared to those of a control sample.

Scanning down the tables rapidly, Lorna could already guess some of the findings. She didn't meet all the kids who came into Zonmark, but she knew some of them well and had an intuitive feel for the way they were responding. In some cases, kids would respond immediately to NP3 – within three months the improvement in their physical state was easily observable. In other cases, there was no such evident change, though measurements including dehydroepiandosterone analysis, thyroid, melatonin and other biomarkers always showed that deterioration was significantly slower than control figures.

Glancing down the tables at the latest figures, she saw that the results of NP3 therapy were better than she had expected. Certainly they were way ahead of forecast. Most promising of all, she realised as she went through each row one by one, was that the longer kids were on NP3, the slower the rate of retardation.

But then she came to Matthew Norton's results. Matt who had been the last panel member tested – and whose results formed the last row of the schedule. And unlike those in every other row, his results in almost every column were negative. These were not just minor variations easily dismissed; they showed a huge deterioration in his condition since six months before. 'We need to speak about these results!!!' recalled Lorna. Damned right they did!

Concentration suddenly focused, Lorna checked through each of Matt's figures, one by one. What the hell was going on? They just didn't accord with her own impressions. Matt had been in just a fortnight before. He'd been wheelchair-bound after a fall. But talking to him in the waiting area she had been impressed by his energy, his physical agility. He'd come over with his mother, Jess, and the time Lorna had spent with them had been wonderfully uplifting – one of those precious moments amid her frenzied timetable when she felt that all the hard work was worthwhile.

But she was alarmed to see how badly he'd deteriorated, according to all the ageing indicators. Her instinctive reaction was to pick up the phone and call Greg, but she knew he was visiting a facility and his cellphone would be switched off until lunchtime. Instead she stared, unseeing, out of her window across the science park.

These were the first negative results in the whole of her

NP3 programme. And it didn't take a lot to anticipate the reaction she'd get from the executive team – especially Drake. She could just imagine him suggesting they should strip out Matthew's results, when they released the findings to analysts. The alternative was guaranteed to shake investor confidence, he'd say. But however they played it to the media, Lorna knew the scientific reality. On top of her recruitment difficulties and panel shrinkage, it was the very last piece of news she needed.

Picking up the phone, she tried Krauss again. It would sweeten the pill if she could give them some good news, some positive story to distract them. But Krauss's phone just rang and rang.

When Gail arrived at the office a short time later, she saw that Lorna's door was shut – a cue that she didn't want to be disturbed. The door remained closed for the next two hours as Lorna worked through the quarterly results in detail, increasingly vexed. From time to time she'd try Krauss again – but always with the same response.

Just after ten, Gail caught her eye through the glass panel of her office door and gestured a mug. Lorna nodded. When Gail brought in coffee a few minutes later, she found Lorna hard at it.

'Thanks.' Lorna nodded as Gail put the drink down on her desk.

Gail had been working for her for more than two years and realised Lorna's intensity was about more than just hard work. Catching her expression, Lorna explained, 'I had a pretty awful time in New Orleans yesterday. Only got back late.'

'Barnett give you the runaround?'

'Barnett was fine. It was other stuff . . .' she trailed off, before glancing over at Krauss's contact details. 'Look. This is really important. I urgently need to speak to this guy, Albert Krauss. Ran the Neuropazine trial at St Augusta Hospital. I've tried his number a few times already. No reply.'

'Okay.' Gail took the sheet from her.

'Keep trying as long as it takes. Put him through to me wherever I am.' She met Gail's eyes with an imperative expression. 'It's *very* important.'

'I'll stay on the case,' Gail reassured her, before asking, 'Are you okay?'

Lorna averted her eyes as she nodded. 'Fine,' she grunted. She didn't want to talk about it.

The second shock of the day came only a short time afterwards, when she received the e-mail from Andrew Norton. They hadn't been in touch since his phone call with the shocking news of Matt's death. It had been her intention to write the Nortons a condolence letter, but like so many other of her current plans, she just hadn't had time to follow it through.

Andrew's message was only two short paragraphs, but it left her aghast. Evidence had emerged, he reported, that Matt's death might not have been accidental. His fear of water – something that Lorna herself had been aware of – had always made the manner of the 'accident' seem incomprehensible. Then a neighbour had reported seeing two men with Matt shortly before his death. Her testimony might not be reliable – she was an elderly woman with a wandering mind. But Andrew couldn't let things rest; he was already looking for supporting evidence.

The question he couldn't begin to answer, however, was 'why?' Able to think of little else, he still couldn't imagine anyone who might hate him or Jess enough to want to kill their son. If it had been murder, he was sure there was nothing personal about it. Could Lorna possibly imagine what a motive might be?

Closing the e-mail, she stared at her screen which still displayed Matt's quarterly results, all preceded by minus signs. And as she gazed at the rows of negative figures she reflected on Andrew's question.

The only answer she could think of was deeply disturbing.

5

Minutes later, she was standing in the entrance of Kuesterman's office. 'I have to see you,' she announced.

'I'm on my way to meetings in five minutes—'

But she'd already stepped inside, shutting the door behind her. 'You've seen the quarterly results?'

He nodded once.

'Well, I've just got an e-mail from Andrew Norton. It seems that Matthew's death wasn't an accident after all. There were suspicious circumstances. Quite a coincidence, wouldn't you say, given his last results?' Stepping closer to his desk, she studied him closely for a reaction. But his face was inscrutable.

'And there've been other coincidences,' she continued, heated. 'You made it quite clear last week that you were against my pursuit of the Lafayette trials data. Well, blow me down if there isn't a snake in my hire car when I come back from St Augusta. How many people know I have a snake phobia, Armand? Just tell me! Then it turns out my hotel reservation has been deliberately cancelled—'

'The point you're making?' he interjected.

'Don't patronise me, Armand.'

'I'm just wanting—'

'And don't play the innocent!' she flashed angrily. 'You know perfectly well *the point I'm making*. You couldn't continue the deception without my suspecting a thing. Surely you credit me with more intelligence than that?'

'All I credit you with, right now, is an impaired sense of propriety.' Kuesterman's face was stony. 'These are non-urgent issues—'

She stood her ground. 'I'm not going,' she raised her voice.

'Fortunately, I know the stress you're under—'

'This has nothing—'

'—damaging your judgement,' he continued, talking over her. 'Leading you to ludicrous conclusions. Believing non-urgent issues to be more important than my impending round of presentations in Wall Street.'

'I'd hardly call the murder of a child non-urgent!' she exploded.

'The *what?*' His expression was furious.

'No doubt you have some sanitised expression for it.' Her lips curled. 'But you can't hide the truth from me!'

'If what you are suggesting weren't so completely ridiculous,' he was shaking his head, 'I'd be grossly insulted. What, in Christ's name, are you on about? And what would I have to gain from the death of NP3's biggest success story?'

It was Lorna's turn for shock.

Getting up from his desk, Kuesterman made his way over to the meeting table on which his laptop was running. Ditching the screen-saver, he accessed an e-mail attachment – Greg Merrit's quarterly figures. The same figures Lorna had spent hours going through. But the last row, Matt's results, showed all the figures as positives instead of negatives. According to this version, Matt's performance on every age indicator showed a highly favourable response. Cumulatively they presented NP3's best ever results.

Lorna stared at the screen, dazed. How was it possible the minus signs had all been reversed? Was this just another of Kuesterman's tricks?

'These figures,' she gulped, feeling Kuesterman's eyes on her. 'They're different from the ones I got. They're the opposite.'

'These are the results your deputy sent me.' He was testy.

As he continued staring at her, she felt her confidence begin to crack. He'd taken her completely by surprise. Suddenly less certain, she knew she couldn't pursue her suspicions till she'd spoken to Greg.

Detecting weakness in her silence, Kuesterman continued, 'As for all the talk about snakes in cars and hotel reservations, you must believe, surely, that I have better things to do with my time than adolescent japes?'

Meeting his severe expression, her conviction was slipping away – until she remembered what Jack had suggested. 'Those weren't the only coincidences.' Her tone retained its edge. 'There's also the curious fact that not a whisper of my programme reached the ears of the media until a few weeks after the AGT collapse.'

Kuesterman turned away from her, hands in his pockets. 'Yeah. Well, I'm not pretending that was our finest hour.'

'So you're not denying it?'

He shrugged. 'Ask me a straight question, I'll give you a straight answer.'

'Yeah, right,' she snorted. 'It didn't stop you setting Schwartz on me with all his accusations of leaking—'

'Schwartz didn't know. Drake and I were the only ones in on it.'

'You and the good doctor of spin decided to make me your sacrificial lamb?'

'That's not quite the way I look at it.' Kuesterman shot her a sideways look. 'You were as much a beneficiary as I was.'

'Except for the fact that I don't own twenty-five per cent of the company's shares, you mean?'

'Don't get smart-assy with me,' snapped Kuesterman. 'Our backs were to the wall. You know perfectly well what's happened to the biotech sector since the AGT collapse. Half of it's wiped out. Zonmark was under serious threat from a hostile takeover—'

'And no one else would have had any interest in NP3.' Her tone was facetious.

'They would have, but NP3 belongs to Zonmark. Whoever bought Zonmark would have been perfectly within their rights to keep the programme and fire you if they felt so inclined.'

Though she was shaking her head, she recognised a part of the truth. And that, along with her new uncertainties about Matt's test results, made it hard to know what to believe. Bitterly, she turned to go.

'Look, Lorna—' he began in a conciliatory tone, reaching out to her arm.

'Don't touch me!' She drew herself away from him – only to realise the door had opened and they were being watched by a saucer-eyed Beryl. Eyes averted, not trusting herself to speak, she stormed directly past Kuesterman's secretary, into the corridor and out of the executive wing.

Slouched behind the steering wheel, as she returned across the science park she felt suddenly tearful and foolish. Was it possible she had imagined a conspiracy where none existed? Apart from the media leak – which was serious enough but driven by commercial imperatives all too believable – had everything else been nothing more than her over-fertile mind? Having set out with such certainty and created such a big scene, she was beginning to wonder if she had succeeded only in making a complete idiot of herself.

The biggest riddle of all was the question of Matt's results. And only one person could resolve that. Turning to her car-phone panel, she pressed a memory key. Instantly, the phone was speed-dialling Greg's cellphone. It wasn't yet eleven. Chances were he'd still be out of contact. *Please, Greg, please*, she willed him, *have your phone switched on*.

At the other end, the ringing tone sounded just twice before he answered it.

'Thank God!' Lorna exhaled heavily. 'Matt's results. What in Christ's name is going on?'

Embassy Row, Washington, DC
Friday, 14 April

Jack Hennessy strolled down the corridors of his Palladian villa, scanning each room with the critical scrutiny that came as second nature to the son of a hotelier. Diagonally opposite the British Embassy in one of Washington, DC's most exclusive enclaves, his home epitomised all that was most gracious about architecture in the nation's capital, with its soaring columns, elegant porticos and sweeping, landscaped gardens. More White House than the White

House, inside it was exquisitely appointed. And outside its landscaped gardens were protected by high walls, elaborate alarms and a well-trained pack of six Doberman pinschers.

Making his way towards the front of the house, in a *mélange* of Ralph Lauren shaving lotion and single-malt whisky, Jack conducted the familiar inventory, checking that his housekeeper had fully plumped the silk cushions on the sitting-room sofas, ensuring the damask curtains were neatly drawn, scrutinising the newly lit wicks of the hall-way candelabra.

He'd spoken to Lorna late in the afternoon and was expecting her in the next half hour. He knew about the aborted stay in New Orleans the night before – and of her horror at discovering a flathead snake in her hire car. But when they'd talked, he'd realised something else was disturbing her, too. Something to do with NP3. Which was why he intended her welcome here tonight to be as warm and relaxing as possible. She had a lot to unburden. He wanted her to unburden it all.

As he glanced through the house he tried to see it as though through her eyes. Did she find it a welcome sanctuary from the cut-and-thrust of the corporate world? Or was the opulence overwhelming? Although they'd never discussed money, she must be aware of the scale of his wealth. His lifestyle was certainly expansive. Perhaps Lorna, like many others, imagined he'd never known any different. But while many believed he'd been born with a proverbial silver spoon in his mouth, the financial reputation of his family was far more myth than reality.

His father, Thomas, used to say that the Hennessy family had moved from steerage to suburbs in just two generations. When Jack's grandfather had arrived off the boat from

Ireland in the early 1930s, like so many of his countrymen escaping the Depression, he'd arrived in New York City with nothing to his name but the contents of a scarred leather holdall and the address of a cousin once removed. Finding work where he could, he'd followed a series of dead-end jobs with a period of tenure as a hotel doorman. It was there he'd come to the attention of the patrician owner of the establishment, Dominick du Cane.

The story of how Patrick Hennessy had risen from bell-hop to *maître d'hôtel* to owner of The Du Cane was usually recounted as yet another realisation of the Great American Dream. But in reality, Patrick and his family of five lived most of their lives cramped in four basement rooms of the hotel, living off tips and leftovers from the kitchen. It was only in his mid-fifties that Patrick was promoted to *maître d'*. As a Catholic, Dominick du Cane had always had a soft spot for the Irish, and in later years, as he withdrew from the world, he became increasingly dependent on Patrick, calling his manager to the penthouse suite every evening for a pre-dinner bourbon, and a talk about the old days. Alienated by the complete uninterest of his own children in the family business, when old man Du Cane died of a heart attack, he left the hotel and all his financial assets to his loyal servant, Patrick.

Discovering himself the owner of a substantial Manhattan hotel, Patrick had wasted no time in relocating to old man Du Cane's quarters on the penthouse floor, while grooming his eldest son to assume his own role as hotel manager. The apple of his father's eye, Jack's father Tom had been a handsome young man, self-assured in manner and possessed of an engaging Irish charm. In his mid-thirties, he'd taken to his new-found affluence as to

91

the manner born, quickly acquiring a new wardrobe, a swanky Cadillac, and a lifestyle beyond his dreams. He attended the kinds of parties he'd only ever waited on before. Names of bright young things he'd read about in society pages began to appear in his personal address book. And it wasn't long before the family experienced its second flash of 'Hennessy luck', when his proposal of marriage was accepted by society débutante and tobacco heiress, Cornelia van Haven.

In a single stroke, the Hennessy family's social standing was transformed from parvenu landlords to must-have invitees. The van Havens, who owned a cigar factory in Mississippi and a sprawl of tobacco estates in the Honduras, were not only fabulously rich, they were as establishment as it was possible to be. The van Havens' gift to Tom and Cornelia on their wedding day was a six-bedroom apartment with a panoramic view over Central Park.

Younger than her husband by twelve years, when Cornelia's engagement was announced in the *New York Times*, the difference in age as well as background scandalised society salons. But there was reason, as well as passion, in her choice. Quickly realising that her own business instincts were more acute than Tom's, in marrying the heir to the Du Cane Hotel, Cornelia saw an opportunity to stamp her own mark on Manhattan. She would emerge from the long shadow cast by her family name, to become a woman of stature in her own right.

Growing up between Manhattan and the weekend home in Old Saybrook, Connecticut, Jack had never doubted that even though his father had the title of Managing Director, it was his mother who was the ultimate strategist. And never was her influence more apparent than after Patrick died, leaving the hotel to Tom. Within weeks, architects had been called in with briefs to upgrade. Within months, the entire building was undergoing a transformation, from the famous 'Windsor's' restaurant – so-called because it had been a favourite of the Duke and Mrs Simpson's – to the ballroom, the Palm Court, and each of the individual bedrooms and suites.

The grand opening of the reinvented Du Cane Plaza had been as much a triumph of social engineering as it was of lavish expenditure. Jack, thirteen at the time, vividly remembered the steadily mounting excitement as his mother orchestrated the grandest party in New York that season. It was attended by visiting European royalty, Hollywood stars and business tycoons, and invitations were in short supply – their rarity only serving to underline the point that the new Du Cane Plaza provided an exclusive entrée into a rarified world of glamour and privilege.

From that night on, the Du Cane Plaza became the backdrop for Cornelia's tireless party-giving, as she grew into her role as society doyenne. Its guest list reading like an international *Who's Who*, and its ballroom booked up to five years in advance, there was no question it had been established as one of the most sought-after playgrounds of the shiny set.

Jack was also aware that beneath the daily tide of invitations, gossip columns and social intrigue, there was a growing tension between his parents that was rarely, but explosively, expressed. For while Cornelia had inherited her parents' opulent tastes, she hadn't – yet – inherited the money to pay for them. Her no-expense-spared revamp of the Du Cane Plaza had been paid for only by remortgaging the hotel. Jack's father was uneasy about this, but Cornelia was dismissive; whatever they had to borrow now would be more than compensated by her family inheritance. Why constrain their lives and their spending when they knew they were about to come into a fortune?

Born into wealth, Cornelia had a rich person's way of thinking. She was as untroubled by large figures appearing in the debit column of her cheque account as she was unsurprised by significant deposits into the credit ledger. And there was an undeniable logic to what she said – the van Haven fortune ran to hundreds of millions.

But Tom had known the reality of living in a cramped basement flat. And as its Managing Director, he knew how much financial pressure the hotel could take. Seeing the weekly takings, it was easy to imagine that Du Cane Plaza was hugely lucrative. But, as Jack became increasingly aware as a teenager helping his father, the outgoings were equally astronomical. It wasn't only the loan for the makeover, requiring large monthly interest payments, or the ongoing running costs of a de luxe hotel. Cornelia's spending continued unchecked as she planned ever-more lavish hospitality, designed to move the Hennessys and their hotel to the very epicentre of American high society.

Most of the time, Tom suppressed his financial worries behind his genial nature. Perhaps he reassured himself with Cornelia's confidence. Perhaps he saw the continued inroads into their remaining capital as the price he had to pay for his trophy wife. But he worried and ached and became ill over money. When Jack returned home late from parties as a young man, he'd often find his father bent over a bureau with his calculator and the hotel accounts. Once at university, working in the office during vacations, he saw for himself just how badly their position had deteriorated. The Hennessys no longer had any real wealth – they only had the illusion of it. Living as they did off borrowed money, it wouldn't take much for the entire palace of cards to come tumbling down in a heap.

The final straw had been his parents' twenty-fifth wedding anniversary. Cornelia planned to turn the entire hotel into their private home for a weekend, climaxing with a costume ball on the Saturday night. Tom had protested that they couldn't afford it. Cornelia wouldn't countenance refusal for this, of all celebrations. Jack was convinced the worry of it had killed his father. Just weeks after hosting the big night, Tom Hennessy died of a heart attack.

Jack had returned home from his business studies and helped to arrange the funeral. He and Cornelia had always been close – she saw in her elder son so many of her own aspirations, and he held her in awe for her social achievement. But after the funeral came the double blow; Cornelia's by-now very elderly father confessed that most of the van Haven family fortune had gone. Taken in by a firm of futures traders several years before, he'd been persuaded down a course of speculation over which he'd lost control. The van Haven inheritance would be only a fraction of what was expected. His only comfort, Jack's grandfather said, was that Tom had so obviously left Cornelia well off.

Neither Jack nor his mother could bring themselves to confess to the reality. Jack now faced a more formidable dilemma than any case study he'd encountered in business studies. With their assets heavily outweighed by their liabilities, even selling off the hotel would leave the family in debt.

It was then that Jack had first shown the acuity of his business mind – and his capacity for surprise. After several

95

weeks of intensive preparation, he flew first to New Orleans, where the van Haven family were still held in high regard, and then to Boston, where the Hennessys held some sway. Presenting bank managers with developed proposals, he had soon negotiated significant loans for the establishment of Du Cane Plaza hotels in both cities. When he returned to New York, he gave Cornelia a full account of the family finances and explained his recovery plan. For the next five years she would have to rein in her spending. She would also have to go to work, creating in both New Orleans and Boston, hotels of similar character and stature to the New York flagship. Although they didn't have any assets at all, what they did have was a brand. Thanks to Cornelia's relentless socialising, the Du Cane Plaza had acquired the status of a national icon, with Cornelia herself regarded as the arbiter of glamour and good taste. If this same magic could be bestowed on other hotels, the Du Cane brand could be transformed into a credit balance.

Which was precisely what they did. Over the next two years, suitable properties were acquired and, under Cornelia's direction, were given the Du Cane Plaza treatment. They were launched with the same fanfare as the New York hotel, while the indebtedness of the newly formed Hennessy Family Trust had never been greater, nor had its turnover. Excesses of the past were studiously avoided, and through careful management, the hotel income streams were turned to profit. Continuing aggressively on the acquisition trail, Jack expanded the Du Cane Plaza group to Los Angeles, Dallas, Miami and Chicago.

Within five years, Hennessy Family Trust assets outweighed its liabilities. Within ten, the tide was turning in its favour. On paper the Hennessy family were still worse off than at the time Tom and Cornelia had married – but the potential for growth was dramatically improved. Every successive year saw the value of the hotel group strengthen, its profitability boosted when Jack extended the Du Cane brand even more by launching a range of skincare products, used in its beauty salons, onto the open market.

By the time he'd reached forty, Jack had turned a disastrous inheritance into one of the most prestigious business empires in America. With his mother firmly centre stage, he worked behind the scenes, which was the way he preferred it. For he hadn't reached his position without making plenty of enemies. Accusations of sharp accounting practices, of deceiving investors about company accounts became impossible to shrug off. Creditors from west coast to east were infuriated at having to wait months for accounts to be settled while Jack siphoned off hotel revenues to present inflated cashflows. Increasingly in business circles, as well as the media, Jack became associated with deception bordering on the fraudulent, the flipside of his towering ambition. And there were also rancorous attacks concerning his mother whom critics said he had manipulated, abusing her social influence to swing deals that would never otherwise have been countenanced.

Jack once again showed his capacity to surprise when, shortly after his fortieth birthday, the Hennessy Family Trust announced the private sale of the Du Cane Plaza Group to Inter-Global Hotels. The undisclosed sale price was a source of fervid speculation. Industry analysts suggested a likely figure of between two and three billion dollars. A former Du Cane executive was quoted in the papers as saying that figure was altogether conservative.

Jack Hennessy and his mother remained mute. At the family apartment on the Upper East Side, Cornelia enjoyed her *grande dame* status while, to the surprise of many, Jack settled in Washington, DC, where he managed personal investments and became involved in what he described as philanthropic causes. Jack and his mother continued to be close. She'd phone him several times a week for long conversations and insisted he visit her regularly. Meanwhile the Hennessy connection with Du Cane Plaza Hotels wouldn't be severed entirely. As part of the sale agreement, the family retained, in perpetuity, a penthouse suite in the flagship Park Avenue hotel, with access to similar-status apartments in other hotels available for only a nominal rate.

Jack had encountered Lorna shortly after she came to the attention of the national media. Their first meeting had been entirely contrived – Jack gatecrashing one of the roadshow seminars she had given on NP3. He'd invited her out to lunch within a week and had been gratified to find her interest in him went further than the purely professional. They'd gone to bed within a fortnight and since then the course of their torrid, physical passion had been matched only by her developing trust in him. Lorna had told him everything about herself, from her childhood in Mannofield, Aberdeen, to her short but disastrous string of boyfriends, and her work on NP3. Jack had taken it all in, comforting her when frustrated, reassuring her during the increasingly tough times at Zonmark. The flourishing romance couldn't have suited his purposes better.

When the gateway intercom sounded, Jack got up and made his way to the hallway console, glancing at her car on the CCTV screen before pressing a code to let her in. He had sent his housekeeper off for the night and only the cook remained to prepare their meal. He intended this evening to be an intimate one.

He was standing at the front door as she pulled up the gravel driveway, which curved round a floodlit fountain spuming four magnificent arcs into the night sky. He noted with satisfaction how much care she'd taken preparing for the evening. In a scarlet, off-the-shoulder chiffon dress, hair perfectly coiffed and a bejewelled choker glinting in the night, she was radiant.

He stepped forward to greet her under the portico and they embraced for a long while.

'I've really needed you,' she murmured.

He smiled, hugging her even more closely to him. Then he was showing her through the house to the sitting room where a bottle of Dom Ruinart had been left out in an ice-bucket for his customary aperitif.

'Another tough day?' he asked sympathetically, taking the bottle from the ice-bucket and removing the wire netting with ease of practice.

Lorna needed no further prompting. Although she'd already mentioned it briefly on the phone, now she told him all about her visit to St Augusta Hospital and the peculiar sensations she'd experienced there, together with all the trauma that had followed.

Jack twisted the cork from the bottle with a muted pop, before pouring out their drinks and handing her a glass. 'At least the week's over,' he murmured reassuringly. 'Here's to things getting better.'

Their glasses clinked and Lorna took a sip before confiding, 'I reckon they *can* only get better.'

'Well, after all that stuff—'

'That was yesterday,' she pulled a droll expression, 'I've had another dose of it today.'

'What exactly—?' he began before she cut him off.

'You don't want to know about it,' she sighed.

Wordlessly, he led her to the sitting room where they sat together on a deep-tufted damask sofa. There, he fixed her with an expression of deep concern before murmuring, 'I don't want you to shut me out of your life, Lorna. Whatever is troubling you, it troubles me too.' He squeezed her hand and met her eyes reassuringly. 'Now. I want you to tell me *everything.*'

Lorna did want to share her worries and was grateful for his interest. As soon as she'd started, it all came tumbling out. How she'd arrived at work to be greeted with the quarterly results – and the discovery of Matthew's serious deterioration. How Krauss, and all he knew, had proved impossible to get hold of. She wasn't supposed to talk shop outside Zonmark; a gagging clause in her contract specifically forbade her from confession outside the company. But she knew she could trust Jack. He hadn't accomplished all his success without being able to keep confidences. And during the eight weeks they'd been seeing each other, she had increasingly come to respect his judgement – and to rely on all the support he gave her. So she told him about her further alarm that day on receiving the e-mail from Andrew suggesting that Matt's death was suspicious. Her embarrassment at the fool she'd made of herself in front of Kuesterman before Greg had confirmed he'd made a mistake. Working under pressure as great as the rest of them, he'd sent her the penultimate version of Matt's results, prior to negative indices being replaced by positives.

Jack regarded her with a concerned expression. 'You

mustn't think you're the first executive in the universe to have reached premature conclusions—'

'I know. I know.' She took another sip of champagne. 'But in front of Kuesterman!'

'And you did score a hit with the media leak.'

'Only thanks to you.' She met his eyes. 'I doubt I'd have worked that one out on my own.'

After a pause he murmured, 'At least you got any conspiracy theory out of the way – about Matt, I mean.'

'I don't know what I'm going to tell Andrew.' She shrugged. 'You know, he isn't the kind to get carried away. He's a fund manager. He's paid for his judgement.'

'Though professional judgement is one thing. Coming to terms with something in one's personal life . . . that's a lot different.'

'I guess.' She took another sip of champagne. She didn't need to think any further than her own life to see that. Her choice of boyfriends had been less than impressive.

'If Matt died when Andrew was supposed to be looking after him, he'd be experiencing terrible guilt,' Jack told her.

'Looking for someone to blame?'

'Probably.'

She pondered this for a while before saying, 'All the same, it just sounds sinister, doesn't it? Matt slipping into the river when he's so fearful of water.'

'I don't think so.' Jack was shaking his head. 'Accidents happen all the time.'

6

There was only one word to describe Julius Lupine; a word that might have been created especially with him in mind. 'Sensualist' came close to it – though its emphasis on carnal indulgence and fleshly pleasures was altogether too limiting. 'Hedonist' was also near the mark, but failed to capture the glorious extravagance – the finely honed discernment, the magnificent excess – of his pursuits. No, there really was only one word which, in every lip-smacking, wine-soaked syllable described the very essence of his venal heart: Julius Lupine was a voluptuary.

He'd discovered his true instincts at Yale. A scholarship boy from Midwest suburbia, all he'd arrived with, apart from his Mensa-grade brain, was a talent for the oboe. Already an accomplished performer, his vast repertoire included baroque composers like Telemann, Handel, Bach, and his all-time favourite, the Italian Vivaldi. But within weeks of communing with his Ivy League peers, he'd been awakened to an entirely different dimension of pleasure. And besides the obvious rites of passage – the earthy satiation of libido, the euphoric alcoholic highs – he'd quickly learned of other gratifications. In particular, the giddying pleasures acquired through wealth and privilege which had remained the object of his considerable cunning ever since.

As his career advanced, he'd surrounded himself with all the experiences and *objets* that filled life with pleasure, such as his home in the Upper West Side brownstone in which he was currently standing; the emerald-green velvet smoking jacket, tailored for him in Savile Row, in which he admired his mirrored reflection; the Davidoff cigar resting in the malachite ashtray, filling the room with its darkly expensive aroma.

As he paced the sitting room, a glass of Luigi Einaudi Barolo in one hand, and cordless phone in the other, he chose his opening words with special care.

'I thought I'd update you on progress since the last time we met.' He always exercised the utmost discretion when placing calls to either McIntyre or Pollos. He reckoned that if he operated on the assumption that someone, somewhere was listening in and recording the conversations, he couldn't go far wrong.

'So there's been progress?' McIntyre, working late in his Fort Lauderdale offices, was his usual downbeat self.

'Oh, yes.' For a moment Lupine paused to regard himself in the Louis Quinze mirror, reaching up to touch the silk cravat tucked about his neck. 'I've secured the services of an informant. We now have a direct conduit who will update us on developments on an ongoing basis.'

McIntyre digested this in silence for a moment before responding, 'That's all very well, Julius, but I don't see how it helps.'

103

Lupine's face clouded. McIntyre was always so damned ungrateful.

'The phrase you used was "Shut the programme down",' the other reminded him.

'Right,' Lupine replied mildly, 'but information has to come first. Intelligence.'

'Hmm.' McIntyre sounded unconvinced. 'And what is the reliability of this source?'

'Impeccable.'

'And the cost?'

'Nothing that the shareholders of Mayflower can't bear.'

'I see.' He was mollified.

Lupine had considered carefully how much to say. But McIntyre's reaction made him believe he could reveal slightly more of his hand than he'd envisaged. 'The role being performed is more than that of informant alone. Our man has considerable leverage – especially on her thinking. State of mind.'

'This . . . person,' McIntyre wanted to know, 'he's someone inside the programme?'

'Let's just say he's close to her. Very close.' On a need-to-know basis, McIntyre didn't. And the denial of information instantly aroused his curiosity.

'I'll be very interested to hear what comes back.'

'As will I, Campbell.' Lupine's air of innocence was not, on this occasion, entirely convincing.

'You've told George?'

'Not yet. I wanted to discuss it with you first.' Whether speaking to McIntyre or Pollos, he always conveyed the impression that he gave his listener special preference.

'When do you expect to know more?'

'Don't know. But you will as soon as I do.'

104

'Right.' McIntyre muttered something to himself at the other end, before realising he could have been more effusive about Lupine's efforts.

'Good progress,' he managed, eventually.

'Thank you, Campbell.' It was as great a compliment as he was ever going to get from McIntyre. Ending the call, he replaced the receiver on its handset and picked up his cigar, drawing on it contemplatively.

He had to exercise extreme care in how much he revealed – but he must carry the other two marketing men with him. At present McIntyre and Pollos regarded him as the ringleader of a cartel in which they voluntarily participated. That was the illusion he wished to maintain. There was nothing to be gained from revealing that the two men were only being used to rubber-stamp decisions that had already been taken.

For Julius Lupine was considerably further down the line than he had let on to McIntyre. He had recruited not just an informant, but a committed and active operative. He had given orders to expedite the end of the NP3 programme through all available means. Shutting down NP3 was, indeed, an objective close to his heart. And for reasons that went beyond his role as head of marketing at Mayflower. Only a few months before, he had come to an arrangement with Mayflower's majority shareholder – one which ensured that his protection of shareholder interests took on a very great significance. The understanding involved large, monthly credits to a deposit account in the Cayman Islands; a flow of income designed to ensure he could sate his every sense, express his every instinct, drown himself in all the pleasures that made his life worthwhile.

'Julius!' his wife called him through to supper, intruding into his reflections.

Age and three children hadn't treated Martha Lupine kindly. Plump and soft, her grey hair scooped back in a bun, she had no interest in keeping physically in trim, let alone in the skiing, or luxury travel or the other sensual pursuits that so engaged him. As she clucked over her grandchildren and recipe books, there were frequently times when Lupine would look at her as though at a complete stranger, marvelling at how they'd ever got married. The truth was that his motive for proposing had had much less to do with romance than with Martha's family trust fund, an eight-figure whopper that regularly disgorged interest payments on which his lifestyle was all too dependent. Not for much longer, he vowed. And in the meantime, he was all the more appreciative that his arrangement with Mayflower's shareholder wasn't purely pecuniary. Other important benefits were on offer too.

Walking through to the dining room, he remembered, the trace of a smile about his lips, his visit to that particular boudoir just hours earlier. It had been over lunch, as it usually was. Private, discreet and all thoroughly civilised. Immaculately prepared salmon and scallop carpaccio with lashings of sheep's yoghurt dressing, accompanied by a particularly lively Chablis, and followed by an even livelier romp. Her body had been slim, firm, vigorous. As important was her appreciation. It was as though she could barely wait to tear him out of his clothes and get him onto her satin sheets, beneath her as she straddled his body. Their couplings were never anything but highly satisfactory. Her climaxes were always noisy and unrestrained. Either she really did relish the afternoon delight, thought Lupine, or she was a superb faker. Whichever was the case didn't trouble him.

'I do wish you wouldn't bring those in here before supper,' Martha chided as he arrived in the dining room, Davidoff still in hand. 'Such a fug!'

Stepping into the kitchen, vexed to be wrenched from his reverie, he stubbed out his thirty-dollar cigar in the sink.

Once he was sitting across the table from her, she served him a portion of Boeuf Bourguignon, explaining that she was trying it out with a view to serving it at their next family dinner. Lupine had little time for his grandchildren and even less for his three children. The mere thought of all those leeches suckered up round his table darkened his mood.

Glancing over at him, Martha correctly divined the cause of his displeasure. She looked up at him with that motherly expression he found so irksome. 'So, my dear,' she asked him brightly, 'tell me about your day.'

Washington, DC

Making amends had never been something that came easily to Lorna, but she had no choice. That morning she waited in the Chief Executive Officer's ante-room, presided over by the perfumed Beryl, until Kuesterman arrived at the office. The moment his eyes met hers, she felt he sensed her shame.

'Come on through.' He waved her into his office as though expecting her.

'I'm here about last Friday,' she told him, the moment the door was closed behind them. Her expression had said it before she did. 'I really am very sorry.'

She told him how her telephone conversation with Greg had quickly resolved her – confusion – how the table Greg had mistakenly attached to her e-mail had been an earlier draft, the data in Matt's row expressed in relation to the control sample – the step before the final figures.

She'd had plenty of time to reflect on her mistake over the weekend and she told herself she should be relieved. If she could swallow her pride and live through this particular humiliation, at least the only problems she faced at work were of the scientific variety. Kuesterman's cynical media 'leak' had been driven by commercial realities, but at least she wasn't being sabotaged from within. From now on, she told herself, she would keep her overactive imagination in check. Whatever problems arose at work, she wasn't going to let them fuel her paranoia. First and foremost she was a scientist. She would stick with reason and fact. No more trying to read significance into unrelated events. No more connecting the unconnected to create some menacing conspiracy.

Kuesterman listened to her apologies as he unloaded a handful of documents from his briefcase onto his desk. As she delivered the most abject apology of her career, she tried to judge his mood. She knew that her behaviour last Friday had been both gauche and professionally reprehensible. Her boss was perfectly entitled to tear strips off her. But when he looked back up at her there wasn't so much as a flicker of acrimony in his expression. Instead, he was quite matter-of-fact, 'Like I said on Friday, you've been under a lot of stress. It's getting to you.'

'No it's not!' was the reflex reaction, which she held in check. This was no time for protest. Besides, what if he was right?

'Why don't you take a holiday? A few days in the Florida Keys would be great this time of year.'

'I'll think about it.' Lorna nodded, trying to conceal her lack of enthusiasm. With NP3 in the state it was, a holiday was the very last thing on her mind.

Kuesterman delivered a brief discourse on the importance of keeping a fresh, enquiring mind, when engaged at the cutting edge of genetic research. Then he repeated his commitment to the success of NP3 and to her as its architect. Instead of a dressing down, Lorna found herself on the receiving end of a pep talk. As he spoke she found herself thinking that, quite apart from financial machinations, Kuesterman was also an astute psychologist. Despite his tousled appearance, he knew exactly how to play people.

There was also the question of what to do about Beryl. When Lorna had left Kuesterman's office last Friday, she'd known exactly how things might look to his secretary. And although she hadn't cared about it then, things had soon looked very different. But when she offered to speak to Beryl, Kuesterman shook his head. 'That won't be necessary,' he allowed himself a sardonic smile, 'she has two teenage kids. She's used to far worse.'

Back in her office, Lorna opened her electronic 'In' tray and scanned its contents. Andrew Norton's e-mail from the week before was still listed as unanswered. She hadn't known how to respond when she'd first read it, and had decided to mull it over for a while before replying. As she opened it again she read through Andrew's announcement that Matt's death might not have been accidental . . . the fear of water . . . the elderly neighbour . . . the need for a motive. Only this time, as she read through it, she remembered Kuesterman's words about how stress impaired judgement. And what Jack had said about the power of guilt. Andrew was even more vulnerable to conspiracy theories than she had been. He must be desperate for some form of vindication.

Now she regarded his request for a motive with a sense of pity. And having just suffered the effects of her own paranoia, she felt she should dissuade him from making any hasty assumptions.

Clicking on 'Reply', she drafted a carefully worded e-mail repeating her sympathies, but also urging caution. There was no motive that she could offer for the murder of a progeria panellist. For while there was a whole movement ideologically opposed to genetic technology, it was quite a different matter from setting out to murder a child.

Lorna debated whether or not to mention Matt's last set of results. In any other circumstances she wouldn't even have considered it, but given Andrew's current train of thought, perhaps it was better that she tell him. Eventually, though, she decided against it. Passing on the news was an avoidable cruelty. And besides, there was no evidence that Matt's death had been suspicious, except for the remarks of a senile old woman.

At ten o'clock that morning, the NP3 team held their regular fortnightly update, in the room next to Greg's office at the other end of the ground floor. As Lorna made her way through to the meeting room, fixing a coffee on the way, she felt a reassuring sense of normality after the turmoil of the past forty-eight hours. Things at NP3 might not be going so great, she realised, but now at least she could dismiss any idea that there were sinister forces working against them.

The NP3 meeting room was a functional venue,

dominated by a polished, imitation oak table surrounded by eight black office chairs, and equipped with whiteboards and a range of bright pens. Fortnightly meetings were informal but tightly run, with Gail taking notes that were circulated to everyone by the end of the day, and which formed the agenda for the next meeting.

The main preoccupation today, as it had been for the past two months, was panel recruitment. With only twenty-nine on the panel, getting numbers up was more critical than at any other time. After Greg and Chen had said their pieces, Lorna turned to where Steve Manzini always sat several seats away from her.

'So, where are we, Steve?' she asked.

His deep-set eyes blinking behind their glasses with unnerving intensity, Manzini handed out stapled sheets of paper summarising recruitment progress. 'We've thirty new members under review.'

'*Thirty?*' Lorna was pleasantly surprised. Scanning down the list of territories she noted that, in addition to the handful of potential cases in the USA, UK and Europe, there were larger numbers listed for South East Asia, and twelve in the Middle East.

'Several medical associations we've been talking to for a long time have eventually come on board,' he reported. NP3's first approach was always to the medical association of each country. Only once it had indicated approval could individual doctors be canvassed directly, through professional journals, direct mailing, or conference meetings addressed by one of the NP3 team.

'Turns out there are medical practices in Riyadh, Amman and Kuwait who have seen a higher number of progeria cases than we might expect.'

111

'Twelve current cases?' confirmed Lorna.

'Having said that,' Manzini quickly cautioned, 'we'll almost certainly run up against specific cultural problems.'

'Such as?'

'In conservative Arab cultures, women are forbidden from travelling alone with children. Just getting them over here would be a major undertaking.'

'I'm sure we can find them escorts,' offered Lorna.

'Have to be family members,' Manzini shot back. 'And even if we could find them, their fathers might not be supportive of treatment.'

'What about getting them on the control panel?' prompted Greg.

'No problem there.'

Expressions around the table were sober. The control panel of children who for various reasons couldn't take part in NP3 already stood at over sixty. It was a cause of despair to Lorna that in many of these cases she knew she could help – but because of cultural suspicions or parental refusal, she wasn't able to.

The recruitment list showed a scattering of children in South East Asia. Manzini took them through each territory, one by one. In some cases, NP3 had only just identified the existence of a progeria patient. In others, doctors and parents had been contacted and had expressed willingness to be involved. But after this step came testing. The NP3 team had to ensure they could intervene in progeria cases before they were too far advanced. Once children had reached the equivalent age of seventy, degeneration was too far gone for NP3 to be effective. Some children reached this stage by the time they were only seven. Others reached the age of nine or ten before they were too old to be treated.

Even if they were identified soon enough, there were other disqualifiers. Some of the drugs doctors prescribed for heart disease had proved to be incompatible with NP3. And there were all manner of hormone therapies, usually prescribed out of pure desperation, which, once combined with NP3, would trigger an adverse reaction. In such cases, a child would need to go through a clear 'window' period of three to six months before beginning on NP3.

Going through the recruitment schedule, it fast became apparent that despite having thirty potential new panel members, there were cultural problems associated with some, others had yet to be contacted, while still others had tested negative.

'What you're saying,' Lorna clarified at the end, 'is that, as of now, we have no confirmed new recruits?'

'That's the way things stand as of this minute,' Manzini glanced at the table, 'though I gave Greg letters to three candidates inviting them onto the panel.'

The attempt to shift responsibility didn't escape her. But Greg and she had agreed that, until Steve proved himself, all final confirmations should be made by Greg.

Her deputy nodded briskly. 'Those letters went out ten days ago.'

'No feedback?'

'Not as yet.'

She didn't disguise her frustration. 'Seems to me looking at this list there are a lot of cultural disqualifiers.'

'It is disappointing,' Manzini agreed, 'but pretty much in line with expectations.'

They had frequently discussed the problems of recruiting panel members in the developing world. There would be less readiness to take part in drugs trials than in Western countries where the concept of testing was better accepted.

'What about the programme going forward?' Lorna wanted to know.

Manzini outlined his contact plans – continuing liaison with the American Medical Association, British Medical Association and their peer groups in Europe, together with contacts with new territories that hadn't yet been tried. As he read through the list of new prospects, Lorna couldn't avoid the feeling that they were scraping the barrel. They had deliberately left small countries with low population groups till last. Reading her expression, once Manzini had finished, Greg suggested, 'What about revisiting US and UK lists to see if any of the patients have come out of their window period?'

'Good idea,' chimed Lorna, glancing over at Manzini.

He nodded. 'Will do.'

Just two more panel members would help her get to sleep at night, thought Lorna. Two would get her out of the psychologically daunting twenties. Twelve new cases would be a huge load off her mind – NP3 would be fully back on track. They were targeted to reach the full panel of fifty members by the end of the year. Right now that was looking well-nigh impossible.

Returning to her office after the meeting, she closed the door, picked up the phone and dialled a four-digit number.

She watched through the internal window across the lab as Greg picked up the phone in his office. 'So what did you think?' She didn't need to explain herself.

'Thirty love,' he mused, 'the odds do seem a bit long. But like he said, there is the cultural factor.'

'D'you think he's going as fast as he can?'

'Believe me, he's working his butt off,' Greg defended his assistant. 'He knows his performance is being judged on this, and so far it's been less than impressive.' Then after a pause, 'Let's hope we get some success reviewing the AMA lists.'

'Yes. I just would have preferred the idea had come from him.'

'And there is the new recruit joining us. That should speed things up.'

'I suppose.'

Then, responding to her unease, 'He's still on probation. I mean, we can review his position any time you like.'

Lorna looked through the glass window towards where Greg was leaning back in his desk chair. Eventually she said, 'Let's give it another fortnight. See what comes of the current list of candidates. Meantime, you'll keep hands-on?'

'You betcha.'

After putting down the phone, she looked outside her office to where Manzini was heading down the corridor to his office. She remembered how excited both Greg and she had been after his interview. He'd seemed to have all the answers off pat, and his references had all, without exception, been glowing. And he'd seemed genuinely enthused about the prospect of working on NP3. But so far, none of this wonderful potential had been realised. What had happened to all the methodological brilliance that had so impressed them? It was almost as if he had deliberately slowed their recruitment programme right down.

But Lorna stopped her thoughts right there. She wasn't going to project her imaginings. She would deal in facts alone. She didn't need to go through all that again.

Just before lunch, Gail put a telephone call through to her office. 'Hope you're sitting down for this one,' her tone was caustic. 'I have Ray Barnett on the line. Turns out he knows how to use a phone after all.'

Moments later, Lorna and Barnett exchanged greetings, before the hospital chief enquired, 'You made it back to Washington, DC okay?' If it was anything more than a polite enquiry, thought Lorna, it didn't sound like it.

'No problem,' she replied. She was in no mood for a blow-by-blow recitation of her post-St Augusta experiences.

'I'm calling about Doc Krauss.'

'I've been trying to contact him.'

'I thought you might be. I have some sad and quite . . . shocking news. He and his wife died in a fire.'

'*What?*' She was stunned.

'I know,' he empathised. 'One of his former colleagues down here, Ian Parry, told me this morning. They used to speak every week and Ian and his wife visited. Apparently a neighbour phoned to tell Ian that Krauss's cottage was razed to the ground, with Doc and Mrs Krauss in it.'

Lorna absorbed the news in silence, before she managed, 'Couldn't they have—?'

'Escaped? That's what everyone's asking. But it happened in the middle of the night. They used to burn a log fire in the grate. It's possible they were killed by carbon monoxide poisoning.'

'Really?'

'Ian was telling me they had the most elaborate security bars and grilles. They might have found themselves locked in.'

'My God!'

Barnett continued for a few minutes, telling her about the isolation of Krauss's cottage, and its complete destruction; the horror of his older colleagues who had worked with Krauss. Lorna took it all in, and when he'd finished, could think of only one question to ask: 'When did it happen?'

'Well, let's see . . .' At the other end, Barnett was evidently consulting his diary. 'Ian got the call on the Saturday, and it happened two nights before, so that makes it . . . do you know? It happened on the evening of the very same day you visited us at St Augusta.'

7

Andrew woke at his usual 5.59 am – just in time to switch off the alarm clock. Even before he stirred, during those first moments of wakefulness, he remembered. Turning his head, he looked across at the empty pillow and bed beside him. Jess was still sleeping in the spare bedroom, and had been since their row last week. For the first time in eighteen years of marriage they were sleeping in separate rooms. It left him hollow to the pit of his stomach.

He climbed out of bed and went through his usual morning routine like an automaton. After showering he returned to their bedroom and opened his wardrobe door. Usually, he would be into his suit and tie within ten minutes, clicking in his cufflinks with ease of habit, adjusting the Windsor knot at his neck.

But this morning was different. He slipped on a tracksuit and trainers, making his way down the corridor, where the spare bedroom door was still closed. Picking up his mobile phone and a few dozen of the flyers he'd printed out the day before, he was soon heading out of the kitchen and down towards the river.

Last Thursday, Langley Taylor had told him about two men he'd seen, making their way quickly along the riverside path away from the Nortons'. It was quite probable he wouldn't have noticed them at all had it not been for the fact that they were both wiping their hands on their trousers. Taylor remembered thinking it slightly odd. Neither looked the rowing or fishing type. He couldn't recall much of what they were wearing. He was pretty sure they had been in dark anoraks, but whether they were in trousers or jeans he couldn't say.

Another call from a Millie Watkins, the day before, also reported a sighting of two men, still further down the path from the Taylors'. A mother of three, Millie had been checking the washing on her clothes-line when she'd caught sight of the pair. She'd thought it unusual, she told Andrew, to see two men in their mid-thirties out on a workday afternoon. They'd been moving quickly, but weren't jogging or looking out for someone on the river. Like Taylor, she couldn't give Andrew any detail, having only given the men a moment's attention.

It was no longer Mrs Hayes alone who had seen the two men – although hers was the only testimony to link them with Matt. Neither Langley Taylor nor Millie Watkins had been at home when the police had visited to make enquiries and both, it appeared, were sufficiently distant from the scene of the crime to be considered too far removed to merit a return visit. So much, considered Andrew, for police resourcing. But the fact was that he now had three independent witnesses. Admittedly, none of them gave much detail. But together they told a story.

Where would the two men have been heading? The Weyside Shopping Centre was a mile and a half further down the river. He supposed they might have left a car there. Much closer, a footbridge crossed over the river to Weybridge Rowing Club, which was frequented in the early mornings and evenings, but was quiet throughout the day. The club car park, secluded and bordered by a hedge, would make an ideal location to leave a getaway vehicle.

Now he made his way along the riverside path. It was a bright, sunlit morning – the clear blue sky and scattering of crocuses along the riverside were cheerfully incongruous with the way he was feeling. By 7.45 he was at Weybridge Rowing Club. Half a dozen cars were parked outside, but the clubhouse itself was locked. Built on two floors, its upper floor comprised the main entertainment area – an extended bar and lounge which stretched along the riverside of the building. He and Jess had been invited by a friend, years before, to watch the club heats from the lounge, and now he remembered its panoramic vista, up and down the river. From the changing rooms and showers, also on the upper floor, a set of concrete stairs led down to a row of sheds in which all the boats and equipment were stored.

Glancing round the car park, Andrew realised that a team must already be out on the river. Uncertain when they'd get back, he decided to leaflet the immediate area so that he could watch out for their return. He also kept his eye on the time, and shortly after eight took his mobile out of his pocket and pressed the memory dial button for Ruth. 'I won't be coming in this morning,' he told his secretary when she answered. It felt strange saying the words – this was the first time he'd ever missed work unexpectedly.

'I'll let everyone know,' answered Ruth, imperturbable as ever.

'Something's come up . . . to do with Matt.' He felt the need to confide. Last week he had mentioned Mrs Hayes's comments to Ruth. Unlike everyone else, it seemed, she hadn't reacted as though he was on some deluded self-justification trip.

'You mean, more evidence?' she confirmed.

'Yes. I need to follow it up.'

'Good for you!'

It was the first encouragement he'd received. 'Thanks, Ruth.' They went through a few routine points before he said, 'I'd better speak to Bob Bowler.'

On a Monday morning, they held their weekly allocation meeting to discuss the North American Fund. Although they bought and sold shares for the fund on an ongoing basis, strategic decisions were generally taken at the start of each week when a variety of data – from economic reports and forecasts to federal reserve bank announcements – were discussed.

'Bob, it's me,' he announced himself after Ruth had put him through. 'I won't be coming in this morning.'

'Oh?'

'Personal issues. I want you to run the allocation meeting.'

'Right.'

'You can debrief me when I get in.'

'When will that be?'

It was Bowler's tone as much as what he said that irked Andrew. He recalled Bowler's expression when he'd left early last Thursday afternoon, and how he'd looked at Andrew as though he were going soft.

'Can't say,' he returned, crisply. 'But any movements five per cent plus, let me know.'

The rowers, two crews of six men each, returned shortly after 8.15, and around the same time several wives and girlfriends drove up to the clubhouse. Amid a general scramble of activity as the building was opened, boats were lifted out of the water, and rowers headed to the changing rooms, Andrew made his way inside.

'Mind if I put a notice up on your board?' he asked one of the men. He felt something of a fraud in his pristine tracksuit and trainers among men who were doing what he'd always intended to do, but never had.

'Go ahead.' The other waved through to the lounge area, where two large notice-boards were mounted on a wall.

He pinned up the notice under the curious eye of one of the wives who was rocking a baby as she watched him.

'You'll want to speak to Terry about that,' she told him as he stepped back.

He raised his eyebrows in enquiry.

'Security,' she explained.

'I didn't know you had a security person.'

'Have to.' She motioned in the direction of the car park. 'Theft's been terrible. The lads are out forty-five minutes at a time – it's like an open invitation to break into their cars.'

Andrew recalled seeing kitbags in several of the cars parked outside. Despite the thefts, he reflected, the rowers didn't seem to have learned. Aloud he said, 'So how do I get hold of Terry?'

'That's him, right over there.' The woman gestured. 'Navy tracksuit.'

Terry Saddler recognised Matt from the photo. Like most locals he knew all about the accident, and fixed Andrew with a sympathetic expression. Taking him aside, Andrew explained that Matt's death might not have been accidental; that on the afternoon concerned, two men had been seen, first with Matt, then hurrying in the direction of the clubhouse. It was possible they had used the clubhouse car park. 'If I could get one of these leaflets out to all the members,' he told Terry, 'it's just possible one of them might have seen something.'

Saddler regarded him with a significant expression before telling him, 'I have a much better idea.' Motioning Andrew to follow, he led him past the changing rooms and showers through to a storeroom which was crammed with crates of beer, cases of wine, toilet rolls and a variety of other stock. Leading the way over to a small window, he pointed to a camera immediately behind the glass.

'Twenty-four-hour surveillance of the car park,' he announced.

'I didn't notice a CCTV sign.'

'That's because we want to catch the little bastards, don't we? Give them a nasty shock. Look, we've got a pretty shrewd idea who it is. Local gang, still just schoolkids. It's the inconvenience as much as anything – having to repair windows, worry about insurance excess. One of our lads works for a security firm. He set up the camera about three weeks ago—'

'And that's why you left kitbags in the cars.'

'Bait.' The other nodded, before turning to face several shelves of videotapes, neatly labelled in a row. 'What date are you looking for?'

They returned to the club lounge minutes later, Saddler

123

having identified the correct tape. 'If they used the car park, they'll be on here.' He spoke with conviction, slotting the tape into a video player and using a remote control to fast forward. The time of day was displayed in blue digits on the top right-hand corner of the screen. Andrew watched the digits race towards 15.00, incredulous to be finding himself in this position. If anything showed up on the video, he thought – before stopping himself. He mustn't do that. He was only setting himself up for disappointment. Best take every step one at a time.

At 15.00 hours on the afternoon of Wednesday, 5 April, there had been three cars outside the Weybridge Rowing Club. Saddler quickly identified the large Rover, parked with its side to the camera, in the middle of the screen, as belonging to the club treasurer. Obscured behind it was a blue Volvo. In the far corner was parked a shiny red Citroën.

There was no movement at all to begin with; Saddler pressed the fast forward for as long as the scene remained static. Then at 16.08.20, two dark-clad figures appeared from the left-hand side of the screen. Reacting to their appearance, Andrew stepped closer to the screen, staring at it intently. The men were making their way swiftly towards the Volvo, then climbing in, one on each side. In moments the car was pulling away.

Without his having to ask, Terry Saddler pressed the Pause button, catching the Volvo as it drove out of the car park. They were both looking at the car's registration plate – but the number was concealed by a blur of mud.

'Christ!' Terry Saddler was shaking his head.

'It's more than I expected when I came here,' Andrew told him, 'a lot more.' Then, following a pause, 'Could I borrow the tape?'

124

The other walked over to the video player. 'Take it.' He handed it to Andrew.

'I don't mind paying—'

'Just take it,' he insisted. 'I'll go through tapes from earlier that day. See what I can find from when they parked the car.' Then, squeezing Andrew's shoulder, 'Good luck.'

Andrew made his way home briskly. Just after nine, he could hear the buzz of traffic on the nearby main road. It felt surreal to be walking by the river on a normal working day. At the office they'd already be in the weekly allocation meeting, which had always held top priority in the past. But now, as he paced home, video in hand, he knew what was more important.

When his mobile rang, he assumed it would be someone from the office. But Jim Jones announced himself. He was a local reporter, he said, and had got Andrew's leaflet in his postbox. He wanted to do a piece for the paper.

Andrew's first instinct was to shy away. But as he thought about it, he realised that a piece in the local paper would be read by people he could never get to by leafleting. Fresh information could come to light. Those who read the local rag were, he assumed, the kind of people with time on their hands who might have noticed something out of the ordinary.

Jones started with the questions reporters had always been interested in when asking about Matt: when had they first noticed something was different about Matt? How had progeria affected him? And how had he been responding to NP3? Then he wanted to know more particularly about Andrew's notice. Chief Inspector Hardwick had told him to anticipate tough questions about the notice so Andrew felt prepared.

'It's an information-gathering exercise,' he told Jones. 'All we want is to be able to put things to rest.'

'What kind of information would do that?' the journalist wanted to know.

'As things stand we don't know if anyone actually saw the accident happening. It's possible someone might have seen something and assumed it was just some kid messing about.' He was careful to avoid any question of blame.

'Who was looking after Matt at the time?'

'I was,' he replied evenly. 'We were out on the landing feeding the ducks. I had to go inside to answer the phone. There was nothing unusual about that. But when I came out . . . there was just his wheelchair.'

'And you assumed there was an accident.'

'The police did. The coroner's report found water in his lungs, consistent with drowning.'

There was a pause as Jones digested this. Then he remarked conversationally, 'The police assumption may be wrong.'

'That's why we need witnesses.'

'So you agree the police may have got it wrong?'

'Well . . . I suppose so,' replied Andrew. Then, concerned he may have overstepped the line, 'But it would be premature for me to comment until we know more.'

'I see.' Jones had evidently finished his line of enquiry. 'Tell me, Andrew, are the police involved in this information-gathering exercise?'

'No, it's something we're doing ourselves—' then, correcting himself, '—myself.'

When he got home, he let himself in through the kitchen door. He could hear that Jess was in the shower. Going

126

straight through to the sitting room, he put on the video and watched the sequence he'd already seen at the rowing club. Mesmerised, he sat playing it over and over. This was the moment, he reflected, when perspicacious detectives in TV dramas spotted some tell-tale clue. Something in the appearance or behaviour of the men should provide a flash of insight that would enable identification.

But in the real world, things didn't happen like that. All he could see were two figures entering from one side of the car park, crossing to a car that was mostly obscured from the camera, and leaving. Shot from a distance, there was little, if anything, to distinguish the two dark-clad men. Both were built like bouncers, and wearing anoraks and trainers; one was taller than the other. The shorter one, barrel-shaped, had a red 'V' on the back of his jacket collar. Hardly a reason to call Scotland Yard. And the whole thing was on screen for less than seven seconds.

As he watched, he knew he could do more with this video. Having been on the receiving end of numberless multimedia presentations, he realised that technology existed that was able to enlarge minor details and freeze frames. Perhaps there was something in these particular seven seconds that would yield a lead – only not in the video's current form.

He was walking over to take the video out of the machine when he heard a noise behind him. He turned to find Jess. Dressed in black jeans and a dark green jersey, she looked wan and tired. 'I thought you'd be at work,' she said, as his eyes met hers.

'Something I had to do.' He nodded towards the video. Then, as she paused, regarding him in surprise, 'This video. It came from the rowing club along the river. They got the two men on camera. Look.' He pressed the Play button.

Surely she couldn't deny what she saw with her own two eyes? Surely she wouldn't doubt him then?

But after watching the sequence, she simply shrugged.

'That's the two men Mrs Hayes saw,' he told her. 'And I've had calls from other people who saw them.' Then, when she still didn't react, 'Don't you see, Jess? We've got them on tape!'

'There's no law against parking at the rowing club, is there?' She regarded him coolly.

'No, but there's a pattern forming!'

She was shaking her head, her eyes filled with sadness.

'It may look like nothing to you, but I'm taking this into the office. The multimedia department has stuff that will blow up the size to get more detail.'

'It's no good, Andrew.' She wasn't listening. 'You can't go on like this.'

'Like what?' He was incredulous.

'Chasing after phantom criminals.'

'So you'd rather we let them get away with murder?' he snapped back.

'Just listen to yourself. You've changed. You've become obsessed!'

'I have *not* become obsessed!' he yelled, wagging the tape at her angrily.

'It's as though you've become a completely different person.'

'What in hell is that supposed to mean?' He couldn't bear the way she just stood there, coldly lecturing him. 'I know you think I'm to blame. I know you think it was *all my fault*!'

128

'I never said that.' Her voice cracked.

'Might as well have. But the fact of the matter is that I was there that day. I *know* what happened!'

Meeting her eyes, though, he could see she was no longer listening. She seemed to be staring straight through him, and down to the landing.

Washington, DC

Judith Laing slammed down the phone, shoved her chair back from her desk, and marched across the office suite to the corner fridge. Grabbing an open bottle of Chalk Hill Chardonnay, she splashed out a glassfull and took a deep swig. Christ, she hated this job, she thought. Not just the job – the profession. Profession, huh! The day she was treated like a professional, she'd pass out from shock.

Sometimes she wondered what she'd done to deserve it. In her last job, on the business desk of *The Herald*, she'd found herself working for Alex Carter, the most noxious business editor in Britain. Carter's constant cajoling that she should increase her editorial output had prompted her investigation of global sportswear giant Starwear – a story in which Carter had himself been implicated. It appealed to her wry sense of justice that the man who had done so much to make her professional life a misery had found his own career suddenly blighted. It was some consolation that he now lived in much reduced circumstances in Brighton, flogging advertising space in a timeshare magazine.

The Starwear exposé had done Judith the world of good at *The Herald*. But the prospect of staying on at the paper just hadn't appealed – too many unhappy memories. In the meantime Washington-based polling company US Forecast had hired her boyfriend, Chris Treiger. And when Chris had proposed marriage, she'd happily accepted.

With no idea what she'd do once they arrived in Washington, she'd been busy arranging domestic removals and flat-letting when she'd got the call from the *Daily Sentinel* asking her in to talk.

They'd sold her this job on the basis of editorial freedom. Her brief was as broad as she cared to make it, they said – anything that happened in America of interest to readers in Britain. That was the big picture. The reality, as she'd soon discovered, was that she was just as limited by editorial dictates as ever. And having been on the receiving end of yet another ear-blasting from Canary Wharf on the vexed subject of the presidential elections, she was reaching the end of her tether.

Since her arrival here, the focus of attention had been the up-coming election. With an incumbent Republican President contending for a second term, all the action was in the fight for the Democrat nomination, where the party's former favourite, James Gallagher, had rapidly been overtaken in the polls by popular Louisiana Governor, Grayson Wendell.

Scion of the New England Gallagher clan who had, in the past hundred years, given the nation a president, an attorney general, and two silvering senators, the youthful Jimmy Gallagher had until six months ago seemed virtually certain to receive the nomination. With magazine-cover good looks, a family that was the closest thing America had to royalty, and the most bankrolled campaign of any presidential candidate in living memory, Gallagher had enjoyed a lead in the polls that had appeared unassailable.

And then Grayson Wendell had come out of the

political woodwork. Immensely charismatic, his hypersensitive antennae finely tuned to the swell and ebb of public sentiment, Governor Wendell had emerged as an inspirational speaker, tapping the mood of the nation in a style unseen since the days of Ronald Reagan. He was also an adept at playing the anti-Washington card, the area in which Jimmy Gallagher was vulnerable.

Governor Wendell's performances on the stump were soon outstripping the valiant but ultimately lacklustre efforts of Gallagher. Viewing this *éminence grise* on their TV screens, card-carrying party members began to ask if it wasn't perhaps too soon to wheel on their favourite son – perhaps a few more years in the wilderness would do him good. Wendell had the capacity to transcend the party divide. He had a brave, new vision. Women voters loved him. And right now he had pulled ahead to a double-digit lead over Gallagher.

The trouble for Judith was trying to get to see him. Since she'd arrived in Washington, her bosses had been increasingly insistent she write a piece on him. A big piece. A 3,000-word profile to run in the weekend magazine. But just trying to get five minutes of Wendell's time was proving well-nigh impossible – let alone the luxury of a fireside chat.

She'd just explained all this to London, or tried to. She could do an extensive profile, she'd offered, based on a wide variety of sources. But her bosses weren't buying it. They wanted a face-to-face exclusive splashed all over the weekend paper. What about interviews with Democrat insiders, she'd asked. She'd already conducted several, throwing up unexpected new angles on the charismatic Wendell. But no, that wasn't good enough either.

Swigging her wine, she returned to her desk. Just as her erstwhile *bête noire*, Alex Carter, had been single-mindedly obsessed with her output volume, so her current bosses seemed interested only in her interviewing Grayson Wendell. This was despite everything else she'd done. Despite the stories and exposés that had produced such strong reader response back in Britain.

The world of biotech, in particular, had prompted a flurry of readers' letters. Her recently published profile of Lorna Reid, and the development of anti-ageing therapy had struck a deep, collective chord. People had been fascinated by the work of the high-octane Scotswoman – and Judith had been gathering more material to play the story out.

One of the fastest-growing grass-roots movements in America, Free to Choose, was lobbying Congress to pass laws so that gene therapies such as NP3 would be made available to all. Judith was intrigued by their reasoning. The way things stood at present, said Free to Choose, treatments like NP3 would be affordable only by the rich. And because gene therapy modified not just the people being treated, but their children and children's children, what would be created was a vast, and permanent, divide between society's haves and have-nots.

Social tensions would erupt into fully fledged class war, as those who couldn't afford gene therapies retaliated against the 'superhuman' species, more resistant to ageing, cancer and heart disease. The only fair way to deal with genetic therapy, said Free to Choose, was to make it free to all on Medicare. But the implications of doing this for the nation's tax burden were dire.

Judith found these arguments absorbing. When it came

to reversing the ageing process, most people, she reckoned, never got beyond thinking how wonderful it would be to live to 120. She was keen to write up a piece spelling out all the other implications. But the response from London had been lukewarm. Sure, write a follow-up piece to the NP3 story, she'd been told – but deliver on Grayson Wendell first.

She'd already tried getting access to Wendell via his spin-doctor, William Barbett. But even gaining access to Barbett had proved as difficult as speaking to the candidate himself. Despite persistent calls, she'd been held off by Barbett's deputy. Yes, she would be called back, he kept telling her – only, she never was. No, he couldn't confirm if she'd be granted an interview. As for making an appointment with Wendell – that was out of the question.

Glancing out of the window to where the Capitol building dazzled in the noonday sun, she took another sip of wine. Following her latest bruising telephone encounter with London, she was in a provocative frame of mind. In her *Herald* days she'd have reached for a pack of cigarettes right now, but since arriving in the Politically Correct States of America, a land crawling with those she disparagingly termed 'the safety police', her smoking had become more hassle than it was worth, and she'd recently given up. Which made her current mood only spikier. Yeah, she reckoned, picking up the receiver, she hadn't got anywhere going the spin-doctor route with William Barbett, so she'd dial right through to Wendell's campaign manager and give him a whirl.

She knew of Bryan 'Hatchet' Hulquist by reputation. One of the shrewdest operators in the business, he was also said to be the most charmless. But she could deal with charmless. She'd already dealt with far worse. And what did she have to lose?

On dialling Wendell's campaign headquarters, she was surprised to find herself put through to the Hatchet man himself. There was no personal assistant, or other executive minder to get past, just a short 'Yes' from the other end.

'This is Judith Laing. Britain's *Daily Sentinel* newspaper,' she said. It had been a useful calling card elsewhere. Even William Barbett's 2IC had sounded deferential after she'd introduced herself.

When there was no response from Hulquist, she'd pressed ahead. 'Our editor would like to do a major interview with Governor Wendell.'

'Not at this time.' It came as a knee-jerk reaction. There was no thought to it. Just instant denial.

Thinking quickly, she tried an alternative. 'Then, could I make an appointment for some time in the future—'

'No.'

'—or take part in a joint interview.'

'No.' The tone was completely uncompromising. So bloody rude! What was it with this guy?

'Do you have a problem with the *Daily Sentinel*?' she had to ask.

'Our priority is domestic media.' He begrudged even the explanation.

'But surely a substantial national newspaper like the *Daily Sentinel*?'

'Not our priority.'

'We have international and online editions.'

There was a pause at the other end before he told her, 'Foreign papers don't deliver votes.'

Judith was momentarily taken aback by his bluntness.

Then she was challenging him on the importance of overseas votes in the 2000 elections. But it was too late. As she was speaking, he hung up on her.

The bastard! Dismissing her with such easy contempt. Clearly he regarded her, the *Daily Sentinel*, the whole nation of Britain, as a total irrelevance. Even more evident was the policy of having nothing to do with foreign media. The endless dithering and procrastinating of Barbett's 2IC had disguised what Hulquist had had no difficulty telling her in the baldest terms.

She could forget about seeing Wendell. Not now, not even further down the line. As adamant as her bosses were for an interview, Wendell's minders were equally insistent it wasn't going to happen.

What, for God's sake, was she to do?

The rendezvous was in one of the executive meeting rooms of the Du Cane Plaza on Pennsylvania Avenue. Alerted by the concierge to the arrival of his visitor, Jack Hennessy took the elevator down from the penthouse floor and moments later had swept into the room.

The other man, tall, slender, suited, was standing looking out of the window with an intense expression on his face. They shook hands briefly before Hennessy handed him the large brown envelope with an air of ceremony. 'You'll find all the data you need in there,' he said.

'Very good.' The other opened his briefcase, placing the envelope carefully inside. 'We'll take action on it immediately.'

Hennessy nodded. 'It's absolutely critical that . . . Dr Reid doesn't suspect—'

'Rest assured she won't from our side.' Then, eyes

narrowing, 'As of this minute, she hasn't made any connection at all.'

'Nor should she ever do so.' Jack was severe.

'Of course.' The other man nodded then turned towards the door. 'It's a pleasure doing business with you, Mr Hennessy.'

Jack offered his hand. 'Way I look at it,' his grip was firm, 'we're in this together.'

8

As soon as she was back in her Georgetown apartment, Lorna changed out of her work clothes and into trousers and a sweater. Sweeping her hair back off her face into a pony-tail, she removed her earrings, took off her make-up, and slipped into a pair of fleece-lined sheepskin slippers before padding through to the sitting room. There she flopped down onto a sofa and turned on WGMS, the local classical music station. Mahler Symphony Number 5 was playing – just perfect, she thought, closing her eyes.

She'd never felt more in need of a quiet night at home. After the stress and trauma of the past four days, all she wanted was to unwind. She'd promised to give herself the night off from all thought about Zonmark and NP3. She'd even declined a dinner invitation from Jack. She hoped he'd understood her need for solitude – though he'd reminded her about their date the following Saturday night, when they'd be attending his mother's sixty-fifth birthday party. The significance of his invitation to the event hadn't escaped her. It signalled the seriousness of his intentions. But despite all that, and her own growing feelings for Jack, right now all she wanted was to curl up on the sofa alone and lose herself in the lyricism of the symphony.

Her 30th Street apartment was close to the heart of Georgetown, only a few minutes away from her favourite restaurants, boutiques and the Blues Alley Jazz Club. It was modest in size – property costs round here meant it had to be – but perfect for her needs. Downstairs was a small entrance hall and her study. Upstairs was her main living area.

Her sitting room was a glow of warmth, its rich, mustard-gold walls bedecked with black and white architectural sketches. Sumptuous cream sofas were complemented by antique mahogany furniture, and beautiful elephant lamps which she'd bought from one of her favourite shops on London's King's Road, India Jane. A side table was cluttered with silver-framed photographs of family and friends commemorating all the usual milestones – her parents' wedding day in sepia; her brother Dougie's graduation; family holidays; friends she'd known from Aberdeen, London, then Cambridge. As she opened her eyes now, and looked across at all those pictures, not for the first time she regretted having lost touch with so many friends since coming to Washington. Belonging as she did to the cash-rich, time-poor generation, during the very few moments she had to herself, such as now, she just didn't feel capable of conversing with anyone.

The Adagietto came to a close and she got up from the sofa and went to check the contents of the fridge. She glanced through the boxes of convenience foods stacked in the freezer without much relish, and wondered about ordering something in. Then she caught sight of the jar of pesto in her fridge door. She'd cook some pasta, she decided, and prepare a salad. Something simple and nourishing that wouldn't take much time.

Emptying a sachet of pasta shells into a pan of water, she dug out some vegetables for a salad. As she commenced cutting up an iceberg lettuce her thoughts turned automatically back to work, and in particular, to the afternoon's shocking news about the death of Albert Krauss. Since her visit to New Orleans, Krauss had been a much-needed source of hope for her. She'd so wished that it was only a matter of time before he confirmed that the Lafayette trials had exclusively used black patients. But the news that he had gone, and with him any remaining testimony, was more than a shock – it was deeply disappointing. The Lafayette trail had, it seemed, gone cold.

But surely, *surely*, Lorna kept wondering, with 150 patients treated over a five-year period not everything could have been expunged from the face of the earth? Not every record, not every staff member could have disappeared, even if the trials had been thirty years ago? The problem was, she didn't know who had been involved, much less how to set about tracking them down.

She caught herself thinking about work and immediately stopped. She'd given herself the night off, hadn't she? Too much thinking wouldn't do her any good – she needed to give her brain some down-time. She continued preparing the salad, before getting out the jar of pesto. Focus on the matter in hand, she told herself.

On the radio, the symphony came to an end and a Mahler expert was talking about how the composer had grown up near an army barracks. Bugle calls and other military motifs were, as a result, a recurring theme in his music.

The military reference triggered the memory of an armed truck driving along the road towards her. She remembered 'Wilson State Penitentiary' emblazoned on the side, the glimpse of an armed guard in the passenger seat. She recalled reading about St Augusta's 'secure ward', her association with 'the criminally insane', and Barnett's casual cast-off, 'We even do Wilson State Penitentiary – almost all as outpatients, for obvious reasons.'

What, wondered Lorna now with a flash of excitement, if Wilson prisoners had been among those taking part in the Neuropazine experiment? The prison would have a record of their treatment. Even if only a handful of the 150 patients had been at Wilson, there would still have had to be a paper trail, a link to someone who could tell her more about the Lafayette trials.

Next day at work, during her first free slot, Lorna logged onto a Net search engine and tapped in 'Wilson State Penitentiary, Louisiana'. Within moments she found herself on the home page of Louisiana's Department of Public Safety and Corrections. It provided a full list of all the 'correctional institutions' in the state, along with their admin and rehab programmes. Clicking onto 'Wilson', she had to wade through tables of performance indicators showing the cost per day of incarcerating prisoners, rates of reoffending, and other data. There was no staff list. Though that would have been just too easy, she thought, scanning down the home page again before selecting 'Office of Management and Finance'. The link led to an organisation tree which showed elected and unelected senior officials within the department, including the current Governor of Wilson, whose name she made a note of. But there was also an

140

archive section, and scrolling through all the different Louisiana prisons, she eventually came to Wilson, and its list of former officials.

She could remember the years that the Lafayette trials had been held. The dates 1968 to 1973 remained indelible in her mind. But as it turned out, there had been only one governor for almost twenty years, from 1960 through to 1978. His name was William Gore.

Printing off the page, Lorna wondered where to go next. She'd never played detective before. But in a way she supposed her whole career had been built out of analysis and deduction. There was no reason she couldn't bring those same skills to bear on the Lafayette trials – and get some answers.

William Gore would have been of the same vintage as Albert Krauss. Given their respective links to St Augusta Hospital, the two men might even have had dealings with each other. To find out if Gore was still alive and track him down, she could go the institutional route. But remembering Mrs Lane down at St Augusta, and the malaise of ineptitude and hostility she'd encountered at the hospital, she doubted that Wilson State Penitentiary would be any better.

Instead, she used directory enquiries to track down the only registered 'Gores' in Wilson, and twenty minutes later, with the assistance of a cranky daughter-in-law, had located the former prison director, now a resident of Merrywood retirement village.

It wasn't much longer before she was waiting for the old man to answer the phone.

'Mr Gore?' she confirmed when there a sound at the other end.

'Yeah?' He was wheezy.

'The name's Lorna Reid. And I'd be very grateful if you could help me, please. You see, I'm doing some research on Louisiana and I understand you were Director of Wilson State Penitentiary?'

The only response at the other end was a grunt. Decidedly taciturn, thought Lorna. 'Is now a good time to speak?' she asked. 'Or would you prefer me to call back—'

'Keep goin',' he ordered.

'Right. Good.' She was in no doubt he could understand her. 'I realise this is a long time ago, and you may not remember the full details. But in the late sixties and early seventies Lafayette State University conducted the trial of a drug called Neuropazine. It was administered at St Augusta Hospital. What I really want to know is, were any prisoners from Wilson involved in the trial?'

The pause that followed was so long, and Gore's breathing so laboured, that after a while Lorna wondered if he had fallen asleep. 'Mr Gore?' she prompted, politely.

'Where you from?' The tone was prickly.

'A company called Zonmark Laboratories.'

She'd barely ended when he cut in, 'A reporter, hmm?'

'No! No – I'm not a reporter,' she tried to reassure him. 'I've nothing to do with the media.'

'That's too bad,' he said. Or had he? She couldn't be sure she'd heard him right.

'The implications of my research could be of very great interest to the media,' she continued, trying to cover herself. 'You see, I'm a medical researcher.' It was a shorthand term she always used with the uninitiated. 'The Lafayette trials could have a very great significance—'

'Yeah, yeah. I knew that.'

'You do?' Once again she couldn't help wondering how lucid he was. Though he sounded in control.

'Sure. I've been expecting a call,' he continued. 'I'm surprised it's taken you people so long.'

What on earth was he talking about? It was hard keeping him on track. 'Mr Gore, are you saying you can remember the Lafayette trials?'

Once again he hesitated. Then he told her, imperiously, 'If you want something from me, you're going to have to come here to get it.'

He seemed to be speaking literally. 'I was only after some information.'

'Believe me, I know *exactly* what you're after. But I don't know who you are. I don't know anything about you.'

'I'm Dr Lorna Reid. I'm Research Director of the NP3 Programme at Zonmark Laboratories, Washington, DC.'

Judging by the silence at the other end, Gore was unimpressed. Lorna began to wonder if she was wasting her time with a senile old man when he asked her, 'You been speaking to Krauss?'

The question came out of nowhere and was instantly illuminating. However bewildering, it seemed that Gore did indeed know what she wanted. 'I wanted to speak to Doctor Krauss,' she said, 'but he died before I had the chance.'

'Hmph.'

Gore's brusque response was strangely unsettling. She tried to conceal her feelings beneath a businesslike pragmatism. 'Mr Gore, with all due respect, how do I know you'll be any more . . . forthcoming with information if I come to see you in person?'

'"Ask and ye shall receive",' he quoted. '"Seek and ye shall find. Knock and the door will be opened."'

'But will it?'

Her question hung in silence for another long pause, before he told her, huskily, 'I've been waiting to tell this story for thirty years. Come down and see me. Tomorrow.'

The death of Albert Krauss had occupied William Gore's thoughts constantly since he had read about it in the local paper two days before. He'd known Krauss from the latter's days as a clinician at St Augusta. He'd had to deal with him over a period of many years. He'd always despised Krauss and all he stood for.

The timing of the man's death, however, had him wondering. It seemed way too coincidental that he should die in an unfortunate accident at this of all times. Maybe Krauss and his wife *had* just gone to bed leaving the fire on, as the papers reported. But maybe not. And maybe he himself was only suffering the paranoia of old age. But after his conversation with Lorna Reid, his gaze fell on the telephone and he grew even more apprehensive.

Though Lorna Reid didn't realise it, the Lafayette trials had been the turning-point of William Gore's career. Up until 1968, he'd been a rising star in Louisiana's public service. Belonging to that rare breed of men able to combine clarity of vision with meticulous attention to detail, he was an administrator first, and an officer in the Department of Public Safety and Corrections second. 'Fast-tracking' hadn't been a term in currency in those days, but that was what had happened after he joined the civil service. His administrative skills were quickly recognised by his superiors, as was his ability to establish cordial relations with subordinates – and inmates – without compromising his authority. Quickly rising through the ranks of the service,

144

he had been appointed Director of Wilson State Penitentiary at a youthful thirty-five, a full ten years before such seniority was conferred on most of his peers.

Wilson had been through a tough time by the time Gore had arrived. Jail conditions were deplorable, overcrowding rife, staff stretched to the limit, their morale at an all-time low. Applying his well-honed abilities, it hadn't been long before he'd begun to see improvements. And at that point, for the first time in his career, he'd received an instruction from his superior in the Department which met with his vehement opposition.

His boss showed little interest in his concerns. Unusually, when he argued his case before more senior officers in the service, they too dismissed him out of hand. Pragmatic though he was, and well-skilled in the art of compromise, he felt that this was an issue too big to ignore. When he'd continued his protests he'd been swiftly taken aside by a high-ranking colleague who'd told him bluntly to shut up and get on with it. This instruction, he'd been assured, had come from the top. Any further rebellion would damage his career.

As it turned out, the damage had already been done. Reluctantly following orders, he had risen no further. Somewhere in head office, a black mark had been put against his name. Applications for more senior jobs at the Department were never advanced. More senior colleagues, once his champions, distanced themselves from him. He even suspected his activities were being monitored; mail addressed to him frequently appeared to have been opened. On several occasions he'd heard unfamiliar clicking noises on picking up the phone.

Gore had had no choice but to bide his time. He'd

learned from experience that administrative fashions came and went. It had given him no pleasure to make copies of all the paperwork pertaining to the dispute, in which he'd stated his concerns in stark black and white – only to have them overruled. Conscientious as ever, he'd secured a full set of the original documentation in a fireproof safe in the basement of Wilson State Penitentiary.

By the late eighties, sufficient time had elapsed for his former superiors to have moved, gone, or forgotten about the dispute. Gore made a comeback of sorts. He appeared at several Departmental conferences, and was appointed to a handful of task forces. But by the time the offer of a job at headquarters was forthcoming, it was too late. Facing retirement in just a few years, Gore had already come to terms with seeing out his career at Wilson. Alienated and embittered, he had no wish to work at close quarters with those he held responsible for snuffing out his career.

He'd forgotten about the file of copied papers by the time he was due to retire in 1993. But as he was clearing the basement safe at Wilson prior to his departure, he came across it, and knew immediately that he must take it home. His original reason for securing copies of the papers had been the desire for personal vindication. But events had moved on since then, in a direction he could never have possibly guessed. Two nights before driving out of the gates of Wilson State Penitentiary for the very last time, Gore had removed with him, in a sturdy cardboard box, the file he'd copied over twenty years earlier. What's more, he'd been through it, and updated the records. He had a strong hunch they'd turn out to be useful.

By the time of Lorna Reid's phone call, there was every indication that his hunch was about to be proved spectacularly correct. The file, which he now stored in a steel trunk under his bed, contained information that would have major repercussions, not only in the Department of Public Safety and Corrections, not only in the state of Louisiana, but at the highest level of American life.

From time to time he'd take out those yellowing pages to read, and reread them, realising that he had, in his hands, evidence that could alter the course of national history. The question that had been so vexing him of late was: had anyone worked out that he still had them?

In the long days at Merrywood, he'd had plenty of time to contemplate this. It was on his mind a great deal as he walked, or gardened, or simply dozed in the sun, but he had never spoken to anyone else about it. Keeping himself to himself had always been Gore's style.

But then he'd read about Krauss's death. And wondered. If the doctor's demise had been less accidental than it seemed, where then did that leave him? He had been involved in the implementation of the Lafayette trials just as much as Albert Krauss – and unlike Krauss, he had every reason to bring to public attention this unsavoury chapter of Louisiana history. For while Krauss had been one of the trials' staunchest advocates, he had been their most bitter opponent.

He wondered if he was being watched. Considering who he might be up against, the possibility was more than likely. He would be an easy enough target to monitor. He had few visitors outside a small circle of regulars. Modern technology being what it was, it would be the easiest thing in the world to record his telephone calls. Which is why he sat staring at the receiver with growing apprehension. And along with his fear there was determination.

147

Kneeling down on the carpeted floor of his bedroom, he hauled out the steel trunk with some effort, undoing two padlocks, using keys from the set he kept in his pocket at all times. After opening the lid, he had to remove layers of tightly packed folders and papers and photograph albums – all that remained of a forty-year career and even longer marriage – before getting to the cardboard file. It wasn't a particularly thick file, but the top half dozen pages alone would have been sufficient for him to wreak total and devastating revenge. Slipping the box under his arm, he left the cabin, making his way along a gravel path to the main building.

Even before Lorna's call he had been wondering what to do with the file. He had considered sending it to someone anonymously. A high-profile media person would be an obvious recipient, and he had already begun making a mental short-list. The problem with that approach was that anonymity would make easier subsequent denials and evasion. Gore realised this, but nor did he want to have every damned reporter in America tramping through Merrywood, disturbing his treasured privacy. In a way, he reflected, Dr Lorna Reid was providing him with a very elegant solution. As a scientist, her interest in the material was professional. She would face no difficult questions about motivation when she revealed the facts – but the truth would be out there. She'd make the perfect vehicle to deliver the evidence he had assembled all those years ago. No one would need to know how she'd come by the information he'd give her, or where precisely she'd found it. Meantime, he would be watching it all from the wings.

Up at the main block, Merrywood residents could take meals if they preferred not to cook for themselves. A communal lounge and dining hall provided the social focus – along with a games and a TV room. The management and administrative offices were based here too, and it was in their direction that Gore made his way. A PIN-code-operated photocopier had been set up in one of the corridors for use by both staff and residents. Gore was soon standing at it, working his methodical way through the file of papers, careful to arrange originals and duplicates in neat, separate stacks.

Bureaucratic caution was engrained: never give away original documents; never put all the copies of valuable evidence in one place. After making a full duplicate set, Gore proceeded along a corridor and knocked on the door of Val Henderson, Admin Manager of Merrywood. He knew he could trust Val, not only because she'd proved herself reliable in all their past dealings, but also because she was, coincidentally, one of his daughter's closest friends. He'd known her all her life. She smiled as he stepped into her office.

'Val, I'm expecting a visitor tomorrow. A lady doctor.' She didn't need all the details.

'Oh.' The smile was replaced by a look of concern. 'Are you all right, Mr Gore?'

'Nothing to worry about,' he assured her. Then, 'Her name's Lorna Reid. I've got something here she'll want to see. Do you have an envelope?'

She reached under her desk for a large manila envelope into which he slipped the duplicate set of documents, before printing Lorna's name on the front. Then he handed the envelope to her. 'Will you see she gets it when she arrives?'

'Don't you want to give it to her yourself?'

He shrugged. 'I could do,' he said vaguely. 'I'm not sure when she's coming and if I'm out in the garden it could take a while to find me. I'd just as soon leave it with you.'

The garden wasn't that big, thought Val. It never took more than ten minutes to locate anyone. But she'd long since learned not to argue with old people about things that didn't really matter. 'Of course,' she replied now, putting the envelope in a desk drawer. 'I'll make sure she gets it.'

'It'll be safe in there?' His brow furrowed as he nodded towards the drawer.

'Safe as houses,' she assured him, patting her desk.

That evening, William Gore had a glass of beer with his meal. It wasn't every evening he indulged in this way, but he felt a strange and unexpected ease, as though relieved of a burden he hadn't even realised he'd been carrying. In the old days, for the many, many years that he and his wife had sat together at their kitchen table, supper had been a time to reflect on the day's events. He so wished she was here with him now to share in all that had happened. For he had no doubt at all that, at 74 years of age, he had done something today that would eclipse every other achievement of his life. If he would be remembered for anything, then it would be for this.

The paradox of it didn't escape him. Here he was, a tired old man in a nursing home, long past his prime. And yet all his years at Wilson and before, trying to raise standards, introduce new management techniques, make some kind of impact on the world around him – all that would be as nothing compared to the effortless activities he'd undertaken during the past few hours and which would find their full expression tomorrow.

He'd finished his supper by 7.45 and tonight, as usual, he went over to the TV room to watch the eight o'clock news broadcast. He stayed for a coffee in the lounge, while his contemporaries made halting conversation, played a few hands of bridge, or fell asleep under their newspapers. Then he made his way back across the lamp-lit gardens to his cabin. Reflecting that he'd have an early night before Lorna Reid's visit the next day, he fished his keys out of his pocket, opened the cabin door and stepped into the darkness.

As his arm reached out for the light switch, something suddenly clamped to his mouth. In the next instant, he was being forced to the floor. Hands on his shoulders, impossible to resist, powered him down like a pair of vices. Struggling against them, he heard the door click shut behind him. Even in the pitch black he realised he was hopelessly overpowered. It wasn't just one man behind him; there were at least two.

They had him on his stomach, face to the floor, arms wrenched behind his back. Then the light went on. Craning his neck, he saw a young man in jeans and a red checked shirt staring down at him with impassive foreboding.

That moment lasted an eternity as Gore stared up at his assailant. His heart pounded in his chest as the image of the smooth, sullen face became emblazoned on his mind. The intruder couldn't have been more than thirty, with short, brown hair combed in a fringe across his forehead; dark, deep-set eyes; pale skin; a cold, bland featurelessness – with the exception of a mark under his left eye. A deep red cicatrice.

The other made no effort to hide his face. 'You can do

'this the easy way,' he began, 'or you can make life hard on yourself.' Gore was tugged from behind, onto his knees.

'Just do as we say, and you'll be all right.'

Dragged over to his desk, he saw that the other was gesturing he should sit on his chair. In the surreal timelessness of the moment, Gore recalled how he'd thought about this possibility – not only since Krauss's death. It had occupied his worst imaginings for years. He'd only ever considered it the most remote of prospects – so remote he'd never bothered doing anything about it. Besides, what could be done?

'I want you to write.' The other pointed to the pile of blank Merrywood stationery on his desk. 'Your wife. When did she die?'

'What the hell kind of question is that?' The anger burst up in him.

Instantly, the vice grip was round his neck, squeezing down on his windpipe with such punishing force he began to choke.

'Just answer the question.' His interrogator remained cool.

He coughed, a deep hacking cough, before he managed, hoarsely, 'Three years . . .'

'Perfect.' The other delivered a thin smile. Then, gesturing to Gore's pen, 'My wife died three years ago,' he dictated in a flat, smooth voice. 'Since then, I've been so incredibly lonesome . . .'

9

Protocol among the band of early-morning commuters was well established. Many had been catching the 7.05 from Weybridge to Waterloo for years. Most took up fixed positions along the platform in readiness to get into their preferred carriage – and woe betide anyone who encroached on their territory. Usually, their faces would be obscured behind newspapers, or bent over books. Occasionally one would make eye contact with another and deliver a nod of recognition. Most avoided even this limited communication, holding on instead to every last moment of solitude before being overwhelmed by the inevitable overcrowding.

As usual, Andrew made his way to the far end of the platform, so that when the train pulled into Waterloo, he'd be close to the station concourse. But this morning he had the curious sensation of being watched. Was it his imagination, or had several of the newspapers rustled as he walked past, their readers peering to catch sight of him?

Strolling to the end of the platform he wondered about it for a moment, before deciding that if he was being surreptitiously observed, it probably had to do with the flyer. No doubt several of his fellow commuters lived in houses he had leafleted. Perhaps they were connecting him with his appeal for information.

Opening his copy of the *Financial Times*, which he always picked up on his way through the station, he hadn't long been scanning its front page when he was approached by a man in his fifties in a drab suit and grey overcoat. He was one of the regulars, and Andrew knew him to be a member of Weybridge Council. Now he exchanged a nod with Andrew before sidling up to him.

'Quite the media star!' he muttered.

Andrew didn't know what he was talking about, or what to make of his tone. 'How d'you mean?' he replied, bemused by this unprecedented advance.

The paper the other was opening was that day's copy of *The Globe*. 'You mean, you haven't seen it?'

Andrew could hardly believe his eyes as the man opened up the tabloid. There, on page five, was a large and deeply unflattering photograph of himself, and above it in enormous black type, the headline, 'J'Accuse! Police Got It Wrong, Says Dead Boy's Dad.'

'What the . . .!' Andrew had taken the paper from the Councillor and was quickly reading through the article in a state of horrified absorption. Andrew Norton, said the paper, father of progeria child Matt who had tragically died two weeks before, claimed the police had got it wrong about his son's death. 'Pouring his heart out' to *The Globe*, Andrew had told of his mission to find the two men he believed had murdered poor Matt. 'Somebody must have seen something,' he was quoted as 'begging'. 'I'm just asking them to come forward.'

Andrew had launched a crusade, the piece went on, he wanted to bring his son's killers to justice. He had published leaflets and distributed them widely around Weybridge, 'a posh suburb in Surrey's mink-and-manure belt'. Andrew was appealing to people with any information to call him.

But Weybridge police were denying Andrew's allegations. 'The Coroner's Office reported accidental death,' a police spokesman was quoted as saying. 'We've closed the case. We don't believe there is anything more to be said.'

Next followed a description of Matt's funeral, together with all the well-known facts of his life, rehashed in the nauseating tabloid mix of mawkish sentimentality and crude hyperbole. The article ended with a gushing appeal to *Globe* readers to 'help Andrew find out the truth about our little hero, Matt'.

Even after he'd finished reading it, Andrew stared at the page in a state of shock. Numbed, he remained transfixed as he caught sight of the by-line at the top of the page: 'Jim Jones'.

As the Councillor was taking back his paper, Andrew became aware that the train was coming into the station.

'I didn't know,' was all he could think of to say.

'Good luck.' The Councillor's expression remained veiled as he moved back down the platform to his usual spot.

After climbing on the train and finding a window seat, Andrew stared out, unseeing, at the passing countryside. Stunned, he began to realise how he'd been misled. He went back over in his mind the conversation he'd had with

Jones. Jones, who had introduced himself as a local reporter. Andrew had taken that to mean he reported for a local paper. Jones had been all too happy to create the illusion – and sustain it. They both knew that Andrew would never knowingly have talked to a representative of *The Globe*. He certainly would have been a lot more guarded in what he'd said.

Andrew remembered Chief Inspector Hardwick's stern warning: 'Whatever you do,' his tone had been severe, 'there must be no suggestion of wrongdoing. Asking the public for more information is one thing; hunting for murder suspects is quite another.' Andrew had tried to heed the policeman's warning. But Jones had caught him by surprise, and twisted his words.

Or had he? Jones was only saying what Andrew really believed. He *did* think the police had got it wrong. He *was* on a mission to find out the truth. But the article would make things even more difficult than ever. He had no doubt how the police would react. Hardwick would be livid. Any chance of co-operation now seemed ruined. Worse, would the article give the police grounds to take some kind of action against him?

As for his reputation at work, he could hardly bear to think about it. There were no rules at Glencoe about extra-mural media appearances – none were needed. Senior fund managers understood, implicitly, that discretion and responsibility went with the job. But *The Globe* presented him as a man unhinged; a man who 'poured his heart out' to the gutter press and accused the police of getting it wrong; who was on a single-handed crusade to find motiveless, unknown killers. Was this the kind of person in whose judgement could be safely entrusted a six-billion-pound fund?

Outside Waterloo, he rose and walked towards the nearest door. Already standing next to it was Mrs Turton, a secretary in Glencoe's legal department, who also commuted from Surrey. She waved her copy of *The Times* at him. 'I see you're in the paper, Andrew. Good for you!' she congratulated him.

He tried not to cringe. Christ Almighty – *The Times* as well! 'Do you mind if I . . .?' he asked, taking the paper from her. It was a much shorter piece, without the hype, accompanied by a photograph of Matt. But the message was the same. Looking round the carriage at his fellow commuters, he saw that most of them were carrying that day's papers. He supposed that once the early edition of *The Globe* had been published, there was nothing to stop all the others pouncing on the story too. Little had he known, as he'd slept last night, that his life was about to be trailed through the national press. And how many other papers had the story?

He didn't have to wait long to find out. After making his way swiftly across Waterloo Bridge, along The Strand and into Chancery Lane, he arrived at Glencoe headquarters. No one in the lift paid him any attention. Getting out on the eighth floor, he kept his head down and walked straight to his office. Like that of other senior executives, it was glass-walled and across a corridor from the main, open-plan area.

Standing behind his desk, he reached over to his 'In' tray and retrieved that day's press cuttings. They were prepared and circulated each morning by Glencoe's media department. Always among the first things he read each day, they didn't usually contain anything of such intense personal significance as he discovered in them today.

He was mortified to find *The Globe*'s piece at the top of the pile, his own name highlighted in bright orange. Flicking back the page, he saw that the cutting that followed was a variation on the theme from a rival tabloid, claiming to have interviewed 'a source close to Andrew Norton' who said he had 'become obsessed with his son's death and determined to find someone to blame for it'. Several shorter pieces, that had appeared in the broadsheets, followed. Then there were the news wire versions, and even several mentions in regional dailies.

As he was scanning through these with mounting outrage, Ruth knocked on his office door and brought in his morning coffee. It was one of their daily rituals.

'Andrew,' she greeted him.

'Ruth.' He met her eyes briefly before glancing out of the glass wall of his office to where a group of colleagues were standing in the distance, staring at him.

'Why're they all looking at me?' he demanded, unnecessarily.

'I expect they're wondering about you speaking to the papers.' She was matter-of-fact.

'Well, I didn't speak to the fucking papers!' he snapped, angrily. It was rarely that his self-control slipped at the office. He'd certainly never used the 'F' word in front of Ruth. Remembering himself suddenly, he raised his hands to his face. 'Ruth, I'm sorry. I *am* sorry . . .'

He gestured for her to sit, before telling her about being duped by Jim Jones the day before. He didn't have to justify or explain himself to his secretary, but he felt the need to talk to someone who'd understand. And, nodding sympathetically across the desk at him, Ruth left him in no doubt that she was on his side.

But whatever reassurance he took was short-lived. Bob Bowler was striding crisply across the floor towards his office. Knocking just once, he swung the door open before telling Andrew importantly, 'You're wanted in the Boardroom.'

There was the slightest curl of a smile about his lips.

New Orleans, Louisiana

Lorna hadn't planned to return to New Orleans – certainly not in the near future, after her last traumatic visit there. But Wednesday morning shortly after 11 am found her disembarking from American Airlines Flight 105 at New Orleans airport. Her only luggage a lightweight laptop, she walked through the airport concourse, directly for the Deluxe Car Rental kiosk. She'd hired from Deluxe on her previous visit, and despite the still unexplained snake incident, she'd decided to return on the basis that lightning didn't strike in the same place twice.

After signing a car rental agreement, she was taken out to the car rank by a perky young woman in Deluxe livery to complete a damage check. Indicating a few minor marks on the car, the woman gave her a form.

'Before I sign this,' Lorna said, glancing at her sharply, 'I want you to confirm there are no snakes in the car.'

'You're kidding, right?' The young woman giggled.

'Do I look as if I am?'

'Oh my God!' Recognition dawned. 'You're the lady who—'

'Yes.'

'Oh, ma'am! None of us can work out what happened there.' She was opening the rear door behind the driver's seat and getting down on her knees, chattering about the consternation of the Deluxe staff. Having confirmed that one side was snake-free, she checked the other, then inspected the glove compartment and finally the boot, all the while apologising to Lorna for what had happened to her. Unnecessarily, Lorna felt, she even flicked down the sun visors, before stepping out from the car with a bright-eyed smile. 'You've got the all-clear, ma'am!'

'Yes. Thank you.' Lorna put her laptop and handbag on the passenger seat, before walking round to the other side of the car.

'Have a nice day!' The other saluted her breezily as she started up the engine.

'Don't tell me what to do,' growled Lorna, as she sped away.

She had already consulted a street map of New Orleans. Merrywood in South Rialto wasn't too far – less than an hour's drive, she reckoned. She had considered taking a taxi, but dismissed the idea, not being sure of availability at the other end, and not wishing to hang around waiting. This way she was independent.

Taking the map out of her handbag and laying it on the passenger seat, she followed the route she'd already planned. Having to watch for road signs and follow turn-offs demanded her full concentration. But once she'd got onto Route 103, a secondary road that curved its way first through the suburbs, and into rural Louisiana, her thoughts turned to NP3.

Her decision to come down had been impulsive. But she'd felt strongly that this was the most important thing she could do. Her telephone contact with William Gore had been more promising than she'd dared hope and she'd

160

fully updated her Zonmark colleagues – and Jack. In fact, it had been Jack who had convinced her she should make the trip down here right away. 'Gore's there and he's willing to speak. It could be very big news for your project. What are you waiting for?'

South Rialto was an expansive farmland area of cane fields and rolling pastures with the occasional rambling Southern homestead in the distance. The turn-off to Merrywood was well signposted. Lorna wondered if she'd find a classic *Gone With The Wind*-style mansion at the end of the driveway, but instead discovered a settlement of modern bungalows set in tranquil parklands – a copse of woods, an ornamental lake – conveying an impression of quiet affluence. Speed humps and frequent reminders of the 5 mph speed limit necessitated slowing down, so that she had plenty of opportunity to take the place in.

As she drew near the main building, she allowed herself to feel some of the anticipation she'd been suppressing. In just a few minutes, she thought, she'd be speaking to William Gore, a man who not only knew what she was interested in, but also had something specific to tell her.

Merrywood's Reception was spacious, light-filled and decorated in warm colours. Although there were a lot of grey heads in the sitting room, and out in the gardens, there were no nurses' uniforms – the place didn't feel like an institution.

'I've come to see William Gore.' She approached a pleasant-faced woman behind the Reception desk.

'Certainly.' The other picked up her phone. 'Who shall I say is here?'

'Dr Lorna Reid.' She nodded. 'He is expecting me.'

The woman dialled the number. It rang without reply for

some time so she hung up and reached for a microphone to page Gore. Her message sounded throughout the main centre. 'Why don't you take a seat?' The woman waved Lorna in the direction of some well-padded armchairs. 'I'm sure he won't be long.'

Sitting as suggested, Lorna picked up a copy of the local newspaper from a coffee table and flicked through it without interest.

When there was still no sign of Gore a few minutes later, the receptionist got up from behind the counter and came round beside her. 'Mr Gore's obviously not in his cabin, or the centre,' she said. 'Perhaps he's out in the garden. He does like his walks, you know. Let's go and find him.'

Lorna followed the woman, who introduced herself as Mary, as she led the way along a path that wove through the manicured flowerbeds and over a wooden bridge that crossed a gurgling stream.

'Very pretty,' she remarked conversationally.

Mary nodded. 'Guess that's why Mr Gore spends so much time out here. He's one of our most committed walkers.'

'Is he?'

'Uh-huh. We encourage that kind of thing, you know. Healthy body, healthy mind.' They went on a rapid tour of Gore's favourite areas, Mary surveying the gardens as they made their way past several bungalows.

'Mr Gore lives just over there.' She gestured towards Gore's home.

Lorna looked over. It seemed no different from the rest. Though as they approached, they saw the door was ajar.

'Ah! Looks like he's just got back in,' confirmed Mary, turning to her. 'He always locks up behind him when he

leaves – very security conscious, you know. Maybe not surprising – he used to run the local jail.' She chuckled at her
own humour as they approached the cabin and she
knocked on the open door.

'Mr Gore!' she called out cheerily. 'Your visitor!'

She beamed expectantly at Lorna. Lorna raised a hand,
automatically tidying her hair. Then, after a few moments
when there had been no response, Mary knocked again
more loudly. 'Mr Gore?'

The smile faded when there was still no sound from
inside, and her expression turned serious. After she had
knocked a third time, she told Lorna, 'He may still be outside, but it's not like him to leave the door open. Rather be
safe . . .' She gestured inside. 'Mr Gore, I'm coming in!'
she announced, pushing the door fully open and stepping
inside. Lorna heard her walk down a short corridor and
halt, before the footsteps quickly returned. Hands raised to
her face, she slumped against the door frame, breathing
heavily.

Alarmed, Lorna squeezed her arm before deciding to go
inside herself. A short, tiled hallway led to a lounge area
where a few armchairs were arranged in front of a television. There was also a large writing desk and sturdy chair.
But it was the scene inside the bedroom that soon shook
her too. Limp, white, contorted in death, an old man was
hanging from the wardrobe, a noose of electric flex around
his neck.

Lorna and Mary returned quickly to Merrywood's centre,
both working to recover their composure. The moment
they were back in Reception, Mary turned and said, 'I think
you'd better wait', before making her way down a passage.
Standing at the counter, Lorna could hear the sounds of a

muted conversation before Mary returned with a tall, suited man, a stethoscope around his neck, and another woman who was evidently her senior. 'You go on ahead,' the other woman was telling the doctor, before looking over at Lorna.

'Dr Reid?'

She nodded.

'Valerie Henderson,' the other introduced herself, 'I'm the administrator. Won't you step into my office for a moment?'

Her office was a short distance down the corridor. She closed the door after Lorna. Her expression was grave, as she walked over to her desk. 'This is an awful shock.'

'Yes.'

'You didn't know Mr Gore.' It came out more as a statement of fact than a question. Then, as Lorna was shaking her head, 'You see, Mr Gore, quite apart from being resident here, was also a family friend.'

'I'm sorry.'

'His daughter and I . . . we're very close.' Her face was etched with emotion as she sat behind her desk. 'In all my years at Merrywood, nothing like . . . this has ever happened. I'm very sorry you had to find him this way. Dr Harkeness is going over there to confirm, you know. I'd better call the police.'

Lorna sat in Valerie Henderson's office, watching her pick up the phone. Her own feelings were strangely detached – as though she were watching a television drama play out around her. Like the hospital administrator she too was deeply shaken, if for a very different reason. It wasn't so much the discovery of Gore's hanged body, though that had been macabre; it was rather the recognition that his death, like Krauss's, had followed within twenty-four hours of her efforts to make contact with him. And determined though she was not to invent conspiracies where none existed, this was a coincidence simply too great to ignore. Hadn't Gore said only yesterday afternoon that he'd been waiting to tell this story for over thirty years?

Having explained to the police what had happened, Valerie was asking them to park, when they arrived, outside William Gore's cabin rather than in full view of the main building. Replacing the receiver, she looked over at Lorna. 'I guess you'd better stay, just in case they need some kind of statement. By the way, do you have a business card?'

Lorna reached into her handbag and removed one from its holder.

Valerie took the card and looked at it curiously. 'Biotechnology. That's interesting. Do you mind my asking why you came to visit Mr Gore?'

'It was business,' she replied, trying not to appear too cagey.

'Uh-huh?'

'Mr Gore had some information he wanted to give me.'

'Lord, yes!' She was opening her desk drawer and retrieving the large manila envelope which she handed over the desk. Lorna's name was hand-printed in large letters across the front.

'Bill gave this to me last night – he said for safe-keeping. I have to say I found it a bit strange at the time. He said I should give it to you when you arrived. When I asked why he didn't just give it to you himself, he said something about how he might be in the garden, taking a walk . . .'

Their eyes met in mutual acknowledgement of the significance of what she'd just said. William Gore had evidently planned his suicide with some care.

'Do you have any idea what might be in there?' Valerie was nodding in the direction of the envelope.

'None at all.' Lorna shook her head. 'But if it has any bearing on . . . what's happened, I'll let you know.'

'Please do.' Taking one of her own business cards from a box on her desk, she handed it over to Lorna. 'Shall we go up to the cabin? The police shouldn't take long.'

Nor did they. Less than five minutes after the two women had walked back through the gardens, the first blue and silver police car bumped up the driveway and towards Gore's bungalow. Valerie Henderson, flanked by Dr Harkeness, Mary and Lorna, was soon greeting the officers and going over the details of the discovery again.

Acutely conscious of the large manila envelope under her arm, Lorna tried her best to conceal her impatience as the policemen disappeared inside the bungalow for several minutes. Valerie Henderson obviously observed her foot-tapping, though, because as soon as the policemen had emerged she was asking them if they saw any reason why Dr Reid needed to stay.

Notepads out, the policemen asked her once again to go through the discovery that morning. They fired off a few supplementary questions she felt unable to answer – had she noticed anything unusual about Mr Gore's home that morning? Had she known the deceased very long? – before quickly ruling her out as a useful witness. She was free to go, they told her, taking down her contact details.

After saying goodbye to Valerie Henderson, it was all Lorna could do to walk, rather than run, to her car. Opening the driver's door, she flung her handbag on the passenger seat and quickly climbed in, ripping open the envelope. It contained a large wad of papers, some of which

166

had been individually stapled, all neatly held together by a bulldog clip. There was no note of explanation attached. She didn't waste a moment speculating why. Instead, she was immediately scanning through the papers.

The top page was an internal memorandum to William Gore from someone in the Department of Public Safety and Corrections. It was dated June 1968 and, although it had been copied from a document that seemed to have faded with age, it was still quite legible. The memo was an instruction to Gore to ensure that certain prisoners took part in 'pharmacy trials' run by Lafayette University. Lorna felt a flush of excitement. Gore hadn't been leading her on. It looked as if certain Wilson Penitentiary prisoners *had* taken part in the Neuropazine trials.

Flicking over the page, she found a list of the prisoners selected for the trials. Typed in single spacing, it took up an entire page. This was more than just a handful of prisoners. They had comprised a large part of the sample. Turning over, she discovered the list continued on a second page. And a third. On the fourth and last page of the list, a final paragraph confirmed a total of one hundred and fifty prisoners.

The entire Lafayette sample had consisted of inmates at Wilson State Penitentiary!

Aghast though she was, Lorna had to keep reading. The next document was another memo, this time a response from Gore. It was a methodical and vigorous questioning of the order he'd received. And as she scanned through it, line by line, her astonishment deepened to near disbelief as she realised the significance of what Gore had been ordered to do – and the implications for the Lafayette trials. She began to sense, for the first time, the predicament Gore had found himself in.

But over the page was another memo from Gore's bosses, countermanding his arguments and curtly ordering him to proceed as first directed.

A meticulous record-keeper, Gore had included next the transcript of a conversation he had had with one James Barnley. It was dated April 1968, and stamped 'Strictly Private and Confidential', and it seemed that Gore had made the transcript for his own purposes. The document was over six pages long, and Lorna realised she'd need to give it her detailed attention, but she couldn't resist glancing through it, page by page.

As she did, different phrases caught her eye. One, which had been underlined for extra emphasis, was in a section where Barnley was advising Gore he should do as he was told for the sake of his career. 'I personally agree with you, Bill,' Barnley was quoted as saying, 'but sometimes you just have to put what you think to one side. Pick the battles you can win. And you can't win this one. The order hasn't come from just nowhere. It's from high up.'

'How high up?' Gore had asked.

'Very high up.'

'You're talking about the Department Chief,' was underlined.

'I am.'

Further into the conversation came the line Gore had used himself: 'the fact that they're all black . . .' he had said to Barnley.

Lorna halted. There it was, documented – *the fact that they're all black*. In other circumstances she'd have been thrilled by the confirmation. But she had no doubt now that this was a truth someone wanted to suppress. And glancing over in the direction of Gore's cabin, as a further two police cars pulled up outside it, she realised that the pressure Gore had been under when he took his own life might have had everything to do with the very documents she held in her hands.

After the transcript came a list of the prisoners who'd taken part in the trials, compiled in order of their prison ID numbers. Against each name was a date of birth, date of imprisonment, and first treatment of Neuropazine. Next to these, a handwritten column was headed simply '1993'. Why that date, Lorna wondered? Had it been just before Gore retired? The fact that he had bothered to revisit this list so many years after the Lafayette trials had been scrapped showed he attached some kind of importance to it. Under the '1993' heading, against each name he had printed an update. In the majority of cases it was 'Deceased'. In some cases 'Released' and a date. Running through the four pages, she noticed that two prisoners were asterisked in the left-hand column in a different colour ink. A note in both cases read 'Trans. Masden, MI' giving a date in September, 1993.

One of the prisoners, Jeb Livingstone, had been born in 1910. What, she wanted to know, was an eighty-five-year-old man doing in jail? The other, born in 1921, was a Ronald Moffat. Livingstone and Moffat. She connected the two names. They were the same as two famous Scottish missionaries in Africa.

Of all the Lafayette trial participants, the only ones whose whereabouts were known, twenty years on, were Livingstone and Moffat. The date of their 1993 transfer must have been after Gore had already retired from Wilson State Penitentiary. But he'd continued to track their whereabouts. Why had it been of such continuing importance to him?

The rest of the papers consisted of individual records of each prisoner involved in the trials, including photographs with prison identity numbers, and full details of charges, jail terms, medical and other records.

Shoving the papers back in the envelope and onto the passenger seat, Lorna started the engine and pulled away from Merrywood. As she drove slowly up the winding driveway she noticed several more police cars arriving outside Gore's cabin. Uniformed officers were making their way towards it, one of them carrying a body bag. Reaching over, she touched the envelope, to reassure herself. She couldn't wait to get back to DC.

She'd been travelling less than two minutes, heading towards New Orleans on Route 103, when she glanced in her rear-view mirror and noticed the car. It was large, dark and travelling at high speed. Someone was obviously in a hurry to get somewhere.

Although Lorna was travelling at the speed limit of 70 mph, the car behind her was quickly gaining ground. With only a single lane going in each direction, she expected the other car, now almost upon her, to go tearing past. When it didn't, she looked across to find it travelling alongside her car. A man in the passenger seat, large, dark-haired and wearing sunglasses, was shouting aggressively, demanding that she should pull over.

10

She realised what was going on with a rush of panic. In that same instant she knew she didn't dare stop. Instead, she jammed her foot on the accelerator. The speedometer needle curved sharply as her car pulled away. She expected a gunshot at any moment. Pushing herself down and back in her seat, she stared ahead with sudden intensity of purpose.

A car was up ahead, where the road rose to the crest of a hill. It was a blind rise, but she knew she couldn't cut her speed. She had no choice but to overtake. Usually she'd have thought this an act of madness. But she veered left, directly into the face of whatever oncoming traffic there might be.

There *was* a vehicle coming up the other side, but it was just far enough down for her to cut back in lane. Car horns were blaring furiously. She raced down the other side of the hill, glancing in the rear-view mirror for her pursuer. Temporarily unable to overtake, he'd been forced to brake. But he had soon swung out and was once again behind her.

She'd put two hundred yards between them. With both cars racing faster than ever, the other was gaining steadily.

171

A set of traffic lights loomed. They were red, but she slowed only momentarily, to check for a break in the crossing traffic. Then she jumped them. She had no idea what she'd do once she got closer to the city. There was no safe haven she could head for. This was foreign territory.

Now the road was curving sharply. She barely slowed and soon had to swerve onto the other side between a slow-moving truck and a car coming in the opposite direction. Pumped up on adrenaline, her focus had never been more intense. But she was disorientated. Nauseous. She kept looking in the mirror. She didn't see them. She knew though that they weren't far behind.

She couldn't keep this up. But where would it end? Another set of traffic lights came up, this time much busier than the first. They'd only just turned red, but she raced across, accompanied by another blasting chorus of horns. Traffic was getting heavier now. She had no choice but to slam on her brakes.

At that moment she heard the distinctive wailing of a police car. Looking up in her rear-view mirror, it was with relief that she saw a Crown Victoria pulling out of the traffic. It was heading directly towards her, lights flashing.

She tugged the steering wheel while continuing to brake, guiding the car off to the side of the road. Watching the police car come closer, she raised both arms to the top of the wheel and for a short while leaned her forehead against them, feeling a wave of gratitude. Someone, somewhere had been looking after her, she decided. She would never have made it otherwise.

Not one, but two police cars materialised through the traffic, one pulling up alongside her, the other behind. Opening the door and climbing out, she walked towards the police car behind her. It seemed the worst thing she could have done.

'Hands in the air!' Screaming, a policeman had emerged from the first car and was waving a pistol at her.

'Okay!' Were they expecting some kind of shoot-out?

'Turn round! Hands on the trunk! On the trunk!'

She turned, as requested, lowering her arms. Four policemen were rushing towards her from all directions. They were treating her like some fugitive drug dealer – not someone who'd just fled a hit squad. She'd soon put them right.

One of the policemen was behind her. 'Legs apart. Don't move!' he ordered. While his colleagues covered her with pistols, he began frisking her for concealed weapons with more vigour than was necessary, pressing roughly around her arms, her breasts, running his hands all the way down her body and between her legs. After he'd finished she was standing up straight when he shouted, 'Don't move! I didn't say you could move!'

'But—!'

'Shut the hell up!'

Looking up towards the other officers, she was horrified to see her pursuers pulling over directly beside them. And now the car had a flashing blue light stuck on its roof. The man who'd threatened her was emerging from the passenger side. Tall, swarthy and wearing reflector sunglasses, he wasn't in uniform. But without a word to the other policemen he walked directly past where she was being held, to her car. Through the window she saw him retrieve William Gore's envelope and check her handbag for other material.

'You can't do that!' she screamed. Then, when everyone ignored her, 'That belongs to me!'

Behind her she heard a muffled conversation between a

policeman and the driver of the dark car. Then it was driving away.

In that moment, Lorna realised, appalled, that she'd just been set up.

At the police station she was marched in handcuffs to the charge office. One of the policemen barked out a list of offences. They included removing evidence from the scene of a crime; evading police arrest; several serious road traffic violations. The keys to her hire car, her handbag, cellphone, watch and jewellery were confiscated.

Scarcely believing what was happening, she demanded her right to make a telephone call. A flint-eyed officer told her she'd have to wait her turn. Then she was led through sliding steel doors into a concrete passage.

The first thing that hit her was the fetid stench. The rank closeness of body odour, urine and faeces which pervaded the place almost made her gag. On both sides of the passage, angry men's faces were pressed against the narrow grilles of cell doors, screaming out abuse. Most hadn't had access to a lawyer or even a telephone since their arrest.

Further down the corridor, the women's section seemed less crowded, though the stench was no less repulsive. One of the policemen was removing her handcuffs while the other opened the cell door. Realising this was her last chance to appeal she told them, 'Look. I run a major biotechnology programme in Washington, DC. And this is an abuse of my democratic rights. I'm warning you—'

She never got to finish the line, as she'd already been shoved into a cell, the door slammed behind her with a loud clank.

Two black women lay on narrow, stained mattresses.

One had rolled with her face to the wall; the other, half-sitting, was staring up at Lorna with large, glazed eyes.

'Warn all you like, sweet-pea, they never listen.'

Lorna looked over at her. Tight black skirt, skimpy red top, stilettos; there was no doubt what she was in for. Ditto the other woman who lay clutching her stomach, moaning in low, hoarse pain. A third mattress occupied the small cell, a rough blanket folded on top of it. In the corner, a toilet offered no privacy – nor even a seat. Up on the ceiling, two strip lights emitted a low, blue-white light, with the only ventilation provided by a circular fan far up the wall, whirring in lethargic cycles.

'What's a nice girl like you doin' in here?' Her fellow inmate was watching her surveying the squalor of her surroundings.

'Long story,' Lorna replied.

'Ain't it always?'

'We should be able to make a call. It's the law.'

'There's only one phone.'

'I could have used my cellphone.'

'He-heee!' The other found this wildly amusing. 'Couldn't we all! "Officer," she tried to mimic Lorna's accent, "I want to use my cellphone."'

Lorna ignored it. Her sense of humour, right now, was rock bottom.

'How long have you been here?' she asked after several minutes spent watching the groaning, sobbing form of the second woman as she came down from whatever trip she'd been up on.

'Since last night.'

'You mean, more than twelve hours? You still haven't made a call?'

'Can take two days, sometimes.' The woman regarded Lorna with bleak resignation. 'See, I'm a regular. Take it from me, best thing you can do is sit back and enjoy the scenery. Gonna be a long, long wait.'

London
Tuesday, 18 April

The ninth floor of Glencoe House was very different from the eight floors below. It accommodated not only the Boardroom, but also the offices of Sir Stuart Jamieson and his fellow executive directors, as well as a hospitality suite. Deep blue walls, so dark they were almost black, lent an aura of brooding power. Against them, Glencoe's own art collection, illuminated by down-lighting, augmented the effect of long-established affluence. Elegant deep-pile Persian runners sank under foot, and all the doors were of panelled mahogany with solid brass handles. The whole place seemed calculated to exert a humbling effect on those who were excluded from its hallowed chambers.

Andrew already had plenty of reasons for trepidation as he made his way swiftly towards the Boardroom. While early-morning summonses such as this were not unheard of, they usually followed a significant announcement by the Chancellor of the Exchequer, or the Federal Reserve Bank, or a major market correction. He'd never been ordered here on personal matters. The subject of crisis had never been himself.

The Boardroom door was already ajar when he got there. Pushing it further, he stepped inside. Sir Stuart was in a huddle with three other directors – Bradshaw, Carter and

176

Johnson. Were others to join them too? It seemed not, as Sir Stuart waved him towards the table, before he and his colleagues sat on the other side, placing their coffee cups on the vast, high-gloss slab.

'Time for a frank exchange of views.'

Andrew had used the phrase himself in the past. It was diplomatic talk for something a lot less polite.

'I know I speak for all present, indeed the whole Board, when I say I am extremely disturbed by this morning's papers.' His gaze met Andrew's, eye to eye, betraying nothing; no heat, or coldness. But it was unflinching. 'As you know, you have our full sympathy over the tragic loss of your son, and I don't want anything I say to take away from that.' His words were measured. 'Also your private life is entirely your business and we have no desire to prescribe how you manage your personal affairs. Nevertheless, talking to the national press isn't something we can ignore.'

'May I say—?' Andrew wanted to put him straight.

But Sir Stuart wasn't having it. 'Let me finish and you'll have ample opportunity to reply – I promise you.' He regarded Andrew solemnly before continuing, 'Having one of our most senior and respected executives associated in the media with a personal loss or tragedy is one matter. But wild accusations suggesting police incompetence – or worse – is quite another—'

'If I could just—'

'We have in our trust,' Sir Stuart bulldozed on with one of his favourite maxims, 'over thirty billion pounds of investors' money. It is the duty of every one of us to ensure that nothing we do suggests that their trust is misplaced. If our judgement is called into question, we're no longer in

177

business. It's as simple, and brutal, as that.' He glanced at his fellow directors, who wore serious expressions.

'As of now, no connection has been made between your personal situation and Glencoe. But if that were to happen,' he shook his head sombrely, 'it hardly bears thinking about – does it? We can't have a Glencoe versus Scotland Yard scenario in the media. I couldn't countenance it.'

Was this a prelude to being fired, Andrew began to wonder? Had that single conversation with Jim Jones proved fatal to his career?

'In the circumstances, I don't think it unreasonable to ask you to explain yourself.' Sir Stuart's eyes were boring into him. 'What provoked you to speak to the national press, and principally a tabloid from what I can gather, without so much as mentioning the fact to our media relations people, let alone taking their advice?'

Relieved by the opportunity to defend himself, Andrew needed no further prompting. 'In the first place,' he began, 'I never agreed to speak to a tabloid reporter. And in the second, the comments attributed to me by *The Globe* and others are deliberate misrepresentations—'

Sir Stuart and his fellow directors sat back in their chairs, regarding him intently. This was, Andrew realised, a battle for his job. 'The facts of the matter are as follows.' Calm and succinct, he took them, point by point, through what had happened: the questions in his mind ever since the day of his son's accident; the conversation with a neighbour after the coroner's verdict; the discussion with the local police and how he'd set out – with their approval – to find further witnesses. Then the call from Jones, posing as a reporter for a local paper. 'He knew very well I'd never have spoken to him if he'd told me where he was really calling from,' declared Andrew, 'and I never used the words "the police got it wrong."'

By this time Andrew detected a change in mood across the table. Sir Stuart was sitting forward in his chair, hands folded in front of him on the table. The three other directors seemed less impassive. Johnson was even nodding in support.

Andrew explained how his first knowledge that a piece had even appeared in *The Globe* had been while standing on the platform of Weybridge station, just over an hour before. He was, he told the directors, still shaken by the discovery.

After he had finished there was a moment's silence before Sir Stuart cleared his throat. 'A salutary lesson,' he murmured, 'to us all about speaking to any journalist.' Sir Stuart had a fundamental distrust of newspapermen.

'Perhaps we should consider grounds for suing *The Globe*,' intervened Bradshaw, a qualified lawyer. 'Obtaining information by deceit. Misrepresentation. Gross distortion—'

'At least demand a retraction,' Carter chimed.

'As I said,' Sir Stuart reminded them, 'so far there's been no connection at all between Andrew and Glencoe in the media. Nor do we wish there to be one. What do you think, Basil?'

Basil Johnson, whose workaholic reputation was exceeded only by his worldly cynicism, was swift to respond. 'The best course of action is to do nothing at all. Today's news wraps tomorrow's fish and chips. Don't give the bastards any more information, and the story will just be a one-day wonder.'

There was a reflective pause round the table as this was considered. Had the situation been retrieved, wondered Andrew? Had he held the storm at bay?

'I think Basil's judgement's probably right.' Sir Stuart looked over at his fellow director. 'But I'd like to discuss it further with our media people.' Then, looking back at Andrew, once again holding his gaze, 'There is, of course, the much larger question that is still a concern. This activity you're undertaking – which seems to me like dereliction of duty on the part of the police – it must be making considerable demands on your time. Are you able to assure me, and my fellow directors, of your undivided attention as manager of the North America Fund?'

'Yes, Sir Stuart.' He tried not to blink. 'On the few occasions I've been out of the office, I've made specific provisions for my absence.'

Sir Stuart was nodding reflectively. 'Safe pair of hands – Bob Bowler.'

Although the appointment of Bowler had been Andrew's own, it turned out that the Bowlers and Jamiesons were family friends – no doubt why Sir Stuart was more positively disposed to Andrew's second-in-command than he might otherwise be.

'I don't want you to take this the wrong way, Andrew,' Glencoe's Chairman had evidently not finished, 'but the hard questions have to be asked. With all the stress you've been under are you sure, absolutely certain, that right now you're up to the job? It would be entirely understandable if you felt you needed time out—'

'That's definitely not necessary,' responded Andrew. Nor desirable, he thought. While the importance of all his usual preoccupations had suddenly diminished, the idea of giving up the last vestiges of his daily routine was something he didn't even want to contemplate. 'I like my job.' He smiled weakly.

'Good.' Sir Stuart was brisk. 'I trust there'll be no more unexpected headlines, then?'

Returning downstairs, Andrew found Ruth waiting for him with a handful of telephone messages. While he'd been up on the ninth floor, half a dozen radio and newspaper journalists had called. It was infuriating that they'd tracked him down to Glencoe so quickly. After Sir Stuart's lecture this could prove to be yet a further embarrassment. 'Call them all back and tell them I've no comment,' he instructed Ruth. 'The same goes for anyone else who rings.'

Ruth nodded. 'Have a look through these anyway. There are a few other calls there.'

'Right.'

His first priority was to put his colleagues right about the situation. Summoning the department together for a five-minute meeting, he repeated what he'd already told Sir Stuart and the other directors. Explaining the deception, as well as his own embarrassment at finding himself in the national press, he was at pains to emphasise – while keeping a close eye on Bowler – that he and the Board were unanimous in their response to what had happened. Outraged as they were by *The Globe*'s behaviour, they had decided against provoking any further coverage of the story.

It took only a short time to clear the air. And after that Andrew received several sympathetic glances and encouraging half smiles. He hoped he had stopped the crisis deepening further.

Settling behind his desk, he tried to turn his mind to the business of the day. Ruth always had a complete list of fund holdings ready for him by the start of each day's trading. Scanning through these, he picked up what he assumed to be a reporting error. There were two large movements of identical amounts, out of the fund's blue-chip mainstays and into financial services. He called Ruth from where she was busy fielding calls.

'This switch yesterday. It's been reported twice—'

'That's no mistake.' She guessed what he was thinking. 'There *were* two separate transactions carried—'

'Authorised by . . .?'

'Bob made the call.' They glanced out of Andrew's office to where Bowler was barking at one of his colleagues.

'I see.' Tight-lipped, he picked up his phone and began dialling Bowler's extension.

'That's all, thanks, Ruth.'

By the time Bowler got to his office, Andrew had worked out the game. Each switch was the equivalent of 4.5 points. Combined they amounted to nine per cent of the fund – significantly more than the five per cent movement that required his specific authority. But because Bowler had made the transfers in two separate actions, he was technically in the clear.

'What the hell d'you think you were doing yesterday?' he demanded as Bowler appeared.

The other feigned puzzlement.

'Drop the act, Bob. We both know what you did. I want to know why you did it.'

'If you're talking about the move into financial services, I took the only prudent course of action in your absence.'

'Prudent? You sank nine per cent of our fund into just four financial institutions.'

'That's a lot less than most of the other North America

182

Funds,' he asserted confidently. 'And the point is, every single one of those companies is the target of a potential takeover.'

'No. The point is that you've pulled us out of a twenty-four-company spread and tied our fortunes to just four.'

'But when those four start to rocket—'

'That's not the way we do business here and you know it! This is a managed fund – not the Futures Exchange. We're looking for consistent profits, not bang or bust.'

As Bowler fixed him with a contemptuous sneer, he felt anger rise up inside him. 'We both know damn well I'd never have given my consent to this – which is exactly why you shifted the cash in two tranches—'

'I thought we were supposed to be "opportunistic"?' Bowler quoted from the North America Fund prospectus.

'There's a difference between opportunism and rampant speculation.' Andrew's voice rose. 'All the four stocks you picked are way up on where they were just a fortnight ago. They're wildly overpriced.'

'They've got a lot further to go.' Bowler was unrepentant.

'That's a matter of opinion.' Andrew glowered across his desk. 'I leave you in charge for less than five hours and you put us in the most exposed position we've been in for the last five years.'

'You could switch back again,' the other challenged him, facetiously.

'Yeah? And how much would that cost us?' They both knew that every time they moved in and out of different shares, commissions and the bid/offer spread meant a loss of between two and ten per cent per share. Which, on hundreds of millions of pounds, amounted to a colossal figure.

Andrew seethed. 'We might have to work extra hard for months just to pay for your error of judgement.'

'I can only see the upside.'

'That's because you're young.'

'Yeah? Well, maybe in this business you need to be.'

'Just what the hell are you implying?' Andrew found himself rising to his feet. It was Bowler's arrant disrespect, as much as his rash overconfidence, that he found so intolerable.

Bowler realised he'd overstepped the mark and a look of alarm crossed his face. 'Just an observation, that's all.' He tried backing down.

But Andrew was approaching him till his face was only inches from Bowler's. Eyes blazing into the other man's, his voice was barely more than a whisper. 'You may think you're something special because you're twenty-eight and you've never made a bad call. That's because you've never been *allowed* to make a bad call. When it's your name up on the door,' he pointed, 'that's when your "observations" count for something. Right now, I'm stuck with your judgement, and I'm not happy about it. Now get the hell out of my office and, make no mistake – pull a stunt like this again, and you're out.'

No sooner had Bowler departed than Ruth was putting her head round the door. 'Jess called again. She's desperate to speak to you.'

'Again?'

'One of the messages I gave you.' Ruth nodded.

He glanced at the pile of telephone messages on his desk. He still hadn't got to them. 'I'll phone her now,' he confirmed.

Dialling home he guessed he'd have to tell her about

what had happened. She might even have heard about the newspaper reports – her friend Sally would have relished passing on that particular news.

'Where the hell have you been?' Jess left him in no doubt about her state of mind.

Andrew took a deep breath. He had no wish to provoke further hostility. 'Look, I'm sorry I haven't called back before now. I didn't get to my messages – I'm having a crisis over here—'

'*You're* having a crisis?'

'Why? What's—'

'I'm besieged by bloody journalists!'

'Oh, Christ!'

'They've been banging on the front door. Now there are four of them up the driveway. The least you could have done is warn me—'

'I didn't know about it myself.'

'Then how did it get in *The Globe*? You "poured your heart out", it says.'

'It didn't happen like that at all! This reporter called me up saying he was a local. I thought he meant—'

'Oh, spare me! You've had plenty of time to come up with a story by now!' She was contemptuous. She evidently believed he'd not only collaborated with *The Globe* behind her back, but was now trying to deny it.

'You have to know,' he couldn't let it pass, 'I never wanted all this media interest.'

'What did you expect when you started leafleting the whole country?'

'So it's all my fault, I suppose?'

'I don't see who else's it could be,' she responded icily.

'What are they wanting to know?'

185

'Oh, don't worry, I'm not saying anything. I'm just telling them to phone you at work.'

'I'd rather you didn't drag Glencoe into it.'

'Suit yourself.'

'It's not just about myself.' As much as he was trying to keep his temper under control, she would provoke him just by her tone. 'I've just been summoned to the Boardroom because of what happened. My job's on the line. If things go flaky here, it'll affect us both.'

'Not any more, Andrew,' she responded, flatly. 'I've packed two suitcases already and put them in the Rover. I'm going.'

'You can't just up-and-off without even talking!'

'It seems to me that the only time we ever talk, you end up getting aggressive.'

'That's just not true!'

'Like you are now.'

He paused before responding, 'Jess, I know we've been through a bad time lately. But you can't run away from it.'

'You've left me no choice. I'm not staying here, barricaded by journalists.'

'But we've been married for nine years!'

When she replied, her voice cracked with emotion. 'You're not the man I married. You've changed so much I hardly recognise you.'

Outside his office, Ruth was waving for his attention, gesturing towards the phone and pointing upstairs. Evidently one of the directors was trying to get hold of him. Looking down at his desk, he asked, 'Where are you going?'

'Becky's.'

Her sister lived in Chester. He suppressed his protest at

how far away she'd be. There was no possibility of them seeing each other to talk.

'I haven't worked things out after that. I'll arrange to get my stuff out of the house.'

'I thought you said you had two suitcases?'

After a long pause she replied, 'This isn't a holiday, Andrew.' Her mind was evidently made up. 'I'm not coming back.'

'As you both know, we've successfully planted a conduit of information inside Zonmark.' Julius Lupine had taken the precaution of not only closing, but locking his office door before his teleconference with McIntyre and Pollos. Now he stood contemplating his immaculately manicured fingernails, directing his voice towards the phone placed at the centre of his desk. 'I've just learned some invaluable things as a result.'

'What sort of things?' Pollos was eager to know.

'The current status of the NP3 programme. Trial test results. Panel recruitment – the whole shooting match.' He was expansive. 'I'm having it put into a report which I will, of course, pass on to you.'

'The intelligence might be interesting,' Campbell McIntyre was his usual, jaundiced self, 'but what about the chances of actually *doing* anything?' Regarding Lupine as an industry peer, he found his competitive instincts hard to suppress. Lupine had been quite clear about wanting to 'close down NP3' when they'd met in Zürich. He wasn't going to

187

lose the opportunity to remind him of that fact now. Little did he realise he was playing directly into Lupine's hands.

'I'd say our chances are better than you might imagine,' Lupine responded. 'Zonmark's main problem right now is panel recruitment.'

'You mean, of progeria kids?'

'Correct. They need fifty. But as of this moment –' he paused for dramatic effect, 'they only have twenty-nine.'

'But the newspaper reports have said close to forty,' interjected Pollos.

'PR puffery!' Lupine told them. The sample had been higher than twenty-nine, but the less said on that subject, right now, the better. 'The point is, until they have a full sample, they don't have a clinical trial. And our ally is turning off the recruitment tap.'

'So this guy's inside Zonmark?' McIntyre asked.

The same question, Lupine remembered, had come up at their last conversation. And he had no intention of giving the answer. 'Let's just say he has considerable influence. Recruitment is already down to a trickle. We'll make sure it dries up altogether.'

'Won't Reid look into it?'

'She already has. Repeatedly. But our approach is bulletproof.'

'And that approach is?' persisted McIntyre.

Lupine had anticipated being pressed for more information than he planned to divulge. As he had agreed with Mayflower's controlling shareholder, from whom he took all orders, there was to be a drip-feed of information to the two other PR chiefs. But he might have to go a little further this time as he would soon be turning conversation to the subject of budgets.

'Well, the position is as follows . . .' He stood in the centre of his office, looking out of the window at the soaring arches of the Chrysler building, and behind it the vast, anonymous sprawl of the city. Folding his arms so that his dark Gieves & Hawkes suit pressed snugly to his body, he explained more about the operation he currently had underway.

Silence greeted his revelations – which he knew meant support. Both men had always been quick to voice their reservations.

'Not only are we enjoying success at containing the panel size,' he told them, 'there's also been a breakthrough with the Lafayette trials.' As a PR veteran, Lupine was a master of presenting the facts of any given situation as though they were entirely of his own making. 'NP3's not going well so Zonmark's trying to find something positive for the marketplace. In particular, they've been trying to get hold of the Lafayette trials records. The only problem is, all existing records were destroyed in an archive flood five years ago. Dr Reid decided to do some super-sleuthing in Louisiana.' Lupine felt like an illusionist building up to the climax of his act. 'But she went too far. Now she finds herself in jail.'

'Arrested?' queried Pollos.

'For removing evidence from the scene of a crime,' confirmed Lupine. 'And other things besides: evading police arrest; various traffic violations. Nasty array of charges. They'll keep her distracted for quite some time.'

There was a pause while the two others digested this before McIntyre observed, 'I suppose this is all costing a lot of money?'

'Ah, Campbell. Always so concerned with pecuniary matters!'

189

For several minutes they discussed the critical issue of budgets. As ever, Lupine appealed to the big picture: they wouldn't be in business in a couple of years if they didn't take action now. But there was no escaping that both McIntyre and Pollos needed to find money. There followed the usual hand-wringing and teeth-grinding about the cost of the exercise, which was considerable, and how much prime-time television could have been bought instead. They talked of squeezing advertising budgets, or appealing to their respective CEOs for increases in their 'market intelligence' budgets.

Lupine pretended to take an active interest in the conversation although it bored him completely. He focused instead on the very attractive *portière* draped on his office wall. It was a Jean de la Croix *père*, dating back to 1705, and a tapestry of which he was particularly proud. Attention to detail was exquisite – and the colours! Even after three centuries they were magnificent.

Although he was an avid collector, the *portière* was the only antique he'd brought into the office. A few of his treasures furnished his home. But the majority, the most prized *objets* in his collection of French rococo, were in special storage, locked away in a secure, temperature-controlled bolthole for his rare delectation.

McIntyre and Pollos schemed on about their budgets. Little did they know that the shortfall created by the cost of NP3 would soon be offset by additions to their funding – something both men would be told by their respective bosses during the next few weeks. Lupine never ceased to be surprised that two men so obviously intelligent and capable as McIntyre and Pollos were so unquestioning of the *modus operandi* of their respective chief executive officers.

Today, as he often did, he asked towards the end of their teleconference: 'So, how are the powers that be?'

'On a golf course, as usual,' responded McIntyre. 'Not as though there's a shortage of places to choose from. I'm sure that's why we're headquartered in Florida.'

'Not seeing much of mine either,' Pollos followed. 'Real e-commerce entrepreneur. Got bored with e-insurance years ago – he's probably half a dozen companies ahead by now.'

'Hmm. At least they're not breathing down your necks.'

'Mine leaves me to do pretty much my own thing,' remarked McIntyre.

'An excellent judge of character, Campbell.'

The three men chuckled at the obviousness of it, before McIntyre asked a question he never had before: 'And what about you, Julius? You never talk about your great leader.'

For a moment, Lupine was genuinely perplexed. His first instinct was defensive. He had no intention of revealing anything about *that* particular relationship, he thought. However, he quickly realised he'd misinterpreted the question. By 'great leader' McIntyre was of course referring to Mayflower Chief Executive Officer Dan Wright, whom Lupine had recruited following the departure of Wright's predecessor.

'Oh, yeah, Dan's fine,' he replied eventually. 'I keep him on a tight leash.'

The other two men laughed. They thought he was joking.

11

Jack Hennessy was taking a late-night stroll through the grounds of his home, his six, well-muscled Dobermans thundering across the lawns, when the call came through on his cellphone. Spencer Drake was on the other end, and the news was greatly displeasing. In the darkened shadows of a hedgerow, Hennessy listened intently before bursting out, 'What the hell do you mean? William Gore left *what* for her?'

At the other end, Drake tried to explain. Hennessy cut in, 'Did she get to read any of it?'

Drake continued. Hennessy was waving an arm. 'What in Christ's name are you guys playing at? This is a disaster!'

The other tried to placate him. Zonmark was making arrangements, he said. But Hennessy interrupted, 'Forget it! Call off the lawyers. Leave this to me.'

Abruptly pressing the 'End' button, he was immediately dialling another number from memory.

'Hugh, it's me,' he announced himself to the pilot of

the Du Cane Plaza Group's corporate jet. 'I've got to get down to New Orleans. Pronto.'

Lorna recognised the cause of her problems. Unwittingly, she'd stumbled into a cover-up. Someone didn't want her near the Lafayette papers because of what they showed. It would be hard to come up with a more damning indictment not only of the Department of Public Safety and Corrections, but especially of the Director who'd taken the decision to use Wilson's black prisoners as human guinea pigs.

Once she found out who that was, she'd know exactly who was orchestrating the hush-up campaign. It might also solve the other riddle that perplexed her. William Gore had retired from the service in 1993 – twenty years after the Lafayette trials had ended. Yet he'd continued to monitor the movement of each and every one of the trial participants. Even after he'd left the service, as his handwritten notes in the margins indicated, he'd still charted their destinies. What Lorna wanted to know was: why?

Her mind had been going round and round in circles as she tried making sense of it all. Like her two other cellmates she'd been slumped on a rough blanket, staring up interminably till she knew every inch of the cell: the graffiti on the wall; the concrete floor, stained and scarred with despair. She sat vacantly watching the four blades of the fan turning round and round in a vent clogged with cobwebs, its bars caked with grime. As for the toilet, even though she needed to urinate, she couldn't bring herself to go near it. She would postpone that horror as long as she possibly could.

She had tried to reason with one of the prison guards

who patrolled regularly. She'd explained her dilemma; begged for help. But he'd ignored her.

Anger had followed desperation. Then, in turn, despair. But even as she lay in strange semi-consciousness, she couldn't stop the questions. There were so many dark concerns from the past few hours. Such as why had her pursuers not put the police light on the top of their car from the beginning? Why had the police outside Gore's cabin told her she could go – or were the local police not a part of the conspiracy? Was there a connection between Gore and Krauss – and also a connection with her own first visit to Louisiana?

She'd been dazed when the cell door had suddenly opened and a guard gestured to her to come out. Handcuffed, she'd been led back up the corridor amid a chorus of catcalls from female prisoners, wolf-whistles from men, and screams of indignation that she was getting preferential treatment because she was white.

Her two guards ignored the clamour, the spitting on the floor, leading her into a small room which had a table, but no chair, and gesturing towards a telephone.

She had already decided whom she'd call. She dialled straight through to Kuesterman's cellphone. Although it felt to her as if it was past midnight, the clock on the wall had said it was just after 9 pm. The phone rang three times before switching over to the answering service. Speaking slowly and clearly, she had outlined her situation. She knew Kuesterman always checked his phone for messages last thing every night before going to bed. He was a creature of habit, and Lorna had no reason to think he would do anything different tonight. And even if he did only get the message in the morning, she supposed there was nothing he, or Zonmark's lawyers, could do overnight.

All the same, she'd felt an anticlimactic weariness as she was returned to her cell. It would have been good to speak to someone, to receive the reassurance she wanted right now. In her heart she had wanted to talk to Jack, to be swept up by his unwavering confidence and told that everything would be all right. But she was only in jail because of Zonmark business. Phoning Kuesterman first was her only real option.

She'd been forced to walk the gauntlet back to her cell, and by the time she was pushed back inside she'd felt emotionally fragile. Sliding down against the wall she crouched with her face pressed to her knees, arms wrapped around her legs, hugging herself.

'Least you got somebody to call,' a voice came from the corner.

The cell lamp had remained on all night, casting a surreal blue-white haze, making it impossible to sleep without using the blanket to block it out. Crouched in the foetal position, her face to the wall, she tugged a corner of the rough fabric over her eyes and tried her best to imagine she was back in her childhood bed in Mannofield, Aberdeen, safe, secure, with nothing to trouble her.

Reality was to prove inescapable, however. Somewhere in the middle of the night, the woman who'd been semi-comatose when she'd arrived woke up from her drug-induced sleep and picked a fight with her other cellmate. Both women had, it seemed, been working the streets to feed their heroin addiction, under the control of their pimp and dealer, Bobby. The hooker who had just woken was accusing the other woman of not warning her about the police – she'd been arrested in possession. The other woman responded bitterly, accusing the first one of hiding her real earnings from Bobby to score drugs from a rival.

The argument went round in circles, loud, vindictive, repetitive. The crass stupidity of it all made Lorna want to scream. But that would only provoke them. And she had no desire to attract their attention. Instead she lay wishing for sleep, while her mind continued its crazy jumble.

She realised she must have passed out at some time, though she had no idea when, because she awoke to the sound of one of her cellmates vomiting. Disorientated, she'd lost all sense of time, but as she blinked up towards the fan vent, she saw that the sky outside was lightening – she reckoned it must be just before dawn.

For a long while she lay, disheartened and unmoving, between sleep and wakefulness. Then the loud crash of a metal trolley outside marked the arrival of breakfast. Up and down the corridor outside, slots in the bottom of cell doors were being opened and trays banged across the concrete. The chorus of angry voices started up again.

Raising her head, Lorna looked over at their tray out of curiosity. Although she hadn't eaten for eighteen hours, and her stomach felt hollow, she didn't think she could ever bring herself to eat in here. Not in the midst of this stench. And definitely not the disgusting swill of brown gruel in each of the three dented enamel bowls that stood on the tray.

The two other women were less particular. Scrambling out from under their blankets, bedraggled and bleary-eyed, they helped themselves to a bowl of porridge and a plastic spoon, and began slurping noisily.

Once again Lorna closed her eyes, trying to block out reality. This would come to an end soon, she told herself.

Kuesterman would have someone over here during the morning, then she'd be out of this god-awful hell-hole.

'Better eat up, honey – it's a long day,' one of the women called out to her. She knew what was implied, and shook her head. Within moments the other two had helped themselves to her bowl.

Before they'd even finished, from outside came the sound of the trolley rattling down the corridor again as guards collected breakfast bowls. They would pause outside each cell demanding the tray be returned with bowls and spoons. Sometimes there'd be an argument, and threats would be made or a cell door opened. Usually there was noisy clatter as trays were shoved across the floor, then stacked on the trolley. One by one the guards progressed up the corridor till they came to their cell.

There was talking outside between the guards, as the breakfast run temporarily ground to a standstill. Then the cell door was being opened and a guard came in and looked over at Lorna. 'Dr Reid?' he asked, gesturing her outside. Her two cellmates were immediately whooping with envy and excitement. '*Dr* Reid,' they were crowing. 'Been a bad girl, have we, *Dr* Reid?' Ignoring them, Lorna again found herself handcuffed and led back along the corridor.

She had no idea what was going on, but tugged along beside one of the guards she felt almost somnambulant, and strangely indifferent to whatever was coming next. She guessed the time was somewhere between six and seven – far too early for Kuesterman to have ordered a lawyer to her rescue.

They passed through several gates, and eventually the guard unlocked the final steel door that led into the office where she'd been charged.

As the door opened she saw him standing there. Instantly, she became aware of how dishevelled and unattractive she must look. Part of her wanted him to be anywhere except here. But she was rushing forwards to hug him – until held back by her handcuffs.

'There's no need for *that*.' Jack Hennessy glowered at the charge officer, pointing to the handcuffs. The latter nodded at the guard to release her. Soon, she was pressed to Jack's shoulder.

'How did you know—?' she began.

'Shh.' He stroked her hair. 'Plenty of time to talk later. Let's get you out of here.'

'But they charged me—'

'They just dropped the charges.'

'What?' She turned to the charge officer.

She was wide awake now. Not only that, but she instantly realised that as far as the police were concerned, the past fifteen hours just hadn't happened.

'That's right, ma'am,' the charge officer was saying. 'The first two charges have been dropped. Charges for the road violations will be mailed to you.'

She looked from him back to Jack in disbelief. He was nodding, with a reassuring smile while, behind him, they had brought out her belongings in a box. Her jewellery, watch, phone, handbag, purse and the other items she'd had to hand over. A ledger was produced in which were detailed her personal items and she was told to sign it. Taking the Biro offered her, she was about to do so when she looked up. 'What about the envelope?' she asked.

'What envelope?' the charge officer wanted to know.

'The one you took out of my hire car.'

'*I* didn't take—'

198

'One of your colleagues did. Plain clothes.'

The other was shrugging. 'Was it signed in with the rest of your things?'

Lorna flashed a glance between the charge officer and Jack. 'You know perfectly well it wasn't.' The anger was rising inside her.

'Then that's not inside my control, ma'am,' he said. 'I can only give back what you signed in.'

'But it's my property!'

'You'll have to take that up with the arresting officer.'

'Who's that?'

He shook his head. 'Can't say. The case officer can tell you.' He was looking at his watch. 'He won't be here for another two hours.'

Lorna fixed her gaze on Jack. 'They took this stuff from my car,' she told him. 'It's really important.'

He nodded. 'I know. Doesn't seem like we can do anything about it right now.'

'Are you saying I should just forget about it?'

'No!' He was vehement. 'Absolutely not! We'll speak to whoever it is when they get in.'

'You mean hang around here for the next two hours?'

'We can phone,' he replied.

'I'm just scared if I sign this, I'll have no way of proving . . .'

'I really don't see you have much choice.'

Her eyes met his, with a questioning gaze, for a very long while. It wasn't that she didn't trust him. She trusted him completely. He was here, wasn't he? He was getting her out. And his judgement in the past had always been faultless. But, this was a big step. What if it was a mistake?

Eventually, she leaned over the ledger and signed it.

Then she was strapping her watch back around her wrist, slipping on the gold rings she wore on the third finger of her right hand, the little finger on her left. Jack already had her handbag, purse, and other items. About-turning, she couldn't get out of the place fast enough.

'I need to get to the nearest hotel,' she told him as he held the police station door open for her.

'My poor darling! You haven't eaten?'

'It's not that.' She shook her head. 'I could really use a clean toilet!'

It was Lorna's first trip on a private jet – a Gulfstream IV-SP that carried every convenience that might be demanded by senior executives of a prestige hotel group, from a luxurious bathroom and wood-panelled bedroom suite, to an onboard *cordon bleu* chef. Not that she was exactly in a receptive frame of mind to make the most of it. Instead, after they'd left New Orleans, and she'd had a chance to shower and change into an onboard terry-towelling dressing gown, she and Jack talked through everything that had happened.

She told him about the discovery of William Gore hanging from an electric flex in his chalet; the envelope she'd received from Val Henderson; the car chase; all the questions that had plagued her mind throughout a semi-wakeful night, especially the biggest question of all: who had given the order to use Wilson State Penitentiary inmates for the Neuropazine trials?

Meanwhile, Jack described how he'd taken a late-night phone call from Spencer Drake. Drake had, minutes earlier, been contacted by Kuesterman after the Zonmark boss had picked up her message on his cellphone. Kuesterman intended getting Zonmark's lawyers on the case first thing next morning, but Jack explained how he'd stood them down. Hennessy family connections in Louisiana were strong, he explained to Lorna now. No sooner had he arranged for Hugh to fly him down in the early hours of the morning, than he was on the phone to one of New Orleans's most prominent lawyers, who had in turn put in a late-night call to the Chief of Police. While Lorna had been driving herself crazy on a filthy mattress of a jail cell, it seemed the phone lines had been burning red hot between Jack's lawyers and the Chief of Police.

They discussed the envelope and how to ensure it was returned to her quickly. If the police had dropped the charges that she had removed evidence from the potential scene of a crime, they couldn't justify holding onto that 'evidence' for a moment longer. Since Jack's lawyer had been dealing with the matter, they'd ask him to ensure the envelope was quickly returned. Jack promised to put through a call to him at the start of the working day.

In the bedroom of the plane, leaning against the bed-head, Lorna reflected on how suddenly things could turn around. Less than two hours earlier she'd been enduring the most degrading conditions of her life. Now, here she was in an executive Gulfstream, jetting back to Washington, DC. And all thanks to Jack.

'You know,' she reached her hand out to him, 'I don't know where I'd be without you.'

Jack took her hand in his with a smile. 'Waiting for Zonmark's lawyer, I guess.'

'It's not just that. You know what I mean.' Leaning over she kissed him. 'Nothing like this has ever happened to me before. The whole car chase and jail thing . . .' She was

201

shaking her head, before fixing her gaze on him. 'It's so reassuring, knowing you're there.'

'My darling,' he stroked the hair back from her face, 'I plan to be here for a long, long time to come.'

'This plane – it must be costing you a fortune.'

Smiling, he cocked his head to one side. 'I'm only doing it for my own, selfish purposes.'

'Oh, yes?' She fixed him with an expression of wry enquiry.

'I couldn't have you festering in some jail cell. Cornelia's big birthday bash on Saturday, remember?'

'Oh! Of course.'

Cornelia had been on the phone to Jack for weeks before, pleading with and cajoling him to help with various arrangements.

'You could always have taken someone else,' she teased. 'I'm sure you have plenty of pretty blonde friends.'

'It's *you* I want on my arm, Dr Reid.' He grinned. 'Does wonders for my ego.'

'Oh, Jack Hennessy, you flatterer!'

Exhausted after her restless night in jail, she managed some sleep on the aeroplane. They flew in to National airport, then Jack dropped her home, before heading to his office in the Du Cane Plaza. He'd made her promise to take things easy. She didn't have to worry about the missing envelope – he'd see to it. After the trauma of the past twenty-four hours, everyone would understand if she took time off from work today.

But sitting around at home had never been an option for Lorna. Quite apart from getting the envelope back, she had that other, equally urgent, enquiry in mind. And she intended getting to it right away. Stopping only long enough to pick up a long black from Starbucks, she went straight to her office at Zonmark, closed the door behind her and logged onto the Net.

She knew exactly where to go once she was logged on. She'd already added the Department of Public Safety and Corrections to her list of 'Favourites'. And once the Department's home page came up, she found her way quickly to the list of current title bearers, and from there to the archives.

She scrolled down the list of Directors, from the present day back to the late sixties. When she got to the correct date and read the name listed against it, she simply didn't believe it. Her first reaction was that this had to be some kind of mistake. She hadn't expected to recognise the name; she certainly would never have guessed it to be that of someone extremely well known. This just didn't seem possible.

She was so disbelieving, she knew she had to double-check. How could she verify his résumé? *Who's Who*, she decided. Armand Kuesterman kept a copy in his office.

Sweeping out of the NP3 building, she'd soon driven across the science park to Zonmark HQ, and made her way through to the executive offices. Beryl, it appeared, was absent from guard duty, and Kuesterman wasn't in, so she made her way directly to the bookshelf in his office. Pulling the volume down onto a table, she quickly flicked through the pages until she found his entry. And, sure enough, the confirmation.

Staring at the name, mind reeling with the full, devastating implications, she caught the scent of perfume before she heard the voice.

'Can I help?' Beryl asked in a decidedly unhelpful tone.

'Yes.' Lorna didn't look up from where she was staring at the book. 'I need a drink.'

The Grayson Wendell problem hadn't gone away for Judith. It had only got worse. Since her call to 'Hatchet' Hulquist there'd been no let-up at all from London. They still demanded a major interview.

With increasing desperation she'd considered her options. She could pretend to be an American reporter, she supposed, and try to get to Wendell that way. But his staff would be sure to check her press accreditation card before any interview, and the game would be up.

She wondered about proposing that the *Daily Sentinel*'s owner, a wealthy Canadian media baron, lean on Wendell's advisors to get them to relent. But that, she decided, would have to be her last resort as it was a virtual admission of defeat.

The only alternative she could see was high-risk. But she didn't have much choice. So, Hulquist reckoned the overseas media were an irrelevance? Then let him suffer the consequences. Drafting a piece on how the 'special relationship' was likely to suffer under a Wendell presidency, she hauled out a long-forgotten remark from Wendell's pregubernatorial days, during which he'd disdained Britain as 'an overpriced theme park with bad weather'. In an interview with a former friend of the candidate with whom he'd travelled round Britain as a teenager, Judith revealed how contemptuous Wendell had been about the parochialism of the people he'd met, his scorn for the country's dilapidated railway system, its twee seaside resorts and absurd class-consciousness. After three weeks in a succession of B & Bs, Wendell had apparently vowed never to return. And bringing the piece bang up to date, Judith highlighted Hulquist's recent trenchant riposte about how 'foreign newspapers don't deliver votes'.

Back home in London, her article appeared on page three of the newspaper, and was automatically syndicated in its weekly international edition, in Canadian newspapers and online. Within a day, the piece had been picked up by US newspaper bureaus and was being replayed in America. The reality of global media was never more apparent as Judith started being interviewed herself on US radio stations. It was all going wonderfully to plan. As a foreign reporter she was considered a waste of time by Wendell's minders. But as a thorn in their side, they'd have to take notice of her. What happened once they did, remained to be seen.

In the meantime, her interest in the Free to Choose lobby group had grown further after her visit to the local shopping mall over the weekend. Touring the boutiques in search of a few new items for her wardrobe, she'd been enjoying the retail therapy when she'd passed by a gleaming new four-wheel-drive being raffled off to raise funds. Behind it was a large and striking black and white photomontage of elderly people being given nursing support. It was a powerful appeal, Judith had thought wryly, simultaneously playing on people's altruism and their cupidity. Despite her cynicism, though, she bought a couple of raffle tickets herself.

Hundreds of others had already done the same thing, judging by the bulging stubs of tickets strewn across the table – but then the shiny new Jeep Cherokee was an enticing incentive. Noting that the draw was less than a month away, Judith had put her tickets in her wallet and continued her tour of the mall without giving the raffle another moment's thought.

It had been only much later when, laden down with boutique bags and contemplating her next MasterCard bill over a latte, she'd taken out her wallet to check on a receipt. Then she'd read the fine print on the raffle tickets – and discovered that she'd just helped raise funds for Free to Choose and that her purchase of the tickets confirmed her support of the organisation's objectives.

There might have been no great significance in that had it not been for the countless media releases she'd received claiming massive increases in support for the organisation. What was actually being supported, she'd suddenly realised, had nothing to do with genetic technology. Instead, it had everything to do with the desirability of a four-wheel-drive. She remembered giving her name and postal address to the girl behind the raffle table, and how people had been queuing up to buy tickets. She marvelled at the duplicity of it all; what a surefire way to recruit 'members' by the thousand! No doubt about it, an investigative visit to the lobby group was well overdue.

Free to Choose offices, in the gleaming Apex Building, were glass-walled and modern. Everything, from the highly polished leaves of the indoor plants to the gleaming fittings and fixtures, conveyed an impression of well-manicured prosperity – unusual for a grass-roots lobby group.

Posing as a new recruit, Judith was given a volunteer application form to fill in at reception. Clearly laid out, with plenty of space for answers, it was more exhaustive than any of the forms she remembered filling in as a student activist at Oxford. She was still working through it when a power-dressed man in his mid-thirties made his way vigorously towards her.

'I'm Eugene Kennedy. Member Supervisor,' he announced himself.

As she stood, he was pummelling her hand forcefully, before handing her a sleek-looking plastic satchel in transparent blue. 'Welcome to Free to Choose!'

'Thank you.' She glanced from his bright expression to the satchel.

'That's our welcome pack,' he told her. 'Leaflets, stickers, buttons, a CD about our crusade.'

'Right.'

'If you'd like copies for distribution, just let us know.'

She nodded. This had to be the best-organised campaign group she'd ever encountered – suspiciously so.

'I had trouble finding you,' she told Eugene.

'Address, you mean?'

'Yeah. Wasn't on any of your material.'

'That's because we discourage drop-ins. Though of course,' he reached out, touching her arm, '*you're* very welcome. If footfall traffic gets too high, it can distract our staff.'

'But, surely, it's a good thing if lots of people sign up?'

'Absolutely.' The other nodded vigorously. 'But there are far more effective methods of volunteer recruitment than passer-by sign-up.'

Like raffling off cars, she thought caustically, taking note of his marketing jargon. Gazing over his shoulder she commented, 'Looks as if you have a big team here. Would you mind giving me a new volunteer's quick tour?'

He hesitated momentarily, before regarding her bright-eyed eagerness. 'Oh, sure. Fine.' He turned, leading her past the reception desk. 'Where did you hear about us?' he asked over his shoulder.

'In the papers, to begin with. Then you seemed to be just everywhere.'

'We're trying.' He nodded soberly.

The first cluster of open-plan offices was dominated by a large map of the United States, with different-coloured flags in most states indicating, Eugene told her, which activities were being held during the next month. This was the strategic planning department, and the closest thing to it that Judith had ever seen was during a visit to the Labour Party's headquarters in Millbank, London.

Next was the graphic design area, where all the Free to Choose publicity material was produced. Half a dozen designers worked at a row of brightly coloured Macs, while others rushed to and from colour photocopiers, or scrutinised transparencies. The buzz was inescapable. This operation was running at full tilt.

Judith and her guide hardly paused before moving past media relations. 'These guys are highly specialised,' Eugene confided as they passed an expanse of desks awash with paperwork, their occupants talking into strap-on headsets as they juggled media releases, research reports, mugs of percolated coffee.

The whistle-stop tour continued to celebrity endorsement. Posters of Hollywood icons and sports stars ran down the sides of the walls. A group of serious, suited men, silvering about the temples, was sitting around a meeting table at which large sums of money were being bandied.

'And, finally, our telemarketing team,' Eugene told her, as they returned in the direction of Reception, past banks of teleworkers sitting at computers as they dealt with calls as efficiently as any employees of a telephone exchange.

'Rotating team of thirty from noon through midnight, working the time zones across the country,' he said.

'Very impressive.'

'All state-of-the-art technology,' he hardly needed to add, 'supported by dedicated staff using best-practice techniques.'

'You mean all these people here,' she gestured, 'they're not just volunteers?'

'Oh, no.' He smiled at the naivety of the idea. 'The core staff have to be trained professionals. It's the only way you can run an operation as big as this.'

'I've been involved in a few campaigns in Britain,' she said. 'They always had the same problem; there was never enough money.'

He nodded. 'We have the financial support of a huge membership base – right now, over five million people nationally. We're building up to a huge March in the Mall in a few weeks' time.'

She raised her eyebrows. 'These five million people. They're all . . . informed supporters?'

'How d'you mean?' He affected puzzlement.

'Last weekend I was out shopping and there was a raffle—'

'Highly effective recruitment method.'

'But a lot of people buying tickets wouldn't have known they were supporting Free to Choose.'

'No shortage of visual imagery,' he countered. 'And it's printed there on the tickets in black and white.'

'*I* know that and *you* know that.' She didn't want to risk arousing his suspicions by pushing this too far. But she couldn't resist another try. 'But do all the five million people even know they're members of Free to Choose?'

He regarded her carefully for a long while, before putting a benedictory hand on her shoulder. 'You're obviously a highly intelligent person, Judith,' he told her, 'and of course you're right that lots of people on our books aren't what you'd call "committed". But when you're trying to get noticed by the media and on Capitol Hill, only one thing counts.' He nodded emphatically. 'It's all about numbers.'

She was back at her office later that same day when the call came through for her. It was Grayson Wendell's spin-doctor himself, William Barbett. 'We're very concerned about the statements you've been putting out about foreign policy—' he began.

'You should be.'

'You have no evidence,' he boomed, 'for all these allegations about our candidate, except hearsay.'

'I spoke directly to Hulquist.' She was defiant. 'He left me in no doubt as to the importance of foreign affairs—'

'He's denying he ever said anything of the kind.'

'I bet he does.' Judith grimaced. Evidently, she'd been the subject of discussion.

'Well, we won't tolerate mud-slinging.'

'I hope that's not a threat.'

'I'm warning you, there'll be serious consequences—'

'Before you go any further, I should explain that all telephone calls to this office are recorded. Including my talk with Mr Hulquist. I'd be happy to give you a copy of our conversation.'

The effect was instant.

'Well,' Barbett was suddenly emollient, 'I can only say that Mr Hulquist must have misstated himself.'

'He what?' Of all the weasel-word self-justifications she'd ever heard, this one had to take the cake.

'That being the case,' he continued, 'I can only apologise.'

Judith had counted on precisely this reversal. And once presented with it, she needed no further urging. 'Are you saying that Governor Wendell is prepared to speak to the UK press?'

'Of course he is.'

'Good. When can I see him?'

'The Governor's on an extremely tight schedule.'

'Sounds to me like I'm being turned down again.' Her voice was sing-song.

'You're not being turned down.' He was emphatic. 'I promise you, you'll get your chance to speak to him.'

'When, exactly?'

'I'll be in touch during the next few days.'

'That's what your deputy kept telling me. And I never heard back.'

'You will this time.' He was wry.

'Is that a promise?'

'Of course it is.' He paused. 'You've got it on tape.'

12

It was shortly after 8 pm when Lorna stepped into the lobby of the Du Cane Plaza Hotel. As she made her way towards the Cliveden Room, heads turned to admire her striking features, her Valentino gown, her flawless skin. Few noticed the hotel security guard following, a few steps behind. She'd asked Jack for special protection at the event. After her discovery of the day before, she'd never felt more threatened.

For Jack's sake, she tried to contain her feelings. She knew his mother's sixty-fifth birthday party was a big night for him too, and she didn't want to spoil it for him. Vulnerable though she was, she'd decided against telling him the identity of the former Director of Public Safety and Corrections until after the party. Tomorrow, she reckoned, was soon enough.

In the meantime, she'd tried to block the fear from her mind, brought about by the deaths of Krauss and Gore under highly suspicious circumstances; the knowledge that she now also knew the secret that the erstwhile Director was determined to bury.

Instead, she'd spent the past two hours getting ready for this evening in Jack's penthouse suite. Before leaving her alone upstairs, Jack had produced a jewellery box from the suite safe. It contained the most magnificent emerald necklace Lorna had ever seen – part of his grandmother's collection, he'd told her. His mother had agreed to let him give it to her, and hoped she might wear it tonight.

It was the most extravagant gift she'd ever received. Flushed with appreciation, and fully understanding its significance, she'd tried it on immediately, studying her reflection in the mirror, the bedazzling arc of green light about her neck.

'Oh, Jack,' she'd turned to kiss him, 'I don't know what I've done to deserve you!'

A moment of tenderness had passed between them, and as she'd held onto him her gratitude had been all the more intense in the knowledge of all that she faced in her world away from him.

Now, arriving at the Cliveden Room, she caught sight of him standing at the entrance. She reached up, self-consciously touching her necklace.

'It's so beautiful.'

'Only because of who's wearing it.' He embraced her, their mouths opening briefly as they kissed.

'And you're very dashing,' she complimented him. 'First time I've seen you in a tux.'

'Oh. There'll be many more, don't you worry.' He was taking her hand and leading her into the room. 'I can't wait for you to meet Cornelia.'

The Cliveden was decorated in lavish style. Large round dinner tables were bedecked with starched white tablecloths, gold cutlery and crystal, and in the corner a string

213

quartet cut crisply through a Handel Concerto Grossi. Waiters in elegant Du Cane Plaza livery, bearing trays of champagne and cocktails, circulated among the guests, while towering vases containing lavish floral bouquets glistened, vivid and exotic beneath the chandeliers.

Lorna instantly recognised the elegant figure in the distance, from the photographs she'd seen in Jack's home. As they drew closer, she observed how Cornelia Hennessy was, every inch of her, the society matron. Tall, stately, her youthful glory had transformed with age into a poise at once graceful and imperious that conveyed her status as doyenne of New York's *haut monde*. She retained a svelte figure and her hair was big and blonde, the jewels at her ears unmistakably expensive.

The first thing that Lorna noticed about Cornelia's features as they approached her were her clear blue eyes – they didn't miss a thing.

'How lovely to meet you.' Even to Lorna's ear, there was more than a trace of Southern colour to her voice.

'Mrs Hennessy.' She smiled.

Cornelia grasped Lorna's hand between the bejewelled fingers of her own, while her left hand remained poised, mid-air, holding her trademark cocktail sobranie. The two women stood, taking one another in. Cornelia had evidently been a great beauty in her day. And while her youthful bloom had faded, she looked nothing like sixty-five years of age – a fact that Lorna wasn't slow to remark on.

'Are you sure this isn't your fiftieth?' she said, smiling.

Cornelia flashed a droll glance at her son. 'We like her already.'

Still holding Lorna's hand she led the younger woman

away from the group she'd been with, leaving Jack to take her place. 'I've been looking forward to this moment so very much,' she told Lorna.

'Me too.' Lorna felt uncharacteristically subdued – but was quite happy to be dominated by Cornelia. This was Jack's mother, after all.

'Very, *very* much,' the older woman repeated. Then, reaching out to the stones around Lorna's neck, 'They *do* suit.'

'Yes, thank you, Mrs Hennessy—'

'Cornelia, please.'

'I'm so grateful to you for letting Jack give them to me. I know how much they must mean to you.'

They exchanged significant smiles, Cornelia holding her gaze for a long while, before saying eventually, 'I really am fascinated by your work.'

It was the last thing Lorna had expected. Questions about her family, perhaps, or personal life. But maybe Cornelia was merely trying to put her at ease.

'What aspect in particular?' she asked.

'The effectiveness of NP3.' That clear blue gaze was penetrating.

Was this more than just polite interest? A personal involvement seemed implied in the question. Perhaps Jack had told his mother about her work. Was Cornelia considering the potential benefits for herself?

'It's still very early days.' Lorna used her standard phrase for dealing with overexcited enquirers. 'We've still to finalise our panel before testing—'

'I thought you'd been testing for some time?' Cornelia took a sip of her Bombay Sapphire gin and tonic.

'That's right.' Lorna nodded. 'But for tests to be valid,

they have to be repeated on a large sample over a long time.'

'Quite so.' Cornelia appeared to think of this as a technicality. 'What about your results so far?'

'They've been extremely good,' admitted Lorna.

'How much longer are your people living?'

Lorna began to feel somewhat uncomfortable standing before this grand inquisitor. 'What we measure,' she tried to explain, 'is the rate of ageing, rather than longevity. But from that rate, we can impute life span.'

Another burst of guests flowed into the room through the door at the other side. Glancing over at them, attention momentarily distracted, Lorna felt a hand on her shoulder.

'Don't mind about them,' Cornelia instructed. 'Please. Carry on.'

'Well, the rate of ageing has come down quite a bit. We reckon we've slowed it down by about thirty per cent in patients who've been on NP3 for three years or more.'

'So its effect is . . .?'

'Cumulative.' She nodded.

Then as Jack's mother absorbed this, drawing on her purple sobranie, she explained.

'Very simply, our life spans are genetically determined. Each of us has what you might call an expiry date written into our DNA. All I'm trying to do is push that date back. But it's still,' she felt obliged to emphasise, 'very early days.' The last thing she wanted was to have Cornelia ask her for her own personal supply.

She felt Cornelia's eyes upon her. 'Don't worry.' Her gaze was intuitive. 'I'm not going to grill you all evening.'

Lorna nodded a relieved smile.

216

'But you must come to visit so we can talk about this more.'

'I'd love to.'

After reaching out and squeezing her hand in what Lorna took as a mark of approval, Cornelia sashayed across the room, to meet her newly arrived guests. Released from her presence, Lorna felt unexpectedly relieved, as though emerging from an interview with the Headmistress. Cornelia Hennessy was a powerful presence, no doubting it. She could quite see how Jack had come by his unwavering self-assurance. Growing up as a boy, it would have been sink or swim.

The people attending tonight came from a wide variety of backgrounds, she discovered, as she was guided round the room by Jack, who knew them all. Many were familiar faces, several were instantly recognisable. Telling Jack not to worry about her, but to help his mother instead – not, she supposed, that help was required by the eminently capable Cornelia – Lorna found herself in a group with Hilton Gallo, Chief Executive of Hollywood agency GCM, and the famous gossip columnist Inky Mostyn, bow-tied and as dapper as he appeared in the glossy pages of *Vanity Fair*. The world's most syndicated gossip columnist, Inky was here to set Cornelia's sixty-fifth in purple prose for the benefit of his global audience.

From time to time, Lorna would be distracted by a fresh arrival at the door. There was one man in particular whose presence she found curiously disconcerting. Tall, imposing, with an air of well-fed opulence, he had a touch of the dandy about him, in his magnificent brocade cummerbund. She probably wouldn't have given him a second glance – except that he noticed her. It wasn't just the

217

momentary hesitance as she caught his eye – a fact of life she had become used to since her frequent appearances in various newspapers. Nor did she think it was the interest of an older man of a certain kind in a much younger woman. It was a different look from that; it seemed almost carnivorous.

Having stepped into the Cliveden, the man paused for a moment, surveying the room. Then, to her further surprise, Lorna saw Jack break away from the group he'd been with and stride over to greet the newcomer. She observed him shake the man's hand, then briefly put his arm round his shoulders. She'd seen that gesture before, when Jack had been dealing with the manager of the Washington Du Cane Plaza. It was, she had supposed, Jack's way of asserting himself among subordinates, to create a feeling of camaraderie. But even as Jack talked to the other man, the newcomer continued looking over at her with undisguised curiosity.

Although distracted, she tried to concentrate on Inky Mostyn's account of the flamboyant lives of Scotland's Highland aristocracy. But only moments later she felt her arm being squeezed – and turned to find Jack standing beside her. Next to him, his hand already outsttretched towards hers, was the new arrival.

'There's someone I want you to meet.' Jack was smiling.

The other man was already shaking her hand as their eyes met. Though his mouth formed a smile, the expression in his eyes was one of detached enquiry, thought Lorna. He seemed to be summing her up.

'This is Julius Lupine,' continued Jack. 'Julius, the light of my life, Dr Lorna Reid.'

'Delighted.' Lupine nodded.

Glancing at Jack, Lorna tried a smile. 'How do you know Cornelia?' she asked.

Lupine looked over at Jack, as though for direction. 'We go way back,' he said, nodding. 'I guess you could say—'

'Friend of the family,' interjected Jack.

'Oh, really?'

'Yes,' the other concurred. 'Years and years.'

An awkward pause followed as they held each other's eyes. What was it about this man, thought Lorna, that made her blood run cold?

Fortunately, Jack was being summoned by his mother. Lorna was relieved when a short while later, he led Lupine away to meet an aunt of his who'd flown in for the big night from Palm Beach.

Mixing and mingling continued before the assembled guests were called to their tables. Seated next to Jack, she found herself at the head table, just a few seats away from Cornelia herself. It was a gathering that was as much about being seen as anything else, and as an outsider Lorna was amused by the posturing and attention-seeking of her fellow guests. She felt Jack squeezing her hand under the table as he watched her taking it all in, and knew that he shared her amusement too.

After hors-d'oeuvres of blinis and crabcakes came the toasts. Jack stood to deliver a brief speech, embroidered with entertaining anecdotes about his mother, before proposing her health. Other close friends followed suit, reflecting on her roles as a hotelier, socialite, confidante and friend. Then, amid much ceremony, main courses were brought on under silver cloches – baked Atlantic salmon and marinated veal. As the Chablis and Cabernet flowed freely and the conversation level increased, there were gales of laughter from around the room as everyone relaxed into the festivities.

In the corner, the string quartet had been joined by a pianist and drummer; there followed a swift transition from baroque to Bill Haley and other fifties music, reflecting the era of Cornelia's social début. Dessert was followed by dancing, with the band augmented once again – this time by electric instruments and a brass section – and floor-to-ceiling dividing walls pushed back to reveal a ballroom beyond. No sooner had the band struck up 'New York, New York' than Jack was gesturing in the direction of the dance floor.

'What about your mother?' asked Lorna.

But Cornelia Hennessy was already being escorted to the dance floor by a distinguished Wall Street financier.

They moved and circled about the floor, other couples quickly joining. It wasn't ballroom, but Lorna realised it was the first time she and Jack had danced together. With one hand at her waist, his other steady and guiding, Jack was firmly in control.

'Oh, Jack,' she met his eyes with ironic appreciation, 'so masterful!'

'Isn't that what every woman wants,' he responded with a provocative grin, 'the man to take the lead?'

'I don't know about that,' she replied. 'Some men do, though.' She was looking over at where Lupine was dancing with the daughter of one of Cornelia's friends, a dazzling young blonde in her early twenties.

'You don't like him, do you?'

'That obvious, huh?' She met his eyes. 'There's just something very . . . predatory about him.'

'Oh, he's all right. Known him for years. He's a business friend of the family's.'

'Not married?'

'Oh, yes. Yes, he is.' Then by way of explanation, 'Mrs Lupine isn't what you'd call a social butterfly. This sort of evening – it's not her scene.'

'Doesn't your mother think it rude?'

He shrugged. 'Don't think it bothers her, really.'

It was a different world from the one she'd been brought up in, that was for sure, thought Lorna. Back in Aberdeen, that kind of thing was unheard of. Her own father would never have dreamed of going out to a black-tie dinner without her mother. And if her mother had had reservations about accepting, he would have stayed at home.

The dancing continued with a change of partners, Lorna finding herself opposite Hollywood *über*-agent Hilton Gallo who, she was amused to see, despite a client list star-studded with rock icons, had no sense of rhythm. His tall, ascetic frame moved uneasily to the music.

When the tempo slowed and the lights dimmed, she returned to Jack. They held each other in the midst of other moving couples, dancing among the celebrity faces: Hollywood stars cheek to cheek with fashion designers; business tycoons and their immaculately upholstered wives. 'Sometimes, life just feels like a dream.' Lorna nuzzled into his neck, trying not to think of the world outside this room.

'Good dream, I hope?' he murmured.

'It is now.'

'Good.' He guided her around the floor. 'For me too. The envy of every man in this room.'

She smiled, still unused to being complimented in this way. None of her partners in the past had had Jack's romantic extravagance. If they'd come out with a line like that, it would have been quickly followed by some deprecating witticism. But Jack was different.

'You're very romantic,' she told him tenderly, holding him closer. Then, sensing his arousal, 'You don't have . . . some ulterior motive, do you?'

He chuckled. 'Even if I did, it wouldn't make it less true.'

She felt his hands descending her back and closed her eyes with an involuntary shiver. 'Don't start anything you don't mean to finish,' she murmured as their bodies moved together.

'Oh, I mean to finish it,' he whispered. 'I always do.'

She awoke to the grey light of an overcast Sunday morning filtering between the curtains of their bedroom suite. Blinking her eyes open for a moment, she registered where she was before closing them again. Jack was already up – she could hear him in the shower next door. Remembering their lovemaking of the night before, she smiled. It had been their best ever.

Jack had always been a more than satisfying lover. And perhaps it was her own response this time; perhaps it had taken her a while to completely relax and be uninhibited with a man. Whatever the reason, she'd never experienced such utter abandonment, such blissful release, as she had the night before.

She reached out for her watch, tucked under the pillow, and opened her eyes to check the time. It was just after nine. What an indulgence to be in bed so late, she thought dreamily. Cornelia's party hadn't finished until around two. And she and Jack had gone to sleep quite some time later.

After a few minutes, Lorna propped herself up in bed,

looking around the room, and eventually got up, slipping into one of the silk dressing gowns laid out for them. Hair mussed, and still only half awake, she made her way over to the window, where she brushed aside the curtain and looked down at the street, forty floors below. Up here on the penthouse level, behind double-glazed windows, it was a still and silent Sunday morning. But out there, it was already a busy New York weekend. Yawning, she stared down at the scene as though at a movie. So much of her life, in recent weeks, had taken on this dimension of unreality. Only a short while before she'd never have guessed she'd be dating a billionaire philanthropist; making herself at home in a penthouse suite; under threat from one of the most famous men in America.

She wandered through the suite, the deep-pile carpet sinking beneath her naked feet. The trip to New York, and last night in particular, had come as a much-needed relief; respite from all the pressures of Washington. But she'd known she couldn't escape from reality for very long, and in particular she had to face up to a situation which nothing in her scientific training had prepared her for.

She found a small kitchen off the private dining room, filled a kettle with water and switched it on. Locating fresh milk in the well-stocked fridge, as well as Twinings Lady Grey tea bags, she was taking two mugs out of a cupboard when Jack appeared in the doorway. Freshly showered, and in his royal blue bathrobe, he was every bit as desirable as he'd been the night before, his dark hair wet and tousled and a broad smile on his face.

'Sleep well?' he asked as they embraced.

'That was the best insomnia treatment ever!' she told him as he picked her up, squeezing her tightly.

223

'Delighted to be of service!' He chuckled. Then, looking over at the kitchen bench, 'What's that?'

'Morning tea.'

He was shaking his head. 'You're so English!'

'I've warned you before—'

'Sorry,' he corrected himself hastily. 'Scottish. You're so Scottish.'

'That's better.' She pulled away from him.

'You could have ordered from downstairs,' he told her.

'I know. I didn't want to have to see anyone. I just want it to be us.' As their eyes met, her expression turned serious. 'There's something I've got to speak to you about, but I wanted to wait until after the party.'

'What is it?' His expression was changing.

'I can hardly believe it myself—'

'This is to do with New Orleans?'

She nodded. 'Remember I told you about how William Gore used Wilson prisoners?'

'Yeah.' He nodded. 'If it's the return of the envelope that's worrying you—'

'No. It's not that – though I do have to get it back pretty quick.' She was determined. 'The point is, Gore was *ordered* to use the prisoners. It wasn't some idea he came up with on his own. This wasn't a low-level deal between Wilson and Lafayette State University. A hundred and fifty prisoners were involved.'

Folding her arms, she was pacing up and down the small kitchen. 'So, Gore gets this command to make prisoners available for the trials. He objects. But he's ordered to buckle down.'

'How d'you know this?' Jack followed her with a sharp-eyed intensity.

224

'One of the documents in the envelope. It's the transcript of a phone call between Gore and some guy in the Department of Public Safety and Corrections. This guy told Gore if he didn't shut up, his career was over.' She met his gaze with a significant expression. 'Deciding to use Wilson prisoners wasn't some arbitrary order out of the department bureaucracy. It came from the very top.'

'When you say the top—'

'The Director.'

'You didn't tell me this before.' Jack's expression was perturbed.

'That's because I didn't have any idea how important it was. I thought the Director was probably some small-town official no one had ever heard of.' She was shaking her head, her disbelief still evident, as she continued, 'On Friday I got onto the Department archives – they're on the Net, anyone can go through them. I checked out the list of past departmental directors.'

Jack raised a hand to his lowered face and was pinching the bridge of his nose in a gesture that made her pause for a moment before continuing.

'The Department Director in 1968 was Grayson Wendell.'

When Jack finally looked back up at her, there was an unexpected heat in his eyes. 'I had no idea you'd gone so far.' He seemed to be rebuking her.

'What d'you mean?' She was taken aback. His reaction couldn't have been more different from what she'd expected. 'I haven't gone anywhere yet. I've only done the fact-finding—'

'If I'd known this had anything to do with Wendell—'

'I didn't know myself until Friday!'

But he wasn't listening to her. Instead, he stood staring

at her, seeming to get angrier and angrier. 'Christ, Lorna! Have you any idea what you're getting into?'

She regarded him, aghast. In the two months she'd known him, she'd never seen him come anywhere near losing his temper. She'd come to believe he wasn't capable of it. But there was no doubting, he was furious. Worst of all – he seemed to be holding her responsible!

'I'm not "getting into" anything!' she retorted, her own voice rising.

'You'd better not be.' He was sternly shaking his head. 'You'll have to walk away from this.'

'From what exactly?' She suddenly resented him telling her what to do.

'From anything to do with Grayson Wendell.'

'I don't give a damn about Grayson Wendell. Or the Democrat Party. Or American politics. I just want to get on with my job.'

Glowering, Jack was adamant. 'Well, you'll have to drop the Lafayette trials—'

'I've no intention of doing that!' she snapped back.

He regarded her, flabbergasted.

'The fact that all the patients were black has huge implications for NP3. You surely don't expect me to ignore that?'

'You have no proof they were black.'

'I will when I get my envelope back.'

'But you're not getting it back,' he roared.

'That's not what you told me a minute ago.'

'That was before I knew Wendell was behind this.' He was furious. 'Can't you see what's going on? What do you think happened to Krauss? To Gore? It's a cover-up. If you know what's good for you, you'll get right away from this as fast as you can.'

'Why do you think I asked you for some security?' she barked. 'And I can't believe you're standing there, ordering me about.'

'It's for your own good.'

'Isn't it always.' She stepped away from him and stood staring, unseeing, out of the window.

Quite apart from her bitterness, she was also in a state of shock. This was the first time they'd argued. And it concerned what mattered to her more than anything else. She was fighting for composure, and when she turned back to face him, she spoke in a calmer voice. 'You of all people advising me to give up?'

'Only because I know what'll happen if you don't.' He was uncompromising. 'For all I know, it might already be too late.'

'I don't care if it is.' She resented his obduracy. 'I've come this far. I'm not about to throw it all in now.' Eyes blazing, she strode over to where he was standing in the kitchen doorway, face dark with disapproval. 'Will you get out of my way, please?'

He stepped aside to let her pass. Then, as though realising how badly he'd miscalculated, for the first time he spoke in a conciliatory tone as she stormed back to the bedroom. 'What about the tea?'

'You can do what you like. I'm not having any!' Slamming the bedroom door shut behind her, she marched to the cupboard, pulled out her overnight bag and hurled it on the bed. Grabbing her clothes out of the cupboard, she threw them in a pile beside it.

Ten minutes later there was no sign that she'd ever been there – except for the emerald necklace, glittering on the bedside table.

13

All day volatility on the South East Asia markets had kept Andrew glued to his desk. In particular, two of the four financial institutions into which Bob Bowler had so precipitously switched nine per cent of his fund had risen on the back of fresh rumours. In both cases, the rise had exceeded the bid-offer difference, meaning that both shares could be off-loaded without losing money. The question was, could they rise further, or was it time to bail out?

He'd consulted with colleagues in New York the moment they'd got into work, and it had become clear that the latest increases were the result of pure speculation. No fresh announcements had been signalled, to generate a price hike. It was a scenario Andrew had seen countless times before. Prices would rocket on the basis of a late-night drinking session. When, after seventy-two hours, nothing new had materialised, they'd slump right down again – frequently to a lower level than before the rise. Now was an ideal opportunity to climb away from Bowler's rash decision, unscathed.

Calling in Bowler, he told him to sell both companies. They'd make no money – but nor would they lose it. They'd reduce their financial services exposure to four and a half, instead of nine per cent. The North America Fund would regain its former balance after the aberration of the past seven days.

Bowler was surly and argumentative. Both companies had a long way to go before the bull run was over, he complained. The rewards of staying in the game could be dazzling. But Andrew made it clear he was not for turning: Bowler must close their positions immediately. After a short, bitter meeting, Bowler left his office, face dark with anger. His deputy had become a liability. Another problem he'd have to fix, Andrew realised, taking a large brown envelope out of his briefcase and making his way downstairs to Marketing.

Late the week before, despite *The Globe* fiasco, he'd managed to get the Weybridge Rowing Club video to Jenny Watson, who ran Glencoe's audio-visual department. Enlisting her services, he'd asked her to produce photograph enlargements of the two men climbing into the Volvo.

This she'd done with brisk efficiency. But despite poring over the resulting photographs, he was no further on than when he'd watched the video, unable to find any clue, not one identifying characteristic of either the car or the men, except for the red 'V' on the back of one jacket collar, and a golf umbrella lying in the rear window of the car. But how far could he get with that?

Returning to Jenny, more in desperation than hope, he wondered if she had any further suggestions. Jenny was sympathetic. She wanted to help, but couldn't conjure up something out of thin air. There was no more to be done to

229

enhance the detail of the photographs. But she did wonder if it was worth his talking to her colleague, Patti, who was in charge of marketing procurement; if there was anyone who knew about golf umbrellas, it was Patti.

As Jenny led Andrew over to where Patti was standing by the fax machine, his expectations hardly improved. With hair dyed bright scarlet, and wearing an orange and green tartan skirt, Patti was tapping her Doc Martens in time to some bubblegum music on Capital Radio. As Jenny introduced them, he caught the glint of something silver in her tongue.

'Let's have a look, then.' Patti soon seized the envelope from his hand, after Jenny explained the problem and left the two of them together. She went over to her desk, pulled the photos out of the envelope, picked up a magnifying glass and looked, one-eyed, at the first, a grainy enlargement showing the back of the car with the umbrella resting on the back shelf.

'Oh, yeah. You want some umbrellas like that, then?' she asked, breezily.

Andrew hadn't explained why he wanted to identify the umbrella, only that he did. 'It's more that I'd like to know if there's any way to find out where that umbrella came from. I know it's a long shot.'

But Patti was shaking her head. 'I can easily find *that* out.'

'Find what out, exactly?' He felt they must be talking at cross purposes.

'Supplier's name. That's what you want, isn't it?'

'Yes.' He was momentarily distracted by her bright green eyes – were they coloured contacts? 'But don't all golf umbrellas look the same?'

' 'Course they do. But Canadian Mutual just go to one supplier.'

'Canadian Mutual?'

'That's who it is, isn't it?' She was looking at the photograph again with her magnifier. 'The logo, I mean.'

'Are you sure?' Astounded, he bent over her desk, borrowing the glass for a moment and staring at the mostly concealed logo on the umbrella. It hadn't meant anything to him the night before. But, staring at it now, he wondered if it just might be as she said.

'I'd recognise it anywhere.' Patti glanced back at the photo, casually. 'It was me who had to scan it onto all our stationery for the roadshows last year.'

Andrew looked up at her, momentarily transfixed. She had no idea about the significance of her revelation. Until a moment ago he'd thought he'd reached the end of the road. There hadn't seemed anything more he could do. But what if the logo *was* Canadian Mutual?

He realised Patti was frowning at him strangely. 'Sorry.' He shook himself from his thoughts. 'I was just thinking . . .'

'You want me to find out who supplies the umbrellas, right?' she confirmed.

'How would you do that?'

'Remember Kelly – used to work here? Short blonde hair? Anyway, she and me is mates and she's got a job at Canadian Mutual. Just down Holborn.' She was already opening a Filofax and scanning down its index.

'Can you find out how many they had made?'

'Sure.'

'When they made them. And what for – was it some hospitality thing?'

231

'Yeah, yeah. Kelly'll dig it all out.' Having found what she was looking for, she began dialling, before reaching over to a small radio to turn up 'Bachelor Girl'. 'Don't worry, love.' She turned to dismiss him. 'I'll phone upstairs soon as I have something.'

He'd barely got back to his office when his phone rang.

'Canadian Mutual made them for a golf day last September,' Patti told him. 'Corporate hospitality. They ordered three hundred. Economies of scale. But two hundred are in storage. That's exact, right? Kelly counted them herself. The name of the manufacturer . . .' She went on to give him the manufacturer's details, in which he affected an interest.

Putting down the phone a few minutes later, he leaned back in his chair for a moment and stared out through the glass wall to where the North America Fund office was a hive of activity. Patti's sharp eye had given him the most unexpected breakthrough. But it also presented him with a dilemma.

The reason she'd recognised the Canadian Mutual logo was because she'd used it so many times before. And that, in turn, was because Canadian Mutual and Glencoe Asset Management had a business relationship that went back years. It was a reciprocal deal by which Canadian Mutual managed Glencoe's Pacific Ventures Fund, while Glencoe looked after Canadian Mutual's European Fund. The two companies had operated the informal partnership for as long as Andrew had worked at Glencoe. He'd met John Barlow, Canadian Mutual's London director, frequently in the past. They had a smooth, professional relationship. The question was, should he be phoning Barlow to ask about a corporate hospitality event, completely outside his area of professional interest, for motivations that were purely personal? He had every right to ask him about anything to do with Pacific Ventures, or seek advice on his own North America Fund. But talking to him about golf umbrellas was altogether different.

He wouldn't have been so self-conscious about it if it hadn't been for the Boardroom session with Sir Stuart and the other directors. There'd been no doubting the consequences for him if there was any further evidence that his mind wasn't on the job. Sure, he could pick up the phone to John Barlow. But what if word of their conversation got back to the all-knowing Sir Stuart? What if Barlow mentioned, even in passing, that he'd received a strange call from Andrew Norton asking about golf umbrellas? It might not be enough to tip him out of his job. But with everything else that was going on, could he afford to risk it?

He got up from his desk, moved over to the glass wall of his office, and turned round the blinds, to give himself some privacy. Standing looking across at the row of certificates on his wall awarded to Glencoe's North America Fund, he wondered how much he'd be compromising himself. How much harm could really come of it? Of course, it had been made clear that he was being closely watched, but he could make his call an innocuous enquiry. Or was he just rationalising his own wishes?

What really made up his mind was the idea of not calling Barlow. If he didn't follow this lead, where else did he have to go? Maybe something would still emerge from his local leafleting. Maybe the Weybridge Police would stumble on some unexpected evidence. But he couldn't count on it. If he didn't pursue this one, he knew he'd always ask himself, what would have happened if he had?

At the other end of the line, some minutes later, John Barlow greeted him cordially.

'I guess I'm calling about a personal matter,' Andrew began. He'd worked out how to run with this. His line of attack. How much he'd reveal if he had to. But he'd try keeping things light. 'Your golf day last year . . .'

'Basil told you about it, did he?' Barlow chuckled.

Andrew quickly made the connection. Basil Johnson was an avid weekend golfer. He'd evidently attended the Canadian Mutual day on Glencoe's behalf. 'I believe it was a great success?' he risked.

'Yes. Very good. And I suppose you want to come along this year?'

'Well, it's not so much that—'

'Of course you must. Didn't realise you were a golfer. We're planning to expand, seeing it went off so well last year.'

'Actually, I was thinking about doing something for Glencoe. Smaller scale.'

'Uh-huh.'

'Only, I'm new to this. Could you tell me who organised the CM day?'

'I did.'

'Right.' He grimaced. 'And would you have any advice?'

Barlow was soon talking about club memberships and group concessions. Evidently a keen golfer himself, he spoke about timing, numbers, catering – all that was required for a well-run corporate event. Everything, except what really interested Andrew. 'I believe,' he asked, when Barlow paused for breath, 'you gave out some very nice umbrellas?'

'Yes. People seemed to appreciate those. Good quality. Still see quite a few of them around the office.'

234

'You gave out, what, about a hundred of them?'

'About sixty to guests. The other forty were CM people.'

'Drawing up the guest list could be tricky?'

'I just sent a memo round our senior staff asking for suggestions. Good balance of staff and guests.'

'Mm.' Andrew appeared to be absorbing this before saying, 'I don't suppose you'd let me have a copy of your guest list, would you? Just to spark some ideas.'

'Don't see why not.' The other was unconcerned. 'We had a guest list available on the day. I'll have my secretary e-mail a copy over.'

'That would be wonderful.' He tried not to sound too relieved.

'I don't care what you say,' Barlow's tone was mischievous, 'I'll bet Basil's behind this.'

Andrew tried to sound light-hearted. 'No. Really. But if it comes off, I'll make sure you're invited.'

Half an hour later, the Canadian Mutual golf day guest list arrived as an e-mail attachment. Andrew quickly sent it to print. It was three pages long, with names arranged in groups of four, experienced golfers teeing off first. About half of those listed were asterisked, signalling that they were employees of Canadian Mutual. The others had company names listed next to them, and it was these that Andrew scrutinised.

Eyes narrowed in pure concentration, one by one he checked off each company name. There were financial institutions like the Royal Bank of Canada, Bank of Scotland and ANZ, independent financial advisors, private banks and accountancies. And there were other suppliers too – IT consultants, back-office providers, change management advisors. But as he went through the list the first time, one firm immediately caught his eye, even though he'd never heard of it. The words alone sent off signals. Picking up his red pen he drew a circle around the name 'Executive Protection'.

Armand Kuesterman and Spencer Drake listened with growing astonishment as Lorna told them about her visit to Merrywood, the discovery of William Gore's body, her scanning through the contents of the envelope he'd left for her, and the car chase culminating in her arrest and imprisonment. It was her first opportunity to debrief the two men, and in contrast to many of her previous visits to Kuesterman's office, there was no conflict today, no recriminations as they discussed what she'd been through. On the contrary, both Kuesterman and the ever-silent Drake, resplendent in his purple shirt, matching tie and dark suit, regarded her like the survivor of some appalling accident. In particular, the heavy-handed treatment she'd been meted out in New Orleans was a source of very evident outrage.

She told them all she'd absorbed in her car outside Merrywood, starting with the memorandum from the Department of Public Safety and Corrections, ordering Gore to use Wilson prisoners for the Lafayette trial. The whole sample, she reported to her two astonished colleagues, had comprised normal, healthy prisoners. And as Gore's memo had confirmed, all the prisoners were black.

It was the card she'd kept up her sleeve since returning from New Orleans, and she relished playing it now. 'You know what that means, of course?' She looked from one to the other. Then, as they urged her to explain, she lectured on how the shorter life expectancy of a black, compared to a multicultural American sample, meant that her Lafayette-based calculations had been significant under-estimates. NP3 extended the human lifespan even more than she had first thought. She had still to recalculate, but she was thinking forty to fifty years.

Drake was excitedly taking notes. Even Kuesterman had abandoned his customary slumped posture and was leaning forward in his chair. As they listened with total concen-tration, she told them how Gore had left her the entire list of prisoners' names, and how he had continued to track the progress of both Livingstone and Moffat, even after he'd left the prison service.

But she kept the ultimate revelation for last. Explaining about the conversation transcript, and how Gore's order had come 'from the top', she told the two men how she'd researched the name of the departmental director at the time of the Lafayette trials. And how she'd identified him as Grayson Wendell.

Kuesterman was unable to contain himself. He burst out of his chair and was striding about the office, his portly form tugging the shirt untidily out of his trousers.

'This is . . . incredible!' he exclaimed. Then, in the next instant, 'We've got to get the envelope back!'

'Tell me about it!'

Eyes glinting with excitement, Drake wanted to know, 'Where are we with that?'

'We left it for Jack's lawyer to handle,' she explained. 'He did a great job getting the police to drop charges and me out of jail. But I want to get control back.' Without going into the details of their weekend row, she explained how Jack had been scared off by the Wendell connection.

Kuesterman's reaction was explosive. 'That's ridiculous,' he burst out. 'No man is above the law!'

'Spectacular publicity,' was Drake's all-too-predictable response.

'Whatever Jack's reasons,' Kuesterman continued energetically, 'the best form of defence is to get this out in the open.'

'I agree.'

'And to do that we've—'

'—got to get the envelope,' they chimed.

'I'm telling you,' Kuesterman pointed a stubby index finger, 'I'm going to get the best goddam law firm in the South on this case. I want that envelope back inside twenty-four hours.'

Lorna nodded. She couldn't begin to describe how relieved she'd be to get all this out in the open, and to put the Lafayette trials behind her. Ever since discovering Grayson Wendell's name on the roll-call of Departmental Directors, she'd been living with the harrowing certainty of who she was up against. All the security, the sense of safety she usually took for granted had deserted her. Instead, she felt permanently at risk.

The meeting ended with her telling them about her reservations about Manzini. It wasn't just his singular lack of progress on the recruitment front. It was also that the previous afternoon, on her return from New York, she'd come into the office, workaholic that she was, to find him skulking in Greg's office. He'd acted as if he'd been caught out, standing guiltily in the midst of a scattered chaos of files. He'd tried to make out that he hadn't been able to get to the files all week as Greg had been in his office. But Lorna hadn't liked it. And nor, it seemed, did Kuesterman. They both decided it was time to let Manzini go.

Returning to the NP3 block, she called Greg into the meeting room first to tell him what she had planned. Despite her suspicions, Greg was still defending his deputy. He was disappointed with recruitment too, he told her, but Manzini wasn't entirely to blame. He did add though that there was no truth to Manzini's explanation that access to Greg's office during the week had been difficult. In fact, Greg had spent all Friday morning in the lab – why hadn't Manzini gone through the files then?

So, Manzini had lied to her about his reason for being in the office on a Sunday afternoon. That was enough for Lorna. Calling him in, she sensed, the moment he walked through the door, that he'd already guessed the reason. His eyes darted from one to the other. When she invited him to sit, he fidgeted nervously across the table from the two of them.

'Steve, you know I've not been happy about recruitment for some time. The problem, as we all know, is that there hasn't been any.'

Behind those thick lenses, Manzini regarded her darkly.

'We also know it hasn't been for want of trying on your part. I appreciate all you've done – the long hours, the perseverance. It hasn't been easy. But at some point,' she leaned back in her chair, 'I have to draw the line. I have to say, "This isn't working."'

'If you go only by *numbers* it's been difficult.' He glanced from Lorna to Greg and back again. 'But there are plenty of other measurements—'

239

'And I know exactly what they are,' Lorna stemmed the argument, 'because I developed them. But I'm judged by results. *I* can't go to Kuesterman and the Board and all Zonmark's shareholders and say, "We're making great progress – only you can't see it." *I'm* judged on numbers. They want to see positive figures. Upward trends. At the moment, all we have on recruitment is a nose-dive.'

Opposite her, Manzini's features were inscrutable, though she noticed his foot tapping under the table.

'Steve, there's no nice way of saying this.' She met his gaze. 'We're letting you go.'

He didn't move in his chair, nor did he miss a beat. 'On what grounds?' he demanded.

She paused, surprised he had any wish to prolong the agony.

'On the grounds I've just mentioned. On your failure to recruit a single new member to the NP3 panel in the past six weeks.'

'You're throwing me out before I've even had a chance?' His voice was thick with indignation.

'That's not true.' She was calm. 'Believe me, this isn't the result I was hoping for. It takes time and money to recruit and train the right person. One doesn't dismiss staff on a whim.'

Manzini's spectacles once again flashed in Greg's direction before he looked back at her with a deepening intensity. 'I just can't believe you're doing this,' he was shaking his head, 'before I've even had time to deliver—'

'Steve, did you, or did you not, promise to have a list of three new panel invitees on my desk by the end of last week?'

'Yes, but—'

'Then where is it?'

'I got two of them, right? The third needed the final okay of their doctor. It's just a technicality . . .' It sounded lame, and he knew it.

'And what were you *really* doing here yesterday?'

'I told you, I needed to access files—'

'Sure you did. You said you weren't able to get into them when Greg was in his office. But I've just checked with Greg, and it turns out he worked in the lab all Friday morning.'

Manzini's indignation turned to anger. Scowling at Greg he snapped, 'That was only part of the reason.'

'What was the other part?'

'That's something I want to speak to you about.' He fixed her with a baleful stare.

'You are speaking to me.'

'One to one.'

'I have every confidence in Greg,' she responded smoothly. 'Anything you want to tell me, you can say in front of him.'

'Then just forget it!'

'One other point I wanted to raise,' she continued grimly. 'At the last update you reported that three letters had gone out to potential panellists. You haven't mentioned any acceptances so far—'

'Don't ask me,' he pointed at Greg, 'ask him!'

Greg looked bewildered.

'I don't understand,' Lorna pressed him.

'*You're* supposed to be chasing them up,' he snarled at Greg.

'Now wait a minute. I agreed to help if you ran into problems.'

'*You said you'd do it!*' he roared, shaking in his chair. For a moment Lorna wondered if he was going to attack Greg, physically. Looking from his fury to Greg's shaken expression, she allowed a few moments to pass before she asked coolly, 'Do you mean to tell me that there are three people out there who've been waiting for the phone to ring for the past seven days?'

'He told me *he* wanted to phone them!' Manzini repeated the accusation while across the table from him, Greg shook his head slowly.

Lorna gasped with frustration. 'Whether this is incompetence, or a communications breakdown, whatever the hell it is, it can't go on!' Then regarding Manzini with undisguised impatience, 'We recruited over thirty people before you joined. There were others in the line. Since then, the panel has shrunk. And I've lost all confidence in your ability to deliver. I want you to leave the building now. We'll bag your personal belongings and bike them to you later.'

She felt no obligation to spend a minute longer in Manzini's presence. She'd heard his attempts at self-justification and they hadn't impressed her. Pushing her chair back, she stood up, headed to the door and straight through to her office. Once there, she saw Greg returning to his.

As for Manzini, she watched him make his way towards his office, collect his jacket and briefcase and start towards the security door, before about-turning. He was heading up the corridor directly towards her. Stepping inside her office, he closed the door behind him.

There was no mistaking his angry turmoil as their gaze met. His eyes glowered dark and unnaturally large behind their thick spectacle lenses. She had hoped that she'd

242

finished with Steve Manzini. But she realised now that he certainly hadn't finished with her.

'You're firing the wrong guy,' he told her, approaching her desk.

She had already drawn heavily on her reserves of patience, listening to Manzini blame Greg for all his failures. But she needed to deal with Manzini's own fury which was already boiling over. She paused reflectively for a few moments before saying, in a calm voice, 'Steve, I know this is hard for you. And maybe you don't feel it right now, but it's for the best. For both of us. Things just aren't working out.'

'Yeah. Because of him.' He jerked a head in the direction of Greg's office. Then, as she regarded him in silence, 'Shall I tell you the real reason I was in yesterday? He's been fixing test results to disqualify candidates.'

'Now really.' She was shaking her head. 'That's absurd.'

'Just the same as he said he'd phone those three new panellists, then didn't.'

Sitting back in her chair, she tried to convey disappointment more than anger. 'I think this is a classic case of projection. But really, I can't let you hold Greg responsible for your problems.'

'He's a snake in the grass, that one,' persisted Manzini. 'You don't see it, because he doesn't show that side of himself to you. But believe me, you're in trouble with him on board. He's an evil bastard.'

Lorna pulled a droll expression. 'Well, it may interest you to know that the "evil bastard" argued vigorously in your favour. He wanted me to keep you on.'

'Why d'you think he did that?' Manzini seemed unfazed.

Lorna shrugged. 'You tell me.'

243

'I'm the perfect cover, aren't I? You push all the blame onto me for recruitment failure, meanwhile it's him who's sabotaging the programme.'

'You're being utterly ridiculous!' Patience snapping, she could no longer abide his accusations. 'Everything you've just said only confirms that I made the right decision to let go of you.' She rose, walked to her office door and reached for the handle.

Watching her every move, Manzini regarded her dangerously. 'Don't think Zonmark can get rid of me that easily.' His voice was low.

'Steve, I think you've said quite enough.' She opened the door.

'Believe me, I've hardly even started!'

For a long while she regarded those dark, magnified eyes, filled with fury. She couldn't think of a single thing to say.

Not so, Manzini. 'You're too blind to see it,' he jabbed an index finger in her face, 'but you've just made the biggest mistake of your life.'

Across Zonmark science park, Spencer Drake had remained behind in Kuesterman's office after Lorna left. Listening in while Kuesterman phoned Mitchell, Curtin, Zonmark's company lawyers in Washington, he heard his boss instructing them to seek out the most powerful law firm in Louisiana, a company with heavyweight clients, with clout, and get them on the case of the missing envelope asap. Minutes later came the recommendation to hire Blake Hampton, Louisiana's top attorney.

Still keyed up from Lorna's revelations, Kuesterman was evidently finding it hard to keep still. He bounced up from his desk and paced the room while the two of them discussed the contents of the envelope: how to package the revised ageing figures that would come out of Lorna's recalculations; what angle would play best to industry analysts and the market as a whole; and what to do about the much bigger issue of the Grayson Wendell revelation. As Drake remarked, going out to the media with that would be like lobbing a hand-grenade into a fireworks factory. The results would be instant and massively explosive. Zonmark would find itself pitched into the midst of presidential politics. The point was: would that benefit the company?

They discussed the issue at length, coming to no firm conclusion, before Kuesterman had sufficiently calmed to return to his seat. Then, looking over at his media advisor, he asked, 'And how's the other operation going?' There was evidently no need to refer to it by name.

'Unstoppable,' confirmed the other, with a half smile. 'We're building to a high-impact climax.'

The other grunted. 'Though, after this envelope thing, you wonder if it's needed.'

'How high do you want the share price?' Drake asked rhetorically.

'You reckon she's still in the dark?' Kuesterman gestured to where Lorna had been sitting minutes earlier.

'I know she is.'

The Zonmark boss regarded him for a while over the top of his glasses. 'You sound very sure of yourself?'

'I have it,' said the other, 'on the very best authority.'

245

14

Ruth knocked on the open door of Andrew's office. 'Tony Faber says your visitors are here,' she told him.

'Thanks.' He pushed his chair back from his desk.

'How long will you be?'

'Forty-five minutes. An hour, max.'

He headed towards the stairs and three floors down to the Vector offices. Tony, who was talking to a colleague, broke away as Andrew approached. 'I'm putting them in the Sorrento,' he said.

Andrew nodded. The Sorrento was not only an internal meeting room. It was also used for market research groups, as it was furnished with a large, one-way glass viewing panel concealed behind a net curtain running along an end wall. Stepping inside the theatre-style viewing chamber on the other side of the glass, Andrew took up his position.

'You okay?' Tony turned to the net curtain.

Andrew knocked on the glass to confirm. It hadn't taken him long to track down Executive Protection. They weren't in the London phone book, but he'd located them out in Richmond. He'd asked Ruth to phone requesting information on their services. The leaflet that had appeared in the post was a bland list of services – security patrols, bodyguards, advice on corporate and personal protection. The name 'Executive Protection' was printed on a sticker that covered part of the leaflet. Holding the brochure up to the light, Andrew made out the original name of the firm underneath it – J & G Security. What, he wondered, had prompted the change?

Now Tony's secretary was showing in the two men from Executive Protection. Just feet away, Andrew studied them intently, straining for some kind of recognition. The older man, short and wiry, wore a neat, pin-striped suit and brown seventies-throwback tie, his grey hair carefully Brylcreemed down against his pate. There was nothing about that sharp, vulpine face that Andrew could identify from the video of the two men outside the Weybridge boathouse. He seemed too slight of build – but it was hard to tell from the distance at which the video had been shot. Similarly, he could find no distinguishing feature about the younger man whose dark, swarthy looks suggested Mediterranean descent, though his shape and size certainly fitted.

After shaking their hands, Tony seated them across the table from him, so that Andrew had a full view of their faces. Andrew was profoundly grateful to Tony for doing this for him. Always a supportive colleague, Tony hadn't hesitated when he'd asked him the favour.

If the two men found anything untoward about the meeting room, they didn't show it. If anything, their behaviour suggested an awkwardly formal self-consciousness, as though they weren't used to this kind of encounter.

247

'Thank you both for coming in,' began Tony. 'Your services were referred to us by Canadian Mutual.'

The two men nodded.

'We're thinking of reviewing our security arrangements here and were wondering how you might help.'

The silence that followed seemed interminable, as the three men sat, staring at each other, until the older man finally realised this was his cue to speak. When he did, it was in a South London accent, with a curious rasping tone. 'You mean, something like Canadian Mutual have got?'

Tony had been expecting a fuller answer; some kind of explanation about Executive Protection's services. He tried to follow it through. 'That could be a useful starting point,' he said.

Once again, a tense silence pervaded before the older man said, 'They just have guards, really.'

Tony nodded, waiting for further elaboration and receiving none. 'Round the clock?' he asked after a further pause.

'If that's what you want,' retorted the other with a shrug, 'or a nightwatchman only. Depends what you're after.'

It was clear that if Andrew and Tony had been expecting a well-rehearsed sales pitch for Executive Protection services, they were very much mistaken. Anyone would have thought these guys had never made a corporate pitch in their lives.

'Our problem,' Tony was telling them, 'is that we don't know what we need, exactly. You're the security experts. We hoped you could advise.'

'Oh, we can do that.' The older man nodded. 'It's just this office block, is it?'

'That's one of the things we need to sort out.'

'Well, you've got security barriers, alarms, CCTV, guards, or any combination of those four. Depends on what level of security you're after and how much money you have to spend.'

One by one, Tony went through each of the options, though it was a desultory business. The older man was terse in the extreme; the younger man said absolutely nothing.

Less than ten minutes after they'd arrived, there seemed nothing more to discuss. No progress had been made whatsoever. Watching intently from behind the glass, Andrew chewed his lip with frustration.

Then Tony was looking down at the Executive Protection leaflet in front of him.

'Executive Protection,' he said. 'Couldn't find you in the book.'

'Name change.' The younger man spoke for the first time. His accent was East End with a dash of something foreign. Dressed in a tie and leather jacket, he conveyed an air of self-importance. 'It was just Reg before. But we're now part of a big American company. We're still waiting for the proper brochures.'

'I see.' Tony nodded. 'Why did you join up with them?'

'*They* asked *us*,' the younger man corrected him. 'They needed help. One of their clients is a big company. Lots of sites. All hush-hush. Can't say a word about them.'

The older man was nodding.

'But you can talk me through the kinds of things you do for them?' Tony asked, reasonably.

'Confidential,' the younger man retorted.

'In broad terms?'

'We do the whole lot,' the older man stated as though Tony had somehow missed the point. 'Alarms. Patrols.

Personal protection for visiting executives. Offices and res-idential . . .'

'That's . . . the lot, is it?' Tony looked from one to the other.

The two visitors remained silent. At which point Tony decided it was time to change tactics. Two could play this game. He'd see what happened when he turned the tables.

'Well, thank you both for coming in.' He sat forward in his chair, as though preparing to leave.

The two men exchanged surprised glances.

Standing, Tony was picking up his notepad and pen, before making his way to the door. There was a bewildered silence in the room as the two visitors followed him. Behind the glass, Andrew was as confused about what was going on as the two men. Then the young man came out with his awkward question. 'You said your office block was . . . one of the things you need to sort out.'

'Did I?' Tony had his hand on the brass doorknob.

'Yeah. Like there was something else.'

Tony stepped back, looking from one to the other. 'Don't think it's your bag,' he said doubtfully, shaking his head.

'Like he says,' the younger man gestured towards his col-league, 'we do whatever's needed.'

'Seems to me you're more about protective measures.' Tony was adamant.

'Other stuff, and all.'

It was the moment of truth. Next door Andrew strained to catch every word, every gesture. He observed Tony take his hand off the doorknob and lean against the wall, regard-ing the two men with elaborate circumspection.

'If a company came to you with a . . . difficult situation,

something needing direct action . . . discreet but effective action . . .?'

'Someone's giving you trouble?'

'I was only speaking hypothetically,' Tony quickly corrected him.

'Yeah. 'Course. We are too.'

'And,' Tony fixed the younger man with a steel-eyed gaze, 'if it wasn't just putting the frighteners on people?'

'We understand.' He was nodding. 'We handle all kinds of contracts.'

Tony's expression was severe. 'The company couldn't afford to be compromised in any way.'

'No connection to you, mate,' the younger man assured him. 'I mean, the company.'

'What sort of money?'

The younger man was about to say something before his associate gestured to him to keep quiet. He met Tony's look of enquiry with a hooded expression. 'We don't know who you are, Mr Faber,' he said in that strangely contorted voice. 'We've never met before.'

'Indeed, we haven't.'

'If you want to talk more, we'll need full instructions. And ten thousand pounds.'

'Ten thousand?'

'Think of it as a deposit on the final amount.'

Tony looked perturbed. 'It's the final amount that worries me.'

'Oh, don't be worried,' the other reassured him. 'Nothing to a big company like you.'

'Yeah,' agreed his partner with a smirk. 'Besides, you'll appreciate the benefits of our work long after you've forgotten how much you paid.'

From behind the glass Andrew regarded that smug self-satisfaction with cold fury. Though it was what happened next that had him rooted to the spot in horror. As the three men were about to step out of the Sorrento, Tony's PA arrived with the two visitors' coats – a camel-coloured trenchcoat for the older man, and for the younger, a navy anorak emblazoned on the back of the collar with a scarlet 'V'.

Washington, DC

It was shortly after lunchtime when Lorna got the call from Beryl Hattingh. The courier delivery had arrived for her. She drove straight across to Kuesterman's suite. There her boss and the ubiquitous Drake were sitting with a large DHL delivery bag on the table in front of them. Both were eyeing the bag with undisguised anticipation.

Before exchanging a word with the other two, Lorna ripped the seal open and removed a large white envelope, stamped in the private office of Blake Hampton, Louisiana's hard-hitting attorney. Kuesterman handed her a letter-opener which she used to slit along the edge of the white envelope. She reached inside.

She took out the plain, brown envelope William Gore had left for her with the Merrywood administrator. She recognised it instantly: her name, carefully printed by Gore on the outside; the flap at the top which she'd torn open when reading through the contents in her hire car. Flashing a look of excitement at Kuesterman and Drake, she grabbed the contents of the envelope and put the small pile of papers on the table in front of her.

In the undiluted excitement of the moment, both men

watched her in total absorption as she leaned over the papers and began to read. The top document, just as she remembered, on Department of Public Safety and Corrections letterhead, was a memorandum. Glancing down she picked up the phrases she recalled about the prisoners being used in the trial. Flicking over to the next page, she found the longer memo. That was right, she thought, remembering Gore's protests to the Department. Though she was puzzled as she looked back at the top and found that this memo was *from* the Department *to* Gore. Scanning down, she confirmed the various objections that were raised. But the objections were coming from the wrong source.

Feeling suddenly weak, she grabbed a chair. She had to sit down. She must have been mistaken, she thought, confused and deeply self-conscious that her every move was being followed by her boss. When she'd read this in the car, there'd been no doubt in her mind that the prison Governor had been objecting to his superiors in the Department. Had she misread it?

'Is it all there?' Kuesterman could contain his impatience no longer.

Unable to tear her eyes away, she held up her hand, while rapidly going through the memo again. Yes, there were the phrases that registered, but it was Gore who was being held responsible.

Her bewilderment deepening, she turned over to the next document. It was the list of prisoners, with annotations in the margin, just as she remembered. She checked down for the two asterisked ones, Livingstone and Moffat. She remembered their names distinctly. Since coming back from New Orleans she'd had flashbacks to her time at her school, St Margaret's. She remembered how her eccentric history teacher, Mr Holmes, had surprised the class by wearing a pith helmet while lecturing on Scottish explorers in Africa.

But neither Livingstone nor Moffat were on the top page. Shooting a look of alarm at Kuesterman, she flicked over the page, continuing down. Had she been mistaken? Had the names been on page two? Three? Four?

But they weren't there. She wondered if she should check the list again. But she knew she could not have missed them. It wasn't only the names themselves. She remembered, distinctly, how they'd been halfway down the page, each with an asterisk beside it.

The next document was the prisoner records, a page for each and every one of the 150 prisoners. She fanned through the pile, to confirm there were no papers caught up in them. And there weren't. The document she'd been looking for, the transcript of the conversation between Gore and his superior, had been removed. In that instant, what had happened became all too clear.

'They've tampered with these documents!' she burst out.

'How?' Kuesterman lurched out of his chair to join her.

'They've taken out the main one. The one that shows how the order came from Wendell. And they've changed the others to make it seem as if it was all Gore's idea.'

'What about the prisoners being black?' Drake wanted to know.

'Oh, that's still there.' She met his look of enquiry. 'Yeah, they've given us that – though they've changed the identities of the only two who lived into the 1990s.'

Drake looked up at Kuesterman. 'Isn't that all we really wanted?'

Lorna was shaking her head. 'Don't you see what's going on?' Her voice rose. 'Wendell's got his guys on the ground to airbrush him out of history.'

'After what you've told us about him,' Drake shrugged, 'that sounds like par for the course.'

'Par for the course that a candidate for the presidency should be a total crook?'

Kuesterman looked from one to the other before making his way ponderously to his desk. As Lorna went back over the paperwork, he stood poised, looking for a number amid all the paperwork spread across his desk, before putting his telephone on 'speaker' and speed dialling.

At the other end, the phone rang just twice before being answered by Blake Hampton.

'Blake. Armand. We have a problem.'

'It hasn't arrived yet?'

'It arrived okay. I'm sitting here right now with Dr Reid, going through it. Thing is, she says they've tampered with the papers—'

'—and taken out a document,' Lorna reminded him.

'—and taken out a document,' he repeated.

There was silence for a while before Hampton responded. 'What do you want me to do about it?'

Kuesterman cocked a quizzical eyebrow as he met Lorna's angry expression. 'I would have thought that'd be obvious.'

'Yeah, well I can talk to the Chief of Police, but I have to tell you, you're on shaky ground.'

'How's that?' Kuesterman and Lorna were still holding each other's gaze.

There was a wry laugh from the other end. 'First, you accuse the Chief of Police of stealing property. When it's

255

returned, after the due process of the law, you accuse him of tampering with it. I mean, is there anything else you want to accuse him of?'

When Kuesterman hung up a few minutes later, he stared at his phone for a while before looking back at Lorna. 'You heard what he said.' He shrugged. 'I reckon, let's go with what we've got.'

'And quietly forget Wendell and the two prisoners?'

Kuesterman's expression turned stony. 'You got it.'

'Just walk away from it,' she could hardly believe they were asking her to do this, 'as if nothing ever happened.'

'We've got to stay focused, Lorna.' Raising his hands to his face, Kuesterman made a tunnel gesture. 'Our business, your business, is NP3. We've got all we need for a big media announcement about the Neuropazine trials.' He looked over at Drake who was nodding vigorously. 'Why get caught up in the alleged involvement of a politician?'

'Nothing *alleged* about it.' Lorna was defiant. 'It's the truth. Doesn't the truth interest you?'

He met her fiery gaze with a conciliatory expression. 'Of course it does,' he responded smoothly. 'But I'm running a business here, not a political crusade.'

Lorna returned to her laboratory with orders to recalculate the impact of the all-black sample, while Drake worked on media strategy. Kuesterman wanted to go out with revised figures before Zonmark's next Annual General Meeting in a fortnight's time. It would help take the heat out of awkward questions about panel recruitment.

She had already completed the recalculation. She wouldn't have been able to sleep without working out that one. She could already show that instead of adding an expected thirty years onto the average lifespan, NP3 would extend life by forty to fifty years.

She could see all the headlines: 'Life Expectancy Leaps to 120'; 'See You in the Twenty-Second Century'. There'd be more journalist interviews, more TV time. Zonmark's share price would climb even higher. But she cared less about that right now than about the injustice of what had happened. In her head she knew Kuesterman was right. They were in the biotech business. She, more particularly, was a research scientist. Political shenanigans had no place in her world. But it was hard just to turn away from what she knew – the conspiracy of silence that she was sure explained the deaths of both Albert Krauss and William Gore. How could she pretend none of it had ever happened?

Even if she did forget about Grayson Wendell, there was still the issue of the two prisoners who had lived into the mid-1990s. And whatever names had replaced theirs on the forged list, she knew their true identities. Grayson Wendell might have wanted to delete them from the records, but she remembered who they really were.

Back in her office she recalled Gore's scrawls in the margin of the original list. His reference to 'Masden, MI', which she'd assumed was the name of a jail. Examining the revised list, she tried to work out which names had replaced the originals. But she soon gave up. A photographic memory wasn't something she was blessed with.

She mulled things over for a while, wondering what to do, before deciding that, for the sake of a few minutes, it was worth making just a couple of calls. She'd always believed in the direct approach. What about phoning

Masden Penitentiary to ask about the two prisoners? She didn't know anything about the disclosure rules on convicts who she assumed were now dead – it was over thirty years, after all, since the Lafayette trials. If she found out what had happened to them she would at least have the final pieces to her jigsaw.

It didn't take her long to get Masden Penitentiary on the line.

'I'm phoning about two prisoners—'

'Are you a visitor, ma'am?' The woman at the other end was terse.

The question took Lorna by surprise. 'Well, I suppose, yes, I am. But I lost track of both men some years ago.'

'Names?'

'Livingstone and Moffat.'

'Please hold.'

She could hear letters being tapped out on a computer before the woman returned to the phone. 'Mr Moffat died on 15 October 1995.'

'Soon after he was transferred from Wilson?' prompted Lorna.

'I don't have that information.'

'And Mr Livingstone?'

'There's nothing here about Livingstone.'

'But he transferred from Wilson the same day.'

The other repeated, louder, 'I have no documentation of Livingstone.'

'Isn't there anyone else—'

'Access to Records is restricted.'

'Right.' Lorna hung up, but her expression was defiant.

Exactly what the hell was going on? Why did they have records of the one, but not the other. Gore had made the

258

same scribbled reference against *both* prisoners' names. This whole Gothic tale was becoming more and more bewildering with each turn.

She was gazing out of the open door of her office, watching Gail working at her computer, when she was struck by a thought. What she needed was a different voice; an American accent. Calling her PA through, she briefed her quickly before handing her the phone and pressing the Redial button. Moments later, Gail was asking to be put through to Records, introducing herself as Gail Lowe from the Federal Department of Public Safety in Washington, DC. Once through to Records she gave the assumed identity again before saying: 'I'm calling about the transfer of two prisoners from Wilson, Louisiana to Masden on 15 September 1995.'

'What about them, ma'am?' asked a clerk.

Lorna came round to stand next to Gail, so that she could listen in.

'I need to confirm their names and the dates of their incarceration period. I have one name here as Moffat, but the other has gone astray.'

'Yeah.' The voice on the other end was typing on a computer before saying after a while, 'The other was Laurence.'

Lorna seized the list of prisoners received that morning and was rapidly going through it. She could find no mention of Laurence.

'Paul Laurence, Prisoner 550323, was transferred from Wilson to Masden on the date you mentioned. Then Masden to Brooklyn on the third of February 1997.'

Lorna hastily scribbled a note for Gail, who then asked, 'When was his incarceration due to end?'

'Life sentence, ma'am. No parole.'

When Gail put the phone down, Lorna was shaking her head. 'I don't believe this!'

'Why? What?'

'Livingstone, or Laurence, or whatever the hell his name is – he was born in 1910. That made him eighty-seven years old when he was transferred to Brooklyn!'

'What was he doing in jail? Surely an eighty-seven-year-old man—?'

'That's not all I'm wondering.' Lorna's thoughts were racing. 'You've also got to ask – why the name switch? And why was he sent up to Brooklyn after spending his whole lifetime in the South?'

'Get him out the way?' suggested Gail. Then, as the same thought occurred to them both, she asked. 'You don't think he's still . . .'

'Worth a try, isn't it?'

A short while later, Lorna was dialling the number of Brooklyn Penitentiary.

'I want to visit a prisoner—' she began.

'Mondays, Tuesdays, Fridays, one till two, first come, first served,' came the reply.

'Okay.' She paused. 'Can you confirm a prisoner's there?'

'Putting you through.'

It was a while before she was routed through to the prison register. 'Laurence,' she told the officer. 'Paul Laurence.'

She met Gail's eyes again. The wait seemed interminable. Then a voice was saying, 'Yeah. He's here.'

'He's an old man, right?'

'I can't give information on convicted felons.'

'It's not a mistake?' Lorna hardly dared to believe this. 'You don't have another Paul Laurence?'

'He's here,' insisted the other.

'And I can visit him?'

'Mondays, Tuesdays, Fridays, one till two, first come, first served.'

Lorna hung up and the two women met each other's eyes with expressions of excited incredulity. At ninety-two years of age, prisoner Livingstone was languishing in a Brooklyn jail. Though Grayson Wendell had changed his identity, and transferred him out of Mississippi, he hadn't been able to conceal his entire existence. The last imprisoned patient of the Lafayette trials had survived. If he was still *compos mentis*, his testimony would be devastating.

15

___

Jack quickly realised how badly he'd blown it. He felt stupid about the way he'd behaved. Losing his temper had been foolish; inexcusably inept. Up till that moment he'd been at pains to show support for Lorna's work, including her investigations of the Lafayette trials, never dreaming for a moment she'd get as far as she had. But she'd proved him wrong. And he'd blundered.

He knew there was no point chasing after her. Besides, within minutes of their row, she'd packed her clothes and left the suite, slamming the front door on her way out. It was going to take her a while, he realised, to cool down. Determined though he was to talk her out of her pursuit, he knew she wouldn't be in a receptive frame of mind right now. Best he give her some time.

Back in Washington, early on Monday morning he took the call from his lawyer in Louisiana telling him that Blake Hampton, acting for Zonmark, had taken over the case of the missing envelope. According to his lawyer, the Chief of Police down there was apoplectic about being accused of theft by some slick Washington yuppies. Up at Zonmark, meantime, it appeared that tempers were getting increasingly frayed. With the release of the envelope not expected till the following day, Jack realised that if his next approach to Lorna was going to be any more successful than the last, he'd better hold out another day. In the meantime, he reflected, it wasn't as if he didn't have plenty to keep him occupied.

It was Wednesday evening before he felt his moment had come. Lorna would have taken delivery of the envelope that day. He was intensely curious to learn her response to its contents. Returning to Washington, having at Cornelia's insistence had a private lunch with his mother, now he drove by Lorna's apartment. He could see the lights on. He parked the car nearby, walked up to her front door, and knocked. He hoped she'd let him in, though he wasn't counting on anything.

When she opened the door she stood, arms crossed and expressionless. She was still in her work clothes.

'Lorna, I'm so sorry.' He shook his head regretfully. 'I've come to apologise.'

She regarded him, unmoved.

'I acted like an idiot and I'm really sorry I lost my temper.'

Despite his pleading expression, she remained silent.

'There was no excuse, okay?' He held up his hands in surrender. 'I was way out of line and I want to make it up to you. Won't you at least let me in to explain myself?'

Still saying nothing, she stood aside, but remained in the hallway. Evidently she wasn't inviting him up.

'I can understand how you must be feeling.'

'I don't think you can,' she retorted.

'Well, perhaps I can try to imagine. I know how important all this is to you. What made me go off the deep end was—'

'Grayson Wendell.'

'Exactly.'

'So, what's the big deal with you and your mate Grayson?' she queried, eyebrows raised.

'It's not that way at all.' There was a pained expression in his eyes. 'Quite the opposite.'

'You had me fooled.'

'There's a story about Grayson Wendell that you should know.' He leaned back against the wall, regarding her soberly. 'His father, Crawford Wendell, and my grandfather, Otto van Haven, used to be the best of friends.'

'Oh, aye?'

'They were both high-rolling Southern businessmen from well-to-do families. They moved in the same circles and went into business together, building WenHaven Sugar Refinery. At one time it was the biggest cane factory in the whole country.'

'What's any of this got to do with the Lafayette trials?'

'Hear me out and you'll see,' he told her. 'The two men bought WenHaven – forty-five per cent shares each, the remaining ten per cent going to Paul Huey, a golfing buddy they wanted to help out. Crawford Wendell was Chairman and got a stipend. Otto and Huey were sleeping partners.

'When old man Wendell died of a heart attack, all his business assets went to Grayson. Not long afterwards, my granddad, Otto, realised he'd squandered the entire family fortune on the futures exchange. He was desperate to sell his assets. WenHaven was the only thing big enough to keep him out of bankruptcy.

'But when he announced to Grayson that he wanted out, Grayson told him to take a hike. Grayson couldn't afford to buy him out, but he didn't want a less accommodating sleeping partner. Otto and Huey had let him carry on in his father's footsteps, running WenHaven exactly how he liked.

'So Otto goes to the company lawyer and asks him to dig out the paperwork of the original agreement. It said any partner could sell his shares on the open market at any time, after first offering them to his partners. But, what do you know?' Jack's eyes narrowed. 'The only agreement they found said that shares could be sold on the open market only with the *approval* of both other partners. Not exactly,' he pulled a face, 'how Otto remembered it.'

'Hadn't he kept a copy of the agreement himself?' Lorna wanted to know.

Jack shook his head. 'Hadn't seen the need for it. The three men had been the best of friends when they set up WenHaven. They were gentlemen. The company lawyer had the agreement. What more was needed?'

Lorna was following him intently.

'Otto gets desperate. He needs a huge cash payment to settle his creditors. Everyone's trying to close him down. So he goes to see Paul Huey who is running a tourist paddle-steamer operation on the Mississippi. He wants to ask if Paul will testify that the agreement the company lawyer is holding isn't the original one they signed. Problem was, when he drove out to Huey's offices it was too late. Huey had just died in a bizarre accident. He'd fallen into the wheel gears of one of his steamers and had been crushed to death.

Jack was shaking his head. 'That was fifteen years ago.

But I doubt Wendell's *modus operandi* has changed. And if that's what he'd do just to keep things cosy at WenHaven, think how far he'd go to protect his chances of becoming the next President of the United States.'

Meeting Lorna's eyes with a pensive expression, he tried to gauge the effect his words had had on her. She'd been caught up in the story all right, but did she believe him? 'Maybe now,' he ended, 'you'll understand why, as soon as you mentioned Grayson Wendell . . .'

Whatever was going through her mind, Lorna wasn't showing it. The references to Wendell switching documents and getting rid of obstructive witnesses sure rang bells. But she was undecided about Jack. She shrugged, unhelpfully.

'It's only because I'm so concerned for you that I don't want you going anywhere near him. That guy will stop at nothing.'

'Yeah? Well, I'll remember that.'

'Please, Lorna, promise me you'll stay away from him.'

'You're not the only one wanting me to do that. Kuesterman and Drake are also telling me to forget it.'

'On this occasion, perhaps they're right. It's only—'

'For my own good. Yeah. Thanks a lot. Now, if you'll excuse me, I have work to do.' She was opening the front door.

'Does that mean . . . you and me . . .'

'It means I have work to do,' she repeated firmly.

'So, where do I stand?' He fought to control his temper from flaring.

'I don't know, Jack. Really I don't!' She sounded exasperated.

'You don't think you're being unreasonable?'

'I don't see what any of this has to do with reasonableness.' She closed the door firmly behind him without so much as a goodbye.

Standing motionless, Jack stared at it for a few moments, before turning and slowly walking away.

Before he'd come here, he'd thought he'd managed his own expectations. But even so, he couldn't help the disappointment. She'd let him in, she'd listened to his story, and for all that she'd shown no sign of budging. He didn't know what was going through her mind, what plans she had to pursue Grayson Wendell. But if reason wouldn't stop her, he'd have to come up with something else that would. There was no more time for talking.

Steering Committee meetings were scheduled for 6.30 pm to accommodate members arriving straight from office jobs. The buzz of anticipation built steadily from six onwards as various members arrived in suits, jeans, nurse's uniforms, taking their place at the circle of tables in Free to Choose offices.

Arriving just a few minutes before the 6.30 start, the quiet, well-groomed figure in the matching royal blue shirt and tie chose not to take one of the few remaining places in the circle, but instead sat in a chair set slightly behind, its back to a wall. Inconspicuous, his presence barely noticed by inner-circle members who talked animatedly among themselves, he had an excellent view of the proceedings. With pen and notepad at the ready, his expression was inscrutable as he watched Ed Dieter call the meeting to order, and proceedings begin.

The main committee members reported, in turn, about their activities over the previous fortnight, Dieter keeping a tight reign on discipline to ensure one update followed smoothly on from another. As always it was slickly run, quite unlike the majority of voluntary-sector meetings, which would ramble incoherently from one subject to another without any measurable progress. But the simple fact of the matter was that all the core members of the Steering Committee were highly paid consultants. There wasn't a single volunteer among them.

The man who chaired the Steering Committee, Ed Dieter, had no official position in Free to Choose. His name didn't appear in any meeting notes – in which he was simply referred to as 'the Chair' – letterheads, or other Free to Choose documents. Introduced, in the early days, as coming from a professional fund-raising background, his dominance at committee meetings had been established from the beginning and accepted unquestioningly. It was a *fait accompli*.

In the same way, the absence of the organisation's high-profile Director, former White House staffer Dennis Penno, whose name was as widely bandied about as Dieter's was invisible, seldom drew question. The notion that someone as high-powered and important as Penno might be kept away by pressing affairs of state was readily accepted.

In fact, much about the workings of Free to Choose was understood by bona fide volunteers as simply the way things were done. In most cases they had little experience of grassroots movements, and no yardstick against which to judge the operations of Free to Choose. Quite apart from that, the sheer dynamism of Free to Choose, its success in generating a massive groundswell of public support, was so self-evident that few questions were asked about how it operated.

Tonight's Steering Committee meeting comprised just forty volunteers along with the consultants. But they were the most important forty. Their performance was of critical success to the movement. Having been through each of the committee functions in turn, Dieter had to pull it all together – and to get committee members to redouble their efforts in the build-up to the March in the Mall.

'What we've heard this evening is extremely encouraging,' he observed, to nods of agreement round the tables. 'Speaking personally, I find it simply inspiring.'

Judging from all the expressions round the tables, noted the man in blue, the volunteers were agog to hear Ed Dieter speaking personally. He'd seldom seen attention so rapt.

'Free to Choose,' continued Dieter, 'has assumed a size and national importance barely conceivable for a campaign that only came into existence four months ago. As you've heard, it has a massively growing membership in every state. Media hits have gone from zero to four hundred a week nationwide. Every hour that goes by we're taking calls from high-profile celebrities, sports stars, businessmen and politicians. They're all signing up to our cause. So, why's that happening?' He paused, glancing slowly round the room, his expression one of shared intimacy with his most trusted cadres.

'First and foremost, it's happening because of you.' His eyes continued to roam the gathering as he launched into a paeon of praise. Of course, he didn't make eye contact with all those present. The core staff, the executive team, didn't merit so much as a flicker of a glance. And certainly not the man in blue. No, it was the volunteer workers, those who'd come to the meeting from factories and offices and homes around the capital, on whom Ed Dieter lavished his praise.

'It is your commitment, your vision which drives this movement. Each and every one of you has, in a very personal way, made sacrifices. In a time-starved society, you have given up recreational hours to come to meetings, to manage recruitment activities, to spread the word among friends and strangers. You've drawn from your own disposable income to buy rail tickets and petrol to come to meetings.

'But there are plenty of people,' he continued to spellbound gazes, 'who make big sacrifices and never achieve anything. And do you know why that is?' He didn't leave the rhetorical question in the air for long before answering. 'Because they don't have a plan. A strategy that works. Free to Choose has a strategy! We've had it right from the start.' He was gesturing to a whiteboard behind him.

'Grassroots and treetops!' called out a volunteer, on cue.

'Exactly,' he nodded, encouragingly. 'We started off with grassroots, mobilisation at the mass level. And then, when we had enough energy behind us, we headed for the treetops. The most influential, visible, well-respected leaders of our society. And have they been willing to listen, or what?' He beamed, as a wave of agreement rippled round the room.

'We've got Courthauld, the most famous IT tycoon in the world. We've got Dennis Penno.' Portraits of both men were on the wall behind him, as were others mentioned as he listed the roll-call of celebrity names. 'From every sphere of human endeavour, have you ever known such a rapid, headlong rush by superstars to sign up to a cause?'

Once again, there was an excited buzz which Dieter

allowed with an indulgent expression before holding up a hand for silence. The talk soon subsided as his audience leaned forward in their seats, eager for what he had to say next. Dieter deliberately waited for the anticipation to build before continuing. 'So what do we have?' He held up a finger. 'One: the most effective, committed volunteer force in the history of mass action.' As he glanced round the room, none could doubt him. Then, holding up a second finger, 'Two: grassroots and treetops. The strategy for success.'

They were ready for it now. Galvanising all the energy about the tables, he knew it was time to head for the climax. Raising his voice he told them, 'The third thing we have at Free to Choose, the essential core of any campaign, the reason for being where we are today, the reason we have created such massive and inescapable momentum' – around the room they were, quite literally, on the edge of their seats – 'is because we have right on our side!'

This time there were whoops and cheers from around the room, a brief flurry of applause as Dieter exchanged broad smiles with the volunteers. 'You don't think Courthauld or Penno or any of those others would be giving their names to something which isn't good and fair and true?' The fervour in the room became even more palpable. Expressions on the faces of the volunteers were urging him on. And far be it from Ed Dieter to disappoint. 'Those people, and millions of others like them, are waking up to a new threat. Free to Choose is the alarm clock of the nation. It's our purpose to ensure every single American knows what genetic modification means. It's our historic duty. We're not talking here about some minor infringement of civil liberties. We're not squabbling over the rights of a tiny minority. What we're fighting against is the greatest threat America has ever faced. Biotechnology threatens to rip our nation in two!' His eyes blazed vehemently as he caught up his audience in a single purpose. 'When we march in the Washington Mall, we're doing it to say, "No!" "No!" to a divided society where the haves live to be healthy and a hundred, and the have-nots die of heart attacks aged sixty!'

Unable to contain themselves any longer, volunteers thumped their tables in support.

'"No!" to the creation of two species of human beings – super-species and sub-humans!'

This time the drumming and shouted cheers were even louder.

'But we're not a negative movement.' Face colouring with passion, Dieter abruptly turned the tables. 'We're not about resistance and victimisation and threats. We want our representatives in Congress to say a big "Yes!" "Yes!" to free access to all for genetic treatment!' Around the room, the tide of support had grown so intense that eyes were glistening as he continued amidst a steadily rising background of excited chatter.

'"Yes!" to quality of life! And "Yes!" to NP3!'

There was no holding back the yells of encouragement and thunderous applause now.

'When we march on the Capitol,' Dieter had to almost shout to be heard, 'we're saying "Yes!" to being Free to Choose!'

As the room erupted all about him, the man in blue, whose expression had been muted throughout the proceedings, could no longer suppress a grin of pleasure. *He* had been Free to Choose, he thought, and he'd done well.

He'd chosen Dieter – and Dieter was about to hand him victory on a plate.

The call came into the car-phone of Julius Lupine's Aston Martin Lagonda. He was slouched in his seat, listening to a favoured piano piece – Moriz Rosenthal's spectacular transcription of *The Blue Danube* – and as soon as the voice came through the phone speaker, he hitched himself up, assuming a more attentive pose.

'It's our Scots friend.' The deep, gravelly voice required no identification.

'What now?'

'The strategy's just not working.'

'Don't you think—' he began, defensively.

'I'm not inviting debate.' The other was firm.

'What are you saying?' Swallowing his considerable pride had never come easily to Julius Lupine.

'Desperate times require desperate measures.'

Glancing up, he met his own eyes in the mirror of the driver's sun visor. He was under no illusion about what was shortly to follow. 'A new activity?' he confirmed.

'The last. For her.'

They had, of course, contemplated the final solution in the past. Discussed it in detail. How final would it be, they had pondered, if they got rid of Lorna Reid? Wouldn't it be only a matter of months, possibly weeks, before someone else popped up in her place? Cut one head off, and another would surely appear. He had no idea what had happened to persuade the shareholder to change course. Only that he daren't question it – not if he treasured the continuation of his many creature comforts and offshore cash.

Finally, he replied. 'This is a . . . considered instruction?'

'Very considered.'

'And you're sure—'

'Next time I read about her,' the other was insistent, 'I want it to be in the Obituary columns.'

Weybridge, Surrey

Andrew first saw the news in the *Financial Times*. The train had left Weybridge and was en route to Waterloo when he found his way to the United States business news pages. A three-paragraph article at the bottom of the page instantly caught his eye. 'Shakedown in US financial services,' ran the headline. Engrossed, he devoured the contents. The paper was reporting on the flurry of takeover activity, as globalisation and rationalisation saw major insurers and banks gobble each other up.

He knew all the background. Of particular interest was the report of overnight activity in which none of the four companies Bob Bowler had bought with such alacrity had emerged as a takeover target. In fact one of them was a hostile bidder.

Both Griegson and Metrapax, which thankfully he had offloaded the day before, had seen their highly inflated share prices crash as it became clear that they weren't on anyone's shopping list. Not only had they lost their recent gains, they were down twenty-five per cent on where they'd been before the rumour mills had kicked in.

Andrew registered all the company names and figures as

he read the piece, and even though he'd closed his positions on two of the worst-affected companies, he couldn't avoid recognition of a narrow escape. It was the same hollow nervousness he felt during market meltdowns.

He certainly didn't take any pleasure from proving Bowler wrong. The North America Fund was his baby – not Bowler's. Like travelling past the scene of a gory road accident, he was reminded just how easy it was to fall.

As he reached the office, he was even more eager than usual to check the fund valuation. He was still in his coat when he leaned over his desk to the 'In' tray where Ruth always left him the print-out of fund holdings, correct as at the start of that day's trading.

His reaction was one of undiluted shock. The North America Fund value was down by 500 million dollars! Glancing through the stock holdings he instantly identified the cause. Both Griegson and Metrapax, whose shares had collapsed overnight, were still on the list.

'Ruth!' he called her through. 'What's happening? Griegson and Metrapax went off yesterday.' The provisional list she'd produced the day before had carried neither company.

Aghast, he threw his coat off, staring at the figures again. It wasn't like Ruth to be careless. She usually went through paperwork in meticulous detail.

At his door, she was shaking her head. 'Those figures were correct, as at midnight last night.'

'But they can't be!' His voice was heated. 'I want you to check with Registry.'

'I just did.'

Striding past her to his office door, he looked directly over at where, less than three yards away, Bob Bowler was on the phone. Glancing up, Bowler met his expression of fierce enquiry. Andrew gestured towards his office. Bowler nodded. Andrew returned inside, while Ruth went back to her desk. Pacing up and down he still thought there must be an error; that somehow it had taken time for the sale of Griegson and Metrapax to be registered. It had happened once or twice in his career – delays like this. But never in an emergency scenario. Never with consequences anything like this. The worst he'd been hit in a single day's trading was 50 million – and that had been bad enough.

He saw Bowler hang up, and immediately dial again. Desperation rising by the instant, he burst out of his office again and right over to Bowler's desk. There was no question that Bowler had seen and acknowledged him. Now Andrew stood over where his 2IC was sitting, dark-faced and eyes fixed in concentration. After a while Bowler put his hand over the mouthpiece. 'I'll be with you right now.' His eyes met Andrew's for a fraction. Andrew couldn't place the emotion in them. But the moment he saw it, he knew he was in trouble. Guilt, anger, whatever it was that Bowler felt so strongly, its meaning was the same.

'What the hell's going on?' he demanded from his desk chair the moment Bowler stepped in his office.

'That's what I'm trying to find out.' Bowler gestured towards his desk.

'You mean there's a back-office problem?' He hoped against reason.

'The information coming out,' Bowler's voice was strangled. 'It's all wrong.'

'What information?'

'About Griegson and Metrapax.'

276

'Wrong, as in they shouldn't be on the list?' he tried again.

'Wrong, as in they were both takeover candidates.'

'I don't give a damn what they were, or are.' Andrew thumped his desk, furiously, 'I told you to sell them on Monday. I gave you instructions to act immediately. They were off the provisional listing yesterday—'

'I held off when—'

'You *what?*' Andrew leapt to his feet.

'I thought they had further to go.' Bowler's features had flushed several shades darker. His eyes burned with indignation and guilt.

'You directly countermanded my order?' Andrew could scarcely contain himself.

'It wasn't that!'

'Then what was it? He was aware of faces turning towards the raised voices, though he could still only focus on Bowler.

'They had further to go!' Bowler repeated.

'According to who?'

'Everyone in the market.'

'Everyone except me, you mean?'

'They had huge support from the institutions—'

'I don't see any of our competitors with fifteen per cent exposure to financial services!' roared Andrew. 'I don't see anyone else down half a billion dollars!'

Bowler's eyes flashed with guilt. Terror. 'I don't know what went wrong,' he whined, raising a hand to his face.

'You know bloody well what went wrong. Those shares always were a bad buy. When we had the chance to sell them, when I explicitly instructed you to do so, you didn't.'

'But I was told—'

'This is where being "opportunistic" gets you! This is the advantage of youth, is it?'

Bowler was deflating in front of him, like a blow-up figure with the air escaping. Suddenly the hard-nosed ruthlessness had gone, crumpled in desperation.

'Is my job on the line?' he pleaded, his voice pitiful.

Andrew pointed at the door. 'Just get out!' he yelled.

As soon as Bowler had left, Andrew sold the shares personally. He had no choice. The two stocks would never recover and would only spiral further downwards. As he hung up from issuing a 'sell' instruction, he put his face in his hands, fighting to control the tumult of emotions.

This was a disaster impossible to contain. Portfolio holdings for all the funds were circulated to Board members every morning. It was an administrative requirement. Usually the procedure was for information only – there was seldom any comment from on high. But any movement above two per cent, in any of the funds, would be highlighted. Paperwork would be given priority treatment. Looking at his desk clock, he saw it was a quarter to nine. All the Board directors would have been in for almost half an hour by now. It was certain that they would have seen this. He was astounded no one had phoned down yet.

When the call came, it wasn't from one of the upstairs hard-ballers. It was from Sir Stuart himself.

'Come up to see me,' he ordered, foregoing his customary etiquette.

When Andrew stepped into his office, he looked up from behind his desk over a pair of half-moon spectacles. 'When I got the print-out this morning, I assumed there'd been a mistake.' Sir Stuart's tone was sharp. There was no mistaking his extreme displeasure. 'What's behind it, for God's sake?'

'Our exposure to the financial services sector was far higher than it should have been.'

'I'd worked *that* out!'

'I tried to reduce it only yesterday afternoon.'

'*Tried?*'

Andrew shuffled, embarrassed. 'It's obviously not the result I was looking for, but I do have plans in place to recover our position.'

'Sounds to me,' Sir Stuart was livid, 'like bolting the stable door.'

'It's the best I can—'

'Well, it's just not good enough.' He'd never heard Sir Stuart so provoked. 'Half a billion dollars!'

Across the desk from him, Andrew tried to contain his own anger. As much as he felt like exploding right now, he knew he had to keep the lid on his emotions.

Sir Stuart was removing his glasses and coming round to his side of the desk. He gestured to Andrew to sit in one of the leather wingback chairs opposite him. 'My reading of things,' his tone was grave, 'and not only mine, is that you haven't given yourself a real chance to come to terms with the death of your son.'

Andrew shook his head, adamant. 'This has nothing to do—'

'Normally,' Sir Stuart spoke over him, 'I would agree that personal lives must remain personal. But let's be candid: you've gone off the rails.'

He hardly needed to elaborate. Andrew's appearance in the newspapers was still fresh in everyone's minds. And Andrew wondered what else Sir Stuart knew.

'My concern has got to be the good of Glencoe. It's what the shareholders pay me for.'

'If you're saying there's some kind of connection—' he started again.

'Come, come, Andrew.'

'I've not *let* my personal life get in the way.' He was defiant.

'You know that's just not true,' the other remonstrated. 'What about all the time you've been spending trying to track down the men you believe killed your son?'

Andrew regarded him, surprised.

'Not just your own time, but staff time too. There's Jenny Watson down in Marketing, she did some work for you, I believe. And her colleague in Procurement.' Andrew had always known of Sir Stuart's reputation for omniscience, but he had never, for a moment, considered that the man would find out so much. 'I understand you had a meeting with Tony Faber down at Vector on an extracurricular matter.'

Andrew raised a hand to his forehead, and closed his eyes wearily.

'And are you telling me Ruth hasn't helped at all with your investigations?'

Sir Stuart was making it easy, so easy, just to admit it all. To say, 'Yes. I lost the plot. We're down half a billion dollars because of my obsession.'

'At our last meeting, in the Boardroom,' he was continuing, 'we offered you time off.'

Andrew nodded.

'You didn't take it.' He paused. 'In my view, that was an error of judgement.'

When Andrew looked up, Sir Stuart met his eye. 'You

haven't been coping. You haven't had your eye on the ball.'

'A convenient theory, Sir Stuart, but just not in accord with the facts.' He tried to contain his exasperation. 'The North America Fund was compromised last night because of holdings in two companies. I told Bob Bowler to close our positions on both of them yesterday afternoon.'

'So it's all Bowler's fault, then?'

'Exactly right.' His voice was firm. Then, before Sir Stuart could reply, 'We wouldn't have held these shares at all if it hadn't been for Bowler's insubordination.'

'What on earth do you mean?'

'Bowler bought the stock behind my back.'

'How could he have exposed the fund—'

'Two separate purchase orders, just below his authorisation limit.'

'I would think,' Sir Stuart challenged him, 'that constituted grounds for summary dismissal.'

'Bowler was under no illusions about where he stood. But the damage was done. We had to wait for the bid-offer spread to close before I gave the sell order. That was yesterday afternoon.'

'And Bowler didn't sell?'

'No.'

'You didn't think it . . . prudent to confirm he'd sold?'

'I don't usually check that routine instructions—'

'Hardly routine.' Sir Stuart was withering. 'And given his previous insubordination . . .'

'Bowler knew what he had to do,' Andrew burst out, able to contain himself no longer. Leaping from his chair, he stalked across Sir Stuart's office. 'I gave him the order to sell, just like I give sell orders every day of the week.' He gestured furiously. 'I resent your suggestion that I'm some-how losing it when the simple fact is—'

'That you've lost my company half a billion dollars!' Sir Stuart roared over him.

'What I'm trying to say,' Andrew turned to face him, 'is don't confuse my state of mind with the most reprehensible insubordination I've ever experienced.'

'What you're trying to say,' rising from his own chair, Sir Stuart trembled with anger, 'is that I should hold Bob Bowler responsible for the management of your fund.'

'That's not fair and you know it.'

'Well, are you, or are you not, in charge down there?'

The men's eyes locked in long, silent fury before Sir Stuart announced dryly, 'We're putting you on gardening leave.'

Andrew's gaze fell away. Gardening leave. What a euphemism for the death sentence. 'Gardening leave' meant three months' suspension from the office on full pay, leading to termination. It was written into the contract of every senior staff member. The idea was that three months away from the cut and thrust would leave him with no trade secrets, no close clients, nothing to take to a competitor firm. It would also dramatically reduce his employability – especially when the half-a-billion-dollar débâcle became known.

Reeling from the knockout blow, he hardly knew what to say. What he did say was bizarre it was so pedestrian. 'Wh-what about the fund?'

'I've asked Gary Atlin to take over.'

Christ Almighty, they hadn't wasted time. In the last hour, it was now clear, they'd evidently poached Atlin from a rival fund, and agreed terms.

'From tomorrow,' Sir Stuart added.

'And Bowler?'

There was a pause before Sir Stuart replied, 'I'll have to consider that one.'

There was no point continuing. Andrew could see it was a done deal. Striding out of Sir Stuart's office, he left without another word.

Returning downstairs, he was reminded of the same unreal feeling he'd experienced after Matt's death. He'd found himself in the midst of normality, but his whole world had turned upside down. He was in turmoil – but all around him, life went on as though nothing had happened.

He walked straight to his office. On the way past Ruth's desk he asked her to collect two plastic archive boxes for him. By the time she'd appeared with them, ten minutes later, he had already moved all the personal items from his desk to one corner, and was clearing the shelves.

She looked over at him, shocked. She hardly needed telling.

'Your new boss is Gary Atlin. Starts tomorrow.' His tone was subdued. 'I've met him a couple of times. Seems a nice guy.'

'Oh, Andrew.' Coming over, she put her arms round him, hugging him for several moments before stepping back, self-conscious. 'I'm sorry,' she apologised.

He shook his head.

She went over to draw the blinds of his office so that no one could see inside. Then she was helping him pack.

He was surprised how little time it took to clear away his personal effects. Less than twenty minutes and everything had been stored in one of the boxes. He stood in an office stripped of any sign of his presence, Ruth standing opposite him looking as though she was about to burst into tears.

'Do you know what you'll do?' She was solicitous.

He shook his head. 'I get three months' pay, so there's time to think.'

'If you need any help – secretarial work, you know.'

He pulled a rueful smile. 'That's very kind. But you've already gone beyond the call of duty.'

'No, I mean it. Anything I can do to help you and Jess.'

He glanced down into a box. 'Actually, Jess left me.'

'What?'

'Last week. Staying with her sister.'

Her concern was even greater. 'You sure you'll be all right?'

He reached over, squeezing her hand, trying to convey his gratitude. Then, as they both looked at the boxes, she told him, 'I'll have this sent down to you.'

He nodded.

'You'll stay in touch?'

'Of course.'

She nodded her head in the direction of Bob Bowler's desk. 'What about him?'

'Christ knows,' he grunted.

He'd left the office by 10.30 and found himself making his way, automatically, to Waterloo. Still hardly able to take in what was happening to him, he got on the train, drove home, and changed out of his work clothes into corduroy trousers and a sweater. Without thinking he made his way through to his study, where he cast an eye over all the paperwork. Some of it would have to be collected up and returned to Glencoe. Most of it could go through the shredder, but he couldn't be bothered to do anything with it all now.

Restless and unable to concentrate, he wandered through the house. There was no shortage of domestic chores, he realised. He had a pile of laundry he'd already put into bags waiting to be taken down to the local launderette – a woman there washed and ironed. In the kitchen, dishes were piled up from numberless meals. The bin was overflowing with empty Marks & Spencer ready-meal packaging.

But he couldn't bring himself to do anything. Instead, he was benumbed, paralysed by shock. He thought about going for a walk. He even started towards the bedroom to get his trainers. But he changed his mind halfway there and returned to the kitchen. He couldn't be bothered to do that either. Instead he put the kettle on and stared at it as it began to boil.

So this was how it felt to be fired. During the course of his working life, he'd known plenty of people who'd been put on gardening leave, or out-placed, or whatever term had currency at the time. He'd never been so arrogant as to think that it could never happen to him. But as long as he had been riding high in the league tables, it hadn't seemed a very likely scenario. Now that things had changed so abruptly, he felt shaken to the core.

He spooned some coffee into a mug, poured in the boiling water and added milk. He had to use the long-life stuff, having forgotten to buy a fresh pint on the way home. As he looked at the strangely coloured brew, he thought that now there was nothing normal left in his life at all. He'd lost his son. His wife. Now his job had gone too.

He walked through to the sitting room, which looked

dishevelled and untidy, with several days of national news-papers piled up, local rags mixed in. Crumbs from a meal lay scattered on the coffee table, along with two used mugs. He was about to raise the coffee to his lips when he changed his mind. He didn't know why he'd even bothered making it. He hated the taste of that long-life stuff.

Instead he went over to the drinks cabinet and pulled out a bottle of whisky. It was single malt from Macduff, and he poured out a generous measure, taking a first tenta-tive sip, before downing the rest in a few swallows. Then he poured himself another. Bottle and glass in hand, he wan-dered over to the piano, the top of which was cluttered with silver-framed photographs, under a light patina of dust. The piano had come from Jess's parents – she'd learned as a young girl and was always intending to go back to lessons but never had. Instead, the piano had become the repository of family history; photographs of all their years together, with the most recent ones at the front. There was one of Matt and himself last Christmas after they'd built a snowman in the garden. He remembered now how they'd used a plastic bulb from Red Nose Day, and squash balls for eyes – they were still lying in the corner of the room, next to *Scrabble*. It was all so recent, just a few months ago, yet he felt as though it all belonged to a dif-ferent age.

Pouring out another Scotch, he reflected that it didn't take very much for the fabric of life to unravel. Just a single tug of its close weave, the events of one afternoon, and everything had come apart. He wondered what Jess was doing, what she was thinking right now. He and her sister, Becky, had been good chums. Becky was a lot like Jess except more extrovert, something of an attention-seeker.

He wondered what advice she was giving Jess – and whether Jess was taking it. Becky was one of the few people Jess listened to, but she was at home with three kids so Jess would have little time for quiet contemplation. But perhaps that was no bad thing. Where was contemplation getting him now? As he sat down he realised it wasn't even twelve o'clock. Time, usually so precious, so fleeting, weighed heavily upon him.

He decided he wanted to speak to someone – the effects of the Scotch were beginning to kick in. But who could he call? His friends at Glencoe would already know the news, and working hours weren't a good time to talk – their schedules were every bit as hectic as his had been. Other friends, outside the office, were mostly parents of kids who'd been at school with Matt. And he just couldn't face them.

The only one he wanted to speak to was Jess. They hadn't spoken since she'd gone. Perhaps, by now, she'd be feeling differently?

When he dialled up the number on the cordless phone, Becky answered. Her usual friendly voice turned perceptibly cooler when he announced himself. 'Is Jess there?' he asked.

'She doesn't want to talk to you.'

'I'm not ringing to cause trouble or anything,' he reassured her.

There was a pause before she repeated herself. 'She really doesn't want to talk to you. That's what she's told me.'

'But I have news for her. Something important.'

'I'll pass on the message.'

'It's not that kind of news.' He tried to reason. 'It's too big for that.'

287

'Just tell me what it is.' Her tone hardened. 'She'll decide if she wants to phone you back.'

'On the other hand, she might not.'

'I can't speak for her, Andrew.' The voice cut through him. 'You *must* realise.'

'Oh,' he sighed wearily, emotions vacillating between fury and despair, 'just forget it.'

He threw the receiver onto the sofa, feeling so very weary. He just wanted the floor to open up and swallow him, to make him disappear without trace. Looking across at the CD player, he wondered if he could lose himself for a while in music. There was the aria he'd been playing recently, the haunting melody that captured so well his feelings about Matt's death. Using the remote unit he switched it on, before making his way slowly over to the window and staring out. Purcell's 'When I am laid in earth' flooded through the room, poignant and aching. He stood by the picture window staring down the lawn to where the landing was raised and empty at the water's edge. Low clouds swirled in a dark tumult overhead. Sky and river were drawing closer and closer together. It began to rain.

16

Arriving at the Georgetown Health & Racquet Club, Lorna pulled up in the members' car park, and walked briskly to the entrance, glancing over her shoulder as she did. Gym-bag in one hand, she looked about her as she stepped inside, making her way past the juice bar, sportswear shop and lounge. She felt safe here, in a familiar environment, surrounded by other people. Slipping her card through a turnstyle, she let herself through the members' entrance, and carried on to the women's changing room.

The room comprised a series of U-shaped sub-sections, divided by walls of lockers, each with a wooden bench at its centre. Private changing rooms were also available, though Lorna had never bothered with them. And now, more than ever, vigilant about her safety, she wasn't going to shut herself away and out of sight.

It was nine o'clock – later in the evening than she usually came here – but it had been a long start to the week. Until Steve Manzini was replaced, there'd be extra work for

289

all of them. Greg especially. The two of them had worked late, ordering in a noodle dinner around seven, and carrying on at their respective desks. By half past eight she'd had enough of being cooped up in the office since seven that morning. She'd decided she needed a good physical workout. Collecting up the gym-bag she always kept packed and ready in her office, she'd waved goodnight to Greg, before heading here.

There weren't as many people around as earlier in the evening. She'd soon slipped into her swimsuit and put her clothes in one of the lockers, securing it with a key which clipped to her costume. Towel rolled under her arm, she walked to the front of the changing room, lined with basins, hair-dryers, and a wall-to-wall mirror. There were a couple of other women, seeing to their hair and make-up. Lorna surveyed herself critically in the mirror, sweeping her shoulder-length hair back off her face and under a swimming cap, before turning right, past the showers and up a short flight of steps to the swimming pools.

Her routine these days was very different from the rigorous training of her teenage years at St Margaret's in her home town of Aberdeen, although it followed the same format. She'd do two lengths each of butterfly, breaststroke, backstroke and crawl, in eight-length cycles. On a good night she'd do thirty-two lengths. On a great night, forty. The effect, however, was always the same. During the time she was in the water, she switched off completely to the world outside.

The swimming pool area reminded her of a cathedral. Its sandstone walls curved upwards in gracious arcs to a high, vaulted roof, which ran the full length of the main pool, a junior pool and a diving well. Reflections from the floodlit waters dappled the ochre walls, giving them the patina of age. There weren't too many people around, which meant she'd have a lane to herself and her swim would be uninterrupted.

Approaching the water, she dipped in her toe to test the temperature, before stepping back, flicking her fingers around the elastic where her swimsuit met her legs and then arms, in an automatic gesture. About to throw her towel over a nearby stone bench before taking to the water, she glanced over towards the hydro-pool; maybe that was a better idea, she reckoned. She could do with a bit of a loosen-up.

The hydro-pool room was off the main swimming pool area. The pool itself was a quarter the size of the main pool and only waist deep. In it, six steel harnesses on which to lie were positioned just above water level, half a dozen nozzles poised to deliver powerful blasts of water at one's body. It was like a Jacuzzi, but better, and the perfect therapy after a sedentary day at the office.

Lorna could see a couple of people already in the room. As she made her way over she gave no thought to the accident that had happened there several weeks earlier. A young man had slipped on the steps leading into the hydro-pool. As he'd fallen, he'd hit his head on the bottom of one of the steel harnesses, knocking himself unconscious before falling, face down, into the water. It had been late afternoon and the area had been teeming. Fortunately, within moments he'd been rescued by a lifeguard and had soon returned to consciousness.

After the incident, the gym's management had erected large signs throughout the pool areas, warning about slippery surfaces and disclaiming all responsibility for accidents resulting from them.

She stepped into the hydro-pool room, and was surprised to find it empty, having been sure that she had seen figures inside. She didn't realise that the two men she'd noticed were now behind her, on either side of the entrance, their backs pressed to the wall. As she approached the pool steps, they sprang silently forward.

Suddenly, something was covering her face. She was dragged to the ground. Caught completely by surprise, she crumpled. Then her instinct to fight kicked in. She writhed furiously, trying to scream – but found she couldn't. Her throat was choked in silence, her gasp soundless. Then came the smashing pain in her forehead. And that was all.

The two men lifted the body, hurrying it down the steps of the pool. Their lookout, stationed at the entrance, kept watch while they removed the cloth bag from round her head and held her, unconscious, face down in the water. It didn't take long.

They kept her there for half a minute after she'd breathed in water, careful not to squeeze arms or legs or leave other evidence of bruising. Then one of the men pressed his ear to her chest. With a single nod, he confirmed.

They secured the body under one of the steel harnesses in the pool. It would seem as if, having been struck unconscious, her body had drifted under the harness where she'd been trapped. They left her bobbing, face down, in the water.

New York City

Although a serial philanderer throughout the twenty-two years he'd been with Martha, Julius Lupine had rarely allowed himself the indulgence of a full night away from the marital bed in the pursuit of sexual pleasure. That made it all the more enjoyable when he did. Like a fine vintage wine such occasions were to be savoured and enjoyed. Each and every moment was to be lingered over and relished. In contrast to hurried lunchtime trysts or athletic *soirées*, a whole night leisurely exploring sensual pleasures appealed to him immensely. Now, as he loosened the knot of his Versace tie and poured liqueur into two cut-crystal tumblers, he contemplated the evening ahead with a particular pleasure.

Although he wasted no thought on his wife during these interludes of fleshly delight, he was nonetheless meticulous in planning around her. For despite Martha's irksome domesticity, she was no fool. And he couldn't afford her suspicions to be aroused – at least, not till he was ready to drop the bombshell. Her family trusts were still too valuable. Collecting up the two liqueurs and putting them on a tray, he reflected on the unexpected dénouement that his extramarital relations had led him to.

Until just three years ago, he had assumed that the long-established shape of his life would remain as it was into the foreseeable future – or at least until old age dulled his passion. His two sons had long left the family nest to fend for themselves. His wife ran the home and fiddled with her domestic hobbies. For pleasure, he took mistresses. It was an arrangement that had served him well over the years, and one that he could see no reason for ending.

But fate had surprised him. Without any effort on his part, he'd found himself in an extraordinary position at just the right moment. As Marketing Director of a pensions provider, his experience of financial services in America was long and encyclopaedic – in fact it encompassed everything that was required by a major insurer, according to a management consultant who'd been appointed to headhunt someone for a senior role.

Lupine, always on the lookout for ways to fund his increasingly lavish tastes, had agreed to a meeting with alacrity. It had all been very cloak-and-dagger. The management consultant had sworn him to secrecy, and made him sign confidentiality papers before even revealing that his client was Mayflower, America's most up-market health insurer. A series of meetings had followed during which the broad scope of the job was discussed, first with the consultant, then, only after Lupine's interest had been confirmed, with the client.

What quickly became apparent, at that point, was that he was being offered much more than a simple move up in his career. The new position promised change in every area of his life. Quite apart from the serious-dollar pay-packet, and generous offshore bonus entitlement, were all the corporate toys. And also this other side of things.

In the past, his extramarital affairs had taken a wide variety of forms – but never anything like the present, highly satisfactory arrangement. His first dalliance, eighteen years ago, had been with the account director at the advertising agency he used. It had been a torrid, dangerous adventure that had ended in a bitter stand-off – her unprofessional conduct and his infidelity providing each party with a weapon of mutually assured destruction.

Second time round he'd gone for something a lot tamer. The relationship with Tammy, his Personal Assistant, was the oldest cliché in the book, but it was manageable. She, having married too young, had been looking for excitement. He had relished her youth and eagerness to please between the sheets.

But confronted by Martha, after carelessly mislaying a credit card statement, he'd been forced to abandon the novelty of her lithe-limbed body, transferring her, at Martha's insistence, to another department across town.

The affair with the Italian waiter had caught him by surprise. Before then, he'd never believed himself to be anything other than heterosexual. But late one evening at Postetino's, when all his work colleagues had left him to see to the bill, the irredeemably gay Marco had flirted with him quite shamelessly. Well oiled by Chianti, he had reciprocated. One thing had quickly led to another, and soon he was drowning in Marco's Kouros, clutching feverishly at that gym-fit torso, and groaning with lust amid the sides of veal in the restaurant meat pantry.

There had been more meetings after that night. Trysts in Marco's downtown studio during which he'd gape at the young man's casual nakedness, awestruck by the grace and vigour of that body, enthralled by his prodigious loins. He had come to reflect that perhaps the Greeks had got it right. Maybe boys *were* for pleasure. Or was it more simply that he took beauty wherever he found it, and slaked his instincts wherever they were aroused?

In between these star turns had been the regular succession of more commercial transactions. Simple, unambiguous, free of encumbrances, they seemed the best solution to his rampant libido. But even so, he was worried by the 'little black book' disclosures that surfaced in the papers from time to time. Now a senior figure in the insurance world, who was to say his own name wouldn't come to light if a madam's directory fell into the wrong hands?

Within weeks of taking up the new job at Mayflower, he was involved in a relationship unlike any before; a benefit that came as an intrinsic part of the package, his new superior having perfectly understood his instincts even before he'd been hired. This new woman was more than attentive to his sexual needs. She was also a lot smarter than any of his previous lovers, and had more business savvy than many of his peers. More than simply a lover, she also quickly became his confidante. And for the first time in his life, with his offshore accounts filling up rapidly, he began to think seriously about leaving Martha. Dull, dumpy Martha. Martha of the cheesecake recipes and double chin.

In the past few weeks he'd done more than think about it – he'd begun active planning. But the final act in the drama was all about timing, and he wasn't ready yet. There were just a few last issues he needed to sort out first. Personal financial transactions. And of course, the professional niggle he would like resolved too.

That didn't mean that he and his mistress couldn't sate their senses in the meantime. And relish the thrill of the forbidden. Tonight, while Martha believed him to be at a public relations awards banquet, they had run the risk of dining out at one of New York's most exclusive restaurants. It was one that Lupine and Martha had never frequented, nor had he heard any of his friends or colleagues mention dining there. Nonetheless, it gave the evening a decided *frisson*, which remained after they had returned to her apartment.

Carrying the tray of liqueurs through into her bedroom, he thought, not for the first time, that this was every inch a mistress's boudoir. Its walls were fuchsia-pink moiré, bedecked with velvet curtains and gilt-framed portraits. Its scent was hers – the rich, redolent tones of Paloma Picasso. But it was the antique four-poster that dominated the room, with its red damask curtains and Porthault sheets. Bedside pedestals and a dressing table in ornate Chinoiserie lent an exotic flavour. Tonight, as on previous visits, her chamber was lit only by an elaborate candelabra on her dresser.

Having changed out of her evening wear, she lay beneath the sheets, a tempting, succulent morsel, awaiting his pleasure. Physically, she was quite unlike his previous women. In the past he'd always been attracted to petite nymphets, women he could dominate both physically and intellectually. But the long-limbed beauty of his current mistress was altogether different, her breasts pert in a black lace brassière, blonde hair brushed back from her face, her eyes large and dark in the candlelight. As he came towards her, she wore an expectant smile.

No sooner had he handed her her drink than the cell-phone rang in his trouser pocket. He checked the number on the display, before answering.

The caller took less than ten seconds to pass on the message. When Lupine ended the conversation, it was with a satisfied smile.

'Good news?' she asked, eyebrows raised.

'Very good,' he rumbled, with a sip of his liqueur.

Taking his hand, she tugged him onto the bed. 'Another mission accomplished,' she murmured, in a tone of admiration.

She knew about his more important work concerns – though none of the detail. He didn't trouble her with that. It was enough for her to know that he'd succeeded in solving a vexing issue.

'I like a man who can stand and deliver,' she purred, as he knelt astride her.

'I know that . . . only too well,' he responded.

'Oh, Julius!' she gasped, her hands roving down his body. 'Where would I be without you?'

Washington, DC

The swimming pool lifeguard had returned from the men's toilets, where he'd gone during a lull in activity. There'd been only a few people around. Walking back towards the raised guard chair, from which he could survey the whole area, he stepped past the hydro-pool and glanced through the entrance, in a routine check.

He immediately noticed the shadow under one of the harnesses.

He stepped inside, and what he saw triggered his instincts so that his next actions were pure reflex. Immediately he was heading for the pool, hitting the alarm button on the wall as he went. He tugged the body out from under the harness. In moments he had her out on the concrete. He checked her pulse – though he knew she'd already gone.

He'd been drilled for exactly such contingencies. The training took over. Tilting her head back, he was opening her mouth, making sure her tongue wasn't blocking her throat. Then he was pumping her chest vigorously, to clear the water in her windpipe.

Every second counted. He must bring her back. He couldn't have her drowning on his shift! Water gurgled from her mouth with each powerful pump action. Christ, how much had she swallowed? This was nothing like the dummies they'd drilled on, but he remembered to set up a rhythm – and stick to it. Three hard thrusts. Clear the water. Check the airway. Three hard thrusts.

When her trachea was clearer, he began mouth-to-mouth. Please, God, let her come back! They just couldn't lose her. Even though she had a deathly pallor, emphasised by the dark, wet hair clinging round her face, he still recognised her. She was young – and a looker. He remembered watching her in the pool during previous visits, wondering if she was something in the fashion industry.

All these thoughts raced through his mind as he took in great gulps of air, forced it into her lungs, and pushed it out again. He wondered how much time she'd been trapped under the harness, face down in the water. It couldn't have been that long. He'd only been off duty a couple of minutes.

He tried remembering times and procedures from resuscitation training. How long before mouth-to-mouth stopped working? Would she need cardiac massage? Ventricular defibrillation? Getting her breathing was one thing, but what was happening to her brain in the meantime?

He didn't recall anything, from training, about the sound; the deep, primordial groan that seemed to emerge from her very core, just as he had begun to fear he was losing. But no sound could have been sweeter than her gasping for air, coughing up more water, her eyes blinking open. Spluttering for life, she was bewildered to find herself lying on the concrete, the lifeguard over her.

Events moved swiftly after that. An ambulance was summoned and arrived within minutes. Still dazed by what was happening, she was stretchered away to hospital, an oxygen mask strapped to her face, and an intravenous drip in her arm.

On arrival at the hospital, the doctor examined her, monitored her breathing, her heartbeat, her circulation. He asked her questions, a lot of them, and she remembered her approach to the hydro-pool; how she thought she'd seen figures in the area – but its emptiness when she arrived; then the flicker in the corner of her eye, the cloth covering her face as she struggled.

By the time he was through, the doctor seemed satisfied. But he wanted her to undergo more tests, including a brain scan. Even though she was starting to feel normal again, he told her, in a voice that would broach no argument, that she was to spend the rest of the night in the High Dependency Unit under observation. He prescribed her a mild tranquilliser to help her sleep.

If she could manage it – but it was entirely up to her – the police wanted to speak to her. It seemed they had some questions of their own.

17

Embassy Row, Washington, DC
Monday, 1 May

When Jack Hennessy was told that Lorna was lying in an observation unit of George Washington University Hospital, he was more than simply upset. He was furious. Despite all his intentions, all the carefully set plans, she was now the victim of a botched murder attempt, cordoned off behind police and hospital security.

Leaping up from behind his desk, he paced the passageways of his majestic home and considered his options. After his last attempt to see her, he was under no illusions about her feelings for him. Indignant at his insistence she back off Wendell, she felt betrayed, perhaps even disgusted at his lack of support for her all-consuming programme. If he turned up at GWU Hospital now he might not get near her private ward. There was every chance she'd refuse to see him.

But he felt driven to go. He must look into those deep blue eyes so recently acquainted with death. He had to speak to her, at the very least find out what the police were doing. Without information of any kind, it was impossible to move forward. If he was certain of anything, it was the need for swift action.

Glancing at the hands of his Patek Philippe, he saw it was eleven at night. Way past ordinary visiting hours. Not that there was anything ordinary about the present situation. After freshening up his appearance in his marble bathroom, he was soon behind the wheel of his 450 SLC, driving through the Washington night.

It was the first tranquilliser Lorna had taken in her life, and she'd found its effects weirdly wonderful. Tranquillisers, she'd always imagined, made you feel sleepy, or at least calm. But that wasn't her experience at all. Instead, it was as though her thoughts and emotions, like two cogs in the machinery of her mind, had been drawn apart so that no observation or reflection, nor anything that happened in the outside world, could have any effect whatsoever on her feelings.

Right now she felt wonderfully protected and safe. It was as though she was caught up inside a cloud of warm, good feeling impossible to disturb. She could even remember back to what had happened at the pool without a moment's disquiet. In fact, she'd had to when the police had arrived. She'd been able to give Detective Bradley a full account of all she remembered – which wasn't much – after arriving at the Health & Racquet Club. And when inevitably he'd asked if she knew anyone who might want her dead, she'd been unflinching. She knew it would be wrong to tell him about Grayson Wendell. If she did that, she'd quickly lose control of events – and there was something she needed to do first. She'd known it before her visit to the gym, but she realised it now with an altogether greater sharpness of intent: she must get to see prisoner Livingstone. He was the last piece of the jigsaw; the final, indisputable evidence she needed before she went public. And going public was the only way she was going to put this all behind her.

Late at night, she lay in the semi-darkness of the hospital ward. No one knew she was in hospital right now. When she'd been asked the usual questions about next of kin, she'd explained that her parents lived in Scotland, where it was currently the small hours of the morning. She didn't want to disturb them with something they could do nothing about. Besides, she was fine.

Painkillers had reduced the blinding headache from the blow to her forehead to a background pain. She'd checked her appearance in the mirror. Raising the hair from her forehead, she'd realised the ugly strip of inflammation would take weeks to heal. But she had survived without any lasting harm or disfigurement. She'd phone her parents the following day and speak to them herself. In the meantime she'd given the hospital Armand Kuesterman's cellphone number as a contact point. As she did, she remembered their last encounter, how adamant he'd been that he was running a business, not a political crusade. Tomorrow, perhaps, he'd realise the impossibility of that distinction.

Jack's arrival was unexpected. Would she like to see him, a male nurse asked, curious about the darkly handsome visitor the patient hadn't included on her contact list. Still anaesthetised from her feelings, Lorna said yes.

The police debriefing she'd so recently gone through had given her cause to reflect on Jack's angry warning about Wendell. Events at the hydro-pool had given it all a very different perspective.

He stepped into the room bearing roses, a massive bouquet of twenty-four stems, so extravagant and typically Jack. Despite the hour – it was close to midnight – he appeared as cool and fresh as if he'd just stepped out of his dressing room. Though as he made his way across the shadows, his face was filled with concern.

'How're you feeling?' he whispered as she smiled up at him.

'Oh, I'm floating.' Her throat still weak, she managed a rueful smile.

He handed the roses to a nurse before turning back, shaking his head. 'I came over as soon as I could.'

He was standing right next to the bed and she reached out her hand and took his. 'I'm glad,' she murmured, pulling him towards her. As he perched carefully on the edge of the bed, she didn't notice his shoulders ease back with barely perceptible relief.

'Do you mind talking about it?' His enquiry was gentle.

She shook her head on the starched hospital pillow. 'Not a lot to say. I was going into the hydro-pool. There's this flash out of the corner of my eye and a cloth over my face. They're dragging me to the ground. Next thing, I'm laid out on the concrete getting mouth-to-mouth.'

'It's terrible!' His voice was soft in the quiet of midnight. 'And just bizarre. I mean, why the hydro-pool?'

'Accident there last month. Guy knocked himself out. He was quickly rescued.' She met Jack's eyes seriously. 'It was a lookalike.'

Jack appeared surprised, as though he didn't know about the previous incident. Then he was saying, 'I guess the police will be round tomorrow morning.'

'Been already.'

304

'Yeah?'

She glanced behind him at where her police protection was sitting outside. 'I didn't tell them about Wendell. Not ready yet.' They exchanged a long gaze before she squeezed his hand. 'I . . . I realise, now, why you tried to warn me.'

'I should have handled it a lot different,' he confessed. 'Only, as soon as you mentioned that guy's name—'

'I know.'

'I've been so worried about you.' His voice was tender.

'Believe me, I've been watching my back. But after tonight—'

'They won't give up,' he ended for her.

'Not unless they have nothing to gain.'

'How d'you mean?'

'When I go public about Wendell. They won't touch me then.'

Alarm flashed in Jack's eyes. 'When would you do that?'

'Very soon.' She remembered Livingstone, ninety-two, languishing behind the bars of Brooklyn Penitentiary. Last remaining participant in the Neuropazine trials. The senility of grand old age might have corroded his mind completely. But if he was lucid, if he could remember anything at all about that time, she wanted his final testimony.

'When you get out of here,' Jack was saying after a pause, 'I want you to move into my place. I've got Grade 5 security and I'll arrange a personal bodyguard.'

She looked up at his grave expression. 'Not a bad idea,' she murmured. 'At least, until everything's sorted out.'

'Good. I'll make the arrangements.'

Still cocooned by chemicals, she smiled at his impatient concern. 'I'll think about it.'

'What's there to think about?' he queried. 'You're the

target of a hunt-to-kill operation. You have the choice between maximum-security protection, or a Georgetown apartment that doesn't even have a burglar alarm.'

'When you put it like that—'

'Because that's how it is.'

They held each other's eyes for a long while in the darkness, before she drew him down to her, closing her eyes and scenting the strong, incisive fragrance of his Polo in her nostrils. 'Jack Hennessy, you can be very persuasive,' she murmured.

'Sometimes I have to be.' He kissed her with a smile.

Weybridge, Surrey

The ceiling of Andrew and Jessica Norton's bedroom was a rectangle of white plasterboard, edged by a plain, curved cornice, like a framed, empty canvas. During daylight hours, the canvas would become an intricate frieze of shadows cast by the light passing through the patterned net curtains, increasingly blurred as shadows fell further away from the window. By night, the same elaborate web of curve and counter-curve was cast in the eerier white of the streetlamp fifty yards away, though interrupted by the crude, asymmetric 'Y'-shaped shadow of the elm out at the front of the house, stretching across the ceiling like a hangman's gallows.

Andrew had had ample time to study the repeat warp and weft that trailed across the ceiling, having spent much of the past four days lying motionless, and staring up.

He had never understood depression before. In fact, he'd believed it to be a weakness of character, an indulgence arising from excessive self-concern, and resulting in sloth.

Now, for the first time in his life, he was reduced to a terrible passivity he'd never experienced before, a numbed paralysis that left him oppressed by the thought that any movement would be futile.

Since Matt's death there had been moments when he'd been overwhelmed by grief. And Jess's departure, or was it desertion, had dragged him down to his knees. But even so, there had still been an imperative to get out of bed every morning, to continue the routine, to carry on through the daily misery that his life had become. Now, having lost even that, he spent days feeling there was nothing. No reason to move, to think, to breathe.

As though to confirm his irrelevance, the phone had rung only once since his sacking from Glencoe. Ruth had called to say his personal effects had been dispatched to Weybridge. He hadn't bothered taking the call, listening to her message on the answerphone with the same lethargy with which he'd already heard the courier firm dumping two cardboard boxes on the front verandah.

For a while he lay there, willing Jess to return his call, thinking that just the sound of her voice, however stripped of tenderness, might perhaps be a lifeline out of this pit of despair. But of course, no one rang; not Jess, nor any of his colleagues from Glencoe. Not even Tony Faber, who must have heard the news by now. It was as though the whole world had given up on him.

There was, however, one image looming out of his crippling reflections, capable of stirring him. In real life it had been only momentary, but he had replayed the scene in the cinema of his mind so often that he'd felt a part of it for hours. Not a word was said. It was, instead, the memory of a single expression that provoked an anger in him, his only alternative to depression. The scene was the Sorrento Room in Vector offices. Tony Faber was showing the two men from Executive Protection out of the door. The younger of the two men, the dark-jacketed one with the red 'V' on his collar, was turning and looking in the direction of where Andrew sat, behind the one-way glass. He had repeated that old cliché about Executive Protection services being valued long after their cost was forgotten. Then, across his face has passed that look of smug satisfaction. A killer's smirk, thought Andrew. The complacency of one who thought himself beyond the law of man and nature, who believed he had got away with murder.

It was a smirk that haunted him in his sleeplessness and, when back pain from lying down became too much, that curled back at him when he caught his reflection in the bedroom window. It was a smirk that goaded him from the early-morning mist, as he sat outside in his bathrobe, staring down the garden to where the posts of the empty landing formed a dark silhouette against the shroud of funereal grey. And it was the smirk that, when he could take the hopeless impotence no more, led him back on the trail of his son's killers.

The encounter in Vector's offices had been all that Andrew needed to convince him that Executive Protection had murdered his son. What he still missed completely was a motive. Why would anyone want to do away with a terminally ill little boy? This was no personal vendetta. It had been a surgical attack carried out by hired professionals. But what organisation, what company could have ordered Executive Protection to carry it out? And why?

He thought about how he might uncover Executive Protection's client list. That might provide some clues. The most simple way would be to phone them, under the auspices of Glencoe, dangling a security contract in return for a complete list of references.

No sooner had he considered that option, however, than he dismissed it. Even if he did convince them to hand over client names, there was no guarantee that among the list would be the organisation or individual who had commissioned Matt's execution.

Perhaps he'd get further by investigating the American owners of what had, until recently, been J & G Security. Could it be that the new owners had brought with them the client responsible for Matt's death? Certainly couldn't hurt to look, he decided.

Still in his bathrobe, he sat behind his computer, searching the Net for Executive Protection. His first attempts to guess a web address having failed, he tried out the company name on several search engines. In rapid succession he tried out Google, Alta Vista, HotBot and excite – but to no avail. Executive Protection didn't seem to have any presence at all in cyber-space. But if their business was anything like what he suspected, thought Andrew grimly, zero visibility should hardly come as a surprise.

Even their telephone number proved elusive. Calling international directory enquiries, he asked for their number in New York before, getting nowhere, prompting for a listing in Los Angeles, Miami, Chicago, Boston. But he drew a blank each time. Just how 'big' was this 'big American company', as claimed by their UK associates?

Staring out of the window to where the mist was rising off the river, Andrew wondered how else he could get some kind of handle on Executive Protection, before remembering back to his conversation with John Barlow on the subject of the company's golf day. The golfing guest list that Barlow had e-mailed him was a composite mixture of brokers, professional advisors and office supply companies. And then he wondered, for the first time, who had put Executive Protection on the list? Perhaps Canadian Mutual had a security officer. Or was there some manager whose remit included the management of its various properties? If so, how much did *that* person know about Executive Protection?

Picking up his cordless phone, he'd soon looked up the number of Canadian Mutual in his electronic organiser and had dialled through to the company switchboard. A receptionist told him that property security was handled by Facilities Manager, Jeff Broadwick, to whom she connected him. Broadwick, evidently not high enough up the organisation to merit a secretary, answered the phone himself.

'The name's Faber.' Andrew had no intention of breaking cover. 'Vector Fund Management.'

'All right?' The voice at the other end was pure estuary.

'We're reviewing our security arrangements and had a firm in called Executive Protection.'

'Reggie Bennett, eh?'

'That's right. And another, younger chap.'

'Yeah.' The other was clipped. 'Yeah, that Stan Fenelli or Ferelli or some such.'

'Uh-huh. What I'm looking for is a reference—'

' 'Course. Me and Reggie, we go back years.'

'You do?'

'Sure. Back in them early days, 'bout fifteen years ago, we did everything for this firm. It wasn't Canadian Mutual then, it was Linton Frobisher. We did the security, courier deliveries, chauffeuring the top brass to the airport, you name it. Then Canadian Mutual took over and they had this change of management. We had to tighten up. I stayed in-house, but Reggie went and started his own security firm which we outsourced. Load of cobblers, if you ask me,' he couldn't resist. Then, adding hastily, 'But he's a solid man, our Reg.'

Andrew was scribbling notes in his ring-bound pad. 'Tell me, what kind of work is he doing these days?'

'Same he always did. Puts guards in buildings. Protection for VIPs.'

'And that's it?' Andrew pushed.

The question hung suspended for a long while before Broadwick acknowledged, 'That's Reggie's bit, yeah.'

'So there's another . . . bit?'

'Y'see, Reggie was ticking along very nicely, like. We've grown a bit in the past few years, now he's got five buildings to contend with. Then along comes this Executive Protection crowd offering to buy him up, triple his business overnight. They had their own client contract, right?'

'You mean, Reg Bennett didn't have any clients besides Canadian Mutual?'

'Nah. Never needed it. We kept 'im busy enough.'

'So why didn't Executive Protection just set up shop themselves?'

'Didn't have the connections. Getting staff in this game isn't easy.'

Not when you're hiring killers, thought Andrew.

'You can't just walk into a new country and set up from scratch. You need connections. Someone who knows the lie of the land. Reggie's an old hand.'

'And this Italian chap, Stan Fenelli, he's with Executive Protection?'

'Too right.'

Andrew noted the diffidence in his tone. 'Reg Bennett

must be very pleased,' he probed. 'Sounds like he's on a good wicket.'

'There's that to it,' agreed Broadwick. 'But it's a different culture, like. The Americans, they have a different way of doing things. More . . . hard-nosed.' Then, remembering himself, 'Not that you must let that put you off using them. I'd recommend Reggie any day of the week.'

His antipathy for Ferelli and Executive Protection couldn't have been more pointed, thought Andrew, before getting to the main purpose of the call. 'I just want to clarify one thing, Mr Broadwick. Executive Protection – they came with their own client list, did they?'

'Y'could call it that.' Broadwick grunted. 'Point is, there's plenty of sites, but only one client.'

Andrew's eyes widened momentarily. 'And do you know who that is?' he queried.

'Oh, yeah. That American hotel group, what's their name . . .?'

There was a pause at the other end before Andrew ventured, 'Marriott? Hilton?'

'No, it's that luxury group. The one with the logo – I know. Du Cane.'

'Du Cane Plaza?' Andrew confirmed.

'That's them. Charge the punters top dollar, they do,' observed the other, 'but, Jesus, they screw their suppliers!'

'And what sort of stuff does Ferelli do for Du Cane Plaza, d'you know?'

'Can't say for sure, but I can find out. Fingers in many pies, I'd say.'

'I'd be very grateful if you could get back to me,' said Andrew. 'What I do next could depend on it.'

*

312

Clicking his phone off, for a moment he rubbed it contemplatively against his chin. He knew about the Du Cane Plaza Group, having followed its fortunes, along with those of other major private companies in America with a marked potential for a stock exchange listing. It was a textbook case: single-site hotel grows to national leisure chain, then the sell-off to Inter-Global Hotels – a classic exit strategy for the founding family whose name currently escaped him.

Going through to the bedroom to change into jeans and a jersey, he thought through what Broadwick had just told him. If Executive Protection only had two clients, a fund manager and a hotel chain, that still left him very much without a motive. What interest could a luxury American hotel franchise have in a child with progeria? Or, for that matter, someone like himself on the other side of the pond? None of it made sense.

Back in his study, he had soon gained access to the financial news service, one of the few Glencoe intranet services to which he'd have access till his 'gardening leave' came to an end. He clicked on archive, and rapidly entered 'Du Cane Plaza'. Within moments he was presented with several hundred items, the most recent being newspaper pieces documenting new hotel openings in Edinburgh, Munich and Moscow. Scanning back in time, he saw the news pieces went all the way to that intensive period of several weeks when Du Cane Plaza had made its appearance in news sections of the major US business press, during its sale to Inter-Global. Throughout this period the news focus had been on Jack Hennessy, the controversial entrepreneur who'd turned the family business around.

As he surveyed the coverage, including photographs of

the good-looking Hennessy, Andrew was reminded of some of the unsavoury allegations which had done the rounds about him at the time. They mainly centred, he seemed to recall, on how Hennessy had fiddled the books. Highly inflated revenue figures had been leaked into Wall Street around the time that Hennessy had been looking for a buyer. While his creditors, including many small businesses, went to the wall because of payment defaults, Hennessy was reporting generous cash flows.

There had also been reports about political manipulation. His socialite mother had many friends in high places whom Hennessy had courted assiduously, swinging deals involving city planning approval and state subsidies that should never have been allowed to happen. The number of allegations made about Jack Hennessy suggested he was less than squeaky clean. And it seemed an astounding volte-face, that he claimed to be bowing out of the grimy corporate world to become a Washington, DC-based philanthropist.

The new owners of Du Cane Plaza Group, Inter-Global, were listed on the New York Stock Exchange and had a Board weighed down with eminent non-executive directors, each of whom held other executive and non-executive jobs. As he ran down the roll-call of corporate warriors, Andrew kept thinking how wildly improbable it seemed that any of them could be involved in the death of a small boy. Trying to uncover a possible motivation for involvement in Matt's murder wouldn't just take forever, he thought disconsolately, it also wouldn't prove a thing.

Clicking open a few of the more recent news pieces, he found a headline from the New York *Tatler*. Up came a spread from the society pages celebrating Cornelia

Hennessy's sixty-fifth birthday celebrations held at the flagship New York Du Cane Plaza Hotel.

Glancing through the photographs without much interest, Andrew couldn't help noticing the glittering presence of Hollywood luminaries, business tycoons and politicians of a certain generation. Jack Hennessy, the son, was there too, of course.

But the image that struck him with sudden and overwhelming force was the one in the bottom left-hand corner. There among a group of Cornelia's ageing relations, standing directly between 'the birthday lady' and her son, was none other than the woman who had given the Norton family its greatest cause for hope in recent years: Dr Lorna Reid.

Washington, DC
Tuesday, 2 May

Judith hadn't told Canary Wharf about her conversation with Barbett. Until she had a firm date in her diary, she didn't want to build up false hopes. But she was determined to make Wendell's spin-doctor deliver on his promise. She'd go and doorstep him if necessary.

As it happened, she didn't have to go that far. Shortly after arriving at work, she received the unprompted call from William Barbett.

'Don't sound so surprised,' he quipped. 'I promised you an interview.'

Keep up the sweet-talk, baby, she thought, it won't change a thing.

'Thursday the fourth. Eleven am,' he told her. 'Media briefing room at Wendell Campaign Headquarters here in Washington.'

'How long do I have with him?'

'He'll give a briefing of about five minutes. Then questions for twenty-five.'

There was something cagey about the answer. Something she didn't trust.

'Why the briefing?' she asked. 'I've got enough questions for a whole hour.'

'He always likes to start with a briefing. A few issues he wants to cover.'

That was when she twigged. 'This interview. Will other journalists be there?'

'I never promised you an exclusive.' He was Mr Firm But Reasonable.

'You never promised me oxygen either, but I'm assuming the interview won't be underwater.'

'That's a rather . . . extreme metaphor.'

'So how many others are coming?'

'We haven't had confirmation yet.'

'Christ! You're talking about a whole goddam media conference, aren't you?'

He didn't respond to her protest.

'I suppose you've got fifty journalists with only twenty-five minutes of questions?'

'You'll cover the ground, Ms Laing—'

'I don't think so,' she was uncompromising, ' 'cause I'm not coming. This isn't the deal we discussed.'

'It's the only deal on offer.'

'I've just been looking at the Governor's record on health services,' she threatened. 'Are you aware that Louisiana hospital queues have doubled under his administration?'

There was a gasp at the other end before he told her, 'Look. I'm putting you in front of him. You can deliver the interview your editor so desperately wants. I'll promise you the chance to ask a question—'

'A question?' She was incredulous.

'Governor Wendell just doesn't have any other available time.'

Should she blow him out of the water, wondered Judith, or take what she could get? Disillusioning as it was to find herself so marginalised, she was also desperate to get whatever face time she could with Wendell. It was the prospect of remaining empty-handed that tipped the balance.

'Well, you've come way down from the exclusive you promised me,' she hardballed him. 'I'd need at least ten questions.'

'Let's get some perspective.' Barbett was smooth. 'Ten questions is half the question time. I couldn't justify it. I'll give you two, and you'll be doing as well as any news organisation in America.'

'Five and I'll consider it.'

'I couldn't deliver. There'd be a revolution.'

'Five,' she repeated.

'I could say five, just to keep you happy. But I'm only prepared to offer what I know I can give you.'

'How very principled of you, Mr Barbett.' Her tone was acid.

'Look,' he sighed, 'I know you're disappointed. I know you want an exclusive. I wish I could create an extra hour in the day for Governor Wendell to see you personally. But you have to accept, that's simply never going to happen. No matter how many unhelpful articles you conjure up. I can give you three questions and that's my best offer. Do we have a deal?'

It was a long while before Judith murmured, 'I guess.'

18

Brooklyn Penitentiary
Tuesday, 2 May

As a late-nineteenth-century penal establishment, Brooklyn Penitentiary isn't the oldest jail in New York. Nor is it the largest – that dubious honour belongs to the 16,000-strong jail complex on Rikers Island. But Brooklyn does have its own point of distinction; it's notorious for being the most miserable hell-hole in the entire US Federal Bureau of Prisons.

Built on the banks of the East River, a forbidding silhouette of stone wall and scrambled razor wire, inside it is a dark pit of deprivation and despair. Hated, not only by long-term lags, but also by its jailers, for whom transfer here is career suicide, Brooklyn is a place where human life has been reduced to its basest existence.

The prisoners are all lifers. Locked up for twenty-three out of every twenty-four hours, they subsist on brown food and grey light, and pass their long, caged hours inflicting vile degradations on those inattentive enough to fall prey. Convicted murderers, rapists and violent criminals, they are men for whom the judicial system has no answer but incarceration for stretches of twenty or thirty years, until every energy and evil purpose is worn out of their lives.

Lorna knew nothing of the prison's reputation, though as she sat in the visiting room she couldn't avoid the malevolence of the place. Her only prior experience of jail had been her overnight stay in New Orleans, and that had felt like a momentary unhappiness compared with what she found here. It was more than just the monstrosity of the building. It was also the hostility of the staff that was so oppressive. As she surveyed the banks of warped, wooden visiting tables, the plastic chairs and naked neon strip lights, there was a quite palpable sense of wretchedness about the place. Human misery seemed to sweat from its very walls.

She'd found her way here after her discharge from GWU Hospital. Slipping out of the hospital in the back of an ambulance, after explaining her position to the Hospital Administrator, she'd been driven directly to Union Station, where she'd had to wait only fifteen minutes for the first direct train to New York. At Grand Central Station, she'd caught a taxi directly here. All morning, she'd kept her cellphone determinedly off.

Visiting hours at the jail, she remembered, were from 1 till 2 pm and she arrived in time to join the queue outside the gates – one that was surprisingly short given the vast, decaying sprawl of pitted concrete and steel.

Inside, the visitors were taken through clanking sets of gates and subjected to the indignity of a body search. Interminable waiting was followed by the inevitable paperwork before more gates were opened and visitors were driven, like goats, deeper into the jail, through a dark cavern to the visiting chamber.

In TV shows, jail visits always occur in brightly lit facilities, with visitors and prisoners communicating through glass windows with microphones and speakers, and Lorna had come to Brooklyn half expecting reality to match the TV image. But as they were herded into the visiting room, she realised this place was nothing like that, and neither the setting nor her fellow visitors bore any resemblance to her preconceptions. Directed to their separate tables, the other visitors were a ragged assembly. Middle-aged or older, they were, without exception, poorly dressed and down at heel. Lives as ravaged as their faces, they sat, in cowed silence, facing a wooden door in the corner through which prisoners were evidently expected.

Lorna was directed curtly to a desk and told to wait her turn. Glancing round, she felt her apprehension growing. Trying to control her feelings, she told herself she should be excited. She was about to have confirmed the truth about the Lafayette trials. She'd also soon know a whole lot more about Jeb Livingstone.

But instead, she felt hollow dread in the pit of her stomach. She hadn't anticipated that she would be directly facing a prisoner she'd never met, with no protection, no bars or plastic wall between them. Nor had she prepared herself for the full, baroque horror of this jail.

After all the visitors were seated, the clanking of locks and chains reverberated through a maze of windowless corridors in the bowels of the jail beyond, before finally the wooden door was opened and a group of inmates appeared. Lorna had no idea what Livingstone looked like, though as a ninety-two-year-old black man he would surely stand out?

Another mistaken assumption, she realised, as the first prisoners came into view. None of them looked anything less than retirement age, and a few considerably older, their short hair grizzled, and figures stooped. Hobbling across the floor with difficulty, many were black. Most seemed spare and broken, survivors of a lifetime lived inside cages. But despite the unimaginable privations etched into their faces, every one of them, Lorna noticed, was sharp-eyed, alert. No matter how gaunt their appearance, they had the heedfulness of prey.

One after the other they appeared through the door, most making their way purposefully towards where their visitors sat in regimented rows, surrounded by prison officers. Each of the visitor desks was assigned a number, so there'd be no question where Livingstone was to go. But as inmate after inmate appeared, and still no one edged towards her desk, she wondered if perhaps she'd come here under a mistaken assumption. Prisoners weren't obliged to see visitors. But until you came, there was no way of finding out for sure whether you would be seen. She guessed Livingstone might have reasons for not coming out. Infirmity, for instance. And, as she'd known all along, there was the question of his mind. He might not be in a fit state to speak to anyone, visitor or not. There was every chance that he might be very senile. Even if he wasn't, would he be able to recollect events that took place over thirty years before?

More stooped and elderly men appeared at the entrance, some with the sharpness of stoats, others shambling wrecks. Making their way over to waiting visitors, their eyes would dart about the room at the other tables, feasting on the faces of all present. Lorna could feel their eyes pausing on her face, scrutiny incisive and unwavering as headlights. Gaze fixed on the wooden door, she avoided all eye contact as she wondered, and waited, and hoped.

After still more time had passed every visitor's table in the room was occupied – except her own. Talk, low and furtive, hissed all about her and the empty seat opposite. The wooden door leading to the cells remained open, though no one had come out of it for some time. Prison officers, scrutinising the rows of tables, were impassive as they surveyed the vacant chair.

Waiting for what felt like an eternity, Lorna glanced from the door, to the clock on the wall, to the prison guards, to her own watch. On the point of raising a hand to summon an officer, she became aware of a shadow at the door, half in the darkness beyond, half in the light, lingering uncertainly. Realising she was being studied she became self-conscious. She tried to adopt an unthreatening demeanour, leaning back in her chair, brushing a fallen lock back from her face.

Unable to help herself, she looked back at the door, straining as she gazed into the depths beyond it, trying to make out the watchful, motionless figure. Then he stepped forward, and she caught sight of him properly for the first time.

It was his height that took her by surprise, as he came into the strip-white light of the visiting room. His height and his bearing, too – even at ninety-two he held himself with an almost regal poise, his bearing that of an elderly aristocrat as he made slow, measured progress towards her. It was as though he remained untouched by the diminution of ageing, there was no bend in the neck or sinking spine, and his walk, though laborious, was unaided.

The moment he made eye contact she knew his mind, too – his face communicated intelligence, a perspicacity undimmed. Though lined, it was nowhere near as ravaged as might have been expected of someone of his years, and he was completely shaven – no grizzled whiteness to accentuate his longevity. His lips, smooth and well-formed, were slightly parted as he breathed heavily – evidently the journey from the cells had tired him. But for all that he still bore himself proudly upright, wearing his prison jumpsuit as though it were robes of office.

Slowly he came forward till he was almost at the table. Lorna rose from her chair in a gesture of automatic respect. Eyes locked into his, she was aware that at that moment they were taking the measure of each other, both of them held in a timeless moment of mutual enquiry. She was about to raise her hand to shake his when she remembered the warden's instruction: no physical contact of any kind with the prisoners. Instead, she gestured towards the chair opposite and said unnecessarily, 'Please. Sit down.'

Facing each other again, she found the knowledge that this was him, the last surviving participant in the Neuropazine trials, sitting facing her, almost overwhelming. The last survivor, who also happened to be a life-sentence convict. A man who, sometime in the past, had been found guilty of the most heinous crime. She didn't even like to speculate about what that might be. It was the first time she'd been in the company of such a person, though she could find no trace of violence in his face. Instead, the calm, level gaze was strangely disconcerting. There was no hostility or reserve or emotion of any kind in that expression. The emptiness of it made her nervous.

'I was worried you wouldn't come,' she started. Then immediately wondered if she shouldn't have said that. Perhaps the delay had been caused because he simply couldn't walk fast.

But if he took offence, he wasn't showing it. 'I made them check.' His voice was deep and reverberant as a well. 'I'm not used to visitors.'

'You haven't seen anyone for a while?' The words came babbling out.

'Not for nine years.'

Nine years! She couldn't begin to comprehend such isolation. That was just about as long as her entire professional career.

Trying to let go of her own reactions, she marshalled her thoughts. 'I'm Dr Lorna Reid. I work in the pharmaceutical industry,' she began her introduction as planned. 'I'm developing a product which has shared properties with a drug called Neuropazine.'

If he had any recognition of the name, he wasn't showing it.

'It was tested on outpatients at St Augusta Hospital, Louisiana, between 1968 and 1973. I believe you were one of those patients.'

Eyes still bearing into her own, opposite her he puckered his lips. 'You've got the wrong guy.'

'I'm sure I haven't.'

'I'm Paul Laurence.'

'Prisoner number 550323,' she recited. 'Yeah, I know.'

'I ain't never been near St Augusta Hospital.' His expression was unchanging.

'You haven't?'

'Don't even know where it is.'

'I'd like to assure you, Mr – um – sir, I'm *not* here in any official capacity. I'm *not* working with the authorities, or the prisons, or any government or political organisation or individual. I'm here as a scientist following up on an

324

experiment some people seem determined to cover up.'

Her credentials, intended to reassure him, appeared to have no effect. That unnerving gaze lasted a long while before he responded, 'Look, ma'am, I'm sure you're well-meaning and all, but best leave me be.' His speech was plain and clear. 'There's been a mistake. Happens all the time.'

She raised her eyebrows, questioningly.

'Look at my record. Never been anywhere near Louisiana.'

'That would be the record of Paul Laurence. But what about Livingstone?'

'Never heard of him,' he replied, a fraction too quickly, pushing himself back from the table.

'Please . . . Mr Livingstone!' she urged him. 'You have to help me!'

Once again it was a long while before he replied, 'Every time you move in these places it takes time to set yourself up. There's gangs and guards and it's hard on a man, especially an old man, to be left in peace. I've got that now. It's taken me since when I arrived to work up to it. But I've got my quiet place. You want to take all I've got away from me?'

For a long while she said nothing, but simply held his gaze. She felt sure he was Livingstone, she was convinced of it. But it was impossible not to sympathise with his position. For the entire duration of his prison life it was probable that the only treatment he'd ever received at the hands of authority figures – among whom she'd no doubt be included – was rejection and disappointment. If she had it right, betrayal of the worst kind. How could she convince him she was different?

'Taking away something from you is the very last thing I

want to do.' She was shaking her head. 'What I want is to help you all I can.'

'Why,' he asked simply, 'would you want to do that?'

'Because I think you've been the victim of a grave injustice. Because I don't see how incarcerating a ninety-two-year-old man can possibly benefit society.'

'Mighty fine words, Dr Reid.' It was the first time he'd used her name, and he delivered the words with an unmistakable irony. 'But why does a lady like you want to help a man like me?'

He'd cut to the chase – and she knew this was her opportunity. So she told him about Zonmark and her NP3 programme. How initial success had turned into disarray as she found herself besieged with problems on all fronts. She explained the connection with the Neuropazine trials, and her discovery of its unintended side effects. How, to divert attention from her own difficulties with NP3 she had searched for full Neuropazine records – and had quickly found herself with a powerful enemy.

Opposite her, still wearing that inscrutable expression, he took this all in before asking, 'How far did you get, looking for these records?'

It was the first sign of any interest on his part, though she tried to keep hope reined in. 'Far enough to know,' she replied, 'that on the fifteenth of September 1993, William Gore listed two prisoners transferred out of Wilson to Masden, Mississippi. Those prisoners were Livingstone and Moffat. Masden only registers the arrival from Wilson of Moffat, who died within a month. But there was another transfer that day.' She nodded towards him, her voice barely a whisper. 'I believe that other transfer was given a new identity and sent out of state to erase the evidence of the trials. I believe your real name is Livingstone, that you were born in 1910, and that you have no place being in jail.'

Still, his eyes betrayed nothing. But she observed that he was breathing more quickly. The truth had registered, she was sure she'd got it right, but caution and the reserve of many years' bitterness made it hard for him to trust.

'You say you're being . . . harassed?' he asked.

'That's right.' Lifting her hair up, she showed him the bandage. 'This happened just last night,' she said, before describing what had happened.

After she'd finished, he asked, 'This . . . powerful enemy. Do you know who it is?'

'Oh, yes,' she leaned forward, 'Grayson Wendell. He's doing all he can to make sure the Neuropazine trials don't come back on him.'

At mention of Grayson Wendell's name, a sudden, unconstrained fury flashed across his face.

Yes! thought Lorna. There could be no mistaking the anger in his face. He knows all about Wendell – he'll talk now.

But despite the emotion, he still said nothing.

'If my theory is correct,' she pressed further, 'you and Wendell should be swapping places. But I need your help. I tried to speak to Albert Krauss, but he and his wife burned to death in their house the day before I tried to make contact. I tried to speak to William Gore, only he supposedly committed suicide the day before we were due to meet. There's no one left, Jeb. I'm out of every other option. Wendell's put out the order to have me taken care of. I'm in this as far as you now, and I need your help to get us both out of it.'

327

She could see the acknowledgement in his face. But still there was a reserve.

'Even if I did know anything about the stuff you just mentioned, what would you do with the information?'

'Get it out to the media.' She didn't hesitate. 'Wendell will stop at nothing to contain it. But once it's out there he'll have far bigger things to worry about.'

The other regarded her carefully. 'That sure would make you a big hero.'

'Believe me, I've had all the TV I want in one lifetime. I'm not after fame. I just want to get on with my job.' Then, realising how self-absorbed this all sounded, 'And is it too much to believe I actually want to help you too?'

'Get my life back at ninety-two, you mean?'

'Why not?'

He was shaking his head again with a wry smile. 'Where would I go? What would I do? Everyone I know died twenty years ago.'

'You'd have payout money – wrongful imprisonment. You must have some hankering to go back to your roots.'

'The sweet wind in the cane fields? The rolling blue of the Mississippi?'

'Something like that.' She regarded his sceptical expression at length.

Then he surprised her. 'Seeing Wendell go down. That would be better.'

Lorna caught her breath. 'So you'll trust me?'

He pursed his lips reflectively, 'I don't trust no one. But way I look at it, at my time of life a man in my position don't have too many options.'

'I can promise you I won't let you down, Mr

Livingstone.' Her voice was firm with conviction. 'It is that, isn't it?'

He looked down at the worn wooden desk, the darkly scarred no-man's-land between them. 'Yeah'm. Jeb Livingstone. And those transfers you said before,' he nodded, 'they're right too.'

Moving her chair closer, she leaned forward across the desk. 'Can you confirm you participated in the Neuropazine trials at St Augusta?'

'I can.'

'Tell me, who else participated?'

' 'Bout a hundred and fifty of us from Wilson.'

'All black prisoners?'

'There weren't any white ones. Least, not in them days.'

'Did you know where the order for the trial had come from?'

'Most of us put it down to Gore. He was a hard man. Some folk reckoned the order came from higher up.'

'What did you think?'

'I didn't much care. Back then I was in it together with everybody else. I was just one in a hundred and fifty. 'Course, by the early nineties, there was only two of us left.'

'You and Moffat?'

' 'Sright. I was counting down to my parole, fifteenth December '93. Moffat, he was out two years later. By then Wendell was Governor of Louisiana. There was talk of him running for the White House. I still wasn't connecting him to the experiments. But that sure changed quick.'

'The transfer to Masden.'

Fire returned to his eyes. 'You got that right! He wanted to wipe out Moffat and me. He knew if it ever came out what he'd done back in St Augusta, well, he wouldn't stand a chance. Like you said earlier, he had to get rid of the evidence.' He fixed her with a penetrating stare. 'One day I'm called into the Governor's office. He tells me I'm being transferred to Masden. I object. It's less than two months till my parole. Less than two months to the day I've been countin' down to for the past twenty-five years. Every Early Parole Board I ever applied to, and by Jesus I applied whenever I could, every Board turned me down with any excuse. The one thing they couldn't take away from me was the end of my sentence – least, that's what I thought.

'So the Governor's goin' on about a transfer and I just can't understand it. Why send me to the next state for eight weeks? I didn't know the plan, see. If I had, I'd have killed one of them.' His fingers were shaking with anger.

'Next thing I know, I'm on Conair to El Reno – that's where all prison transfers have to go through. Which is when I work out something funny's going on here, something unofficial. It's the fifteenth September 1993, like you say. Friday the fifteenth. I'll never forget it, 'cause by the time I get to Masden, suddenly my number's changed and they're calling me Laurence. I don't know nothing about this Laurence, who he is, what he's in for. Turns out he's seven years younger than me and he's on a murder sentence with twenty more years to run! Twenty years!' Anguish choked his voice. 'Nothing I do or say is gettin' through to these people – they reckon whatever I say is just the rantings of a crazy old man.'

For a few moments he halted, to check the powerful emotions close to the surface, before he continued, 'I'm in my new cell, the day after the transfer, and word gets round that Moffat has also come over from Masden, same day as me, only they haven't changed his name. Everyone in Wilson knows about Moffat.' He met Lorna's eyes. 'He's seventy-two, and he's got cancer. The transfer pushes him over the edge. He gives up the fight and it's only weeks before they're carryin' him out under a blanket.

'Which was when I got to figure it all out. They push Moffat over the edge deliberately. And me, because they know I'm going to be around for a while, and they want to keep me locked up and out of trouble, they have to fix a new identity. Later I get to hear the real Paul Laurence died on a workers' gang in a plantation. Arm came off in a sawmill and he bled to death. So I get his identity, and I'm trying to work out what it is that Moffat and me have got that these people, whoever they are, are so desperate to keep under cover. Moffat and me, we hardly know each other. We've never been in anything together, no prison gangs, nothing like that. And the more I think about it, the more I see. The only thing we've got in common is those drug trials. And the guy in charge of the department at the time was Grayson Wendell. I get to thinking, Wendell's the guy behind all this.' He studied her with a lengthy gaze. 'It was only a theory up till today.'

Sitting facing him, absorbed in his story, Lorna felt a powerful mix of emotions – a welling up of sympathy for Jeb, the victim of pitiless machinations. And deepening outrage at how Wendell had been so willing to bury him in the living death of jail.

After a long pause while he eyeballed her, she said, 'Let me get this right. You've now served thirty-four years for a twenty-five-year prison sentence.'

'You got it.'

She raised her hands to her face. Words were wholly

inadequate to express her feelings. Though there was still a part of the drama she didn't understand.

'The move from Masden to here in '97.' She spoke quietly. 'Why was that?'

'To get away from Wendell.' He nodded.

'But he could track you down here. Probably has.'

'Oh, sure. He knows I'm in here. But he can't do much about it. In the South he's got friends, influence. Up here they never even heard of him till he threw his hat in the ring.'

'You were worried he'd . . .'

'Wipe out the last remaining evidence?' He cocked his head slightly to one side. 'It might sound kinda pointless to a young lady like you with a full life ahead o' her, that a man of my age should want to last out another year in jail. But the will to live, you know, it's a strong instinct. Stronger even,' he glanced about him, 'than the worst jail in the system. Stronger than the chance of "85" passes.'

She raised her eyebrows sharply.

'Rule 85?'

'Never heard of it,' she confessed.

'After age eighty-five, prisoners with clean records on the inside are allowed out under supervision – six hours at a time.'

'And Paul Laurence isn't eighty-five?'

'Sure he is. Thing is, because Paul Laurence doesn't exist, he don't know any responsible citizens on the outside.'

'But you do.'

'I have nephews, nieces. Only they're all down there in New Orleans. They don't have money. They never been to New York. And this old guy, he's just the skeleton in the family closet.'

Heart pounding as an idea began forming in her mind, Lorna studied him closely for a few moments before asking, 'Are you saying that some . . . responsible citizen could sign you out of Brooklyn Penitentiary for six hours?'

'Sure could,' he confirmed. Then, after a pause, 'But who'd want to?'

19

The revelation that Jack Hennessy and Lorna Reid were intimate changed everything. For a while, Andrew had stared at the photograph of the two of them together which had appeared in the New York *Tatler*, with sheer disbelief. According to the caption, Lorna was Hennessy's 'partner'. Exactly what that meant, he couldn't be sure. But judging by the way her body folded into his, she was more than just his squeeze for the night.

Andrew found it hard to take in. He'd met Lorna many times; every six months Matt had had to go over to Washington for monitoring, and usually both Jess and he had gone with him. Over the years they'd got to know Lorna on a personal as well as professional basis. Because of his job, Andrew followed the biotech sector on Nasdaq; he knew not only what was going on at Zonmark, but also what was happening among some of their direct competitors in the industry. There'd always been a lot to talk about. They'd even got into the habit of going out to dinner one evening during each visit. He and Jess always extended the invitation to Lorna *and partner* but, for all the time they'd been going to Washington, she'd claimed never to have a partner. Her working hours were too long and she didn't seem to meet the right people, she'd always said – and they'd had no reason to disbelieve her. It looked as if that had changed, thought Andrew, still staring at the photograph. But had she any idea about the kind of man she'd got herself involved with?

The photo made him rethink the direction of his investigations fundamentally. For he realised the assumption he'd been making. In chasing after Executive Protection's current clients he'd hoped to find some clue, some motivation which would lead him to the door of those who'd ordered his son's death. Du Cane Plaza Hotels had seemed an unlikely proposition from the start. He realised now, however, that as Executive Protection's former paymaster at the hotel group, Jack Hennessy would be intimately acquainted with the security firm's *modus operandi*. In fact, if Executive Protection only existed to service Du Cane Plaza Hotels, Hennessy would have been directly responsible for the company's massive growth. Which meant that whoever ran Executive Protection would be greatly in his debt. If Hennessy needed something done, he knew where to turn for it. So what exactly was Jack Hennessy up to these days? And what was Lorna Reid doing on his arm?

Trawling through the press cuttings on Hennessy from Glencoe's archive, Andrew saw that most covered the sale of Du Cane Plaza for $3.5 billion. Hennessy was described as a philanthropist who'd retired to Washington, DC, but to Andrew that really didn't ring true. A man like Hennessy, a deal-maker who lived, ate and breathed business, didn't retire to philanthropy in his mid-forties. It wasn't in his nature to bow out of commercial life – at least, not for long. Studying the more extensive pieces that had appeared in the *Wall Street Journal*, and the *Tribune*, he looked for details, anything that might suggest what Hennessy had done after Du Cane Plaza.

There were few clues in the mainstream press, so he started on trade journals. This was exactly the kind of corporate detective work his job at Glencoe had required of him – tracking down information that could prove critical. And as he knew from past experience, the trade press, though tedious, usually carried a level of detail missing in other media.

America's hotel and catering magazines were every bit as boring as he had anticipated. Scrolling back to the time of the Du Cane Plaza sale, he had to work through screeds of articles repeating the same well-worn detail. After half an hour of reading, he wondered if his efforts had amounted to anything – Hennessy's PR minders had, it seemed, held the media on a tight rein.

Then he came across the diary piece in *American Hotelier*; a page of light-hearted gossip about industry players. In one of the paragraphs it was jocularly reported that a group of merchant bankers had been spotted performing the conga, late one night by the swimming pool of an up-market hotel in the Bahamas. Stand up, Jeffrey Plantel, of Plantel Stewart merchant bank. Could it be that he and his colleagues had been celebrating the bumper fees they'd just earned from the sell-off of Du Cane Plaza?

Plantel Stewart. Andrew had had ongoing dealings with several analysts there. At Glencoe he'd subscribed to their information feeds. Checking his watch, he saw that it was just after 8.30 am in New York – they'd be behind their desks by now. He had to pause only a moment to recall the Plantel Stewart phone number, before he commenced dialling.

Pete Brewer, the Leisure and Entertainment analyst at Plantel Stewart, wasn't someone Andrew had had a huge amount to do with in the past, but they knew each other. Andrew called under Glencoe auspices, explaining that he needed to find out what Jack Hennessy had invested in after the Du Cane Plaza sell-off. Brewer, a soft-spoken New Englander whose mental acuity was matched only by his laconic style, had replied simply, 'Financial Services took care of him.'

'They're your personal investment arm, right?'

'Uh-huh.'

'That would mean trust funds, that kind of thing?'

'No question.'

He could have worked that out for himself, thought Andrew. Of course Hennessy was going to protect his capital gains in a trust, probably offshore, to maximum tax advantage. And once the cash was safely routed into some tax-free territory like the Caymans, British Virgin Islands, Liechtenstein or Sark, it would become untraceable. The whole point of the exercise was to put money out of reach of tax authorities, creditors – and the wiliest of investigators.

But that didn't mean the trail had run cold. Money protected in even the most elaborate of trust arrangements still had to be invested. There was no point in leaving it lying around in a bank account earning five per cent a year – especially if it was controlled by someone with the entrepreneurial instincts of Hennessy.

'Your Financial Services people – they'd have advised on investments.'

'Sure.'

'Would there be any way of finding out—'

'Closed book.' The other paused before observing, 'You're pretty serious about this, aren't you?'

'Deadly.'

'Let me try.'

Minutes later, Brewer had called him back on his mobile. 'The way they operate over there is recommendation, not prescription – gives them an out if it all turns nasty,' he observed with a cynical chuckle.

'Would they tell you their recommendations?'

'Big-picture stuff,' he confirmed. 'You'd have to work the detail yourself.'

He didn't care how much detail he had to plough through, thought Andrew – if he could just get a lead. He felt sure he was onto something.

'The sectors they were recommending to clients at the time were aircraft, health and construction.'

Writing these down, Andrew murmured, 'Construction was never flavour of the month for Hennessy. He lost out badly building in Texas.'

'As aircraft analyst at that time, I can tell you there weren't many opportunities around.'

'So, by elimination . . .'

'Over to you.'

'Yeah.' Andrew knew he'd gone as far as he could with Plantel Stewart. There was no point in pushing things. 'Well, Pete, I appreciate your help.'

Andrew fixed himself a caffeine hit – a cafetière of his favourite Kenyan coffee which he took through to his study. While he had a fair overview of the US health sector, his knowledge was concentrated on publicly listed companies.

And it was almost certain that Hennessy would have avoided the stock market – that wasn't his style. The way he'd run Du Cane Plaza showed him to be a man who shunned the limelight. Unlike his socialite mother, he preferred operating from behind the scenes. If he'd bought into the health sector, it was likely he'd have done so privately, his identity probably concealed by the vehicle of an investment trust. Even the companies he'd bought into might have no idea who their controlling shareholder really was.

It didn't make things easy. But there couldn't have been too many three-billion-dollar investment opportunities in the health sector, the year following the disposal of Du Cane Plaza.

He called Ruth. It was the first time they'd spoken since he'd been put on gardening leave. And when she answered, she was highly solicitous. How was he coping? Was he taking care of himself? Had he heard from Jess? They were all questions he preferred avoiding. Swiftly assuring her he was doing fine, he got down to business. He needed a rundown of all the major private transactions in the US hospital and medical supply sectors, for a one-year period after the Du Cane sell-off. Could she pull it off the Glencoe deal-list archive and e-mail it to him?

She assured him she would – no questions asked. Within minutes her e-mail had arrived, and he started with the chunkier deals, working his way downwards. In most cases the buyers were well-established competitors in the same industry, most of the mergers and acquisitions involving no new external investor, unseen or otherwise. But there were others requiring further investigation – any one of them, he realised, could hold the key to what had happened to Jack Hennessy's billions.

As the afternoon wore on, and he drank his way through the first cafetière and started on another, he began wondering where this was heading. He had, by then, checked through all the biggest transactions, and was down to the smaller deals. It was conceivable that Hennessy had spread himself across a range of investments, but Andrew's instinct was that he'd prefer to control a major slice of the action. He'd developed Du Cane Plaza into a premier chain. Andrew didn't see him receding to virtual fund manager status just yet.

But he was missing something, he knew, scrolling down the Glencoe deal-list. He had every major private hospital deal here, every medical equipment supplier. He was confident in the integrity of the lists. So why wasn't he getting anywhere?

Pacing his study, as darkness fell outside, he wondered where to go with this. What else came under the 'health sector' heading that he should look at? Hospitals and equipment were in the mainstream, but he guessed there were other industries too.

He briefly considered pharmaceuticals before dismissing the idea. That was such a massive industry, it was considered a sector all of its own. Surely Plantel Stewart would have said 'Health & Pharma' instead of only 'Health' if that had been their recommendation?

Biotech was another industry, but a three-billion-dollar deal didn't seem in keeping with Hennessy's preferred business practices. His track record suggested it was altogether unlikely that he'd move from an established old-industry environment to one that was at the sharp end. Would he sink all his hard-earned billions into one or two high-risk deals?

It was only some time later that he came up with health insurance. What if that was Hennessy's game? Checking his watch Andrew realised that Ruth would have gone home by now – he wouldn't be able to pull health insurance deals off the archives till tomorrow. But he was in no mood to stop.

Within minutes he'd found his way to the on-line archive section of the main US trade title, *Health Protection Week*. There was no ready-catalogued list of major transactions, so he had to scan the news pages of each individual edition, starting from the time of the Du Cane Plaza sell-off onwards.

It had, by all accounts, been a busy time in the industry, in terms of mergers and acquisitions. There'd been a spate of activity – hostile takeovers, share-swapping and other corporate activity. Making a meticulous list of every significant transaction – the money, the players, and special note of unknown investors – he paused when he got to Mayflower. The mainstay of America's upper-end health insurers, Mayflower was reported as having carried out a private capital-raise thought to be worth in the region of $1.5 billion. Mayflower was saying nothing about the raise, except that it had happened. There were no details about what shares had been issued and whether or not they constituted a controlling interest, although industry analysts seemed to believe they did. Considerable mystery surrounded the identity of the investor, though there was no shortage of speculation, with at least three commentators citing a family trust.

A grainy photograph of Mayflower's CEO had been taken around this time, climbing into a car at Mayflower headquarters, accompanied by a corporate minder, one Julius Lupine, who was grimly eyeing out the photographer.

As he stared at the photograph, the more Andrew thought about health insurers, the more obvious the motivation seemed. If Lorna Reid developed NP3 all the way to the market, the hardest hit companies would be health insurers. Claims for hip replacements, major surgery, prosthetics and drugs would increase exponentially. It was hard to see how insurers would cope without hiking their premiums way beyond what the market would possibly bear.

NP3 spelt disaster for Mayflower. Had Hennessy decided it must come to an end? And how better to penetrate the very heart of the drugs trial than to develop an intimate relationship with its creator? Andrew couldn't but admire the audacity of it. Jack Hennessy had used his masculine good looks, and considerable powers of persuasion, to whisk Lorna off her feet and into his arms, where she'd no doubt told him everything he could want to know.

Certain he'd come to the truth, but still incredulous, Andrew glanced down the list of transactions he'd recorded. It was possible that Hennessy had bought into more than only Mayflower. If the deal had been worth $1.5 billion, that would still have left him plenty of capital with which to do deals with two other insurers, H&S and Virtual Health, who had also seen their controlling shareholdings move to an anonymous private trust.

He clicked back to the photograph that had sparked his astounding discovery – the picture of Hennessy and Lorna at Cornelia Hennessy's birthday party. The society page was crowded with photographs from that night, focusing on the society matron's star-studded guest list. But something else had just registered in Andrew's mind. Going from the photograph of the Mayflower CEO and Julius Lupine in

Health Protection Week to the *Tatler* photo-spread, he glanced through every picture individually.

He didn't suppress the gasp of triumph when he found what he was looking for. There was a photograph of Jack Hennessy and, to his right, Julius Lupine. Both men were resplendent in their evening wear, and one of them had evidently just made a wisecrack. The two seemed like the very best of friends. As Andrew stared at the image, his reflections were interrupted by his mobile phone ringing. He answered, to find Jeff Broadwick, Canadian Mutual's Facilities Manager, on the other end.

'Had a word with our Reg—'

'Oh, yes?' Andrew hadn't really expected Broadwick to pursue it, but maybe he wanted to help an old mate win some new business. Maybe there was a cut in it for him?

'Ferelli keeps Du Cane Plaza business pretty much to himself.'

'Uh-huh.'

'It's mostly routine hotel security, but he does special projects too.'

'Did he tell you—?'

'There was something, recently, but he wouldn't say much about it.'

Andrew's expression was intense as he stared at the picture of Hennessy and Julius Lupine.

'Just,' continued Broadwick, 'they had to get rid of some unwanted research material.'

Brooklyn Penitentiary

As soon as Lorna emerged from the dark maw of Brooklyn Penitentiary, standing in the shadows of the forbidding

343

gatehouse, she switched on her cellphone and called Jack. Now that she'd done what she'd come to do, she wanted to tell him she was safe and well. She felt she owed it to him.

At the other end, Jack sounded agitated. Without going into details, she told him she was in New York and heading home. She'd planned to make the return trip unescorted, but he wouldn't hear of it. After what had happened the night before, he lectured her, she should be taking no chances. At his insistence she was to go to the Du Cane Plaza Hotel on Park Avenue. By the time she'd taken a cab there, he would have arranged for a chauffeured car to take her back to Washington. She was staying at his place, there was an assumption in his tone, though he left the question hanging.

'You mean,' she said, 'your place, or mine?'

At the other end there was silence. Jack Hennessy was in no mood for frivolity – her disappearance had evidently had him worried, which she found touching.

'Yes, Jack.' She smiled as she reassured him. 'Your place.'

The Mercedes, the guard from Executive Protection told her, was generally used to ferry officials to and from the United Nations headquarters. It was hijack-proof and its bulletproofed windows were so dark it was impossible to see inside. As Lorna climbed into the back of it, in the basement of the Du Cane Plaza Hotel, she felt strange sitting in such a vehicle, bristling as it did with security equipment, telephones, a bar and satellite TV. As they purred up Fifth Avenue, though, she closed her eyes and exhaled a long breath.

She was relieved that she'd achieved all she'd hoped to

344

at Brooklyn Penitentiary. More, in fact. Jeb Livingstone's testimony had surpassed whatever she could have expected. She now had all she needed to take this story into the public domain. Within twenty-four hours she would have the full story of the Neuropazine trials out in the open, with Grayson Wendell's dark secret laid out for full, public view. Then she'd be able to put all this behind her and carry on her work without being perpetually shadowed by fear.

Until that time, she had Jack to thank for her security. And as she travelled down the freeway to Washington, DC, she reflected that she'd never felt safer in her life. She recalled his face when he'd come to visit her at GWU Hospital, bringing those beautiful roses – how his eyes had filled with such concern. He'd been her only visitor and it touched her that he had showed how deeply he cared. She'd also come to realise how badly she'd misjudged his own opposition to her pursuing the Neuropazine trials. How foolish she'd been, thinking he'd somehow been trying to protect Grayson Wendell!

She was mulling over her meeting with Jeb, starting to work out exactly how the Neuropazine story should best be presented to the media, as she checked through the messages left on her cellphone. She was never able to leave it switched off for longer than twenty minutes without the messages banking up, and today was no exception. She found twelve. Several were from colleagues at Zonmark. Gail had called, as had Greg Merrit, twice, wanting to know where she was. Kuesterman had wanted to speak, as well as a couple of external suppliers. There were the usual media calls, which she noted on a pad on her lap. She didn't usually consider these a priority, but one of them gave her pause for thought. It was a brief message from Judith Laing – just a quick question, she'd said.

Lorna remembered that the last time they'd spoken, Judith had told her about the pressure she'd been coming under from London to set up an exclusive interview with Grayson Wendell. She wondered curiously what had come of Judith's efforts. Had she managed to schedule a time to meet him? Was it possible that the interview had already taken place? She and Judith had been in touch several times since her profile had appeared in the *Daily Sentinel*. It had been a positive piece, and conversation between the two of them had been relaxed.

Within moments, Lorna had dialled a number and was announcing herself.

'Thanks for getting back to me.' Judith was appreciative. 'I wanted to ask you about this lobby group, Free to Choose. You know much about them?'

'Sure do.' Lorna nodded. 'They're big and getting bigger by the day. Haven't they got a march—'

'March on the Mall,' confirmed Judith, 'that's right. They're very vocal about NP3.'

'All gene therapies. That's their rally cry, isn't it?'

'Yes. But NP3 in particular.'

'To be honest, I hadn't really picked up on that.' Lorna paused. 'I've had no direct contact with them.'

'You've not met anyone from the organisation?'

'Lord, no! Waste of time.'

'One can't help wondering who's bankrolling the operation.' Judith was frank.

'Not Zonmark,' Lorna retorted. Then, recalling Kuesterman's line, 'We're running a business, not a political campaign.'

Judith was pondering this before Lorna continued, 'On the subject of political, have you booked to see Wendell yet?'

Judith responded with a groan. 'Yes and no,' she said after a while. 'I'm guaranteed three questions – but it's at a press conference.'

'How come?'

'According to his media minders, it's the only time he's got. The place will be packed with journos – the big networks, foreign media, you name it. Hardly the kind of fireside tête-à-tête I was hoping for.'

'But that's fantastic!' Lorna didn't conceal her excitement as she thought about her nascent plan. 'When's it happening?'

'Two days' time.'

'Judith, would you mind visiting me tomorrow evening?' Her tone was urgent. 'I promise, I won't be wasting your time.'

'This is about Free to Choose?'

'Grayson Wendell.'

'You know something relevant?' She was surprised.

'More than relevant.' Lorna's eyes glittered. 'What I've got will blow his campaign right out of the water.'

By the time the car pulled up inside the portico of Jack's mansion he was already at the front door, waiting to greet her. As she emerged from the back seat, he collected her up in his arms.

'My darling, am I pleased to see you!' he said with feeling.

After they had kissed, she clung to him tightly, her eyes closed. 'Not as glad as I am to be here,' she whispered.

'I've been so worried about you. After last night—'

'I know. But there was something I had to do.'

'In New York?'

'I'll tell you all about it.'

He was leading her through the house to the sitting room, where he turned. 'Is there anything I can get you? A drink? Hot tea?'

She was shaking her head. 'All I really want right now is a shower and change of clothes.' She gestured towards what she was wearing. 'I've been in these things for two days, but all my stuff is across town.'

'Well, let's see what we can do.' He took her hand and led her upstairs into a guest suite. Although she'd explored his house on a previous visit, she had never spent time in this room before and was bemused at his taking her there. She stopped wondering though when he opened a cupboard door – to reveal all her clothes.

She shook her head with a smile. 'Well, that's service for you! How did you get into my apartment?'

'The same way any hired gun could have. With a credit card.'

'I know,' she mused, shaking her head. 'It's not secure, is it?' Then, glancing out of the window at the high wall that ran around his property, the gatehouse with the guard, she murmured, 'I feel safe here, though.'

'Oh you are.' He was holding her again. 'Very safe.'

'And I've never felt such relief.'

They held together in silence for a few moments before she asked, 'So, didn't you want to give up any of your precious wardrobe space for me, Great Protector?'

'It wasn't that.' He pulled back, regarding her with a wry expression. 'I just didn't think I should make any assumptions about our . . . sleeping arrangements.'

Glancing over to the bedside pedestal she noted that the books she'd kept by her bedside at home had been transported here. And the quilt cover from her bed. She looked back into his eyes. 'You are an old-fashioned charmer, aren't you?' Then, as he opened his mouth to protest, she raised her finger to his lips. 'Say nothing. I like it that you . . . don't make assumptions. Right now I'm feeling very grubby. But who knows how I might be feeling after a shower?'

Minutes later she was in the shower cubicle of his capacious bathroom, savouring the warm water blasting all over her body. His bathroom was a huge 'L' shape, with the shower room occupying one leg of the 'L' and the larger, capacious sweep of Egyptian marble that was the other leg furnished with a ball-and-claw bath, washbasins and, in the corner, a spa. From his toiletries she'd selected liquid soap and shampoo and as she caught the scents of them on her body, she smiled.

It amused her that he'd put her in a guest room instead of his own bedroom. Under that superconfident veneer there was more reserve to him than she would have guessed. But then he'd always been attentive to her, both outside the bedroom – and between the sheets. She recalled the last time they'd made love, the night of his mother's birthday party in New York. She remembered the thrill of it, the anticipation that had built through the night as they'd held each other on the dance floor, bodies pressed together, wanting each other so much. Just thinking about him now made her tingle. She turned so that the stream of water washed the soap foam down her breasts, her torso, her legs. The erotic tug between Jack and her was as potent as ever.

When she emerged from the shower she didn't notice, at

first, that the bathroom was in near total darkness, except for a dim light from the other end. Instead, she towelled herself dry and slipped into the white bathrobe Jack had laid out for her. Never having showered here before, nothing struck her as unusual. She was still absorbed in her thoughts when she stood in front of the mirror next to the shower and, choosing a brush from the collection ranged in front of her, ran it through her hair. She didn't want to look a complete mess when she emerged from the bathroom, to use the hair-dryer Jack had no doubt had sent over from her apartment.

The significance of the darkness was even lost on her when she emerged from the shower area. Until she noticed the flickering candles at the other end. There were half a dozen of them placed around the spa, which was switched on, its bubbling waters giving off a soothing fragrance. Sitting next to the tub, in a dark bathrobe, was Jack. Meeting his eyes with a smile, she stepped over wordlessly to where he stood. Clasping her to him, he kissed her, his intentions unmistakable. 'I thought you could do with some . . . total relaxation,' he murmured in that dark, gravelly voice of his. He was tugging the cord of her bathrobe so that it fell open.

Her eyelids flickered, and over his shoulder she gazed into the swirling waters of the spa; the rising steam; the all-engulfing darkness.

Then his arms had slipped around her and she was firmly in his grip.

Upper West Side, New York City

Martha Lupine knew that something funny was going on from all the muffled calls Julius had been making from behind closed doors. Her husband prided himself on being the very model of discretion. But while she paid heed to the image he had of himself, in reality few of his activities remained hidden from her for very long. All those hours over the stove hadn't completely frazzled her brain.

After he'd left for work that morning, after another behind-closed-door session on the phone, she was dusting the sitting room when on impulse, she picked up the telephone receiver and pressed 'Redial'.

Very quickly she found herself in the telebanking service of the First National Bank, Cayman Islands. Prompted for a code word, she had no difficulty providing one. A creature of habit, Julius had used 'cor anglais' for everything as long as they'd been together; just as he always used the number 0001, on the basis that he'd never forget it. So there were no surprises as she negotiated her way through the prompts. Where the surprise came though was when she requested the current balance of his investment account. This turned out to be slightly in excess of four and a half million dollars.

As she carried on with her dusting, Martha had cause for thought. Money had never interested her in the slightest. Thanks to the family trust funds, she'd always had what she wanted and, besides, she was hardly what the glossies referred to as a 'high-maintenance woman'. That said, though, her discovery wasn't exactly on a par with finding loose change down the back of the sofa. Especially with Julius constantly pleading poverty. And even more so, given the many signs that all was not well in their twenty-two-year marriage.

'Be Prepared,' Daddy had always drilled her. And Daddy had been right about most things. So when she'd finished the dusting and vacuuming, had taken off her housecoat and was relaxing over a coffee and biscuit, she used the cordless phone to call First National Bank again. This time she waited for a 'client advisor'.

'My husband has an account with you,' she told him, 'and I'd like one too.'

'Certainly, ma'am.' The other was eager to please. 'I can arrange that right away.'

The advisor wanted to know what kind of account would suit her needs.

'Just somewhere to put money in,' she told him vaguely.

After some discussion it seemed that a current account would suit her best.

'Now, if my husband or I want to move money from his account to mine, that's something we can do, is it?' She wanted to be quite certain.

'Do you use Internet banking?' prompted the other.

'No, I'm sorry.' She'd never really been a computer person. 'What about using the telephone service?'

'We need written authorisation, ma'am. Unless, of course, you use our telebanking system. But then you and your husband would have to exchange your secret passwords.'

'Oh, I think that could be arranged,' Martha reassured him. 'There are no secrets between us.'

20

Andrew had taken the last flight to Washington, DC the night before. Arriving at Dulles Airport, he picked up a hire car and drove directly over to Zonmark. It was 8.30 am when he arrived.

He had no doubts about what he was doing. He needed no further confirmation that it was Jack Hennessy who was the ultimate master of events; that it was Hennessy who, to protect his financial interests, had ordered Matt dead. Were there other progeria victims elsewhere in the world who'd died in mysterious circumstances? Having betrayed Lorna's trust in him, was Hennessy attempting to destroy NP3 in other ways too?

More important than anything right now was Lorna's safety. She clearly had no idea at all about the true nature of the man she'd become involved with. Little did she realise that his veneer of charming self-assurance was nothing but an illusion.

Lorna was irritated by Andrew's unexpected arrival. When

353

Gail came through to her office to tell her he was sitting in the waiting room, she didn't hide her displeasure. As if she didn't have enough to get through today! Having been out of the office, she had double the usual paperwork and banked-up e-mails to deal with. Her afternoon was blocked out with meetings. Early evening she had her critical meeting with Judith Laing.

Gail asked if she should put Andrew off. 'I can tell him you're in a meeting,' she offered. If he had been just about anyone else, Lorna would have agreed. But she knew Andrew well enough to realise he wouldn't just show up, unannounced, unless it was important. Besides, he wasn't simply another NP3 client's father. He was also the grieving parent of a dead child. And she regarded him as a friend. She *had* to make time for him.

Checking her appearance in her compact mirror as she retouched her lipstick, she caught the glow in her cheeks – and recalled the night before with a smile. Her reunion with Jack had been more wonderful and thrilling than ever. Like something out of a romantic dream, it couldn't have been more perfect. She felt closer to him now, more intimate, than she'd ever known it was possible to be.

She greeted Andrew warmly in the waiting room, before leading him past the bodyguard who'd accompanied her into work today, to her office. There, they sat together in two of the armchairs, remembering Matt. Gail produced coffee, and it was only once they were alone that Andrew regarded Lorna carefully.

'You remember the way I reacted to Matt's death – my suspicions that it might not have been an accident?'

As she nodded, Lorna also recalled her reply to his e-mail. She had urged him towards an acceptance of Matt's death, however difficult, instead of chasing after demons. That had been some time ago. She wondered how he'd taken her advice.

'Well, I followed up my suspicions.'

His expression was subdued, and cautiously she prompted, 'And you found . . .?'

Looking her in the eye he told her, 'They were true.'

Her eyebrows shot up. 'You're certain?'

'Couldn't be more sure.'

Although his gaze was even, she wondered what kind of evidence he really had. Was it the kind that would stack up in court, under cross-examination, or was it the evidence of a grief-filled, guilt-stricken man seeking self-justification?

'That's why I'm here,' he continued. 'You see, I don't believe Matt's . . . death was an isolated incident. Have there been other deaths of panel members?'

'Well, yes.' She nodded, thinking of Ouyang Wing in Beijing, Darryl Barker in Australia. 'But there's been no suggestion that their deaths—'

'And what about the panel? Are you fully up to speed?'

Lorna got up to close the door of her office before returning. When she did, she told Andrew in a low voice, 'Confidentially, we're short on our projections. But that's a long way from saying . . .'

'I believe,' he told her gravely, 'and it is only a belief at the moment, that there is a systematic attempt underway to derail the NP3 programme. Matt's murder was carefully planned and meticulously executed. It was a professional job.'

He had considered carefully how best to break the unpalatable news about Jack Hennessy. And he'd decided to show her the evidence from the ground up. She was a scientist, after all – that was how her mind worked.

355

So he told her about the several witnesses of the two men his neighbour had seen with Matt, and how they'd actually been captured on video climbing into their car outside Weybridge Rowing Club. He explained how he'd tracked them down to the private security firm, Executive Protection.

The name sounded familiar to Lorna, though she couldn't place why. Listening to Andrew, her bewilderment tempered by reservations, she asked, 'How can you be so sure about these men?'

'I've got them on video,' he replied.

'And why do you think the . . . murder had anything to do with NP3?'

'They virtually said so.' He repeated his conversation with Broadwick, Facilities Manager of Canadian Mutual, explaining how the latter, without any idea of the significance of what he'd said, had confirmed Executive Protection's activities; their efforts on behalf of a client to 'dispose of unwanted research material'.

Nothing could have landed the problem more firmly on her doorstep. But the more he spoke to her, the more disbelieving she felt. Could there not be some other explanation for all this? A far less sensational set of factors?

Trying to think clearly, she asked, 'Do you know who's behind it?'

'I don't know the chain of command,' he approached this carefully, 'but your enemies are in the health insurance industry.'

She frowned. 'Look, I know about the actuarial debate about gene therapy. But that's a huge leap away from some kind of sinister plot to derail my programme.'

'You'd better believe it's true,' he replied calmly.

His cool certainty was both unsettling – and aggravating. 'Seems to me as if you've pulled together a lot of factors to build a theory that might not be valid.' She was blunt.

'I wouldn't have come here if it wasn't.'

'You've been to the police with this?' She met his eyes.

'Not yet.'

'Well?' She raised her hands as if he'd confirmed her reservations. 'If what you're saying is rock solid, why didn't you?'

'I felt an obligation to come to you first.'

'These "enemies in the health insurance industry".' She wasn't listening. 'It sounds very vague.'

'I can be more specific,' he said. 'The lead organisation is Mayflower.'

If she knew about Hennessy's controlling shareholding in the company, she wasn't showing it.

'Know anything about them?' he probed.

'No more than the next person.' She shrugged.

There was a pause before he asked her, 'Tell me about the new man in your life.' He sat back in his chair.

Lorna glanced up, taken aback by the *non sequitur*. Maybe Andrew really was losing it. Maybe he needed help. 'We met a couple of months ago.' She couldn't have been shorter.

'After NP3 hit the headlines?'

She nodded.

'You probably talk to him about NP3 a lot?'

'We share confidences, as in any other . . . relationship.' She fixed him with a hard expression now. 'Where are you going with this, Andrew? What's it got to do with Matt?'

'I'm not sure how much you know about Jack Hennessy's business life.' His tone was conciliatory.

'I know some of the charities he works with.'

'There's more to it than that, I'm afraid. You see, the Hennessy Family Trust is the largest shareholder in Mayflower.'

'What *are* you saying?'

Andrew looked down at the floor. 'I'm sorry, Lorna. I really wish this wasn't true. But Mayflower stands to lose more from NP3 than anyone else. And the Hennessys virtually own it. What's more, the people who killed Matt, Executive Protection, are the Du Cane Plaza's security firm.'

'Are you crazy?' She jumped from her seat.

'I understand how you must feel.'

'You couldn't possibly *understand*!' She was scornful. 'You don't know the half of it!'

She realised, now, why the name Executive Protection was so familiar. The bodyguard right outside her office was from Executive Protection. And the idea that Jack could be so duplicitous was an outrage!

'You have my sympathies regarding Matt,' she sounded far from sympathetic, 'really you do. But to come here accusing Jack—'

'You met him only after NP3 became public knowledge, right?' he persisted.

'And you're suggesting—'

'As Mayflower's biggest shareholder, you have to question his motives.'

'I don't even know he *is* Mayflower's biggest shareholder!' she blazed.

'Why don't you ask Julius Lupine and see?'

Recalling Lupine's carnivorous expression from Cornelia's party, those hungry eyes, she demanded, 'And who is Julius Lupine?'

'Mayflower's Corporate Affairs Vice President and a business associate of Jack Hennessy's.'

She couldn't deny that, she thought, turning to conceal her face. And she couldn't forget her own visceral response to Lupine's predatory inspection.

'Is it, or is it not, the case,' Andrew was asking, 'that your difficulties with NP3 all began after you got involved with Jack?'

The significance of his question wasn't something she could deny. The answer, of course, was yes. The shrinking panel, the recruitment slow-down; it had all happened in the past two months.

For the first time, her certainty began to crack with doubt. She remembered Steve Manzini's outburst after she'd fired him; how he'd stormed into her office, accusing Greg Merrit of fixing test results to disqualify NP3 candidates; saying that Greg was claiming to be inviting potential NP3 panellists on board – but not doing so. *You're firing the wrong guy!*

Finally, she turned back to Andrew. 'It's true that the panel problems have all been recent. But I've put them down to an incompetent team member.'

Meeting Andrew's enquiring expression, she tried to get a grip. She needed to take things one step at a time. She was too shaken to work it out, right now, but Andrew must have got it wrong. She didn't doubt the sincerity of his motives, but Matt's death would have played havoc with his judgement. She couldn't dispute all his revelations right at this moment, but there must be an entirely different explanation for the way things seemed.

Deciding immediate action was called for, she stepped over to her desk and picked up a file, before turning for the door of her office and striding down the corridor towards Greg Merrit's, Andrew trailing in her wake.

'You reckon there's sabotage going on in my panel?' She was curt. 'Well, let's see, shall we?'

She couldn't do much about Andrew's other allegations right now, but she could do this. Greg was away at a seminar. His office was open. And she had his latest update on panellists.

She started at the top of the latest round of rejections. Andrew watched as she opened the drawers of a filing cabinet and searched through names from those on her list. They were in alphabetical order and quickly checked. Within minutes she'd gone through the paperwork of three of them – the correspondence, test results, interview transcriptions, final letters – all was in order. Greg had neatly annotated, in the margins of letters, the content of any phone conversations he'd had with parents. In light of what Andrew was saying, these notes might be completely meaningless, she realised, as many of them related the reasons why parents had declined to go ahead with the trials.

But after checking five cases without coming across irregularities, she ran spot checks going back a week, a month, two months. What she found was the same well-maintained paperwork. Nothing was amiss.

Watching her growing exasperation, Andrew asked, 'Most of the progeria kids who come in for testing – they don't make it to the panel, do they?'

'The majority test okay. There's a large minority who're on drugs incompatible with NP3, or who have other conditions—'

'If you wanted to, how could you create results to disqualify them?'

360

She flashed a glance in his direction. More and more she was convincing herself he'd invented this whole fantasy.

'Easily enough.' She removed a computer print-out from a folder. 'Just put the wrong numbers in here.'

'And would the right numbers ever have been recorded?'

'On individual tests. But that,' she gestured towards the archive room, 'would be like looking for needles in a haystack.'

'Even if one made just a few spot checks?'

She was regarding him evenly as he persisted, 'These letters to parents and guardians. Don't they ever reply in writing?'

She nodded. 'Written permission is required by law. We get that when they bring their kids in for treatment.'

'What about the ones who decline treatment. They never write?'

'No need.' She shrugged. 'Greg follows up with a phone call.'

'But if they did?'

'If they did,' she was sharp, 'their letter would be put on file.'

'Unless Greg didn't want it found.'

'In which case . . .' she pointed facetiously to an industrial shredder in the corner of his office.

Andrew had never had any doubts that it was going to be hard winning Lorna over, persuading her to reject everything in which she'd placed her faith. He realised her patience was wearing thin. But he couldn't let her walk away. He had to convince her to continue – even if he had to search through all the detail himself.

'How's this for an idea?' he asked as she continued rifling through one of Greg's cabinets. 'Can you show me how to cross-check the lab results with the stuff in the archives? That'll save you wasting any time. Meanwhile, it might be worth your calling some of the parents he said he spoke to, and who declined.'

'You mean, check he didn't make it all up?'

'Basically.' He nodded.

Her expression was tight. 'Not very professional, is it?'

'In what way?'

'Phoning these people again just to get them to repeat what they've already said.'

He paused, regarding her with a challenging expression.

'But what if they don't?' he asked.

Reluctantly, she took Andrew into the archive room and, armed with a set of twenty failed case results, showed him how to check the paperwork kept in the files against the handwritten codes written on lab test papers. She was doing this, she decided, to prove to herself, as well as him, that the whole basis of his conspiracy theory was flawed.

But within minutes of her return to her office, Andrew appeared in her door. 'There's something I'd like you to have a look at,' he said, putting a filed result and a single lab test paper on her desk. 'The DHEA level.' He pointed. 'On the lab paper it says 0.368, but on the filed copy 0.863. Is that significant?'

Pulling both towards her, she stared at the figures, from Greg's hand-written number to the one he'd transcribed onto the test paper. There was no doubting, the filed number was wrong. And that alone would have been enough to disqualify the candidate from taking part in the NP3 test.

After a long pause she handed the sheets back to Andrew. 'Looks like a transcription error,' she admitted.

'Important?' he asked. 'To the outcome, I mean?'

She nodded.

'I'll put it to one side.'

She watched as he stepped back out of her office and made his way down the corridor. Transcription error, or deliberate fraud? She didn't like even asking the question.

Professor Fernandez of the University of St George in Lisbon was standing on the balcony of his Sintra home, watching his daughter playing in the garden, when the phone rang. Poor Rebecca had deteriorated even more in the past four months. She was six years old now, and the differences between her and her friends at the local Montessori school could no longer be so easily dismissed as in the past. There were questions, so many questions, about what they should do. Where should she be sent to school? Should she be sent at all?

He'd tried not to allow his hopes to be raised by his family doctor, who'd been told by one of the top paediatricians in Portugal about the NP3 trials being pioneered by Dr Reid in Washington. He knew though that the new therapy seemed the only alternative to patient acceptance of what God had ordained. The family had, of course, been in touch with Dr Reid. And after initial screening in Lisbon, they'd flown to Washington where Rebecca had gone through exhaustive tests.

But within weeks they'd received the call they'd hoped and prayed most fervently to avoid. For reasons to do with thyroid functioning, picked up in Zonmark's automated biochemistry analyser, NP3 was almost certain to provoke a reaction strongly detrimental to the child's metabolism.

The salvation they had sought was not to be. All of which gave Rebecca's carefree antics in the garden a poignancy the Professor found almost unbearable.

Hearing the telephone, he went inside. When he answered it, there was at first no reply. Then a voice enquired, 'Is that the Fernandez residence?'

He recognised the international delay on the line. 'Fernandez speaking,' he responded in English.

'Professor. Lorna Reid calling from Zonmark in Washington.'

They had met, though only briefly, during the family visit to Washington. The Professor had been impressed by her authoritative presence. If Rebecca had been accepted onto the programme, he had no doubt she would have been in capable hands.

'I apologise in advance if I'm repeating a discussion you've already had with my deputy, Greg Merrit.'

'I spoke to Mr Merrit, yes.'

'This is really,' she had formulated her words carefully, 'a routine follow-up call.'

There was silence at the other end as she continued, 'We like to give people time to reflect for a while after receiving our letter. It's a major decision, after all.'

'We received no letter.' Fernandez spoke hesitantly after a pause. She sensed confusion. 'But we did get the news from Mr Merrit.'

She was looking at the date-mark on Greg's letter. It had been posted ten days before. Surely the mail service from Washington to Lisbon wasn't that bad?

Deciding to put the letter to one side, she continued, 'I suppose the question I have to ask is – could I say anything that might make you reconsider?'

'Reconsider?' She couldn't place the other's tone, but it seemed irritable. 'I don't follow?'

'Your daughter. Rebecca.' She read from the file. 'Might we not persuade you to enrol her in the programme?'

'Dr Reid, we were praying for just such a miracle!' He was exasperated. 'Mr Merrit told us it was out of the question.'

'He did?' She felt the blood rush to her cheeks.

'Her thyroid reading,' said the other. 'He told us it made her inclusion on the panel impossible.'

A short while later, Lorna made her way along the corridor to where Andrew was squatting on the floor of the archive room, going through a records box. Sensing a movement in the doorway, he glanced up to find her watching him, wearing a strange expression.

'I found two more . . . transcription errors,' he told her.

She leaned to read over his shoulder as he held out each lab test paper for her to see, along with the filed paperwork. Sure enough, in each case, the 'error' was such that it rendered the patient unsuitable for panel inclusion.

As he stood, she met his eyes, her own expression still hard to read. 'I've just been on the phone to the father of a potential candidate in Portugal. According to Greg's notes, he said no. But when I spoke to him a moment ago,' she was shaking her head, 'he told me it was the other way round. He's desperate to get his little girl on NP3. Now these—' She gestured towards the files scattered about the archive floor. 'Another three.' Raising her hands to her face she murmured, 'I'm just finding this . . . so hard to believe!'

Greg had convinced her he'd left nothing to chance in

365

his efforts to recruit new panellists. Both of them, she thought, had been desperate for new panellists. But she couldn't deny now that there were simply too many 'mistakes' for them to be accidental. And while that was betrayal enough, far worse was what it meant about Jack. Because, if Andrew had it right, Jack was far more culpable; Jack was at the centre of it, the mastermind. The man to whom she'd given herself only hours before had, it seemed, only engaged her affections in order to destroy her career.

The realisation filled her not with any extreme emotion; it was almost too big for that. Instead, she felt a growing numbness, which held all emotion at bay. Standing in the doorway, stock still, she had no idea what to think.

Judith couldn't deny that Lorna had her intrigued. She'd been speculating like crazy on Lorna's promised revelations about Grayson Wendell. What, for God's sake, had Lorna Reid, a biotechnologist, uncovered about Wendell that was so sensational? And how, in the course of her Zonmark duties, had she uncovered it? Of course, Lorna could be hyping up things, but she didn't seem the kind. From their first meeting, Judith had detected in Dr Reid a strong streak of Aberdonian reserve.

After letting her head spin for quite a while, Judith realised there was nothing to be done about the problem. She'd simply have to wait until she met Lorna. In the meantime, it wasn't as if she didn't have her other story to pursue.

Her research into lobby groups in America had revealed a phenomenon she'd never before encountered: the Astroturf movement. These were grass-roots organisations boasting the kind of massive memberships that made Congress sit up and pay attention – but were secretly funded by industry. While indistinguishable from genuine grass-roots organisations, Astroturf movements were well managed, usually by professional consultants. Free to Choose fitted the description perfectly. The question was, which company stood to benefit most from its activities?

Having examined the lease agreement for the Apex Building, available as a public record, Judith had discovered that the third-floor offices were rented, not by Free to Choose, but by Dieter Ross. The name meant nothing to her, but working on the theory that Dieter Ross was some kind of lobbyist, she put a call in to one of the less reptilian spin-doctors she knew on Capitol Hill, to ask if he'd heard the name – he hadn't – and also enquired if there was some association to which lobbyists could belong. There was. It was based in Florida, and she'd soon made contact with it, obtained an e-mail members' directory and struck gold: Dieter Ross was an 'Issues Management Consultancy' in Chicago.

Next, she'd posed as a potential client and phoned the consultancy asking for information about its services – and clients. The company website, to which she was referred, was of the all-singing, all-dancing variety with links all over cyber-space. Dieter Ross described itself as 'a new paradigm communications consultancy', whatever the hell that was, and blathered on about how 'top down communications practices are being replaced by stakeholder consensus'. An organisation could best achieve its objectives, it pointed out somewhat obviously, if it carried the support of all its stakeholders – employees, customers, shareholders etc.

Glancing down the list of services, she scanned across the extravagant tapestry of 'new paradigm' vernacular – environmental audits, issues management, stakeholder consultation. But the one that caught her eye was 'advocacy campaigning' which, the consultancy promised, enabled organisations 'to attract widespread public support for corporate objectives'. Pretty much, thought Judith, what Free to Choose was all about.

Working through the site, she checked out the Dieter Ross client list. A large part of the work carried out by the consultancy, it was explained, was only effective if conducted behind the scenes. For this reason, many clients did not appear on the list. But as she glanced down those that did, one name immediately caught her eye: Du Cane Plaza Hotel Group.

It was no secret that Lorna was dating Jack Hennessy, the former Du Cane Plaza CEO. Could it be pure coincidence that the consultancy orchestrating the Free to Choose campaign was the same group that had worked for Lorna's lover?

As an investigative journalist, Judith didn't much believe in coincidence. But Lorna's denial of any knowledge about Free to Choose had either been brilliantly deceptive, or quite genuine.

Now she sat at her desk, trying to pull it together; Free to Choose was a Dieter Ross production, its offices rented by the lobbyists, and its operation far too slick to be a genuine grass-roots organisation. There was no doubt that if it wasn't for whoever was bankrolling Dieter Ross, Free to Choose wouldn't be even a tenth its current size – if it existed at all. But who was doing the bankrolling? And where did Jack Hennessy fit in?

She clicked through the staff list – there were photos and blurbs about each of the senior consultants. Checking out the link from advocacy campaigning, she came across an Ed Dieter, Managing Partner of Dieter Ross, who also headed up the firm's advocacy campaign practice. Judith couldn't help smirking at the titles. All the 'partners' and 'practices' were clear references to legal firms, whose dubious stature Dieter Ross was clearly trying to imitate. The photograph of Ed himself was, in true PR style, not of a man in a suit, but rather was a folksy shot showing him fishing with his son in gumboots and a checked shirt. The blurb explained that Ed found it soothing to commune with nature. Yeah, soothing, thought Judith, so long as you weren't the fish.

According to the notes, Ed had directed strategy for every major advocacy campaign the firm had handled. New clients could be guaranteed of his strategic counsel. Sitting back in her chair, Judith began to think . . .

It was some time later that she decided to wing it. The way she saw it, she didn't have anything to lose. Dialling up Dieter Ross, she asked to be put through to Ed Dieter.

'Kerry Atkins, calling on behalf of Jack Hennessy,' she announced after being screened by two of his gatekeepers. 'We help with his personal media relations and we'd like to do more to publicise his commitment to Free to Choose.'

There were so many assumptions embedded in those two sentences that the conversation could blow up in any number of directions. But at the other end, the Managing Partner was clearing his throat. 'We'd welcome that,' he seemed perplexed, 'but Jack's always made it clear he wanted to stay out of sight.'

369

'Exactly.' She thought quickly. 'But I think we're turning him.'

There was a long pause before the other responded, 'He's never mentioned . . . your involvement before.'

'Quite probably.' She was prepared for this one. 'We mostly do charity PR. We met him in connection with some of his charity interests.'

'Ah.'

'Do you think,' she was really pushing it now, 'we'd have any problem from Zonmark, if Jack became more visible?'

'No. They're very grateful to him, all the celebrities he's put onto the campaign.' Then, after a pause, 'There is the issue of Lorna Reid.'

'Yes. Do you know why that is?'

The pause at the other end this time was even longer. 'Where did you say you're calling from?' he wanted to know.

Judith glanced about her office. 'Atkins . . . Packard,' she said.

'Before we go any further,' his tone had cooled considerably, 'I think I should discuss this with Mr Hennessy directly.'

She didn't care when he hung up on her. In fact, she burst out of her seat! What a story! What a coup! Free to Choose bankrolled by biotech buccaneers Zonmark. Lorna Reid, the glamorous wunderkind being kept in the dark. Her billionaire lover, pulling strings from behind the scenes.

The fallout would be a spectacle indeed! But before her story appeared, there was one encounter she didn't relish. Later today, when she met Lorna, how would she break the news about her lover, Jack Hennessy?

21

——

'I'll cut to the chase.' Armand Kuesterman glowered across the Boardroom table at Greg Merrit. 'What's this?'

He flicked across a copy of the letter, date-marked ten days before, addressed to Professor Fernandez; the copy on which, in his own handwriting, Merritt had recorded a conversation in which Fernandez had declined the offer of a panel slot on NP3 for his daughter, Rebecca.

Merrit took one look at the page, and knew in an instant. Having just arrived back at Zonmark, he'd been hastily escorted to the executive suite. He now faced the assembled suits – Kuesterman, Lorna Reid, Drake, Adrian Mitchell, Managing Partner of Mitchell, Curtin, Zonmark's law firm, and some anonymous, thousand-bucks-an-hour sidekick.

Some kind of slip-up had always been a possibility. They'd already discussed what he should do if this happened. He knew just how to play things.

'NP3 panel offer.' He nodded helpfully. 'We send out several most weeks.'

371

'And your conversation with Professor Fernandez – do you recall how it went?' asked Mitchell. Large and amiable-looking he might be, but Merrit knew that behind the benevolent exterior was concealed a rapier-sharp legal brain.

'Looking at the note, I see—'

'I didn't ask you to look at the note.' The half-smile playing about Mitchell's mouth was far from reassuring. 'I asked if you recalled how the conversation went.'

Merrit stared into space as though trying to remember, before admitting after a moment, 'I'm sorry, no, I can't.' He looked over to Lorna with a rueful expression as he tried reading her mood. But it was as though a steel barrier had slid down over her eyes.

'That's unfortunate,' Kuesterman was saying, 'because when Lorna spoke to Fernandez a couple of hours ago, he had a very different take on the conversation from what you noted.'

Merrit was shaking his head, looking appropriately grave. 'If I got something wrong, I really do apologise. I know it's not much of an excuse but the pressure, you know, we're working under—'

Kuesterman was about to continue when Mitchell silenced him with a hand. 'Are you saying that you got yourself in some kind of muddle?' he continued with the same deceptively sympathetic tone. 'That you transcribed your phone conversation with Professor Fernandez on the wrong letter, perhaps?'

'Yes,' agreed Merrit. 'That was probably it.'

'But you'd have noted your call with him on one of the letters?'

'Definitely.'

'Well, then, we should be able to resolve this quite simply.' Leaning back in his seat he regarded Merrit thoughtfully. 'It's only a question of identifying on which of the letters you made notes of your conversation.'

'I . . . suppose.' He glanced from Mitchell to Kuesterman to Lorna, who was still determinedly blanking him out.

'As it happens, I have all the letters you've sent out in the past two months right here.' Mitchell shoved a file across the table to him.

He instantly recognised the trap Mitchell had talked him into. Fernandez wasn't one of the two panellists he'd put through in the past week. For each of them he'd ensured excited language in the margins of their letters.

Sorting through the correspondence file, pretending to inspect his own margin notes, didn't take him long – there weren't many letters. Most of them were only a sentence or two. As he came towards the end he said, 'It's possible I made the note somewhere else.'

'Where?' asked Mitchell. 'Your organiser?'

He didn't want to get too specific, he thought, his mouth starting to dry. 'I – I can't say.'

'That's too bad.' Mitchell pursed his lips. 'Tell me, Greg, how many panellists have you recruited in the past month?'

'Not many,' he replied, 'that's why we've all been under such pressure—'

'But how many *exactly*?'

'If you're talking strictly the past month,' the other met his eye, 'I'd have to say two.'

'Two?' repeated the other. 'You're under this huge pressure you keep telling us about. You're trying to recruit like crazy. You speak to a guy in Portugal who says yes and *you can't remember the conversation*?'

'Well, actually, it's coming back to me now.' His eyes flickered across to Lorna. 'I did get excited at the time, very excited. But Lorna was out of the office that day, and by the time she got back I'd moved onto other things.'

'You forgot to mention it?'

'It's more just that there was so much going on . . .' It wasn't convincing and he knew it. But what other line was there?

'Not only that,' persisted Mitchell, 'you also forgot to put it in your report. According to this,' Mitchell was fingering his latest update, 'you recruited two members in the past four weeks. But as you've just admitted, that figure was, in fact, three.'

He was getting hard looks from everyone around the table. He realised there was little point talking about pressure again. He'd just have to brazen it out.

'Look. I've already apologised. I made a mistake. I overlooked that one conversation. Like you say, it *was* a big thing when Fernandez said yes. Going back through the paperwork I would have remembered. I would have sorted it out. It's not like permanent damage has been done. It was a one-off.'

Mitchell was nodding as though accepting what he'd said. 'If someone makes a mistake, a one-off, as you put it, well, he's entitled to a bit of slack. We all make mistakes, after all.'

The others, Merrit noticed, weren't showing any agreement.

'What makes it tough, is when people knowingly lie.'

Merrit glanced across the table, fiercely. 'What are you implying?' His tone was aggrieved.

'I'm implying nothing, Greg. I'm saying that you're lying to everyone in this room.' Mitchell's expression had turned stony. 'You've just told us it was a big thing when Fernandez said yes. But he never said yes. You told him his daughter didn't qualify for the panel. He spoke to Dr Reid about this just a short while ago – she's got the whole conversation on tape, just as this meeting is all on tape.' He pointed in the direction of a Dictaphone on the table that Merrit had failed to notice. 'You've also said your "oversight" was a one-off. So how do you explain,' he produced a sheaf of letters from a folder, 'the comments you wrote about the Marchettis' child in Italy; the Duguids' son in Scotland; Muriel Macmanus in Donegal, Ireland; the Wititos' child in Japan; Maria Cook in Australia?'

Merrit couldn't conceal his alarm at this turn of events. They'd checked out all his correspondence for the past three months!

'That's five extra panel members,' Mitchell hardly needed to emphasise this. 'Including the Fernandez child that makes six in all, representing one fifth of the current panel size. Do you really expect us to believe that these are all work pressure errors?'

There was an age-long silence in the room before Merrit said sullenly, 'I want a lawyer.'

'What for?' demanded Kuesterman.

'This is getting heavy.'

'Damned right it is.'

'All this recording of conversations – it's illegal. I won't have you try unlawful dismissal on me.'

'Believe me, Merrit,' Kuesterman snapped, 'unlawful dismissal is the very least of your worries. Right now you're looking at breach of contract, misleading conduct, fraud—'

'This is . . . unbelievable!' He looked to Mitchell with a shaken expression.

Kuesterman cut in before Mitchell could respond. 'A jury won't think so when presented with all the evidence.'

'So I made a mistake.' He was suddenly a lot less cocky. 'Maybe a few mistakes—'

'At least *ten* mistakes,' said Mitchell, 'if you include those kids you blocked from the panel at test stage.'

Merrit swallowed. So they'd got onto the lab tests too!

'And those are only the result of a spot check. A far more comprehensive analysis will be carried out.' He fixed Merrit with a severe expression, and it was as though he could read the other's mind. 'There's a clear pattern, and it doesn't look good for you. I'd say you'd be looking at a custodial sentence of at least five years. Good behaviour and a bit of luck, you might get out after two.'

Merrit glanced at all the expressions around the table. He'd never been the focus of such concentrated animosity in his life before.

'Two years,' Mitchell was continuing. 'It's tough on a college boy like you. Career down the pan – no one's going to hire you with a record. Meantime, for the next two years you're locked up most of the day with uncongenial company. Gangland stuff. Sodomy. Drugs.'

Another long silence followed, as Merrit absorbed this. Mitchell hadn't said it, but he realised the game now. They wouldn't all be sitting here, reeling off evidence, unless they wanted to cut a deal. If their intention was to go legal, it would have been far better if they hadn't shown him their hand.

Eventually he said, 'So where do we go from here?'

Across the table, Mitchell turned to Kuesterman who eyeballed Merrit bitterly. 'That's up to you. We can pursue you through the courts. The evidence we have, the quality of our legal counsel, we could tie you up for months, maybe years, with the certainty of jail at the end of it.'

'Or?' he prompted.

'You tell us who put you up to this. Why you did it. We wave goodbye.'

'What makes you think anyone put me up to it?' he tried.

'You were a good worker, until not so long ago. People don't suddenly turn for no reason.'

'Maybe I was getting pissed off at where she was taking the programme.' The sudden heat in his voice caught Lorna by surprise. Meeting his eyes she was aware of a resentment in his expression she'd never seen before.

'Her obsession with the Lafayette trials. And all the publicity,' he whined. 'She made out she was such a big deal, like she ran the whole fucking programme single-handed!'

In contrast to his raised voice, Mitchell's response was cool. 'Jealousy and bitterness could have been motivators. But that doesn't explain why you'd destroy your own livelihood.'

'That's for you to say!'

'Well, if you want to play it like that,' snapped Kuesterman, 'we'll see you in court.' He began shuffling his papers into a single pile.

'The court will sure want to know what a cock-tease she is!' Merrit wanted to prevent Kuesterman from leaving.

'A what?' spat Lorna.

'Played me along for weeks, didn't you?' he sneered. 'Like you think it's fun? Gives you a feeling of power, does it? You'd like that. But when it came to the crunch, it's "Oh no, not me. I don't sleep with the help."'

'That's so utterly absurd!'

377

'So what d'you expect me to do?' His voice once again rose in self-justification as Kuesterman stood up and gestured to Mitchell that they should leave. 'They were only wanting me to slow things down a bit. Suited me just fine.'

'How much were they paying?' Kuesterman demanded.

'Twenty grand. A month.'

'And who – exactly?'

'I only met intermediaries. No one from the company.'

'Which company?' Kuesterman leaned over the table.

'A deal's a deal?' Merrit confirmed.

'Only if you give us everything you know.'

'Oh, I do know.' He flashed a sly look at Lorna before returning his gaze to Kuesterman. 'The name you're looking for is Mayflower Health Insurance. Their Mr Big is a spin-doctor. His name is Julius Lupine.'

Lorna returned to her office, sick to the stomach. She was more than simply shaken by Greg Merrit's snide confession. She felt her life unravelling into surreal nightmare.

The betrayal of her trusted second-in-command was cause enough to feel traumatised. But it wasn't Greg Merrit who occupied her thoughts. The admission that Julius Lupine and Mayflower were behind the destruction of her programme confirmed her worst fear of all: things had come full circle back to Jack.

If it hadn't been for Andrew's earlier revelation, the name 'Mayflower' would have meant nothing more to her than just another major insurer. But 'Julius Lupine' was a different matter. She'd instantly remembered him from Cornelia's birthday party – and her memory was vivid. She recalled the grand bearing of a blue-blood, and the very evident refinement combined with a disconcerting rapacity in those intelligent, clear blue eyes. She'd wondered why he'd taken such an interest in her that night. Now she knew: he had been like a predator surveying its next meal.

She also recoiled from another memory: that of Jack, observing Lupine's arrival and immediately going over to greet him. There'd been a warm cordiality between the two men. At one point, Jack's arm had been around his shoulder. Jack had described him as 'a business friend of the family's'. It all made hideous sense.

Back in the NP3 building, Lorna went through to where Andrew was still working in the archive room. He glanced up at her, questioningly, as she stepped in.

'You were right.' She nodded, sombrely. 'He was working for Mayflower. Julius Lupine.'

Perching on an archive case, she told him everything that had happened in the meeting. As she did so, she reflected on the irony of her situation. Days, even hours before, if someone had told her she'd be adding at least ten extra progeria kids to her panel, she'd have been ecstatic. But now that it was on offer, she was in a state of horror.

When she'd finished talking, Andrew wanted to know, 'Where's Kuesterman going with this?'

'He's in with Adrian Mitchell right now. But you can be sure they'll be taking Mayflower to the cleaners.'

'And Merrit?'

'They'll tie him up so he won't say a word to anyone, on pain of imprisonment. He's a Zonmark witness now.'

Meeting Andrew's pensive expression, she thought about the sacrifice he'd made searching after Matt's killers when everyone – herself included – had thought he was only doing it to assuage his own guilt. He'd worked his way inexorably to the final truth, got on a plane and flown all the way here to break the news to her, in person. And she'd reacted with angry disbelief.

'I guess I have an apology to make for this morning.' She lowered her eyes. 'I just didn't believe you.'

'That's why I flew over.'

She was nodding. 'I know your job is seriously demanding. For you to take time off—'

'Things have changed.' Raising a hand to his face, he squeezed the bridge of his nose. Fatigue from the sleepless overnight flight was beginning to catch up with him. 'I was fired last week.' He took in her shaken expression before confirming, 'And, yes, I had my eye off the ball. Was too busy chasing after Executive Protection. One morning when I was out of the office, my deputy made a . . . rash decision. I ordered him to reverse it, but pride, you know, comes easily to the young. The fund took a hammering. I had to go.'

'I'm so sorry.' She shook her head, emotion clearly visible. 'I had no idea.'

'No reason you should.'

'But Jess. She's been supportive?'

He grimaced. 'She got tired of me before Glencoe did. She left me, couple of weeks ago. She doesn't even know about Glencoe.' Looking down at the floor he murmured, 'You know, I think she blames me for what happened to Matt.'

Her face filling with concern, Lorna asked, 'So what are you going to do? You've got the evidence you need to file a lawsuit?'

He shrugged. 'No amount of money can make up for losing Matt. I did all this to prove I wasn't going mad.' Meeting her clouded expression he told her, 'I've done that now. The journey's over.'

380

Reaching out, she took his hand in hers and, for a long while, held it in silence.

Later she was racing across Washington behind the wheel of her TT. In the passenger seat beside her, Andrew followed their manic progress with alarm. Several times he'd tried to calm her, but Lorna would not be calmed. Having just spent the past half hour closeted with Judith, she was no longer in a state of frozen shock. She'd worked through that, just as she'd got over her denial: right now, she'd never been more furious with anyone in her life than she was with Jack Hennessy.

Having briefed Judith on the Lafayette trials, and agreed on a plan of action, she'd been stunned when Judith had turned the tables, revealing her discoveries about Free to Choose; the fact that the Astroturf group was bankrolled by Zonmark; that Jack had been pulling strings from behind the scenes.

Hearing yet more revelations about Jack, she finally snapped. Furious, she was determined to confront the lying bastard. It was a showdown that had been inevitable since Andrew's arrival early that morning. But now there was no holding back.

She swung her car into the Du Cane Plaza Hotel on Pennsylvania Avenue, and stepped out of it at the valet parking desk. Then she led Andrew across the hotel foyer, into the lift, and directly up to penthouse level. After storming along the corridor and finding the door of his office ajar, she strode right in.

Jack Hennessy's smile of greeting froze as he caught her expression.

'I can't believe you think I'm so bloody stupid!' she began.

381

'Now, darling—'

'Don't you "darling" me!' She couldn't contain her anger. 'Did you really think I'd never work out—'

'Lorna, I have no idea what you mean.' His tone was placatory. 'And you haven't introduced me to this gentleman.'

'He's an intelligence agent from Britain.' They'd agreed on that line in the car. 'And what I've discovered about you today—'

'You're obviously upset, but there's really no reason.' He was leading them across to where his Chesterfield and a couple of armchairs were arranged in the corner of his office. 'There must be some kind of . . . mis-communication.'

'Oh, really?' Hands on her hips, Lorna was in no frame of mind to sit. 'Then how exactly would you care to "communicate" your involvement in Free to Choose?'

'So *that*'s what this is about?' He seemed almost to suppress a chuckle. 'Spencer Drake spilt the beans, did he?'

'I don't see what's so damned funny about your running some phoney operation—'

'Hardly "running", my dear.' He was droll. 'And there's nothing funny about it. What I find . . . difficult is your reaction. Over-reaction.' He shot a self-conscious glance at Andrew. 'That Scottish temper showing through.'

'Don't patronise me,' she snapped. 'Answer the bloody question!'

'If you're asking me why I've been supporting Free to Choose, the simple answer is – to help you. I didn't want you to feel in any way obligated which was why I kept quiet about it.'

'So I'm supposed to be grateful, am I?'

'My intentions, all along, have only been benevolent.'

Perched on the arm of the Chesterfield, arms folded, he looked relaxed.

'Then why in God's name Free to Choose?' She was having none of this.

'Because they're the most powerful advocates in the country for NP3. They've already achieved more than any PR programme, any multi-million-dollar advertising campaign could have. Look what they've done for your share price.'

'Pity they're just a bunch of phonies.'

'That's not true!' His expression turned testy. 'They have legitimate arguments—'

'How can you sit there and say that! You know damned well they wouldn't *exist* if it wasn't for Zonmark's money.'

'I don't know that, Lorna, and nor do you,' he lectured, wagging his hand at her. 'You might not approve of the advocacy technique, but business is business.'

'And I suppose you're going to tell me that destroying the NP3 panel was also in my own best interests?'

'What the hell are you talking about?' he exploded, leaping up from where he was sitting.

'About Greg Merrit's sabotage.'

'I've no idea—'

'About your hired guns at Executive Protection,' she persisted, 'murdering panel members.'

'Are you out of your mind?' Gone was any pretence of mollifying her now, replaced by raw anger. 'I'm disgusted you even think me—!'

'Oh, so smooth, Jack. Always so smooth. You're not denying you control Mayflower?'

Blood rising to his cheeks, he was mighty in his fury. 'Hennessy Family Trust is a major shareholder in

Mayflower.' He shot a furious glance at Andrew. 'But the whole world doesn't need to know about it.'

'Just like they don't need to know about you and Julius Lupine?'

'Julius is an old family friend.'

'Who's just been fingered for sabotaging—'

'That's bullshit!' he bellowed.

'I'd expect that from the chief architect.'

'I might have been prepared,' he thundered, 'to make allowances for your ... lively temperament. But I don't have to stand here listening to these contemptible accusations!'

Lorna turned to Andrew. 'Should've known he'd try brazening it out.'

'There's nothing *to* brazen out except for your bizarre fantasies.'

He turned to Andrew, fixing him with a lowering fury. 'I don't know what sort of muck you've been filling her head with.'

'Only,' returned Lorna, 'that at least one of my panel members was murdered by Executive Protection.'

'You can't be serious!'

'But no doubt you have *a very simple explanation*.'

'I have no explanation for something that was nothing to do with me!'

'You're saying,' Andrew couldn't resist demanding, 'that the company you control sabotaged NP3 without your knowledge?'

Jack Hennessy pulled himself up to his full height and fixed Andrew with a look of sneering disdain. 'That's exactly what I'm saying. I've never heard such preposterous accusations in all my life.'

Lorna was tugging Andrew's arm, gesturing towards the door. 'Let's get out of here,' she said. 'Listening to his denials just makes me sick!'

Though as they left the office, she couldn't resist the parting shot, 'And what about me, Jack? I suppose I was just an added bonus. Bit of fun on the side?'

'You'll regret this!' he roared after them as they moved down the corridor. 'Tomorrow morning you'll wake up and you'll realise exactly what an idiot you've made of yourself.'

They paused at the lift doors, facing him. 'Oh, I am an idiot, Jack, we're agreed on that,' she shouted back at him. 'I must be ever to have trusted you.'

22

Judith was more excited today than she had been at any time in her career. And it was not because she thought Grayson Wendell would set the world on fire – no doubt he'd come out with the same high-sounding verbiage of politicians the world over. Nor did she expect any great departure from his campaign platform. She noted with satisfaction, as she glanced at her watch for the hundredth time in the past ten minutes, that all the news channels in America were here – every major network, the best-known political commentators, senior reporters from the press. And the international media were also well represented with news agencies and stringers from several dozen countries.

She had been to Democrat Party media briefings before, but never to any so crowded. Today the journalists were arranged eight deep from the desk at which Governor Grayson Wendell was due to be seated in just three minutes' time. When her objective had been an exclusive briefing by Governor Wendell, the thought of being crowded into a room with every other political hack in Washington had come as a sharp disappointment to Judith. But since her meeting with Lorna the day before, all that had changed. Now it was a case of the more the better! She had no doubt that within an hour William Barbett would wish that he'd set her up for a one-to-one exclusive with the Governor for as long as she liked.

Barbett had scheduled the briefing for maximum television exposure. The 11 am media conference would provide fodder for all the lunchtime news broadcasts on the east coast, and breakfast news in California. It would be flighted through the day and no doubt an additional announcement would be made in the afternoon to give the briefing the legs it needed to carry it into the main evening news. It was a tried-and-trusted formula for delivering air time. And that could not have suited Judith's purposes better.

The usual mêlée of cameras and cellphones, hasty note-taking and last-minute arrivals grew to a buzz of anticipation as the eleven o'clock start time came – and went. Wendell was now officially late, though no one would have known it to look at the media scrum. An Agents France Press reporter was gesticulating wildly into his cellphone. An ABC anchorman was standing, his back to where Wendell would be arriving, wisecracking with a counterpart from CBS, while a surly-looking creature in a black leather mini and tank top was perched on the front desk, manicuring her dark maroon nails.

But the general raucousness was transformed by the arrival of the men in suits. Three of them appeared through the door and trooped directly to the front. Wendell was flanked by 'Hatchet' Hulquist and Barbett, both redolent with self-importance.

Within moments the untidy mass of assembled reporters had taken to their seats, conversations halted mid-sentence and concentration focused on the familiar features of the grand old man from the South. Then, to Wendell's left, Hulquist was standing up and introducing himself. He was sorry they were slightly late, he said, but they'd been delayed in Philadelphia. Now Wendell was here, however, he was sure they wouldn't be disappointed. (They sure won't be, reflected Judith wryly.) 'Ladies and gentlemen,' his voice rose to the occasion, 'I give you the next Democrat nominee and the next President of the United States of America, Governor Grayson Wendell.'

The build-up, more suited to a public meeting, fell flat when it failed to provoke applause. Wendell moved awkwardly in his seat before, mustering all the presidential stature of which he was capable, he bade them all 'Good morning' in that lilting, Southern accent. 'I do have a short, but important statement to make on equal opportunities,' he told them. 'And afterwards I'll be happy to take any questions you may have.'

The focus on equal opportunities was an attempt to shake off the Southern conservatism that had been stuck to him since he first threw his hat in the ring. Minority-group voters, blacks in particular, took one look at his patrician features, or listened to a single sound-bite in that Southern drawl, and turned right off him. Wendell needed to shrug off the 'good ol' boy' image and reassure those people that he stood for them too – 'the People's Democrats' was the phrase Barbett had conjured up.

It was hard to think of a better backdrop for what was to occur, thought Judith, although – unlike her peers in the media – she paid little attention to any of the detail of his statement. She was the only one in the room, after all, who realised that none of what he said would have any news value at all in just half an hour.

Sitting, as instructed, at the end of the third row from the front, she made sure she caught the eye of William Barbett. Standing on the Governor's right, he acknowledged her with the half nod she supposed was all she merited as a mere foreign correspondent whose news organ failed to deliver votes.

Wendell's statement was short. It ran to just over five minutes – though to Judith it felt like an eternity. She turned her head to her left, towards the door leading out of the media room, and was reassured when she caught a glimpse beyond it of Lorna Reid.

Eventually Wendell ended, and announced that he was ready for questions. Barbett, who was fielding, quickly opened up to the major networks. They were the ones, after all, who carried the most sway with voters. It was they he'd been courting assiduously since day one of Wendell's campaign.

Judith knew she would just have to practise patience. Barbett knew she was there. He'd promised her three questions. But as question time ran from ten minutes towards fifteen, and Barbett still wasn't making eye contact, she began to worry.

Several times she glanced to the door to see Lorna outside, arms folded, ready and waiting. Meantime, back in the room, hers was just one of a sea of hands and chorus of voices that erupted every time Wendell had finished a question.

Working systematically, Barbett was covering the US media, base by base. After the networks came the main syndications; the commentators whose political musings were carried across the nation, coast to coast. Air time and column inches were what he was after, and today Wendell was in cracking form as he worked the room.

After more than twenty-five minutes, Barbett was holding up his hands. 'Just a few final questions please!' he told them. At the end of the third row, just yards from where the men were sitting, Judith stood up. She caught Barbett's eye as she did so – he couldn't ignore her now. 'Yes. You'll have a chance.' He waved her to sit down. Wendell glanced over at her petite frame with interest, before Barbett directed him to a question from the other side of the room.

She had more agonising waiting while another handful of questions were taken. There was still no sign of her promised 'slot'. Now Hulquist was saying something over Wendell's shoulder to the spin-doctor. And the campaign manager was wrapping up.

'That's all we have time for today.' He was waving his hands. 'Governor Wendell is heading for a fundraiser in Florida.'

'But you promised me a slot!' Judith leapt to her feet again, eyeballing Barbett.

Wendell looked to Barbett to identify her before turning to Judith and repeating, 'The British *Sentinel*.' He was both condescending and inaccurate. 'You have a question?'

'I was promised three questions.'

'Well, let's not be greedy.' He swept the room with a benign smile. 'But I'll see if I can help.'

Judith looked back to the door, where Lorna was nodding, before she asked, 'Can you confirm that in your time as Director of Public Safety and Corrections you ordered the involuntary participation of black prisoners in a drug trial held by Lafayette State University between 1968 and 1973?'

The beneficent glow faded from Wendell's face as a flurry of sudden interest passed through the assembled news corps. Barbett was speaking quickly in his ear. Then Wendell was clearing his throat.

'I would hope the statement I made today set out, quite clearly, where I stand on minority groups and discriminatory practices. I have no knowledge of events which you say happened thirty years ago.'

'Then let's get right up to date.' Judith continued standing, defiant. 'Did you order the murder of Dr Lorna Reid,' she had to raise her voice above the growing furore, 'when she tried bringing the Lafayette trials to light?'

'That's an outrageous accusation.' Hulquist was on his feet, shaking his finger.

Several network cameramen had broken out of their rows and were climbing to the front to catch the exchange.

Waving his arms, Barbett tried to regain control of a media briefing that had jolted right off the rails and was ploughing towards dangerous terrain. But reporters weren't interested in Barbett. They were clustering quickly around Judith and the towering, wrathful Grayson Wendell who had yet to reply to her question.

'I don't know what you're playing at, Ms Laing,' he snarled, his menacing anger captured in a blaze of flash cubes and on every digital feed in the room. 'But you have no right to disrupt this conference.'

'And you have no right,' Scottish cadences cut above the rising frenzy, 'to destroy the life of a man just because he was the victim of your own racist agenda.'

Stepping in through the door, Dr Lorna Reid was followed by Jeb Livingstone. Tall, ancient, but possessing a self-contained dignity now completely absent from the presidential nominee, the effect of Livingstone on the media was yet another hasty refocus. No longer a media conference, the gathering had turned into pure theatre.

Barbett hurried over to Lorna, gesticulating angrily that she leave the room on the basis that she didn't carry a media pass. Wendell's voice rose in an indignant yell as he tried to command attention. Lorna Reid, already known to many reporters, was authoritative above the fray as she announced, 'This man, Jeb Livingstone, is ninety-two years old. He has served thirty-four years for a twenty-five-year sentence. Despite good behaviour, he's had every opportunity for early parole refused. Nine years ago he had his identity taken away from him, and was given a new one so that he'd stay behind bars till the day he died. And all because he is the last surviving participant in a racist drug trial authorised by Grayson Wendell.'

Wendell had to get out. This was an ambush of overwhelming proportions. If it was even possible to retrieve his position, he wasn't going to do it here and now. With as much dignity as he could muster, Hulquist was leading Wendell and Barbett towards the door.

But Livingstone was still standing in it, and showed no signs of moving. And as Wendell approached the tall black man, bristling with confrontation, he merely provided yet another photo-opportunity, another moment of drama to be played across the nation's TV screens that day.

'Will you step aside?' he demanded.

'He's been locked in jail for nine years, thanks to you,' Lorna retorted sharply. 'I think you owe it to him to stay for five minutes.'

Wendell's humiliation could not have been made more complete. Forced to retreat to one side, face contorted with fury, he had to listen while Lorna read out a joint statement. Providing a blow-by-blow account of why he was unfit for public office, it covered the Lafayette trials and the cover-up that followed; Jeb Livingstone's private torment; the Krauss fire; the Gore suicide; the murder attempt on her own life just days before.

As the media excitement all around him rose to feverish new heights, Jeb Livingstone stood with a serene and silent dignity. Turning back to Wendell, reporters shouted out, in a chaotic flurry of demands. What was his response to Dr Reid? Who had authorised the drug trials, if he hadn't? Since he had always been so big on minority rights, why hadn't he intervened?

Wendell was no longer capable of controlling his savage anger. Face contorted with fury, he jabbed his finger at Lorna, threatening to sue. Then he yelled at the media pack, refusing to answer any more questions, and demanding they leave. But none of the reporters had any intention of going. On the contrary, Grayson Wendell had never before been the focus of such intense excitement. He was jammed between Jeb Livingstone and the wall, with TV cameras crowding over him, questions being screamed out. Particularly aggressive was the female reporter with the tank top and deep red talons. Thrusting a microphone in his face, she repeatedly demanded that he admit to being Grand Master of the Ku Klux Klan.

Never had a presidential contender looked so unpresidential. And never had one been confronted so directly by his nemesis.

Now journalists were turning their attention to Jeb Livingstone. For the ninety-two-year-old man, having spent the past thirty-four years of his life in jail, the experience might have been overwhelming, but he stood wearing a serene expression, politely answering questions. It was when he stepped forwards to hear one of the reporters more clearly that a gap between him and the wall appeared, and Wendell didn't hesitate, pushing precipitately behind him, while Hulquist and Barbett trailed in his wake.

Instantly, a ruck of the major news networks followed in hot pursuit. 'We have no further comment at this time,' was the only platitude Barbett could manage as they hurried to a waiting limo.

But the part of that day's media conference that was to be played and replayed many times was still to come. It lasted only three seconds, yet it cost Wendell not only any chance of nomination, but the possibility of remaining in politics one day longer.

It was to become a piece of television iconography, as notorious as Bill Clinton's 'I did not have sexual relations with that woman – Miss Lewinsky' or Nixon's 'There will be no whitewash at the White House.'

For in his haste to leave the media behind, Wendell had forgotten to remove the microphone pinned to his lapel. It was an oversight that few viewers would ever forget. He strode out to his car, and the bevy of cameramen following caught his lips at the same time as his furious voice boomed through the media room loudspeakers.

'They must be crazy,' he exploded at Barbett, 'if they think I'm quitting the race over some goddam nigger!'

In the four-poster bed of his mistress's fuchsia-pink boudoir, Julius Lupine, like the rest of the nation, watched Wendell's fall from grace in a state of mesmerised concentration. Naked beside him, propped up on a Continental pillow, his mistress watched it too. Having stopped by at her apartment for some afternoon delight, his decision to watch the lunchtime news had been made on the spur of the moment, something to tide them over what he termed his reload time, along with the Semillon blanc and some interesting New England cheeses.

'Never seen anything like it in my life!' he exclaimed after CNN ran Wendell's soundbite for the third time in five minutes. 'Must have been Barbett's worst nightmare – the past coming back to haunt him.'

'I only wish he'd got a lot further.' Beside him, she reached over for her box of cocktail sobranies, selecting one in daffodil yellow. 'Like as far as the White House.'

'You mean, the higher they fly, the harder they fall?' he enquired with a roguish smile.

'Exactly,' she chimed in that gravelly smoker's voice, as she prepared to light up with her gold Cartier lighter.

Cornelia had never disguised her hatred of Grayson Wendell. There'd been some family feud, Lupine knew, in which Wendell had cost Cornelia's father both his name – and a great deal of money.

'Oh, you are ruthless!' He grinned, reaching over and removing both sobranie and lighter from her fingers and returning them to the bedside pedestal.

She made no protest as he put his hands on hers and leaned down to kiss her. 'That's why you like me,' she murmured. 'We're like . . .'

Pulling the sheet back, he kissed first one bare nipple then the other. 'Two peas in a pod?' he enquired.

Closing her eyes, she sighed.

As he feasted on her, Julius Lupine had little thought for anything else. It wasn't only that Cornelia was remarkably well preserved, with no expense spared to defy the laws of both age and gravity. In addition, her money, power and social standing had the effect on him of the most potent aphrodisiac. It was as if, in possessing her, he possessed all that she had.

And she had some. After the sale of Du Cane Plaza, the Hennessy Family Trust had been set up with herself and Jack as the principal beneficiaries. Jack had involved her in shortlisting the executive who would look after the Hennessys' controlling interests in three separate health insurers. Enter, stage left, Julius Lupine.

The spark between the two of them had soon ignited. They had both become more hands-on than anyone around them would ever have believed. And when he'd warned her of the dangers of Lorna Reid's NP3 programme, she hadn't hesitated to order him into action.

Now he collected her up in his powerful arms, and flipped her over on the bed.

'Sometimes,' she gasped, on knees and elbows, 'I feel you can read my mind.'

Sliding down on her he whispered in her ear, 'Sometimes I do.'

Later, the doorbell sounded just as Lupine was slipping into his Turnbull & Asser shirt, a satisfied glint in his eye. In her dressing gown, Cornelia adopted a puzzled pout, before making her way out of the room. 'Stay here,' she commanded. 'I'll get rid of them.'

Closing the bedroom door behind her, she made her way to the front of the apartment. She was only partly self-conscious at answering the door in her state of *déshabillé*. It wasn't unusual for her to change in the middle of the day, between lunch and afternoon engagements. And her visitor must be someone she knew very well, or perhaps a neighbour, otherwise the porter would have phoned.

'Jack, dear!' Standing in the doorway, she leaned forward to accept his kiss.

But Jack, it seemed, wasn't in a kissing frame of mind. Sweeping past her he stormed into the hallway. 'I'm getting alarming reports from Mayflower.' He was angrier than she'd seen him in years.

She hurried him through to the sitting room at the other end of the apartment, and well beyond earshot of where Julius was dressing.

'What's going on?' She looked surprised.

'That's what I'm here to ask you!'

'Good heavens, Jack!' Sitting in her favourite armchair, she drew on her sobranie. 'You're the business brain in the family.'

'You're not exactly short of schemes yourself!' He confronted her, hands on hips.

She looked taken aback, before adopting an expression of disarming innocence. 'Nothing I don't discuss with you,' she retorted.

'Is that so?'

'Of course it is! Jack, what's got into you? Your behaviour is, quite frankly, boorish.'

'I'll tell you what's *got into* me,' he flashed. 'But there's something I need to ask you first.'

Approaching her, he put his hands on the arms of her chair, his face just inches away from hers. 'Julius Lupine,' he said. 'What's going on between the two of you?'

She pulled her well-practised Gallic shrug.

'Nothing?' He was disbelieving.

'Nothing . . .' she replied carefully, 'of any consequence.'

Turning away from her, he struck his own forehead. 'So I'm right!'

'I won't deny finding him attractive. We see each other socially from time to time.'

'An affair?' he confirmed. 'The two-backed beast!'

'And there's no need for the possessive charade. I'm not only your mother, I'm also a woman with my own private life.'

'It's not your private life that worries me. It's what you're no doubt . . . persuading Julius to do.'

'As you well know, I find talking shop so very vulgar.'

'You're telling me you know nothing about the NP3 programme?'

Her eyebrows twitched. 'No more than Lorna told me—'

'You have no knowledge of her programme being sabotaged?'

'Good Lord, what do you take me for?'

That was precisely what had preoccupied him since Lorna had exploded in his office the evening before. Deeply upset by her accusations, his first reaction had been to assume that the pressure of the past few weeks had combined in her mind to create this bizarre, deluded confection.

But this morning he had been woken by Dan Wright, Chief Executive Officer of Mayflower, and the babbling recipient of a letter from Zonmark lawyers Mitchell, Curtin, alleging corporate sabotage. Allegations of criminal wrongdoing were already in the hands of the police. In addition, Zonmark was seeking compensation for industrial espionage and damages in the order of $250 million.

So the accusations weren't just an invention of Lorna's hyperactive imagination. And the Hennessy Family Trust, on which his many philanthropic interests depended, risked swingeing damage. Whether or not it ever came to a $250-million payout, if policyholders believed their insurer was failing, they'd desert Mayflower in droves. The value of the family holding would collapse.

Jack knew that Dan Wright could have played no part in any conspiracy. Despite his title, he was nothing more than a figurehead. Julius Lupine was the real power at Mayflower, the custodian of the Trust's investment. The question was: would he have got involved in the activity? And why?

Jack understood the threat of the NP3 programme to health insurers. He'd gone to one of the early seminars at which Lorna Reid had presented, to find out just that. The fact that they'd discovered a mutual attraction had been a surprise bonus.

But he'd never considered NP3 a threat to the Trust. Jack had already met representatives from Plantel Stewart to discuss diversifying, to give the Trust a better spread. So why would Julius Lupine have acted independently? Why would he have carried out clandestine operations without any reference to his controlling shareholder? Unless, of course, Cornelia had put him up to it.

It was at this point, just hours earlier, that the appalling scenario had begun to unfold. Although Jack was a dutiful son, he was by no means blind to his mother's weaknesses. They weren't a subject he cared to dwell on, but he knew perfectly well it was her heedlessness and extravagance that had reduced his father's once-profitable hotel to the debt-ridden wreck he'd inherited. It was her impetuosity that had created the money worries that had eventually killed Tom. Recklessness and greed are not traits any son wishes to find in his mother, and during Jack's revival of the family fortunes he had tried to rein in her impulses.

Now, it seemed, they had resurfaced. He could just imagine Cornelia reading about NP3, imagining the worst, and concocting some ludicrous scheme to protect her money.

Now, in her sitting room, he was shaking his head. 'Julius has always been like putty in your hands.'

'It's not like that at all!'

'Then what is it like?'

'We're only friends.'

'Then you should know that your *friend* has been implicated in the murder of one of Zonmark's panel children in England.'

Cornelia's shock was genuine. Sobranie poised in mid-air, she blanched.

'And Zonmark's suing Mayflower for $250 million for industrial sabotage.'

Trembling, she dropped the sobranie in an ashtray, and tried to speak. But she could only gape, stupefied. For the first time in her life, Cornelia Hennessy was dumbstruck.

'Do you realise,' Jack had no intention of letting up, 'this could be the ruin of the Trust? If the media get hold of this, and God knows they will, Mayflower's policyholders will defect by the thousand. Our holding in the company will crash.'

'But . . . there must be *something*,' she managed eventually, her voice breathless, 'we can do?'

After showing Jack to the door she went to the bathroom where she had a drink of water and pressed a flannel to her face and tried to regain her composure. Then she returned to the bedroom where Julius was, once again, immaculate in his tailored elegance, ready for business.

'Sorry. That took longer than I thought.'

Julius regarded her carefully. He suspected the visitor had been Jack – he'd heard a male voice in the hallway. And, though she was trying to hide it, Cornelia was evidently flustered.

'Jack?' he enquired.

She nodded.

'Something up?'

'Just a family thing.' She turned away from him.

'You seem upset.'

'I'll get over it.' She was still avoiding his eyes. 'Nothing, really.'

He paused, considering whether to pursue the subject. There was no doubt at all in his mind that he was implicated in the contretemps, or why wouldn't she look at him? But she wasn't admitting to it, nor could he force her to speak. Instead he said, 'Well, I'd best be going then.'

She saw him out to the front door in silence, her embrace a muted version of her usual endearments.

401

'Till next time,' she murmured, as she always did, opening the door.

'Yeah.' As they exchanged a final glance, he couldn't fail to observe the emotion in her eyes, correctly identifying it as fear. And at once he knew there wasn't going to be a next time. Not for the two of them. Not ever.

She walked through to the home office she rarely used, except to file the occasional bank statement or service accounts. The large, leather-topped desk at which Tom had sat so often, long into the night, was completely clear, except for a green-shaded banker's lamp which she now switched on.

Helping herself to a sheet of letterhead and a rollerball pen from the desk drawers, it didn't take her long to compose the single paragraph. She read and re-read it, checking for errors before signing her name in full underneath. Then at the top she wrote the words 'Jack Hennessy'.

In a cupboard of the office, on the second shelf, a fax machine stood on permanent standby. In its day it had spewed out messages round the clock. Now it was used even less frequently than the office.

She had to look up the fax number of the Hennessy Foundation. And after watching the page go through the machine, she waited for the confirmation slip, which she stapled to it, before filing it with her personal papers. She had little choice but to do what she'd just done, she told herself.

Anyone else in her position would have done the same thing. It was a matter of survival.

At the other end, Jack received the fax with mixed feelings. He'd left Cornelia to reflect on the action, and she'd responded swiftly. That meant he could now pursue the only damage control available.

But what did it say for his mother? She hadn't admitted to an affair with Julius Lupine – but nor had she denied it with any vehemence. Which meant his suspicions were probably true. And the alacrity with which she'd been prepared to betray her lover was dizzying.

For as he prepared his own statement and faxed it, along with hers, to Dan Wright's office, he knew the result would be one from which Julius Lupine would find it impossible to recover. Within the hour, Dan Wright would issue an announcement that Lupine was suspended from duties. Mayflower would be conducting its own investigation into allegations of corporate espionage made against its Corporate Affairs Director. Both his mother's statement and his own made it clear that Mayflower's controlling shareholders were shocked by the allegations against Lupine, and would ensure that, if they proved to be true, retribution would surely follow.

Mayflower would be seen to have acted swiftly and with honour. Confidence in the company would be retained.

Julius Lupine was the fall guy.

23

White Collar Crime Chief Sheehy of the FBI's Manhattan office barely looked up from his computer when Special Agents Ross and Jessop stepped into his office. Focused on a budget spreadsheet, he gave no indication that they had his attention other than a slight tilt of his chin towards them.

'It's Zonmark,' said Ross. 'We've been through the paperwork. We've spoken to Merrit. We want to interview Lupine.'

'So soon?'

'All the stuff we got from the English guy, Andrew Norton, pretty much ties this thing up.'

'Ties it up, eh?' mused the other, before breaking away from his screen to face them. 'Then why not an arrest?'

'We want to see where Lupine goes after we speak,' replied Jessop. 'Who he's taking orders from.'

Sheehy shrugged, turning back to his screen. 'Just don't lose him,' he warned.

*

Martha Lupine had come thoroughly prepared. Her ample handbag contained a Dictaphone, street map, low-denomination banknotes for taxi fares, a zoom-lens camera, cut sandwiches – her favourite roast vegetables and caramelised onion with just a dab of pesto – and of course, her knitting. Private eyes could spend hours at a time staking out properties, but she couldn't be doing with such waste. At least if she found herself having to watch a building or restaurant, she could get on with the jumper she was knitting for her baby granddaughter.

She was dressed as though for lunch, elegant but not over-stated. If she found herself having to go into a hotel or apartment block, she could do so without feeling self-conscious.

She'd given all this some thought when she'd first followed Julius, just over a week ago. On that occasion, he'd gone nowhere more eyebrow-raising than the barber shop he visited just round the corner from Mayflower. The second lunch hour she'd followed him, he'd ended up in some corporate raiders' trough off Wall Street with three other men in suits.

She'd be patient, thought Martha. She'd watch and she'd wait. If her suspicions proved unfounded, no one would be more relieved than she. But every instinct told her that Julius was, once again, being unfaithful to her. And after eighteen years of unfaithfulness, if she could prove it, this would be an infidelity too far.

Although Julius thought she'd only ever found out about that sordid business with his PA, she knew about all his affairs. For the sake of the children she'd kept silent, however, about the girl at the advertising agency and the affair with Marco, the Italian waiter, which she had put down to

405

mid-life crisis. The other extra-marital activities – one-night stands and a catalogue of other sweaty wrestles – she didn't wish to think about.

For the most part she'd been able to dismiss all these as the straying of a tomcat. In many other ways, Julius was an ideal husband, and following his nocturnal – and, for that matter, diurnal – emissions, he'd always return home.

But this time, it was different. She had the feeling that whoever he was seeing had a hold on him that went beyond hormones. At home he'd become cool and more distant. He'd spend hours absorbed in thoughts to which she was no longer privy. Any sense of partnership between them had become so reduced that for the first time in their marriage, she'd begun to think he might leave her. With their first two children married and off their hands, and Hayden away at college, perhaps he had decided the time had come to trade her in for a trophy wife. He was making all that money at Mayflower, both on and offshore, so perhaps her trust funds were now dispensable. He'd bought his dream car, the Aston Martin. Maybe now he was looking for a piece of arm-candy to complete the picture, someone half his age to hang off him, confirming his alpha-male status.

Martha had decided she ought to find out. The idea of hiring a firm of private detectives to follow Julius had crossed her mind – but only briefly. There was something so furtive, so calculating about commissioning a private eye to spy on one's husband. If, on the other hand, she happened to be in town, and 'found' him where he wasn't supposed to be, she'd feel in no way morally compromised. Besides, her own cautious nature made her wary of entanglement with some firm that could run up bills of thousands of dollars without anything to show for it.

The job was best done herself, she reckoned, which was why for two lunch hours during the past week, she had stood in the glass-fronted foyer of the building next to Mayflower headquarters, waiting to see if her husband would make an appearance.

Unlike both previous occasions, when he had not emerged from the building until after one, today he was very early. No sooner had she taken up her position, shortly after 11.30, than he was striding out of Mayflower and stepping into a yellow taxi. Feeling, not for the first time, like something out of *Cagney and Lacey*, Martha flagged down a taxi and ordered it to follow his, throwing herself and her voluminous bag on the back seat.

This could be just another wasted venture. Maybe he was on his way to a business meeting? Though the further his taxi headed away from the financial district, the more things began to look interesting. And once they were on Fifth Avenue, heading towards Central Park, she felt sure this was no insurance business meeting he was attending.

His taxi pulled up outside one of the smart apartment blocks on the Upper East Side. Zoom camera carefully focused, Martha clicked as he went in, straight past the porter and towards the lift. Once he'd stepped inside it, she emerged from her own taxi and crossed the street, looking inside the lobby to check which floor the lift had stopped at. It was the twelfth.

She had little doubt now. This was classic Julius. He'd had lunchtime trysts with all his women before, and was doubtless at it again. Crossing to a bench on the fringes of Central Park that provided a direct view of the apartment block lobby, she couldn't resist scanning the twelfth floor

407

with her camera. But, even with the powerful lens, at that angle nothing was visible.

She pulled out her knitting and was soon clicking the needles at a ferocious pace as she tried working out the deal. Was this some love nest he rented specifically for the purpose, she wondered? But surely not even Julius could justify the expense of it just for the sake of fornication. Perhaps Mayflower had a place in town for visiting execs? Perhaps he had use of the apartment when some business friend or contact was away? One thing for sure was that he'd never mentioned an Upper East Side apartment to her. And when it came to Julius, she could think of only one reason why that might be.

Keeping a close watch on the apartment lobby, she waited for the arrival of whoever it was Julius was seeing. By 12.15 no one had shown up. By 12.30, she decided the woman must be there already. At one o'clock she opened her sandwiches, fresh and moist thanks to her generous layer of shredded iceberg.

The tedium of surveillance was something she'd come prepared for, but even with her knitting, the minutes passed slowly. Her granddaughter's jersey was coming on nicely – she had already done both the arms, and was presently working on the front of it, a complicated ribbed pattern requiring the careful counting of the stitches. Several times she put her work down, stood up and stretched her legs, or massaged her finger joints for a few minutes' respite. But she never took her eyes off that lobby for more than a few seconds at a time.

Just before two, she stashed her knitting away and, camera at the ready, put herself on high alert. If he'd left the office at 11.30, he couldn't take off much more time, surely?

She noticed other comings and goings, of course. In particular, a man who looked darkly handsome from a distance, and who'd arrived and departed within the space of fifteen minutes. His driver had waited for him in a Mercedes, and he'd come out of the building at high speed. There was something about the way he moved that made Martha think he was having a very bad day.

Finally, a few minutes later, Julius emerged from the lobby – alone. Disappointed, Martha moved behind the protection of a bus shelter as she watched him wave down a taxi, just ten yards away, and head back downtown. Emboldened by his departure, she made her way directly to the lobby, and stood across the road from it, waiting for the woman to appear.

But after fifteen minutes there was no sign of her. Nor even after twenty-five. After half an hour's further waiting, still no one who might remotely pass for a mistress had emerged. A thought seeding in her mind, Martha seized the moment and walked inside.

She strode to the elevator wearing her no-nonsense expression, and when the porter asked who she was visiting, she didn't even look at him. 'Twelfth floor,' she barked, pressing the lift button. 'Sister.'

'Shall I let her know—?'

'She's expecting me.'

She was partly surprised not to be interrogated further. But the doors were opening and she stepped inside.

As she headed upwards, she reflected on the exchange. Whoever Julius was seeing was known to the porter. Did she live here, she wondered? None of Julius's other mistresses had had any money – at least, not Upper East Side apartment money. Perhaps he was seeing a married girl. One who lived in the family home?

The doors slid open and she was in a lobby with Apartments 23 and 24 on opposite sides. Taking 23 first, she decided on the line she'd use, before pressing the buzzer. It was only moments before a short, oriental woman had opened the door on a security chain. She wore a housecoat and carried a duster.

'I'm looking for Terry,' Martha told her.

The other screwed up her face. 'He go Sweeza-len.'

'She is home now?' she persisted.

'He go Sweeza-len. He come back Monday.' The house-keeper closed the door in her face.

It could be a ruse, thought Martha, though it seemed genuine.

She pressed the buzzer of number 24 and waited for what seemed an eternity. When, finally, the door was opened, her shock could hardly have been greater.

Martha recognised her instantly, of course. Anyone who'd lived in New York City as long as she had couldn't fail to recognise Cornelia Hennessy – even in her bathrobe.

'I'm looking for . . . Terry.' Her words were scrambled.

'Not on this floor.' The other delivered a hooded glance. Then she was shutting the door.

Martha didn't remember anything about how she got downstairs and into a cab. And the journey home passed by in a blur. Her suspicions had been confirmed – yes. But in the most horrible way. She might have understood Julius being lured into adultery by some svelte young thing with a pert butt and breasts round her neck; someone with whom she couldn't possibly compete in the pin-up depart-ment. But Cornelia Hennessy was several years her senior. Hadn't she recently turned sixty-five? Cornelia Hennessy, the self-obsessed society *grande dame*, contrived and

410

manipulative, represented everything that Martha most despised.

All kinds of unexplained riddles began falling into place. The money in the offshore account – was that some kind of payout from the spectacularly rich Cornelia? The intuition she'd had about Julius leaving – he was planning, no doubt, to spend some of the Hennessy billions on his expensive and increasingly grandiose tastes.

But, she decided, fighting back the tears as she returned home, if Cornelia Hennessy wanted her husband, let her have him. Let her have the lies, the cold detachment, the endless suspicions of infidelity.

But there was something Martha intended doing first.

Back in their bedroom, she retrieved the envelope she'd received from the First National Bank in George Town, Grand Cayman Island, which she'd hidden at the back of her lingerie drawer. Just as well she'd taken the precaution, she thought, of opening her own account only days before. Next, she was dialling into the telephone banking service to check on the balance of the account Julius had kept secret from her. There was even more money in it than the last time – just over 4.8 million dollars. A good deal less than he'd spent of her family's money over the years, but a substantial sum nonetheless. Listening carefully, she followed the 'transfer' instructions.

She moved the lot. Every last cent of it went into the First National Bank account of Martha Lupine. Then, to make sure the transfer couldn't be reversed, she faxed an order, with a bank authorisation code, to have the money wired immediately to her own Citibank account in Connecticut.

That done, she changed out of her clothes and into a

411

comfy housecoat. Going through to the kitchen, she put on the kettle and prepared to make herself some Earl Grey tea, which she'd always found soothing.

In times of stress, especially when there was nothing to be done but wait, the only remedy she knew was to throw herself into some other task to create an absorbing distraction. Taking down her Martha Stewart cookery book, she looked up the Damson and Cinnamon Crumble recipe on page 534. Yes, she thought, that did sound nice. She had all she needed to bake it. And she could take it out to her grandchildren when she went upstate to see them at the weekend.

When FBI Special Agents Ross and Jessop arrived at the Lupines' front door, they found his wife Martha in her housecoat, sleeves pushed back to her elbows, and hands dusted with flour. Although domestically engaged, she seemed slightly dazed – and had she been crying? – but, she told them, her husband was most assuredly not at home. Nor would he be. Between three and four in the afternoon, he should be at work.

Would they tell her why they wanted to speak to him, she asked. They declined. They only wanted to interview him briefly. But they did leave behind their cards, with the request that Julius call them as soon as he was able.

Martha was surprised they'd even bothered coming to the house. Fine detectives they were to go looking for a businessman at his home in the middle of the afternoon! What she didn't know was that they'd already phoned Julius's office, to be told by his PA that Mr Lupine was at a lunch engagement. He was expected back by four.

As it happened, however, Julius Lupine had changed his

plans. When, at four o'clock, Ross and Jessop presented themselves in the ante-room of his office, his PA told them her boss had returned sooner than expected, only to go out again. Unusually for him, he hadn't said when he'd be returning.

The two Special Agents exchanged glances. What about his cellphone, they demanded. But she'd already tried him on that, and found it diverted to voice-mail. Then they asked about his schedule – what appointments did he have set up?

His PA explained that Julius's Outlook calendar didn't always conform to the arrangements he kept in his personal diary. Would she check his office, they asked, in case he'd left his diary, or any other information behind? Rising from her chair, beady-eyed with doubt, she led them into his office.

While she searched over his desk and in his drawers for the diary she knew he only ever kept on his person, the two agents glanced out at the panoramic vista with the Chrysler Building at its centre, and noted the office's wood-lined walls and Chesterfield furniture; this was clearly the den of one possessed both of considerable wealth and importance. It was also scrupulously tidy.

'Empty-desk policy?' Ross enquired, nodding at the gleaming expanse of mahogany, vacant but for a few papers stacked in the right-hand corner.

'Mr Lupine is meticulous,' she said.

Then, noticing a large area of wood panelling which looked as though a picture had been hanging against it until recently, he asked, 'Empty wall, too?'

Glancing up, she saw that Julius's magnificent *portière* had vanished. Suddenly perturbed, she glanced back at the

413

paperwork he'd left behind. There were the usual documents that needed to be returned to their files, the final draft copy of the upcoming Mayflower Annual Report. But it was the envelope on the top that made her hesitate. It was a regular white envelope with the Mayflower logo in the top left-hand corner. Sealed, it felt like the envelopes in which he often left her Dictaphone tapes to transcribe. But instead of her name on the front, with the usual 'Confidential' printed in neat capitals, this time he'd written just three words – 'New York Police'.

Jessop was watching her expression as she paused, holding the envelope, before glancing over at them. 'Have you found something?' He stepped over beside her.

'You're not the New York Police, are you?'

'We're working with them,' he replied smoothly, hand outstretched. 'Looks like your boss had something he wanted us to see.'

Actually, it was something to listen to. As the two men discovered when they'd returned to 26 Federal Plaza, Julius Lupine had helpfully recorded all the telephone conversations in which Cornelia Hennessy had given him orders. The recordings included revelations about Executive Protection and action she had taken, on her own, to dispose of panel members in England, Tokyo and Perth, Australia. They also revealed that Julius had persuaded her to change direction. She couldn't annihilate the entire NP3 panel, he had reasoned, and even if she could, with new panel members being added all the time, it would serve no purpose. Better, by far, to slow down the recruitment process from within.

The tapes in no way mitigated his own involvement. But it seemed that he'd calculated that there was already sufficient evidence to tie him up. What they did show was that he'd been taking orders. And there was no question where those orders had come from. To help their investigation along, he'd thoughtfully enclosed Cornelia Hennessy's visiting card, with all her private contact details.

Georgetown, Washington, DC

Lorna poured out two glasses of Gallo White Grenache, which she took through to her sitting room.

'Thank you.' Andrew accepted one, waiting for her to sit opposite before raising his glass. 'And also for having me to stay over tonight.'

'Believe me, I'm so glad you're here.' She delivered a wry smile, before glancing about her apartment.

After last night's encounter with Jack, she hadn't thought it at all wise to return home, so she and Andrew had both spent the night in neighbouring rooms at the Four Seasons.

And although she'd had time to prepare herself for today's media circus, even she had underestimated the furore that would accompany the revelation of Grayson Wendell's past – and Jeb Livingstone's stepping into the limelight. Since then, every news bulletin had been full of Wendell's machinations. Jeb Livingstone had had hours of prime-time play. Mid-way through the afternoon, the announcement had come out of the Wendell campaign that their candidate was withdrawing from the nomination race. This in turn provoked a new media frenzy as Jimmy Gallagher, the establishment favourite, was virtually handed the Democrat nomination on a plate.

Jeb Livingstone had been taken back to Brooklyn Penitentiary by Spencer Drake, with whom Lorna had signed him out that morning. Several news crews had followed him all the way back, while others were doorstepping the Director of Public Safety and Corrections, who'd promised an urgent review of the prisoner with whose case, until that day, he'd been completely unfamiliar. Most had predicted that Livingstone would be released within days, and there was great speculation about the level of compensation he could expect. What precedents were there for payouts after wrongful imprisonment? Were these anything to go by when the prisoner was a ninety-two-year-old man? TV stations were running chat shows on the subject to cash in on public hysteria, with viewers being urged to vote for a suitable payment. Jeb Livingstone had captured the public imagination.

After returning to Zonmark, Lorna had spent most of the afternoon closeted in the Executive Suite with Andrew and Kuesterman and lawyers from Mitchell, Curtin. Extensive legal actions were being prepared against Mayflower Health Insurance, and her participation was obligatory. When she'd emerged shortly after five, feeling drained, she'd decided to give herself a rare early night. The trouble was, she had no idea what to expect when she arrived home. Despite Wendell's withdrawal from the race, and despite the fact that things were now on a proper legal footing, she still felt at risk, still worried about her safety. So when Andrew had offered to stay over, she'd gratefully accepted.

They'd arrived back to find all her clothes and other possessions from Jack's house returned. She was astonished. With all she knew about Jack now – and he couldn't carry on the pretence any longer – it just seemed so unexpected, so out of character.

She'd hardly had a moment to take all this in, however, when Special Agent Ross had called her on her cellphone. He and a colleague had just tried to interview Julius Lupine. Lupine hadn't been available, but they had recovered tapes of conversations showing that he'd taken his orders not, as first thought, from Jack Hennessy, but from Jack's mother, Cornelia. Lorna had put down the phone in a state of shock.

Now she and Andrew faced each other across her sitting room which was warm and tranquil in the falling night.

'So they're saying,' he nodded towards her telephone, 'Jack really had nothing to do with the operation—'

'That would be hard to believe.'

'But what if I got it wrong? I'd feel so bad—'

'You're not to apologise,' she responded to his contrition.

'But he's . . . he was . . .'

'My man. My lover. Sure he was.' Lorna sipped her wine, pensive. 'But the trust just isn't there any more. He admitted going behind my back with Free to Choose—'

'Though his intentions were honourable. And as an issue it's nothing compared to sabotaging your programme.'

'But important to me. You can't build a relationship where there's no trust.'

'Yeah,' he reflected, looking into his glass. 'That was where things went wrong for Jess and me. She blamed me for Matt's death. Thought I should have taken more care looking after him.'

Lorna was following him closely.

'When I became convinced it wasn't an accident, she just thought I was trying to find excuses. Ways to justify myself. Even though I'd started getting evidence – the witnesses, the video from the rowing club. I s'pose,' he met her eyes, 'that was all about trust, too. Before . . . Matt died, she'd have accepted anything I told her. She'd have trusted me.'

It was a long while before Lorna asked, 'What if Jess knew the truth now? Do you think that trust could be repaired?'

'I honestly don't know.'

'But . . . would you like it to be?'

Andrew thought of all the nights he'd lain awake and alone in their bed, watching the patterns on the ceiling moving and dissolving with the wind; the evenings when he had returned to the house, to find it empty and forlorn. The loneliness he'd felt since she'd left him had been overwhelming.

'Of course I want her back.' His voice was choked with emotion.

'She's staying at her sister's, you said?' Lorna confirmed.

He nodded.

'And you have the number?'

New York City

Several times a year, Inky Mostyn, raconteur extraordinaire, and the most widely syndicated gossip columnist in the world, would invite several of New York City's leading ladies to a slap-up dinner at one of the city's smartest eateries. Diminutive, dapper, bow-tied and bespectacled, Inky had for years been in the habit of extending such invitations to Cornelia Hennessy, and for years she had been in the habit of accepting – despite the abominable way in which he had treated several of her society friends. For although an assiduous networker, and a *bon vivant* seldom seen without his trademark glass of Taittenger in hand, if Inky came across some truly scandalous piece of gossip about one of his intimates, he would never hesitate to publish it. No matter that he'd dined at their table a hundred times, that he was godfather to their pampered darlings, or even that they'd made their confession in the strictest confidence. As soon as their newsworthiness outweighed their social usefulness, Inky's 'friends' would find their lives retailed to countless millions across the globe – and in the most unflattering light.

Unsurprisingly, Inky had been blackballed by many of Cornelia's circle, but she felt no compunction to follow suit. She didn't advertise her meetings with him, though some must have wondered about the provenance of some of the stories that appeared in his column within days of his visits to New York City. For Cornelia, Inky was *such* fun to be with, *such* an outrageous flatterer – and even more outrageous gossip – that she could never resist spending time in his company. Besides, she believed herself to be safe from his scrutiny should he turn to the details of her own life. What did she have to hide, anyway?

So it was that on the evening of Thursday, 4 May, Cornelia found herself at Inky's corner table in L'Escargot, sitting in the company not only of Inky, but also of two other senior members of American gossipocracy – the Serbian ex-wife of one of the nation's biggest property developers, and the English editor of a leading glossy magazine. Everything was set for a big night out with Inky, as all present sought to establish their social importance, with increasingly daring intimate revelations about the rich and famous.

However, they were barely halfway through the first round of Martinis when there was, for Cornelia at least, a most unwelcome turn of events. It began with something of a *contretemps* at the restaurant door, as the *maître d'* tried, but failed, to halt the entry of two unlikely-looking diners. The whole restaurant had, it seemed, had its attention distracted by the commotion, and turned to see what happened next. Having broken into the Holy of Holies, the two men were making their way past the tables. Inky and his guests regarded them with disdainful amusement, as the glossy magazine editor passed unfavourable judgement on the shininess of their polyester-blend suits. Then their expressions froze as – was it possible? – the men headed directly towards them.

An expectant hush had fallen upon the restaurant, all eyes upon the two intruders, who seemed impervious to the effect they were creating. They were now bearing down directly on Inky's corner, and he and his guests were completely mystified. The men seemed so sure of themselves, so purposeful.

Cornelia's own surprise deepened to shock when the two ended up directly opposite where she was sitting next to Inky, and fixed her with steel-eyed expressions.

'Cornelia Hennessy?' said Ross, as both produced badges from their breast pockets. 'Special Agents Ross and Jessop. FBI. We need to speak.'

Acutely aware of the audience she was playing to, Cornelia quivered with indignation, her expression one of curled-lip contempt as she responded, 'I suggest you call my secretary for an appointment.'

'Now.' Ross ignored the attitude. 'We need to speak *now.*'

Cornelia drew on all the *grande dame* stature for which she was famous. 'Can't you see I'm dining, you silly man!'

Special Agent Ross had, in his time, done duty in the Bronx, and been abused by the most contemptible dregs that had ever crawled out of the sewers of the city. So nothing that came out of the mouth of Cornelia Hennessy had the slightest impact. 'Sorry to interrupt,' unruffled, he glanced about the table at the others, 'but it's urgent.'

'You can't just march in demanding to speak to me.' She was imperious.

'I just did.'

'But it's . . . it's . . .' she blazed about the table at her fellow diners '. . . monstrous!' Then, as the Serbian glamour-puss egged her on, 'This is a free country. I won't have our dinner disturbed.'

'If you like, I'll come back in half an hour with an arrest warrant.'

'Arrest?' she derided him. 'What on earth do you mean?'

The moment she uttered the question, she knew it was a mistake. But in her rage she hadn't been able to contain herself.

'What I mean,' Ross replied in that infuriating calm, 'is three charges of third-degree murder, corporate espionage, sabotage and related white-collar crimes.'

'I've never heard such absurd nonsense!' she exploded, now painfully aware that her fellow diners were staring at her like spectators at some kind of freak show. Everyone in the restaurant was looking at her as though she'd just grown two more heads. At her own table, the Serbian blonde had stopped nodding. The pale, English cheeks of the magazine editor had drained of the last vestiges of colour. And the muscles round the mouth of Inky Mostyn were twitching in

421

the way they always did when he caught the pungent odour of social disgrace.

The two FBI agents stood opposite, hands in their pockets, biding their time. And as Cornelia stared up at them she realised, to her complete mortification, that her only choice was to go with them, or risk even deeper shame later on. But that didn't mean she had to go quietly. Incandescent, she rose to her feet. 'This is an outrage,' she brayed. 'My lawyers will have the pair of you fired before the week is out.'

She glanced around the room for a sense of shared indignation – but there was none. Instead, the faces of her fellow diners betrayed the kind of disdainful triumph she herself had reserved for those who fell from grace. As for Inky Mostyn, sitting right beside her, he could barely contain his gleeful disbelief at being present at this most public of humiliations. No doubt already mentally penning the devastating phrases that would appear in his next column, he was unable to prevent his whole mouth from trembling.

It was all too much for Cornelia. Unwisely, she turned to vent her wrath on Inky. 'And what are you cackling about?' she demanded ferociously, 'you vicious little shit.'

'Like a wrathful demon, *grande dame* Cornelia was duly led away to the dungeons, from which she is unlikely to return for the rest of her natural life,' Inky Mostyn reported to at least three million avid readers in his next syndicated column. 'It's not every day – not every year – that New York society sees one of the most glittering social stars in its firmament plunge so spectacularly into darkness. But that night at L'Escargot was – game, set and match – the burnout of the decade!'

422

24

Washington, DC
Six weeks later

Lorna had spent most of the afternoon clearing her desk and packing away the contents of her office. She'd never been one for framed photographs on her desk or other personal memorabilia, so there were only a few items to store away.

Paperwork had been carefully filed, and could be easily found after her departure. Besides, Gail was staying on, and knew her way round the system as well as Lorna.

All that was left for her to do was to go through the few remaining items that had collected on the shelves behind her, such as the stacked copies of the paper she'd presented to the World Biotechnology Institute at its conference in Toronto a month before. The timing of her appearance had presented the perfect opportunity to announce the full results of the revised Lafayette trial life-extension estimates. Working on the knowledge that the sample had been a black, rather than mixed-race group, her new calculations showed that she'd been overly conservative in her original forecasts. NP3 could conceivably add not just thirty years to the average human lifespan, but forty to fifty.

As a result, confidence in her programme was at an all-time high. The problems of panel recruitment behind her, she'd become once again the darling of the media, more interviewed, photographed and lauded than ever before.

However, none of her successes was able to solve her problems at Zonmark. Confronting Kuesterman and Drake about their secret funding of Free to Choose, she'd provoked yet another major row. Believing they'd been acting in the company's – and therefore NP3's – best interests, the two men had been as unrepentant as they had been about leaking NP3 to the media in the first place. The purpose of Free to Choose, they had argued, was to raise awareness of NP3 not so much on Capitol Hill – that was only the purported aim of the group – but more importantly among Nasdaq investors who would recognise the next big thing when they saw it.

As it happened, though, Lorna Reid had gone one better than anything that could have been achieved by Free to Choose, with her much-hyped hijacking of Grayson Wendell's media conference. 'The biggest PR stunt in corporate America!' Spencer Drake had congratulated her, much to her chagrin. For even though her intentions had had nothing to do with publicising NP3, that was exactly the effect of the Wendell showdown.

With media attention more clamorous and demanding than ever, in the furore she'd persuaded Kuesterman and Drake to withdraw their support for Free to Choose, a movement she considered illegitimate. She achieved this not through any appeals to higher values or corporate ethics, but more simply by invoking the name of Judith Laing.

Judith had yet to write about Zonmark's sponsorship of

the lobby group – but, as Lorna pointed out, who was to say she wouldn't? Realising they had more to lose than to gain, Kuesterman and Drake quietly turned off the tap. Free to Choose offices in the Apex Building mysteriously closed down overnight. Ed Dieter and his staff returned to Chicago. And although a few genuine advocates of the movement remained, with the wind taken out of its sails, the group quietly fell out of the headlines. The March on the Mall was postponed indefinitely.

Privately, having talked to Judith over a drink, Lorna thought it unlikely that she'd turn her attention back to Free to Choose. In London she had already been nominated for a 'Best Foreign Correspondent' press award, for her work at the Wendell circus. Few journalists were privileged enough not merely to report on, but actually to change the course of, political history. No longer on the receiving end of terse demands from London, Judith had had the *Daily Sentinel*'s editor on the line to congratulate her, and had even been the subject of a cartoon in *Private Eye*, caricatured being held back from a political rally as she wheeled a skeleton-filled wardrobe behind her. She and Lorna had laughed about the trepidation with which her interviewees now met her. In recent weeks she'd had some of the big men in Washington quaking in their boots.

As she continued to clear her office, Lorna picked up a copy of that morning's *Washington Post*. On page seven there was a piece about Washington philanthropist Jack Hennessy who had launched a new Species Ethics Institute, in an attempt to challenge the treatment of apes and other close relations to man. Why, he asked, should they be treated any differently from humans? 'The days of species-ism are numbered,' claimed Jack, under a photograph of himself with the gorilla Kayla, who could sign two thousand different words and had a demonstrable IQ of over 110.

Earlier in the day, Lorna had read the piece and studied the photograph with the same powerful, contradictory emotions she'd felt ever since Andrew's revelations. She couldn't deny that she was still drawn to Jack. It was much more than the pure, physical tug of him. It was also the world of ideas he inhabited. He was always on the edge of new thinking, which made him a stimulating companion to be with.

But equally powerful were her doubts. Even now, six weeks after his mother's arrest, Lorna was as uncertain as ever. Jack had put out a statement, clear and unambiguous, that he'd had no involvement in the 'alleged' sabotage. And Cornelia's lawyers hadn't challenged it. But knowing how close they'd been, was it really possible he hadn't had any idea about his mother's scheming?

Lorna could never go back to trusting him completely, implicitly. And though she told herself it was as well that this had happened early in their romance, instead of later, there were still times when she was left feeling bereft. At such moments, especially late at night, when her apartment was soft-lit, and the streets outside quiet, she felt engulfed by that same aching solitariness she'd been wishing, it seemed for her whole adult life, would go away.

She was mulling this over when there was a movement at the door and she looked up. Steve Manzini was holding a folder. 'Panel update?' he offered.

'Shoot.' She threw the *Post* in her waste-paper basket.

She'd offered Manzini Greg's job the day after her once-trusted 2IC had made his confession. Although he'd been interviewing for other positions, Manzini hadn't yet been offered another job. When Lorna had explained the rapid turn in events at Zonmark, and apologised for her previous suspicions, she'd quickly won him over. She'd never had any doubts about his diligence. And she needed someone, fast, who knew the system.

'We're now at sixty-four,' he told her, as she put a few loose papers in her desk drawers. 'Another four letters are going out – the ones you signed earlier. We're coming to the end of the lab checks, finally. Those may wash out another five or so candidates, max.'

'Pretty much there?' she queried.

'I'd say so.'

The panel target had always been set at fifty. Lorna had wanted to build in plenty of room for inevitable shrinkage. Mid to high sixties gave them plenty to work with.

She regarded his earnest expression with a smile. 'From thirty to sixty-eight in six weeks is fast work,' she said.

'Like picking plums,' he replied. 'They were all just hanging there.'

She knew that well enough. On Manzini's very first morning back he'd discovered a further eight progeria children whose parents had been told by Merrit that they were disqualified for trials. Archive searches had revealed even more.

'So, are you going somewhere interesting –' it was the first time he'd asked her a personal question, '– on your holiday, I mean?'

'Oh, just back to Scotland.'

After the past few months, she thought, she didn't need 'interesting'. She'd had plenty of that to keep her going for a while. Instead, she'd be returning to the small coastal village of Whitehills where her parents had retired. She was looking forward to long walks in the lengthening evenings, across the sand beach to Banff, or up to where the land rose in gorse-covered cliffs above the ebb and swell of the Moray Firth. And there'd be single malt in front of a log fire at night. Welcomed back to the warm reassurance of her family home, she reckoned that for the next two weeks at least, quiet would do her just fine.

Weybridge, Surrey

Jess had been persuaded by her sister to join her on holiday in Greece. It had done her the world of good, or so her sister said on a crackling line from Athens. Andrew had offered to collect them from Gatwick, but Becky had declined. She'd left her car at the airport in the long-term car park. It wasn't too far out of her way to drop Jess back home.

Andrew had been awaiting their arrival, curiously nervous. For the past few days he'd caught up on every last bit of housekeeping that needed doing, cleaning the place out, tidying the garden, restocking the pantry and fridge. It seemed peculiar that the arrival home of his wife, something he'd once taken for granted as a daily occurrence, should cause him such dry-mouthed concern. But it wasn't as if she'd just been out at the office; she was coming home after eight weeks away.

The flight was due in at 2.30 pm. Realistically, that meant they wouldn't be home much before five. All afternoon he'd fussed about the details, changing the bedclothes and putting out a fresh set of towels, going down to the local florist's for two bunches of her favourite tulips, glancing at the clock every few minutes.

When, finally, the green Rover crunched up the gravel driveway, he waited till he heard their voices before opening the front door. He went out to greet her shyly.

It was Lorna's phone call to Jess that had been the breakthrough. After she'd explained to Jess how Andrew had not only tracked down Matt's killers but also saved the whole NP3 programme from destruction, the tide had turned.

All the same, they'd spoken only briefly on the phone and he was unsure what kind of reception Jess would give him. Would she be standoffish and distant? And where was she planning to sleep tonight?

But the woman outside looked nothing like the wife who'd left him. Deeply tanned, her sun-bleached hair cut short, she was wearing a white cotton dress which showed her bronzed skin to perfection. As he approached her, she also seemed unsure, though he took her smile as a positive sign. Coming together, they kissed and hugged each other briefly, before he collected up her suitcases and carried them into the house.

Becky wouldn't stop, wanting to drive straight through. After waving her down the driveway, they turned to go back indoors, closing the front door. Alone together, they stood in the hallway before he offered, 'A drink?'

She nodded, glancing around as he left the room, noticing the changes he'd made. Matt's crutches and cricket bat were gone from the corner barrel, but the photograph of him receiving the chess award, which used to be kept in his bedroom, was now framed and hanging on the wall. She noticed the newly dusted surfaces, the vase of fresh-cut tulips.

He returned, bearing a bottle of champagne and two glasses. He'd only ever bought champagne when there was something to celebrate, and her emotions, so close to the surface, welled up. For the first time in what felt like an age of misery, she dared to risk happiness too.

'So. What have you been doing?' she asked, sticking to the safety of the mundane.

'Nothing much. Few projects round the house. A bit of gardening.' He gestured out towards where she could see the flowerbeds on either side of the lawn bright with colour.

'You've been industrious.'

'Yeah.' He met her eyes with a small smile. 'I've enjoyed it.'

Easing the cork out of the bottle, with a gentle pop, he began to pour.

'Have you thought about what you're going to do next?' Her tone was open.

'I've thought about what I don't want to do,' he replied, handing her a glass. 'That's the City.'

Then, responding to her surprise, 'One thing about these past weeks and months – it's made me realise what's really important. I've rearranged my priorities.'

'What are your priorities?'

As he looked into her eyes, he experienced again the emotions that had made him want to lose himself in that beautiful blueness when he first met her. 'My top priority is you.' His voice was soft with feeling.

She reached up to wipe her eye.

'Our future.' He raised his glass to hers.

Not daring to speak, she smiled.

Mary-Jean, the woman who took Jeb in, was a distant relation. Sketching out the family tree with charcoal on the back of an old sugar sack, she explained how, the way she reckoned it, he was her great-uncle. And some great-uncle too! His fame had preceded him, in the small rural community of Jackson Creek, Louisiana, and there were plenty of folk wanting to see him all the time, though Mary-Jean took it upon herself to chase off uninvited visitors.

The smallholding where she'd spent her whole life had a cottage down the back, where her father, Jeb's nephew, had lived until his death, more than ten years ago. It was only four rooms, but after thirty-four years in jail, it felt like a palace. Just being able to get up from his chair and step out of the room whenever he pleased was a novelty Jeb still hadn't got used to, a month after his release. There were times when he'd walk through the door and back again, into the cottage, then outside it, with a heady thrill that no one around him could possibly understand. And nourishing home cooking, after all those years of jailhouse stodge, reawakened pleasures he'd long since forgotten. He had his life back again, his freedom. And it dizzied his senses.

Every morning he'd wake up at jail time, 5 am. And even though he could roll over and go back to sleep till eight, or nine, or ten, he wanted no part of that. There was too much of the world to enjoy and how much longer would he be in it? He'd get right up out of bed and go out into the dawn, where everything was fresh and new.

The roosters would be crowing and hens out in the yard. He'd catch aromatic ribbons of freshly ground coffee, percolating up at the homestead. But nothing could hold him back. He'd walk into the surrounding farmlands, and carry on walking through sugar cane fields that rolled down a hill to the slow curve of the river. Cane grew the full height of him, and more, forming a swaying, whispering arch over where he trod. Often a shower of early-morning rain would scatter across the land, and he'd look up and feel the drops against his face. And when he came to the river he would stand there looking at the place where the first light appeared on the edge of the horizon. There was a clear emptiness about it that held a kind of perfection. And each time he looked at it, he could contemplate the day ahead without fear – and that, for him, was the greatest liberation of all.

Ever since he came out he'd been asked about Wendell. That was all some folk wanted to talk about. Louisiana's Governor had been forced to step aside while being investigated, not just over the Lafayette trials and his own treatment, but other things that had crawled out of the woodwork. If he was found guilty – and Jeb was sure he would be – there'd be no doubt he'd land himself a long stay behind bars. And by a quirk of fate, the chances were high that he'd end up in Wilson State Penitentiary. The media had made a great deal of this. Though, to his own surprise, Jeb hadn't thought about Wendell as much as he'd imagined. In jail, consumed by bitterness, the Governor's evil had been the heaviest burden he'd had to bear. But things were different now.

He'd spoken on the phone to Lorna Reid since his release. And he would often remember the encounter that was to transform his life – his first visitor in nine years. In the mornings, especially, he'd replay the scene with a thankfulness so great he could hardly contain it. Gratitude came as a physical force that would rush through him, putting purpose in his step, generating an energy so strong he felt like a young man again.

And sometimes, when he thought back to that first conversation with Lorna Reid, he'd realise how he'd got things the wrong way round. She'd asked him what would make a difference to him, and he'd told her that seeing Grayson Wendell go down was what really mattered.

Well, Grayson Wendell had gone down now, and that felt pretty good. But standing on the banks of the river in those clear, summer dawns he'd feel the sweet wind in the cane fields and look out on the rolling blue of the Mississippi, and he'd realise, no doubting it, this was so much better.

Epilogue

The villa overlooking the ocean was sumptuous by any standards, though no different from a thousand other Caribbean bolt-holes. For years the super-rich had operated bank accounts and private trusts from this exotic locale, attracted not so much by the balmy climate and other tropical delights as by the island's tax status and battalions of well-armed lawyers.

It was for this precise reason that Julius Lupine had established not only an offshore bank account but also a residence on Grand Cayman. Though by the time he'd arrived, via private charter, it was to make the appalling discovery that the homely Martha had transferred his secret nest-egg well beyond his reach.

Even in anger, he hadn't been able to suppress a grudging respect. He'd never have thought she had it in her. Picturing her shut away in her kitchen, red-faced and perspiring over some new culinary experiment, he wouldn't have imagined her capable of suspecting he had a private stash of money offshore – let alone working out how to wrest it from him.

Robbed of the funds on which he'd been counting to start a new life, he did however have certain compensations. No one knew about the villa itself – imposing, isolated, the perfect retreat from which to plan his next move. Nor could they have guessed about the antiques that furnished the high-ceilinged rooms and sweeping galleries of 'Summer Place', as he'd named his island home, with mischievous understatement.

Yes, the loss of his £4.8 million had been an undoubted setback. But he had a gift for making money. He might have to reinvent himself, take on a different guise, a new identity, but that was of little consequence. He'd done it before, and he'd do it again. As a spin-doctor his life's work was, after all, the mastery of illusion. And while he maintained a scrupulously low profile until he was decided on a fresh course of action, he would have the very great pleasure of enjoying his villa and all its contents at leisure.

By necessity, his past trips here had been brief: snatched days on his way to and from foreign conferences; midweek sorties during which Martha had believed him to be visiting Mayflower offices in other parts of the United States. Simply contemplating the uncluttered days that stretched endlessly ahead of him was a source of unalloyed delight.

Living in seclusion might have been a burden, had he not had the foresight to install a computer and modem, several months earlier. Accessing all his favourite news sources online, he'd kept right up to date with events in the world he'd left behind as he surfed the Net beneath the magnificent *portière* that had once graced the wall of his New York office. It gave him the greatest satisfaction that he'd correctly second-guessed the purpose of Jack's visit to

Cornelia's apartment on that memorable afternoon – and, more to the point, what Cornelia would do next.

But when it came to remorseless expedience, Cornelia had met her match, as the discovery of the tapes had quickly proven. Lupine digested, with wry amusement, Inky Mostyn's account of the night she was taken away. He could just imagine the furious ranting, the high-profile humiliation. For Cornelia, ending her life behind bars now seemed inevitable. It would be a difficult adjustment after her lifelong reign as society queen. But Lupine wasn't completely lacking in sympathy. Once she'd been tried and sentenced and her fate settled, he might even send her a memento. Nothing too cumbersome, of course. One couldn't fit much inside an eight-by-six-foot cell.

In the meantime, he loved nothing better than to stroll amid the fountained majesty of his hillside retreat, his Savile Row suit replaced by more casual clothes, a Marinella cravat at his neck, pausing to savour his private collection of treasures with the relish of one whose every quivering fibre was finely tuned to the principal purpose of pleasure.

These, he used to think, were the things by which he defined himself. There were his cabinets by André Charles Boulle, the salon side tables by Charles Cressent; and the pride of his rococo collection, the celestial globe dating back to 1730, dedicated to the Comte de Clermont. He'd bid for them, along with other favoured *objets*, at the auction houses of Sotheby's and Christie's, whose intrigues and stratagems he knew well. There were also the pieces Cornelia had loaned him for safe-keeping, after selling her parents' property in the Honduras: Impressionist paintings whose style he didn't much care for, but which would fetch a tidy sum when traded. As traded they would be. It wasn't as if Cornelia had any need for a Manet – or, for that matter, a Cézanne – where she was going.

His pleasures weren't constrained to the visual. Down in the cellar he'd taken special care to lay down a dazzling array of cabernets and merlots, chenins and champagnes, all of which awaited his gustatory delight. And in the kitchen his chef, previously in the employ of the Belgian ambassador, would conjure divine fantasies out of the local seafood. Even more succulent were the fantasies performed by the young man who worked in his gardens. While crimson bougainvillaea raged out of control over the courtyard walls, and flowerbeds teemed with the purple trumpets of deadly nightshade, the snake-hipped mulatto youth would appear each day at siesta time. Stripping out of his clothes, as unselfconscious as though alone on one of the island's white beaches, he'd brush aside the mosquito netting over the bed where Lupine lay in greedy anticipation. Looking up into those pale, corrupt eyes with mute watchfulness, a knowing smile would appear on his full lips as he knelt to indulge his master.

Of an evening, with the sun sliding down over the ocean, Lupine would go out onto his balcony with an open bottle of Louis Latour – nothing too heavy, and just fruity enough for interest without any residual sweetness. Pouring himself a generous glass, he'd take out of its case his beloved oboe.

It was like being back in his student days, when he'd driven his fellow Yale scholars wild, throwing open his windows and practising his scales. Once again, he would carefully tune the instrument before working his way, somewhat rustily, from C major all the way through to B minor.

Warm-up completed, he'd conjoin the twin delights of the very finest wine and the most transcendent baroque – a little Handel, or Bach, or his alltime favourite, Vivaldi.

Holidaymakers travelling south on the road out of George Town, had they wound down their windows while passing the towering walls of Summer Place, might have caught the rising cadences of the Adagio from Vivaldi's *Concerto in D Minor*. But would any of them have possibly imagined that this achingly beautiful tenderness was being played from the dissolute heart of one of America's 'Most Wanted Men'?